Perhaps the most majestic feature of our whole existence
is that while our intelligences are powerful enough
to penetrate deeply into the evolution
of this quite incredible Universe,
we still have not the smallest clue to our own fate.

~ Sir Fred Hoyle

The absence of evidence is not evidence of absence.
~ Carl Sagan

Also by Scott K Bywater

eVOLUTION
The Genesis Makers

EMISSARY

by

Scott K Bywater

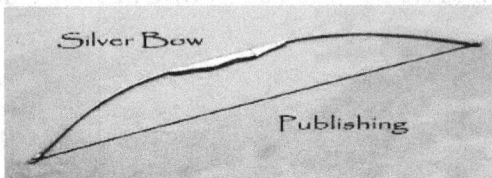

720 Sixth Street, Unit # 5
New Westminster, BC V3L 3C5
CANADA

Title: Emissary
Author: Scott K. Bywater
Cover Art: by Joshua Nicholas Bywater
Layout and Design: Candice James
Editing: Candice James

ISBN 9781774031476 (softcover)
ISBN 9781774031483 (e-book)
© 2021 Silver Bow Publishing

Library and Archives Canada Cataloguing in Publication

Title: Emissary / Scott K. Bywater.
Names: Bywater, Scott K., 1962- author.
Identifiers: Canadiana (print) 20210109335 | Canadiana (ebook) 20210109394 | ISBN 9781774031476
  (softcover) | ISBN 9781774031483 (EPUB)
Classification: LCC PR9619.4.B99 E45 2021 | DDC 823/.92—dc23

For Mary, Joshua and Alysha
My Universe

Also … For Dr Sagan

Contents

Prologue

Dawn

'In all our searching, the only thing we've found that makes the emptiness bearable,
is each other.'~ *Carl Sagan*

In an orbit stuck between hellish acid and crimson dust, it was approaching the end to the second Millennium of the modern age. Having crawled planet bound for eons, Man was about to take his first unsteady steps, to complete his first real adventure and leave his permanent mark on a new world. It was the beginning.

Like hairy apes that ambled around on all fours, millions of years ago, humanity was about to stand up and finally be counted.

A primitive craft glinted in the unimpeded sunlight of space, freefalling toward the surface of Earth's lifeless sibling. One then two, three then four of its sprung metal limbs caressed the scorified talcum. The golden pod padded onto the scarred worldlet with a thump and brought life to it for the first time in nearly four billion years.

Despite its desolation and sterility, the lunar pioneers were instantly dazzled by the exquisite panorama of rich browns and myriad tonal greys. From Earth it was barren and bleak, but up close, on its surface, it was an unimaginably beautiful world. Most of Earth thought it was pig-ugly, with no atmosphere and no prospects. Little did they know, it was the only reason they were there.

A static breath escaped the craft soon after landing, '...Houston...er...Tranquility Base here, the Eagle has landed.'

Precisely eighty-four minutes after this broken verse was murmured, an altogether different Earthly voice met a thunderous destiny, after arrowing through the cold loneliness for almost forty-nine years. It was an icy, desolate ride for Earth's microwaves. A distant listener inhaled the ancient syntax from an unwitting planet that had uttered it and then promptly forgotten it.

'...KDKA Pittsburgh, we're on the air, this is public radio.'

Prosaically human. Dispatched in 1920, no one could have guessed that these humble words would become Earth's emissary to an extra-stellar intelligence. The faint syllables were the first burblings of a planet come to cognition, to leave the world and speed into space.

Some of these microwaves carried the power to punch through the ionosphere and careen into the cosmos at the speed of light. They instantly girdled the Earth with the first shell of distinctly human, palpably intelligent radiation. It screamed *Aloha* to anything bothering to listen closely enough. *Hello, we're here.*

At 11:38 GMT, in the spectacular northern summer of 1969, a metallic structure penetrated the third spiral of the Milky Way Galaxy. It was the first time this beautiful Galaxy of a trillion stars had been breached by something alive and non-human. The finely sculpted form slowed to a halt only a few tens of light years from a solitary yellow star called Sun. The local intelligence had looked for radiation from others for decades, but found zip. *Where in God's name were they?* Enrico Fermi said it best, they should be everywhere around us, but they weren't anywhere to be found. Until now.

The strange beast was hedged with slender polyps and skeletal limbs that ringed its torso like fabulous crystals. Most looked turgid and sturdy but some were tenuous and narrow and seemed to drift and flow as though responding to a gentle breeze. It looked a little like something you'd tread on in the shower.

The vessel remained unremittingly still as it studied the accretion of a gas planet from a luminous dust shell that clothed a single crimson star. As its visual brain watched, the first tendrils of a feeble cosmic wind swept over its delicately hewn contours. Finally, an intelligence had met the outworking of another mind. Momentous and historic, two asymmetric technologies had made contact.

Chattering. One of the intruder's soft full compass limbs caught something that made its prime agenda ganglia literally bounce to attention. Within a heartbeat, every one of its ears was cocked toward the impossibly weak current that washed through space. The gentle flow of microwaves dribbled over its malleable exo-skin, provoking every pore of its elaborate carbon cortex. The ancient sneeze of energy gave humanity its first appointment with destiny.

The probe had scored the most unlikely of victories, catching faint broadband sprays that were wafting from the 'burbs of a yellow star less than fifty light years away. It immediately recognised the melody as artificial and significantly, as not of their own. The signature of others.

Fifty thousand years of venturing through space had suggested that their minds were unique. That their worlds were born with a silver spoon of such improbable rarity that it qualified them as singular...as a miracle. Disproving this ancient absurdity was their obsession, a deep seated intractable desire, fed and fattened to thumping obesity by millennia of failure. Each year that went by, only intensified their belief they were there. They were never disheartened. The hunt was never abandoned because they knew they were there. Others were just difficult to find. Like detecting the proverbial black cat on a dark night. Much, much harder as it turned out.

The vessel listened with ears erect to the burblings and chatterings of another culture, of another civilisation that was so incredibly close. The weak breath of radiation that had escaped Earth fifty years before had less power than a firefly, yet to the probe it was a blindingly precise and unequivocal beacon.

The fragile echoes were a cognitive supernova that nothing in the inanimate cosmos could have created. It knew and it silently rejoiced. The vessel explored space but it could think and make decisions by itself if it had to. It had the most incredibly intuitive autopilot imaginable.

In the first seconds they realised that the cosmic porism had been unriddled, laid bare like the most exquisite cerebral erotica. The justification for their eon long search had come in a heartbeat of thundering, wondrous understanding. It meant that after all this time, they hadn't been wasting their time. They already knew that, but now it was finally confirmed.

It meant they were not the only ones to feel the agony and the ecstasy of consciousness, not the only ones to savour the wonder of self-awareness. They knew now that they were not alone in an ocean of inanimacy, a sea of dead worlds and primitive mindless life. The greater Universe was alive with more than one voice.

Clever life could claw its way up from the everyday chemical shufflings around them, shufflings whose ultimate prize was the animate born of the inanimate. Simply, geochemistry grown into biochemistry. No miracle required, that was now proven beyond doubt. They had theorised for millennia that by the sheer weight of numbers v and sheer planetary plenitude, the cosmos could not have reared but a single wisdom. They were simply hard to find. The Universe had so many opportunities to experiment. Unless it was a miracle. And now they knew ... Now they knew.

The probe was organically cybernated, operated without physical effort by its single occupant who laconically interfaced with its organic neuroaxial net. It was an artificial but thoroughly biological and intelligent cortex, engineered to control every function of the titanic craft down to its finest subsystem. It was conscious but not self-aware. As far as the craft was concerned, it was the craft.

The vessel had been fully briefed on the nature of the mission. It was to take hold of the black hole that gave it passage to the Galaxy and drag it through space to its rendezvous with the outermost world of the earthly system. From there it was a short hop to Earth in non-Lorentzian space.

Quite literally, it knew what it had to do. The collapsed star, once positioned, would offer it a slip through forty million light years of space in less than an hour.

1

AASSA

'Extinction is the rule. Survival is the exception.' ~ *Carl Sagan*

'Please...fucking...please,' he whispered, feeling the desperation in his own voice. The dread was stuck in his throat like a rusty railway spike. 'Come on you sonofabitch,' Mitch mouthed almost silently, looking daggers at the thing in front of him, hating the gilded beast that blocked his horizon. His fists were shaking and pale he was holding them so tight. 'Piece of shit...blow up, see if I care...I dare you.' He was still glaring at the rocket as it made its way slowly into space.

The loathing was absurd, Mitch knew that, but it refused to be soothed by any conscious act of will. The irrational dislike had been permanent baggage for well over a year now. Mitch was sick of the sight of the damned thing, sick of being reminded of its pivotal role in the future of New Commerce in shallow orbit. 'Yeah, yeah,' he would respond, rolling his eyes, trying to downplay its importance in his mind, but knowing better. Hoping for better.

It was a shiny, malicious symbol of pain, that he knew. The scrawny beast rose in the sky like a blazing Phoenix, covering the earth with an exhalation of acrid vapour that licked at the window only inches from Mitch's nose. He peered at the thing with an intense, fevered stare, eyes slightly narrowed. He was weary just looking at it, tired thinking about it. He frowned at it through spread fingers. He'd forgotten his sunglasses, yet again. He pictured them on the table by the door in his dorm. Fat lot of good they were doing there. It was so bloody bright, he thought sourly, glancing up and trying to block out the Sun.

Beyond the soundproof glass, the world was a canvass of ochre, a cracked and lethal killing field to all but the best prepared. Weeks of unrelenting heat had descended on the ancient plateau and tortured it with a haze of fire and dust. For a landscape exposed for billions of years without interruption, it was nothing unusual, but for the human inhabitants it was an unbearable hell, more like Hades than Earth. In the near distance, a dust devil was churning the dusty alluvium, whipping saltbush and desert pea high above the bohemian contours of the satellite range.

Mitch Taylor was rigid and sweating, his eyes almost closed against the Sun, in the final, gut wrenching moments before departure. He was watching terrified as an Austek rocket exploded skyward from the heart of the Aust American Space & Shuttle Agency (AASSA). The stark geometry of the Agency sat on the lip of Menzies village, a tiny shelter that cowered on the brink of an endless red desert in bullseye Australia.

For Mitch it was the coup de grace of a mentally crippling year. The new Dieter Orbus project had nearly fucking killed him, and with the birth of its first offspring he could feel his mindset slip a cog. Mitch felt a vein in his neck start to throb as he considered the year he'd struggled through, and what was coming up in the next few months. He could almost hear the quaking in his sinews and the pressure in his brain, feeling like it might suddenly burst in a bloody spray of mental decompression. Although he'd never concede it to an outsider, he knew he needed out. Out of this place called AASSA. Somewhere far away from the arid heartland that surrounded him like an infernal prison. He wouldn't concede it because he knew it wasn't possible. Mitch was AASSA. He was a hero to Earth and a God to those at AASSA. If he wasn't there to hold the walls up, the whole bloody lot would fall apart and vanish under the desert, or so he reckoned anyway.

Mitch was proud of his achievements, but there was little ego, at least not outwardly. He'd been plucked from a University postgrad in 2004 and elbowed into the Agency's astronaut program in the States, where to nobody's surprise he'd killed 'em for years. Seventeen Shuttle missions were his, and he'd occupied the big chair on all but two of them. Mitchell Taylor had been around, but there was one thing that set him apart from the rest of his kind. Something that chiseled his name in gold and made him forever unique. Forever in this case, truly meant forever.

Mitch had been the first from number three to set a human footprint on Mars. The first to see the plumes of sparkling dust shine and ripple in the light from a distant Sun. As famous as Neil Armstrong, in fact way more famous, for he didn't simply stumble around like a goose for an hour on a stillborn seed of Earth. He was the first to take stride on a truly different world. On another of Sol's major family, a rock in a totally different and distant ecliptic. Finally, Earth inhabitants had made it to Mars, and Mitch was the man who made it so.

The planet had tantalised humanity for over ten thousand years. The United Space & Planetary Agency (USPA) had grabbed him, trained him, then thrust him into the fabulous surface photos snapped by the Martian probes, the Vikings and the Pathfinder missions. Those same dazzling photos had sparked his love affair with space so long ago, and with the red rebel in particular. But every time he thought of Mars, of those stupefying months he spent on Chryse Planitia, that cajoling image of his father, Zach, came crashing back. And so did his loathing for the galloping horror that had stolen him, before Mitch's left boot had sloughed into the crimson corrugations of Mars.

Ten months after the hypergolic ramjets had cut his team free of Earth orbit, and just before aerobraking in the Martian ether, Zach had fallen to the tumorous bastard in his head. It was torturous, bitter irony, and it never failed to weigh on him, an ache no less physical than a knuckled fist to the solar plexus. His father had missed it all. All his achievements were accomplished after he died a horrible death at the hands of what was a miserable disease.

Cancer had lined up his family and mown them down, and along with them, the memories that should have been so precious. It had a hell of a lot to answer for. Fucking piece of shit disease, he thought over and again feeling a suffocating sensation tighten his throat.

Fighting what seemed like constant adversity, Mitch had somehow seized the destiny he'd always hoped would be his. The achievement was there, certainly, but the memory of his parent's agony, left his mind's eye tainted with pain. The memories should have been golden but they weren't. The memories weren't nearly as good as they should have been. They were terrific and horrible in equal measure because he knew what was going on back on Earth. Now, Mars reminded him of his Dad, death and pain, and they shouldn't have. Mitch tried not to think about them, which, in itself, was a fucking travesty. He tried his best to play down his achievements, but it was difficult sometimes; most times.

Despite having been Director of AASSA since it was hatched by the USPA in 2055, he still flew on occasional missions, most of them joint runs with the Americans or the Russians. Mitch was the closest thing the Agency had to a living legend, and few, probably none, considered the tag unearned. He was a pioneer in the most glorious sense of the word. None of the one hundred billion souls that had ever trod the planet had accomplished as much as he had. Not just a mountain or a dead satellite, he'd conquered another fucking world. Mitch stood atop an apex of humanity so slender, it only had room for one...him. He tried to be humble, but that wasn't easy either.

An inch of glass held back the evening heat that was more like the belly of a blast furnace than a landscape waiting for the shawl of night. Although comforted by air conditioning, he and Jessy Truman were both sweating crazily as they watched Austek slide spaceward after a flawless launch. Mitch had one eye on Jessy and one on Austek, blinking like a madman, only partly because he'd forgotten his sunglasses. Their desert port for Aust American insertions had finally gotten Dieter Orbus up and running. They were ogling the first of twenty planned Austeks, watching a hundred billion dollars of future income claw its way Moonward, every one of those dollars hanging on the success of this humble little rocket. No pressure. He was well known for achieving his best when under pressure. A damn good reputation to have as head of anything.

Sean McKay and Rhys Volkers stood like mannequins near the massive, blue washed wall. Overlords of chemical momentum for Dieter, they waited in white knuckle terror for something to go horrendously, explosively, wrong. Surely, it had to happen; it was long overdue, given space industry standards. Both were fully certified cosmonauts with long hours spent in space, and each longed to resume their love affair with the darkness that had touched them so deeply. But growing responsibilities on Earth, with AASSA in particular, had stolen them away from their favoured field. Their dreams remained though, passionate and incessant fantasies that craving any luck that might grant them a reprieve from their dusty terrestrial prison here at AASSA.

Mitch looked like hell and he had the voice to match, a rough, low bark wobbling under the weight of numbing fatigue. 'I need a holiday as far away from this goddamn place as possible.' He hacked out a cough and angled his head back. As the shining beast hit the first wisp of Cirrus, his jaw was still grinding with the venom of the statement.

Jessy glanced at him and hesitated, opening her mouth but snapping it shut just as quickly. Mitch's comment stunned her, not so much in what he'd said but the way he'd said it. Intent, that was it. She continued to eye him warily, seeing the agitation flickering behind his normally calm expression. Mitch rubbed the back of his neck hard. He felt like saying something but clamped his lips closed, saying nothing, which he reckoned was best at this point.

A bit surprised maybe, but Jessy knew what was wrong with him, and perhaps even agreed with him, sympathised certainly, but equally she felt like walking up and punching him in the nose and telling him to snap the fuck out of it. Her eyes burned with irritation. 'If I didn't know better, I'd reckon you were ready to toss it in,' she finally mustered, remembering how distracted he'd seemed lately, which was also unusual. He was normally so intense and focused. Mitch was like a fucking computer when it came to AASSA. Taking it all in, her mind was doing the sums and arriving at answers that seemed entirely unthinkable. No way, she thought, tossing hair out of her eyes with a deft head flick. Mitch turned slowly to face her, finding Jessy meeting his gaze, piercing him with eyes that fairly bespoke surprise. She was bug eyed, staring at him, waiting for him to respond.

'Actually, I was kidding, but the administration of this place and the constant begging for funding, Jesus, it's a nightmare Jess. The Americans, the USPA, even our own people, they're out of control, goddamn bureaucratic juggernauts. Sometimes I wonder why I bother? Do they want any R&D? Do they want any forward thinking at all, or should we just roll up the footpaths and bolt the doors?' Mitch's voice dropped to a whisper, and his narrowed eyes darted everywhere, 'do they know what they're doing, do they know what sort of sapping effect their ignorance is having? Shit, their funding criteria are tighter now than they were ten years ago.' His eyes narrowed as he thought about it, running a hand across his face. 'Crazy?' He continued, with eyes slowly widening at Jessy. 'The really crazy part is that it's fucking true.'

Mitch turned his head and looked through the window to the gantries below. 'I never intended to get so involved in administration. I've taken ships to other worlds and walked where no man has walked before, or had walked when I was there.' He couldn't help but grin at Jessy after that comment, although he needn't have bothered, she ignored his piss poor attempt at humor.

'For Christ's sake Mitch,' she said too loudly, watching him closely, 'look around you; you fought and bled for this place, dragged it together from dust, singlehandedly swayed Canberra, Paris and Washington. You can't walk after all that, you can't.' Jessy stopped talking and looked away, daring him to respond. Daring him to confirm what she would never believe. Would he walk from AASSA, no way she figured. But after what he'd said, well, who knew? He sure sounded serious. Scarily serious.

Mitch clenched his fists and said nothing, firmly clamping his tongue between his teeth. She was horrified at the suggestion that he'd finally had enough of the Agency's bullshit. And whilst he hadn't actually meant to give that impression, the basic premise was about right. The stress and the frustration was destroying his motivation piece by piece, sloughing away his passion like a worn out husk. The humdrum of everyday administration was getting to him. Turning him into a fucking mainframe. He could feel it, but he couldn't do anything about it. Turning around, he sighed heavily and gazed back at his old friend, and despite himself he smiled. Mitch couldn't help but like what he saw. Actually, he admitted grudgingly, he loved what he saw. Jessy's profile always seemed to strike a chord with that part of his mind that looked after the more basal instincts.

Workmates and professionals, they were, but his hormones would not be denied. And each of his, he knew, had tiny little minds of their own. Minds that were stubbornly indifferent to reason. He shoehorned his gaze back to Austek, but the image was burnt into his mind like a copper etching. He could still see every detail, could still see the green cat's eyes, shining as though the energy of star life lay rumbling and sparking somewhere beneath. Jessy was way too attractive to be an astro-tech, and he knew everyone on base thought the same thing. He'd been privy to the tavern talk, and witnessed firsthand the lust so poorly disguised in the eyes of the men, and even a few of the women. She had a dark, straight bob cut that framed catlike eyes and the body of an athlete. But Jessy's brain was the clincher. She was genius par excellence, an undeniable space sciences guru, and it even managed to outshine her intensely sexy feminine symmetry. She was a rare jewel indeed, that rare cut of physically and mentally supercharged humanity, brilliant and beautiful. A killing montage to the weaker sex. A killer to Mitch in particular, who held his chin high and continued on.

With a familiar twinge, he remembered her body, so perfectly formed that even the loosest space wear couldn't hide its real form. Mask it perhaps, lessen its impact maybe, but hide it, no. Like trying to hide Eiffel with a layer of sandwich wrap, he mused, thinking hungrily about her physique. She was dressed in a loose T-shirt and baggy chino's, and happened to glance up and catch Mitch's lingering gaze. He snapped his eyes back to the sky. He glanced at her from the corner of his eyes, and chastised himself silently. She was looking straight at him, he could tell. He'd been sprung, big time. Both were unmarried and invariably made flippant claim to being married to the cosmos. At best that was only partly true. The partly bit was getting smaller, the longer he spent with Jessy, and the more he saw her the smaller it got. They watched Austek as it arced smokily toward space, keeping a close eye on the progress and attitude of AASSA's latest and most expensive toy.

Rhys and Sean were idling in the far corner of the Com tower and were also watching the ascent of their joint creation. At the same time, they were straining to catch the exchange between Mitch and Jessy. Sean inched around and watched through the metal fibre window.

'Who's she trying to fool?' he murmured to Rhys, 'I know she feels the same way he does. Both of them should still be in R&D, if not here then at NASA or ESA or USPA, not in admin. for God's sake.' His frown dug a network of canali in his forehead, making him look a hundred years old. In reality Rhys was only half that, just well baked, second time it was here at AASSA in the middle of Australia, first, back in the good old Lone Star State of America. That's where he did his training as a pilot, which led him to Houston, eventually becoming an astronaut, and then working here at AASSA, and of course where he was now. 'That work they did on the Interstar was groundbreaking, decades ahead of anything else in the field.' Sean was getting fired up by the sound of his own voice. And even though Rhys had heard it all before, he let him continue on.

Trying to interrupt him, he knew, would only spur him on to louder and longer, more painful proclamations on the Agency. So, he kept quiet, hoping that Sean would eventually run out of air, which was a fruitless hope in itself.

'...the science community, almost views interstellar travel as a scam, some boyish predilection ... something totally beyond our reach.' Sean's head was thrust forward. 'Maybe they're right, but maybe they're wrong and if they are wrong it's the Interstar that'll fucking prove 'em so.'

Rhys watched as Sean drank in a deep breath to fuel his voice. 'USPA thinks it'll be a couple hundred years before it might become a reality. They don't give a damn, they're not even interested. Criticism is all we hear, the Interstar is too revolutionary, uses too much untried technology, is too ambitious to risk committing scarce funding dollars to.' Sean's eyes were large and fierce. 'And that's despite the fact that there's no other designs anywhere near the level of technical completion and theoretical certification as Cygnus. They're scared shitless it might fail, blow up during testing or detonate near Earth and stuff up future funding from Uncle. Limited funding...it's all we damn well hear. God forbid they should say anything positive or encouraging.' Sean's eyes were dark and assessing, his expression a deadpan stare.

'Limited funding?' Rhys's eyes were straining. 'You mean fucking extinct don't you, and not extinct by transformation either, just extinct!' He couldn't help but grin briefly at Sean but quickly

14

turned serious again. Although the sentiments were familiar, Sean's tirade had pressed his buttons once again. The situation with the USPA really ticked both of them off, and he was the first to acknowledge it.

Sean knew he'd opened a rotting wound, but he continued anyway, snarling through a mouth that was barely wider than a text a line. He was blinking fast and shaking his head, revealing how much it pissed him off. He struggled to believe USPA'S ignorance. '...with recent fiscal tightening, NASA quit Cygnus funding, AASSA refused to pick it up and USPA naturally agreed with their decision, pointing to the recent golden bloody rule, their so called Global Objectives in Space.' Sean's mouth was flecked with saliva. 'But the team continued their work on conceptual grounds, mostly on their own time. I know I've harped on this, but the Interstar should work, it hasn't been built and hasn't been tried, but technically it's all there, it's beyond brilliant. I know it'll work. Revolutionary, radical, complex, yes, absolutely. But all the same I think it has to work, certainly in principle. Not taking account of the million variables that space might throw at it of course.' He took a long, shuddering breath. 'You don't have to convince me, I'm with you. Hell, maybe you should've gone with 'em to address the last funding meeting, you're quite compelling. Nevertheless, no one will fund it, you know it, I know it, and Jessy and Mitch certainly know it.'

Rhys kept nodding, agreeing with everything Sean was saying. 'Fucking NSF,' Rhys barked to himself, letting out a long sigh of displeasure. Sean continued rambling, 'How could we not know it, the Agency decreed that theirs and therefore our goals would be focussed locally until further notice. Funding for any manned initiatives that look even a kilometre outside the inner planets will be rejected outright without discussion.'

Rhys's brow was seriously furrowed as he spoke, a vein in his neck throbbing with the pressure of the statement. 'Fucking rednecks,' he spat, wondering how the hell space got so stuffed up. He shifted his weight and scowled downward at the floor. 'Goddamn it,' Rhys spat as he thought about the whole space industry and the clowns funding it. He didn't want to think about those that actually directed it.

They were absolutely precise in their assessment of Mitch and Jessy. Both were tormented by their inability to take their plans for extrasolar travel further. The worst part was the pigheaded stance taken by the USPA, a joint venture between the USA, Japan, Australia, Russia and the Euro Confederation (ECON). It meant seeing the project come to fruition would likely not occur within their lifetimes, if ever. Sean expected to never see anyone go beyond Mars, ever. He opened his mouth to continue, but closed it, thinking better of it. He reckoned he'd said enough.

Above them, the Austek rocket would deploy a Euro Nippon satellite into geostationary freefall above South America. Known as Xanadu, the orbiter was a state-of-the-art remote sensor dedicated solely to scanning the cosmos for X-rays and other high energy radiation. The only other decent satellite in the field, the Nightglow, had suffered a fiery death over Greenland eighteen months earlier when its orbit was destabilised by an apparent collision with space junk. It was the same fate handed out to ROSAT and EUVE years before. It was becoming an occupational hazard, a bloody expensive one. Sean's jaw clenched and he narrowed his eyes as he continued to think about NASA's bullshit.

Seven members of the AASSA executive including Mitch and Jessy watched Space Shuttle Sagan via deployment bay video as it successfully released a gently rotating, jet-black Xanadu into its precise spatial coordinate high above the broken Brazilian cloud tops.

2

Nemesis

'I don't want to believe, I want to know' ~ *Carl Sagan*

Soon after Xanadu was set free, Earth's celestial backyard witnessed an extraordinary event. It occurred almost forty trillion kilometres away but would eventually have a profound impact on the distant cradle. And on its people who clung to its soil mostly oblivious to the possibility of a global killer. More than four years would pass before Earth would receive any hint that something unspeakably lethal had been spawned in nearby space. The light and X-rays and other radiation, the mark of apocalypse, would take that long to span the trillions of vacuous kilometres.

The vessel was gliding through a steadily thickening stellar breeze, with the dead star rotating behind it. It was hauling ballast of the highest gravitational order. The black hole was invisible, but only in the human spectrum. Every dimension of space was feeling the passing of the great sphere, being crushed for a split second into a dimensionless gutter, bereft of any space whatsoever. The collapsed star was like a cosmic kidney stone in reverse, rupturing and then strangling the backbone of light, space and time. A trio of brilliant stars dominated space around the craft, lighting it and warming it, and all were now so close that their glare washed out much of the star scape beyond.

The vessel's path to Neptune was obstructed by these exquisite pyres. One of them was only a few million kilometres from the tug and was similar in almost every way to Earth's small sulfurous Sun. The other, a magnificent burning orange, shuffled around its yellow comrade in an apparently perfect alliance.

Between the two stars was a haze of reds and blues that was being swept in a turbulent bluster of seething stellar wind. But the most dazzling feature of the star scape was a small third sun which skirted the twin Alpha Centaurians. The massive craft had accidentally ventured into the busy inner system domain of a three-way stellar ballet. The third star was tiny V645 Cen, Proxima Centauri.

The tug's course toward solar space had been favoured by only a cursory reference to its end point by the single occupant, a fleeting synaptic spasm that guided the craft's carbon-based cortex. Stellar sized objects or for that matter, any sized objects, had never before presented a problem. That was about to change.

Their astrogation record was faultless. It was premised on organically aware technology that had not failed its creators since its carbon cortex had been born centuries ago. The makers had presided over a living transit system that was totally without accident or fault of any kind, for a long time. It thought, it calculated and it was successful. Although it had never, not once, located technical life, before now.

The colossal vessel thudded through the cool stellar corona and struck Proxima's rapidly brightening equator in a fantastic annihilation. Travelling at close to Luminal speed, the vessel pierced a flocculi on the surface and punched right through the flaming orb in much less than a heartbeat. It exited in a stream of primrose star stuff that leapt away from the fiery wound like a spray of pale blood.

The ruined ship flashed away and vanished amongst the background of stars as though it had suddenly winked out of existence. But not before its dying attractor had grabbed Proxima and given it a stupendous tug forward, ripping it from the orbit it had so obediently trodden for almost five billion years.

16

Catastrophe. The black hole, though free of the dead vessel's grip, continued to eat up the void that separated it from the now galloping star. Within minutes, the gravitational colossus had edged past Proxima, in the process ambling so close as to inhale some of its boiling rivers of flame, not close enough to spaghettify it. Shadowed by an almighty vice, the red star had no hope of escape, its star napping was as good as fact.

In an instant of unimaginable fury, Proxima found itself clamped in a maniacal dance around a rotating black hole. The invisible beast was already clawing at the corona of its new companion, ripping away its life stuff and gorging on it, inhaling it from a swarm of gas that had forged a gorgeous belly hoop around the vortex. Eventually, the entire star would be consumed.

As the gas was snatched from the plasma ring, massive bursts of X and radio waves flooded away into the rapidly darkening void and formed a distinct particle jet. The new noise signalled the birth of a brilliant new energy source in the constellation Centaurus. Its nursery was already empty, the pair had already bolted.

***

It was like a finely hewn cogwheel, the platinum contours tumbling across the face of the exquisite globe that stretched from horizon to horizon beneath it. Cyclonic storms casually swirled and gyrated across its intensely stippled hemispheres.

It had finally been built. Named and designed fifty-five years earlier, the reluctant planet had finally mustered the foresight and the collective inertia to actually build it, and do it properly.

Apart from Mars Platform it was humanity's first decent effort to colonise its own space, to permanently tread the concentric dimensions of deep orbit. The massive structure in stationary orbit was Earth's first decent scale cooperative space city. Freedom was completed in 2057, a joint funding and operational venture between the USPA and NASA which boasted the gamut of space capable nations. After decades of stalling and politicking, for those with the dream, success was as magnificent as it was unexpected. Congress and the UN had actually said yes!

The piecemeal construction of a smaller space station was started in 1999 but failed before it was finished when Alpha's oxygen cycler detonated. Thirty people were killed and the floating habitat was fatally dissembled, and later abandoned. The Russians continued to remain alone in permanent Earth orbit, until The Awakening.

By the dawn of the second decade of the twenty-first century, humanity had finally started to rouse itself, gradually waking up after years of introspective slumber. Mankind was finally returning its consciousness and focus to the dazzling potentials of space, mainly due to Congress conceding that something interesting actually existed above their heads. Something that had slipped their collective mind, despite the glorious frontier days of a generation prior. NASA had lost its way following Apollo. Why? They had no one to compete with.

But things were changing, in fact had changed. There was a slowly swelling desire to get re-acquainted with space, not remotely, but re-acquainted personally. Since the Remington Decree in 2013, Man had made leaps in rocketry and infrastructure on a scale that rivalled the Moon era sparked by JFK more than half a century before. The imagination of the world was suddenly refocused, ogling the greatest adventure of all. Finally gone was the fiscal rigor mortis that had cursed the Post Apollo period like a choking melanoma.

Of course, there were reasons for the change. Private enterprise had gotten involved in space, together with China and Europe, which propelled the entire industry into a new space race to get to Mars and back to the Moon. There were even substantial plans for space tourism. Global economies had strengthened almost across the board, particularly in the West. And the wasteful dedication of funds to defensive and offensive hardware had largely evaporated in the wake of formal global consent and hard resolution. The focus for science had once again spun outward, not only to the possibilities of near Earth orbit, but beyond the inner planets, toward the dappled titans. Toward the plump sentinels and their precious families that sat distant and forgotten. Not unmanned missions either, that was old news. The wonders those remote friends had delivered were stupefying and groundbreaking, but their aim was for human missions. Multiple ventures using rapid transit vessels that would ride on the back of the data gathered by the old NASA robots. For the USPA, the stars literally beckoned. Hallelujah and about bloody time, most said.

By the end of 2022, there were permanent and self-sufficient human habitats on Luna and Mars, and there were two space towns in deep orbit. Freedom, in deep La Grangian transit around Earth held a permanent population of six hundred, while the two hundred on Copernicus enjoyed a geo-stable orbit above the beautiful Proclus crater.

The Lunar Gravinet Platform had a stunning view of the brilliant little moon mark that punctuated a tiny lenticular ridge between Mare Crisium and Mare Tranquillitatis. Times had definitely changed.

By Christmas of that year there were even sporadic passenger flights to the Moon. The Luna shuttles were 1900 series Boeing jets, highly specialised, tougher aircraft with a dozen fully rotating epoxy cellulose boosters strutted into the fuselage. When required they could thrust the jets into hyperbolic orbit and eventually cut them free of Earth's gravity altogether. Flying once a fortnight from Kennedy, and from special USPA docks in New York and LAX, they could dock with either of the floating space towns. The Luna Boeings were flexible, go anywhere, land anywhere excursion vehicles known colloquially as spaircraft (space going aircraft).

The latest achievement in space was the small Tranquility Base Sheraton, designed to service a very select and wealthy clientele. This was no basic Holiday Inn, it was an octagonal lowrise of pure indulgence, for $200,000 US dollars a night it had to be. And despite the cost there was a two year waiting list for rooms, not to mention a thriving black market where accommodation trading was rife.

The American flag and the descent stage of the LM Eagle left on the Moon by Armstrong and Collins was the centrepiece of a laser illuminated historical park, lying almost conjoined only a hundred metres from the hotel's Vacudome foyer. The vista through the silica bricks of the Viewing Turret was impossibly poignant. Three hundred and sixty degrees of dazzling skyless panorama, punctuated by a stunning sapphire cradle suspended in dead blackness, rich and emotional beyond description.

Exploration of the solar system was now focussed on the planning stages of a dozen manned flights to the deeper family, to pass close by Jupiter and Saturn, to caress the partly organic asteroid Chiron and to land on the minor planets of Europa, Enceladus, Ganymede, Callisto, Titan and possibly even Triton.

With the intriguing data from the Pluto and Charon probes, the USPA was also pondering an eventual manned mission to the Pluto system. To coincide with that part of Pluto's oblate and oblique shuffle where the planet's unique ether was a gas and not a collapsed frost. To achieve these ambitious plans, much had to be accomplished.

Space was the new real thing. Prodigious amounts of energy were being heaped on the preliminary stages of an advanced space domain on farside Luna. One that was capable of engineering, mining and launching craft to these distant worlds and ultimately, in the future sometime, sometime soon hopefully, boosting Man to the closest planets.

Plans were also on the board to quadruple the size of Mars Hab 1 and splice into it a similar, though smaller, launching and construction facility.

The Martian reconnaissance undertaken by USPA with these goals in mind had led to one of the most stunning insights of all time, to one of Man's most sobering moments in space, and on Earth. By pure accident, they stumbled onto something astonishing that lay long hidden beneath the crimson wadis of Mars. Something incredible.

Stage 2 geophysical surveys conducted around Mars Hab in 2015 led to the chance uncovering of deeply buried, pseudo-morphed fossils of ancient marine Martians. Tiny exoskeletal organisms, highly segmented and wormlike, were found embedded in the limonitic gristle of the ancient river gutters in Kassei Vallis. Similar finds, including bodyprints and casts of cyanobacterial

18

colonies and pseudo-ammonites, were made later on the rim of the Chryse Basin and in eastern Mangala Vallis.

They all knew what it was. Extraterrestrial life. The poignancy of the find hit the population on Earth almost as one, stunning them with a thunderous, humbling spasm of sudden realisation. *Other life!* If it had happened twice, it wasn't a miracle, it was everywhere! It was widely believed that life was common but intelligence rare, Bayesian logic said so, more proof that they were right.

The Mangala find boasted hundreds of exquisite, highly divided worms that were totally replaced by silica, and sat in beautifully crystallised magnetite. Some of the "silica worms" were entirely transparent, almost glasslike, and were as near to faithful as anyone could have hoped. Some were stunningly fluorescent under longwave ultraviolet light and many carried sparkling inclusions of native gold, as druses of tiny, suspended crystals. They made stunning specimens. Earth was slobbering with awe. It wanted more. It needed more.

The finds were cause for profound celebrations, the scientific community finally confirming what most of it had always believed. That life was not somehow peculiar to Earth, that it had occurred elsewhere.

Of course, they couldn't be sure that the Martians weren't seeded from Earthlife that had been swept to Mars on impact meteors, or that Mars life hadn't in fact seeded Earth. After all, the tenuous suggestions for life on the red planet had already been found in Antarctica, inside the gizzard of an ancient meteor hawked from its dusty belly.

But as far as Earth was concerned it was other life. That was the scientific jury's historic ruling. A magnificent, momentous step forward, it was a singularly historical moment in Earth's history. And it was rightly assumed that the nature of philosophical thinking on the planet would never be quite the same again.

***

In the middle of the year 2020 Mitch and Jessy had been invited by the National Science Foundation to present a fifth submission to the USPA. A fifth attempt to secure funding for full scale development and proving of a prototype Interstar engine. Or perhaps a fifth chance to endure the soul destroying agony of rejection and setback. In any event, the work had gone as far as it could without massive long term funding. Theory was fine up to a point but that point had well and truly been reached. Like Keynesian Economics, it was fine in theory, but had to be proven in real life.

Out of nowhere, they were invited to proffer what they had. It had always been a matter of pushing and prodding and almost begging to front the NSF and Congress. To be invited was totally unexpected; to Mitch and Jessy it was almost incomprehensible. They knew it had to mean something. Something positive maybe? They were too scared to consider their own question for fear of jinxing themselves. But still, they could taste the possibility of a life's dream at hand, but they put it aside, or at least they tried to. The unsolicited letter from J Elliot Pratt had simply turned up, and it asked them to do the same.

After five minutes with the Funding Executive it was obvious that something deep within the ponderous heart of the USPA had changed. Grim faced they remained, but there was something softer and more supplicating in their tone.

The familiar presentation wasted two hours of everyone's time and was followed by another hour of what they thought was useless question time. Then it was over and they were dismissed. Gently clicking the door shut to the Agency boardroom, Mitch found it difficult to conceal his delight. His mind was swimming with disbelief. The taste had blossomed into a gastronomical orgasm.

'You're fucking joking, it must be a dream, has to be,' Mitch exclaimed, feeling like running a victory lap up the runway. Or screaming at the top of his voice. Perhaps a dance of some sort. M itch tried to calm down and caught Jessy's eye, his voice hitting her like a rush of hot wind. 'Jesus, we've done it, we're on our way, we got it, we damn well got it!' He paused and revelled in the words he'd just spoken. 'Full funding for three years with an option on a further five years. And not a three month wait for a decision, the NSF made it on the spot. They said yes on the goddamn

19

spot. I didn't give us a chance, well not really, shit I can't believe it! They've had a complete change of heart.' Dumb fuckers, he thought, grinning evilly. They should have made the same decision years ago. Why now and not before, he wondered? He gazed at Jessy with piercing yet thoughtful eyes.

He fell silent and kept staring at Jessy, feeling suddenly uncomfortable, waiting for the words he could see were coming. He could see them written in her expression like black ink splashed on fresh snow. He watched her top lip quiver slightly. Not long now he thought. He watched her face closely, waiting for it to happen.

Jessy was dressed impeccably, makeup perfect, but her composure was clearly entering the final stages of terminal collapse. She swallowed heavily and added hoarsely, 'it's terrific Mitch, an unbelievable opportunity, but now that we've got the mandate I, er...feel a little dazzled at the task in front of us. Jesus Mitch, I'm not sure...I can go on with it, I'm not sure I'm up to it.' She shrugged and peered down at the featureless ivory floor, feeling the familiar needles burn into her mind, feeling them dig deeper with every self-defacing thought. Her misgivings had been swelling since the verdict was delivered, a verdict they both realised had been reached well and truly before they'd even stepped through the door. Before they'd stepped in the bloody car to get there actually.

Mitch paced along the bone white corridor and gaped through the dusty safety glass to the manicured gardens below. His voice was harsh and tortured and started with a guttural sigh, all pointers that those who knew him would have instantly recognised. They telecasted the depth of Mitch's frustration, more clearly than any overt display of temper. As a tell sign, they were quite distinct.

'We'll be backed by twenty five of the finest technicians and engineers on the globe, which includes Rhys and Sean. And we'll have the combined intellectual, not to mention engineering, grunt of NASA, USPA and AASSA. We're hardly on our own here Jess, they've rated Cygnus a Priority 12 project, that's as high as a nonmilitary op gets.' He looked at Jessy with a concentrated stare. 'They believe we can deliver the bird they're after, the one that will finally take us beyond the threshold, although I think they've always believed that.'

He paused and couldn't help but ponder what he'd just said. Why the sudden change of heart from USPA? Mitch assumed it stemmed from a legitimate belief in their PND technology, together with a rather furious rethink by Congress on the value of manned space initiatives. The latter, he knew, was largely due to the pressure applied by the President and his band of "Senatorial Persuaders" who came to be known around the nation's capital as Wilson's Military.

Under considerable coercion, Congress, wanted back in space. They were convinced of such by the technical merit of Mitch and Jessy's rapid transit machinery as "explained" to them by POTUS. He believed it would work and he wanted to push it. It had to be as simple as that. But why now and not before? He wondered, rubbing his chin hard, continuing to ponder what had been at the root of Wilson's brand new mindset. He had never once shown any interest in noncommercial space exploration, and that worried him. Mitch just hoped the President's "Many Worlds Bill" wasn't the result of naked desperation. That it didn't stem from one man's hunger to do it first, to be the presiding force at the moment when humanity laid eyes upon, and perhaps even touched, another world.

Other worlds in other stellar families would be well within reach inside the lifetime of an average human being. But even if it did follow from some blind unscientific lust, who really cared? Not them, if it meant they had a contract. Right? He knew he shouldn't, but he did care, despite trying his best to put it aside. He wanted the decision to be based on pure logical scientific assessment of their creation. To be the result of a thoughtful process voted on unanimously by a jury of world class scholars, without a thought for anything but the calibre of what they'd built. Of course, he knew that if it had been, it was probably the first time in history it was so. Mitch thought of Kennedy, and knew the US wouldn't have put their Apollo on the Moon until the 1980's without him, well and truly after Russia had slid the hammer and sickle into the soft talcum. Manned sojourns into space, by their very expensive nature, always seemed to need the propelling force of some charismatic and motivating leader. Situation normal, Mitch thought, thinking about Kennedy and the Moon, Jackson and Mars. Someone, and that meant POTUS, had to get hold of the dream and run with it.

Jessy glanced at her Geramo shoes and swallowed hard, 'maybe you should look for another co-designer.' She pursed her lips and narrowed her eyes, then backed away looking down at the tiles.

Mitch stared at her blankly, brows almost knitted together. 'Shit,' he barked, still staring at her. Jessy had all but designed the Cygnus engine herself. She was at least half of the intellectual property, probably more. Mitch needed her on board. Jessy was a required asset.

Everything seemed suddenly too bright, tilted somehow. Grabbing her, he walked her slowly down the corridor. 'Jesus, fuck,' he said out loud. One minute she was confident and self-assured, the next she was like a tubby teen in a tight outfit, scared, self-doubting and self-conscious. He stood back and struggled to believe it. In front of USPA's Funding Executive she was the epitome of an assured rocketry scholar, but now, he thought, now, God she was fucking frustrating.

Mitch looked at her and took a slow, deep breath. He knew what he had to do, he'd been there before. He pushed his hand into Jessy's and spoke softly, 'we're due in Florida in ten days to start refining and proving, and meeting with specification and material design engineers.' He paused again and moved closer, staring into Jessy's eyes from only a foot away. 'Think about the last fifteen years of sweat we've poured into this project. You can't turn your back on it now.' With that, Mitch turned on his heels and left and kept walking. Without looking back. He hoped to God she'd see sense, but wouldn't count on it happening.

Jessy watched him walk toward the elevator and punch the button with a clenched fist. She knew he was right, no doubt about it. She'd wanted this moment for as long as she could remember, had obsessed over it, dreamt about it, craved it with an almost sexual passion. And now that it was here, she felt distinctly unsure. She fingered her necklace and shook her head slowly. She needed more confidence, she'd known that for years, that was her. Take it or leave it.

Jessy toed toward the elevator and felt the rumble of a small Kasein IV rocket, pausing as its hypergols shook the building with a massive pulse of sound. She stopped and leant against the wall, feeling the power of the plasma boosters shake every cell in her body. Jessy gradually felt some of her energy returning. She knew she had to meet this thing head-on, or just give up and walk away, leaving everything behind, everything that ever meant anything in her life. Stay or go, the decision was pretty easy. Jessy was sweating even though her body was cold. Jessy knew what that meant.

The choice was straightforward but the decision was hard to make, because she could visualise the tiny ice flake it would create, the ice flake that would rapidly snowball into something she wasn't sure she could handle. At the moment, she was sure she couldn't handle it. Jessy couldn't let Mitch or the space agency down though, she knew that much also. But she was equally terrified of disappointing them, of committing to it and failing miserably. Imploding like a neutron star. In fact, she was absolutely mortified by the idea of failure and just hoped they, she, didn't fail.

By the middle of 2020, the flood of radiation from the dislocation in Centaurus was only a cosmic stones-throw from Earth. The photons were currently darting between snowballs in the Oort Cloud, that flimsy crown of comet stuff that pimpled the solar system like a shell. Nemesis itself was still almost three light years away. Thirty trillion kilometres. And incredibly, it was hurtling through the void at more than half the speed its own radiation was travelling at. More than half the speed of light. Bloody fast!

Despite being freed from the gravitons that had guided it so precisely through space, the path of the black hole remained almost identical to that of its tractored course. The dead star was still slicing toward the orbital plane of the planets, edge on; a path that would be occupied, at some time or other, by all but one of the Sun's family. Like wood ducks in a shooting gallery, many would be in for the shock of their lives … sitting ducks rife for annihilation.

The worst luck imaginable had dropped like a rare tumour on the inner worlds of Sol's precious family.

***

21

The Cygnus Interstar Program celebrated its first anniversary of full production. The Foundation Phase, forecast to take ten months, was on time and budget, and expected to wind up in less than three weeks.

Mitch and Jessica headed the project that had taken root near Woomera in Australia and would soon possess the focus of more than four hundred senior United Space personnel.

Unfamiliar technologies and exotic materials had elbowed the project to the barren hub of middle Australia. To one of the more isolated and dismal regions of the planet, hundreds of kilometres from any settlement and not far from the geographical bull's eye of the continent. The possibility of a massive fusion explosion or a major gravitational blow-through, whilst remote, was a threat that politicians and the USPA, not to mention AASSA, and the Alice, simply could not ignore.

A really rotten problem with the drive system, those in the know realised, would make Tunguska in Siberia look like a four-penny-bunger. If the worst happened, then Australia could look forward to its heartland being vaporised and replaced by a fractured red crematorium...an earthly Valles Marineris forged by technology gone horribly wrong.

Of course, the National Coalition immediately saw the fiscal benefit of the project and almost fell over itself in consenting to the USPA proposal. They blithely ignored the protests of the Greens and Native Title campaigners, not to mention the thunderous howls of local landowners. As one, they pointed a finger at the British snow-job that ruined adjacent Maralinga and Emu Field and killed a thousand Aborigines. To no one's surprise though, the Nationals got their project. Big money always wins. You have concerns? Okay, we'll give you another truckload of cash. That'll do it. Good boy, off you go.

***

The quantum and material basis of the Interstar engine was worthy, most believed, of a Nobel Prize. Of several of them in fact. Mitch and Jessy's creation had stunned the world of science into childlike disbelief. Most of them had placed the hopes for interstellar travel with some derivation of normal fusion energy. And while the Interstar certainly used fusion energy, it was anything but normal. Anything but simply detonating nukes to send a vessel on its way. Most reckoned the chances of an effective fusion technique were in the same box as trans-warp drive and safe antimatter engines. Quite simply, it wasn't going to happen. Ever. Or so they thought.

The revolutionary transit system that gave dazzling new hope was christened almost two decades before by Mitch and Jessy, as Pseudo-Novae Drive or PND. It was the quantum vault in technology which they and everyone else in the field knew was at the crux of making extrasolar travel feasible. They well realised that current boosters would simply not do the job. Travelling to the limit of conventional technologies it would take forty thousand years to travel to the nearest star, considered by most as a tad on the long side.

The superphysical marrow of PND was the Thermo gravity Breeder. A device with a similar outward guise to the miniature fusion reactors recently developed. The Breeder joined staccato pulses of extreme pressure with several billion megawatts of power from millions of exactingly aligned laser tubes. Within the almost perfect vacuum of the Breeder, superheated plasma collapsed into basketball sized artificial suns or pseudo stars. Nuclear fusion came and went inside these stars within thirty minutes. After fusion died, the Breeder's hundred million kilograms of pressure (per square centimetre) caused the dead stars to collapse inward to form tiny cores of ultra-condensed neutronium. From there, using femto timed neutrino bursts, an explosion was engineered along the lines of the greatest power source in the cosmos, the supernova.

The ceramo-carbide armor shield was designed to deflect the flow of particles away from the ship and offered the forward acceleration that in theory could propel the ship at close to Luminal speed. Deceleration would be achieved by simply reversing the direction of the ship. Brilliant and unimaginably super advanced; many thought this might be its major problem. The thing that would unravel everything. Maybe it would just explode. Few seriously believed that humanity had the nous to properly control the mechanics of supernovae, albeit very small ones, or the intense gravities and

22

densities of the collapsed neutronium. But they were wrong, because in theory at least they could handle it. Cygnus theory told them so.

On September 12th, preliminary testing of the Breeder kicked off at Woomera amid a fanfare worthy of an Olympic opening ceremony. Development and testing of a complete prototype would not commence until the Cygnus project was relocated to its own dedicated construction range near Moonbase II on the lunar farside. There, they could access the outer solar system and to limit danger to Earth when Cygnus was built. At least that's what they thought.

On farside Luna, the piecemeal construction of the first Interstar would begin early in the lunar summer of 2022. Assuming of course that all testing went to plan and there were no major delays. No disasters.

An entirely new USPA space technology facility was needed and indeed was well on the way to completion inside the post maria crater Mendeleev that hid on the side of the Moon that permanently shunned its cloudy blue parent. USPA took advantage of a moon that rotated synchronously with its mother, leaving 41 percent of it totally concealed from those on Earth, including the Mendeleev Crater which sat across the Lunar equator on the farside. The Earth would be totally protected from any goings-on within the crater.

Not only would Mitch and Jessy be confined there permanently for three years but so too would Rhys and Sean and four hundred other United Space specialists. They would eventually construct the first Interstar, concurrently designing and refining the innovative biological systems that would be needed for the hauntingly long stays in space they were planning.

Their maiden journey was scheduled to the red runt, toward the red dwarf known as Barnards Star in 2024, to eyeball the world they knew was there, a Super Earth, bigger than Earth but otherwise very similar. The round trip would take more than twenty years Earth time. A lot better than using conventional "plodding" technology which would take several thousand years to get there.

Humanity had finally committed itself to visiting some of the more interesting star systems on the outskirts of the Milky Way Galaxy. To journey to some of the friendly suns in the next suburb that blazed with the promise of untold revelation and discovery. They had no idea and would have had serious trouble accepting the fact that one of their neighbouring stars was coming to visit them.

***

During early August of 2020 a mighty river of ultraviolet, X-Ray and photons penetrated the solar system and speared toward the Sun at the speed of light. The first tendrils of the hard cosmic wind had punched through Neptune's bright methane clouds several hours ago. Engulfing the Moon, the hurricane would reach Earth in a little over a second.

Spanning forty trillion kilometres of space, the high energy gale had arrived, flooding the Earth with a potent but mostly invisible particle storm. In the bright afternoon sunshine of March 6th a fantastic new object blossomed in Earth's sky, a blinding beacon to the robotic eyes on Earth and in space that were staring permanently spaceward.

***

His eyes suddenly felt like ball-bearings, as though they might exit their sockets and dig holes in the terracotta floor. Ross Munro spun his head back to the screen and conceded that the crimson numerals were real. A glitch? He wondered, instantly knowing they weren't. Whatever it was, it was real, he could tell that much. It looked at first glance, correct. Way too strong, but right. Everything about the data was on the money, it was just the location and strength of the emanation that was difficult to reconcile. Still, the images being beamed to his visual cortex just didn't seem possible. Confusion stalled his senses for long seconds as he tried to digest what was dancing so casually in front of his eyes. He finally managed to organise his thoughts a bit and speak.

'Sonofabitch, what is…er, that?' Hardly an Einsteinian response he thought, pausing and moving his head closer to the monitor, pondering the crazy data. It was amazing, he drew in a breath as if drowning. 'Christ, check out the zeros on the EM counter...er, Hank?' His eyes were mortared to the real time display sprawled in front of him. He felt like all the fluid in his head had surged into his eyes. Ross felt his mind surge as he chewed on the figures being spat out by Xanadu. Munro was a microwave astronomer based on long term contract in Woomera, the high priest of the Xanadu census. Whatever he said, was right. About anything. He peered at it, the data looked right but it was too close...surely.

Knowing Ross rarely asked for an opinion on anything, let alone spoke with something approaching emotion, Hank almost jumped to the bank of computers that towered in front of him like a tremendous state of the art cockpit. His eyes gleamed with excitement.

Louder this time, Ross said, 'these, er...this radiation has just been picked up.' His nose was almost touching the terminal, so close his breath was frosting the screen. 'The interesting thing is that Xanadu was surveying this area for several hours before it sensed it. Er...what I'm saying is that this massive dump of energy has only just appeared in our region of space,' he looked around at the sea of eyes, 'like in the last forty-five minutes. Before that, well, nothing...it simply didn't exist. Wherever it came from, it's just arrived,' he said, raising his eyebrows and arching them, still glued to the monitor, seemingly waiting for it to change or to stop...or something.

Ross turned away from the console and stared dumbly at his comrade, too stunned to put his remaining thoughts into words. He needed to know the meaning of what was being delivered to them by their golden beetle that sat high above the forests of Zaire. And he needed to know right now. Any patience he might have had was lost on first sight of the astonishing data from Xanadu.

Hank had never seen Ross so patently bewildered and felt compelled to say something, anything, to break his frozen expression. His eyes were massive and staring. Munro was hovering above the terminal like a gull above hot chips, still gawking at the data. Now he was scratching his head.

'Well...okay, so what do you think we've got, neutron star, Xray binary, Seyfert cluster, what?' Hank knew it was none of those, but he said it anyway.

Ross swallowed and hesitated, his eyes staying wide and fixed. All of a sudden, they focussed and narrowed, like a lens suddenly resolving an object. 'No um...Hank, you're not hearing me.' Ross looked up at him and without blinking or making the slightest demand on his facial muscles, he said, 'Xanadu is telling me that the source is only a few light years away, right in our own backyard, and I'm telling you its huge...massive.' His eyes were like circular chunks of limestone. 'Xanny is being blinded by this thing, it's quite incredible...intriguing.' He whispered the last part of his sentence through lips pulled into a taut line, so tight they looked as though the blood had been entirely expelled.

Twenty other technicians in the Comtower had crowded around the incoming data. Ross and Hank were agog at the prospect of an awesome new discovery in their part of the sky, literally in *their* part of the sky. Hank was elbowing Ross, trying to best position himself in front of the data. Of course, they realised that every Xray detector in the southern hemisphere would be swamped by the gale from space. One that would no doubt kindle a massive surge of enquiry. Major cosmic discoveries were rare, discoveries so close to Earth, on the same street, were unheard of. The words Unique and Singular and Fame rifled through their minds like a wondrous, pulsing headache. They all knew they had something without peer here, something totally out of the box. Finally, something amazingly interesting.

Ben White looked as though he'd just fallen out of bed, from a great height. Head of radio astronomy and second in charge of the whole facility, he could've quite easily passed as a homeless vagrant. Unshaven and distinctly untidy, he entered the complex in a hurry and pushed his way to the front of what was now a pressing crowd, raising his voice to be heard above the racket. His first voice was more of a hack so he coughed to clear whatever was in there.

'Um...have you heard from Tom or Ray at NASA? Carl at United Space? They'd be receiving this from their online diagnostics.' He rubbed his forehead hard as he tried to think.

'They're probably still trying to fathom it,' Ross answered without looking away from the luminous numerals. 'I mean, what can it be? It's so damn close, but the radiation is almost pure Xray with a bit of gamma length and some radio. There doesn't seem to be any visible light, or at least not much. We're waiting on the okay to get Hubble's main widefield scope locked onto it, er…to confirm any visible lengths.' Ross stretched and held both arms above his head, pushing at the air.

Ben looked dumbfounded. The telltale creases pocked his forehead like contours on a steep cliff, his voice still raspy, 'um, yeah okay, good,' he offered, running a hand though his tangled hair, like it made a difference. 'We need optical confirmation of the source. Do we know exactly where it's located, you said it was a few light years away…' Ben looked unblinkingly at Ross, still trying to clear his throat, waiting for the answer he knew would blow his mind.

'Xanadu is telling us that it's coming from Centaurus, in the vicinity of…in fact right next to Rigil Kentaurus. Hubble will confirm it, assuming that whatever it is, is actually radiating something we can see. I assume it is from the data, but we'll need to wait and see.'

Ross finally looked away, stood up and walked toward the massive panes of steel reinforced glass, rubbing his eyes with clenched fists. Jesus Christ, he thought to himself. He looked out at the stunning early morning landscape, taking in the hundred different shades of chestnut and ochre. His eyes flicked up to the sky. What the hell are you, he puzzled?

'If it was a supernova, we'd know…I mean we'd be blinded and probably fried by it, given its proximity.' Ross said. 'It'd be brighter than the Sun for God's sake, so I think we can safely rule that out. Ross grinned but he quickly lost it when confronted by the sea of dour faces. Shit, he thought, what is wrong with them? They looked like mourners at a frigging funeral. 'Um…besides there's only stable, er…main sequence stars that close to Earth. It'd be billions of years before any of those blew their tops.' There was only shrugs and head shakes for as far as the eye could see. Ross shook his head, seemingly in sympathy. Nobody had any ideas they cared to voice, that was clear. Silence gripped the Comtower as the questions and the scenarios joined in an air of almost psychedelic expectation.

Mitch had been summoned from the scaled down Cygnus facility that now resembled a ghost town of empty compartments. Virtually all the technical and support infrastructure had been hauled to Kasakhstan for relocation to Mendeleev on Luna. He and a good many of the AASSA specialists were due to leave Earth next month to join Jessy and the others who were already enjoying the notorious "comforts" of Moonbase II.

Having been briefed on the situation in near space, Mitch was stunned. Like the others, he could only imagine what this new and very close celestial neighbour might be. Seated in the AASSA communications centre, Mitch was in animated discussion with his NASA and USPA counterparts, Tom Stewart and Ray Clarke. Having pinpointed the location of the source, tentatively named CX1 (Centaurus Xray source 1) all agreed that both facilities should immediately begin hard analysis. They knew they had something out of the box.

Optical, microwave, and specific Xray and infrared eyes in the southern sky began detailed observations and assessments of CX1. Along with the networking of AASSA and United Space, the Global Institute of Astrophysics and the Super coms at NASA/AMES were all monitoring, detecting, collating and interpreting the data to fast track the identification of the astonishing object. The global space network was quickly smothered by an almost surreal feeling of nervous excitement. It was the new and the unexplained and the extraordinary that most within the industry sought, and many believed t their dreams had abruptly materialised, right there at the end of their telescopes.

Mitch and a number of others had a fair idea what they were dealing with, or at least they thought they did. All but a couple of possibilities were quickly ruled out by collective studies of its radiant qualities and mass. Continuing analyses would doubtless, he thought, define the fantastic new object beyond any question.

He and his colleagues were stunned by the unexpected birth of this wondrous radiation blizzard in very adjacent space. By stunned he meant shocked to the core.

25

3

Centaurus X1

'Intellectual capacity is no guarantee against being dead wrong.' ~ *Carl Sagan*

'Mitch, this is Brian Gates from United Space, are you ready for us?' You fucking better be, he thought, tapping his fingers on his thigh, wondering how the hell he got roped into this bullshit. Mitch stepped to the head of the massive AASSA boardroom table and fingered the image activate button. A picture of the NASA/USPA boardroom in Washington dropped into view on a high resolution two metre square Mercury screen.

'We're all here Brian,' Mitch toned as he motioned everyone to their seats. 'Be seated gentlemen.' He could feel the sweat break out above his top lip. Christ, what a frigging nightmare. A bunch of fuckers, the whole lot of them, he thought grimly. He looked for a friendly face around the massive table and couldn't find a single one. Fuck, he thought again, staring at them. A crowd of massive indifference stared back.

The United Space facilities of AASSA and NASA were linked for a debate on the "Nature and Implications of Object CX1". Senior scholars and diplomats from the USPA nations were waiting nervously to ferry details back to their respective Governments. As were numerous Heads from the Agency's network facilities at Stennis, JPL, Toulouse, Capetown, Toyama, Ningpo and Gorki.

The director of the Astrophysical Council was there as were four members from the SSEC and eight controllers from Spaceguard. Not to mention the Assistant Secretary of Defense and chiefs from the National Science Foundation, the Science Advisory Committee and the National Security Council. The interest was intense, the concern global.

Few of those present knew much about CX1, only that it existed, was somewhere close in space, and had an odd, catchy name. The Russian Consul thought it sounded like a new age smart weapon, like some laser guided biological horror. He was a fuckwit in the truest sense of the word. It was a predictable response most thought, given the effect of decades he'd spent buried like a dog in a Soviet Gulag, carrying out covert EMP research. The dick could barely see a few inches in front of himself, and had glasses so thick they put a Coca-Cola bottle to shame.

The USPA had already alerted the United Nations, in particular the Security Council, to the possible need for a delicate global release on the implications of the almost naked eye object. Thus far they'd managed to counter the information, most of it misinformation, that had crept into the public domain. Anything, and that meant anything, related to the object's attitude was classified by the recent Curtain Raiser Protocol, restricting it to the few heavyweights who were cleared for Level 12 intelligence.

But despite the penalty for disseminating the data, and the relative few who knew the real face of CX1, some fragments had clawed their way into the media that were pretty much on the money. At this stage they merely spoke of a mighty Xray source, nature not certain, but known to be highly mobile, and very likely to be a black hole that had somehow taken up an intimate residence about Proxima Centauri and was currently shredding it. The star would take millions of years to disappear. Faint gravitational waves were also detected by LIGO and other detectors in the US and Europe when CX1 was born, when spacetime itself alternately squeezed and stretched according to a small law called general relativity devised by Albert Einstein.

The hows and whys of CX1 had stirred a horde of bizarre theories. If one cared to look on YouTube there was plenty to see. All of it wrong. Most assumed it was moving as a result of a supernova kick. No one could have guessed that its arrival near Sol was owed to something more

26

preposterous than even the wildest guesses. The second most accepted idea was the Catapult Thesis, that the black hole had been disgorged at high speed by the explosion of a binary companion, from another area of space. From another galaxy probably.

The fact that the Agency was being vague and evasive had injected it with an irresistible inertia, one they could have done without. USPA knew it had to act quickly to avoid not only a catastrophe should the precise nature of the object become known, but also to avoid a massive embarrassment to itself, one from which they would likely never recover. After all, they were trying to hide the truth. The former was their biggest worry, but not by much. Their reputation was very important to them. And it was being eroded, bit by bit.

Mitch remained standing behind the podium, facing his AASSA colleagues and the grim image of Brian Gates and the USPA Executive in Washington. The light in the room increased a notch and he gulped, a dry painful swallow of thick atmosphere. Fuck me, he thought. Here we go. Looking at them, it was like exchanging stares with statues, arranged around a massive oak table.

'Welcome to the subject of CX1,' Mitch started. 'I remind you all that this information is protected by Curtain Raiser Protocol and Government Act. Dissemination in any form is punishable by life imprisonment. Sorry to be so formal but I know you understand.' He made eye contact with no one. He didn't really give a toss if he upset anyone, which he knew he would. He'd been called a "fucking Aussie prick" before, and was sure this wouldn't be much different, probably no different.

Mitch opened his folder and shuffled the contents nervously. He felt his heartbeat increase, could feel it throbbing painfully below his Adam's apple. Clearing his throat, he continued in a voice that was ominous and low. From NASA's perspective, Mitch was sure he looked like a lunatic, with long eyebrows and a number two up top.

'The aim of this meeting is to exchange views on the nature of this object and importantly, on its implications for us, and Earth as a whole.' He shuffled papers and took a deep breath again. Fuck me, he repeated silently, peering at them. He wished he hadn't. They looked like they wanted to kill him.

'Whilst we've all gotten the same data, it's likely that different ideas and theories have emerged, although our previous briefings seem to suggest that we're pretty much in agreement. For the benefit of those who aren't familiar with what we are dealing with, I'll commence with an overview.' He continued to look around the mighty table at the sombre faces.

The smoke-filled boardroom at NASA abruptly assumed a new air. Those previously reading or talking, all stared as one at their AASSA counterparts. Mitch hesitated and peered down at his red folder titled "Centaurus X1". He glanced up and saw a forest of wooden faces, and continued. 'Shit', he said quietly but emphatically to himself, just discernible through the Zoom audio.

'CX1 was found by Xanadu three months ago and was noted as an entirely new and extremely close, and mighty galactic Xray source. Not only previously undiscovered, CX1 was previously not there, that is to say the Xray source in Centaurus literally only turned on a few years ago. Xanadu was looking at that part of space when the first threads of electromagnetic energy struck Earth.' He paused briefly, swallowed, then coughed and resumed, slightly more confidently and louder than before. 'The radiation is pouring from a close stellar region a bit more than a light month from Alpha Centauri A and B, only a few short light years from us. Of course, the entity itself is closer than that due to the time taken for its radiation to get to Earth...and the fact that CX1 is very obviously moving.'

There were a few scattered exhalations after Mitch's last comment. Not everyone knew it was moving and by moving they correctly took it to mean moving radially, not orbitally. 'Dumb fucks', he thought, although this time they seemed to have cottoned on. If these guys were in charge of global security, God help us all, he thought, thinking of NASA taping over the Moon Landing or the Austrian army attacking itself. Then there was putting flammable gas in the Hindenburg history was littered with monumental fuck ups, that should never, ever be repeated. These guys needed to be kept away at all costs. Otherwise, history might be repeated, right here.

Mitch continued, 'Analyses have shown that it is a huge producer of rapidly variable sinusoidal X-rays with lesser gammas, some visible light and the occasionally violent radio flare. Clearly a catastrophic and energetic object, although no gravitational waves have been detected. Several ideas were considered as current candidates for the powerhouse.'

Surveying the myriad faces in front of him, he saw all eyes were fixed on him. No one was talking or reading or writing. There was only the drone from the straining air conditioner that was doing a piss-poor job of providing fresh air.

'Several observations have led us to an inescapable conclusion. We've determined the mass of the unseen companion, noted its gravitational wave and massive Xray production and are aware that it turned on without prior detection. All these factors taken in conjunction with optical studies by Hubble and James Webb have enabled us to reach an assured conclusion.' Mitch could feel the collective, unblinking gaze from his colleagues tearing into him like red-hot pokers. Waiting for him to say it.

'Gentlemen...what we have in our very own piece of space is a black hole that for one reason or another has taken up a short period orbit around the star V645 Cen, Proxima Centauri, and is trying to eat it but won't complete its job until it well and truly leaves Earth vicinity.' Take that, he thought, looking at the pensive faces, stepping away from the podium, seeing the shocked look on some of the faces. It was classic. *Take that you fuckers*, he repeated silently.

Whilst half those present knew what they were dealing with, both boardrooms broke into animated discussion. To hear the news within the formal USPA confines seemed to add weight to its significance even for those who already knew what had moved into the neighbourhood. Both rooms were a cacophony of amorphous racket, voices that summed to nothing more than a jarring clatter. It was rapidly turning into a circus.

'Brian...er, can we continue?' Mitch asked loudly. Both rooms quickly fell silent. They all wanted more, despite the collective anxiety about what that more might be. Mitch felt nervous about the rest of the information he had to reveal. Very few of those present knew it, at least to the extent that he did. He spoke slowly and deliberately, trying to keep his voice level and even, failing, he reckoned. He was sure he sounded like a goofball. Still, he had little choice other than to continue, to try and sound and appear like he was in control of the situation.

'We can detect the invisible companion for the same reasons we've been able to detect the other two hundred confirmed black holes, the closest of which was several thousand light years away. Gas is being torn from the star and wrestled through a narrow La-Grangian exit and into the domain of the black hole, detected first by the Event Horizon Telescope and later, Hubble and various other detectors. The captured gas forms a rotating belly-disc and when the inner rings slow down, they spiral inward...into oblivion and heat up. It's the flood of X-rays from this annihilation that have allowed us to "see" it. And so it is with our Centaurian source, which has somehow grabbed V645 and is forcing it through a full revolution every two days.' Mitch looked up to make sure they were listening. All eyes, like a sea of shining china plates, were glued on him. Silence was absolute. Even the noise from the air conditioner seemed to have evaporated.

'The most confusing aspect of the source, one that we have only recently detected, is its movement. CX1 has a radial velocity of over half the speed of light and its trajectory, should it remain unchanged, will eventually carve a path through the solar system.' He knew that'd get 'em.

There was commotion now. Few knew of this precise interpretation apart from Brian, Mitch and two or three others. They'd been told to remain silent. Members of the NASA Executive began rifling questions at him along with several of his own AASAA people.

Most of them were demanding to know why they hadn't been forewarned. The meeting was starting to turn ugly, and only emphasised what they could expect if the release of the information wasn't handled in an appropriate fashion. In fact, the decision to release information at all, was anything but assured. What in God's name would the consequences of such a release be, especially if it wasn't sweetened? Mitch shuddered.... Disaster.

28

Order was restored and Brian Gates took over. His deep set eyes, grey as a naval warship peeped through mounds of wrinkled flesh that were hairier than his cranium. His expression bespoke drama. His voice was slow and deep, full of gravel.

'We don't have to tell you that CX1 will have a catastrophic impact on our solar system. If its current path remains stable and we have no reason to believe it won't, CX1 will impact the plane of the planets, cutting it at only one or two degrees.' He paused, apparently contemplating what he was about to say. We're fucked, he thought to himself. 'In other words,' he continued, 'we've been dealt a mountain load of bad luck because it's heading toward the solar system almost directly edge on and will pass beneath Pluto and Charon at the farthest edge of our planetary group.

No doubt it will affect them, maybe disrupting their orbit, maybe destroying them. The position of Neptune and Uranus on their ecliptics should leave them unharmed. CX1 will then comfortably miss Saturn and Jupiter but will probably, almost certainly, come extremely close to Mars. The planet will probably be hit directly and annihilated.' Do you get it now, he felt like screaming? They all looked so damn calm. Grim but calm.

Mitch was struck by a sudden crystal-vivid image of asteroids and dying dinosaurs. He could see millions of burning, asphyxiating animals suffering the excruciating wrath of space. Extinction. They've got nothing on us, he thought. This time the whole damn world was in trouble. And they were sitting there like rows of Howdy Doody puppets.

Brian was all too aware of the next planet in line, although at that point it would be on the opposite side of the Sun to Mars. He hesitated and looked down. Grabbing at a glass of water he missed and knocked it to the floor. It smashed with an emphatic crash. He'd deftly managed to add to the tension. Good one, dickhead, he thought instantly.

'Sorry about that,' Brian quipped.

Feeling more composed, with a cough and a half sidestep, Mitch continued. 'Having passed, at best, extremely close to Mars, it will miss the Sun by about thirty million kilometres and pass out to the other side of the great circle. Here it will miss Mercury, pass close to Venus, and then CX1 will encounter Earth.'

He sucked in a deep breath of superheated air. 'Having taken account of likely perturbations imposed by planetary masses and assuming its trajectory stays the same, all our computations agree that the black hole and Proxima will pass within approximately half a million kilometres of here.' He raised both arms to forty-five degrees, adding fearful emphasis to what here really meant. *Really fucking close*, he actually wanted to say.

Sweet Jesus Almighty. Those unaware of the danger glanced at their colleagues, locking eyes here and there, mutely conceding a fathomless, disbelieving terror.

'...the likely scenario is that we will lose Mars, maybe Venus, maybe Pluto and Charon and I would suggest, the Earth Luna system. The entire solar system will probably be shattered by the profound distortion that we can expect simply by it passing reasonably close to the planets. And it looks as though it will come far closer than reasonably close. You must remember that this thing brings with it an unimaginably cavernous gravity well that will buckle all dimensions of space in every way conceivable. Earth might be devoured and annihilated outright, or if luck is on our side, we might be spun off into space to die a slow, freezing death. Or take up an orbit around the black hole and be fried by Proxima. There is no point diluting the situation we face. These are the facts according to the Super coms, no more, no less.' 'We're fucked,' he repeated to himself, so no one else could hear.

Brian's expression was as bleak as a lunar mare. 'Gentlemen, the picture for Earth looks grim. His eyes were fixed on his AASSA counterparts. A close encounter with a black hole such as that at the heart of CX1 will rip the planet apart. Tidal forces, the thermal impact of V645 and a radiation hurricane leaves us with very little hope. Failing a change in its trajectory, Earth is terminal unless we can come up with a way of deflecting or destroying it. And doing it while it remains in deep space. I mean doing it as soon as we can.' Brian looked at his own people, then at Mitch, his face tightening, with the hint of a shrug.

29

The planet had long known the risks of a nemesis from above, a rogue asteroid or a comet that could erase life in a heartbeat. It had happened before. Earth's history was pocked with monumental extinctions wrought by celestial death chunks. They all knew that. But now they had Spaceguard and Legacy looking out for the planet. Dedicated orbiters that were watching for potential Extinctors, mapping their trajectories and doing all they could, but who the hell could have foreseen this? This was out of their league. Comets maybe, asteroids possibly, but black holes and stars? There was no avoiding those.

How the hell do you shift something like that? He wondered. The most prodigious force in the Universe. His mind pulsed with a depthless horror. Was there any way out? Were they really fucked? Equally, he realised that they couldn't just concede the planet, the solar system.

Mitch stood back up quickly and cleared his throat. 'We know our enemy and realise it is something unutterably powerful. We face the greatest test of all, the greatest test of our technology in history, and if we fail, then quite simply we are lost. The stakes could not be higher gentlemen.'

The balding Chinese Consul Yuan Bo jumped from his chair. 'Correct me if I'm wrong, I'm not a scientist, but a black hole is just that, invisible, and has the weight of what, ten suns or more maybe? Is there any hope at all, or should we perhaps prepare our people for the end?' He looked truly mortified. Shit-scared actually. Yuan looked ridiculous with his hair slicked back, and appeared genuinely insane with his wild eyes and long beard. He was, however, to be respected.

The Japanese Ambassador Kamasiki nodded animated agreement, more in the hope of eliciting a positive response, some sort of answer. He was looking for a panacea to their talk of doom, instead of the horrible explications that were flowing like an alpine rapid in thaw. None were forthcoming. The presidential aid from ECON, Jeffrey LaHore, started speaking as he was moving to stand. He directed himself toward Brian Gates. He wanted answers, assurances if possible, anything positive no matter how small. Something to grab hold of. Anything encouraging to report back to POTUS.

'Does your USPA have the technology to deal with this situation? Is there a plan in place or being developed to defend Earth against this thing? His eyes were initially closed, then gaped at his AASSA counterparts. 'I think you should speak frankly here, everyone present has security clearance for G12 information.' His eyes roamed the sea of faces as he waited for a response. Yes? He felt like screaming. They all looked like they wanted to ask something.

Mitch motioned to Brian that he would field the question. Discussion of Earth's response to the threat was next on his agenda anyway. Mitch started speaking but his voice failed him, catching on his thickened throat and dribbling out as a floury rasp. He took a sip of water and carefully replaced the glass, apologising as he did so.

'We have a plan that could nullify the threat. Tom Stewart and Ray Clarke of NASA and myself, Rhys Volkers and Sean McKay have developed a strategy that could work, that we believe will work. The Supercoms at Marshall and Discover at Goddard give us a thirty-five percent chance of success.'

LaHore jumped back to his feet and was joined in a chorus of splutterings. '...thirty-five percent,' he exploded, 'you're saying that you will probably fail and Earth will be destroyed...terrific, a whole thirty-five percent, good plan, perhaps we should release that to the public!'

'Christ Mitch, we need more hope than that,' Trent Harmon pleaded, wiping sweat from his brow.

Australia's Vice President pried his ample rear from the Pelto chair. 'We need a better plan... this is unacceptable, tell me there's more to the idea. None of us will agree to it, there has to be a better solution, thirty-five percent, forget it.' His straining eyes and bulging forehead said it all, as did the ruby red flush that covered his face. He looked unhappy to say the least.

Mitch boomed, 'okay, enough! The story is not as bad as you think. Once we've built the vessel and successfully booted PND, the Cray odds blow out to almost sixty-five percent. As far as we're concerned the odds for success of this mission are sixty-five percent. They're the figures that should be released, if any figures need to be released.' He glared at Brian.

'What are the specifics of your plan Mitch?' LaHore groaned. He wasn't sure he wanted to know, hoping like hell this guy was as good as he'd been told.

Mitch's eyes narrowed to slits, he grabbed the side of the podium tight. The light in the room was suddenly blinding. 'You're all familiar with the Cygnus project. Some of you are scheduled to begin transport to the Moon in a few weeks to join the Generation Phase. The Cygnus vehicle will form the infrastructure for the project we have designated as Earthshield, our primary defense.' Only defense, he knew. If it failed, they failed.

Kamasiki from Japan spoke softly, '...if this CX1 is travelling toward us then shouldn't we be building the rocket now, I mean how long have we got, it makes me feel nauseous knowing this thing is out there and heading straight for us.' Like everyone else his mind was besieged with numbing images of global apocalypse. 'Shouldn't we be doing it now?' he added. Kamasiki was rigid and wobbling, apparently ready to drop.

'I'll give you some figures on that Massey,' Mitch soothed, loosening his grip on the podium a bit. 'For reasons entirely beyond our understanding, CX1 is travelling at almost sixty percent light speed. Clearly it was disgorged by a very energetic something. The object we see in the sky, the X-rays and so on, are about four lightyears away and although its actual location in space is closer now, we do have time. We are currently seeing the radiation produced in the first few months after the birth of CX1 but the object itself has travelled for a further four years at over half Luminal. It's now only about two lightyears from Earth.' Fuck me,' he thought, it sounded close. Really close. He'd managed to scare himself, so God knows how the population generally would react.

Moans and groans were audible from both camps. Holy God, Kamasiki thought bleakly. Despair and dread continued to wash over him. It was getting closer…fast.

Mitch countered, '...we still have a further four years before impact gentlemen and perhaps longer, er... hell it may deviate, who knows.' Like pigs will fly, he reckoned.

Most looked decidedly unimpressed by his last comment. Mitch glanced down at the plush pile, unable to hold the gaze of the staring masses in front of him.

'And for this vain hope we should be thankful?' Yuan asked, bounding to his feet, looking like a crazy version of Jim Carrey in The Mask.

As much as he disliked Yuan, he was correct.

Mitch continued. 'It is planned that Cygnus will have a close encounter with CX1 at a lateral distance of twenty million kilometres. It is also planned that this encounter will happen a full lightyear from home. We have until 10 November to construct the vessel and depart Luna. From there the trip will take seventeen months at sixty percent Luminal. With time to accelerate and decelerate this will put Cygnus where it needs to be, one light year from Earth. By November 2051 the craft will be close enough to deploy its phalanx pod that will deliver four hundred individual three-thousand megaton auto-track warheads. The plan is to detonate the nukes a thousand kilometres above the inner-coronal equator of the star. With the radial speed of CX1 in mind, the necessity for an exactingly precise delivery of the fusion weapons cannot be overstated. Weapons delivery will test our technology equally as much as the construction of Cygnus and its successful piloting across the threshold of the heliosphere.'

'And this will work Mitch?' Harmon asked. Mitch just stared at him. He resisted saying 'fucked if I know'…just.

'Even the Discover Supercomputer at Goddard doesn't understand the complexities of CX1 because we don't, so they can't really provide an accurate judgment. However, we believe the shock front from a million megatons of TNT if precisely directed at Proxima will shift the trajectory by a significant fraction of an arc. Such a change will be more than enough gentlemen. The Sun's family will be spared, but of course there can be absolutely no guarantees here you understand.' They didn't have a clue, but the suggestion of something positive was welcomed.

Brian took over, and gave Mitch a small salute. 'We are entering brand new territory, black holes and humanity have no business doing business, but we should at least thank God that we're as advanced as we are. If we weren't, we would be irresolvably doomed.' He paused and drew in a deep breath. 'The USPA has the ultimate say on any course of action involving space so I can tell you that what we have outlined here is the course of action that will be instituted to fulfill Earth-shield to save our planet. You are all reminded that the information discussed here can only be conveyed to those that hold the appropriate security status. We know the penalties for breaching these laws. The United Nations Priority Team will be advised of our discussions. It will be strongly suggested that a general release be made by USPA to the effect that the Cygnus mission is scientific and investigative only. The real nature and trajectory of CX1 will be kept under wraps for as long as possible. All observatories, optical and microwave, and all Spaceguard facilities in both hemispheres including McMurdo Sound will be data suppressed and networked, of that you can be sure.' Everyone present had "heard" rumours of sanctions required to maintain the ruse, and everyone knew the rumours were probably true, despite the furious denials.

'The Cygnus Interstar Project or CIP is now priority 1,' Mitch said as Brian resumed his seat and sipped from a new glass of water. All personnel involved in the project, including those who will soon be added, will be advised of the new date for lunar relocation. Cygnus must be up and running on Mendeleev within seven weeks. Jessica tells me that all external vacu-structure is complete and extra accommodation is already available at Moonbase II and on Copernicus.' He looked at Jessy and nodded.. Mitch then gazed back at the suits. He distractedly thanked all those present and stressed his confidence in their ability to deal with the celestial nemesis, although he found it difficult to muster any real enthusiasm. The meeting was closed and the video link terminated.

'Christ almighty.' Mitch muttered as the screen went blank and he took his seat. He was staring at Jessy, exhausted. Both camps were left to ponder the possible extinction of Earth and everything they called home.

32

4

Mission

'Somewhere, something incredible is waiting to be known.' ~ *Carl Sagan*

Hugging the dead talcum, its geometricity was alien to the barren meteor sculpted moonscape. Mendeleev was an oasis of life that cowered in the midst of an airless and sterile desert; desolation born from the same dusty cloud as the hidden terrestrial cradle. This was Earth's poorer, not so lucky cousin.

The base was a low rise of silver and gray that shimmered in the glare from a Sun that hung almost directly overhead, naked and dazzling. Not bad for the dark side of the Moon.

Inextricably bound to Moonbase II was the new Cygnus Interstar Complex that now accounted for more than sixty percent of its total area. The entire facility hid within a massive impact crater, blasted out when a chondrite meteoroid hammered Luna more than seven million centuries ago. Now, the area was stable and flat and in its proximity were some of the most valuable, and unusual deposits of metallic ores on the Moon. Possibly in the solar system. Possibly anywhere. All were crucial to the Cygnus and Earthshield efforts. They desperately needed the metal.

Three mineral deposits were being actively mined within only a hundred kilometres of the base, all of them giving up precious and base metals in the form of extravagantly rich primary sulfides. These were the astonishing Mendeleev 1, 2 and 3 mines that were all linked to Moonbase by the newly upgraded Lunarail Transrail Network.

One of the more exciting discoveries ever made, on the Moon or elsewhere, had been laid bare at the recently topped Mendeleev 3 mine. Located by Tycho's Orbital Gravimet Sensor, the orebody was found to come within thirty metres of actually outcropping on the lunar surface. Most couldn't give a toss, but it was significant.

At some point in the Moon's history, it was assumed, rightly or wrongly, that it rose to the surface. When the lode was cut and broken for inspection, its bizarre nature was revealed. On Earth, Mitch was the first to hear of the astonishing find via AASSA's telemetry link with the geosynchronous Eaglehawk 2. To say he was astounded was an unholy understatement. He was completely and utterly flabbergasted.

The head of the orebody consisted of typical lunar KREEP. No surprise there. But there was a surprise below the surface, because the basalt had been unexpectedly interfered with, found by the first muckers as a weathered and honeycombed parcel of bizarre manganese gossan. Oxides! The question was obvious and the implication thunderous. How had this pile of rock been so eroded on a moon where human theory stated that liquid water and oxygen had never been present in measurable quantities? Mitch's buzzing mind didn't know, but he couldn't help wonder. The cavities in the gossan were brimming with spectacular crystal groups, suggestive of richly oxidized fluids, water and very slow and stable depositional processes. But how could that be?

Mitch had a keen interest in mineralogy and remembered some of the stunning crystal groups he'd seen and photographed. The specimens dragged from this unique deposit were sent on to the Smithsonian, who like everyone else, were clambering for more.

Research into the genesis of this complex chemical wonderland had been suspended by the need to divert all resources and brainpower to the Cygnus Project. But it was clear to Mitch (and most others) that at some time over the past several billion years, the orebody had bathed naked in a watery, even humid environment. It was the how's and why's that were incomprehensibly intriguing. The oxidized zone suggested that Luna may have once, perhaps in highly restricted areas, perhaps everywhere, been somewhat Earthlike. Of course, most refuted the suggestion outright. It was madness! Not on the Moon. Apparently, it was dead and always had been. Like hell it was! At some point, it was alive.

Was it a leftover from a Moon that had a lavish atmosphere billions of years ago? Buried to remain undisturbed for billions of years? Undisturbed that is, until dug up by the curious people from the next rock down. These were the questions that filled Mitch's mind, haunted him and kept him awake at night. But the answers were somewhere beyond his fingertips and always would be. Now they had to wait until, or if, Nemesis was foiled before they could get back to the strange treasure of M3. Mitch still thought about it every now and then. During the depths of night, he sometimes fantasized about being let loose in the mine with his Esuit, his geological pick and his Hardipack knapsack. Priorities, he reminded himself. Priorities.

***

Ecstasy. Jessy could feel her senses gathering momentum as she savoured the chilled champagne. It slid down her throat like nectar. Such delicacies were hellishly rare on any of the lunar colonies, but especially so on Moonbase II on the farside. Food drops or any drops were rare and horrendously unreliable. She was perched in Mitch's quarters along with Rhys Volkers, Sean McKay and Mitch himself. It was early in October 2020. They were all shit-scared.

The pressure hatch made a sound like beer being thrown on a campfire. Kevin Yorke ambled through from a dark corridor. Officially, he was the CEO of the base but he was more than that to himself at least. Kevin's self-image was altogether too healthy, despite greying hair and a decent paunch. Commonly referred to as commandant, Yorke was a power freak with a zealous desire to control everyone and everything on farside. He was affectionately known as the Fuhrer of farside. Less affectionately as Hitler.

The five senior Cygnus personnel were in Mitch's quarters for a final debrief after nine months of stress and frustration that was Foundation on Mendeleev. Kevin slumped into a chair near the vacu-glass plate, catching a fleeting glimpse of a starkly beautiful moonscape.

It stretched beyond the window like a pallid canvass, stippled with a thousand tallow tones. Ishtar B, the bone-white radio telescope was vivid in the near distance, its gigantic ear cocked upward toward the shining cluster of Ursa Major. In the distance was the primary crater lip that led to the uplands of the Aeria plateau. Further away was star filled space with Syrius or the Dog Star on show. It was truly a beautiful sight.

'Kevin, this champagne is wonderful,' Jessy whispered with a measured smile, smiling slowly. 'You must be over the moon to break it out of the vault.' She gazed at the contents of her glass, and then up at Mitch, smiling. She felt good. Jessy also liked the irony of her statement.

Those involved in CIP had been christened by the Press as Cygnans, a name that had instantly stuck and one they'd gradually warmed to. After all, they mused, they belonged to the same extended family, dysfunctional as it might have been at times. Although isolated by the distance of space, they were united inexorably with those back on Earth by a single-minded purpose, like a family of synapses in a collective brain. A brain that had been purpose built to save their species. And like family, some of them really pissed each other off. Some so much so, they wished they'd go back to Earth, and somehow be spaced along the way.

'You've all accomplished great things,' Kevin said, casting his red-rimmed eyes over those in the room. He was stunned. 'I'm still amazed that this engine actually seems to work, or not so much that it works but that we've got the technology to control the energy source. I've gotta tell you I still find it hard to believe.' He shook his head in disbelief. 'The whole damn thing, the principles, the design, the power. Christ, it's is so far ahead of anything we've ever dealt with,' he locked eyes with Mitch for a second. 'Or for that matter anything we've ever thought of before. Guess I'll get over it eventually.' Doubt it, he thought to himself straight away, glancing out the window at the Mel, an escape vehicle that dominated the near distance.

Mitch chewed on what Kevin had said. 'Anything you'd ever thought of,' he corrected, his left eyebrow going up, as if to say "you're kidding". 'The only amazing thing is that we've had so few teething problems during testing.' He felt like touching wood, or signing the cross on himself. Mind you, they had a shitload of time to theorise and think about it, and it was still all he thought about…until this.

Jessy watched Mitch speak and could feel the desire tingling in her toes, the result of several glasses of champagne. She noticed, not for the first time, just how damn good he looked.

Mitch stood as he spoke, running his hand down his crinkled shirt. 'Our revised deadline for lunar egress is November 28th …that's twenty-two days from now. We've scrutinized every atom of the engine's operation and it's passed every test, leading Failsafe to be reasonably confident of its performance in space. Of course, nothing can be guaranteed, we know that. Given more time, perhaps it could be firmed up, but with Foundation so shortened we can only go with best guesses and trust that they're right, that the engine will perform as designed and work as tested.' The slightest hint of uncertainty marred his features, Mitch wondered if he sounded as unsure as he felt. He hoped not. Sounding confident was the least he could do for his crew, even if he felt anything but.

'What about the deflection system?' Rhys asked quietly, blinking as if paying very, close attention to what Mitch was about to tell him.

'Kevin tells me that the hydrogen modules are being loaded as we speak. The whole shebang will be completed inside two days. The Project should be on standby by November 20th. We'll be issuing a further revised launch date tomorrow after we confer with our thermo fusion people. They're working nonstop to meet launch schedule.' The expression in his eyes changed to something a little more pensive. He stopped and let out a long sigh, wondering how it was going to pan out.

Mitch's quarters fell every bit as quiet as the pressure-less vacuum that hung beyond the steel and boron four pane vacuglass. Everyone in the room felt the crushing pressure of the realization. Of the knowledge that the fate of the planet, the fate of their civilization, probably rested with the achievements made during Foundation. Only nine months, Jessy brooded, wondering how the hell they'd managed to finish it, and do it pretty much on schedule, a schedule that was expected to need several air brushings along the way. But incredibly, they'd finished on time.

It sounded impossible, but she knew it was never really in doubt, the motivation for success was existence. Still, it only seemed like yesterday that Lunaway Verne had dropped her onto the colossal ashen punchbowl that was Mendeleev.

The Interstar was ready, what was done was done and they had precious little time to make any significant changes. None really. Jessy just hoped it had all been done precisely. She'd overseen a lot of the work and was sure it had been, but her doubts lingered…serious gut wrenching doubts that stirred something horrible and black inside her. Jessy didn't want to get inside Cygnus. She was sure she'd never see the outside again.

No one was sorry that their work on the Project had finished. Dealing with constant pressure, ridiculous deadlines, the unfamiliarity of the systems, the new techniques (to many, crazy techniques) and the strange multiphase lubricants and odd new alloys. All with the suffocating knowledge of the consequences of failure. It was crushing.

It was a fucking nightmare, and to no one's surprise, more than twenty people had collapsed and been evacuated, ferried to Medi-plex on Freedom, where most of them still remained in varying states of distress. Nine people had died in the nine months, one a month, not from accidents but from stress related disorders. Strokes and cardiac arrests mainly, brought on by long hours, broken sleep and unrelenting stress. Pussies, Sean thought, pretty sure most were bullshitting after the work simply got too hard.

Conflict was daily baggage in the crowded CIP Zone on Moonbase II. Irritability and outright anger amongst the Cygnans had been growing almost exponentially, but thankfully seemed to be easing as the deadline approached. Because with it came the warm realization of completion. And freedom, short term though it might be if they failed. Then it would be death at wholesale prices. Everything would go.

Kevin got up and stretched noisily. 'Okay, that's it then,' he grunted, standing up and nodding toward Mitch. 'I'll see each of you in Cygnus 4 at 1900. We can spend some informal time together before the launch.' He chuckled to himself. 'Won't that be bloody novel.' He smiled widely and moved toward the vacuum plate which slid back and only partially disappeared into the wall of Mitch's quarters.

'I'd really prefer to go to my quarters and sleep,' Jessy said quietly, knowing it wasn't going to happen. The sentiment was echoed by all in the room. A good night's sleep was something none of them had enjoyed for the better part of a year.

'I agree, but we have to put in an appearance. I know you've said your goodbyes but I think we should at least show up, we said we'd be there.' Kevin looked at each in turn.

'I'll bill you for lost down time,' Sean said, half grinning and half scowling.

'Post it to Washington,' Mitch said with a brief smile, glancing at Kevin and grinning.
Rhys and Sean got to their feet and left the room. Mitch watched Jessy from the corner of his eye, she made no move to leave. She shifted in her seat.

Shit, he mouthed silently, looking the other way, pretending to be busy.

'Mind if I stay?' Jessy whispered, raising her brows, searching for a warm response from Mitch. He took a look at her and continued to clear the glasses up.

She'd consumed altogether too much champagne, that he knew. The fuzzy look in her eyes told him all he needed to know. Both were fixed unblinkingly on him. Watching him. Mitch wanted Jessy but he knew that now was not the time to have a physical sortè with his old friend. He turned his head and looked back at his yawning laptop. Leave please, he implored silently, hoping against hope that she would leave voluntarily.

'Jessy, I've got a mass of Agency reports to get through before this function tonight and...'

'Christ Mitch, she said, cutting him off, '...relax will you, stop torturing yourself. The Project is done. Cygnus is out there waiting to go. Take some time off for fuck's sake!'

Mitch looked at her. Any doubt had just been blown away, he was now certain that this would be a mistake. 'No Jessy I can't. The Project is finished but I need to go over the software encryption for Intercept and check the onboard diagnostics. The Cray programmers and those from Goddard need one hundred percent accurate data to feed into Guidance. It's important Jessy and it can't wait. You're part of the team so I know you realize how important all this is.' His eyes scanned Jessy thoroughly as he talked.

She did understand, but the champagne was stifling her ability to think rationally. Besides, she knew all the data had been checked manually and by the Supercoms a dozen times. It was ready. If it wasn't, it never would be, ever. He was fobbing her off, absolutely no doubt about it. She felt deflated, devalued, call it what you like, she felt it.

'Okay Mitch, if you need any help you know where I am.' Jessy kissed him goodbye as she left, a fleeting touch on the cheek. It spoke volumes.

'Damn it!' he said to no one after Jessy had gone. 'Fuck!' he snapped to no one.

Mitch would spend the next few days liaising with his flight crew and going over and memorizing the now familiar details of Earth-shield Things were going so well, egress had been brought forward to November 22nd, a few days away. All plasma fuel modules were fully pressurized, all fusion warheads locked and aligned. Almost time to meet whatever was coming at them.

***

The flight crew were assembled in Cygnus 9, the Medi-lab. All knew exactly what their responsibilities were once they entered the vessel. Six months of hardcore training and preparation hadn't been wasted. None were under any illusions about the importance of the mission, of the leading

36

role they would play in determining human destiny, of ensuring there was a destiny beyond the current generation. The tormenting thought was always there, idling near the back of their minds, permanent, grating baggage they lugged everywhere. End Time. Psychological thumbtacks, Jessy thought, hammered in to the hilt. Jessy felt the blood drain from her face.

If they failed to divert CX1, then they would probably condemn themselves to the status of cosmic curiosity, the last four humans in the Universe. With Earth gone, Cygnus would be a tiny strongbox of humanity, a unique sardine can carrying four doomed bipedal hominids. The final quartet from Earth, floating forever on the dim breath of the interstellar tide.

Their world and their people would probably be wiped out within twenty-four months or so of their failure, and if they did fail, Earth would drink in the grim message from space twelve months before contact. The Cygnan cosmonauts would not return to their planet. Instead, they would remain adrift and alone on the edge of the great emptiness, without a planet and without a future. They would be the ultimate castaways. Like those on Earth, they would die in space. The casualties of truly fucked up luck. Star or black hole, it didn't matter much. Either would do the job. Once again, it would be destruction of a species from without.

Sitting behind the flexiguard glass of Cygnus 10, Mitch and the others gazed at the scene laid out like a surreal tapestry below them. Here was the focus for the entire construction process. Components of the fabulous ship were all manufactured elsewhere in the facility and came together here, all of them eventually conjoining below them with exquisite precision. Each tegument was constructed and relentlessly tested, then shunted to C10 where the Earthshield vessel itself was assembled piece by piece and section by section with an exactness to the limit of human technologies.

And it was backed by complex, rigorous and multiple Failsafe inspection. Engineering, construction, proving, installation, and onboard testing was overseen and checked by three independent Techs. Two had died doing their duty.

Every piece of carbon fibre circuitry was quadruple checked. No one had to be reminded that there were no second chances here. Everything had to be right and operate as planned the first time. Otherwise all was lost. And all had never carried such an encompassing and tangible threat to the planet and to their civilisation.

Surveying the completed beast, the crew agreed that it looked wholly impressive. Its white dermis shone with a vitreous lustre in the light from twelve sodium "suns" suspended fifty metres above. Mitch was reminded of the first time he'd glimpsed a nighttime Shuttle in Canaveral, smoking and floodlit and bursting to go. It was like Apollo 17, but even superlatives or similes didn't seem enough so he was silent. This gleaming phantasm was his, his and Jessy's. A smile tugged at Mitch's mouth as he looked at Cygnus.

The ship looked as it should have looked, like nothing before engineered by the hand of Man. It looked alien to Jessy although the massive parabolic dish on its mid-quarters gave it something of an earthly flavour. Mitch had based the vessel's symmetry largely on the requirements demanded by its propulsion system, and by its singularly rapid transit through the void, that is, the need for colossal frontal protection from the potentially lethal effect of ionizing gas and dust. He also based it on his own cognitive image of what an interstellar spacecraft should look like. His superstructural plans had been massaged and trimmed by JPL but it still looked pretty much like his original blueprint, and he hadn't failed to impress. It looked amazing.

Cygnus was half a kilometre long and a tenth of that wide, looking something like a doubly terminated pendulum, the ends protruding far beyond the gaunt cylindrical biozone. There were also a host of extrusions pocking the surface, the main one being the mighty fifty metre wide radar dish. Hideous beauty, Mitch reckoned, gawking at Cygnus. It seemed an apt metaphor.

Encapsulating the toe of the craft was a massive lithium hydride Xray umbrella that stretched a hundred metres beyond the anorexic midzones. Looking somewhat less bulbous, the front of the craft was similarly cocooned by a metre thick beryllium alloy blanket that would shield the craft from interstellar "collisions".

At their dazzling rate of passage even the humble hydrogen atom would threaten their survival, not to mention dust and ash particles. Some twenty-five hyper (hydrogen peroxide) rockets were just visible as small gray cones along the belly of the craft. These would produce the gentle thrust needed to escape Luna's gravity, and by hinging and gimballing the nozzles, would provide the critical ability to manoeuvre the craft, to pivot it, later in flight. So, it could eyeball CX1, and then hopefully shift its trajectory by enough to save Earth.

'Dear sweet Jesus,' Jessy murmured, overcome by a terrible dread that struck without warning. In a sudden horrid flash, she realized that the exotic edifice would be their home for at least four years, if they succeeded. She already knew that, but doing it here and now added something to its impact. It could be her home for the rest of eternity if they failed. She chewed over the possibilities and shuddered at the prospect of dying aboard their creation. Shaking her head, the horrendous vision only fish-hooked deeper into the fertile pulp of her mind. The thought was now caught by the barb, completely and utterly stuck.

Another deep-seated fear for Jessy was the lack of any Mission Control, either on Luna or on Earth, once they cut Jupiter's ecliptic. There was no one to monitor mission parameters, the ship, PND, or themselves. No feedback on their progress. No external support whatsoever. No one to speak to, to double check with or to confirm with. They would quickly be alone in depthless, unreachable space. Jessy's face twitched with fear but she knew there was no other way.

She immediately thought of the Shuttle Poseidon and shuddered. Where the hell would they have been without Mission Control? Dead, that's where. Completely fucked in the truest sense. The velocity and distances involved with Earthshield required that everything to do with Cygnus, all failsafe's, all astrogation and all verification had to be self-contained shipboard. She felt a great vice squeeze her chest as she contemplated horrendous catastrophe in deep space. Positive thinking, a lack of, had always been the standout chink in Jessy's rather fragile character. She was the proverbial tubby teen. Jessy still looked terrified, seemingly made of steel, she was so rigid. Totally stiff and unbending.

To observers, Mitch and Jessy seemed to come closer together in the few weeks before November 22nd. They rarely left each other's side. Many believed they'd finally become an item although rumours had persisted on that for years. Most thought that if they weren't, then they should be or ultimately would be. Simply a matter of time, most assumed. Maybe they'd go through life and be almost but not quite, who knew. Jessy broke her stare from Cygnus and turned to look at Mitch.

'I can't believe it's arrived,' she whispered hoarsely, 'In less than a day we're going to board Cygnus...and not leave it again for at least four years. It's hard to come to terms with, it's an amazing realization you know.' Her focus dwindled, pupils swelling like ebony balloons as she paused to consider what she'd just said. She was quiet for a long time.

'You'll be fine Jess, I'll make sure of it,' Mitch assured her with a grin. His heartbeat increased a notch. Don't fuck up, he told himself again, glancing at Jessy. She was on a knife's edge, that was clear to anyone who bothered to look. Jessy was anxious and tense. Very tense.

Sean and Rhys were eagerly anticipating the moment. They were career space nuts and even though neither had been beyond Earth orbit for five years they'd both undergone intensive retraining and passed without incident or single negative review. They needed this mission. Both craved anything cosmic, and each had an intimate knowledge of both the Pseudo Novae propulsion system and the general design of Cygnus itself. This and their results on the psychometric tests made them ideal choices for the mission.

The only uncertainty was R.M.L. Truman. There were lingering doubts about her psyche results and her ability to cope with the four year journey, despite much of it being in a state of semi-coma. She was beset with strange feelings of inadequacy even though she had the highest IQ of all the crew. Not to mention an unrivalled knowledge of the quantum mechanical complexities of PND. Mitch refused to consider her not going on the mission, but he too had his doubts about her psyche. He would just have to watch her. Make sure she didn't become a one person mission slayer.

The Earthshield vessel lay like a colossal barbell in Cygnus 10, blithely unaware of the tremendous voyage and profound task that lay ahead of it. Cygnus had the responsibility to save or kill a civilisation. Jessy well and truly realized that self-awareness and wisdom were wondrous things, unimaginably awesome and rare in the cosmos. But there was no escaping the emotions that came along with them as unavoidable baggage. Jessy knew it only too well. They all knew the events of the near future would stretch to breaking point the very plinth of their thinking beings. Jessy looked at the craft and for a second, she envied its lack of mind. Fuck it, she thought, let's do this thing.

***

Time waits for no one, neither man nor machine, there was no escaping fate and they all knew it. Once the celestial jury had delivered its judgment, good luck or bad, time would work unrelentingly to bring its sentence to bear, and when that happened it was either sink or swim.

Only wisdom and technology could be the counter. Dinosauria didn't have it but maybe others did. Humanity perhaps? No one was sure, but the Cygnans would soon confront the question head on. And their answer would come in the blink of an eye. Hopefully, their tech would work as well as it was supposed to.

Would they be the first creatures from spaceship Earth to effectively counter an Extinctor from space, or would they simply maintain the status quo? Another chapter in the book of species ruined from above? Jessy was pondering that exact thought as she stared at the front part of Cygnus. They had to, and thought they had, but probably hadn't, confronted the reality of failure. They all put it realistically, at around 50/50, so they and the rest of civilization had a 50 percent chance of dying, of becoming extinct. Great, Jessy thought, looking upward toward the top of the craft. Hoping like hell for some Divine help. Good luck with that, she thought, knowing she wasn't a good Christian.

Time had indeed reeled in the day. Egress was minus seven hours and the four crew, Earth's pioneer extrastellar journeymen, ambled toward the cylinder that looked so much like a swollen sausage, burst and gnarled at both ends. The crew had farewelled their hidden blue home via the Farside VideoNet, the signal first bouncing off the Eaglehawk satellite and then off the Tycho. Both orbiting relays were deep and geostationary above farside in positions that allowed continuous direct telemetry with Earth and spacetowns Copernicus and Freedom.

For those remaining on Luna, to finally bid farewell to their spaceship and crew was an achingly sad experience. The grim scenario for them and for the eight billion souls back on Earth, should Cygnus fail, weighed heavily as liftoff loomed closer. If they indeed failed, Earth would probably be destroyed and the whole thing would be a fucking travesty. Apart from the four actually making the trip, the rest of humanity could only wait and wonder. And hope like hell.

***

Everything seemed far too bright, like a miner's first glimpse of the noonday sun. Mitch stepped inside Cygnus first, followed by Rhys, then Jessy and Sean. Jessy drank in the silver gizzard of Cygnus and realized with a wrenching gasp that it would be years before she'd see it from the outside again. If, she reminded herself, if. The likelihood was that she wouldn't "see" a bloody thing. And Jessy realised it well.

A myriad of bright-coated engineers and dull-coated technicians were hovering around and indulging in some manner of banal activity. All quite unnecessary, Mitch thought. If it wasn't right now, it simply wasn't going to be right. Particular attention was being payed to the Protocoma Maintenance (PCM) Cylinders. These "naptraps", despite what they thought back home, were not suspended animation. Ageing still occurred.

They were, however, deep sleep chambers consisting of fully enclosed chiro-stretchers banked on one side by a towering array of physiometric monitors. And on the other by large isometric hardware units with newly developed muscle toning Medi-plex software.

Each of the crew when their time came, would be placed in Protocoma or a state of baseline respiration and biological function. It was simply an exceptionally deep sleep, a psychological necessity on a trip of such duration, or so they thought at NASA. No matter what they told Earth though, the Press couldn't get past the notion of suspended animation. Fucking Sci-fi had a lot to answer for.

***

Bleeding over the Lesser Mendeleev plain, the recycled air wafted like fog into the great emptiness, dancing and disappearing within the tenuous helium froth of the Lunar ether. Despite the gentle decompression, clouds of Luna talcum were disturbed and belched high over Moonbase II in a blanket of silt turned brilliant and sparkling in the rays from a mighty Sun. It was supposed to be the dark side of the Moon. What a frigging joke.

Two doors ninety metres high were mechanically winched outward until they formed a tremendous oblong craw to the exquisite plain beyond. Cygnus sat like a supine silkworm atop its seemingly delicate launch vehicle. Slowly ambling out to its departure point four hundred metres away, the strange beast would begin its journey from the magnetic bull's-eye of Mendeleev.

Jessy and Mitch noticed just how relaxed and genuinely excited Sean and Rhys appeared to be. How did they do it? Jessy pondered. How the fuck could they be so calm and composed? So many risks, she thought, so many life threatening hazards. Not to mention the responsibility. What of failure, should it occur? So many things could go wrong. Christ, she felt sick. Get a grip, she groaned silently, looking grimly at Sean and Rhys, wondering why she didn't feel at least a tiny bit of joy. It was the number of things that could go wrong, she reckoned. Her jaw tightened as she tried to reel in her sense of foreboding. Why on Earth would she feel any joy when failure means extinction of the species? Including everything else that called Earth home as well.

'Okay people, EV suits now,' Mitch commanded quietly, feeling his heart jump a bit in his chest.

All Techs and engineering personnel had departed the Interstar. Only the four crew remained. The RLV that would provide Cygnus with a mechanical push was in position and stationery, with the ponderous vessel piggybacking it, like two colossal creatures rutting in the middle of the lunar desert.

The craggy rim of Mendeleev was a dark and distant ledge just above the close horizon, the whole scene slowly brightening as Sol inched its way upward. Dawn on farside was beckoning. Most people really thought farside was dark, but boy, were they wrong. Finer details of the stunning moonscape appeared before them as their precious star rose into view and lit their skyless world. They got a real sense of their world as it brightened, with Earth as the much bigger brother in the background.

Jessy glanced at Mitch and saw him staring through the curved vacuglass of the Compit at the Moon. All prelaunch tests were complete and at E-minus thirty minutes it was simply a matter of waiting and monitoring. Keeping a close eye on the wall of digital displays in front of them.

It also gave Mitch time to look into space and eyeball the faint light they were on their way to confront. They all tried to keep a lid on the anxiety that threatened to boil over and thrust Jessy, at least, over the edge. She tried to focus on what was in front of her. The controls for the Breeder, the PND, the weaponry systems, were all showing nominal. Jessy prayed the bluelight status would continue right up to and through the booting sequence. She spoke to Mitch, trying to loosen visions of extinction and blackness.

'...your thoughts?' Jessy asked, without taking her eyes off the moonscape, watching as it bared its dawn soul in front of her. She needed some positivity.

Mitch whispered, '...just wondering about the planet behind us, the hopes of the billions we're carrying. Fuck a duck, it'd be easy to be crushed by the prospect, Jesus, it's so um…daunting.' He didn't break his outward stare as he spoke, his eyes open wide, unblinking.

'I never thought I'd hear you say that Mitch, me yes, you ... no.' He wasn't helping at all.

'What can I say,' he said distantly, 'perhaps I'm feeling sentimental about ol' blue skies.'

Jessy knew that being in the Big Chair, he felt the crushing pressure even more than the rest of them. She cringed as she realized for the first time that Mitch himself was responsible for the fate of the world and perhaps, no definitely, of humanity itself. He was fucking number one. Again. It was a stunningly emotional realization. Stuck on the Moon, hidden in a farside crater, and engulfed in toil sixteen hours a day left little time for contemplation of the Big Picture. Now that she was doing it, it was nearly too much to bear. What else wasn't she aware of, she wondered? Might be anything. The big picture was dead set scary. Certainly, it was too much to properly digest. Jessy turned her head and joined Mitch's brooding stare. Despite her efforts, her mind continued to spiral.

To Jessy the fitting of her helmet was unwelcome proof that the mission was here...was actually happening. The scope of the voyage was really dawning on her, choking her with a feeling of giddy detachment, a feeling that she was watching as an observer rather than a player. But now she was under no illusions, any doubt that this was actually happening was shattered. The dreadful profundity of the mission suddenly became clear, growing a three dimensional definition that sliced into her mind like a titanium blade. Fucking hell, she thought, not really believing she was here. Jessy was finally in the ship. Perhaps forever.

She looked to her left where Mitch was seated. He was fully suited and ensconced in data transmission back to Cygnus 9 from the so called Steinardt Intelligence System (SIS) which took up most of the nose area of the craft. They relied on SIS for nearly everything.

SIS was the brain of the vessel, a supercomputer with superpower, connected by kilometres of optical fibre to every part of the ship, to every system, large and fine, and to every sensor. To the myriad that pocked the internal workings of the ship and to those external that monitored every square centimetre of the hull, feeling for particle impacts and searching for radiation levels. It was an exquisitely sensitive homeostasis mechanism that made sure everything to do with Cygnus stayed as it was supposed to, constantly probing the operational subsystems and life support network. Looking and searching for problems. Anything with a hint of being illogical and SIS was all over it.

Like them, SIS was responsible for the wellbeing of the only intelligent cradle in a galaxy that boasted more than a trillion worlds. Shit, she thought again, signing the cross roughly on her forehead. And this from a supposed Christian who never goes to church, even on Sunday. If we were relying on intervention from above, we had no hope, she was sure.

A metre further on Sean and Rhys were seated in front of a smaller panel of monitors and were also ferrying data back to Luna. Jessy stared outward and immediately wished she hadn't. 'Oh fuck,' she murmured under her breath, feeling her heart start pounding against her ribs. 'Shit...shit,' she snapped to herself, her brows so tightly drawn, Jessy looked like she had a monobrow.

From their position near the geographical axis of Mendeleev, she could see the wreckage she hadn't wished to see. It gripped her mind with a terrible foreboding. Eight months before, during the early stages of Foundation, a Lunaway Shuttle with twenty-seven Techs aboard had crashed on the Moon only half a kilometre from the base. It was very ugly indeed.

Any landing you can walk away from is a good one, but this had most definitely not been a good one. It was a shocker. Everyone on board had been killed when the craft's atmospheric bladder had been severed on impact. Many of the Techs had been alive when they were exposed to the searing emptiness of daytime Luna. Like poisoned insects, they had writhed and shuddered on the scorified talcum of farside, erupting and exploding like overstuffed sacks. The scene that greeted the Lunavac team was horrendous beyond description, a dusty battlefield of burst bodies and burnt entrails. Somehow the USPA/Boeing vessel had initiated forward instead of retro thrust on its final approach, despite the numerous safeguards that should have made it impossible. 'Impossible'. That word was for fools. If it couldn't happen, it would, be sure of it.

It thudded into the crater bottom and dug another hole in the dusty mafic Mendeleev surface. Jessy looked and pondered. In space, like on Earth, or anywhere else for that matter, anything was possible. With the power of a meteorite, she looked at the few remaining pieces of broken and twisted metal, remnants of the craft she'd flown in a dozen times. Horrified and sickened, Jessy's face was almost bloodless as she thought about the smash. She thanked God she wasn't involved.

Her fears, she was sure, would give biblical demons a run for their money. Worries that she could feel, burning into her brain like a jagged ganglion. What did they really know about black holes? They knew about their physics but did they truly comprehend their power? No way! At least she didn't think so. They terrified her. A stellar corpse squashed by its own weight so that the very configuration of Nature's pixels was demolished. And gravity, the weakling, given the almost supernatural power to stop light and everything else dead in its tracks.

They weren't something, they were nothing but severely warped spacetime and gravity, that was it. She understood their quantum nature almost as well as anyone on Earth, that she knew. But to actually come face to face with one, especially one bleeding such a hail of radiation nasties, was disturbing to say the least. She felt a kind of breathless wonder-terror at the prospect of such an unlikely, unpleasant encounter. Jessy knew the feeling of loathing and terror would worsen by degree as they closed on the terrors from Centaurus.

The booster engines, hydrogen peroxide with a dash of dimethyl, had been smoking for several minutes, the gray mist rapidly losing itself in the near vacuum of the Moon. Eight cones abruptly broke into a blanket of rust and blood, then they arced dazzlingly white. A few minutes later, the RLV threw the craft upward, thrusting it into a controlled tailspin from the surface. Cygnus torpedoed upward in the stodgy pull of the Moon, the gyro boosters quickly grasping and balancing the craft for its correct attitudinal egress. Accelerating to two kilometres per second, they sailed away from the shining and pitted farside at gradually increasing velocity.

Mitch spoke brokenly to Mendeleev as he scanned SIS. Glancing at Jessy, he smiled, one that wasn't returned. Her face was set like a terracotta pot. 'Congratulations crew,' Mitch said, '... first hurdle safely negotiated. 'Well done,' he said, like a good Captain.

Jessy finally broke her stare, smiling briefly at Mitch, then shifting her gaze back to space, the anxiety chiseled in her features. Her mouth was ajar and eyes bulging behind the Perspex visor, expecting disaster, ignoring Mitch's bullshit platitudes.

Mitch had repeatedly questioned the USPA directive that PND only be activated once they reached a lunar distance of five hundred thousand kilometres. He thought they needed a show of strength in support of the viability of the craft, which was certainly not what their directive engendered. It made Mitch feel a little stupid.

But deep down he knew it was the only way. After all, who really knew how successful this immensely complex technology would be. Tests suggested it would be okay but there were any number of gremlins that could afflict any part of the system at any time. It had happened in space and on Earth before, to tried and tested vehicles before. And even to ones using conventional rocketry for God's sake. Where the hell did that leave us? Jesus. His thoughts had suddenly developed teeth. Shaking his head, he looked back at SIS, hoping it knew what the hell it was doing.

There were other reasons for starting PND at a good distance. There had been a howl of protests on Earth at the realization that Cygnus would leave behind a trail of tiny quantum sized neutron cores. Despite the peril of Earth's situation, the idea of polluting the near neighborhood with degenerate matter wasn't a popular one. That is until JPL struck a plan that soothed the protesting masses. Most of them anyway. Assuming SIS maintained the craft's course scrupulously, the collapsed cores would be thrust in the direction of the Sun. The plan was that they would impact the solar photosphere and stay there, taking up motions within Sol's belly. After a thousand years or so, when their orbits decayed, they would find a home right at the solar centre, safely stored out of harm's way. JPL had painstakingly calculated the path of the tiny remnants, taking full account of gravity effects from nearby planets.

Of course, once outside the solar system the atomic nuggets would be liberally sprinkled through space, but in the vastness of space it was considered, rightly or wrongly, that the tiny relics would be insignificant.

***

Jessy padded along the dimly lit corridor that ran from the Compit all the way back to the bowels of the ship where the critical componentry of the Drive lay. She was fearfully pondering the starkill propulsion system that would be booted in a little under an hour. This, she prayed, and by prayed, she meant "based on testing", would boost them by degree from eleven kilometres per second under their current impulse to a hundred and eighty thousand kilometres per second under PND. Her mind shuddered as she grappled with the massive...the exponential jump in speed that would soon occur. Holy shit. She swore to herself as her heart suddenly squirmed in her chest. Over half the speed of light, 'she thought with an intense stare, stiffening until she was almost standing to attention. Jessy put her hands up to push the hair off her face. 'Shit,' she said, taking a step back toward the bulkhead. She turned and walked back toward the Compit and for the first time she felt the effects of the ship that imprisoned her. The confining, cramped feeling, the sense of no way out, was already shoehorning into her brain.

The spaceship felt small and was already getting smaller. The idea of calling Cygnus home for so long was already starting to pick at her being, prodding her phobias like fingernails down a blackboard. More than anything else it was the time aspect of the journey that was stirring her feelings of claustrophobia and anxiety. She couldn't help but wonder whether her psychometric conditioning had worked at all. She knew the ship wasn't small, like a shuttle or a sparecraft. God, Cygnus was huge compared to those. By a factor of ten it was the biggest craft ever built, in terms of the space available to the crew. It was the duration aspect, pure and simple, the infinite corridor of time that clotted in front of her eyes every time she closed them, especially when she was in bed. She wanted out already.

Although the rear hundred metres of the craft was taken up by the Breeder and drive system, almost two-thirds of the entire ship was open to the crew. It was the minimum size for the number of crew and the length of time allocated for the mission. Apparently. What the hell that was based on, no one knew. Each had separate living quarters even though the four of them would only be awake simultaneously for five percent of the voyage. There was a gymnasium, a conference room and a crew room.

The crew room was astonishing. It was brimming with sophisticated entertainment systems, Rom games, four virtual reality chambers, swimming booths, soundproofed music and blue disc cabs, gymnasium equipment and Solarnet data that they could access at any time. And which would continue to be updated from Earth until they slipped passed Saturn. Then Earth and all she carried would become a receding memory as they slid onward in space and forward in time, gradually running down its own radiation until they travelled at more than half its speed.

The ship was lit by pseudo solar light for fourteen hours followed by a gradual transition to a dull bioluminescent glow during the ten hours of night. All these apparently nonessential considerations on Cygnus were there to benefit the crew, to counter the psychological impact of such an unprecedented stint in space. Jessy knew these quasi Earth luxuries would help, but she was still going to have a hell of a time remaining sane over the two years she would be awake. Jessy's eyes were cold and flinty as she considered it .

Avoiding micro stimuli was critical. The way Rhys cleared his throat, fucking continually, it was already starting to really piss her off. At least he'd be asleep soon. It couldn't come soon enough, she thought, letting a small smile drift briefly across her face, thinking of him asleep.

Time would tell whether she'd get used to Rhys and being hemmed in, but there was a strange pressure swelling behind her eyes, and she recognized it for what it was. The enemy, the throbbing, debilitating pressure of self-doubt and anxiety. Voices. Jessy returned to the Compit at slightly under E-plus ten hours.

'I was about to send Sean to look for you,' Mitch whispered as he walked back to his seat. She followed him and took up her position, looking distracted and tense. Her eyes narrowed to slits.

'...needed to clear my head.' It hadn't come close to working, but she'd needed to try.

'We're at N-minus ten minutes people,' Sean said, referring to that which would hopefully pick them up and boost them toward the stars. 'This better work', he said, looking at the N-buttons with eyes that were still tense and staring. Jessy was definitely doing no better.

'Once the sequence is complete and we're running at seventy percent power we can dice the suits and get comfortable.' Mitch glanced at Jessy, hoping to see her eyes uncoil a bit. In the next few minutes her help would be critical, but terror was clearly enveloping her. She looked nervous and sweaty, eyes wide and brows forming a single haunted line. Fucking hell, he said silently, squinting at the buttons; He knew Jessy was bad, but he was still a bit shocked at how jumpy she was. It was like she was made from jointless titanium or some other hard element.

It was N-minus four minutes.

'Okay this is it,' Mitch exulted loudly, 'let's go for the Drive.'

Jessy looked over and hesitated. She eventually swallowed and spoke. Her life was spinning in front of her like some grim digest, family, friends, her dog and cat, they were all there, sitting above her left shoulder. Staring and looking irritated, even the cat. Waiting for her to fail. Fuck me, she mouthed to no one, glancing at Mitch, then at the mountain of controls in front of her. Her mind was fuddled by a lack of sleep.

'Extinguishing thrusters...' With trembling fingers, she pressed a series of squat buttons and turned a tiny altitudinally mounted lever on the daunting panel in front of her. Looking over at Mitch she signalled with a raised thumb that Cygnus was now travelling on momentum only. Mitch swivelled his head to look at Sean who was behind them, then at Rhys and lastly, he looked back at Jessy. She looked terrified, her lips were trembling and her breath rasping a bit as it came a bit harder.

'...activating the sequence for Thermo-gravity, Mitch said, facing the console. Novae will follow in five minutes.' Mitch paused and then nodded almost imperceptibly, investing Jessy with silent instructions. They both manually pushed back the opaque black covers that protected the small 'N' buttons. Jessy was struggling mightily, but she eventually managed to jimmy the key through the minute opening. Both keys were now sitting in their shafts, waiting. Pressure filled the Compit like a solid fog.

'Turning on my mark...3, 2, 1, mark.'

Both turned their keys simultaneously which armed the two buttons. Sean and Rhys were keeping one eye on Jessy and one eye on the digital monitors in front, to the side and the head up above them. They hoped like hell that SIS was paying attention. Goddamn computers, Sean said to himself, watching the whites of Jessy's eyes and wondering who the hell made her 2IC. Fucking bullshit, he was sure. He respected and liked Jessy, but thought he was the obvious choice. He was far more grounded, apparently. She was chosen because Mitch chose her. Her eyes were clouded with visions of Earth.

All of them knew that the next few minutes could decide the outcome of the mission. Successful activation and operation of the Drive was absolutely fundamental to Earth-shield Without it they weren't going anywhere. Failure in the next minute or so would mean that Earth would likely meet whatever was arrowing toward it from the void. This was the planet's first and only reasonable defense, the very best its technology could muster.

'Okay Jessy,' Mitch said smiling at her soothingly, a smile that again wasn't returned. Jessy's face was full of concentration, frowning a bit with uncertainty. 'The buttons are enabled and must be pushed firmly at the same time, you know the drill.' Jessy nodded. Her expression was blue steel, fear flickering behind her eyes, sweating copiously. Fuck, what if something goes wrong, was all she could think of?

Mitch's voice took on a deeper, more ominous tone. The fog suddenly turned blindingly white. 'Pushing on my mark...3, 2, 1, mark!' The deed was done, a perfect choreography of human pressure on metal. One push to save humanity, didn't seem too bad. She only wished it would be that easy. Jessy looked up and hoped against hope it would go as planned. She felt like crossing herself again, but refrained this time. Last time she'd felt a little stupid. And, it probably didn't help anyway.

For what seemed like an eternity, nothing happened. Just silence. Everyone stared straight ahead, too scared to move or look at one another, terrified of what they might see in the other's eyes. They all felt the torturous horror of uncertainty. Of future histories, destinies, global fortunes being made, decided by what was happening right now. Space outside seemed suddenly blacker and distinctly less friendly than it had before.

Then it happened. Jessy's expression was grim. Thank Christ, she immediately thought…noise. At least something was happening. She slowly started to uncoil a bit. The growl of the Breeder erupted from the rear of the ship like a herd of wounded beasts. Sean and Rhys started breathing again as they watched the escalating pressure levels in the Breeder. Jessy's toes were almost snapping from the pressure.

The visual displays were singing the right song, so far. It was showing rapid real time phase changes within the plasma soup, and SIS told them that each of the seventy-six graphical assessments were right on the money. Its score for what was happening on the inside was 9.55 out of ten. Anything above 9 was acceptable. It was looking good…well, pretty good anyway. Laser tubes and pressure pads were being brought to life, parameters good individually to three decimal points.

'PND minus four point two five minutes. Hang on for the ride of your fucking life.' Mitch said, gazing around at his saddled crew. His tone concealed a fathomless terror. He was terrified, despite his outward excitement. He looked over at Jessy, she clearly wasn't doing much better than he was. She was trying to deal with tremors in her hands and fingers.

The plasma soup in the fusion module was rapidly condensing, the rotation becoming more rapid, quickly approaching critical thermo mass. The trillions of watts of power kicked out by the millions of laser tubes began to forge conditions approaching those of the stellar furnaces that hung in space around them. Pressure within the Breeder was increasing on schedule, passing 25,000 g's…it was N-minus thirty seconds. The vessel had been ambling through space on impulse from its peroxide engines but when the Drive kicked in, Cygnus shot forward. At the moment of E-Minus zero, Jessy was visibly shaking, although grateful at being seated and strapped in tightly. Fucking go, she mouthed to herself, going pokerfaced. Sean and Rhys were rigidly expectant, faces like alabaster. Mitch was a canvass of intensity and concentration, his jaw tightening as he frowned at the view ahead.

Although carefully harnessed in their gravity saddles, the crew still felt the excruciating pressure from the initial jump in speed, even though it was structured to be as gradual as possible. Unfortunately, it was like trying to make a nuclear explosion "measured". In fact, it was exactly like that. It wasn't going to happen, although thankfully, there were ways around it.

It was a difficult task given the nature of the propulsion system. The diameters of the pseudo stars started out minute and very gradually grew in dimension until they were the size of basketballs, hence a relatively gentle increase in velocity. 'Fuck me,' Sean yelled mutely, 'I thought it was meant to be gradual.' Rhys glanced at Mitch and arched one side of his brows, 'and when does that start?' Sean said, trying to grin but not really making it.

They were all prepared for the g's but everyone silently queried the accuracy of the simulations they'd suffered through at Dryden. The inertial stress was many times worse than the dozen or so tests that were supposed to simulate the initial jump to Novae drive. Typical balls up, Mitch thought as the skin flattened on his jowls. He was none too happy with any of the tests they'd been involved in. He raised his arms and blew his cheeks out to Sean and Rhys. It was anything but gradual, he concurred. It hurt like hell. Jessy concurred, if only by the raised thumb he could see from his supine position.

At N-plus twelve minutes, Sean and Rhys were studying the crammed instrumentation of PND. SIS's self-assessment modules had just proffered their first hard assessment, and they spun toward Mitch almost in unison as they digested it. 'Yafuckenhoo', Sean said, revelling in the numbers. 'The Drive is operating as planned. All parameters are reading normal…blue status on every system. Velocity is point oh five Luminal.' The first of a series of monumental barriers had been safely hurdled. Now they at least had a chance.

45

Sean unharnessed himself from his saddle and toed over to the vacuglass plate that stretched partly along one side of the instrument panels. He stared at the disc of Mars, watching it recede slowly as they arced toward the emptiness and desolation of the deeper solar system.

Rhys stood stiffly and stretched, 'we need to watch the system carefully, until we've operated at max stress for a sustained period, we need to remain frosty. He peered at Jessy, we need to watch PND closely okay?' Sean then looked at SIS. Der, he thought. Mitch's staring eyes added drama to Rhys's statement.

Rhys glanced at Sean through his visor. 'Take it easy my friend. SIS's self-analysis will tell us if anything goes awry, and at this stage everything looks fine, like a training run.' Rhys's grin turned into a full blown victory smile. He walked up and gently swatted Sean on the shoulder. 'So just enjoy the view for a while.' He followed Rhys's finger and with a huge smile he breathed in the depthless visage that was laid out beyond the viewing plate. The solar system was gorgeous.

***

The suited figure stood up clumsily. 'Okay, er, dice the suits.' Mitch spoke through his EV com as he started to rip away the Velcro from his biosuit. 'Get this shit off,' he said. There was an immediate flurry of movement in the Compit as the lightweight but still bulky pressure suits were slowly and awkwardly discarded. In the slightly reduced gravity of the rotating craft it was difficult to carry out even modestly delicate operations while stuck in the suits. The full suit only weighed in at nine kilos with lockable vents to keep the wearer cool. But getting rid of them still felt great.

They now had time to consider their position, and most of all their speed. Soon, they hoped, they would be the first from Earth to successfully embark on true extra-stellar flight. Several ancient robots were pottering through the void but most would be reeled in by Cygnus in less than a day. Even Pioneer 10 which had been ambling along for close on half a century would be hauled in within a couple of days. Voyager 1's plutonium heart had expired several years ago but not before it had touched the edge of the solar heliosphere, the rim of the dusty zephyr where Sol's power died and true extrasolar space began. In plasma physics terms, it was where the plasma or wind ended the Sun's "bubble" of influence. They would flash past both Voyagers in less than two days and bounce beyond the ebbing and flowing border of the Sun's domain and enter the desolation of the Great Wide Open.

Mitch had an intimate knowledge of the course that had been plotted for Cygnus, a course that would take them on an unprecedented personal tour of the solar system. By design though, they would pass close to only two of its family, Jupiter and the tiny twins, Pluto and Charon, as they arced under the main plane of the planets. The course designed by JPL was precise like no other, manicured and massaged to the centimetre, because it had to be. Some of the rest of the planets would be on the other side of the Sun or at best be several hundreds of millions of kilometres away when their orbits were breached by the increasingly relativistic vessel.

Mitch spoke excitedly to the others, his eyes gleaming with enthusiasm, 'We'll pass Jupiter only a million k's from its south pole. Then we pass Pluto and in just over a couple of days we'll follow frigging Voyager and jump into the truly unknown…we'll be the first!'

'You mean you'll be the first,' Sean groaned, wiping his forehead free of sweat. 'Rhys and I will be in PCM as soon as we pass Pluto. We might as well be in the fucking dorm at Ames for all the sightseeing we'll be doing, Christ, we'll be comatose.' He said, crossing his arms and closing his eyes tight. They all saw the wrinkles in his eyelids as he contemplated playing dead for so long. He wasn't impressed at all but he knew the necessity for PCM both from a psyche point of view and for the conservation of life support aboard Cygnus. That didn't stop him from moaning though. Sean was just being Sean. Moaning and groaning was his thing.

'We'll be sure and take plenty of photos,' Jessy whispered. 'And don't forget we have those high speed Jarrions mounted outside. You'll be able to catch up on anything you missed.'

'Thank you good lady,' he grumbled, lowering his brows and closing his mouth.

46

'There won't be much to see anyway,' Rhys added, seemingly as an aside.

'That's right,' Mitch said, '...once we're past Pluto that's fairly much it.' Yeah right, he thought. What a load of crap...glad it's not me, Mitch said to himself silently, staring at Rhys and trying to smile. Mitch hated the thought of PCM but he acknowledged its importance.

Sean smiled as he turned to look at Mitch. He'd never heard so much bullshit in his life. 'If we happen to be buzzed by something for speeding, or for flying without lights or for going too slow which is perhaps more likely,' he said, scratching his head and creasing his face with concern, 'be sure and wake us, okay?'

'Count on it,' Jessy returned, seeing the frustration hidden behind Sean's humour. Sean's eyes darted to everyone. He knew had to go, but he didn't want to go. No way he wanted to go. Sean wanted to see, but the only seeing he would be doing was the inside of his eyelids.

Sean and Rhys were busying themselves on the two large optical telescopes that dominated the viewing chamber immediately behind and to one side of the Compit. It was pure vacuglass that bubbled slightly outward from the skin of Cygnus to give them stunning, wide angle views of the cosmos. Jupiter was already plump in space before them, a rapidly swelling bladder of stupefying colour that rode a dead black sea.

They were now only a few minutes from their closest approach, travelling at sixty thousand kilometres per second. Jessy watched, astonished as details of the depressingly beautiful planet dropped into view and blossomed before her eyes.

'My sweet lord,' Jessy uttered slowly, closing her mouth then opening it and her mouth stayed open, staring at the colossal weather systems that coated the massive globe. She looked closer at the warring clouds that were stippled and stained with fantastic cyclonic barges. Her eyes were plastered to the glass, staring outward like a statue.

The entire spectacle was banded and choked with ribbons of vibrant colour that were swamped by the stupendous crimson phosphorus spot. The Great Rotation was bigger and more dazzling than she could have imagined. The whole incredible scene was punctuated by ten or so moons that she could see shining brilliantly in the light from a distant, primrose Sun. Jessy was aghast at the depth and clarity of the pigments that danced before her and were momentarily smothered by several almighty flashes of lightning. They lit the dark northern pole of the planet in staccato bursts of glorious white fire. The pure scale of the planet was stunning. It was more massive than all the other planets combined.

Jessy spread her fingers against her breastbone. She was dazzled by the planet that so resembled a giant marble. As they whipped past Jupiter, she saw the belly hugging twin rings of the planet light up and smile as they were backlit by the rays from Sol. Then they were gone, in a minute they were four million kilometres beyond the tessellated Jovian coin.

Sean's hoarse whisper was predictable. 'I wonder if there's life down there?' he croaked as Jupiter receded behind them. 'I know the three probes found nothing...but the water layer that Ryle found blanketing the north pole at depth was a constant thirty-five degrees. You never know do you?'

'Cloud people Sean?' Mitch asked quizzically. 'I doubt it.' Fucking idiot, he thought, almost laughing in his face but restraining himself. Maybe on the Galilean Moons but not on Jupiter, he reckoned. 'Nup, no way,' he said, feeling a little sorry for Sean.

'Don't be so quick to judge,' Sean said, the colour draining from his face. 'Besides, my brain is being forced into neutral in a few minutes so let me dream.' Sean turned his head back to the vacuglass and resumed his stare into space, watching the colourful titan rapidly deflate to nothing, thinking about the long sleep ahead of him, not liking it at all. Mitch was nodding as Sean was talking.

The proximity of Cygnus to Jupiter gave its crew the first real impression of their crazy velocity. Gauging speed in featureless space was impossible, but the reference point that Jupiter gave, made their rapid transit all too real. It was now terrifyingly obvious to Jessy and the others that they were travelling unbelievably fast. The Interstar was now arcing away from a dimming and now distinctly jaundiced Sun, and heading rapidly toward the unguarded orbit of Saturn. They were now the best part of a billion k's from Earth and the Sun looked small but was still the brightest star in their rearward view, although sunshine was at least a hundred times dimmer than that hitting Earth.

It was all a bit of a headfuck to Jessy. The Sun did not look like the Sun. It looked alien. Cygnus resembled a piece of ancient Dorian architecture. A statuesque Greek pillar, gaunt in the midriff like the breach end of a shotgun, but curving outward at each end, as it hurtled through space at seventy thousand kilometres each second. The rear of the vessel was drowned by a blinding white aura that stretched behind it like a colossal cometary coma. Every few minutes there was a mighty stellar flash of bluish-white light that exploded behind the ship and dove hundreds of thousands of kilometres backward into the cosmos. This was starkill supernova drive. It looked less like a means of locomotion and more like a cometary coma.

Sean and Rhys would soon leave the fate of Cygnus in the hands of Mitch and Jessy for the next eleven months. The idea of such an extended cerebral holiday, with so much to look at and so much to think about left Sean and Rhys horrified. They were in the midst of seeing the previously unseen. Hardly the time to sleep, Rhys mused, disturbed by what he might miss.

While the crew contemplated Protocoma, Cygnus cut Saturn's ecliptic and for the first time passed above the main plane of the planets, skimming within fifty million kilometres of the finely ringed worlds of Uranus and Neptune. Their distance and transit left the greenish and blue giants as only brightly coloured motes, spectacular against the darkness of space. The Great Unknown was now only blocked by Sol's last tenuous captive. Apparently, now a dwarf planet. Pluto was an antisocial little snowfield that maintained its shuffle out of synch with the rest of the family, below the disk of the planets and very nearly in line with the path of Cygnus. The little orphan lived life literally in a plane of its own.

Sean had seen the closeup photos snapped by NASA's Pluto Express in 2014 but he was totally blown away by the sheer beauty of this icy little rock. Not viewed through a 1990's TV camera, but with the dynamic perception of the human eye. No comparison, Sean decided. There was little resemblance to the bland PEP Skyboard pictures, closeup though they were.

He stared at the rapidly swelling poles of Pluto which shone as though there were an inner fire burning somewhere beneath. He watched in total awe as the bright nether regions gave way to a pale crimson and in places stippled blue equatorial zones which also boasted a strange fiery white feature. The whole vista was unexpectedly dazzling. Sean watched with an open mouth smile. Slightly to one side of the little disk, almost seeming to beckon to him, was icy blue Charon which looked to be so close to Pluto as to almost touch it. Looking at Charon he couldn't help but think of a dirty snowball. And there were some smaller, oblong moons reflecting the light from a distant Sun.

'Holy sweet Jesus...it's fantastic,' Sean exulted as the craft arced past the embracing sentinels of the outer solar system, on the way to what, he wasn't sure. Well...he knew what it was, but not what it looked like.

In a few seconds they had come up on, and then whipped past the last of the Sun's kin. It was slightly over E-plus twenty hours. Rhys visibly cringed at the sight of the minute worlds. They were beautiful, no argument there, but it was time and he knew it. Time to sleep.

***

Dull strobes sparked to life near the middle of the ship, wrapping the Protocoma pods in staccato tones of saffron and shadow. Mitch and Jessy had already completed the first initialization. As soon as Sean and Rhys were connected to Medi-plex, PCM would automatically entomb them in comastate for just under eleven months or until an emergency required their presence on deck. They ambled slowly toward their separate sleeping chambers, resplendent in blue and white arterial pressure suits that were ridiculously tight. Despite their efforts, Sean and his wife had been unable to bear any children, and he was damned sure these suits wouldn't help any.

Jessy kissed them and tried her best to be casual, but predictably failed. Shedding tears, she apologized, knowing it was cruel and unusual punishment for two hopelessly inquisitive

48

cosmologists. Jessy stepped away and her legs buckled beneath her, definitely not the reaction she was hoping for. She rubbed the back of her neck to try and get the blood flowing.

'Time will fly in there,' Mitch said lightly as he squeezed Jessy's lightly muscled upper arm. Sean looked at Mitch and briefly shook the offered hand. Suck it up, he felt like saying, but he held onto it, looking at both of them, thinking how diminutive they looked among the gadgetry.

'Good luck and for God's sake bring us out of these things if you need to.' His eyes were shadowed and huge. He definitely didn't want to go. This thing wasn't for him.

'Trust me guys, you'll be the first ones I'll turn to, uh…after Jessy.' He offered a wide, forced smile.

'Alright then, we'll catch you in just er…u-u-under a year,' Rhys said quietly, his voice catching on the last few words and ending in a frozen rasp. Rhys felt like he was about to be on the receiving end of some terrible punishment, which in a way he supposed he was. After all, playing dead for more than a year was hardly an indulgence of spirit. Taking the last few steps to their new homes, they got in, squeezing under the airtight domes that were raised to attention. Guillotines, Rhys thought, the resemblance was disturbing to say the least.

The task of connecting them to the snaking tendrils of Medi-plex was Jessy's, who along with Rhys was a qualified Medtech with an intimate understanding of the Protocoma system. Once connected and functioning, PCM took over. The acrylic domes cycled closed with a gentle hydraulic whir, and immediately a bluish-gray mist dulled the aluminized interior of the pods, tiny water droplets already forming on its upper dermis. When the gas had dissipated, Rhys and Sean were clearly gone. They looked dead, Jessy couldn't help thinking. Dead as fucking doornails.

'All lights are in the blue Mitch, they're under.' Jessy's eyes stayed fixed on the status bulbs as her mind drifted. She hoped like hell the system was working okay. But what if it wasn't? Lights were blue but were the sensors operating correctly? Were they relaying the right information…accurate information? Jesus, of course they were. The pessimism and the doubts lingered though, like three-corner-jacks embedded near the base of her brain.

'Goodbye guys,' they said as one.

***

'Alone at last,' Mitch said lightly as they walked the hundred metres back to the viewing bubble near the head of the ship. Jessy walked in silence and was deep in thought, a fact obvious to Mitch. She paced slowly, stroking an eyebrow, eyes troubled.

'Your thoughts?' he prodded, as they entered the viewing area. Mitch could see she was upset. Jessy stood in front of the vacuglass slab and was silhouetted by a dim spark of light, dim but by far the brightest in the sky. She turned around and gazed at the Sun and finally spoke.

'I understand that to keep us busy, the egg heads at USPA have scheduled enough astro research tasks to last us a decade…even if we had nothing else to do. They must think we're on a bloody joyride. Christ, we've got ETI monitoring, interstellar medium and spectral studies, planetary searches…cepheid variable measurements et cetera. And we've got a program for monitoring SIS, PND and PCM. Of course, then there's the entertainment facilities. Jesus fuck. I'm sure all this will keep our minds active, but eleven months. Jesus. It's going to take time to come to terms with it…until I can start living without seeing this endless corridor of time stretching in front of me. Maybe Rhys and Sean are better off than we are.' *No way* was her brain's immediate scream. PCM scared her. She understood its mechanics as well as anyone but it still terrified her. It was that lack of control once you were inside. That's what scared her the most. No way, she repeated to herself. No way she would be put to sleep.

'Well I for one am looking forward to it,' Mitch proclaimed, yawning, suddenly distracted by the point of light that he knew was Eta Carinae, a star, actually two stars, whose flame had surged a thousand fold in the past few years. Although it was incredibly distant, Mitch knew it was one of the two brightest lights in their home skies. His attention snapped back to Jessy who was still staring at him, watching him, piercing him with her intense cat's eyes. She lifted an eyebrow, continuing to stare. 'After all,' Mitch continued, 'think of all the quality time we can spend together.' He grinned broadly and looked away, at the floor and then out the window. Anywhere but at her.

That was precisely the problem she thought as her gaze lingered on his muscled frame. She forced herself to look passed him and into space. CX1 was still trillions of kilometres from Cygnus but with both careering toward one another at more than fifty percent Luminal, their rendezvous in cosmic terms was imminent. Collectively they were eating up the gap at the speed of light. Fuck, they were travelling, she thought, looking beyond the glass, imagining how they must look to an observer. Amazing, literally stunning, she was sure.

Jessy had begun to notice the extraordinary visual effect of their increasingly rapid, now relativistic motion through space. The feeling of wonderment and awe (and fear) was almost complete as she peered through the viewing bubble at the crazy vista beyond. The normal cosmos had been erased and replaced by something quite bizarre.

Behind them, the thick patina of stars had virtually vanished and those that did remain were tiny and fuzzy and all uniformly reddish. Ahead of them was a sea of headlights, all on high beam. In front of Cygnus, the stars had swollen, not only in number but also in brightness. Jessy stared slack-jawed at what had formerly been an ocean of dull stars ahead, pocked with a few bright ones here and there. Now there was a vivid bluish glare of perhaps fifty fold more stars than were "there" before, and all had been somehow stoked to super brightness.

All the light from the stars ahead of them was being squashed to the blue end of the spectrum by the fantastic speed of Cygnus through space. Mitch leant forward against the window, the satisfaction sparked in his eyes as he delighted in the Relativistic cosmos. Very few were sure exactly what the effects of such rapid transit would have on their view of the starscape, but Mitch had predicted it almost perfectly. It looked like he thought it would.

From the viewing bubble at the side of Cygnus, V645 could be seen as a blue-rendered dot, one that was being precisely tracked by the vessel's phased array radar. Mitch noted that its motion sunward hadn't changed at all since its photons, the relics of initial apocalypse, had touched Earth's skies a year ago. It was still doggedly focussed on the edge of the solar plane. A seemingly unshakable nemesis. A fucking cosmic leach.

***

Back on Earth nothing much had changed. The populace was still comfortable and mostly ignorant, unaware that chance had cast a terminal judgment on their world. That is, the cosmic dice had been tossed and Earth had lost bigtime, the destiny of the planet having been shortened by eons. Apparently, it was the worst luck possible, but it had actually happened many times before, it was just the first time we knew of, that a goddamn black hole was involved.

The USPA had successfully quashed the reports made by professional astro-labs and amateur sky-watchers. Bringing every one of them "online", they had threatened and intimidated them with the illimitable fury of the Government and its so called Global Secrets Act which, in actuality, was only recently enacted. The implications of the covert Curtain Raiser legislation were nothing if not militant and brutal. Imprisonment and other more ominous action was guaranteed if compliance wasn't complete and unconditional.

After all, they argued, the stakes involved couldn't be higher. Planetary security was at stake. And there would be no repeat warnings, they were fucking serious, and their demands were backed by the highest possible authority. And so far, their threats had worked. Or so they believed.

Anyone with a decent 'scope' could easily ogle the strangeness in Centaurus. But the average backyard sky-watcher wasn't the problem. None would know what sort of threat CX1 posed.

Simply observing was fine. *Look my lovelies.* It was those that could unravel some of its deeper secrets, its attitude, that were their targets. The Agency had already compiled a long list of troublemakers, in particular that throng of wide-eyed comet hunters who obsessed over finding new comets...and worse, plotting their orbits and position in the ecliptic. Those on the first list had already been effectively silenced. Spaceguard facilities were a bit harder. These advanced watchdogs, some linked to the Legacy and James Webb space telescope, perpetually scoured the skies for rogue comets and asteroids. Looking for the Great Extinctor they knew was out there...that terminal death chunk that their math told them was on its way to Earth. Only its location was in question, they claimed. Spaceguard had detected CX1 almost immediately. Their labs of LONEOS, PACS, DROCO and AANEAS had been rapidly aligned and now formed part of the USPA web of deceit.

All access to Hubble, Xanadu, Spartan and James Webb as well as seventeen other space based remote sensors had been terminated indefinitely. Only those empowered by Curtain Raiser, those with the highest possible security clearance, still monitored the progress of CX1. So far, the public hadn't cottoned on to the problem, remaining blissfully unaware that their destiny was about to be erased by the feeblest of night-time specks. Although still several trillion kilometres away, Nemesis had already reached out to tweak the fragile fibres of Earth. Number three was a planet whose leaders were horrified by their own shortcomings as a species. What terrified them was the knowledge and understanding of their own fragile mindset. Its high tenants knew that destruction from within, born from chaos and panic, were equally as likely as destruction from without. And they realized they only had direct control over one of them. So, they acted accordingly.

The USPA had so far quashed all the rumours of pending disaster. They had managed to pervade the media with a belief that Proxima, whilst heading in their general direction, would in fact miss the solar plane by more than two billion kilometres. What a load of crap that was. Still, it was, at this stage, only a rumour like a thousand other things.

Men of considerable scientific repute had confirmed the claims, and effectively elevated them to fact. Anyone disputing the official stance was methodically discredited, or worse, by Global Security Intelligence (GSI), the USPA's newly formed security arm. Stalin had nothing on them.

This deadly band of seconded coverts from Langley had virtually unlimited powers to deal with the problem. In other words, they were licensed to kill. And kill they'd already done.

Dissemination of data, that in any way disputed the official position of the Agency, was considered a breach of world security and was dealt with immediately. The release of uncontrolled intelligence, the truth, they were sure would see panic of truly hellish proportions break out. No one in the know doubted that; they knew what would happen or at least they thought they did.

The hard-won infrastructure of the globe would suffer terminal breakdown very quickly. Law and order would fail, financial markets would collapse, medical care, business activity, primary production, then politics, the whole goddamn lot would quickly grind to a halt. In short, the fibres that held up their civilization, the politics and the socioeconomics, would unravel and drop them into a sea of crime, death and anarchy. From which very little would survive.

Such was the flimsy nature of the earthly psyche, it simply couldn't deal with the idea of dying, of knowing when it was going to die. Such hideous facts would take root in the human brain like a runaway cancer, excluding everything else. Knowledge of the how and when of mortality would eventually lead to the end of civilization before the actual impending disaster..

Society and culture and infrastructure, they knew, relied on death remaining a distant and hazy concept. Guaranteed certainly, implicit in life absolutely, but untimed and shadowy. Mortem Incognita. If the worst happened and the real story emerged, then all that would change to the serious detriment of the planet. The mindset of eight billion souls would change overnight. The world would genuinely be fucked.

The fight to control the situation was coordinated by a team of ninety agents from the CIA, seconded under private resolution from the UN by Government Act. No one had to be reminded that the CIA were well versed in carrying out covert and unpopular operations. Sanctions had already been required. Citizens who had gotten close to the truth and had refused to accept that global security was of far greater concern than the rights of an individual had been sanctioned and sometimes even worse. Tough times required tough measures, demanded tough justice. Transcend and die. It was tough but fair, given what was at stake.

Their killings had been fully ratified by law. And as that brand new law proclaimed loudly, *'where killings were to the global benefit, to the benefit of millions of innocent citizens, the*

51

implications of the First Commandment will no longer hold. It shall not be murder'. Quite simply, the GSI had an unconditional license to murder its citizens. Even if Earth wasn't destroyed by its gravitational nemesis, the ruination of the planet would still be effectively accomplished if the GSI failed. To avoid the death of millions they would not hesitate to murder whoever chose to oppose them. At least that's what their unwritten mission statement told them.

***

E plus twelve days. The Sun had been reduced to an odd, pathetic relativistically reddened star. No longer their star, it had long since faded to obscurity, a brightish pinpoint amongst the few that remained in their rearward sky. Just a bit brighter than the rest.

Cygnus and its propulsion system had continued to work without fault, carrying the craft at extraordinary speed for nearly ten days. Determining their rate of passage was the job of SIS, which did it by simply looking and listening. Cocking its massive radio ear, it followed the Doppler shift in three nearby stars, Tau Ceti, Barnard's and 70 Virginis. With great aplomb it could then speak to them about just how fast they were travelling. SIS told them that Cygnus was hurtling along at sixty-one percent Luminal. A hundred and eighty-three thousand kilometres per second!

Not bad for Earthlings, Mitch thought with pride. He remembered the months spent in a tin can getting to Mars in '24. Now they were swallowing the same distance in a few minutes! He grasped his temples and rubbed them furiously with a single finger from both hands. The idea of such fabulous velocity was terrifying. and at the same time, fucking glorious, in equal parts.

Even though Jessy and Mitch had designed and engineered the drive system, they still couldn't help but be astounded. They were forced by circumstance to finish the project in less than thirty percent of the original time frame, but it still worked, and did so (so far) without identifiable fault. That will change, Jessy was sure. She was philosophical about the engine, the mission…about everything. If they exploded now, she wouldn't be happy…but she wouldn't be surprised either. Jessy wouldn't know anything about it if it happened. It'd be too quick.

In spite of the flawless performance, Jessy was fatalistic about chances of that continuing. The feeling of looming disaster was unshakable. In her mind she could see catastrophe; a horrendous explosive apocalypse in space. And it wasn't pretty.

All contact with AASSA's Ben White had ceased soon after they farewelled Pluto and the solar system. The time delays from there, even with luminal speed transmissions, was almost five hours. Realtime conversations were a hazy memory. Jessy and Mitch were on their own, entirely at the whim of the super technical space shell that surrounded them. Even though vital stats from PND were dispatched by automation every ten hours, it would take Earth more than seven days, currently, to warn them of any problem they happened to identify which SIS and the crew did not. They didn't expect anything to get past them, but it wasn't impossible.

It was therefore up to SIS and to them to unrelentingly monitor the onboard systems and detect a problem when and if it should occur. If they failed to recognize a warning sign, they were lost...the mission was lost. The responsibility was daunting, a civilization held in their palm. They needed to be very frosty. Very aware of potential signs of disaster. They thought they had it covered.

***

After two weeks aboard Cygnus, Jessy knew she was in deep trouble. Despite trying to avoid it, she finally had to admit her attempts had failed. Her state of mind had gradually declined into something tangibly uncomfortable. She was constantly depressed and it was affecting her ability to concentrate, and above all she needed to concentrate. She knew what the warning signs were. The worst part was the open ended concept of time. She still had the best part of a year to endure before she went PCM and when she emerged there was still another month to wait before they would know the answer they all craved. Whether or not they could return home, or whether they would have to resign themselves to life and then death as cosmic castaways. Twelve months, she considered ruefully. It was a long time. A long time to worry about "things". The strut-riveted walls closed in a bit more. Sometimes it was unbearable to the point she thought she might scream and keep screaming until someone sutured her mouth shut. Christ, she thought forlornly, she was turning into a nutter.

So much for psyche training she mused. What a fucking joke that was. It was supposed to acquaint one with the rigours of lengthy confinement, but it had clearly failed, for herself and for Mitch. She conceded that it never had any chance of succeeding. Time had quickly become the enemy. Now was the enemy. She was chronic. Jessy was becoming more of a nervous wreck the longer the mission went for. The real problem was obvious. In spite of being busy, Jessy still had too much time to think...to dwell on the possibilities, on the negatives of what they were on their way to do. And there were many, many negatives, especially to her creatively pessimistic mind. Conditioning was great for avoiding conflict but that was about it. Apart from that, it was useless.

***

They had numerous specified tasks, but the maintenance of the ship's systems was fully automated and required only cursory monitoring. The vessel was working so well that no manual course adjustments in the form of radial trimming had been required at all. Their course remained within a few distant decimal points of perfect. SIS was doing extremely well, as expected. By vectoring the positions of prechosen stars along the way, it was methodically updating them using its own brand of relativistic mathematics. Navigation in three dimensions, astrogation, had never been tried before using deep space calculations. To their relief, and pride, it seemed to be working beautifully. Thank Christ, Mitch thought, it was originally his suggestion, far better than navigation from online maps, or inertial and radio techniques. Their course needed to be accurate to the centimetre. The astro-research they were carrying out was fun and provided a stimulating outlet. But it didn't solve Jessy's other problem. That problem was Mitch. She wasn't sure when it happened, but to her deep seated horror, she realized that she'd actually fallen in love with him. Jesus fuck, was her first thought in the dead of night. How?

Stupid question, she knew. It had probably happened before they left Luna, but in those chaotic last weeks she simply hadn't had time to notice. Hadn't had time to unravel her spinning mind or knotted emotions. Alone for two weeks in a tin can, she was now under no illusions. Jessy knew. Mitch had caught her staring and although both made light of it, he was no fool. He knew what it meant, but he chose to ignore it for as long as he could. That was his way. Ignore it and it will go away...hopefully. At least until it was a problem.

Shipboard duties had to be his focus, were his focus. And he was trying like hell to maintain it. Keeping discipline was essential to any crew. Both had dropped into a set routine on Cygnus. They would rise and shower at 0700 after the artificial sun had "risen" and light levels rose from nightglow to Cygnan daylight. Each had specific systems checks to perform, involving reviews of life support equipment which they, and Earth, relied on so heavily. Jessy was intimate with the amine cartridges and the electrostatic deletor, the latter having quickly developed the character of a familiar, friendly companion. She'd even started talking to the damn thing, much to her dismay. At some stage during the first few weeks it had somehow grown a personality, as it sang its sonorous tune, grunting and groaning with the pressures of work. She would tell it about her day, and it would grunt and creak in reply. Happily, and effectively so far, it had removed their carbon rich exhalations from the air.

Mitch was cognizant and familiar with the fourteen microbe and organo-chemical burners and the reclaimed water PCDU, the phase change distillation unit as well as the bizarre looking Gravitator. The massive corkscrew maintained the controlled roll of Cygnus, generating the one "gee" of gravity that kept them so comfortable. All of these systems were linked to SIS. Their examinations were a backup only, SIS did the critical examinations and undertook the fine tuning where necessary. Still, they maintained their routine. Discipline was critical. Keeping busy a priority. At 1200 hours they would take lunch in the spartan dining chambers adjacent to the viewing platform. Food consisted mainly of dehydrated and thermo-stabilised soya proteins, corn based meat substitutes and dried vegetables. Considering its muddy appearance, they both agreed that it wasn't all that bad.

The only variation to this fare was the strictly once a week fresh vegetable "pig out" that was orchestrated by their vege-cultural greenhouse. It was a small semi-sealed eco farm that Jessy lovingly tended, and where a variety of seeds were grown to maturity in a rich human waste biome. It also helped in a small way to condition the atmosphere but more importantly it helped their state of mind, especially Jessy, who loved the carrots and zucchini; the look and the taste. Mitch was sure she'd bathe in carrots if given the chance. She said it was the colour and the crunch, but he knew it went a lot deeper than that. They both revelled in the familiar leafy contours and vibrant bio-pigments of home. It was a tiny verdant slice of Earth, the only interruption to the purely geometric symmetry and dull shades of the Cygnan interior. Both of them loved it, but Mitch would never fess up to it.

From 1500 to 1900 hours both would involve themselves in prescribed astro-research, radio/infrared/UV, planetary searches, and follow-up. After dinner at 1900 hours the rest of the night was free to exercise in the gym or do whatever they wanted to do. Free time. Time to think and to contemplate and ponder. Basically, Mitch and Jessy, whether they liked it or not, spent at least half the day in each other's company, doing nothing but looking, mostly at the view beyond the window.

And whilst their psych tests showed them to be compatible types for extended mutual exposure, Jessy knew their compatibility went a lot deeper. How deep, she wondered, well fuck knew. This trip would let them know, she guessed, trying her best not to think about it.

***

Cygnus had been ploughing through space for almost five weeks and was now almost half a trillion kilometres from home. Sol was a truly alien star, as blurry and unfamiliar as any of the distant lights that pin-holed the skies. The Sun was barely brighter than everything else out there. Einstinian physics had painted the Sun with pigments more attributable to Mars, unimaginably strange because it should have been a dominating yellow pyre. It was deeply unsettling, but it was the unavoidable baggage of extreme speed.

None of the Sun's planets could be seen at all. Earth wasn't even a dim speck, it was totally and completely invisible, like it wasn't even there. It sent a deep dread seeping into Jessy's mind, illustrating just how feeble and tiny their little cradle was. And just how incredibly vast the Great Darkness really was. Everyone she ever knew or heard about lived on a rock that was now invisible. 'Shit,' she bellowed, peering grimly through the window. Surely this proved how scarce and isolated intelligent life or even life per se might be. Christ, no wonder we haven't found them, she considered. The scale of things was thoroughly crushing. The distances totally beyond comprehension. She felt the familiar needles of gloom tearing into her stomach as she gazed at the dead vacuum outside, rubbing her eyes with the heels of her hands, leaving stars before her eyes. How fitting, she thought.

Mitch and Jessy had long believed that other clever life existed somewhere in the cosmos. They'd first set eyes on each other at a SETI conference in 1992, and been taken not only by each other but by the elegance and eloquence of the speaker from Brooklyn. He pervaded their souls with vitality as he exulted on his topic with unbridled spirit and confidence, and with captivating and focussed reason. That there were others. They were hooked on the subject in every sense of the word. And on each other. Looking back at their fading star, Jessy's belief was strengthened. She questioned why wisdom would only raise its head near that pinpoint, that inconceivably minor clump of stellar fluff called Sun, that one amongst centillions. Sol was clearly not exceptional in any way. Extrinsically it was special because its third seed was brimming with the energy of life, but nothing of itself set it apart from the trillions of other friendly fires. From her distant perspective it seemed unlikely in the extreme that the swarms of other planets could have been stillborn and been fated to remain that way forever. Her tiny seat, so far out in space, emphasized just how truly small their home was. Literally a grain of sand on a beach profuse beyond dreaming.

One of Jessy's greatest disappointments was the lack of success of the SETI projects, META, OSAL and STAT. But with a major expansion in 2015 and the introduction of new technology and new space telescopes, she was hopeful that the search would eventually succeed.

They had to be out there. The odds were stacked vastly in favour of them being there. She knew in her being that they were there. Somewhere.

***

'I've never tasted chicken and spuds this good,' Mitch said, grinning widely at Jessy. It was 1920 hours as they chewed their way through their synthetic, odorless evening meal.

'My cooking has really come along,' Jessy added. 'If only I could make something that looked as good as it tasted.' She offered Mitch a fleeting smile then resumed her heavy-lidded frown.

Simple addition of water created a tasty and nutritious meal but to their constant dismay it resembled something intimately related to the sewage reclamation plant. It had none of the aroma of proper food but both agreed that one out of three was infinitely better than none. Following their ritual complaints about the food, Jessy fell quiet, once again becoming withdrawn and distant, behaviour that had become her disturbing norm over the past few weeks. It didn't seem to be affecting her ability to perform her duties though, nor for that matter was it effecting Mitch's. So, on that basis he ignored it and stuck to small talk, either leaving it to Jessy to broach or waiting until necessity forced him to bring it up. He still had options, and he hoped to Christ it stayed that way.

Jessy slithered up from the table while Mitch continued to work his way through the brown chicken pulp. She'd lost weight, he saw that, but it certainly hadn't affected her beauty, she was still stunning. Her symmetry was made all too obvious by the nylon and neoprene sweatsuit that hugged her body like a second skin. Jessy had never looked more attractive, strike that, sexy, Mitch decided as his lust grew unconsciously. He never saw her exercise, but she had the look of an athlete. Go figure, he thought to himself. Jessy glanced down and caught him in the middle of an all too obvious leer. Turning away, she padded quickly through the door, smiling broadly as she left.

'Christ, Fuck,' Mitch mumbled to himself. She'd caught him staring. He cringed as he pictured his wanton expression. There would be no mistaking his thoughts. Damn. Mitch was horrified at his sudden desire. 'Damn!' he repeated it out loud this time, directing the comment at his remaining pseudo chicken. At least hide it a bit, he whispered to himself, a half-smile shaping his mouth. Meaningful stimulation on the starship was virtually nil and Mitch knew that this was only adding to the tension he was feeling. There was no doubt Jessy was suffering the same thing. They'd been warned it would happen, that sexuality would become a priority on voyages of extended cerebral confinement. They also knew what the solution was and the recommended solution, that is.

Reclining in the viewing bubble, Jessy watched the Sun, pondering. It amused her to think that she was the first human to look directly at it through a high powered telescope and not be instantly blinded. The massive coma from the Novae Drive made rearward observations virtually impossible but the Sun was now in a position somewhat to the side of the supernova tail, making some examination possible. She redirected the scope onto Barnard's Star. It swivelled obligingly and had just locked into place and beeped softly when her world suddenly exploded. Kaleidoscopic colour and a jarring dissonance stunned her senses for long seconds, making her mind swim like a hellish discotheque. Jessy almost threw up in the moments before she realised what was going on. 'Fuck,' she screamed, throwing her arms out to steady herself, waiting for decompression to attack her from everywhere. Yellow lights were strobing and a ridiculously loud klaxon was wailing. At that moment Mitch came stumbling into the room.

'Proximity Alert!' Mitch just managed to be heard above the sirens. Spinning on his heels, he was already gone, through the hatch and sprinting down the throat of the craft toward the Compit. Known as Prox, the particle sentry was a phased array radar emanating from all points of the massive punchbowl that pocked the superstructure like a metallic pimple. It sat almost directly above them, behind the beryllium shield. It was designed to warn of anything larger than an oversized grain of dust within fifty million kilometres of the nose of the craft along its projected line of trajectory.

Even with the speed of the ship and the amount of space it was covering, it was considered unlikely that a significant object would be encountered. In space though, nothing is guaranteed. Both

55

knew that much. Anything is a given. They could have literally run into anything. They were in uncharted space.

Jessy and Mitch sprinted to SIS and immediately began scrutinizing the sensor. A group of objects, some twenty in all, were spread over ten thousand cubic kilometres of space and ranged in size from pebbles to small mountains. And all were careering in the direction of Cygnus, or more to the point, Cygnus was careering toward them.

'We've got a situation here, er...what's the range on those objects,' Mitch snapped. Jessy was already working on the answer, eyes fixed forward, lips showing signs of a slight tremor. 'Fuck me,' she said, gawking at Mitch. Her eyes were as wide as they could go, without falling out.

'According to Prox, they're twelve million kilometres away, we have to make a course adjustment now, otherwise it's telling us we'll impact with one of those mountains in thirty-two seconds.' Jessy was certain they were about to die. She could taste it.

'Why the hell did it pick these things up so late? We should've known about this two minutes ago,' Mitch barked, glaring down at the goddamn system. 'The ship isn't designed for rapid course changes. Shit...shit!' Mitch was hysterical, breathing like he'd just run a marathon, hesitating and then dexterously fingering the course input button having already thumped the override button.

He finished typing and hit the initiate keystroke. Fucking move, he screamed to Prox.

'Impact in twenty-eight seconds, I can't feel any course corrections,' Jessy shrilled, with eyes that were wide and questioning.

Suddenly, both could feel the inertia as the massive craft fought to alter its course in line with Mitch's instructions. While quick in a lateral sense, any other movements by Cygnus were cold blooded and slow.

Jessy was still glued to the monitor, urging the craft to move. Hoping it would move quick enough. 'It's happening too slowly Mitch,' she tried to speak as calmly as she could but it sounded shrill and harsh in her ears, '...impact in twenty-one seconds, we're not going to clear their path. We need to slow our velocity but there's no way to...'

Both could see the meteoroids at the very limit of their Jarrion vision, growing larger and doing so with staggering speed. It was clear in the seconds before impact that they were the remnants of an asteroid or a small moon shattered by some thunderous collision with something. But what were they doing here? As good as anywhere he supposed, gulping a breath of the suddenly leaden atmosphere. Murphy's Law, he hadn't forgotten.

She felt like screaming. 'Five seconds Mitch, they're going to hit, aren't they?' Jessy squealed. Mitch was hypnotized by the unexpected danger. 'Fuck', he repeated loudly. He glanced at Prox, knowing he was totally powerless to fend off the deadly hailstorm. Whatever was going to happen...was about to happen.

'We're definitely going to avoid all the big fragments,' Mitch whispered as a sound like a shotgun blast filled the craft. Something had penetrated the ship. Fortunately, it was still in one piece. Jessy and Mitch instinctively grabbed each other, watching in terrified awe as several tumbling fragments of rectangular rock the size of small mountains passed within a few hundred kilometres of their precious craft. Jessy's eyes darted from Mitch to space outside and back again. They were there and then they weren't, gone in the blink of the eye. Jessy closed her eyes. She knew she was about to die. She could taste it on her lips like a bitter spray of vinegar. They were big, not that it mattered.

Any one of the larger chunks, had they hit, would have destroyed their ship in a heartbeat...and Cygnus was hit. The entire vessel was flooded with strobing arrows of red energy, meaning it was losing pressure to the bio support area. Yellow meant something was detected, red meant something had hit in the bio zone. Red was the worst. Cygnus had avoided the death chunks only to be maimed by a piece of celestial talus. Structural breach.

'We're losing pressure,' Mitch yelled to Jessy. He immediately started fingering the keyboard. Hull Integrity was flashing on the monitor, revealing two one-hundred percent breaches to the superstructure. Parts of Cygnus were open to vacuum. Life support showed that the nitroxyether was venting at an alarming rate, and he knew they needed to be sealed in the next few minutes. Jessy felt like running to the breach or breaches and fixing them right now, but she didn't know where they were. She was instead doing a herky-jerky walk from one wall to the other, not sure what do.

Mitch hoped to God that the breaches could be reached from inside the ship. To his left, the Hull Integrity visuals showed that both the craters in the hull could be reached from bio support and were located close to each other. One was above the gymnasium and one below. It also showed that the holes were large. 'Bloody hell,' he yelled, staring at the figures being spat out by Prox. Mitch and Jessy could sense the loss of air pressure in the wobbly feeling swelling between their ears.

'I want you in your EV suit, NOW!' Mitch exploded as he ran the few steps to retrieve both their pressure gowns. 'Fucking move,' he screamed, gripping the edge of the window to right himself.

Equipped with a handful of resin sponges and seeing Jessy in her pressurised E-suit, Mitch sprinted the few metres to the gym. The holes, like terrifying ebony eyes, were each about five centimetres wide, and to his horror he noticed that he could see stars through the chasms, as though the eyes had tiny zirconian pupils. They were only partially obscured by the milky atmosphere whistling into space.

'Oh fuck,' he muttered as he peered at the life gasses hemorrhaging into the vacuum. Balancing on top of the graphite ladder, he'd set the first of the pads in place in under two minutes. The other cavity on the floor was fixed in a few seconds. Within half a minute the polycarbonate platelets had swollen to tightly plug the rips. It was clear that they had been hit by a tiny moon fleck that had passed straight through the craft, in through the roof of the gym and out through the floor in a direct line. Like a hot knife through butter. The noise made by the escaping atmosphere had been earsplitting and terrifying. Now there was only silence. Wonderful, redeeming silence. 'Thank Christ,' Mitch breathed, puffing and panting, knowing what he now had to do.

Jessy was similarly gasping for breath at the foot of the ladder, terrified by visions of their mission over almost before it got started. Her immediate thoughts had been a swirling blend of pity and sadness. Sadness for her and Mitch and pity for Rhys and Sean who would never have woken from PCM. And then of course there was the small issue of Earth and all it held. 'Sweet Jesus in heaven,' she murmured under her breath, trying to slow her breathing. Her heart was still firmly lodged in her throat, squirming and knocking above her voice-box.

Mitch descended the ladder in a single bound and grabbed Jessy who responded with a lingering embrace. 'Thank God,' Mitch said. He cleared his throat, grabbing Jessy around the midriff. Hugging was no easy assignment in a pressure suit, no matter how lightweight and manoeuvrable the designers claimed they were. Absolute stitch me up salesmanship, Mitch thought absently. He remembered the slick team from Massachusetts who sold them to AASSA.

Sliding apart and removing their helmets, they stood and stared at each other. He could see the terror flickering behind her red-rimmed eyes.

'Jesus Christ,' Jessy rasped, scrutinising Mitch's face closely.

'I never want to go through that again,' Mitch growled through clenched teeth. 'We should be dead you know, those mountains missed us by a millisecond,' he whispered, holding his thumb and forefinger close together. If Cygnus was slightly further on in space, just slightly, we'd be space dust, a vague cosmic memory.' He was visibly shaken and pale as he coughed and gagged on his own bile, pondering what might have been in altogether too much detail. Thank God that's done, Mitch said to himself, looking around gratefully at the intact ship.

'You performed superbly.' Jessy sat down on the knee-curl exerciser and crossed her legs.

They were both out of their Esuits now. Mitch was talking and Jessy watched him intently. He suddenly paused and looked up sharply. 'We need to check Prox, we should've known about those goddamn rocks minutes well before we did, that was nearly the difference between life and death, for us, for the mission...for Earth.' Mitch hesitated, clearly overwhelmed by the whole thing. He looked at Jessy and tried to smile. Mitch got half way there and stopped. He knew she wouldn't like what he was going to say next. 'Now for the good news.' He paused again, looking at her directly in the eyes. '...I'll need to go EV and weld fibre plates over those holes. The resin pads won't hold indefinitely.'

57

She looked at him blankly, mulling over the statement, feeling the gut wrenching anxiety that bubbled within. Mitch was right, she didn't like it. She fucking hated it.

'It's not a good idea,' she said quietly, shaking her head and glancing up briefly. 'You know we should avoid going outside, the radiation from the Drive...'

'Come on Jess,' Mitch soothed, 'the Peri-shield screens the hull and I'll be wearing the armored E-suit, so I'll be safe, don't worry. I won't leave you. If it wasn't completely necessary, I wouldn't consider it, you know that. I'll be well protected.' He was almost convincing himself. 'If I don't do it, it'll go, eventually. Out here, continuum mechanics will make it so. Might go soon, it could go closer to Centaurus, might be never...who knows, but we need to reduce the risk?' He smiled briefly at Jessy and moved quickly toward the Compit. He needed to do this, no matter what. Jessy followed close behind, heart pounding and palms bleeding icy sweat.

'Maybe we should wake Sean or Rhys?'

'Definitely not.' Mitch wouldn't consider it. 'This is a minimum risk operation, it'll take forty-five minutes tops.' He proceeded to don the Lobster Shell, special E-suit that was pumped with lithium hydride and Dacron, interlaid between the aluminized nylon and marquisette cloth. It was ionising resistance to the limit of human technology. Mitch hoped it worked like it was supposed to.

The USPA had recently redesigned the suit to protect against severe ionising radiation and heat. Lengthy testing in dirty fission furnaces and the new, cleaner fusion reactors suggested that it worked even better than they'd hoped.

Mitch was hopeful that his experience with it here would be just as good as the tests suggested. If it wasn't, then the cost would be his life and maybe that of eight billion others.

Jessy watched as Mitch ambled into the airlock, decked in his crimson exo-skeleton. It was chilling to think that she would soon be the only person conscious on Cygnus. Jessy peered at Mitch with a slack expression and partly open mouth. The inner airlock door closed with a soft whoosh. She could see Mitch through the small plate as he prepared to cycle the rim hatch and reveal himself to the depths of space. She felt her face go cold and ashen as she watched him make preparations to leave Cygnus.

'I'm opening the outer hatch.' His digicom was static. He thumped the CV line to no effect.

Jessy saw the blackness swell like a coal stope in front of him. The last wisps of air swirled in front of him, spiralling like steam into the great emptiness. Although Mitch was an old hand in space, the knowledge that he was so far from home gave this space an extra impact, an extra unsettling dimension he didn't need. It was unsettling already and he hadn't even left Cygnus yet. After hesitating, Mitch manoeuvred himself alongside the great ship with the aid of his rotatable compression thrusters that were attached to both arms and both legs of his Esuit.

They looked like tiny black and red aerosol cans. Jessy ran to the gym so she could see him as he scrambled to the "roof", carrying with him the small sack of patching equipment. She watched him drift quickly past the plate and rapidly beyond her line of sight. He was going fast, she thought. He'll be back soon, she was sure.

Mitch slowly set up the equipment, finding it hellishly difficult to coordinate all the materials. Maybe he should have taken Jessy's suggestion to wake Rhys. He would do this in no time flat. Concentrate, he chided himself. He knew what he had to do. After half an hour, Mitch was well into sealing the last of the external wounds.

'I'd reckon another ten minutes,' he said, taking ragged breaths that sounded staccato-like through the intercom that linked him to Jessy and Cygnus.

'Just hurry up Mitch,' Jessy whispered. 'Just hurry the fuck up!' Jessy was reddening in the face and visibly sweating. 'He'll be fine,' she kept repeating to herself.

He planned to take a two minute breather and then finish the repair work that he guessed would take another five minutes. As he stood motionless on the spine of Cygnus on top of the massive black "U" in "USPA" he swivelled his head and gazed straight up. A stunning nebula, mostly pink but with thousands of sapphire pinpoints hypnotized him. He knew it was light years away but he was choked by its primeval beauty, the colours, and its apparent proximity. Mitch stared, in complete awe, remaining totally still as his mind left his body and wandered into the cosmos. He felt himself totally stationary, like a boulder surrounded by kilometres of rock. Inert.

He knew he was travelling impossibly quickly but who would have known? The fabulous velocity was beyond his grasp, not to mention his feel. Five orbits of the Earth in one second...with no indication of movement at all. A magnificent feeling of tranquility and stupor descended on him as he continued his upward contemplation. He knew the pink points of light surrounded a supermassive black hole.

His wanderings were shattered by a heart shaking jolt.

'Mitch!' Jessy was screaming and he could hear the wailing klaxon over her voice in the intercom.

'Proximity Alert! For God's sake, get your arse back in the ship! She yelled, bringing a shaky hand to her forehead as she barked.

Mitch hesitated as his body swayed like a punch drunk fighter. What the hell was happening? Interstellar debris larger than a few microns was unbelievably rare. What was going on here? He collected himself and spoke rapidly, 'How long have we got, what's its, what's the goddamn trajectory?' He yelled, tensing his body inside his suit.

Jessy was fumbling for the information, swearing to herself as she went. 'We've got an object about a hundred metres in diameter at forty-three million k's. It should miss us Mitch, but Prox is telling me that its course is, er...erratic. For whatever reason it's...um, sort of wobbling. Mitch, you've got four minutes to get inside. Bloody well move. For fuck's sake move!' She screamed, walking in a jerky fashion around the cabin.

Grabbing the cold welder, Mitch continued to melt the final web of titanium fibre over the last tear. He knew that if this thing was going to hit, it wouldn't matter if he was inside or out, but he'd much rather be inside with Jessy. He owed her that much. With welder in hand he started a clumsy but quick as possible retreat. Where the fuck was this space junk coming from? We'd be unlucky if we came within a billion kilometres of anything as big as a finger nail, and now this! He couldn't believe it . Kuiper belt was the thumbtack that pricked his mind.

'Hurry Mitch, are you hurrying? I can't see you...what are you doing up there? Two minutes forty-five to encounter,' Jessy screeched, eyes wild, bulging as though they may burst. Mitch could hear her raspy breaths and was sure she was close to losing it.

'Please don't die,' Jessy pleaded. He had twenty metres to go. She estimated he'd be inside in under a minute if nothing went wrong. If nothing went wrong. Plenty of time, she said out loud several times. Fuck, she thought, she was alone in the craft and didn't like it one bit.

Mitch thumped the airlock toggle and was inside the craft. The outer door cycled closed and atmosphere punched into the airlock. 'I'm in Jess,' Mitch puffed into his helmet.

With re-pressurisation complete, the inner hatch breached automatically with a dull 'pop'. Jessy jumped on Mitch and bearhugged him with both feet off the ground, sobbing quietly, tears squeezing from her eyes. She'd expected him to die. Both remained tightly joined for several seconds.

'Thank God!' Jessy gasped several times, shaking her head and closing her eyes. 'Thank fuck,' she breathed, spitting all over him. Mitch eventually loosened her iron grip and sprinted to the Compit. During the feverish past few minutes neither had noticed that the klaxon had stopped wailing and the yellow strobes had stopped strobing without intervention. In fact, everything had gone quiet, totally, unremittingly quiet. Mitch stooped over Prox and peered at it. It had literally gone blank. The luminous data that had been cycling across its face had vanished.

'What the hell...' Mitch started, 'where's the goddamn data?' He looked closer, flaring his nostrils. His eyes darted from Jessy to Prox and back again.

'We should have visual contact by now,' Jessy said, as she scanned the blackness in front of them through the Jarrion. Both could see nothing. Mitch demanded a status report from the system. Where was the goddamn data? All readouts agreed, there was nothing of detectable size in the search arena...a few hydrogen atoms, the odd helium spiral, but apart from that, nothing. Empty. The hunting parameters were clean. Jessy looked equally stunned and relieved, and although confused she couldn't help but smile. 'There's nothing there now,' she said, gazing with focus at Prox. Jessy was smiling disarmingly.

'Indications were that the close encounter should have been, er...now.' Jessy looked at Mitch who was still demanding information from SIS and getting nothing, neither data nor explanation. He was bending over the display, muttering under his breath, chastising it as though it had the power of mind.

'It must have been a ghost...software glitch, a false echo of some kind. Jesus Christ!' Mitch glared at the monitor, almost daring it to respond. It stayed blank. Piece of shit, he thought.

'We have a backup system, I suggest we switch to it immediately. Piece of shit,' he said out loud, and kept staring at it, wondering what the hell was wrong with it? Mitch pounded his thighs with hands drawn into tight fists. Grunting, he made the necessary keystrokes and ensured that the first task of the second system was a self-diagnostic. It was performed and showed that the backup was operating without fault. They would have SIS assess the other system later.

Jessy and Mitch were done, thankful that they and Cygnus had eluded the potentially ruinous hailstorm. They well realized the craft could have been shattered and spread like metal filings on the edge of the galaxy, had it happened only slightly differently. The false reading that followed only served to heighten their sense of relief.

Jessy looked at Mitch and he at her. Neither spoke for a long time. They stood and pondered what might have been, staring at each other only arms-length away. Jessy felt a little light headed. The lethal game of Russian Roulette with rocks and talus had loosened their emotions, allowing them to fizz outward until only a flimsy layer of skin held them in. Mitch felt his intensity rising.

'I could do with a drink,' Mitch said, trying to speak and breathe as casually as he could. She couldn't believe she'd heard him right. Sorry? Jessy retorted silently. What the fuck was he, Mitch Taylor, talking about?

'I think it would definitely benefit the crew,' she replied quickly, before he had a chance to change his mind. Before he had a chance to take another breath actually.

Mitch knew it was against USPA mission directives for both of the crew to consume alcohol or any other Level 3 drug but he found himself having difficulty recalling the exact directive. 53.C (iv) wasn't it? He couldn't help but remind himself. Fuck it, he reckoned, it was a long time coming. Both could do with a drink, come what may.

The Agency had allowed a case of champagne to be loaded onto Cygnus, after a week of vehement lobbying by Rhys and Sean. They had demanded it under the guise of "social concerns and effective crew interaction". What a load of crap, Jessy knew. Their thesis was a compelling one apparently and the Agency had eventually bowed to the request, probably more to shut them up than anything else. In fact, they correctly realized that crew harmony sat at the very apex of their non-technical mission concerns. In space, happy and effective were indivisible.

The conditions attached to its consumption, Mitch mused, seemed billions of kilometres away. And as commander of the vessel he thought that Jessy and he should take the time to mull over the recent events. So, fuck it, he thought, why not?

'I'll see you in my quarters in ten minutes, I'll put the champagne in the nitrogen store for a few seconds, hope you like it chilled!'

She left, smiling softly to herself. 'Yes,' she said quietly. Jessy had a wide smile and a raised eyebrow as she left Mitch's quarters.

Mitch saw the smile, and he knew what it meant, and wondered if he was doing the right thing. He didn't bother to answer himself because the question was academic. He knew the answer was no, but he was on autopilot, at least he admitted that to himself. Mitch knew he couldn't stop what was going to happen, it was inevitable and probably had been since they'd left Luna.

Thinking about it, he broke into a broad smile. Mitch swore quietly to himself as he walked the forty metres to his quarters, trying to remain calm, but failing badly.

Mitch had positioned his two orthopedic chairs around the glass table in the centre of his quarters. Taking up the entire wall nearest the door was a bed, and above was a panoramic titanium-boron dome that gave Mitch a panoramic view of the Galaxy beyond.

He jumped at the soft tones of Jessy's voice. His hair almost stood on end. For a man who had endured so much, been the first to trek across the deserts of Mars, he was letting this situation get to him. Personal relationships had always been his Achilles heel, the chink in his makeup, and he was the first to admit it. Where the hell was his voice...how old was he?

'Can I come in Mitch?' Jessy repeated, exhaling quietly into the radiophone outside his quarters. Mitch thumped the remote control and the hatch hissed into its narrow wall recess.

'I've been expecting you,' Mitch grinned motioning her to the champagne and the crystal. No expense spared, he thought. The scene looked ridiculously surreal, his mind and other parts of his anatomy were throbbing with excitement. Impressed by Jessy's appearance, he was stunned.

She looked drop-dead gorgeous and patently sexual. Holy shit was his earsplitting thought. She was wearing her only decent outfit, a too short black leather skirt that hugged her body, complemented by a lowcut red top. One that clung determinedly to her breasts, vividly painting the contours of a starkly feminine form. Mitch considered where they were and almost laughed out loud. It was a crazy, unthinkable scenario. Shit, it was fucking insane. But in a flash, he knew it wasn't. It was something that had to happen to cut through the debilitating stress..

Mitch's breath caught in his throat as she padded toward him. Was it the fact that he hadn't seen another woman in five weeks that made her look so good? Christ, what would he be like after four years? Or was it because he hadn't had time to even think of a woman in the last ten months since Cygnus became so important. Mitch knew the real reason and he tried to ignore it. The course they were on was irrevocable. Fated. What to do? Just follow the tracks came the voice in his head.

Jessy moved slowly to her chair and sat down. The skirt was short. God it was so short. Mitch tried not to notice but his gaze was drawn, dragged inexorably to her crossed legs. He had to concentrate on looking at Jessy's eyes. It was difficult.

'I'm thirsty Mitch, pour for God's sake,' Jessy said, the look in her eyes unmistakable. Mitch had seen it before and had always had the sense, and the will, to resist. But now, his will was gone, lost somewhere in the emptiness of space. Uncorking the Vintage Bollinger, he poured the bubbles into Jessy's glass, watching it spill over the top to form a sparkling pool around the base of the glass. 'Uh-oh,' he thought.

'I should be more careful. Rhys would die if he saw that...this French stuff is very dear to him.' Fucking champagne Mitch thought, wondering if he sounded as nervous as he felt. He hoped not, clenching his toes tightly.

Jessy ran her finger through the puddle and tasted it. 'Mmm...perfect, now pour yourself one.' She was enjoying herself immensely, the smile on her face almost stretching ear to ear. Mitch felt like he was in someone else's body, observing the scene through another's eyes. This couldn't be him, could it? He felt uncoordinated, awkward, like he'd lost four fingers and gained six thumbs. Eventually, getting some champagne into his own glass, he downed it in two gulps and slowly began to relax and uncoil a bit. It was amazing what a few drams of alcohol could do. The stilted conversation began to come more easily as time passed. They started on another bottle of champagne around 2100 hours. Talk became more casual and more unconstrained as the liquid flowed.

Jessy wanted Mitch and she was fairly sure, no she was certain Mitch wanted her. By 2200 hours Jessy had joined Mitch in his chair. Both straps were off her shoulders and her breasts threatened to break free. He realized there was no going back now, he ... they were committed.

Mitch kissed Jessy softly at first but the kisses quickly became more frantic and penetrating. She was free of her top now and was tugging at Mitch's clothes, the hunger written in her slightly unfocussed gaze. Picking her up, he peeled off her skirt and carried her over to the bed where he had the rest of her clothes off in a heartbeat. Jessy was naked apart from her long gold Croix chain that hung to one side of her breasts. Lying on the dappled bedspread, she looked up at him, staring at him, provoking him without uttering a word. Mitch stepped out of his clothes. He wanted Jessy with a desire he hadn't expected, nor known before.

Their lovemaking was as intense as it was gentle, lustful and chaotic, and for the next hour Mitch and Jessy immersed themselves in each other. They were the first interstellar lovers, the first human ones anyway. The recent tension, the boredom of routine aboard the starship and their crushing responsibilities were momentarily lost as their tumultuous coupling choked their senses.

***

Cygnus had been riding the energy of exploding stars for more than two months. It was sliding into space at the rate of an Astronomical Unit every fifteen minutes, the Earth-Luna distance every two seconds. Their rapid passage was vividly mirrored by the alien Universe they travelled through, equally obscured and highlighted, daubed and twisted by the bizarre pigments of high speed.

It was a constant reminder of where they were and what they were doing, and how deeply into the unknown they really were. One glance through the vacuum plate window and all that came hammering back in a heart shaking jolt. They were in the midst of the Great Wide Open.

Jessy and Mitch, we're picking through the starchy mulch they tentatively called breakfast, in the spartan dining area. Looking tired and drawn, Jessy sat in stark contrast to Mitch who looked vibrant and ate his meal with gusto and animation. There was something distinctly wrong with this breakfast time picture. Jessy looked wrong. She was drained and weak although she'd slept quite well. It wasn't like her at all, she looked like shit, and didn't want to eat.

'God, I can hardly bear to look at this shit,' she said in a voice dripping with anger and fatigue, eyes red and sore, rubbing and then scratching at her forearm as she pushed at her cereal.

Mitch rarely heard her swear with such feeling, especially about anything as inane as food. He looked over and caught her staring at her bowl. Glaring at it as though it might dare to speak back. Weetabix rarely did that. Mitch's pulse increased a notch as he considered the scene. Something was definitely wrong with her.

'You okay Jess? ...you, uh, don't look so good,' Mitch enquired casually, trying to concentrate on his food, glancing briefly at her and then down again, at his bowl.

She suddenly swatted her bowl to the floor and without looking up, ran to her room, brushing him as she rushed past. Her hand was pressed firmly over her mouth like a steel plate. Mitch's heart began to beat harder and quicker as he really contemplated the picture. A bright white light turned on somewhere near the back of his brain.

'What the fuck…?' Mitch mouthed as he heard her rapid footsteps disappear up the corridor. Racing to the door of the dining room, he peered after her. Jessy had run straight to her quarters and punched the hatch close button.

Totally out of character, Mitch considered uncomfortably. He replayed the scene in slow motion and as he did so, the unease he felt deepened. What had happened in such a short time? She'd recently been so happy. What in God's name had changed so quickly? His mind was reeling, running over the possibilities as he edged slowly toward her room. He was none too happy with any of them. Knocking on Jessy's hatch and receiving no answer, he pressed the release toggle and the plate slid back. At least she hadn't barred the door, that had to be a good sign. The thought was destroyed by what he found inside.

Jessy was slumped untidily over the toilet as though she'd been picked up and dropped there from a great height. He picked her up and carried her to the bed, trying to remain calm and push through a gathering haze of panic. What is wrong with you, he wondered, not happy with any of the options that flashed through his mind, seeing her hand still clamped hard over her mouth.

'Jess...what's w-wrong, what's h-h-happened?' Mitch stammered as he grabbed a towel and soaked it, placing it gently on her forehead. He tapped her cheeks hoping for some sign of life. Jessy slowly opened her eyes which in spite of her sickness were still clear and bright, like twin emeralds with slightly swollen ebony centres.

'I was being sick and holding my sides when I felt myself going,' Jessy said breathlessly. Tears welled in her eyes and started running down her cheeks and onto the pink bed sheet. He'd never

62

seen such massive tears as they still fell from her eyes, and dampened the bed clothes. She was in serious trouble, that's all he could tell. Mitch's heartbeat increased a bit.

'Jessy...you're okay,' Mitch said gently, hoping for the best. 'You've obviously picked up a bug or eaten something not quite right, it's no big deal.' He knew this was more or less an impossible scenario. Jessy pulled herself up to a sitting position and looked directly at Mitch who was almost sitting on top of her.

'Come on Mitch,' she said firmly, 'you know that's not it. Her eyes were suddenly wide as she spoke. The food is synthetic and totally irradiated, no bug known could survive. And the atmosphere is totally sanitized, the microbe burner doesn't let anything survive. You know that. I don't have a virus or a bug or any bacteria and I think you also know that.' You're not a fucking idiot, don't act like one, she felt like saying.

Jessy stared at him unblinkingly until a fresh wave of tears spilled onto her cheeks. Mitch wiped them away and instinctively hugged her. He was afraid. Shit scared actually. Jessy pushed Mitch away and spoke through tightly clenched teeth.

'I'm pregnant, I know I'm damn well pregnant.' She started sobbing again.

Mitch had felt it coming. He stared at her unseeingly until her gaze dropped to the floor. Fuck, he screamed silently. 'But how...I don't mean how...I mean...it's not possible, surely, it's not possible,' Mitch protested feebly. He knew. Everything pointed in only one direction.

'I was sick yesterday, 'Jessy moaned, 'and I was even sicker this morning and I'm having crazy mood swings. Don't tell me you haven't noticed. Christ, my hormones are everywhere, I can't even think most of the time.' Jessy hesitated, 'If my little sister's experience is any indication then I'm pregnant, with your child.'

'Christ.' Mitch couldn't breathe. He swallowed and looked at the floor. Cygnus was caving in on him. He could feel the emptiness outside sucking at his mind. It couldn't be, it wasn't possible! They were both on long-term contraceptives, the so called cosmo-ceptives designed specifically for those who frequent higher than normal radiation environments. It all but removed pregnancy as a reason for an illness. With both of them taking them the chances of conception were supposed to be less than a fraction of a percent. How the hell could this have happened? It simply couldn't be true, but he knew it was, even before Jessy had suggested it. It was the only realistic explanation. All his options had suddenly evaporated before his eyes. Like steam in the wind.

'Okay, so you're pregnant,' Mitch eventually said as quietly and as calmly as he could, furrowing his brow. 'We can't undo it so we'll have to ride with it.' Mitch smiled tightly and nodded hesitantly while still thinking about it.

Jessy's eyes widened. 'You mean you think I should proceed with the pregnancy...take it to term, have the child? You must be fucking joking.' Jessy looked at him as though he'd sprouted another head. 'It'd be born before we even acquire CX1. How the fucking hell would we care for it?' The lack of paediatric facilities was a definite turnoff for Jessy. She glared at Mitch with cold, hard eyes. It was easy for him, she reckoned.

'We're not equipped for either a birth or the maintenance of a baby. And what about your exposure to X-rays? God knows what effect that's had on you...it might be, um...deformed. We've got to abort Mitch, it's the only way.' Tears were dropping freely from eyes swimming with moisture, suggesting that she didn't entirely agree with what she'd just said. Jessy' face was ashen and her hands clammy with icy sweat.

Looking at her, he drew in a deep breath and spoke softly and deliberately. 'We're in space and we're unsure whether we'll ever be able to return to Earth. Our short term survival and Earth's is tenuous at best. It's a less than suitable environment for a child, I absolutely acknowledge that. There will be problems, I acknowledge that too. But the uncertainties can be overcome. This can be done, if you want it to happen.' Mitch was unsure, but he wanted to sound sure at least. Truth be told, he had absolutely no idea what to do. Mitch briefly shook his head and stared into space.

'Tell me how Mitch, tell me how?' Jessy pleaded as she hoisted herself over to the edge of the bed, puffing all the way. She was way less sure than Mitch. She quite literally didn't know what to do. Keep it, don't keep it, Jessy didn't know which was the best way to go.

'Medi-lab and Rhys can cope with the birth of a child. With the four of us on deck at all times we can care for a child. We have the supplies and the nutrients we would require to supplement your own. Life support can and will cope, my exposure to X-rays was minimal, the proportional counter confirmed it. Genetic transmutation is unlikely. If we have the desire...then we can fucking do this.' He looked at her and forced a smile which appeared remarkably genuine. Jessy looked at Mitch, then closed her eyes and immediately reopened them, staring down at the bed, looking sombre.

Her words dribbled out, low and pleading. She looked like hell. Jessy was deeply troubled and staring at her hands, 'God Mitch, why, and why now? This mission can't cope with a pregnancy or a baby, surely you can see that.' She felt like knocking on something. His forehead maybe.

'No, it doesn't have to be like that.' Mitch was sure now and he thought Jessy might be coming around too. Slowly. Deep down he knew she was only looking for support from him. 'I'll help you Jessy. It will eventually become hard for you to keep up your schedule around here, but I will help and if necessary, I'll bring Sean or Rhys or both out of PCM.' Mitch left her and walked briskly to Medi-lab. She'll make the right decision, Mitch was sure of it.

Jessy's sobbing continued unabated. She could only imagine how exquisitely difficult it would be. She also knew that there was nothing more she wanted than to bear Mitch's child. But to bring a baby into this place, fuck me, was it fair on the child, on them, or on the mission that meant so much to so many billions of people? Surely not, but she wasn't absolutely sure. She also knew that Mitch wasn't sure either, despite his confidence. He had no clue. But if it came down to it, she was doubtful whether either could abort the foetus, so the discussion was probably moot anyway.

Jessy had to steel herself to the idea of having a child aboard Cygnus, assuming that it went naturally to term. She had always pictured herself as a professional, dedicated to her work at AASSA, focussed on her career. Having a baby had never seriously entered her mind. Who with, in any event? Perhaps she would settle down and have one later in life, but just what later meant, she hadn't ever been sure.

Starting an unplanned family billions of kilometres into space aboard a unique spacecraft with no paediatric facilities was not, surprisingly, something Jessy found the least bit appealing.

5

Star Child

'Science confers power on anyone who takes the trouble to learn it.' ~ *Carl Sagan*

Over the ensuing months, Jessy's pregnancy became progressively more obvious. It was slow to come but her stomach gradually found a life of its own and forced itself out into a prominent bulge. Despite the knowledge that it was only a temporary condition she could barely look at her newly acquired proportions, and the loss of her hard fought figure, without crying. Her embarrassment was obvious, especially in front of Mitch, notwithstanding his sympathetic and soothing comments, which meant nothing.

Mirrors don't lie, Jessy would often say. She tried to placate herself by focusing on the result at the end of it all, a child. Her's and Mitch's. God, how she hoped it was normal and the birth was easy. Fear of the alternatives, of complications or deformity, lay at the back of her brain like razor wire. There were no MRI's or ultrasounds, so she would just have to wing it. She prayed to God for her unborn child...and for herself and Mitch. If the child was to be born normal, they would need a dose of luck.

Mitch was now shouldering much of the responsibility for monitoring SIS and the numerous Cygnus ancillary systems. He'd not found it necessary to seriously consider pulling Rhys out of PCM, as much as he might have wanted to. That could wait until Jessy was nearer to term. Apart from his extra work load, not much actually changed aboard Cygnus. Jessy had overcome her morning and afternoon sickness and was becoming fully conversant if not happy with the changes her body was undergoing. She was coping well, Mitch decided. Thank Christ for that, he thought, preferring to avoid thinking about the alternative. He could only imagine what Sean and Rhys would think when they crawled out of their coma pods. He laughed out loud at the prospect, he could barely believe it himself. A fucking spacekid! Who the hell would have thought? No-one, that's who. He continued chuckling quietly to himself.

***

It had now been seven full months since Cygnus had departed Luna. Jessy was overtly pregnant but otherwise appeared to be in good health. It was her spirits that weren't so good, they'd recently started to degenerate, almost in reverse proportion with her swelling midriff. She reported frequently to Mitch on the health of the baby, extrapolating its growth and condition from the facilities in Medi-lab that were helpful if not specific to her needs. Her blood pressure had risen over the past few weeks causing Mitch to severely limit her dawdlings around the ship, and although Jessy resisted, he insisted. Most of her time was spent either sitting behind the larger of the two optical telescopes or checking her's and the baby's vitals in Medi-lab. Boredom was becoming a major problem, it gave her far too much time to think, too much time to dwell on likely outcomes.

Peering at the dull speck that was Proxima Centauri, she continued to be stunned by the relativistic voice of the other forestars. Even despite Proxima's dullness, it still scared her senseless, knowing that it was shadowed by an invisible titan, a monster that was destined to wreak devastation on their planet unless they deflected it. Them and their little craft of weapons. It seemed like a laughable joke. It seemed impossible.

Using the Number 1 scope she could see the swirlings of colorful sun stuff being dragged from the star and sucked kicking and screaming into the maw of its dark companion. It was like a fantastic whale shark snorting a star load of phosphorescent krill.

65

She was busy setting the manual focus on one of the brilliant gas spirals, axial to the two objects, when the yellow strobes and earsplitting whoop of Prox startled her. Not this time, she steeled herself. This time she wouldn't be fooled by some fucked up system.

Jessy walked calmly, but as quickly as she could to the Compit a hundred metres away. Mitch was already there, seated in front of the monitor. The monitor he'd already grown to hate, although this was the second iteration. He remembered the analogy of a computer and a car, the crashing and software updates of the former, and the driving activity of the latter, and nodded knowingly. Fucking Prox, he echoed silently. Nothing like stopping on the side of the freeway for no reason and your car refuses to restart, or it starts and goes so slow you feel like pulling your hair out. Prox was the same.

She padded up to him in a gray lab coat that was now her permanent dress, the only piece of clothing she could find that fitted her corpulence with any semblance of comfort.

'I hope to God this system is working as well as it says it is,' Mitch sighed. 'Where the hell is this space crap coming from?' Not the Kuiper belt he thought, maybe they're escapees from the Oort Cloud, the halo of bits and pieces that embraced the solar system at distance. He snapped back to attention, pounding his thigh with a fist as he spoke, more to wake up than anything else.

'...system's located an object thirty-eight million kilometres ahead of us. Indications are it will miss us by five thousand kilometres...a safe margin, assuming it's correct.' Mitch exhaled loudly, looking at the monitor which displayed vitals on the object. He looked again and blinked, 'what the hell...?' he exclaimed.

'Son-of-a-Bitch!' He said slowly. 'How can that be?' He stopped and hesitated. 'It's...wait, how can that be...it's coming toward us at over forty thousand kilometres per second. It can't be.' Mitch's mouth slackened and his eyes were as wide as they could go. 'What is going on here?' He snapped with brows almost completely knitted. After a long pause, he continued, his voice was suddenly soft and uncertain, '...object is thirteen hundred metres in diameter and is...er...showing up as being close enough to spherical.' Spherical, the word burnt into his mind like a cerebral brand.

'What do you mean spherical? How can it be spherical?' Jessy questioned, not believing it for a second. No way.

'According to Prox, this thing is almost perfectly round and has a curiously uniform albedo, which taken together suggests something unusual...something I cannot explain.' He felt the blood pounding in his brain and spoke with a mixture of uncertainty and excitement. 'I'll direct Prox to lock the external Jarrions on it so we can replay it and get a look. Otherwise we'll barely see it, in fact with the combined speeds in opposite directions, we won't see it, at all.' He glanced out the window, wondering about the true nature of the unexplainable object. It sounded strange.

Pondering what the oddly contoured object was, they both tried to ignore the tingling, slightly sharp sensations that crept into their deeper brains. They both had the unavoidable feeling that something very unusual was upon them. Spherical … he hadn't forgotten. They waited in silence. Waited for whatever it was. They tried again to explain the data from Prox but couldn't. Maybe the system was indeed fucked.

'Encounter in twenty seconds,' Mitch said. Oh well, we're about to find out, he thought, come what may. They padded over to the massive clear plate. The entity passed Cygnus in a fraction of a second. Both had a vague impression of a point of light turning on and off to the right of their standing position. It literally flashed passed them. If they relied on their eyes, they were done.

'Christ, I didn't see a thing,' Mitch said disappointedly. 'Not a goddamn thing,' he repeated, with a stony expression.

'It could've been anything, an asteroid fragment or an ordinary meteoroid maybe,' Jessy added. Spherical, she similarly hadn't forgotten. Both were glued to the viewing bubble, eyes still straining at the blackness outside.

'I hope Prox got that thing framed and zoomed.' He had faith in the Jarrion camera, but not necessarily in Prox. Not Prox, no way he had faith in that thing. It was a piece of shit.

'Let's hope so because if it didn't, that might have been Santa Claus sleigh for all we're going to know.' Mitch punched in several commands on the keyboard. The monitor became a high resolution Digital screen. Prox was searching for the footage and would replay it several hundred thousand times slower than it had happened. They both had sweaty palms. Jessy and Mitch were staring at the screen, their neurons straining under the weight of expectation. If SIS was right in its morphological and optical assessments then it was almost certainly something they had never encountered before.

The screen showed black space. The only reason Mitch knew it was working was by the double image of 61 Cygni, shining steadily in the top left of the screen like a pair of silver eyes. A blurry gray object grew rapidly near the upper centre of the screen and disappeared again in a fraction of a second.

'Shit!' Jessy yelped without moving her eyes, 'that thing is moving!' A brilliant scientific deduction, she thought with a laugh.

Mitch didn't hear her. His nose was only inches from the screen. '...surely too reflective to be a chunk of rock...' he mumbled.

Mitch commanded Prox to replay the image, one micro-frame at a time. He just hoped the Jarrion had properly resolved the object on its quantum-disc. Two hundred and fifty thousand frames per second should have gotten something, he reckoned.

'Now let's see what we've got,' Mitch muttered in a voice that was filled with nervous expectation. Both were hypnotized by the screen. Prox started flicking over the frames one by one and gradually, a faint contrast observable against the background of space, appeared at the top of the screen. Obviously artificial, the smudge fattened until it took up almost a fifth of the screen. Blurred but unmistakable.

'Fuck,' Mitch exploded as he paused the image on the screen. He opened his mouth and then closed it without a noise. It was at maximum size in front of them. Indistinct but very distinct. 'Holy mother of Jesus,' Jessy murmured, her expression frozen like the deepest pack-ice. Her eyes were welded to the impossible vision, seeing but unseeing, biting her lip nervously. The screen showed a roughly spherical, palpably alien spacecraft. The image was so obviously alien that it jumped out and landed a belly punch in that special place where awareness and mind were stored. Jessy's mouth was wide open and her pupils huge as she stared at it for long seconds. Taking it all in, she was having trouble believing what was being beamed to her visual cortex. She gaped at Mitch who looked like he'd been hit with a brick, several times.

Alien though it was it had clearly sustained considerable damage. Pockmarked and dimpled, the vessel looked as though it had been through the fires of Hades. A chunk was entirely gone near one of the poles of the craft, giving the impression that some horrendous beast had taken a bite out of it. Jessy and Mitch stood motionless for some time as they scrutinized the image of the alien machine on the screen. Jessy spoke first, the disbelief splashed in her voice like a vivid Mondrian abstraction. She opened her mouth wider and her mind suddenly decompressed in an avalanche of words.

'...an alien spacecraft Mitch...it's a fucking alien spacecraft.' Her eyes lost focus, but not for long.'...this is one of...no is the most significant image...in our history perhaps. God I can't believe it...this is stupendous, staggering. Who the hell would've thought...out here, now...' She paused to savour what she'd just said, still staring dumbfounded at the image. She choked out more words that echoed through the depths of Sean's mind.

Mitch was silent, staring through bloated headlights at the screen, seemingly waiting for an explanation from Prox. Jessy was uncontrollable, her curiosity about the thing insatiable. She spun back toward Mitch who was shaking his head and staring at the image.

'This is the moment we've been waiting for. You know how important this is don't you? It confirms everything...literally fucking everything! Our theories, our beliefs...God, our dreams.' She stared at him, drawing a heavy breath for the next onslaught. ...this snapshot tells us that we're not alone in this massive fishbowl. Mitch, we finally know that we're not a miracle! Unless that's a

Galileo or a Juno all grown up and coming back to visit...then we've solved the greatest mystery there is. Mitch...there are others...they do exist! The mystery of mysteries...laid bare...right here...I can't fucking believe it.' She wiped her face and pushed hair out of eyes, shaking her head. She was totally and absolutely bewildered. Jessy was moved to tears as she stared down at the floor, overcome by the dazzling image that had suddenly been thrust on her. One of her life's dreams, one of humanity's dreams, achieved in this most ineffable of arenas. It was impossible. Had to be a dream. Surely a dream. Jessy glanced again at the screen, knowing it wasn't. But it was amazing on any scale you threw at it.

Mitch brought a shaky hand to his forehead and had teary eyes, thinking of this thing, and all the jugheads back on Earth. Jessy peered again at the picture, 'to think, Earth was on the precipice of being destroyed. 'Jesus, we have to survive.' Her voice was frantic and wild. She thought of Frank Drake and his famous frigging equation, how right he was to include the "length of existence of an ET society" in it, thinking of Earth and its potential death at the hands of CX1.

Mitch thought Jessy might have the baby here and now. She was still spewing superlatives when Mitch instructed Prox to print the image of the craft by hitting 'sys req' and then 'prt sc' which he now held and was inspecting.

'...looks like a busted up spider,' Mitch murmured as he turned the image through three hundred and sixty degrees. 'Mother of God,' he whispered through grinding teeth as the realization started seeping into his brain. Silence was complete as they inspected the photo, locking eyes every now and then in mute agreement as to the immensity of the moment they were sharing. The thought struck Jessy again. Had to be a dream.

Getting out of his seat, Mitch walked over and fronted the cosmic panorama, ogling the pinpricks that pimpled the dead black curtain. Every one of those distant sparks had suddenly gained a new dimension. Which one, he wondered? Which one did they call home? Becrux... Hadar... Capella...? Sure as hell it was one of them out there. Mitch was trying to remember which had exoplanets they knew about.

Trying though he did, he was struggling to believe what had just happened. Christ, it was so unlikely...so totally, deliriously absurd. He pondered the SETI enthusiasts back home. God how he prayed they would survive so he could return home and present them with the data from Prox and hand them the photograph. The photograph. Who would have thought? The whole scenario was unutterably insane. Others.

Jessy's pregnancy was getting very close to term, a fact quite obvious as she sat pendulously, legs apart and uncomfortable in the chair fronting the main bank of controls in the Compit. She was still thinking about the encounter. She really couldn't believe it. Here, now. She looked down at her pregnancy, and almost laughed out loud. Here, now, she thought, it was crazy.

Like Mitch, she was pained by the lack of answers to the tormenting but glorious puzzle. The thought of something insanely hideous unfolding itself from the bowels of the craft dampened her enthusiasm. Her mind's eye was far too vivid at times. It scared the crap out of her actually.

'You could be right with any of those guesses Jessy, but more likely you're wrong with all of them. He stared out to space, pondering the imponderable...wondering about the nature of the unexpected visitor. Wondering again where it came from. What was inside? Now, she was terrified. Like Mitch said, anything is possible.

***

Nearly three trillion kilometres from Cygnus, an apocalyptic knowing was building in the minds of the high tenants. On Earth it was becoming slowly apparent that the USPA had been indulging in deceit la grande. They had been criminally negligent and had been caught out. They were as guilty as hell. Their hands were well and truly caught in the cookie jar.

The GSI had failed to keep a lid on the erupting claims that Proxima and its hellish moon were in reality heading directly toward their fragile home. Reports, many quite accurate, were emerging and growing almost geometrically each day. Far too many for them to control.

68

There was now a body of opinion simply too large for the USPA to effectively deal with. The Agency had been over-zealous in defending its official position, that Earth was in no danger, that Nemesis would miss the solar system by two billion kilometres. The facade built by the Agency was crumbling and cracking like an over-floured pie.

Many eminent scholars of science who initially gave their support to the coverup were wavering. The primary aim of the ruse was to try and preserve the status quo on Earth, to avoid mass scale carnage and infrastructural failure, which they were assured would follow hot on the heels of 'The News'. So, they agreed to add their weight to the argument...to try and preserve the human foundation of the planet. But the USPA had fallen short, had failed to maintain the lie and that was becoming a monumental problem. The plan to conceal and deceive was close to terminal breakdown. It was almost game over. The leaks and the drips had swollen into a deluge that would soon flood every media outlet worldwide.

Signs of panic were already appearing and that was enough to cause many initially pro Agency advocates, including several celebrated professionals, to consider publicly announcing the real story as they knew it. That would force the Agency to reveal its hand, but at what cost to humanity they wondered? The question remained, honesty or cover up? What to do? Which was of greatest benefit to humanity, irrespective of any threats or moral considerations? No one really knew but the fact that the bluff was disintegrating made the choice easy for most. The truth must come out.

With less than eleven months until Cygnus engaged CX1, sufficient pressure had been placed on the Agency by its principal secret holders to force it to openly concede. It had decided to tell the world the truth, although in reality it had little choice, GSI and USPA had been backed into a doorless corner. They had to lay their cards on the table.

At the AASSA facility in Woomera, Ben White had been monitoring the debacle and wasn't even mildly surprised that they'd stuffed it up. It was always going to be an impossible task. He knew that. Far too many unknowns...too many links, there were simply too many of them in the chain. Complexity theory had triumphed again, ruining the most meticulously laid plans. USPA had truly fucked things up and had only itself to blame. A bad situation made worse, if that was possible.

As acting Director of AASSA, Ben had been one of the few people to be taken into the Agency's confidence. He had little choice but to go along with the rort, but was unconvinced of its worth and even less convinced about its viability. Ben knew the coverup was a band-aid measure at best, but they didn't give a damn about his opinions. The decision to deceive had come from the top, from the zenith of world power. The US President sat at the apex of the USPA. And the decision had been made and was unalterable ... until now.

'...always going to happen,' Ben uttered as he walked down the whitewashed corridor leading to the control hub of his Woomera facility. He ambled into the massive chamber. One side was almost pure tinted glass, allowing unimpeded views into the arid heartland of Australia. A stunning chestnut vista stretched uninhabited for thousands of kilometres beyond the gantried complex.

Earlier in the day Ben had taken an intriguing phone call from Ray Clarke at NASA in Washington. He sounded guarded and strangely unwilling to engage in conversation which was very out of character. Ray would only say that he was sending an email through the Armour net system at exactly 1135 hours Australian CST. And he was told to take great care in disseminating its contents, if in fact he chose to do so. Ray wouldn't tell him exactly what it was but he sounded resigned to the fact that the contents would soon be common knowledge amongst the global population.

Ben knew what the email would tell him, something had clearly broken in the global media. The extent to which it would focus on the negatives, he wasn't sure, but he well realized that there was a fucking bucketload of negatives.

Ben's computer gave a sharp 'beep' at precisely the time he'd been promised it would. In Mail were the bold black letters of Raymond Clarke NASA. He accessed the message and opened the attached document. It was a copy of the front page of a newspaper, as Ben had expected. It was the Washington Post which he also expected.

The words gradually took form and gelled in his mind. For several seconds his voice simply refused to come. Then the backpressure forced it out like air from a punctured tyre. 'Oh shit, fuck,' Ben finally uttered. 'Freedom of the fucking press!' The headline fairly screamed at him:

END OF THE WORLD?

It was in print size that was typically reserved for shattering events...world wars and presidential assassinations, and underneath, it carried a detailed and to his knowledge, accurate report on the implications of CX1. The worst case scenario of course. He closed his eyes hoping it would all go away. It didn't of course.

'Shit, it's worse than I thought,' Ben muttered to himself, hair lifting on the back of his shoulders as he started to run. It was truly as bad as it got. Sprinting back to his office in the main building, he considered the consequences of such an inflammatory release. It had finally happened and he would expect newspapers all over the globe to jump on it if they hadn't already done so. Ben was feeling sick, as he peered at the headline again. He was wondering how he'd feel if he woke up and read that. How would he feel?

It was too late for successful damage control by anyone, the seed they'd all dreaded had finally been planted. And they knew it would rapidly take root, and strangle that which had taken thousands of years to build. The United Nations was currently being briefed on the precise nature of the threat and was scheduled to release a so called "unabridged" picture in only a few hours. Social and online media, television, newspaper and radio would be saturated with reports that would take deliberate pains to be as positive as possible. The UN would stress the details and likelihood of success of their countermeasure, Earth-shield.

Ben telephoned Ray at NASA. He answered the phone on the second ring.

'Christ Ray,' Ben barked, 'what's been the response to that fucking headline?' He considered it and immediately wished he hadn't. It would be hell on Earth. Death and destruction.

'The story is global Ben, it's out, well and truly out. We've got a thousand people camped outside Kennedy, Ames, JPL, Goddard and here in Washington. Other centres will be similarly besieged soon enough. All our facilities, the Government and the UN, are taking thousands of phone calls. It's a circus out there, our worst bloody nightmare, and it hasn't even started,' Ray shrilled.

'It's only a matter of time before the same thing happens here,' Ben murmured, 'thank God we're isolated up here.' He held his phone tight, felt like throwing it.

'Yeah, well you can be thankful for that.' There was a long silence.

'You still there Ray?'

'Yeah...still here, I just can't believe they orchestrated such a monumental stuff up. Maybe CX1 will do the Universe a favour,' Ray said without emotion.

'What're your plans?' Ben asked, feeling the tightness in his body.

'President Yorke has been fully briefed and he is, to say the least, pissed. Not because the information was withheld, shit his office knew that, but because it's been released, leaked that is, in such a bloody avalanche. He's going to make a public statement immediately,' Ray explained gruffly, 'and the UNSC will make a detailed address to Earth, and colonies on the Moon and Mars tonight at 1930 hours. Until then we lay low and say nothing to anyone.'

'What about AASSA Ray? I'm supposed to just sit on my hands, do nothing, tell no one after what you've just told me?' He must be kidding, Ben thought, looking at his picture on the wall.

'The Agency will be in touch with all its remote facilities in the next few hours, so just take it easy until then, okay?' Ray stated dryly.

Ben was silent. His mind was pulsing with hellish images of a world doomed beyond redemption. 'Damn it, he snapped, feeling a little bilious.

'There's little anyone can do to alleviate the problem, the damage is done, well and truly. You're in the same boat as everyone else...on a rock in a family which is in truly deep shit.' There was another, longer pause.

They both contemplated the last sentence and it struck them with equal ferocity. Even the big picture was grim, it wasn't just humanity and Earth that was in trouble, it was the whole bloody solar system. It couldn't get much worse.

'Keep me informed Ray, would you? Before it breaks in the media.'

Wishing each other well, they hung up. Ben swore several times to himself and decided he'd call a general meeting to come clean with what he knew. Fuck the Agency, he thought angrily. Ben's eyes were hard and flinty as he thought about the future.

The base would find out quickly and probably in a less than satisfactory way. He wasn't about to wait around for them to contact him. They'd already made a rotten situation worse. Ben knew that the next year or so would be hell on Earth and if Earth-shield failed. He didn't even want to consider the impact of that news.

***

The multipaneled eyes of each beast had locked as one onto her nakedness. She was sure they were ogling her with some sort of grotesque desire as they salivated, gelatinous stringy drool that hung in strands from their splayed gobs. Jessy could feel the heat from their sudden sexual appetite.

She sat bolt upright in bed, breathless and sweating, the remnants of a scream stippled on her lips. She could still taste the panic. 'Just a dream,' she said breathlessly to herself. 'Just a goddamn dream!' Jessy was shaking uncontrollably.

Jessy sucked air through clenched teeth, blood seeping like dark ink from a bitten tongue. She looked like she was having a severe neurological fit. The bizarre dreams had been with her for nearly two weeks and seemed always to centre around the alien visitor they'd eyeballed recently. Was there something aboard that thing, that was the question debated endlessly by Jessy's subconscious at nighttime. Her thin red nightshirt stuck to her body like a wetsuit. 'Jesus...what a nightmare.' she said to an empty and dark room. They were getting worse and she knew it.

It was 0300 hours ship-time. Mitch was fast asleep in his quarters ten metres away. Jessy knew he'd sleep through a supernova without so much as a snuffle. She also knew that getting back to sleep would be impossible so she rose and dressed in her loose Medi-lab outfit. Being alone during the simulated Cygnan night was horrible, so if she had to be awake it was preferable to be out of bed and active. She'd almost worn her own track to the viewing bubble on Cygnus. Being on her own always led to deep contemplation. Mulling over the scenarios of their mission left Jessy empty, cold and alone. Always the negatives, the good for nothing negatives.

Images of her planet devastated and dead, and them expiring in an alien, Earthless, dead cosmos replayed over and over in her mind together with all manner of creatures from the flying whatever it was. She vividly saw herself alive in space while everyone else back home died, leaving them as the final four, the last humans in the Universe. The pathetic, doomed remnants from laboratory Earth. Continually reliving these scenes in her mind was enough to send somebody mad, she was sure of it. And never far away was the realization that it was surely selfish and cruel to consider bringing a child onto Cygnus.

Jessy wondered what she would want if she were the foetus and could choose between life, such as it would be, or no life at all. The answer was fairly clear. Perhaps they were doing the right thing after all. Who the hell knew? Yes or no, give life or not? Jessy walked the ship for hours, returning to her quarters only after she was so exhausted that sleep came immediately. No more nightmares came that night.

Despite the newness of the technology and the radically shortened proving phase, the craft continued to operate flawlessly, hurtling through the void at slightly more than sixty percent Luminal. They were moving more than ten thousand times faster than anything previously sent into space by humanity. Not bad. Cygnus was now four trillion kilometres from home, pushing toward half a light year. Their auto transmissions took nearly five months to reach out to Earth. They were alone in every sense of the word. The vacuum they were travelling through was truly a vacuum. There was barely anything out here, bar a sprinkling of dark energy. Pressure was multiplying geometrically as the moment of truth came closer for Earth, and for them, and their unborn child. But despite their fear of the moment, they wanted it to come, they were both sick of the stress of waiting, and wondering. And dreaming.

Jessy continued to pray to any god who might be listening, any god who might be able to deliver a trouble free birth. Medi-lab wasn't equipped to handle a childbirth emergency so if the baby was breached or developed some other life threatening problem, the likelihood was that either Jessy or the baby, or both, would fucking die. There would be no help in this most isolated of neighbourhoods. Isolated didn't do it justice, she knew, gaping at the darkness beyond the window.

***

Jessy thought the birth was imminent, putting it at perhaps a week, and Mitch agreed if only by glancing at her. He tried to put the thought of an exploding melon out of his mind but he couldn't, the similarities in form were simply too vivid. The image of pips and pulp flying outward in a fruity spray was equally comical and unsettling. Perhaps it was more unsettling than anything else, as he watched her go about her daily duties.

Jessy sat uncomfortably in front of the large monitor that displayed the operational status of all the PCM subsystems. Mitch was standing and looking over her shoulder, quietly issuing instructions as she deftly caressed the half-spherical keyboard.

'All life support data is in the normal range,' Jessy said as Mitch double checked the information flashing over the screen.

'Okay, go for full release.'

The necessary keystrokes were made and she hit initiate. C'mon you bastard, eyes open, she thought, looking squarely at Rhys. Jessy didn't know it, but she was holding her breath. A clear gas flowed into the pods, noticeable only by its ruffling effect on Rhys's hair. PCM was slowly increasing metabolic function, resulting in life support being returned to levels where both would progressively wake up.

'Eyes open in ten minutes,' Mitch said, trying to hide his dread, biting his lip hard enough to draw blood. He knew the first few minutes after they woke up were critical. They moved over to the pods to take a look at their gradually returning friends.

'Jesus, so pale and thin...so bloody hairy,' Jessy muttered, looking at Sean and Rhys who were still totally inert, still asleep.

Mitch gaped at the thick woolly beards they'd sprouted during the long months of Protocoma. Rumple Stiltskin, they were almost perfect copies, as if she knew what he really looked like. Even as they watched, they could see the rosy tones returning, as heartbeats and circulation levels were slowly restored to normal.

Jessy looked on in awe. 'It's amazing, like reanimation, they've gone from dead to alive in just a few minutes. Perhaps we should try it on you,' Jessy grinned widely at Mitch, and he returned her gaze directly, no smile.

After ten minutes of "de-sleep", both the PCM domes parted automatically with a metallic clunk. A soft wheezing noise followed as the covers slid to an upright position. They were already flexing their limbs, trying to shake off the nine months of inactivity and sleep. Although their muscles were worked during that time by the flickering resistors in Medi-plex, they were still hellishly stiff and sore. And hungry, despite the gallons of IV fluids that were pumped through them. Hungry, stiff and hungover, the joys of Protocoma.

'Wakey wakey boys,' Mitch exulted loudly. He patted Rhys's moist cheek above the tangled hairline of his beard. 'There's things to do, babies to deliver.' Mitch continued to prod them toward wakefulness. Their twitchings and shudderings came closer together until both of them, more or less at the same time, woke up.

'Welcome back gentlemen.' Mitch smiled at them from above. Trying vainly to focus, Sean tried to sit up but fell back before he got half way.

'Easy…for God's sake!' Jessy shouted. She realized how valuable they both were, knowing they couldn't afford an accident. Having to deliver the baby by herself or worse, having Mitch try and help, terrified her almost beyond respiration. Jesus, she thought. He could barely cope with a bloodied nose, let alone a birth. Rhys was very valuable property. Even minimal overactivity during exit from PCM could result in a serious cardiac episode. Arrhythmia and death were a vague but, nonetheless, very real possibility. It had happened before when to everyone's horror, the first human tests at Pasadena had killed an over-zealous colleague who'd bounded from his newly opened pod, determined to showcase the wondrous technology. After a dozen steps, he'd collapsed to the floor in a shuddering heap. His heart had detonated like an overblown balloon. Dead. They couldn't bring him back.

After some time, Medi-plex gave the okay and with help Sean and Rhys hauled themselves to the edge of their modules and hungrily demolished their waiting dextrose drink.

'Christ…I feel like I'm detoxing from a, um drinking binge,' Sean growled, rubbing his eyes with both hands and scratching his newly blossomed beard. 'Fuck, what is this? He asked groggily, forgetting that hair would grow on his chin.

'I'm famished…I feel like I haven't eaten for months!' Rhys croaked, sticking out his grotesquely blue tongue and grinning.

'No food for twelve hours, you know the drill. But that mixture you're quaffing is available in unlimited quantities.' Mitch knew that would be of absolutely no comfort, it tasted like salty hell and he knew it. He'd tried it several times and wasn't impressed. Mitch flatly refused to give them any status reports or for that matter any information at all about the past nine months. Or why they were retrieved early from PCM. That would all come later. 'Just rest, okay? I'll update you later.' Mitch had already repeated half a dozen times.

Sean and Rhys were first into the dining room. Neither had gotten any rest, but both were obviously delighted to be awake. They were back in the real world, if what was around them could be considered real.

Amazingly, Mitch noted, neither Rhys nor Sean seemed to have picked up on Jessy's condition. In spite of their disorientation he couldn't believe that her very obvious pregnancy wasn't noticed immediately. It was so in your face, but they hadn't looked twice, or at least he didn't think they had. Perhaps they thought Jessy had simply gotten fat…didn't want to mention it…didn't want to embarrass her. Yeah, right, she thought. Mitch reckoned it was bullshit too.

He couldn't help but grin, that couldn't be it. His smile vanished as he thought that it might not be as stupid as it sounded. After all, who would have expected this mission to yield a child? Not him and equally certainly not Rhys or Sean. The idea was insane. Totally, unthinkably insane. "Anything is possible in space", Mitch's catch-cry was never more relevant than here. Of course, it was supposed to relate to quantum likelihood, not cosmic parenthood.

The answer to his question quickly became apparent though. Mitch watched as the two of them gazed at her with poorly concealed wonderment, they had noticed. Looking at Jessy and then at him, they were now demanding an explanation. Mitch walked over and pushed his hand into hers and clutched it tightly.

Rhys and Sean were staring first at them and then at each other, frowning like cosmonauts suddenly face to face with a million-year-old pyramid on the Moon. He could almost see their minds grappling with the facts, trying to come up with a reasonable explanation. And failing. Fucking badly.

'What the…you mean you're going to have a baby aboard C.C.Cygnus?' Rhys stammered, brandishing an expression like shocked steel. 'You're joking, right? He looked genuinely stunned.

'There are very few medical centres in this part of the cosmos Rhys, but if you can direct us to one…'

73

'I didn't mean that, but hell, what a time to get it on, I mean it's great that you two have finally gotten it together, but shit, your timing is lousy.' Rhys smiled despite himself, breaking into a face-splitting smile. Rhys gave Jessy a crisp nod.

'We know...but some things just happen. It obviously wasn't planned but we want the baby...which may or may not prove to be the smart decision. Time will tell, I guess.' He looked at Jessy and smiled, holding his head high, feeling good about the choice.

'You're the only one with obstetric experience Rhys,' Jessy said, 'so if you don't mind, we'd uh…like you at the birth, to deliver it that is.'

'…be happy to oblige, although I don't think Medi-lab has much in the way of birthing aids, but I'm sure I can improvise.' Rhys spoke with wiggling eyebrows.

She felt better already. Support. The mental comfort was more than welcome.

'The first thing I'll need to do is give you a thorough inspection, check you out and make sure the baby's sitting right, that sort of thing.' Rhys gently patted Jessy's stomach. He was in shock at the revelation, genuine first grade bewilderment, but some things took precedence. 'First things first,' Rhys went on, 'let's eat,' he said, making the okay sign with his thumb and forefinger, 'I could eat a horse'. He smiled boyishly.

'Food!' Sean echoed loudly, grinning widely through a motheaten beard. 'I never thought I'd crave this amorphous mulch, but I stand corrected, I could eat a bucketful,' he chortled. 'Gimme,' Sean shouted, hungrily.

Mitch proceeded to recount the past ten months and refresh their stale memories on the suffering they each had in store in the coming months. One item recounted by Mitch almost stopped their hearts dead in their chests. Sean and Rhys were flabbergasted by their fleeting encounter with what simply had to be an alien spacecraft. They viewed the disk hundreds of times and voiced animated opinions about its origins, its occupants and its method of propulsion, before it was somehow damaged, assuming that in fact it had been which, they decided, they weren't totally sure.

An alien spacecraft, they simply couldn't get past it. Here, now...it wasn't possible, but in their souls, they knew it was...anything was possible. Quantum likelihood, they hadn't forgotten what it meant, it applied everywhere, under all circumstances. Anything that didn't contravene the fundamental laws of the cosmos was possible, somewhere. And here it was…

Everything was back to normal, Mitch thought as he watched the two friends' bicker. Each was frantically voicing theories on the hordes of daunting questions that were raised by the thing in the millisecond it had taken to pass them. Mainly, it centred around who was onboard, and where did it come from? They couldn't agree on any of it.

Life aboard Cygnus quickly got back to normal, rapidly descending into a nightmarish countdown, firstly to the birth of Jessy's baby, and secondly to their ultimate goal. Their close encounter with the monsters from Centaurus.

***

CX1 was now less than a light year from Cygnus which remained doggedly focussed on the narrow plane of the solar system. Incursion into the bowels of warmth and light still seemed inevitable should Cygnus fail.

The dead star continued to consume Proxima's boiling life gasses, spewing torrents of hard radiation into the void as it went. The manic ballet swung like clockwork, little sun and gravitational titan, locked in a savage symphony, bound by exquisite choreography and symmetry. It was like a stupendous hydrogen atom, one proton, one electron, trapped in an unrelenting quantum energy field.

Earth's nemesis was spearing toward it at more than half the speed of light. And should they fail, it would destroy some or all of Sol's family sometime in the early part of February 2024. In the bigger scheme of things, two years to a black hole was only a few flecks of a nanosecond. The gravitational colossus had the potential to live for a billion trillion years. It would still be alive after the cosmos had doubled its present age, a billion times over. Paradoxically, it had the potential to well and truly outlive the Universe.

74

***

Sean was stooped in front of the computer guided altazimuth telescope on the viewing platform. He'd been looking and photographing with the faint object camera and spectrograph for over two hours. He'd also snapped a series of photographs with the infrared camera. His frustration was written in bloodshot eyes. 'Fuck this for a joke,' he snapped, thinking of his soft bed. 'I can't find any evidence of planets around Centaurus A or B. I thought the stellar shield might help, but nothing. And the comparator photos don't show a bloody thing, no close moving bodies at all. I don't think they're there, I really don't. I thought maybe, just maybe...' Sean was visibly disappointed. Proxima had planets, but the larger Centaurians, no.

Rhys's only surprise was Sean's reaction, he should have known better. 'You know as well as I do that most twins like Centaurus probably don't have habitable planets. Or even planets at all. One or other of those stars you're looking at probably constitutes the material that otherwise might have gone into making them.' He smacked his forehead as if it was obvious.

'I know, but I hoped...' Sean put his reddened eye back to the 'scope.

'What's the distance between Proxima and the black hole?'

'It's variable...about half a million k's,' Sean murmured through a mouth no wider than a texta line.

'I would suggest that any planets that may have existed were annihilated on the spot or at least torn from orbit,' Rhys said as he stared at his downcast friend. 'Bear in mind that Proxima was originally not all that far from Alpha, meaning that the hole's impact on any orbiting bodies on the way through should have been substantial. Look at what it did, and for that matter what it's doing, to Proxima. The planets from Proxima were probably ejected into space when CX1 was born.' Rhys nodded at Sean.

'You're probably right, but I wonder...I mean surely if that spider craft came from a planet or planets in the Centaurus region, wouldn't they have been capable of saving their home?' Sean was intrigued now and his voice took on a more subtle tone. Sean's head flinched a bit and his eyes narrowed, suggesting he was thinking about the spider craft a bit more.

'That craft we saw appeared to be way ahead of anything we've got and we're out here trying to save ourselves. So, unless they didn't have time to prepare, which seems unlikely, we can assume they would've deflected or destroyed it without too much drama.'

Rhys was staring at Sean as if he knew what was coming next, 'and what's the alternate scenario?' Rhys prodded with a slight grin.

'I really believe that with this starlight shield I would've detected a planet around the Alpha's if it was there, which suggests that the craft comes from elsewhere. Anyway, we surely would've detected their radiation if they were there, they're obviously intelligent and technical. That's my final conclusion. It came from elsewhere...not from Centaurus.'

'Brilliant, but where?' Rhys goaded. 'There's no other life-likely stars within light decades of here.'

'That's right, so it's either been drifting in space as a dead shell for a long time, or it travelled here from some other star system. So, what I'm saying,' Sean heaved, 'is that we know fuck all, but I reckon that craft came from another system, maybe Barnard's or Tau Ceti, or Christ maybe it came from the Whirlpool Galaxy.' He exhaled loudly. 'Who knows if this thing is robotic or what, it may have been travelling for a million years at close to the speed of light?'

Sean stopped talking and put his face in his hands. He could feel his brain itching for answers, but he knew in his mind that none would be found. Jessy almost laughed at him, seeing his seriously frustrated face. The answers were already a billion kilometres away, and were receding further with every one of his pounding heartbeats. Pure guesswork was the best he could do, and it was killing him. He had no real idea and probably never would, and he hated it. His mind swam with the sparks of wondrous delirium and pulsed with the pain of uncertainty, the certainty of never knowing where the ship came from.

75

Rhys took up the optical telescope and locked onto CX1. Proxima's red colour was tainted deep blue by their relativistic approach but Rhys could now see the disk of the dwarf star. It was no longer just an optical effect, he could actually see the disk through the main telescope.

Not without some pride, he realized that apart from Sol, this was the first glimpse of the actual torso of a star ever made by humanity. Other stars had previously only been pinpoints of light, tiny dots in space, anomalous light obscured by unimaginable distance, but no longer. It drummed home to Rhys just how bloody far from home they were. Among the stars...

'The first,' he whispered to himself with his face still attached to the scope. He could vaguely see how its shape was distorted, Proxima now looking like a small blue egg lying on its side. The cloud of glowing, flowing plasma that roiled between the pair was now disturbingly vivid. Rhys watched as the star's physique, not to mention its brightness, changed before his eyes, one of the stellar poles suddenly flattening and then instantly bouncing back. He swore to himself, staring at the flowing waves on its surface as it was taunted by the tidal pull from the black hole. He could literally "see" the star dance around the black hole by concentrating on the changes in the patterns on its tortured face.

'Christ almighty,' Rhys murmured to himself, his eye still firmly glued to the eyepiece, but both brows riding high. Having seen the fury of the black hole, Rhys could muster little confidence in their ability to deflect it. He looked at Proxima again, eyes bulging, and thought of Cygnus. A tree beetle trying to ward off an elephant with harsh language, he mused uncomfortably, putting the main scope away. It suddenly became too real. 'You must be kidding,' he whispered forcibly, peering again at Proxima and its friend. It looked so powerful. It seemed as though it had been around since the beginning of the Universe, which he knew was wrong. CX1 with its long astrophysical jet streaming into space was terrifying.

***

Jessy was lying on her bed, feeling uncomfortable and restless but knowing she needed the rest...when it happened. A slight pain in her pelvis was followed by an uncomfortably tight feeling, punctuated by a growing wetness around her lower abdomen.

'Oh shit...damn!' She spat through clenched teeth. Her time was near but she'd hoped it wouldn't come now, she was so bloody tired...but it was now, like it or not. Babies come when they're ready...not when the mother's ready. She knew that.

'Mitch,' Jessy yelled. The pain was worse now. 'Mitch!' She screamed this time, too scared to move. He ran in, instantly realising the implications of such a raucous screech. 'It's time Mitch...for fuck's sake,' She spoke as calmly and as quietly as she could but still sounded horrified. Jessy always claimed to have a low pain threshold. On hearing it, Mitch had always smiled and said she should've been born a man. But she was being serious. Jessy had a low pain threshold.

Within an hour they had gently transported Jessy to Medi-lab after Rhys had checked her out and decided that labor had most definitely started. Of course it bloody has, she screeched. In Medi-lab they walked her around the room dozens of times, massaged her, talked to her, and reassured her until she couldn't go on...until she simply couldn't tolerate the pain and had to lie down.

Helping her out of her clothes, they covered her with a sheet, between which on either side of her were the makeshift stirrups that Sean had fashioned under Rhys's guidance. Fashioned from the ship's stainless steel cleaning and maintenance equipment. To Jessy they were shiny symbols of an agony she could barely imagine...the promise of worse things to come. She remembered a video she'd seen with her pregnant sister, "parent classes". She was under no illusions.

Two hours on and her contractions had worsened to the point of being torturous and were now coming less than three minutes apart. And they hurt. They fucking well hurt! Rhys had given her two Prodramon tablets to dull the pain but they hadn't even touched her agony. He'd tried intravenous Inferol, their only opiate, but even that was only dulling her torment. There was no more he could do bar a general anaesthetic but that he couldn't do, he needed Jessy's help with this one.

Rhys just wished he could've given her an epidural, but the nearest facility that boasted such a luxury was several trillion kilometres away. And to think he'd always considered the jaunt between Mercy General and his home in Miami as a long, tedious haul. The absolute craziness of the concept almost made him bellow out loud. It was truly ridiculous.

'Hang in there Jessy, baby's head is just about at the right angle, just a few more minutes.' She looked anything but relieved and was grunting and breathing in short rasping spurts. 'Dilation is eight centimetres and progressing fine...'

Mitch was gently stroking her hand and trying to help her control the contractions, but he looked equally as terrified as Jessy if not more so. Sweating freely, he looked decidedly ill as he steadied himself on the rail of the stainless steel bed.

'Jess, you're doing fine,' Rhys said smiling. 'Don't push, just breathe as normally as you can. Start pushing only when I tell you to. Jessy had felt like pushing ten minutes ago, to get it the fuck over with.

Rhys hoped against hope that it was an easy birth, for all their sakes. If it was difficult and if there was serious bleeding or some other paediatric emergency there could be two deaths, and maybe three he considered, glancing at Mitch. He looked like he might die of fright at any moment.

Satisfied with her progress and the baby's position, Rhys urged Jessy to go with the contractions, to put her chin down and push. The tip of baby's head had just crowned and was thrusting back and forth as the contractions ebbed and flowed. Jessy now had both legs in the stirrups and had abandoned any pretense to modesty.

After another ten minutes of blistering hell, the entire head of the baby appeared, and her guttural moans turned to earsplitting screams as the baby's shoulders locked hard against her pelvis. Its progress had halted and Rhys suddenly noticed the colour of the face. Purple. He saw for the first time that the umbilical cord was wrapped around the child's neck, not loosely, but tightly like a hangman's noose, after the hanging.

He chastised himself for not checking on it earlier, but he had to work fast. In a fully equipped birthing unit on Earth this was no more than a slight inconvenience, but here, it was life threatening. Rhys sprinted the few metres to the surgical array and was back in a flash, clamping the cord and severing it, freeing the child from the choking ligament. Jessy's screams were terrifying and deafening as the baby's shoulders abraded her already burning nerve endings.

Rhys commanded Mitch (wobbling and pale) to talk to Jessy, to calm her and at all costs to keep her still. It was next to impossible but they had to try. Rhys had to get the baby out now. Reaching down with a scalpel he made a small incision. Using both hands he gently guided the almost self-propelling baby from within Jessy who had mercifully fainted.

At 1710 hours Jessy produced a 3.1kilogram star-child, a beautiful and apparently healthy baby boy. After a few stitches she was fine, exhausted, drained and sore, but fine all the same. Mitch was beside himself and having recovered somewhat, was thrilled beyond words to be a father, already doting over both Jessy and child.

The first human born in extra-solar space, the first interstellar tot, he kept repeating to himself. Their grim circumstances had been briefly forgotten. Cygnus was resounding with momentary joy, not only from the cries of the newly born, but from a miracle shared by all. Joshua Rhys became their symbol of hope, new life born in the midst of profound uncertainty.

***

The official UN announcement that the planet might be in jeopardy had been made two months ago. The world media and the entire stock of humanity hung on every word and every communication sent back by Cygnus, uninformative and mundane as they were. The last status report was received by Woomera when Cygnus was E-plus four months. The rest of the communications, nearly six months' worth, were still travelling at the speed of light toward Earth. They were auto transmissions only, sent by SIS and solely dedicated to PND technical data. They didn't reveal anything about how the mission was going.

What would quickly become known as the Great Chaos had begun in earnest on Earth.
And it would get worse, in fact it would worsen manifold, doing grim justice to the name which it was Christened by the Press. A feeling of doom settled over the globe like a ponderous blanket, officiously tucked in by destructionist zealots, doomsday apostles, and writers and orators of all ilk.

Earth's media in all its configurations, social, radio, television, newspaper, and online had been dominated for months by hellish commentaries on devastation and death. On death chunks, extinction and the demise of civilisation. Those opposing the destruction message, who supported and believed in Earthshield, were buried alive by a choking media storm of pending ruination, perdition and death. The official position taken by the UN, that Earthshield would almost certainly succeed, was ridiculed and mocked by most as a predictable ruse. No one trusted the Government, or the United Nations. USPA had ruined all that.

Many religious leaders and spiritual fundamentalists couldn't help but exhort the virtues of End Time...of Judgement Day and God's Wrath on Earth. And they did it without regard. Of course, it was expected, any excuse would set them off and this was easily the finest excuse imaginable. They weren't backward in exploiting the relevance of Nemesis to their teachings. It was at the crux of most, and if it wasn't, then it was now. And it was coming...because nothing could stop God's Will. They promised their followers that much. Repent before it's too late! Not even they realized how terrible the consequences of their apocalyptic explications would be. Because simply repenting wasn't what many had in mind.

Most scientific scholars claimed that Earth was simply unable to deal with such a tremendous and violent force as CX1. Arguing the reverse, the positivists had failed miserably to comfort the terrified masses who collectively wondered what type of hell their planet was going to descend into, even before Nemesis arrived.

Los Angeles, Beijing, Paris, London, Kuala Lumpur, Moscow and Vancouver were ablaze. Massive fires that in places had coalesced into kilometric firestorms were destroying cities. Engulfing towns alive.

Vicious and bloody riots initiated mainly by minority socioracial groups were virtually global in occurrence. Marshall Law was in force in forty-two countries. Thousands had already died as a direct result of *'The News'*, either burned in the fires, murdered in the riots, or killed by careless but seemingly necessary police and military counter-offensives. Looting was occurring on a hitherto unseen scale, law enforcement was hopelessly inadequate and ineffective. Any group or gang, or individual with a beef, was on the streets.

Crime was rampant, and growing exponentially, and worsening in kind. The chaos was snowballing, a chain reaction of panic and confusion had started that was seemingly unstoppable.
To an observer, the infrastructure of the world seemed to be gradually fading, becoming less apparent by degree. Developed over thousands of years, the social fabric on Earth was slowly unravelling.

The justice system had effectively ground to a halt. In New York, three Republican members of Congress were executed in Time Square in front of a cheering mob of thousands, blacks, whites, Latinos and others. It wasn't a race thing, it was a people thing. Similar scenes were being played out in centres worldwide. Police in many countries had simply gone home to be with their families. They couldn't protect anyone else but they were sure as hell going to protect their own. Most had given up.

The Great Chaos was entrenched on Earth and with eighteen months before word of the success, or otherwise, of Earthshield would be received, no one doubted that the outlook for humanity was grim. The social order was breached and there were no immediate hopes for its resurrection.

***

Ben White now lived permanently at the Woomera base, which was more or less deserted. After *The News*, four hundred of the four hundred and thirty staff had up and left, returning to homes in or near one of the coastal cities of Australia. Ben himself had nowhere else to go, his sister had been murdered in Brisbane three weeks ago, bashed and killed by maniacs in her beachside home.

Now he had no family at all. Those who remained at Woomera did so because they either had nowhere else to go or they considered that their isolation from the chaos was their safest bet. For Ben it was the former reason that kept him on base. He literally had nowhere else to go. For him, it was the only home he had.

Those who remained on site had forged a tight sphere of friendship over the past weeks. Since the encompassing mob had disbanded, the last thirty had been alone and isolated in one of the more remote regions of the planet. And they hadn't seen another soul in that time, plenty had left but none had arrived. All services to the base had ceased two weeks before which led those remaining to learn the finer points of self-sufficiency and resource conservation very quickly. Enough frozen and canned food was on site to last several years and there was a natural water supply that was potable after it was run through the desalinator. It tasted like hell, but it sustained life.

None of them were under any illusions about an imminent solution to the chaos though. They had online access to most of the global newspapers and satellite access to television stations and radio broadcasts. If they lost access to the media, or if the media simply stopped functioning, they would be left to guess and to ponder the state of the planet. They all prayed that the news kept coming, bad though it might be. News was news..

They hoped to God that Cygnus was where it was supposed to be and not lying idly somewhere along the way as a dark, powerless and horrible hulk. The mental image was hideous. In his mind's eye Ben could see Earth's best effort gliding like a dead insect on the interstellar breeze, somewhere beyond Pluto. Surely not, he hoped like hell.

Ben still couldn't come to terms with the reaction of the greater population. Earth was facing a crisis without peer, but there was a contingency plan in place. Cygnus was out there now, or he assumed it was, on its way to try and save the planet. He, like most in the know, considered the chances of success to be about fifty-fifty. After all, only the slightest wobble was needed to save the solar system from that distance. What he was concerned about the most, was the depth and the strength of the gravity well the black hole carried with it. Could they shift it? Who the hell knew/?

Having received *The News* and after the initial shock had subsided, it would be natural to be worried. Frustrated with feelings of impotency, definitely. Terrified, probably. But the chaos that erupted after the Secretary General's announcement was deeply disturbing.

The events that followed *The News* sparked a concern, not only for one's self and one's family, but for the planet as a whole which was every bit as real, even a little worse perhaps, than the direct fear of CX1 itself. Many considered that Nemesis was probably easier to stop than the runaway necrosis being inflicted by a human race gone mad.

Like many, Ben realized that deeply rooted social divisions were mostly to blame for the horror. The underprivileged, the homeless, the racially and socially vilified, the oppressed, and the unstable seemed to have risen collectively to rebel against those not similarly afflicted. Not just because of *The News*, but because of the singular opportunity it provided. They rioted, looted and killed because as they saw it, Armageddon was looming...the world was ending, and they wanted what was owed to them before they went. Whatever the hell that was.

They could strike back at the injustices and the pain they had suffered in the past. They could stand up and front their oppressors, executing their own twisted justice by burning, murdering and destroying, and getting away with it. Doing it without apology. It was a terrible travesty. The Police had initially held them back, forcibly in a lot of cases, but not now. All hell was breaking out everywhere.

With that in mind, Ben and the others felt that the AASSA base at Woomera was first choice accommodation. At least until the nightmare resolved itself, one way or the other. He was mortified by the recurring visions he had of humankind devolving into some murderous gang ruled anarchy in the last few years before the planet was obliterated. It would be a less than gracious ending.

Close contact over the years with students and leaders of SETI had given him a deep respect for humanity, despite their all too vivid shortcomings. He knew in his being that real intelligence was exceedingly rare in the Universe, and unlike most of his SETI/OSAL comrades, he felt there would be no other minds within millions of light years of Earth. Certainly, none within the Milky Way.

Life on a much more basic level certainly existed close to Earth. That had already been proven on Mars. But true cleverness, he doubted that existed anywhere close.by But they were there. Other intelligence did exist, Ben was certain. Maybe in a distant galaxy there were other conscious beings that were wondering about others in the Universe. Wondering where the hell they were? Perhaps in the trillions of cosmic homes there was only a handful of technical communities, each separated by impossibly vast tracts of transgalactic emptiness.

We must survive, he thought to himself in his times of contemplative depression. We are special. We might not act special at times, he thought, but we are special, simply by being. Ben was in one of those moods now. Lying on his bunk and staring at the image of the Aztec IV MEX sitting dispassionately on the ochreous surface of Mars. The fantastic rim of Hellas Planitia was in the background and the pink alien sky was everywhere.

'God, what if we're the only ones,' he croaked quietly to himself, pulling at the hair around his ears. Ben never cried but he came very close as his ponderings became too real and too profoundly distressing. The thought delivered a punch as painful as any physical blow. He poured himself a large whisky and downed it in a single gulp. Sitting on the edge of his bed, he wiped his face as he thought of Cygnus and Mitch and the rest of the crew. 'I hope to Christ you guys know what you're doing,' he whispered to no one.

***

The Middle East was almost ruined as the population rebelled en masse. Some Governments had indulged in massive slaughter, murdering their own people in a final bloody effort to douse the rebellions. But still a fair percentage of their populace fought on, over and around the corpses of their dead countrymen, civil wars with no point and no foreseeable end. Stock markets had closed around the globe. Many businesses and primary producers were forced to cease trading for want of labor and supplies, not to mention demand. All their markets had gone. A fair proportion of the permanent labor force simply walked out and others just flipped the bird. In other areas the local business world was essentially unaffected. The contrasts were astounding from region to region.

It was apparent to most that in the coming months the military forces of every country on Earth would inherit responsibility for the safety of their peoples. In certain highly reactive countries this was unlikely to be good news. For most of the rest of the world it was the only course of action that would ensure the survival of its people. And the continuity of the world economy which had virtually ground to a halt. Trillions of dollars had already been shed and hundreds of trillions more would follow.

It was chaos in the truest sense of the word.

6

Rendezvous

'If you wish to make an apple pie from scratch, you must first invent the universe.'
~ Carl Sagan

In the Compit of Cygnus the crew were totally unaware of the chaos that had gripped their home planet. Mission time was E-plus sixteen months and the star of Cygnus, Joshua Rhys, was six months old.

The goal for Earthshield was close at hand. V645 was all too obvious through the Number 1 scope. Its gradual growth in space was a daunting and terrifying spectre that they tried to avoid looking at...where possible. Just a ball of rippling star stuff sure, but to them its malevolence and intent was as tangible as any conspiring killer. Rendezvous was minus thirty days. CX1 was close, less than half a trillion kilometres away, slightly more than a light fortnight. The crew were preparing for the reversal procedure, a delicate, precise manoeuvre, which, if successful, would place them on a complimentary heading to CX1. From this position, and this position only, could the excursion pod be deployed to deliver its load of fusion explosives. If reversal failed, then quite simply they failed.

They all thought the modus operandi of Earthshield was a curious paradox, that Earth's saviour should come in the form of that which had so often promised global ruination, atomic weapons. NASA had complete confidence that its strategy would work. Privately they reckoned 50/50 was about right. Jessy's eyes were wild and wide as she waited for the moment to turn the vessel around, as it ticked toward zero.

Baby Joshua was asleep in his makeshift crib in the corner of the Compit. Despite having gone without the terrestrial comforts normally afforded a newborn, he was patently healthy. Bright chestnut eyes and similar colored spiky hair and he now weighed in at close to eight kilograms.

"He's the image of his father, the eyes, the nose", Jessy would often cackle to the rest of them. Sean was too taken with Josh to tell Jessy to shut it. He would just continue to think it and not say anything. He was like a mute.

Both parents realized immediately that they'd made the right decision. Not only was he a beautiful little boy, he highlighted what was at the very heart of the mission. The aim of the journey was an imperative for their home planet, but the presence of their son gave it a clear emphasis.

It appeared to Jessy that their little boy embodied all the children on Earth and illustrated vividly what the meaning of failure would be for their tiny blue cradle. It was simple, it would mean death to billions just like him. While Josh slept in his crib, the four crew stood silently near the control hub of Cygnus, staring. The view of the star through the vacu-plate was disturbing and compelling, and made them realise just how damn close they were. And just how soon they would know the answer to their fate. Earthshield was about to get serious. Fucking serious.

***

'Reversal procedure in three minutes.' Mitch looked over at Jessy who was intently scanning the primary SIS module, a compressed array of instruments, monitors and readouts. Actually, it was a congested throng of toggles, controls, buttons, VDU's, avionics, exponders, encrypters, tiny levers, digital signal arrays, actuators and several high speed real time linear readouts and simulators. It was made as simple as possible, but the servo-facade in the Compit was still a daunting assemblage of technology, the embodiment and the "friendly face" of the integrated,

81

adaptive, data transport system they knew as Big SIS. It made noises and had flashing lights they were becoming used to.

'PND is at thirty-five percent, velocity is vectored at sixty point three percent Luminal. Hydrogen consumption will zero out in two minutes forty-three seconds,' Jessy said slowly and deliberately, trying to ignore the scrabbling demons that were multiplying in her mind. Her eyes were as rock hard as her expression. She watched out the widow and waited.

There was a tension among the crew that had been absent since the initial firing of Novae Drive sixteen long months ago. Sean couldn't believe they'd been travelling for so long. 'Bullshit...that long?' He said, blinking rapidly. He found it hard to believe.

To Jessy it seemed a lifetime ago, an absolute goddamn eternity. They'd travelled nine trillion kilometres, almost a light year, and she'd had a baby in that time. A baby...the thought rattled around in her head like a mental gumnut. She still struggled with the concept that it had actually happened, the gumnut was trying to find a hole to drop into, but couldn't.

'PND is out, we're kinetic, reversal sequence can be keyed.' Mitch's eyes settled into their sockets slightly. At least they'd stopped the engines, he thought firmly.

They both realized that failure of the gyroscopic thrusters would mean utter disaster. If they couldn't turn the vehicle. Mitch looked a little pale and his left hand, that which would boot the rockets into life, had the suggestions of a slight tremor. Sean had never seen that before. Jessy looked like she was made of steel.

The conventional fuel boosters were scabbed on the underbelly of Cygnus and were designed and now programmed to completely reverse the orientation of the vessel in space. SIS would commence a low grade burn that would reposition the bow of the craft back toward Earth. Jessy's eyes were gigantic as she watched every move they made, and watched every move the craft made, ready to report anything she felt she needed to.

'Hitting hypergols in five seconds...two, one, initialize.' Mitch thumped the small red actuator and waited, looking immediately at Jessy who was glued to the monitor in front of her.

Her voice was ice, 'the rockets haven't fired...no indication of ignition. This was supposed to be the most straightforward part of the system, you said it yourself. Shit!' Jessy's head spun around and she looked pleadingly at Mitch. 'What the fuck is wrong...' She was cut off by Mitch.

'It's a programmed manoeuvre Jessy, ignition is not immediate, there's a self-test sequence by SIS and then...'His voice was drowned out by a dull thundering whoomph within the craft.

'That's it,' Jessy said loudly, 'I've got blue lights on...all thrusters.' Her eyes settled back into their sockets and her face gradually melted into a twisted half smile. Her expression was way too tight as she watched the screen and felt the craft start to move slowly.

Feeling the welcome inertia, they could all sense the craft slowly turning, seeing the changing starscape in the viewscreen and on the three visual simulators. The disquieting view of Proxima was disappearing, a sight no one was sorry to see go.

'Reversal should be complete in one minute twenty-three seconds.' Fucking go, he implored the craft. Keep turning, Jessy begged, clenching her toes and staring at the mock-up of the vessel on her screen. Sean was monitoring the manoeuvre on the VTU in front of him which showed a slowly rotating multidimensional image of the vessel. The rotation stopped after several minutes.

'Rockets are doused, reversal is complete. What do you say Mitch?' Sean was smiling.

'I say we're in position to deploy the pod.' Thank Christ, Mitch thought, wiping sweat from his brow, standing up to stretch. They were now looking good, facing in the same direction as CX1.

The tension drained from the crew. They were all breathing again...they were now ready to front CX1 with all they had, once they restarted PND. Jessy gave a slow smile. They only hoped to God they had enough. If they all hit where they were supposed to hit, it should be enough. That's what the calcs on the supercomputers said anyway.

Earthshield II was the small EV pod that was designed specifically to approach CX1 and personally deliver the fusion heads. Crammed with four hundred hydrogen nukes, it would deliver three hundred megatons of explosive yield. The tiny vessel was literally an overstuffed nuclear mattress. If delivered accurately, if detonated between twenty and forty thousand kilometres above the polar corona of Proxima, Earth's best guess was that it would work, or so Discover and AMOS said. They said that CX1's bearing would be altered by a margin that would eventually equate to enough to spare their family of planets. Gravity well, astrophysical jet and all.

That was terrestrial theory anyway, and to the Cygnans, it seemed like the computers that hatched the theory were a billion light years away. Shaking CX1 was the mission. Do it by enough and we win. They just hoped they had enough and it would hit where it was supposed to.

Given that Proxima would still be travelling at ten thousand kilometres per second relative to the acquired velocity of the pod and the missiles, the shock wave from the explosion would reach the stellar pole within two to four seconds. The delivery would have to be absolutely precise and for that they would be relying on the servo-heart of the pod and the on missile data compressed circuitry. The cryo-fibers would search for, lock on to, and calculate detonation timing. Then the pod would monitor the diminishing distance and transit time to the star at its closest approach.

If there was the slightest miscalculation, CX1 would flash past Earthshield II and be gone forever. There would be no second chances here. It had to be done right the first time. They could only pray their technology was up to the job. Mitch knew it would be lineball. He looked a little pale as he stared at SIS. 'I hope to Christ you know what you're doing,' Mitch said hopefully, gaping at the metallic monster.

If they did fail and CX1 hurtled past unscathed, Cygnus could eventually run it down, but with its payload of weapons gone, it would be a fruitless effort. They would simply be sightseers, watching the destroyer edge toward solar space. Powerless to do anything about it.

With failure, and barring some in-transit miracle, Earth would be lost and then they would issue their statement of doom. Earth wouldn't breathe it in for twelve months, and it would be followed in another twelve months by the arrival of the death stars. And the ejection of earth and the destruction of all its life. In short, it would kill the lot, everything would go. A cosmic fire sale. Sean felt he might be having a heart attack, as he contemplated coming face to face with the beast CX1.

The rumbling of the Breeder was horrendously loud but it subsided to a more bearable dull pulsing. Novae Drive was being used to slowly decelerate Cygnus and then accelerate it in the direction it was pointing. That is, back toward Earth and on a complementary path to Nemesis.

CX1 would be allowed to slowly gain on Cygnus, and after twenty nine days they would rendezvous, travelling side by side at a roughly lateral distance of ten million kilometres. This was considered to be about the minimum safe distance, but with no practical experience or quantitative data, they could only hope they were being conservative enough. Jessy, in particular, was miserably unsure. She had no idea if it was far enough, supercomputers at Marshall and Goddard said it was, but no one really knew. She knew there was nothing in the cosmos with the raw power of a black hole. Were they underestimating it, how far out did its power extend? How much radiation and heat could they expect? These were the riddles that none of them could answer until they were there. Until they were staring at its terrifying blacker than space facade. Of course, by then it would be much too late to change their plans. They were in it for the long haul. They were in it until a decision was made, yes or no to them and to Earth.

***

She knew she was screaming but there was no sound. Jessy saw Mitch through the glass plate and realized she was outside the ship, floating in space, her flesh somehow unfazed by the freezing emptiness. Then she was alone, no craft, no biosuit, just the black hole and light years of extra-stellar nothingness. She knew in a moment of crushing revelation that Earth and all that rode her were gone. She tried to scream again … again she failed. Breath in a vacuum. Jessy felt the tidal forces, strong on her head and gentle on her toes, as it pulled her apart. Watching without pain or emotion, she examined her ribbonesque lower torso as it floated away into space. Her lifeblood formed swarms of tiny planetoids in front of her, perfect centimetric spheres of bright red plasma gliding on the gentle stellar wind... Jessy spasmed and woke, drenched through with the cold sweat that always accompanied her nightmares. She looked down and was half surprised to see she was

83

clothed and whole. The nightmares were getting more intense and more real. It felt like the stuff of psychedelic drugs gone horribly wrong.

She wondered at what point the reality of the frightmares might start to diminish, or at least to level off. Maybe they wouldn't. Jesus, she thought. The idea of the dreams getting worse, continuing to become more detailed and more profoundly unpleasant was terrifying. 'Fuck me,' she said quietly to herself, putting her feet on the ground. Joshy slept on, seemingly unperturbed by his mother's troubles.

Jessy dressed in her white sweatsuit and padded quickly through the simulated night of Cygnus to the observation bubble. It was now only five days to rendezvous. Jessy hadn't looked at Proxima for a few weeks now. When she did, she gasped, making a sound like a deflating balloon.

'Oh fuck,' she exhaled quietly to herself, 'what, is…shit,' she said brokenly.

Proxima was only a few billion kilometres away and now a naked eye horror, despite its size, a red misshapen accident in space, spastic and twisted, promising torturous destruction. The arc of boiling gas being torn from it was all too vivid. The tormented star was small, but it was still bigger and brighter than anything else out there, due largely to the ring of superheated plasma. Jessy cringed at the whopping doses of X-rays and hard gammas that Cygnus and the pod would suffer during the close encounter.

The protective lithium and lead reticulation in the skin and the vacuglass should protect them, but again, what did they know of a feeding black hole? Maybe they'd be fried. Maybe they'd only receive enough radiation to die slowly from agonising burns. Jessy felt reasonably confident because she'd helped design the craft and knew what it carried inside its box-strutted superstructure.

Looking at the cosmic beast did make her wonder though. The technology of the craft seemed more insignificant and inconsequential the closer CX1 came. She couldn't help but concur with Rhys's analogy, the elephant and the three-legged tree beetle. It seemed distressingly apt. It seemed ridiculous in the extreme that they would have any control whatsoever over a black hole.

Jessy returned to her quarters and padded over to Josh's crib. He was fast asleep on his side, sucking his thumb. So peaceful, Jessy thought. 'If only I could be like you, without a goddamn care in the world.' In an instant, she remembered her nightmare and her heart jumped into her mouth and started pounding like a hammer on the pinkness of her soft palate. She eventually relaxed a bit and realized for the first time just how exhausted she was. The nervous energy that had propelled her for the last hour or so had vanished. Jessy climbed back into bed fully clothed and was asleep in seconds. She slept until morning in a deep, dreamless slumber.

***

Walking along the primary corridor of Cygnus, they turned immediate right and ambled the short distance to the cramped elevator that went in one direction only, down to the EEV Bay. Rhys was decked in his shielded environment suit. His wide, swiftly blinking eyes were clearly visible behind the visor.

It was the morning of 22 May. Rendezvous was minus five days three hours and a few minutes. Earthshield II (ESII) was ready and primed for its heady role in the delivery of the fusion missiles. Roughly pentagonal in shape, the pod sat, along with the smaller pod of ESI, in the launch bay of Cygnus near the axis of the craft. The larger of the two pods was stocked with the equivalent of a million megatons of TNT. The most powerful destructive device ever constructed by humans.

Rhys gulped a lungful of atmosphere as he clamped eyes on his diminutive new home. 'Don't light a match for God's sake,' he quipped, gazing at the pod, contemplating the mission in front of him. Daunting wasn't an adequate description. It was fucking insanity he was sure. He had a disconcerting ringing in his ears. Despite tilting his head and banging the other ear, the helmet anyway, it remained.

The Compit of Earthshield II could only fit a single pilot which was always destined to be Rhys. He was copiously trained in the dynamics of the tiny vessel and knew precisely how to manage its most important system, weapons guidance.

It was a unique, state of the art assemblage. A fully adaptive continuous feedback Ranging Delivery System (RADES) which would do everything to ensure the nuclear payload hit when and where it was supposed to. Had Rhys not survived, it would have been up to Jessy who was trained as his replacement. To put it politely, she was ecstatic it was Rhys making the trip, not her.

Rhys was led up the short gantry by Mitch who briefly shook his gloved hand and stood watching. The bulky figure made its way through the yawning hatch and into the shining bladder that didn't look much different from a large Aquanet submersible. Tree beetle, Jessy thought again, this time with disturbing clarity. Rhys looked pained behind the helmet.

Unlike the other pod, ESII was minus an airlock, there was simply no room. Ninety-eight percent of the space in the craft was designated for weapons storage. There was little room for anything else, including the Compit and Rhys himself. Inside, it was smaller than the descent stage of the Eagle, occupied by Neil Armstrong and Buzz Aldrin in 1969.

Mitch heaved at the composite poly-ceramic door, pulled it shut and cycled the locking yoke. He punched the external mainspring pad which was mirrored by an identical pad on the inside.

Jessy took a final look as she and the others stepped through the ponderous vacuum proof plate of the deployment bay, wondering how Rhys must feel. She pretty much knew, but she wondered anyway. Everyone's hopes rode with him. The mission was in his hands now. Jessy knew he was capable, but like the others she questioned the ability of the technology to properly deliver the blast, given the stupendous radial dynamics of CX1.

Rhys's voice was strained. 'I've got a malfunction reading...' A long silence followed. Sean and Jessy looked at each other. Mitch looked at Rhys through the window.

Sean said, '...what the hell's going on?

Rhys continued. 'I had a problem at part three of the self-test on the central proximity ranger, but it cleared as quickly as it appeared. It's showing a blue light now.' Rhys sounded tense and confused. He'd never seen that before.

'Are you sure it's showing okay, do you want to restart the diagnostics?' Mitch asked, looking at Jessy and biting his lip hard. Now, he was scared.

'No time, we'll have to trust it, it's showing three blue's so we'll have to go with it. There's no time for repairs to the main system, even if we found a problem. Let's just hope it had a bit of a hiccup...read a zero that was a one...or something.' He sounded confused and worried.

Mitch ran a jerky hand through his hair. 'Okay, no probs,' he said; feeling way more concerned than he let on. He needed to sound nonchalant, that was the least he could do for Rhys.

Rhys felt the foreboding hit him, a feeling that things were about to go catastrophically wrong. Tension inside and outside the pod increased a notch. They could have done without the suggestion of system failure.

The torso of Cygnus started to grow a double appendage that was slowly rotating and extending into space, like the spawn from some tremendous marine predator. Twin doors of the deployment bay were breaching, arching backward to reveal a spectacular cosmos to Rhys.

Wisps of residual atmosphere were wrenched into the vacuum, disappearing like snow on a griddle. Earthshield II was mechanically winched to the threshold of the void. As it teetered on the edge, Rhys suddenly understood the nature of the mission he was about to embark on. He was going to try and shift a black hole. Rhys rubbed his face hard. He knew that before, but now he really knew.

Struggling to come to grips with the idea, he stared at the millions of furnaces that hung around him in space. 'Fuck.' It was the only word that sufficed. 'You must be goddamn joking...,' he muttered under his breath, still not believing he was about to do. 'Confront a black hole.'

Earthshield II blew its aluminium clamps and jumped into space, rapidly winding up and speeding away from Cygnus. In four minutes, it was travelling at eighty thousand kilometres an hour, a speed precisely controlled by the pod's servomotors which were already in fluid conversation with RADES.

While the lateral speed away from Cygnus was being minutely trimmed, ESII was still travelling in the same direction and at the same speed as Cygnus by virtue of its acquired momentum from the great ship. This would allow the pod to maintain a velocity within about six percent of Nemesis.

Rhys realized only too well the difficulty involved in trying to shoot something travelling toward and past you at ten thousand kilometres per second. Like trying to shoot an F32 Stealth with a bow and arrow...it could be done but you had to get it just right.

Rhys looked back and caught a final glimpse of the white underbelly of Cygnus, bathed as it was in the glow from a still distant Proxima. He could just make out the letters on the spine of the craft "USPA" and it stung him with uncomfortable memories of home. And it filled him with a strangely emotional pride. Pride for humanity. Pride for their distant little planet. After all, he mused, standing akimbo and crossing himself, we're trillions of kilometres from home, frantically trying to save ourselves.

So desperately wanting to endure as a species. Our will to live has elbowed us out here, far beyond our threatened home, to meet head on that which was trying to snuff out our destiny. The immensity of the undertaking hit him again. Dislodge a star. He continued to cross and uncross his suited legs, hoping like hell the warheads were up to the task. He felt tiny and feeble in the vast emptiness around him, realizing that he and his miniature craft were pitted against the binary powerhouse that was growing, visibly, before him.

'Mitch, I've got the figures from Prox, time to perihelion is four days and eleven minutes. Proxima is coming in at ten thousand nine hundred and twenty-three kilometres per second. Trajectory is unchanged and as already stated. Lateral velocity of ESII is precisely twenty-two kilometres per second and missile transit to target from perihelion is thirteen hours, twelve minutes.'

'Good...that's good, any indications of inconsistency?' Mitch held his breath.

'...all systems are functional, no problems so far.' There was a long pause. 'God, stop worrying would you. If anything goes wrong, I'll fix it, I never go anywhere without my Phillips Head, you know that,' Rhys chuckled quietly.

'Fuckwit,' Mitch said, also chuckling. 'Keep a close eye and report any malfunction, no matter how slight, okay?' Mitch knew there was nothing he could do from here if anything went wrong. He could only pray that nothing would go wrong.

'You'll be the first to know, trust me.' The transmission ended with an emphatic squawk.

'He sounds so damn calm,' Jessy remarked.

Mitch grunted. 'He needs to remain alert and also get some sleep along the way. It's our job to make sure that happens. You and I both know how skilled Rhys is. If he's mentally with it, there's no better person to have in that craft.'

***

A massive yellow fireball that was probably an errant star was headed directly toward Earthshield II, engulfing it and melting it like lard on a Tucson bonnet. Inside the pod, Rhys saw his hands turn to goo as his eyes turned to egg white. Then blackness. The viewing plate melted and, although blind, Rhys somehow managed to see his body flow out into space, parts of him remaining stuck like burnt cheese on the broken hull. Rhys woke with a mute burble as he gratefully acknowledged the intact ship around him. Twice he had slept on his sojourn and twice he'd had unnerving, bizarre nightmares. 'Fuck me, he said breathlessly, peering through the pod window.

His hypothalamus was working overtime, jetting neurochems like an Artesian bore, taunting him with vivid images. Just like Jessy. Must be an occupational hazard, he mused, deep in thought about what might happen in the next few hours. Rhys decided he wouldn't sleep again until the mission was over and he was on the way back. 'Wishful thinking,' he muttered quietly within the cramped confines of the pod. *On the way back.* It was a warm and pleasant thought.

He noticed the image of Proxima had become significantly clearer since the last time he'd looked. Christ it looked angry, he said to himself. It was a flare star and it was intensely unstable, but it looked angry, that was his human take on it.

Proximity ranger showed it was now Impact minus twenty-four hours. Missiles would be unleashed in eleven hours, giving them time to chew up space to their target with their optic fibre gizzards making frenetic calculations along the way. Calculations that would be rechecked and updated twenty times each second.

The waiting was filling his mind with uncertainty. A lone figure in a tiny craft a light year from home. Totally, unremittingly alone...isolated...stranded in a ship that would take thousands of years to get back to Earth under its own power. He shuddered, feeling a rush of terror hit him. The limits of human psycho-endurance were being sorely tested. Did they have the right human in this chair? He wondered. Deep in contemplation, Rhys's focus returned when the noise of the rocket boosters suddenly stopped. His heart dropped into his lap and started thumping like a tin drum.

'Oh fuck...not now,' he started to utter, looked at the PWR and LCK and they were fine. The sound of a different noise stopped him and made him close his mouth, an oddly staccato rumble.

'Oh shit, right.' He realized the craft had automatically executed the slowing procedure by shutting off the main propulsion ring. The rim cones were being fired that would bring him and the weapons to the programmed vector in space. Rhys was annoyed with himself for not immediately identifying the manoeuvre. Numbers were flashing over the monitor in front of him. Confirmation of the vessel's position and status would follow within a few minutes. He contacted Cygnus as soon as the computer proffered its verdict telling him where in space he was. He held his breath then spoke.

'Mitch, the pod has reached a position two point one zero three million kilometres from the projected rotational axis of the two bodies. The computer's finished programming auto release of the missiles, now scheduled in, ten point two five hours. All systems are looking g-g-good.' Rhys almost got through the statement without stuttering. He was shit scared. He didn't want to look outside.

***

Rhys hit the transmit button and sent the message. He could only sit and wait for a response, wishing he'd brought something along to help pass the time. He decided to try and rest, without sleeping, which was recommended.

Although the entire procedure was automated, Rhys wanted to be awake when the missiles drifted from the ship. An alarm would rouse him at Deployment minus thirty minutes if he happened to be asleep. In fact, Rhys did fall asleep after he'd convinced himself that he wouldn't. The hours passed and CX1 continued to eat up space between it and Earth's tiny saviour.

A siren began blaring, and with it came a strobing orange light that drowned the sleeper in a dazzling ocular beat. Rhys was woken abruptly and for some time was numbed by the clanging.

He immediately recognized it as the alarm...the one he'd set so meticulously for himself. But after several tens of seconds he realized it wasn't the alarm, couldn't be the alarm. That was off to his left. This noise was coming from the other side...from Prox.

Rhys spun around and was stunned by a blazing stream of light spearing through the thickly glassed portal to his right. He knew this wasn't a fucking dream. He rubbed the back of his neck hard and fixed his eyes on the light.

'Jesus, what the h-hell...,' Rhys stammered as he shielded his eyes with his palms. 'What the hell,' he repeated. His pulse quickened as his sleep thickened mind searched for a reason for the cacophony, not to mention the light that tortured every pore of his body with pulsing needles. Glancing at the monitor, his heart skipped a beat. It was flashing a continuous alert signal which meant it had something to say. It wouldn't be good news, no way it could be good news. Warnings seldom were.

Rhys punched the relevant command codes and downloaded the details of the warning from Prox. The noise and lights were doused as the monitor started to disgorge its message.

87

As it did, Rhys felt a loose sensation in his bowels as the implications of the warning took root in his mind. 'Fuck, fuck, shit,' he screamed, bile seeping into his mouth and he double gulped to try and clear it. Coughing and spluttering, he looked again through red rimmed eyes at Prox. In his mind's eye he could see the end of humanity spelled out on the monitor in front of him. It was laid out like a terrifying Fleur de lis. It was now telling him that CX1 was going to pass within four hundred thousand kilometres of his tiny, naked craft.

There had been a software breakdown. One that had already been found and repaired by the system's self-surgical software. Apparently, the error had just been located and was fixed immediately with barely a sideways glance.

'Shit, shit, fuck!' Rhys roared to no one. 'Goddamn computer, why now, why this?' He ranted hysterically at RADES, with bulging eyes and a spitting mouth, that squarely said, this is impossible. He'd initially hoped that CX1 had somehow wobbled off course, meaning that his problems were solved. It wasn't the case. Instead, it was a software hiccup that was now repaired. Now repaired! Great, good job. His frustration with the ship's ranging system continued although he realized soon enough that his time would be better spent trying to figure out a solution to the mess. Even though he wasn't sure there was one.

Irrespective of what Mitch might say, he already knew the only course of action was to have the computer rework all the parameters for missile deployment, based on the new and correct data. Without receiving base data before departing, the onboard missile systems would be worse than useless. It was telling him that the new calculations would take several hours, which left Rhys in a crippling quandary.

'...you've got to move to a safe distance Rhys,' Mitch was saying, '...minimum safe distance is around one point eight million kilometres, if you're any closer you won't make it. The shielding won't be effective, er...life preserving if you're closer than that.' He wasn't sure how to say it. Move now or die, he really meant.

Mitch wasn't really sure what was a safe distance, no one was, but he said it as though stating a fact. 'Move immediately and radio back to me when you're there and give me the new calculations. I reiterate you must move now or you'll, er...die.' Mitch's voice sounded shrill and emotional, still, Rhys knew he couldn't comply. He already knew what he had to do. 'Fucking hell', he said out loud, thrusting both arms out, can't I ever catch a break?' he was shaking with frustration.

Rhys had made his own feverish calculations and realized that for the mission to succeed, he needed to stay put. To allow the slow thinking computer time to do its cogitations while the craft was laterally stable. Rhys rolled his shoulders violently. Piece of shit, he thought bitterly. The craft had completely failed him, and Earth.

RADES had automatically rerouted some of its learning software and bypassed the damaged sections. But its ability to think quickly was shattered, reduced at least fifty-fold. The required tracking, targeting, computations and multiple triangulations would now take several hours.

Should a problem arise at any stage during the pre-calculations the computer would have to start over. From scratch. The mission was starting to unravel in front of his eyes. A fucking software problem, he couldn't believe it. 'No good piece of crap,' he snapped to no one, rubbing a hand roughly down his face. 'Jesus,' he swore, gazing at the sweat droplets on the floor of the ship.

If he travelled for five hours the pod would still only be one point two million kilometres from CX1's closest approach which would leave insufficient time for computation and downloading the critical data. Even if there weren't any further technical hitches. Rhys couldn't risk it. He knew it, and Mitch and the rest of them knew it too. 'Damn this shit box to hell.' he yelled, knowing it didn't have the power of mind. It made him feel better though, so he did it again.

***

'Is there anything we can do?' Jessy pleaded, hoping that Mitch would find a solution but knowing otherwise. He looked at Jessy and saw tears welling at the bottom of her limp green eyes. She knew it too.

'He's still got an excellent chance,' Mitch soothed through eyes that said otherwise. 'If he moves the pod at maximum burn immediately after deployment, he'll be at a reasonable distance when CX1 hits perihelion. That'll give him a chance, it's gotta give him a good chance.'

'He's got no choice, though has he?' Jessy asked in a whisper.

'If he doesn't stay put, the mission will fail. He doesn't have a choice.'

At missile deployment minus ten hours and thirty-six minutes, Prox was indicating that all computations had been completed and that it now required Rhys to download the data to RADES within sixty seconds. This would "wake up" the weapons system on the craft. If he didn't download it in that time or give a reason why by selecting one of seven options, it would be done anyway, automatically. No doubt that would work. Missiles would be armed at D-minus five minutes and be deployed by automation at Impact minus five hours and three minutes. They would be guided internally by RADES, detonating hopefully, twenty-five thousand kilometres in front of Proxima Centauri. The shockwave would strike the star's northern pole in two point three seconds and would hopefully create a seismic shock sufficient to alter its radial motion through space. Any alteration would probably be enough. Earth would be saved. Or the fear was it would send Proxima on its way but leave the black hole rooted to spacetime, and on the same trajectory through space.

There were a great many unknowns not the least of which was RADES ability to deliver the explosives as precisely as required. A slight meander of the weapons or a minimal miscalculation would see them explode uselessly in space, the most expensive and tragic fireworks display in history. They could see Rhys's pod through the faint object telescope that was mounted to one side of the vacuglass dome on Cygnus. At the highest magnification it was very distinct. Uncomfortably so. Its encounter with CX1 would be easily viewed, which they were not sure was a good thing, given the change in circumstance. Sean had run through a few more calculations and felt that the heat from Proxima and the hard gammas from the black hole might be survivable at a million kilometres, but he really didn't know. If his retreat was at top speed, according to plan, he believed Rhys might make it. Might. He also might be killed.

***

He watched the brilliantly illuminated timer countdown to Deployment minus eight minutes. Rhys was numb with fear which surprised him despite the obvious danger. He thought he'd come to terms with it in the previous few hours of reflection. But there was no coming to terms with the feelings he had for the others. Rhys's chin was trembling as he looked at CX1.

For the billions back on Earth who were depending on what happened here in the next few hours a software error was the commander.. Was Earth to die because of it? The absurdity of the idea struck him like a kick to the solar plexus. The craft in which he was sitting carried the hopes of a civilization. Jesus. It was all he could think about, the pressure was overwhelming. Rhys shuddered and shook his head to try and clear his mind, to try and clear the burning images of Earth's hellish ruination. And here I am in the big chair. 'Jesus, shit,' he screamed at the instrument panel. Like a fucking monkey, he thought seriously, 'press this button, press that button…'

Concentrating on the bright red numbers, he watched them dwindle to D-minus five minutes. The hundreds of missiles instantaneously and silently armed themselves in the freezing vacuum of the fusion hold. Rhys felt the vibration from the weapons bay hatch sliding back. The warheads were exposed to space. It was time for them to do their job.

'So far so good,' Rhys said out loud to himself, still staring unblinkingly at the timer. He looked up at V645 which was twenty million kilometres away and closing rapidly. As it approached, its malevolence became suddenly clear. Rhys had grown to despise it. A crazy emotion he knew, but still, there it was. 'How do you hate a ball of gas?' He had no reply. The emotion was understandable, he knew that much. It was off to kill a civilisation, his civilisation. Rhys drew his hands into fists as he watched space outside.

The countdown slipped to D-minus one minute. Rhys hardly dared to breath as the seconds wasted away before him. His eyes were wide behind his visor, jutting like chicken eggs in a carton. He emptied his bladder at D-minus fifteen seconds. All systems were normal according to the linear readout. Stay normal, he pleaded. Was normal really normal, he couldn't help thinking. He did his best to change his direction of thinking.

Mitch was glued to the telescope on Cygnus. No one on board Cygnus was breathing. Rhys started counting along with the timer as it passed ten seconds...three, two, one, Christ. He felt the thump of the weapons as they were mechanically hoisted into space.

Their liquid fuel boosters ignited the blackness somewhere below him. He watched as the swarm of nuclear pyres arced away from the ship at tremendous velocity.

Rhys hesitated long seconds before requesting a status report from Prox.

With trembling fingers, he eventually did and noted with quiet elation that all the weapons had fired and were travelling on course at requisite velocities, so far. 'Thank you God,' he murmured.' If there was one..

To Rhys, the rockets were a magnificent sight, shapely symbols of technology finally doing what it was supposed to. Each two-metre projectile speared through space, riding fiery white tails, like a cluster of tiny, fabulous comets.

They appeared to be heading nowhere near Proxima but they were nosing toward the star's continually updated future position. He hoped like hell that the pre-calculations done by the malfunction-prone computer were accurate. If they weren't ... well, he didn't even want to consider the implications of that. He continued to assume they were correct. It was all he could do.

Rhys punched in the running codes for reversal of the program which had hauled him to this unenviable point in space. A reversal that would effectively return him, with a few manual adjustments, to Cygnus. Proxima was looming at frightening velocity now, swelling noticeably in front of him, very clearly moving against the background of stars. Just like a goddamn comet. It was nearly time.

'Thrusters in ten seconds,' Rhys said in a useless transmission to Mitch. '...two, one, ignition. Nothing happened. Rhys didn't panic. He'd done that before and felt stupid, despite being on his own. But this time he couldn't think of a reason why he didn't feel the inertial thump of ignition...this time it should have been instantaneous. He'd over-ridden the systems check. Maybe he shouldn't have.

'Oh God...what now?' Rhys moaned, a vein sticking out and throbbing in his neck, 'give me a fucking break,' as he saw that the monitor and all the lights on the control panel had flickered and then gone out. The only light in the cockpit was the dim halo from the emergency beacon that had clicked on, throwing out a dull radiance. His heart was racing and he was sweating on the floor. His hair felt wet. Rhys knew in an instant of unimaginable terror that if something didn't kick on in the next second or so, it probably wouldn't. Ever. 'Piece of shit,' Rhys repeated, yelling at the craft. 'Come on,' he yelled and felt like kicking, or better still, breaking something.

'Rhys...what's going on?' It was Mitch over the intercom, 'you need to proceed at maximum speed on the programmed reversal, immediately, that is, now...is everything okay?' Mitch was peering at the craft, hoping to God that the glow from the propulsion ring would appear. But it didn't. The craft looked obscenely dark and Mitch could feel the prickling terror on his brow from the realization that only one thing would have prevented Rhys making his escape. The deadly silence and the darkened craft suggested that Earthshield II had suffered some sort of system failure, probably a terminal one, certainly a major one.

The Cygnans watched and waited for the lights of escape. They didn't come. 'Fuck', Sean said loudly, 'what now?' Sean was grinding his teeth, waiting. For what, he didn't know.

'He's going to die unless we do something Mitch,' Jessy screamed. She was grabbing fistfuls of her hair and pulling it. He looked at her, trying to think, trying madly to think of something, anything that might help Rhys. She slowly came to the realisation that there was nothing they could do for Rhys.

Loudly Mitch said, 'we don't have time to send the other pod. It wouldn't get there in time, and we can't fire up Novae for such a short trip, by the time we started it, shut it down and reversed the craft we'd be a billion kilometres away. Shit, what to do?'

After several minutes of torture, Mitch sat down and stared at Jessy until she looked at him. Sean's voice was ominously low. 'We can't do anything, not a damn thing. If Rhys can't fix whatever the hell has happened to that fucking tin can, he's going to fry and there's not a damn thing we can do about it...except hope that he can sort whatever is wrong, out.' Jessy continued to look silently at Mitch with huge, moist eyes, virtually crying. Silence engulfed the viewing platform as they each pondered Rhys's plight. Barring a miracle, which became less likely with every beat of their hearts, he would very closely and very briefly observe an extraordinary cosmic duo. That was zero comfort to any of them, they wanted Rhys to return to his family, and by family they meant themselves. Jessy was seated in the red chair, legs folded under her. Tears again threatened. She loved Rhys in her own way, not like Mitch, but she loved him all the same. He'd delivered her little boy for God's sake.

With only slightly over four hours before CX1 reached its closest approach it was starting to become academic as to whether he got the craft going at all. Even if he left at top speed right now, he would still be less than eight hundred thousand kilometres from the rotational axis of the two objects at perihelion. Too close was Mitch's unavoidable thought. Too close. It was a star, a black hole, an accretion disk, and a relativistic jet of energy – Rhys had very little hope. Perhaps none.

'Stranded...isolated, doomed to die horribly,' Jessy murmured, unable to believe it and equally unable to stop her own flow of tears.

***

Rhys removed his E-suit and sat motionless in the crowded Compit of ESII. At Impact minus one hour he'd given up trying to fix the power grid, having taken everything he could think of apart and finding absolutely no flaw, or none that he could detect anyway. It was clearly a massive servo-electrical breach. If that was the case, which seemed likely, he had no hope of making the requisite repairs. No hope whatsoever. He was doomed.

Thank God the missiles were guided internally, he mused. If they'd relied on data being uploaded from Prox, the mission would be finished, Earth would be finished. All he could see was blackness. He stared at the growing star. It was only a few million kilometres away based on the time to impact, which he was forced to count on his wristwatch. Rhys was mesmerized by the insanely twisted belly of Proxima which grew larger as he watched. He was just beginning to feel the heat from it through the vacuglass. Was it from Proxima or the black hole's necklace – he wasn't sure, and did it matter? Probably not.

'Not long now,' he said calmly, stretching both arms up and feeling the heat.

The worst part was not being able to communicate with his friends on Cygnus. He wanted to say goodbye...to wish them luck. He wanted them to take a message back to his wife and child on Earth, if their mission was successful. If it wasn't then it didn't matter if he died now or later, although he definitely didn't want to die at the hands of the approaching beast. No way. Even before he'd left Cygnus, Rhys had given a great deal of thought to the prospect of not returning, putting his chances of survival at about seventy percent in his favour. So much for good odds, he thought glumly. If all that money was on a horse, he'd make a fortune, assuming he won.

The technology he'd handed his life to had failed miserably. The radical new propulsion system and ancillary wonders aboard Cygnus had worked perfectly to date, yet the conventional power grid aboard the pod had suffered total failure, and actually ceased functioning. Earthshield II had been struck dead and now simply drifted like a celestial seashell on the thickening stellar tide.

Through the main scope, Mitch could still see the glow from the rockets that were powering the fusion weapons. Proxima was three million kilometres away and was bathing the pod in a disturbingly royal glow.

From Rhys's perspective, the size of his killer was perhaps that of the Sun viewed from the sulfurous cloud tops of Venus. He stared, morbidly following the flurry of boiling star stuff that was being devoured by the orb's ghostly companion. His eyes bulged as he contemplated his fate, looking upwards, although he wasn't sure why.

Surrounding the black hole was a ring of gas that was so intricately detailed and stippled as to defy description, being almost beyond the scope of human superlatives. Gazing at it, he was awed by the magnificent rotating wheel of stolen, turbulent colour, stunning and vividly Saturnian against the dead blackness of space. Wonder-horror.

The temperature of the hull was more than nine hundred degrees centigrade at Impact minus four minutes, and getting hotter by the second. Life support kept the interior to a bearable thirty-five degrees, but it too was failing. Homeostasis systems would soon stall, making it quickly unbearable and eventually fatal.

Rhys was clothed only in his astro-suit even though he knew his armored E-suit would have at least temporarily protected him from the lethal combo outside. At this distance he knew it wouldn't matter what he wore, Christ, lead-suit, three-inch metal armor, concrete blocks...he was destined to receive the largest dose of X-rays ever sustained, and somewhat sadly, he also knew that that wouldn't be his killer. No matter how good the manufacturers thought their Mylar/Dacron netting and double-aluminized Kapton was, it couldn't shield him or his craft from the heat of an arm's-length fucking star.

At I-minus two minutes the internal temperature had soared to seventy-nine degrees. The alloy and polyplastic surfaces were burning hot, searing to the touch, venting a twisting, shimmying haze of boiling gasses. Rhys was having trouble breathing, his lungs were scorched...bleeding black blood into a parched throat. He knew he was about to die, and only prayed that it would be quick.

Perhaps he should've taken his own life, but how? Catapult himself into space to swell and explode like sheep guts in the sun? He didn't think so. He was terrified by the thought of touching space, of skin contacting the vacuum, perhaps more than death. No, he'd stay in the craft, come what may. Rhys thought he had about a minute before Proxima literally burnt its way into the pod and vaporized him. The orb in front of him was massive and blindingly white, a maelstrom of tortured gas that burnt his skin through the small viewscreen, like a magnifying glass focussing sunlight on a captured insect. Rhys panted and gasped, he was effectively on fire, his main thought was unconcealed contempt for CX1, and pain. It hurt to die. The starscape disappeared as brightness surged around him. So close now. Rhys's face was singed and pocked, starburnt by the hellish radiation cocktail being emitted by CX1.

***

Mitch stopped looking through the shielded telescope and walked over to Sean and Jessy and sat down. What would be would be, he conceded. Either the missiles would do their job or they wouldn't. Irrespective, Rhys would be dead. They all felt paralyzed by the mingling fear of failure, and fear for Rhys. They just hoped his suffering would be brief. Maybe he was the lucky one, Mitch suddenly thought, wondering what their future would be if the nukes missed their mark.

Proxima Centauri was a cool star by stellar standards, tiny, red and very, very long-living. Its surface temperature was only seven thousand degrees centigrade, unlike the cerulean stars whose outer temperatures could reach seven times that. For Rhys it was difficult to acknowledge such a ludicrously small mercy. Par cooked or fried and atomized, he'd still be dead.

V645 would be at perihelion with respect to Rhys's craft in under half a minute. Its catastrophic movement around the black hole had already been calculated, and those calculations put the star as the object that would more closely confront him. The black hole would be on the farside of Proxima and away from the pod.

Grotesque ripples of burnt flesh had begun to eat into Rhys skin like a thermal cancer, but still he clung to life although his brain had given up the fight. The tormented dermis of Earthshield II bubbled and undulated and in several places the hull simultaneously parted. Explosive decompression dragged Rhys through one of the ragged breaches in the superstructure, shredding him instantly, decapitating, eviscerating and gutting his body. Death was reasonably quick. Rhys's remnants floated into the burning void and were instantly fried into molecular charcoal. The last thought Rhys had before he died and while he was blind was for his wife and young son. He was only sorry that his eyes had been fried to white marble so he couldn't shed any tears. As he heard the hull give way, he mouthed goodbye to no one and everyone. A second later he was gone. Back from whence he came…Star carbon.

At Impact minus zero the fusion cluster detonated. Ninety-two of the warheads found their mark. The rest of the weapons, the bulk of them, exploded between fifteen and forty-five seconds later when the beast was already a hundred and fifty thousand kilometres away. Mitch had forced himself back to his position at the telescope in the final moments. He saw the puff of atmosphere depart Rhys's craft moments before impact. Gone.

'Dear sweet Jesus,' he said under his breath, realizing the hull had ruptured and catapulted whatever was inside…outside. Rhys was gone, he knew that. Seconds later he saw the fiery coronal flash slightly above Proxima's corona as it flashed past them in space.

The flash looked almost inconsequential and moments later he saw a second, a third and a fourth series of smaller explosions behind the galloping monster. He swore quietly as he realized that a good number of the nukes had missed their target. 'Fuck,' he spat through tightly clenched teeth. They all knew what it meant. He rarely swore for no reason and never did it with such feeling unless it meant something serious.

Mitch glanced over at Sean and Jessy who were both staring back at him, demanding some good news but knowing it wasn't going to come. Mitch held his stomach as though pained.

He said, '…we had maybe a fifty percent hit rate…we've at least given ourselves a chance.' Mitch tried to sound positive, but his voice wavered and he sounded unsure, catching on the last few words. Acting had never been his strongpoint. He was shaking his head which was a big giveaway.

'What about the pod?' Jessy asked, 'can you still see it, is it…there?' Her shoulders were slumped and she looked down at the floor as she spoke. Jessy knew. Mitch considered her question for a long moment, and wondered how to answer, still shaking his head. He decided just to be honest.

'He's dead. The hull failed prior to impact, I'm sorry, he's gone…' Mitch's voice trailed off to a long silence. Jessy didn't cry this time, she was out of tears but she was angry. Her green eyes shone with an anger and frustration that was quickly turning to blind rage.

'What the hell happened with that pod?' she screamed. We both checked…double and triple checked every system on that thing and it was fine, right up to launch when we had some sort of software no go. That was fixed and then the entire servo-system apparently failed. What happened Mitch, what did we miss…what did we damn well miss?' Her eyes bored into him. 'I feel so responsible for Rhys…' Jessy's voice broke on the mention of his name and she found new tears. Muscles were jumping in her cheeks. Jessy was angry and felt like she was falling apart. She staggered to her feet and walked over, putting her forehead against the window and thought of Rhys.

'It's no one's fault,' Sean said in an attempt to comfort her. We're pioneers in every sense. Rhys wouldn't want us to feel responsible for his death. As Mitch said, he knew the risks … probably better than we did. He's been thinking about this moment for a lot longer than we have.' They sat for a long time in silence. Jessy eventually got up and paced slowly toward the Compit, with Mitch in step behind her. He gently stroked Jessy's shoulders as she wiped away the last of her tears with a swipe of an index finger. Her face went from a sad mess to angry and back again.

He punched in the sequence of command strokes that would start the computations to replot the course of Centaurus X1. Calculations were based on the precise designation of Cygnus' position relative to eight marker stars. The voltaic Xray scanner would then track the motion and trajectory of CX1 over ninety minutes and provide its decision on the fate of humanity. Mitch looked at the monitor in front of him and contemplated the calculations that were already underway. Fuck me, he said to himself. The result would decide the fate of humanity, and perhaps everything else.

***

Sean watched, from where he didn't know, but the chilling images were stifling any sense of caring. He watched the colorful old friends as they wrestled on the edge of town, watching and crying as they were unceremoniously roasted, melted like snowballs in a Microwave. For a single heartbeat in time, he saw Pluto and Charon warm, drenched in roiling chemical seas and accreting nitrogen skies, warmed by a looming sun that looked so bewitching and friendly. But the kindly face was a killer's ruse, masking a savagery that saw the tiny twin's gangraped and shattered, their ashes hawked like burnt peanut shells into the interstellar deeps.

Sean stared at the binary wrecker as it plunged further into the domain of his own birthplace, spearing, he knew, toward the Galaxy's most precious seed. He felt the trembling in his shoulders, could feel the tears, huge and burning as they blew away into space, riding the edge of the Sun's gravity well like tiny watery moons...captured forever.

Sean then saw himself in downtown Manhattan, he knew that because he was leaning against a familiar white and red bricked storefront, gazing over the road at DePasco's sprawling Pasta Time. But where were the crowds, the vendors, the street bums, the twenty-four/seven crush? There were no people, no cars, no noise. Nothing. Just the rustle of swirling rubbish twisting in the cool morning breeze. And the sunlight, Jesus, what was wrong with this place he wondered, feeling suddenly agitated. He felt like he was skating on the surface of a halogen headlight. He ripped away his RayBan's and rubbed his eyes before spinning his head upward. Holy mother of Jesus, he saw himself stammer, seeing his mouth and face freeze like a Manzù sculpture.

The glare that bathed him was everywhere and up in the sky, above the Bank of America was a sight beyond the grasp of his visual brain. CX1, he knew what it was, but the image was impossible...brilliant, phosphorescent whiteness, so close, and all around it colour more vivid, more intricately brush stroked than seemed possible. It was fatter than the Sun which he could see, yellow and impotent near the horizon like a five watt globe. Oh Jesus, Oh God, he saw himself gasp as he drank in the ghostly landscape, seeing it painted in chilling tones of purple and white.

It was nearly here, the cauterizing pre-coronal wind from Nemesis. Fucking extinction, only minutes away, maybe only seconds. He screamed as the apocalyptic rainbow reached out for the Moon, an ejaculation of hopelessness that bounced off the soon to be vaporized city around him. Humanity and its cradle were gone. Consumed, digested and excreted. Blackness. As he fought his way to consciousness, he heard a strange, unidentifiable sound, somewhere in the distance.

***

After what seemed like days of waiting and pondering, they were finally shaken by the noise they'd all been craving. And dreading. The gentle whoopings of SIS shook Sean from his tormented slumber, loudly announcing its readiness, that it had the verdict. All the signature computations had been completed. About bloody time, they all thought, as they made their way straight to Prox. It seemed to take so long, but, it only seemed that way.

None of them felt confident, they were only too aware of the forces they were pitted against. Jessy settled in between the men in the Compit, unavoidably rubbing herself on Sean's shoulder as she brushed past. Mitch sat down next to her and Sean moved in behind them. From his position he could just make out the smooth upper flesh of Jessy's breasts. Sean winced as he pondered his strange state of mind.

Uncountable months of unbearable pressure had been theirs and here they were about to find out if all their suffering had actually been worth a damn. Whether their home planet had some sort of fighting chance...and here he was trying to catch a glimpse of Jessy's breasts, or at least flesh. Holy Mother of God, he thought. He was losing it for sure. Had lost it very possibly.

CX1 was now over ten million kilometres in front of Cygnus and was edging away at a speed differential of just over ten thousand kilometres per second. SIS had tracked its Xray signature over that distance and was now ready to proffer the verdict on CX1'S motion through space. No one

94

spoke. Silence was complete. Sean, Jessy and Mitch watched the final numbers traverse the screen and disappear. The screen stayed blank. Then the monitor sprang to life, flooding with luminous letters.

CENTAURUS X1 TRAJECTORY COMPUTATIONS FOLLOWING...
The screen went blank again. No one was breathing. A split second later it illuminated:

COURSE CHANGE DUE TO SEISMIC WAVE....0%
ANY CHANGE BELOW TWELVE DECIMAL DETECTION LIMITS...

'Oh...come on! Zero percent...surely they had some effect!' Mitch exploded. I saw them hit...well some of them.' Mitch glared at the screen, not believing it was all for nought.

Jessy looked at the screen, not believing it either. 'Can that be right...zero percent, no change at all?' she asked in a shrill wheeze. Jessy was sure she was about to have a heart attack...or a stroke. Sean was staring mutely at the floor, devastated and disbelieving. He too believed the detonation would succeed, after all they only needed the minutest shift in its course at this distance. The screen changed again:

PROBABILITY OF INTERRUPTION TO EARTH
ENVIRONMENT...94%.

They all succumbed to their own private nightmares. The monitor continued to spit out unwanted information. Unwanted verification of the worst possible news. This is what they were waiting for, but not the news they wanted.

END

There was a long silence as they stared at the last message on the screen. Jessy looked at Mitch. *End.* That summed it up nicely. Jessy couldn't breathe and there was a strange brightness in front of her eyes...shapes and forms, strange silhouettes.

'Well that's it then, we've failed,' she offered in a trembling voice, feeling ill. 'The entire bloody mission has been in vain,' she said, shaking her head and biting her lip. 'Christ, I can't believe this is happening, I truly believed we would succeed...what a terrible, shocking waste of time.' She clenched her fists and rubbed her forehead, digging her fingernails painfully into her flesh. She honestly couldn't believe it. Jessy was sure they'd come out on top. She was wrong though...terribly wrong. And Rhys was dead. All for nothing.

'We had to try Jess,' Mitch retorted painfully. 'We gave it our best shot, but no, we apparently haven't been successful. I guess our technology wasn't up to it after all.' Mitch hesitated, then continued, 'look at what we were up against, even a quantum leap in technology which we achieved with PND wasn't enough....let's face it, if there are more potent forces in the Universe, we don't know about them. Well, we do, but that's not the point, the point is, we were up against an incredibly powerful force.'

Jessy thought of the dinosaurs. Humanity would go the same way. So much for technology, she mocked silently. Might as well have rolled up the bloody footpaths and been done with it.

'That's all very well,' Sean added, 'but the bottom line remains...Earth is probably doomed and our mission has been an abject failure. We all know we gave it our best shot, we know that...but our planet will perish, as will we in time. The fact that we gave it our best shot doesn't comfort me at all. We should have succeeded. Our technology was good enough, I know it was.'

Sean stood up quickly and looked despondently out of the window. 'There could be no greater incentive for success than what we had here. Maybe we went about it wrong, didn't bring enough firepower, who knows, but now everything's fucked!' Sean fairly screamed the last word, the intensity and the pain written in his bloodshot, red rimmed eyes.

They realised that the one thing they never really knew was the firepower required to shift the tremendous gravity well that the black hole created in spacetime. It may have been so deeply rooted in the quantum matrix of space that all the firepower possessed by the planet may not have been enough. Perhaps they were so deeply rooted in the fabric of spacetime there was no amount of energy that could shift them.

'So, what now?' Jessy asked quietly, twisting a gold ring on her finger.

'Earth will be waiting for the Word to arrive in a year,' Sean said. 'Meaning that if we decide to send a message, we should start thinking about it...' He glanced at Jessy.

Mitch looked at them both. He caught their drift. 'We have to send the message, and what's more we have to be accurate in our assessment of the outcome. We all agreed to the Resolution, to our mission parameters...and um, sending the message was a very important part of it.'

Jessy looked pained and spoke in a voice that reflected it. 'You mean you're going to send a message to Earth telling them they're all doomed and that there's not a damn thing they or anyone else can do about it?' She sounded dumbfounded. 'Great idea. That'll go down a treat.'

'Yes, I am,' Mitch said defensively, 'you and Sean have known from day one that a message would be sent whether or not we were successful, it's not open to debate.'

'But don't you feel different...now?'

'No, I don't!' Mitch said firmly as he strutted through the open hatch and down the corridor to his quarters. Of course, he felt differently, but those on Earth had a right to know the truth...the very reason the mission requirement was installed. He also knew that the truth would carry a chilling finality, as there would be no time to launch another effective offensive.

The nature of the mission and the time frames involved only ever left a window for one best effort. One thing they all knew beyond doubt was that contact needed to be made with Nemesis several trillion kilometres from home. If it was any closer than that, the change in trajectory hoped for would still leave their planet and their solar system doomed. Mitch admitted that Earth had little hope of survival. Perhaps it had none.

Mitch lay on his bed and gazed at the featureless gray ceiling. His focus lost itself as he slipped into unavoidable contemplation. Man's achievements, scientific, medical, social...the stunning moments in history...Relativity, landing on the Moon, him on Mars, Freedom, Copernicus, MarsHab, the Olympic Games, curing AIDS, Coronavirus, all the discoveries, all the hard fought philosophy...but for what?

The achievements of billions of people over several millennia would be erased forever and the planet, home of cats, dogs and a multitude of other animals as well as humanity itself, would be annihilated. Made extinct forever. It was too painful to consider. But he was doing it anyway. It was the worst possible nightmare...and it was real. Mitch was abruptly shaken from his contemplations by a sharp metallic knocking on the wall near his hatch.

'Come,' he eventually murmured, hauling himself to the edge of his bed. Jessy and Sean walked in and sat on the chairs near his desk, looking grim.

Jessy's mouth barely opened as she spoke. 'Sean and I have been talking and we want to return to Earth, we know we can arrive home at least three weeks before it does.' Sean stiffened a bit and buzzed his lips in agreement, nodding his head.

'We've all got goodbyes to make,' Sean added. 'Our future in this craft is capped at three years. After that we'll either starve or suffocate, and none of us really wants to go like that. Mitch, we honestly thought we'd succeed. We didn't think about this hard enough.' Jessy nodded at him with large eyes and a solemn expression.

'I need to know what happens to Earth Mitch,' Jessy begged, speaking low, 'it's our planet and we should be there at the end...and it's not a certainty that Earth will be destroyed. And how will we ever know unless we go back? We could be up here dying while Earth is down there existing.' They fell silent, waiting for Mitch to speak. To deliver his judgement, or at least his opinion.

'I agree with everything you've said.' Mitch spoke so softly it was difficult to hear him. 'I'd already weighed up the pros and cons of returning and I, like you, believe we have little choice. It's the best option.' They didn't know what to say, neither Sean nor Jessy. Both stared at Mitch taken aback by his response.

Mitch got up from his bed and walked slowly toward them. 'I've computed transit time assuming we push Novae to maximum consumption. If we do, we'll pass CX1 in twelve hours and arrive on Earth maybe a month in front of it. I'd warn you though that once equipped with the news I'm about to send to the UN we can't be sure what sort of mess the world might be in when we get there. Anything's possible. Of course, I'm assuming that they decide to actually release the News. When we arrive, we could be in for an unpleasant shock.'

'You don't suppose we'll be held responsible, do you?' Jessy shrilled, refusing to believe her own idea.

'Anything is possible. They may want a scapegoat, you sure you want to face that?' Jessy looked at Sean and then fleetingly at Mitch. 'We'll er, take our chances.' Sean nodded his head, agreeing copiously.

'Okay, we go then.' Mitch said. The course is programmed, including reversal, we can initiate Novae at our discretion.'

They all felt slightly better knowing they had a firm and positive plan in place. The downside was the sense of the unknown, of the unpredictable. Returning home to an Earth they may not recognize and to one whose inhabitants might rise up and fucking kill them. Scapegoats…

***

On Cygnus, simulated night had been cast four hours ago. They had literally fallen into bed, fatigued by the stress and anguish of the past few hellish days. PND had been successfully rebooted and was again operating without apparent problem.

In twelve hours, Cygnus would be tailing CX1 with a lateral separation of only forty million kilometres. And it would flash past it with a speed differential of what was now only five hundred kilometres per second but by then would be many thousand kilometres per second.

Mitch had just finished composing the two page message he intended to hurl back to AASSA in the southern hemisphere on Earth. Both Jessy and Sean had read the brief and sterile communiqué and agreed it was appropriate. Auto coded by SIS, the message could only be read by those with the "giga-key" to the Tri-stacked encryption.

Whether or not the UN decided to reveal the message to the public was their problem. Maybe they'd sweeten it, or perhaps only disclose part of it. Maybe they'd announce the opposite, that in fact the mission had been gloriously successful. That Earth was saved. All he could do was comply with his orders, orders that required him to pass on, without embellishment or gratuity, a death sentence to the planet. He felt profoundly guilty but his sense of duty prevailed. He had no choice but to send it. Mitch had his eyes cast downward as he considered what he had to send.

97

7

Visitor

'The universe is a pretty big place. If it's just us, it seems like an awful waste of space.'
~ Carl Sagan

As they slept, the dead star was suffering a spectacular seizure. Thirty million kilometres from Cygnus, the black hole started to shed its apron of darkness. First sparking, then shimmering, it gradually brightened until the rotating beast appeared, kicking and spewing tortured light.

The blackness was changing, becoming a mirror image of itself, a dazzling brilliance. For the first time, the companion of V645 rivalled its living twin, finding life and outshining it as though the star were a firefly pressed against a mighty magnesium flare. The sinister face of the black hole was finally revealed to Proxima Centauri in a ferocious orgy of screaming photons.

Within the bowels of the light storm a livid bruise became slowly visible against the whiteness. An ebony smudge was waxing and waning, slowly assuming something more distinct as it clawed its way from the brilliant aura. Illuminated by strobes of gray and white, the gently throbbing sarcoma was the size of a small moon. The brightness diminished and in minutes the bright rotation had vanished from the Universe. All the humans slept on unperturbed.

A Stentzi was raised and Sean was cut down with a minimum of fuss, his black blood spewing over the bitumen like hot oil as he tried to run. Brains and gore and pieces of skull were splattered over the ceramic nose of the Shuttle. Jessy tried to scream but again she couldn't get the sound passed the knot in her throat. A sudden pulse of light exploded around her.

The grizzled man at the head of the group scraped the butt of his .45 across her right breast before raising it. Jessy was staring down its muzzle, held steady only a few centimetres from the bridge of her nose. The gun fired and Jessy had a vivid image of the bullet that would kill her, a millisecond before it pierced her skull and hurtled through her basal ganglia. There was no pain. Just falling. She fell next to Rhys, still alive, only centimetres from his radiation fried face and bone white, boiled egg eyes.

Jessy sat up in bed, breathing hard and clutching her chest, feeling the relief slowly harden into rage and frustration. Another strange goddamn nightmare, she thought. 'Damn.' She wondered not for the first time why she didn't realize she was having a dream during the dream. Wouldn't it be obvious? Why the hell didn't AASSA provide a shipboard psych for times like these she brooded, almost laughing out loud at the prospect. 'Fucking dreams, that's enough,' she snapped to no one.

The dreams were unbearable and were affecting her ability to concentrate on what she should be concentrating on, her shipboard duties. It was difficult to properly focus on anything, anything except finding a solution to her incessant nightmares. She found herself thinking about them during most of her waking hours. 'Damn', she repeated, rubbing her forehead and biting her lip. Jessy was sweating and glaring out of the window, looking for Proxima but not really wanting to see it.

She changed into her loose suit and went for a trundle along the dim nighttime corridors of Cygnus. Jessy had been walking for ten minutes and eventually made her way to the viewing bubble. She glanced up at the hard pinpricks that pocked the emptiness outside. She expected to see the tortured face of Proxima.

Staring through the three inch 4 pane glass, her mouth dropped open like a whale about to engulf a tremendous wave of krill. Her brows jumped up and her eyes filled with cold fluid, looking like they might suddenly explode from their sockets. Her heart started pounding so hard and so fast it felt like someone had attacked her with a rib cutter. Sugary hormones flooded into her blood vessels like glacial meltwater. Jessy's breath came in shallow spurts as she gaped. She was instantly muddled but gawked on. She scratched at her cheek and her temple, having no idea about anything, even who she was. Jessy was visibly wobbling.

Her congested hypothalamus was abruptly thrust into maximum overdrive by the vista being beamed to her straining visual cortex. My God,' she stammered in total unremitting wonder. 'Sweet Jesus in heaven...' She could only continue to stare straight ahead, ogling what had previously been a familiar horizon of jet black emptiness pocked with a few bright pinpoints.

Floating what looked like only a few hundred metres away was an alien spacecraft. A vessel so insanely bizarre that her immediate thought was science fiction. Her second thought was that it wasn't really there. Jessy convinced herself that she must be dreaming and literally pinched herself to make sure. Nothing changed.

If she pinched herself during a dream would she wake up, she wondered absently, or would she only dream of pinching herself? Of course, she would, it would be a dream pinch. She didn't break her stare at the impossible craft. Couldn't really. Jessy was frozen from her toes to her brain. Just blackness with the occasional flash of white stars.

Eventually she scraped up the power of voluntary action. She closed her eyes and quickly reopened them. She turned around and spun back. It was still there, stalking their vessel, or at least taking a very significant interest in it. The thing was almost on top of them for God's sake. Dream. It had to be a dream. Jessy willed herself to move.

Was it friendly, she suddenly wondered? Or were they about to be taken apart by some profoundly destructive weapon? She remembered being told that an intelligence capable of interstellar travel, one that had developed the technology from scratch would likely be docile and friendly in nature, having developed a responsibility and conscience in tune with their progressive technical elevation. Carl Sagan had said that.

She'd always seen the logic in it. What if they weren't though? What about us? she considered. We're plying interstellar space and we could hardly be defined as pacifists, although our goals in space were certainly noble enough. Who the hell knew? Jessy finally decided. They might decide to get rid of the new arrival. Destroy us without notice.

She continued to inspect the mind jarring contours of the fantastic floating beast that seemed to be mirroring their course perfectly. She thought about moving but had no leg strength. At that instant it jumped from view, vanishing in a second and flashing over to the other side of Cygnus. Jessy was panic stricken that the craft had left, and wouldn't return.

And who would believe her? Shit...no one would! It would earn her a one way ticket to Happy Mountain nuthouse. They would think her a nutter worthy of a strait jacket and head restraint.

Pictures, she needed pictures, or better still, she needed to wake Sean and Mitch and get them up here to see this space thing, if it came back. Her mind was spinning. Jessy could only imagine Sean's reaction when he laid eyes on it. He had been almost struck permanently dumb by the craft they'd encountered previously. And they'd only got a few blurry photos of it.

'He'll probably die where he stands when he sees this baby,' Jessy muttered, grinning evilly to herself as she started to move. Her legs were heavy as she ran. Her mind was whirling and impatient for someone to join her.

Jessy sprinted to Mitch's quarters and roused him from what was obviously a deep sleep. He sluggishly dressed and with Sean, he walked behind Jessy to the viewing platform. Both wondered what the hell was so important that it warranted interrupting their sleep. She refused to say. 'Just move, just come with me,' she kept urging, until they moved.

Found a Cepheid variable perhaps? Mitch thought, knowing that Jessy was writing a paper on them, and had a special interest in these luminous yellow super giants. Or something to do with CX1 maybe. He put his brain in neutral as he walked into the bay. What the fuck was so important that she had to rouse both of us in the middle of the night?

Jessy was ecstatic. It was back! The tentacled beast had resumed its position almost immediately outside the vacuglass dome, totally dominating the scene outside. It was ponderous and unimaginable, like a bizarre fish swimming in the blackness of kilometres deep ocean, caught in the spotlight from a robot submersible. Jessy pointed, her composure faltering under that which seemed to be watching her.

Jessy stood back and let them look.

'...wh...what the hell...' Sean's voice geysered from the depths of his belly as he staggered toward the window without for a moment taking his eyes off the thing outside. He almost had his nose against the glass, like a child mesmerized by a lolly shop window. Mitch was rooted to the spot and didn't utter a sound. It was coming though, Jessy could hear it at the back of his throat.

'...in the name of...fuck, what is it...I mean, I can see what it is, but where, who?' Mitch asked with equal amounts of disbelief and stupor. It was absolutely incredible, he thought as he stumbled and staggered toward the window without for a second taking his eyes off that which lay outside. He felt like he needed to sit down, to avoid falling down. Mitch didn't move his eyes from the insane architecture outside.

Sean's voice was similarly thickened by awe driven emotion as he tried to get the words past his palate. Sean was shaking all over. He was holding himself up by grasping the edges of the windowpanes with both hands. 'It must be a r-relative of the craft we s-saw before.' His brain churned almost painfully as he tried to digest the meaning and significance of what was so casually hanging outside. He looked at it from different angles and at different distances, darting this way and that, then coming back and standing next to Mitch.

'It's inspecting us, perhaps as we would an insect or animal,' Mitch suggested softly.

She stared at it fixedly, 'let's hope it doesn't decide to squish us, or by some other means, destroy us,' Jessy murmured, wondering what the hell the lethal looking spines were. She couldn't even imagine what the purpose of the steeply contoured bilges might be. Remote sensing...hopefully.

Sean continued to speak quietly, as though any loud noise might scare it away, '...have a look at it, it's like nothing we could imagine, they must be eons ahead of us.' He sucked in a breath and spoke in an even fainter whisper. 'Are there, er...beings on board...do you think they can see us?'

Jessy gulped instinctively at the suggestion, feeling the vice around her chest squeeze a little tighter. Fuck, what do they look like, she wondered? She hadn't given a thought to that.

'I would almost guarantee it,' Mitch offered, 'They're probably gawking at us right now, trying to work out what the hell we are and where we come from?'

Jesus, Jessy thought. She wasn't sure how she felt about that. 'Those spikes look like massive antennae...why so many?' Jessy asked no one in particular, knowing they probably weren't what they thought. She tried to focus desperately on the vessel.

'They're probably receptors of some sort, the thicker ones might be optical sensors, but I doubt it,' Mitch said, knowing their best guesses would very likely be way off. He knew how unlikely parallel evolution was, even on the most basic of levels. They were probably something they'd never thought of.

They knew the spines could be anything, weapons, propulsion cones, Christ, sex organs, who knew? In this case, anything truly meant anything.

Sean was standing with his head resting on the curved dome, only inches from the dead vacuum outside. This was the greatest moment of his life, of that there was absolutely no doubt. He hadn't moved his eyes from the ship since he sighted it. He stared at it with desperation in his eyes. He looked like he wanted to jump through the glass, freestyle to the ship and rap on its finely textured skin. Hello, are you there...can I come in? The best part was, he'd probably expect an answer...in English. Sean was like that, logic went out the window when he wanted something badly enough.

The three of them didn't return to their quarters at all that night. Sean barely moved from the window. They stayed and watched and photographed, hoping for some sign of movement, or just a sign from the motionless vessel. They even took a few selfies with their phones. There was nothing from it though, no movement, no attempt to make contact, or none they could identify anyway.

They contemplated its origins, its purpose, its method of propulsion, what in God's name was it made of? What would its next move be? Why hadn't Prox detected the approaching craft? The Prox systems on all their craft needed work, Mitch was sure of it.

Who or what was aboard? Maybe nothing they would term alive or animated at all. But then again who really knew? Might be robots? It was a mystery to all of them. Until they knew, they wouldn't know. Jessy had retrieved Josh from her quarters and he too seemed mesmerized by the strange spacecraft. His large chestnut eyes frequently locked onto the cosmic spectacle that was laid out so close to them. The best he could manage was 'goo'. Eventually, he drifted back to sleep, leaving the rest of them to stare shamelessly through the viewport at their bizarre new companion.

***

They sat arm to arm on the plastiform couch, sipping cold coffee turned bitter by the polyfiltrated water. Its original source was their own waste, but still it tasted and felt like a luxury.

They'd dragged the portable air couch over to the viewport where the panorama of space was fully two metres long and two metres high. The alien vessel had literally not made a move since it jumped into position from the other side of the ship a few hours earlier. It simply sat there, dark, motionless and absolutely breathtaking. Real, but in a sense unreal.

Sean used the wide angle planetary facility on the telescope to peer at every part of the craft which faced them. He looked uninterrupted for more than two hours, inspecting. assessing, and he appeared on the verge of collapse. He was making anomalous noises at a higher and higher rate.

No one bothered to ask him to stop though, Sean was Sean and they knew something as simple as words would be useless. They'd need something approaching a sledgehammer. Tired and pale though he was, his red and swollen eyes still burnt with feverish intensity. He was driven, obsessed by the need to know. Who or what was aboard the incredible craft? That was the first of a thousand questions he had.

Cygnus had now moved considerably closer to CX1. The sight of the bright smudge that was Proxima rising above the alien craft was a sight to behold, a sight that burnt into the soft cells of their memories. Fiery and malformed, the corona and then the belly of the star slowly slipped above the craft, its brilliant pyre blotting out details of the visitor's pimpled skin as it slid slowly into full view. The white fire and swirling trail of ionized gas behind the blackened contours was a stupefying sight in the midst of the great blackness.

Sean's throat tightened and closed, and only after several minutes did he manage to emit something better than a muffled croak. Like the rest of them he knew where that star was headed, and exactly what the silhouetted vessel represented. If only Rhys was here to see it, he would be just as stunned as Sean. He wished he hadn't thought of Rhys because it brought with it a stinging sadness.

Sean's observations of the craft continued to be fascinating but unfulfilling.

'What are you seeing Sean?' Jessy asked repeatedly of the silent and distant figure who looked like he formed part of the structure of the telescope. A fleshy appendage not just an observer.

'I'll tell you when I see something,' Sean had said three times, with growing irritation. It was an hour before he spoke again. He had a ring around one of his eyes, as he looked at the others.

'…there's nothing that looks like an…um, entry port so I'm assuming it's on the hidden side, if there is a way in that is. There are no variations or sections in the hull, it appears totally homogeneous through the scope. Sean pointed and glanced at the vessel fleetingly,

'It's slightly greenish gray I think, and it has a texture, like fine parallel lines, that in places are criss-crossed at right angles by other sets of lines. I don't think they're just markings either, they look more like indentations or striations in the metal, if that's what the stuff is. As for the spines, there's no indication that they carry any technical equipment. If they do it's totally concealed within them. Even looking straight down through the top of the ones that are pointing towards us reveals nothing. The crests appear to be solid and made of the same greenish grey substance, no optical or

101

other identifiable componentry.' Sean felt a wave of heat hit him, that made just breathing difficult, so he sat down and took a few decent breaths. He felt better.

'There are three white spots that I can see which aren't visible to the naked eye. The only difference seems to be coloration though, everything else seems identical, including the striations, which look the same.'

Hardly surprising, Mitch thought, we won't learn a thing by just looking at it. He knew what they had to do. 'So, there's no indication of animation or how it moves or what it wants or what these spikes do?' Mitch said, feeling compelled to ask a question. There was little they could accomplish sitting here, he realized that immediately.

'There's nothing at all...what we have is a ship with white spots and geometric indentations and that's all we know. And unless we can get inside or around the other side, that may be all we'll ever know.' Sean gazed at Mitch with massive eyes, 'if it leaves now, I'll never sleep another night in my bloody life!' He meant it.

Mitch believed him. Absolutely, he believed him. He knew that Sean was right. They needed to find out what the hell this craft wanted but more importantly, where it came from and who or what was inside it? Who, what, why? They weren't asking much. The question of what to do next had answered itself.

'No Mitch, absolutely no way, I flatly will not be left here...forget it. No way.' Jessy was less than cock-a-hoop at the prospect of being abandoned, even for a short time. 'What if you're both killed out there, and don't tell me it's not a possibility because it is, remote perhaps, hopefully, but a possibility.' She gaped at Mitch and squeezed her eyes shut. She meant what she said. Jessy crossed her arms and now glared at Mitch. She dared him to argue with her.

'C'mon Jess, that vessel is no place for a baby, and you can't consider leaving him behind,' Mitch protested. Looking at her, he realized he should have saved his breath.

'Oh God, of course I wouldn't leave Josh behind. Shit Mitch, what do you take me for?

'What I mean is that if you don't come back what the...'

Mitch tried to interrupt but Jessy simply spoke over him.

'If we're going to die Mitch,' Jessy spoke loudly. 'I think we should do it together. Don't think you're doing us any favours by leaving us behind because you're not!' Jessy spat the last word at Mitch and looked away. After an uncomfortable silence, Sean decided to speak. He couldn't do any worse than Mitch. He was a little scared of Jessy. Sean changed tack.

'I agree with Jessy, despite what I said before. She and Josh would be better off with us and the pod can seat six people comfortably for a week or more.'

Mitch looked unconvinced and was clearly battling with competing emotions. Jessy pushed home her advantage. She nodded and smiled crookedly at Sean. 'Sense at last! I'll go and make sure Joshy is set to go.' She brushed past and out through the open hatch to the corridor beyond. Mitch said nothing as she breezed past. He looked at Sean who was staring into space. Jessy was briefly beaming, grinning ear to ear. One for me, she thought.

'Thanks,' Mitch said half grinning, knowing that common sense had probably prevailed.

'You know she's right. We can't leave them here even though it'd be safer in the short term for them if we did. We'll all go and hopefully all return richer in knowledge about whatever the hell that thing is...and who or what produced it.' Sean's eyes shone as he pointed at the craft that was suspended in space like a tremendous mobile. The question struck him again. Who were the architects of this fabulous machine? His mind pulsed with a hail of dazzling sparks that crystallized into a host of wondrous, wishful images. What was the reality? Fuck knew, he thought. But it didn't have to be a positive experience, he knew that much too.

Earthshield 1 was ready for deployment from Cygnus at any time with minimal notice. It was all of an emergency vehicle, a go anywhere excursion module and a planetary lander. It could be operated manually and could also be programmed with complex flight instructions and operated remotely from the Interstar by SIS. It was the same as ESII, minus the nukes and a few other things.

Alone in the spacious deployment bay, the pod's insectual dimensions were emphasized by the absence of the other EV craft. It was a depressing and harrowing reminder of failure and death, and of Rhys's absence. They all tried to ignore it, without success. Jessy was sniffing and wiping her nose as she remembered Rhys. She recalled Josh's birth, and wished she hadn't, because with it came the harrowing sadness of Rhys.

Mitch keyed the access code in the six numeral pad next to the pod's hatch. The four entered into flickering light as the internal bio luminants responded. In theory the mission was a straightforward one, so preflight delays were few.

A basic systems check was undertaken which suggested everything was operative. He watched the systems check proceed and the blue lights appear. The same thing had happened in the number two pod. Blue lights. Yet it had suffered terminal technical failure and probably logics meltdown. He hoped to God the problem wasn't endemic to the Earthshield systems. If it was they might end up stranded, stuck for eternity in a tiny metal coffin. By tiny he meant really tiny.

With everything set, Sean fingered the twin toggles to vent the atmosphere from the bay. In zero pressure, the bay's craw doors would automatically breach and reveal them to space.

Little Josh was strapped tightly into one of the converted chairs and looked decidedly unhappy. He was about to cry, of that Jessy was sure, and although he was still an incredibly good baby, he definitely had his moments. When he wanted to, he could put on a show like few others.

What a time for one, she thought as Josh started to wail. Shit. Jessy unstrapped him and nursed him which only made him cry louder. She handed him his pacifier which he took...and then spat at Sean who caught it with a deft left hand grab. Sean was good with Josh.

They were sitting in a dead vacuum with the bay doors splayed in front of them. Releasing the retention latches and blowing the stabilizing bolts, Mitch maneuvered the craft away from its metal guiders and through the hangar doors. He guided the craft outward into the starred chasm that by chance happened to be on the opposite side of Cygnus to the alien vessel. None of them knew what to expect, was there something aboard the craft, something obviously controlled it...but what...or who?

***

Inside the monstrous vessel it was total vacuum and unremitting blackness, frigid beyond imagination. Liquid helium cold. Something was changing though. The walls, floor and ceiling, in fact the entire internal morphometry of the craft started to liquefy. To flow and to move and change. Walls retreated, solid masses of metal evaporated and expanses of free space emerged.

Along with the metamorphosis came a slow and passive illumination, light from nowhere in particular flooding the craft in a soft, pulsing glow. Soon the temperature began to rise through the range of liquid methane and quickly into the range of liquid water.

Within the bowels of the ship an atmosphere was being silently processed through the entire vessel and was promulgated as a gusty alien wind that stormed through the bizarre interior of the hundred thousand year old ship.

8

Gateway

'We are all just star stuff harvesting sunlight.' ~ *Carl Sagan*

Closer now, the vessel's midriff looked unsettlingly hostile, swelling rapidly until it choked their view with tremendous bilges. Jessy was catatonic, dazzled by its size and stunned by its crazy tumorous symmetry.

Like protective horns, the tubercles soared in every direction, looking oddly threatening but equally magnificent in the burgeoning starlight. Whatever material they were made from had a mirrorlike sheen that contrasted starkly with the forebodingly dark fabric of the vessel. No one spoke as they stared in disbelieving awe, at the suspended visitor and at each other, their eyes wide.

Josh had finally stopped crying and was now contentedly snuffling in his makeshift seat, having exhausted himself after several minutes of lusty bawling. He was already fed, toileted and had given up a huge burp, so just why he was crying was anyone's guess. Maybe he was just bored, after all it was only adults milling around, doing nothing much, as usual.

'Okay,' Mitch whispered through clenched teeth, '...let's see what's over the hill.'

They didn't look up, couldn't tear their eyes off the thing in front of them. It simply demanded to be looked at, swamping their senses with a feeling that bordered on inebriation.

The pod edged its way over the top of the ship, gently thrusting to a halt fifty metres from the visitor's farside with respect to Cygnus. Proxima Centauri was now behind them but they could see its reddened light caressing the lonely craft ahead of them. Jessy looked up and almost gagged at the sight that was dancing in front of her eyes. The shadowy spines of the vessel were crawling across the pale skin of Cygnus like a gigantic black beetle. Jessy looked away and then glanced back, it was still there.

Just a shadow she soothed, but the image was a terrible phantasm of what was floating beside them. The alien eclipse eventually slid away and was gone. She looked at Mitch and then at Sean, hoping for a soft face. There was none. Mitch and Sean both had their heads thrust forward, straining to make out any detail.

'Exactly the bloody same,' Sean snorted disappointedly. 'No way in, what the hell sort of ship is this?' His eyes were everywhere at once. 'Maybe it is totally robotic and perhaps it's hermetically sealed. '

'Maybe there isn't supposed to be a way in.' Sean was appalled by the idea and it showed in the furrows that ate into the sides of his mouth.

'Might be right,' Mitch agreed, locking eyes on the craft, wondering what might be inside. 'Perhaps these things are seeded through the galaxy, designed to eyeball anything unusual and report it back to whoever built them. We were unusual out here, so if we didn't come of our own volition, would they have dragged Cygnus and us away? In that case you'd be right, they would be entirely automated and not designed for entry except by whomever or whatever seeded them.' His eyes were bulging like scoops of frozen tapioca. A single thought was choking his mind. Who...Why?

'Take us closer Mitch,' Sean murmured, '...over to one of the white patches. He looked at Jessy and tried to smile. 'They must mean something, an identification of sorts...maybe some sort of cosmic barcode.' Sean grinned and looked intently forward, not moving his eyes from the visitor. He heard alarm bells ring in his head but he ignored them.

Mitch deftly maneuvered the pod and inched it as close as he dared. They were almost nose to nose with its curiously mottled superstructure.

104

'I hope this thing doesn't decide to leave in a hurry,' Mitch whispered, 'because if it does...we're in serious trouble.' Superluminal. The thought sliced into his mind like serrated steel. Otherwise, how the hell did it get here? Sean's eyes were as wide as they could go, a million questions storming through his mind. Maybe it came from a nearby star, but he doubted it. Perhaps it just went fast, Mitch thought, but that wouldn't do it. No way. Fast wasn't quick enough to get anywhere, unless you completely nulled impatience. It was possible that it came from far away.

'Just get as close as you can,' Sean repeated, 'and I'll sweep the sampler arm over the surface and see what happens, see what it "feels" like. Wouldn't it be nice if we could scrape off a few molecules and run 'em through the SEM. See what they are, see if we can identify them...see if its regular stuff. God, it could be something fantastic...' Sean's mind spun as he stared unseeingly ahead.

Mitch guided the tiny pod to within a few armlengths of the beast that blocked space in front of them. Like Sean, Jessy was thunderstruck, hypnotized by its spinous midriff, dazzled by the whole ineffable vista. Others. It was impossible to come to terms with, difficult to think about without wobbling and feeling giddy...like falling down giddy.

She could barely imagine what beings had forged these finely hewn contours, and only hoped that they'd bear no likeness to the scrabbling horrors that haunted her profoundly unsettling nightmares. She was sure they wouldn't, most of the time. Logic, she reminded herself. But what if they were like spiders, would she cope? Logic was fine but what if it broke down, the father you went in space? Jessy was scaring herself, could feel herself trembling and getting cold. Not for the first time, she wondered if she was right for this mission, although who could have predicted it'd take a turn like this? Logic, she debated, what a crock. Absolute rubbish. Complete 'Tish. Applying logic in space was thoroughly illogical.

Sean was at the controls of the pod, trimming the settings on HOLMES, the periscopic gripper that was fitted only after Mitch had steadfastly insisted on it. He'd had enough experience with Boeing Satellite Catchers to know how truly golden the device was, and how unexpectedly it could be needed. Unfortunately, USPA didn't have the same insight, although they'd quickly ceded to his demands. He was right, he knew he was.

Sean was a bit rusty on its use, but he still had a good understanding of the altitudes attainable by the magnetic, thin, lockable metallic member. Depending on which hand control he used, he could rotate the end effector about any of three axes and with the other hand could move up/down or left/right or fore/aft. It was absolutely indispensable in this situation.

Sean chuckled as he considered the reaction of the Agency, of them knowing their hardware was being used to prod and poke an alien spacecraft. Half of them would die laughing at the suggestion, the other half would just die.

Inching the pod forward on a single rim cone, the thing now completely smothered their forward horizon with a tableau of steeples and gently arching symmetry. Acne was the thought that hit Jessy's mind, it looked like it had a horrendous case of acne. One of the fuzzy white spots was directly ahead of them, the parallel lines like a delicately hewn needlework, just visible against the dimness of the hull. Mitch and Jessy watched spellbound as Sean manipulated the controls to send the arm gliding through space. He stared unblinkingly at the target-mounted aim points that were beamed from the video cameras on the end of the arm. The effector could take the form of a snout-like protuberance for collecting materials or could separate into four gripping fingers that could be moved independently or collectively locked to grasp and tether. Sean hands were visibly sweating as he deftly kneaded the hair-sensitive triggers. His eyes were bulging in the direction of HOLMES.

The end of the arm was locked into a pelican-like beak. Jessy watched, then cringed, as the terminus made contact with the ship, striking it soundlessly in the midst of the great emptiness. Sean's face was like chiseled camphor-ice as they kissed, as the outworking of their own world touched the technical wizardry of another species. Jessy just watched with a slack jaw and hands covering an open mouth as true physical contact happened right there in front of her, not more than a few arms lengths away. History. It was an electric moment, and wasn't lost on any of them, except Josh who slept on unperturbed, oblivious to the profundity that was occurring only metres away.

To their astonishment the snout did something totally unexpected. So unexpected it made them wonder if their eyes were relaying the right information to their brains. Hallucination? No way. Whatever it was, it was actually happening.

Glancing at each other, they immediately knew it was real. The end effector had dug into the hull, somehow it was gouging beneath its surface and causing it to momentarily change colour, from white to gray and mildly translucent. They all fully expected it to bounce back like a hammer off an anvil. Mitch snapped his head up from the controls and looked intently forward, not really believing what he'd seen. 'What the hell?' he murmured slowly without shifting his gaze.

Sean's confusion dribbled out in a shallow puddle. '...it can't be metal...but if it isn't...what is it?' His eyes were like a Kadinksian portrait as he contemplated the totally unexpected. 'Some sort of flexible, er...polymer maybe?' Unmagnetic, he knew that much, looking at the controls and the small blue light, which was off. 'This is incredible.' He proceeded to softly and slowly push the snout a small way into the odd material. '...like pushing into gelatine,' he whispered almost incoherently.

'...Soft metal?' Jessy said, not taking her eyes off the partly buried arm. Elastomer filled Sean's mind. It seemed an appropriate term. Sean's face was a mask of curiosity and wonder.

'Anything's possible Jess,' Mitch said without looking at her, '...it could be metal, plastic, a polymer, some sort of plasma alloy, an insulated energy field...who knows, but it's obviously something brand new to us. Something we've never dreamed of probably.'

Sean spoke with eyes that looked ready to bound free of his skull. He was hungry and lustful to know. 'The amazing thing is, that we don't effect the integrity of the material by pushing the snout in and out. It closes in as soon as the arm is removed, and reforms exactly as it was before...complete with the pattern of lines.' Very odd, he thought to himself, to us at least. Obviously to them it was how it was. It was supposed to be like that.

Sean's face was pale and his hands were drawn into fists that looked more like claws. 'So, it's made from something that's at least partially elastic...and has no apparent means of propulsion...or any obvious entry points. We should have expected all this I suppose.' He squinted and rubbed his eyes with the back of his hands. None of it added up, Sean thought, gawking at the strange craft.

'They could be a million years beyond us, and I don't know about you, but I would've been surprised, disappointed definitely, if they'd sidled up to us in an old clunker like Cygnus.'
Mitch and Jessy offered Sean a fleeting smirk, but they needn't have bothered. His eyes were mortared on the darkness that barricaded their view ahead. Calling Cygnus, a "clunker" was a harsh call It was in human terms well ahead of its time, thank you very much.

'Maybe they're not that far ahead of us,' Jessy volunteered, not blinking and looking away from the alien beast, 'perhaps their technology just grew along different lines, based on whatever was available. I mean, maybe metal was rare on their world.'

'Metals are universal Jessy,' Sean snapped. '...and besides I doubt whether they could've progressed to initial space flight without their planet being a significant metal carrier. My guess is what we're looking at is some advanced hybrid mixture, a polymorphic metal or stereo-acrylic...' Sean glanced down at his feet and breathed deeply, knowing he didn't have a clue about the nature of their spiny friend. It could be literally anything. Jessy's eyes were gigantic as she looked on, clearly expecting anything from anywhere.

Mitch was struggling to believe it, the idea of it actually being soft. It simply didn't seem right, not out here, not amongst the stars. Somehow the idea made him feel distinctly uneasy.

Sean returned the proboscis to the white spot that dominated the hull in the middle of the pod's viewscreen. The snout edged below the gelatinous surface as expected but when Sean pulled it free, the dimple not only didn't reform as he'd anticipated, but started to grow deeper, of its own accord. Jessy's face was creased with fear, where the hell was this leading?

'Oh shit,' Sean whispered, stunned by what he was seeing, not entirely sure what he was actually seeing. They'd definitely started something.

'It's growing deeper!' Mitch barked, stating the bleeding obvious. Never wake a sleepwalker he remembered uncomfortably, watching it closely, confused as to what they'd done.

'Look at it, its…it's growing of its own accord,' Sean said, staring barefaced at the visitor through his visor. 'I'm not doing anything now,' he said. Mitch was stern-faced and looked on, ignoring Sean's inane blather, wishing he'd just shut up.

Jessy could only watch on mutely, eyes gawking at the new activity. 'I-I don't like the l-look of this,' she finally stammered. 'I hope we haven't hurt it or damaged it, or made it angry.' Jessy knew the idea was absurd but she couldn't avoid it. They'd sparked something that now possessed a life of its own, had lit a fuse without knowing how, or if, they could stamp it out. What would the result of their tinkerings be? The possibilities were endless, and most of them were unpleasant. They'd clearly disturbed it. Woken it from a deep slumber. No doubt it was interested in them. Jessy wondered how long it had been dormant, if in fact it was dormant at all. She chewed on the question. Maybe it was waiting for someone just like them to come along.

'Hopefully some of our questions are about to be answered,' Sean said, almost without moving his mouth. Mitch had the sudden comical impression of a ventriloquist's dummy as he watched Sean's frozen expression and pancake eyes. He still couldn't believe any of it.

In the precise bullseye of the white spot, a dimple of sorts had started to form, and was growing as they watched. A hole was neatly sculpting itself in the alien skin. Jessy willed it to stop, but it kept going, seemingly gaining momentum as it went, like a fire in a strengthening wind, starting small but growing quickly. She pondered the "other side" …what was on the inside? Was there an inside? She gulped heavily, swallowing a painful breath of uncertainty, expecting anything. This was way outside the brief for the mission. Spider, Jessy hadn't forgotten. She trembled head to toe, as she considered it again. Her eyes were feline and bulging as she measured-up the alien craft.

'…like molecular acid through Styrofoam,' Mitch muttered, alluding to the ease with which the cavity was moulding itself in the alien skin. Initially rough-hewn, the hole almost immediately smoothed itself to a glassy perfection. Only the most recently formed and deepest parts had any coarse texture to it. The rest was slick, like a section of moist human gut. It was like looking at the human digestive system. Jessy shuddered again, thinking no one would enter that…voluntarily.

A ponderous silence settled over them as they contemplated the activity. No one spoke as they gazed at the yawning puncture that led to who knew what on the inside.

'So…what now?' Jessy finally offered. They were all standing in front of the vacuglass with the alien hull seemingly right on top of them.

'…has to be an answer to one of our questions,' Sean uttered, pushing his hair back, 'it must be a means of getting inside.' He moved his head closer, 'although I don't think it's reached the interior yet.'

Or had it? Jessy pondered, willing her eyes to reveal detail that simply wasn't there, hoping Sean was right. It needed more light. She held her stomach, astonished.

Mitch had reoriented ESI so its docking lights shone directly into the maw of the hole, and Sean was right, the pit was at least two metres deep but seemed to stop in a dead end. It didn't look as though it led anywhere and the progress of the shaft had stopped. 'Oh Jesus,' Jessy said, not having a clue if that was good or bad.

Sean stood up, 'I'll put on the suit and get in the airlock. If you can line me up, I should be able to get a better idea of what's happening.' He paused, but only long enough to suck in a breath and blow it out. He looked at the hole with a withering gaze and thought about it. What would they meet if they kept pushing? Probably a tad late to worry about that now.

The fact that the cavity was about man-sized and formed right in front of us, well…maybe it's an invitation to take a closer look.' He gazed squarely at Mitch. 'We haven't got a hell of a lot to lose, have we?'

Mitch was suddenly unsure but he quickly conceded that Sean was right. His last comment was nothing but accurate, they had little to lose and perhaps a lot to gain. He kept falling back on his belief that an advanced community would be benign in nature. But then…what if they weren't? What if they were precisely the opposite? Looking at Jessy's haunted expression, he knew she was pondering the same thought and it was chilling. Nothing was certain, not out here, he thought, raising his eyebrows, drawing them close together. Mitch knew they couldn't let the opportunity slide though. He also wondered if the goings on within the skin of the craft was a welcome of sorts, an overture, an invitation to the new boys on the block, as it were. Come on in, make yourselves at home.

Mitch massaged the gyroscopic thrusters, slowly edging the pod away and repositioning it so the airlock and the alien throat were aligned. Very carefully, he guided the pod back in until the airlock was only a couple of metres away, and occupying space directly in front of the void. Jessy knew as well as anyone how to operate the No.1 pod and took Mitch's position, sliding in next to its tightly packed instrument panel that was squashed behind the titanium-silicon canopy. Fuck, she thought, here we go. Into the alien throat or bust. Bust probably, she felt sure. Jessy always expected disaster and death. And this time, she might get it.

Josh was, thankfully, still asleep in his own personal cushion-padded quarters in the corner. She prayed he wouldn't wake until they were back on Cygnus, but she also knew that might be some time off. He had his little elephant with him, that was option two, should he wake. Option one was back to sleep.

Sean and Mitch were fully suited in their fibercarb exoskeletons, standing and waiting in the airlock. 'Can you hear me Mitch?' Sean asked, testing the digicoms. Mitch nodded and thumped the small blue pad beside him. Fucking thing sounded like shit, he thought.

A fine mist of atmosphere vented from the airlock and wafted against the alien machine, causing its superstructure to briefly flicker and whiten, like a firefly suddenly finding life and just as suddenly losing it. The ship very quickly returned to its former albedo-less pallor.

After sixty seconds they were lolling in the vacuum of the depressurized lock. Without the rotation of Cygnus and the almost one "gee" of gravity, they were forced into their G-clogs permanently. These lead boots kept their feet firmly stuck to any surface they chose to stand on.

Breaching and cycling, the outer hatch withdrew, giving them a slowly swelling view of the vista beyond. The thing suspended in front of them was all they could see and it was more dazzling than they would have thought possible. Alien. Made by other than humans.

They were only a couple of metres away now, and this close, its odd tones and finely hewn form were stunningly pronounced. It was greyish silver-green and to each side of them, above and below, the excrescences spread in all directions, like an implausible cosmic anemone. Only where they were, near one of the poles of the ship, was the skin unblemished by the massive extrusions.

Sean and Mitch hadn't spoken since the outer hatch of their own craft opened. They were both staring through their visors at a sight that was difficult to comprehend. Fucking impossible to grasp, Mitch thought. He struggled to believe he was here. Mitch had eyes that were shadowy and bottomless, as he listened to his own raspy breathing through the suit. His stare was broken by sudden movement in front of him. He looked closer, it was less of a movement than a writhing, a squirming, and it was everywhere.

'...the lines are moving...I think...take a look.' His neoprene glove was pointing slightly to the right of the cavity. Sean looked and he saw the movement.

'They seem to be vibrating, pulsing, changing colour, turning white...or uh…silver. What the hell's happening?' His eyes were mortared to the sudden animation, his mind trying to sculpt answers from nothing. His heart was trying to leap from his chest and his eyes from his skull.

As far as Sean and Mitch could tell, the craft was undergoing some sort of metamorphosis, not structural, but certainly as far as its pigmentation was concerned. Like a Chameleon, Mitch mused uncomfortably, staring at it. It was camouflaging from what, trying to hide from what?

'Oh shit...I hope it's not getting ready to leave,' Sean barked.

Superluminal. The thought hit Mitch again, rising into his Limbus like the product of a serious nightmare. The pulsing lines and paler color started to dissipate. They watched in silence, their own heartbeats all they could hear in their ears.

'...it seems to be stabilizing,' Mitch muttered, out of breath but thankful that the craft seemed to be returning more or less to its previous state. Whether that was good news or bad, he wasn't sure.

Jessy watched the happenings from her vantage point near the Compit. Hearing nothing through the digicom she finally spoke in a rush of hot breath. 'What's happening...can you see what I'm seeing?'

'We can see. It appears to be settling down but just what that means, well, we'll have to wait and see.'

Mitch cut off communication with the pod. Jessy hoped they were getting ready to come back in. She had a bad feeling. 'What the hell have we gotten ourselves into?' She whispered to no one. She meant it, if it was up to her, they'd be back on Cygnus looking at it from the viewing bubble.

Watching Josh sleep, her fears of being stranded and alone fizzed back at her. They were all hopelessly out of their depth, but equally a part of her realized they had to investigate this thing. They had zero choice, mission failure, she couldn't forget it.

Circumstances as they were, what other option was there? By choice she knew they would all remain out of their depth until answers or at least something, was forthcoming. But how long and at what cost, she could only ponder. Her imagination had some ideas, some strong ones, but she was trying to stifle those.

Sean and Mitch, though still within the airlock, were teetering right on its outer lip, trying to get as close to the other craft without actually leaving the safety of theirs. After some minutes Sean decided to tether himself and move the few metres through space to get a closer look at it, to touch it. Sean had his head cocked to one side as the alien superstructure loomed closer.

He would become the first human to finger the stuff of another intelligence, the first to step foot on truly alien soil as it were. He clipped on the umbilical, but before he could cast off, something odd started to happen. The vista in front of him was changing. Again.

'Jessy...is that you? Have you tripped the roto-thrusters?' Mitch knew she hadn't because there was no rumbling beneath his feet. He asked anyway. That was him.

She looked at the vessel and knew instantly what Mitch was suggesting. The distance between the other craft and their pod was diminishing, slowly but distinctly. It was happening gradually, but it was happening.

Jessy's voice was guttural, 'all power to propulsion is off, any movement is not our doing.' She cleared her throat softly as she watched.

They stumbled to the back of the airlock as the ship loomed larger in front of them. A collision was unavoidable, at the last second Mitch realized that he should have cycled the outer hatch. But he was mesmerized by what was approaching him. He thumped the toggle but it was too late, the two ships came together and hit with a vacuum silent thud. It threw both the harnessed cosmonauts first forward and then backward against the rear of the airlock. Jessy was thrust violently against her chair restraints.

Sean's moist eyes mirrored a stunning vista. 'Christ...look at it,' he exulted, as he struggled back to his feet. He gazed in disbelief at the gaping outer hatch and saw that the skin of the other ship was actually inside their craft. Mitch's heavily veined face looked directly at it. Sean's brows knitted together as he wondered about the goings on.

It had somehow crept fluidly at least half a metre inside the yawning airlock of ESI. Both ships were now touching and part of the soft skin looked as though it had deliberately wriggled inside, through the open hatch. 'What is happening?' Sean whispered with complete surprise on his face. He looked at the skin of the alien vessel and the hull of their vessel, and came up with nothing.

Mitch found himself looking straight down the throat of the inky alien hole.

It was like ESI had punctured the other craft, a potato-gun thrust into its kindling potato. An unlikely sexual act between two palpably different celestial species.

'...it's like...um, it's trying to force its way inside.' Sean's eyes were massive.

Mitch edged warily toward the intruder and peered at the material closely while remaining at what he considered was a safe distance … whatever that was. It was obvious the strange dermis had formed a tight seal around the airlock.

Where their craft met the soft membrane, the pliable skin had sort of melted and pushed itself inside the pod to form a thoroughly impervious join.

Mitch turned Sean's attention to the seal and both immediately contemplated the extraordinary coupling. They stood and looked and pondered. Why? Why was it joining with our craft? Jessy looked pained, as though she'd been shot or wounded by means unknown.

After a few minutes of stasis, the alien skin resumed its animated pulsing and vibrating, assuming an aspect akin to a living, respiring entity. More strangely still, it started radiating light, glowing, or what we'd call glowing, in various softly altering shades of green, giving the airlock an almost supernatural feel. It was lit in several shades of green, each blinking slowly and strobing, giving the impression of movement although in reality there was none.

Sean had the same expression of fascination, as he watched the green alien skin do its thing.

The strobing abruptly stopped and the cavity renewed its growth. The increasing depth was revealed by the inner glow which now lit the depths of the cavity in a chilling alien twilight. Mitch watched as the acid like decomposition of the hull proceeded. To his eyes it looked to be a precisely uniform disintegration, as though the skin was collapsing along atomically delineated lines.

Like the formation of a crystal, but in reverse. Decrystallization, he thought as he watched the skin slough away in front of him. 'Amazing,' he said, studying it closely.

'Here we go,' Sean said excitedly, 'I think we're about to find out the nature of this "invitation". If I'm right, and everything points to me being right, this is going to break into the interior. He was sure he was right, glancing at a fuddled Mitch. 'I mean where else would it be leading but inside?' They both looked at each other, their visors almost touching. Was there even an inside? Sean wondered, but said nothing, looking closely at what was happening only a few metres away.

'And then what?' Mitch asked quizzically, '...we just march in...say hello and sit down?'

'Who knows, maybe they don't want us to come in, maybe they want to come out...'

Both of them were still standing hard up against the inner hatch of the airlock, facing straight out at the dim skin of the intruding vessel.

'Shit!' Mitch uttered quietly, but emphatically. He considered Sean's words and wondered why he hadn't thought of it. What were the chances that something would come scrabbling out to meet them? Son of a bitch! His breathing stopped for long seconds as he pondered the likelihood. Fuck, he thought, visualizing something coming toward him. Mitch's look was wary and a little horrified. Hardly that of a seasoned astronaut.

They were both fixed on the steadily lengthening tunnel when the depths of the pit became suddenly brighter. Mitch's breathing became shallow and rapid as the realization struck him. Inside! It had broken through into clear space. He saw something pale and smoky arcing toward him at astonishing speed. Here it comes, Mitch reckoned.

'Oh Christ, something is...'

They both felt it. A buffeting wind struck them and threw them tight against the inner airlock wall, pinning them against the bolstered strut with an irresistible pressure. Then it was gone, they were free, realizing that an atmosphere of sorts had thundered through the void from the other craft, violently equalizing the dead vacuum they'd been standing in. They looked back at each other, curious about the air they were standing in.

Even though the pressure was gone, Mitch and Sean were still glued to the wall, unable to move, waiting with their hearts thumping and knocking in their mouths. Breathlessly, they stared at the end of the dim throat. What the hell? Sean thought, as he fought to free himself, which he'd now done. Both had masks of terror and stared unblinkingly forward toward the tunnel's end.

What was the fucking likelihood? Mitch asked himself again, fully expecting some inconceivable form to be standing there, silhouetted and motionless in the murky light from the tunnel. He tried to focus, but there was nothing there. For several minutes they just stood in unbroken silence...staring. No talking, almost no breathing, just staring. They were all eyes. Only after several minutes did Sean manage to compel a breath of air through his swollen larynx. 'Whatta we do...we

110

can't just stand here like dummies, the first move has to be ours, right? I get the impression that we're supposed to enter, to do something.' He looked at Mitch with eyes that seemed almost frozen open.

Mitch searched for his voice. He coughed and almost choked on bile that bled into his mouth, a potentially fatal mouth-full in a biosuit. He calmed himself and swallowed gently several times. 'You're okay,' he told himself and repeated it several times.

Mitch remembered the moment when he'd touched Mars for the first time, compared it to that exquisite moment, but there was no comparison. He couldn't identify his current state of mind, he wasn't able to sum it up, at least not in one or even a few words. Anxiety, fear, expectation, awe, pride...it was a tangled mishmash of them all. All of them and none of them. The gamut of emotions, rolled into nothing. An uncomfortable and disturbing sensory mosaic.

'...scan the atmosphere with your Majic12, you brought it I assume?'

'Of course, I did,' Sean snapped at Mitch. He was already working on the Velcro lashes.

He quickly unstrapped the cylindrical device from his backpack. It was one of the newly developed CLH's capable of dissecting the atmosphere with extreme precision. He removed the top by twisting it several times, exposing a clear cubic receptor. After a couple of seconds, he replaced it and entered several keystrokes on the base of the cylinder. After a minute the small device gave them a quantitative assessment of what was around them. They couldn't have been more surprised.

'You sure?' Sean murmured, straining to read the symbols on the tiny blue readout. 'If that's correct then it's no coincidence, it can't be, God, if it was pure hydrogen cyanide, I'd be less surprised. The ebony figures told a familiar, yet mind blowing story.

Nitrogen 67%; Oxygen 31%; ;Methane 0.5%; Xenon   0.5%; Carbon dioxide – trace; Water vapour – trace; Ambient Temperature 20 degrees Centigrade.

'...this is unbelievable,' Mitch said as he watched Sean finger the tiny device. 'It includes some of the atmosphere in our ship, but that's only a tiny percent of what's around us, apart from the methane and no argon, this is Earth.' Mitch's mind sprinted over the likely implications of the friendly air. Maybe the craft was a remote envoy, he thought to himself. Sean had a startled fawn expression, as he contemplated the meaning of the atmosphere. He turned his head and looked deliberately at Mitch. 'Someone or something wants us in that vessel. It must mean that we were expected. Whoever they are have generated a breathable atmosphere for us.' His eyes visibly widened as he repeated the last two words. 'For us!' His voice was shrill with a sudden realization.

'Of course, these creatures, whatever they are, could be similar to us, but the coincidence of atmospheres is astounding. I think we should go now, surely it's inevitable.' Sean was fired up and impatient, desperately wanting to see what was inside the alien creation, clearly prepared to go with or without Mitch. He knew Jessy would agree with Mitch no matter what.

Mitch was leery 'The atmosphere might be a coincidence Sean, a simple parallelism. We breathe it, and cows, so why not others, don't jump to conclusions. But I agree we need to take a look inside. He could see Sean was determined and eager to move forward. Mitch continued, 'I can't think of another way to interpret what we've seen other than it being an invitation to enter...a polite request maybe. I just hope that we're right and we're not misinterpreting all this.' He spun around and looked at Sean full in the face. 'Maybe we should think about it some more, it's a hell of a decision you know. I'm not sure we should just barrel in...'

'There's nothing to think about. The ship has opened itself up to us...shown us a breathable atmosphere and an ideal temperature. Hell, we could walk around naked in there, it's perfect for us. It's a sign Mitch, a clear, precise, unambiguous invitation to come on in.'

Mitch stared at the hull of the intruder, trying to come up with another explanation, but he had zero to add. The unavoidable certainty of entering the craft suddenly sank into Mitch's mind like a gold filling through froth. He stared at the craft uncomprehendingly as though eying an abstract painting. He saw himself entering.

Despite her displeasure at being left alone, Jessy eventually agreed that Mitch and Sean had to make an attempt to enter. What else could they do? Turn and leave and return to an Earth that was seemingly doomed to die? Or go back to the pod and mull it over, and then enter. No, it was glaringly obvious that the only choice was to go in and go now, it was logical and it felt right, even to her. The decision was made. Their destiny was within that ship. Serendipity had made it so.

There was still no activity in the tunnel. It was just an empty and chillingly symmetrical conduit to another world. They could see the inside of the other vessel was only faintly lit. It flushed the sides of the alien craw with a soft and slightly greenish sheen. Mitch was reminded of a mine shaft sunk through a vein of silver sulfide, slightly oxidised with some copper thrown in. Sean stared straight ahead. Their plight suddenly gained an extra carat of clarity as they readied themselves for a plunge into the truly unknown of an alien world. Both men were wired on their own dynorphins, freed enmasse by the twenty extraordinary steps that lay before them like an impossible fantasy.

The neuro-heroin urged them on. Alien. Had to be a dream. Perhaps it was a barren craft that would offer nothing and answer little, but maybe, just maybe, it would be fabulously, incredibly fertile, abounding in alien technology and providing answers to questions they hadn't even considered asking. And answering those that had forever remained out of reach. Whatever though, rightly or wrongly, forward we go, they both thought.

Sean wasn't immune to nerves, he just realised that with mission failure, going forward made a hell of a lot more sense than going backward.

Mitch approached the opening to the cavity and placed one foot and then another inside and stopped. He was aboard. Alien, he couldn't believe it.

'It's hard.' Static filled the digicom like water on a hotplate.

His first thought was that the malleable nature of the soft metal didn't extend to that which lay underfoot. Kneeling down, he poked at the material. It was entirely unyielding. Hard, metal like. The wall was soft and able to be intruded upon with only the slightest push, like elastic plasticine.

Mitch's helmeted head was only inches from the ground as he said, '...floor looks like highly polished silica...like agate, but it's not slippery in the least.' He got to his feet and tried unsuccessfully to push his G-clog along the surface. Mitch signalled Sean to follow as he inched forward. They were both taking small, mincing steps along the alien cavity. They saw the roof of the tunnel was well above their heads, in fact it lay at least two metres above the top of their environment helmets and a metre above the level of the pod airlock ceiling. Sean grinned uncertainly ending in a sour smile.

'If these entry ports are made for whoever constructed this craft...then we're talking about some very big people,' Sean whispered. Fucking huge, Sean thought, looking up at the ceiling.

'Maybe they just made a mistake and thought we were bigger...hey maybe they mistook Carlos...er, y'know the Bulls as a prototype.' Mitch grinned at Sean through his visor and watched him run his hand along the wall, awestruck by the glowing finger lines of silvery-green he left behind.

They were two metres inside the tunnel now and about four metres from where they assumed the interior belly of the craft lay. Behind them, beyond the walls of the shaft, they could easily make out the brightly lit airlock of their little craft.

Sean spied the digital entry pad on its extremity, its geometry so Earthly and so soothingly familiar. He was numbed by the realization that he was looking at this piece of humanity from the gizzard of an alien spacecraft. His mind spiralled and then slowed, filling with the fog of disbelief. An uneasy feeling gnawed at him. His mind was spiralling, everything he saw made it deepen.

Continuing to inch forward, they padded slowly and deliberately toward the light, expecting anything and everything. All they could hear was the thudding of their own hearts, mingled with the staccato rasp of their breathing. He'd just about heard enough of himself breathing.

They did their best to ignore the darting phantasms conjured by the dim surroundings. Sean thought of a trapdoor spider. He shook his head but the thought only burrowed deeper. Maybe they were about to be swallowed by an alien vessel that tempted its prey by stroking its curiosity, an intelligence trap. He chuckled nervously and gawped around, steeling himself to focus on the light ahead. Get it together, he said firmly and silently to himself as he took short steps forward.

Jessy was still in her seat and only now realized why the image of the thing that had "docked" with ESI didn't look right. It was somehow out of proportion or at least less in proportion than it had been. She'd thought nothing of it at the time but now, after calming a handwaving Josh, she looked out through the vacuglass and contemplated the view. She saw it immediately, the other vessel hadn't moved at all with respect to Earth-shield. Rather, the hull immediately in front of them had swollen, distending itself like a silken cocoon and reached out to form an airtight gantry of sorts. It was obvious now, but only from her perspective. Of course, Mitch would've thought the whole ship had been moving toward him but wrongly so, it was only an illusion. The pliable vessel clearly had the ability to actuate some sort of partial metamorphosis. But who or what had sparked the movement? She pondered the question nervously as she sat peering through the viewing plate.

Maybe the ship was an intelligence in itself, synthetic certainly, but perhaps it was capable of thought, of reason, of emotion...hell, maybe it had a personality. Jessy's mind corkscrewed. Surely not, she thought, shaking her head. Jessy tried to deliberately empty her mind, to no avail.

Fuck knows, was her final determination. The fact the vessel was so obviously trying to get them aboard worried her. Their situation before they'd met up with the ship was akin to being thrust into hell. They had zero hope. Probably still had none. Surely this must be a break for the better, but her doubts lingered. She shuddered as she considered what the future might hold for her and Josh. Death was all she could come up with. That was her. The negatives.

Mitch and Sean reached the end of the tunnel, glanced briefly at each other, then walked straight through, penetrating into the alien heartland, into soft white light that lit a stupefying vista. Sean's mind refused to register the significance of the moment.

Motionless at the end of the tunnel, they stood on the edge of something totally unexpected. Below them was a drop of at least four hundred metres and above, about a hundred metres up, was a curved amphitheatre-like ceiling. An environment they really hadn't expected. What were they expecting? Well, who knew? Not this. There was so much open room, everywhere. Mitch and Sean were holding their breath, straining to hear any noise they could within their suits, through the noise-enabled grids below their arm patch. They didn't work very well, but it was all they had. The dim light made viewing difficult and judging distances nearly impossible. But they could see enough to know that they were in the midst of something impossible.

Mitch's voice was like barely running molasses. '...holy mother of God,' He heaved, tilting his head back to catch a glimpse of what was above him. His voice continued in a breathless murmur. 'What is this place? We're on the edge of a...uh...bloody cliff.' The place was extremely odd. Not really like a ship at all. He swallowed thickly, continuing to swivel his head, desperate to get a handle on what was around him.

Having looked down in silence for several minutes, Sean finally pulled his head up and eyeballed Mitch through his helmet. 'Those entries must be scattered all over the polar regions of the ship, where the skin is free of those spines, remember the white spots? They must be entry ports, wherever you want to get in, you probably can, by touching a white spot, which in our case has left us atop some sort of metallic cliff.' Strange...very strange, he thought to himself. Of course, he didn't expect anything less.

Looking up, down, and sideways, they silently assessed the strange alien world they had stumbled into. The vista was so unexpected. It wasn't like a ship at all. On first glance it didn't seem to have any utility, any organization that would indicate it was a spaceship at all. To Mitch it was more like a metallic landscape, a tiny part of a planet copied in metal. It seemed ineffably strange and out of place.

'So, what now?' Mitch eventually wheezed. He could see Sean's eyes, swollen and brimming with lust about what might be ahead. He'd seen it only a few times before. It meant trouble, he was sure of it, Mitch reckoned, gulping thickly.

'I think we should try and get down to the bottom, maybe they are down there...' Sean whispered the words as though someone might be listening, looking down, up and settling his eyes on Mitch. His gaze was eventually fastened downward, the intensity painted in his hubcap eyes.

'Christ,' Mitch said, staring. 'And how do you propose we get down ... jump? It must be half a kilometre, straight down for Christ's sake.'

113

It was obvious there was gravity aboard the vessel but they agreed it was perhaps the only non-Earthly part of their environment. It was noticeably weak, perhaps only slightly more than Luna-like which allowed them to move easily, albeit within the confines of their leaden G-clogs. It seemed strange because the ship wasn't rotating, or at least hadn't been when they'd entered, so the source of the gravity was a mystery. If it wasn't generated through spin, how was it generated? Sean felt like scratching his head, but in a suit, it was an impossible manoeuvre.

Far below, on what they assumed was "ground" level, Sean could vaguely make out what looked like a series of openings in the internal skin of the vessel. There were also some wall markings that were suggestive of concealed passageways that led somewhere else, perhaps to open spaces beyond...to rooms. Perhaps to them, Sean thought, momentarily dazzled by sparks that attacked his mind with tiny needles. His mind was finding novel ways to shock him.

The entire "ground floor" was perfectly circular and looked to be made from the same or very similar soft metal as the superstructure. It was around the perimeter of this circular expanse that the walls with what they thought might be "doorways" were located. Some were simply spaces in the wall through which they could presumably walk. Others seemed to be closed off and showed up as elongated patterns, having the same contours and patterning as the voids, but being "shut". The circular floor between the walls looked totally untouched by even the slightest surface imperfection. From where They stood it seemed they were looking down on a huge slab of polished smoked glass. The question of how they would shimmy down the sheer and slightly concave metal cliff was now dawning on them. They had to get down to the floor below to check the rooms out, but how?

'Surely whoever they are, wouldn't have gone to all this trouble if we were going to end up stuck on top of this metal mountain.' Mitch stopped talking and looked at Sean who was turning slowly through three hundred and sixty degrees.

'Where's the light coming from? It seems constant wherever you look.' Sean was still turning. He hadn't even heard Mitch. Sean looked up and down, he was looking for anything that suggested a way down.

'Concentrate on the cliff...we're looking for a way down.' Mitch glanced tentatively over the edge. Sean's thoughts were everywhere and nowhere, his brainpower entirely routed to visual. All other senses were on hold.

He suddenly spun around. 'It's this metal or whatever this stuff is, the light is coming from within it. Can you see the glow, it's faint but it's everywhere? I'm sure it's responsible for lighting the interior. Jesus, what the Agency would pay for a gram of this stuff!' Sean was high, totally stoned on his own adrenaline, eyes glazed, barely half open, pumped with a desperate craving to know.

'I agree, but we need to find a way down, maybe it's an IQ test, who knows. Look for a way down.' Mitch was peering down, pondering what was down there to discover. What could be down there? Damn near anything. He looked nervously over the edge and was shocked to see large grooves hewn in the surface that began near the apex and continued down the broad face for as far as he could see. Fuck, it was so far down.

Nearby, Sean had found some sort of receptacle which he thought looked like a vertical transport of sorts. The thing had the familiar soft metal sides but had a forward facing panel that could be felt but not seen at all. It was totally invisible and was oriented outward toward the cliff. Inside it looked totally empty.

Sean gazed at it as he spoke, his voice had sunk to a whisper, '...this has to be a means of getting from the ground to the different levels.' He was sure there were other levels similar to the one they were on, stacked above them, and probably below them. But from their angle he couldn't tell. If it was the case and even if it wasn't, he was sure that this was some sort of elevator. But there was no indication of any controls, either inside or out.

All the surfaces were totally uniform and unmarked, including the clear outer panel which he couldn't even see. The only reason he knew it was there was by the green fingerprints which he could still see glowing on, or rather in its otherwise invisible veneer.

114

'Why all the empty space?' Sean pondered out loud, seeing Mitch approach him. 'There's so much bare space down there, why is everything so empty? Is it simply unused storage space?'
Empty people space, Mitch considered silently. It seemed logical enough, he reckoned, feeling his nerves ratchet up a bit. He stared at the voids, wondering. Ignoring Sean's question, he showed him the grooves that were about ten centimeters long and four centimeters deep. They were spaced every metre or so down the face of the cliff that ended at the vitreous circle far below.

The grooves seemed to stretch all the way to the ground, although, he admitted to Sean, it was hard to tell. Mitch couldn't fathom why he didn't see them before, when he'd knelt down to look over the side. Did they just appear? He pondered uncomfortably. No way. He told himself they were there before. Mitch felt the breath catch in his throat as he looked at the grooves. He knew they weren't there before, he was sure of it. Mitch looked around...pondering what might have been here before him. When were the grooves placed there? It was pretty obvious what they were for, but were they just built? And if they were, how and by who?

He looked a little closer, wishing he'd taken more notice before. Releasing his helmet, Mitch dropped it beside him and breathed deeply, knowing the air was eminently breathable. He took two guttural breaths and then spoke, 'It smells fresh, it smells like air after a summer rain, fresh...clean...rich in ozone.' It smelt good.

'Thanks Doc.' Sean unlocked and rotated his helmet until it came free of the duo-tracks. He was equally ecstatic at the sensation of breathing freely and unimpeded. He also filled his lungs with the fresh alien air. It did smell good.

Removing their E-suits, they left them along with their helmets and backpacks near the clifftop. They tossed their G-clogs over the side and watched them spiral toward the distant spherical surface below. They fell quite quickly and landed with a decent thump, evidence of what would happen to them if they fell. They both agreed that falling should be avoided at all costs.

Dressed only in their white and blue flexi-suits, they stood and ogled this very strangest of artificial worlds. They felt like they were a billion lightyears from home, as they grappled with the mind bending oddness that surrounded them. Christ, it felt strange, looked strange. Was strange.

They both felt something akin to vertigo and nausea that they hadn't even considered, let alone felt, while shrouded in their E-suits. The unremitting expanse of emptiness was starting to have an effect already, shoehorning into the fragile pulp of their minds. There was just so much space.

Mitch was preparing to slip over the side and inch down underneath the overhang of the clifftop when he heard a soft padding behind him. To Mitch, the sound of his heart beating was deafening. He felt a sudden stabbing between his ears as though the air pressure had suddenly been dialled up. Sean heard the sound too. It was a soft padding, increasing in volume, it was definitely something approaching. He wanted to turn, but his legs were so weak he was sure he'd collapse if he moved. So, he didn't. Couldn't. He could only stand there motionless and listen to the approaching whatever it was. They were facing the edge of the cliff and the padding, strangely echoing, was looming from behind them. From the direction of the tunnel. Sean's eyes were straining in their sockets. Who...what, he thought?

Mitch's eyes were huge, and his mouth went slack, waiting for whatever it was.

'...amazing, unbelievable, my God it's fantastic,' came the shrill voice. Mitch spun around.
'What the hell, Jessy what are you...'
'Oh, shut it Mitch would you, you can't keep me and Josh in there alone while you two gallivant around in here, no way, simply no chance.' She peered closer at Mitch, 'I did some thinking. What if the craft decides to leave? What then...there'd be no catching up you know. This thing probably travels so close to Luminal speed it doesn't matter. We would much rather be here with our family.' Jessy's initial enthusiasm was descending into sadness and fear. She looked like she might cry, the terror of isolation in ESI had quite obviously gotten to her big time. Mitch didn't give a crap.

'Tell me this,' he snapped, 'you opened the inner hatch without venting, right? So, our vessel's flooded with this air. What about its micro-org potential? Did you consider that? The ship will be hopelessly compromised.' He turned and looked away from her.

Sean looked at Mitch like he was a twit. 'We're breathing the air, I can't see that letting it in the ship is gonna be a problem. If it's harmful or even if it's eventually fatal I think we've already consumed enough, all of us, to be thoroughly screwed.'

'Lighten up for fuck's sake,' Jessy whispered as she brushed past. She was equally as bewildered as they were, as she checked out the amazing alien vista for the first time. Strange materials, odd shapes, empty spaces, artificial cliffs and eerie light, even doors maybe. 'It's really not what I expected,' she said to no one and everyone, '...although, er...I have no idea what I expected.' She peered over the edge to the distant surface below. 'Shit,' she continued. She was dazzled by the unexpected landscape, as she peered down.

Over the next twenty minutes they discussed the best method of tackling the cliff. Then it was time to stop deliberating, and to do. If they were going to do this, the time had come. It was time.

Lying on his stomach, Mitch pushed his feet and then his body over the cliff, searching for the first toehold. He eventually got it, and started the slow descent, being careful not to shove too hard against the wall, which, in these conditions, would send him spiralling away into space and by the time he'd crash into the lower surface, despite the weak gravity, he would easily have gained enough momentum to break his neck, well evidenced by the clogs earlier. He pondered the first human fatality on alien soil. He saw himself sprawled on the surface below, dead as a doornail.

Mitch noticed that the toe and hand holds offered excellent grip. No surprise there. The surface was pliable and their fingers and toes could be literally pushed into it to give extraordinary stability. He relayed all the information to the two above while Sean helped Jessy and made sure she was secure in the first of the groove grips. He followed with Josh on his back soon after.

It was slow going in the low gravity but it was easy, even enjoyable. Being so close to the supple surface, the inner glow was very distinct as was the realization that it gave off ambient heat. With their bodies plastered against it, the warmth was pleasurable although by the time they'd passed the halfway mark they were sweating profusely from the effort of descending and the heat from the cliff wall. From top to bottom it had taken just thirty minutes. They all jumped onto the slab and noticed how opposingly hard it was in comparison to the walls.

Mitch took the first steps on the polished floor. It was, as far as he could tell, a perfect circle of opaque darkness, around which on all sides rose the essentially vertical walls of silver-gray. They stretched upward to the similarly round "ceiling" of the craft which was wrapped in a haze of distance and dimness. If the hand of man had designed and built this craft, it wouldn't be anything like this, Mitch was sure. Interstellar travel would be all business, not...this. He watched Sean shaking his head, trying to get fact from thin air. Mitch couldn't help grinning at the spectacle. Sean was amazed, and thoroughly dumbfounded.

Sean was pleased to note that his earlier suspicion had been correct. He'd actually gotten one thing right. On the side of the ship through which they'd entered there were various levels both above and below the one they had initially stood on. He could see that each level had its own individual path to the floor where they were now standing. The series of hand and foot holds were lined up one after the other, each one to their left going slightly higher than its neighbor.

But why a manual path? Mitch wondered, pushing hair behind his ear roughly. Surely with the technology they possess they could have done a little better. Or maybe he was crediting them with too much wisdom. He doubted that. More likely, they catered to the needs of primitives' like us. Staring upward, he tried to ignore his thoughts about the makers of the craft that were multiplying like E Coli in a noonday cow. Eventually, he gave up and just looked.

On the opposite side of the craft to the multi-tiered cliff, a sheer wall rose and disappeared upward, unbroken by the various levels on the other side. It looked like it stretched all the way to the elliptical ceiling that Jessy thought looked like a huge suspended dance floor.

It was all fascinating but why, what was the purpose of the freakishly illogical landscape? There didn't seem to be any usefulness in it. No utility. Sean felt like he was in the middle of the Colosseum, girdled by ancient desolation, deafened by the dead who once filled it.

116

The dead, he wondered again. Who or what had trodden this path before them? What manner of creature had thrust its paw into those grooves? Sean's mind raced again, his thoughts hammering his mind. He saw some godawful beast with huge paws using these steps before him. Was that close to reality, he debated, with eyes wide and inquisitive.

Standing on the hard surface, they gazed at the towering landscape around them. Within the walls on their level were a multitude of imprints stretching around them in a perfect circle. Some consisted of slightly recessed rectangles that, to their minds at least, were suggestive of closed doors. Twelve of them, from sixteen in total, were rectangular voids that allowed views to dimly lit, forebodingly open chambers beyond. So, they had what looked like four closed and twelve open doors...only a few dozen steps away from the centre of the floor. Bully for them, Mitch reckoned, trying not to prejudge anything.

What the hell to do, they wondered, looking at the options? It was obvious, pick a direction, any direction. With that, Joshua started to cry. Loud...louder. The sound of the cries echoing around them was deeply disturbing. Human cries in a setting so exquisitely alien, they agreed, had an appalling effect on the senses.

And to make it worse, their footsteps on the hard, volcanesque surface were resounding harshly in their ears, seemingly broadcasting their exposed condition to all. Hello, we're here. They didn't think they needed protection, but their human frailties came bubbling through anyway.
The feeling of being trapped in very unknown territory was intensely unpleasant. Concentrating on logic and likelihood wasn't always easy, except for Sean of course. Seemingly, he didn't give a toss about the owners of craft. He was as happy as a pig in shit, glancing everywhere.

'Let's go exploring,' he ejaculated, sounding like a little boy in a toy shop.

'...that's what we're here for, I suppose,' Mitch said, hearing less conviction in his voice than he'd hoped for.

'Where first?' Jessy said softly, slowly tilting her head, still overwhelmed by the bizarre alien enclosure. Behind the doors, she mused nervously, terrified by what they might find.

'That opening in front of us is the closest,' Mitch said, pointing with a single gloved finger.

'As good a place as any to start...'

They stared at the opening for long seconds and then clunked over and toward the void, moving sluggishly in their G-clogs, slowed even further by their squirming motor neurons. To move or not to move. The decision was pretty obvious.

'Empty...absolutely empty,' Sean said slowly with mingled frustration and disappointment.

The room was the size of an average bedroom on Earth and had a flat metallic ceiling about three metres above the floor. It was disturbingly featureless and barren. Nothing. They proceeded to check the other twelve openings and found "rooms" identical to the first, all empty and featureless.

Sean was visibly disappointed. 'No stash of artifacts or memorabilia...not even a photo of the pilot and his family,' he uttered, disappointed. 'Damn it to hell.' Speaking of pilots, there was nothing that looked like controls, he thought.

They turned their attention to the linear recesses, the "closed doors" they'd seen earlier, that they thought might indicate a passage or a room lurking behind. To their Earthly eyes they suggested exactly that, a room, but here, well the lines could've meant anything and they well realized it. Probably nothing, Jessy hoped, knowing they were enclosed and shutoff for a reason.

Mitch walked to one of the patterns and peered at it closely, prodding it like a chef working on a delicate pastry. He was now not so sure that the imbedded parallel lines were doors at all. The patterning was about two and a half metres high and one and a half metres wide but there were no apparent joins or gaps, or anything that indicated they opened, slid back or articulated at all. The parallel lines didn't look like lines of articulation at all.

The "edges" of the door were groupings of ten ultrafine parallel etchings that were imbedded within the soft metal, seemingly forming part of its substance. It was certainly not just a surface feature. They stood facing it, trying to figure out how they could open it, if it opened at all, and wondering what the hell their next move should be?

117

Jessy prayed that it wasn't a door and there wasn't a hidden void behind it. If there was...why was their such a patently solid structure protecting it? What manner of thing lay waiting behind it? Maybe whatever was behind there had been waiting to get out for a million years. She was scaring herself, so she stopped thinking. Her mind was drained and empty.

Jessy raked her forehead with the back of a hand, knuckles first, trying desperately to clear her mind. Christmas trees, visualise Christmas trees. Her psych master on Luna suggested it. Apparently, she related them to comfort and stability. Her mind continued to creak with horror even though she thought about bloody Christmas trees.

'If it's not a door then we're wasting our time standing here,' Sean said. 'But if it's not a door and the rest of this area is barren...why were we encouraged inside and once inside, down here? We were encouraged, right?' He looked from Jessy to Mitch and got nothing but raised shoulders and blank looks. 'Hello? Anyone?' He got nothing. Sean paused and looked suddenly worried. 'Shit...maybe it didn't encourage us. Did we read it wrong perhaps?' He briefly considered what he'd said and then continued. 'I know for a fact that those handholds appeared after we looked down the cliff that first time, surely that confirms they want us down here?' Having said it, he wasn't sure. He continued to run his hand over the warm lines and watched as his fingermarks glowed pale green for seconds afterward. Where are you, you fuckers?

Outside, there was sudden movement. Bon voyage. In a heartbeat, Earthshield 1 found itself free, cut off and drifting on an aimless kinetic spiral. It slowly rotated as it glided toward unreachable space, edging away like a spent rocket booster. The alien hull had abruptly retreated, in the process giving the tiny ship a gentle but terminal nudge into space. Bye.

Had Mitch and the rest of the crew been in a position to see, they would have seen their lifeline to Cygnus sliding slowly past them and on into the forward depths of the cosmos. On what would be day one of a multi-billion-year journey to the distant Alta Regis Galaxy. Their isolation was now complete, their reliance on them total. Unbeknown to Sean and Mitch, their worst nightmare was now true. They were stranded aboard the alien vessel, with no way to get back to Cygnus.

Having shed the little pod, the pliable goliath, imperceptibly at first, started to spin until it reached exactly twelve RPM. Sean was still gazing at the glow from his fingermarks when he felt the pull of increasing gravity. It continued to grow until it reached approximately one "gee". Even Mitch's lips felt heavy. 'Do you feel that?' He asked, swivelling his head to look up at the dim circular sky. Their ears popped and their eyes burnt as they suddenly felt incredibly, unabatingly heavy.

Sean was still looking upward. 'The ship must've started turning...gravity is increasing, feels about the same as it was on Cygnus.' Which was almost identical to Earth.

His eyes lit up, realizing what it meant. Sean cottoned on too. Beyond question, was Mitch's immediate thought. '...positive confirmation,' he spouted. 'The environment is now almost one hundred percent Earthlike. They do want us here, there can be no doubt. It's surely beyond coincidence.' They each heard the pounding of their own hearts, suddenly louder and faster, like peals of thunder exploding in their eardrums. They were wanted by this crazy ship.

Just as Mitch was about to continue, the door in front of him opened. Not in the sense that it swung back or slid into a recess, it opened by falling apart. Not all at once, but by a pin hole sized puncture rapidly swelling outward, eating its way in an orgasm of light into an opening through which they could all easily pass. The brand-new sides of the rectangular void were instantly smoothed to a perfection that resembled lead crystal with beautifully rounded edges. Standing there, they marvelled at the strange opening feeling awed, and not a little unsettled, by what they'd seen. Magic.

'Paydirt,' Sean said loudly to the others, his eyes focused on what was suddenly laid open before them. Well, um...at least it was something.

Jessy looked nauseous and almost buckled to the ground in an untidy heap, she would rather nothing changed. She whimpered something incomprehensible after gulping heavily and almost gagging on the acid in her mouth. She could feel the dread swelling in her stomach like a rotting melon and a heavy feeling in her thighs. In front of them was a room, the same as the others

118

but with one clear difference, something solid stretched for about thirty metres along the far wall. A small sound of wonder came from Jessy.

In front of the thing were seven large receptacles. Chairs, Jessy assumed. They had to be. Everything in the room seemed to be made of the same material as the rest of the vessel, externally and internally, the craft seemed to be totally homogeneous. As though it was moulded from a single piece of material, a single hunk rather than from the massing of smaller units. Like the product of an exactingly detailed jelly mould. The opposite of what we do, which wasn't surprising. And the receptacles were all facing…a blank wall.

Jessy eyed the cavity warily as she spoke. 'If that door closes behind us…I don't like our chances of opening it.' She spun around and clenched her teeth, all wide-eyed, staring at Mitch, desperately, irrationally terrified. It wasn't irrational at all. It was quite a reasonable fear.

'I wouldn't worry about it, if they want to stop us leaving, that tunnel to the pod could quite easily be closed I'm sure.' Mitch said. After some hesitation, Jessy nodded manically in agreement. She hadn't even considered that. Now, she was really fucking scared. Isolated and alone on an alien ship where they didn't understand shit. Jessy didn't like that at all.

Sean walked up to what he naturally assumed was a control panel and saw the semi-geometric rows of flush button-like structures, or holes, he wasn't sure, and the small hemispherical pads that traversed its length. He couldn't make out any other detail. All the gadgetry, if that's what it was, was smothered by a translucent layer of God knew what. It was about twenty centimeters thick. It looked something like hardened protoplasm and it was beneath this presumably protective veneer that the apparent controls of the alien ship lay, be they buttons or holes, or whatever.

'…so close yet so goddamn far,' Sean uttered, pulling the back of his hair and shaking his head, frustrated at his inability to eyeball what he assumed was part of the visitor's technical heart. His nose was hovering only a few centimeters above the gray gel surface.

'This is fantastic to be sure, but what now, surely we're not meant to operate this thing.' Mitch looked thoughtful, '…maybe it'll operate on auto pilot,' He said grinning, but he needn't have bothered, no one was looking or listening. Anyway, it was a decent suggestion. 'Maybe these aren't the controls at all,' he continued, 'maybe they only operate the air conditioning or some other minor system.' Yeah, right, he thought, rubbing his brow vigorously with one hand. They knew nothing and it was likely to stay that way unless they received some sort of direction. And he knew that meant only one thing.

Sean had placed Josh on the floor who was now crawling around on the vitreous but definitely not slippery surface. Apart from the long console and the "chairs", the room, like the others, was empty. Every surface was flat, even the presumed control area which was totally encased by the "protoplasm" was dead flat. And by dead flat, they meant exactly that, to the eye anyway. They discarded their G-clogs which in the stodgy gravity made normal locomotion impossible.

Ssslluurrpp. Mitch heard a noise behind him, like someone slurping water roughly through a straw. They turned as one and noticed that the doorway was gone, now replaced by solid wall. No more exit. Jessy's fears had suddenly been realized. She looked around, head bobbing like a turkey, searching for a way out and finding none. Locked in!

'Fuck…fuck, Shit!' Jessy bellowed, realizing that Josh was no longer in the room with them. She screamed again as she realized he must have crawled through the door when they weren't looking at him. He was now separated from her, perhaps separated permanently. Running to the wall, she started smashing at it with her fists, making no real impact but leaving glowing groups of green fist prints where the opening had been. Fist prints that looked like a crazy game of join the dots.

'Oh God, no…please. Mitch, Mitch! Do something! Jessy screamed, clawing at the soft substance. It was now spattered and splashed with green, as though it were bleeding coppery alien blood. Mitch stumbled over as she slumped to the ground with her back against the wall. Just as she turned and was about to lose it again, the lower twenty centimeters of the door ate its way open and Josh literally sailed through and came to a sliding stop about two metres inside the already reformed door.

'Oh, this is too much!' She exclaimed in undiminished panic, her mouth open and curved downward and she felt the shaking in her shoulders that always preceded the tears.

Jessy grabbed Josh and Mitch grabbed her. He spoke as softly as he could. 'Calm down,' he soothed, looking directly in her moist eyes. 'They obviously want us together and have no intention of harming us. There's nothing we can do but wait and see what they've got in store for us, it's totally out of our hands, and it's been that way since we entered. Let's just sit down and wait and see what they've got in mind.' He looked at Josh and got a raised arm and "goo" in return, which meant he was okay. 'He's fine, he looks like he wants to go again, relax.' Relax, he repeated silently. That'll take time, he reckoned, looking at her harrowed face.

They couldn't help but ponder. Should we wait for them? But wait for them to what? To appear...to take them somewhere? Somewhere wonderful maybe...somewhere horrible? The dreamings of the three ran the gamut of possibility...the colorful wonderings of a trio alike in species but very different in mindset, in what they expected and wanted, from this fabulous alien vessel.

Sean had investigated, looked at, examined, reexamined, and touched everything of any possible interest in the prosaic room. With nothing else to do, he sat down with the others in the oversized chairs that were not only comfortable, but warming. Josh lay in his backpack and continued to beat one side with an arm. Thank God, he was a happy child. If he wasn't...well, he didn't want to contemplate that.

'If this is the control centre,' Sean started, 'why isn't there some sort of viewport to space? It must have the capability to be manually piloted or why would these chairs be here...just for us? I can't see a viewscreen anywhere.' Jessy swallowed hard and bit back tears. She was thinking about Josh, and his future. Sean pointed to the almost opaque console, 'but then again maybe I just can't recognize it, or perhaps it's not required.' He was reddening and looked ready to implode. It was obvious from his tone that he was sick and tired of being unable to even remotely comprehend, what he was looking at.

Barren though it was, with unanswered questions everywhere, Sean was confronted by a sea of wonder in every direction, an alien landscape that penetrated to the very centre of his being, making him dizzy with awe. But he was equally frustrated. Sean's feelings were plainly written on his face. He wanted answers to his questions.

An hour passed and nothing happened. Sean was asleep, slumped in the large square seat like a heap of barely arranged clothes. They were all totally exhausted.

Jessy had sighted the vessel almost eleven hours ago which was fairly much in the middle of the Syrian night and since then they'd spent prodigious amounts of physical and nervous energy. Tired, definitely, but they were also hungry, in Jessy's case, ravenous. And what would happen when the call of nature arose, which in fact it already had. Did whoever they were, realize that the human system functioned by burning food, consuming nutrients and evacuating waste? A hundred watts of energy, minimum, were needed to keep the body humming along, and that had to come from somewhere. She dimly considered that question as she drifted off to sleep to join the chorus of unconscious human breathing around her.

Jessy woke with a start and realized in a moment of total recall that she'd suffered another of her intensely unpleasant dreams. She and Mitch had been doing *it* right there in the oversized chair in front of two creatures, bizarre somethings that crouched only metres away and were taking a great interest in their performance.

She could still see them, their appearance was carved into her mind like a horrible retinal sculpture. Closing her eyes, the repulsion and terror returned in a breathtaking rush. Both her and Mitch had been naked and were rutting like animals, but strangely there was no end to her dream.
For the first time she had woken up part way through. Just when the pleasure had started to rise. Dream pleasure, she mused, flicking her hair out at the back with both hands. Jessy blocked her thoughts and looked around, seeing Mitch and Sean were also awake. They too looked like they'd been woken abruptly. Only Josh continued to sleep but she knew that he had an uncanny ability to sleep through almost anything, except hunger.

Sean was the first to see it. 'Check i-t-t er, out-t...' he slurred and stuttered as he jumped from his chair and pointed toward the huge linear panel. 'It's, er…lighting up,' he whispered. Brilliant, he thought, just a brilliant deduction.

The object had indeed obtained some sort of animation and its previously hidden underside was now fully revealed at the surface. The protoplasmic sheath had melted away or perhaps the lower level had somehow risen up through it. In any event it was gone, but even fully exposed, it bore little resemblance to anything they were familiar with. No one was surprised. The thirty metre long panel was pin holed with what looked like flat and slightly recessed buttons or holes that ranged in size from a few millimeters to several centimeters. The smaller ones were abundant and formed distinct parallel linear patterns, while the larger ones were randomly distributed among the smaller ones at a proportion of about forty small ones to one big one. There was a distinct organization amongst the buttonholes but just what it meant or what it related to, they could only guess at. It looked unfathomably simple. There were no switches or monitors or readouts that they could recognize. Nothing reminded them of space flight or human tech, even remotely. The "buttons" looked like small round holes that had been cut into the panel and then covered with what resembled opaque black plastic. They were both searching for the smallest elements of parallel development.

Sean wondered whether the buttons could be pushed or whether they required some other sort of manipulation or maybe stimulation. He felt compelled to find out but hesitated as he continued to scan its length. His fingers on his right hand were moving in preparation for stimulating the supposed buttons. Sean watched the buttons change. Every now and then a button would go from black to clear for a split second and then return to black. This pattern of alternating color (or clarity) was happening with increasing frequency. He was trying to relate it to their tech, but was failing.

'It looks impossibly simple,' Mitch said, looking closely at the patterns.

'Of course, we're still assuming that these are the actual controls for the craft...for the propulsion and astrogation systems. If they only manage some minor system, we'd feel pretty damn stupid, wouldn't we?' Despite Sean's sarcasm they knew that this and anything else they cared to flippantly consider were more than plausible in this bizarre world where questions were everywhere, but explanations and answers were entirely absent. They all felt like toddlers in a grownup world.

'Are we still moving...I mean, has it accelerated?' Jessy asked, staring at the flickering lights that were mirrored by her swollen eyes. She made "go signs" by flicking her head and eyes.

After the console lit up, Mitch wondered the same thing, but he hadn't felt any increase in gravity. The ship's technical animation had to mean something though.

'I don't think so,' he returned, 'unless it happened while we were asleep and we soaked up the gee's in these chairs.'

'Surely we would've woken up. It's hard to believe we'd sleep through something like that,' Sean remarked, looking at Mitch with a sort of lopsided grimace.

'Who knows, but without some sort of view to space we won't know until we start to decelerate and, well...as horrible as it might sound, it might be years away. If we assume that we're not going back to our solar system, then any trip we're making has to be a long one, unless they've got abilities we haven't considered.

They all looked mighty unimpressed, and thought about it, seriously. 'Fuck,' Jessy snapped like a whipcrack. Her mouth went dry and she felt freezing cold as she considered spending years in space. Years sitting here, I don't think so, Jessy mused to herself.

Superluminal. There it was again. Sean knew his physics and relativity inside out, but looking around him he couldn't help but wonder about it. The vessel seemed to demand skepticism about things he considered normal and proven. "Relativity" seemed trillions of kilometres away. He also knew Hubble had confirmed relativity and "Earthly physics" extended virtually to the edge of the Universe. It was everywhere. A few had suggested changing the laws of Einsteinian gravity to discount dark matter, but they had been proven wrong. So, what was the answer? Sean took a quick breath of utter astonishment as he considered it. How the hell did the craft get here? Could they travel superluminal…faster than light in normal space? He thought about it briefly. Of course not, it simply wasn't possible, he knew that. Mass and energy, the laws that pushed us forward and held us back were everywhere. Higgs was universal. Therefore, no they couldn't.

Jessy scowled at Mitch, '...what about food and water, and a bathroom? Without the first two we're going to die and die quickly, not to mention unpleasantly.' Yuck! She thought, dying in a pile of human excrement didn't appeal to her one bit.

Sean looked up from the console he had been intimately studying. 'They wouldn't have enticed us aboard just to watch us starve and drown in our own waste, I'm absolutely certain of that.' He hoped that was true. Having spoken the words, he wasn't as sure as he was a few minutes ago.

'How do you know this isn't some sort of heinous experiment? Like a baby taunting a dumb animal, how do you know?' Jessy whined, giving a fine impression of the child she was referring to. She was shaking her head slowly and her chin was trembling after she spoke.

Mitch walked over and took hold of Jessy and slowly massaged her shoulders and walked her over to the panel. Her muscles felt like a wad of piano strings, matched nicely by the rigid expression on her face. As he was letting his gaze rest comfortably on the flickering lights, something happened in front of him and his immediate thought was hallucination. All of a sudden, he had an unimpeded view of the cosmos in a broad band, gloriously painted above him. Mitch jumped and shuffled back a couple of steps, Sean gave a protective flinch and gasped. Jessy stood behind Sean and just hoped to survive.

In that area of the vessel, the skeleton of the craft had abruptly become transparent, like the clearest glass, affording them a stupendous panorama of space.

'Shit,' Mitch screamed, looking straight at Jessy, ripping his eyebrows up. His second thought was that they were all about to be sucked into the emptiness, such was the extraordinary clarity of the view. His heart was racing.

'This isn't happening, this can't be happening,' Jessy moaned. She wanted out of this crazy, random world. Her voice had risen to a cry of pain.

Without uttering a word, Sean moved from his chair and over to the panel and touched what for all intents and purposes was a massive geometric rip in the hull. He could still feel the familiar softness of the surface even though visually it wasn't there anymore. Where he fingered it, there was a pale green smudge on the cosmos that gradually faded and disappeared.

'This is fantastic,' he exclaimed ecstatically. It was clear they were moving, though at what speed it was difficult to say. 'Fast', he whispered.

'How fast?' Jessy murmured, knowing it was anybody's guess.

'...very hard to say,' he said, pointing, 'but I do know we've almost completely reversed our course. Can you see that bright star out there, well that's got to be Barnard's...if we were still travelling toward Earth that should be behind us. And that's not all,' he said, still pointing, 'that bright star just off centre is V645.' Jessy squirmed in her seat and felt a growing pall of discomfort.

The fear and the confusion were stippled in Jessy's voice. 'The last view I remember from Cygnus was of CX1 in front of us, just like this view...and we were heading toward Earth, so what the hell's happening? We can't be going in two directions at once, can we?' She looked at Mitch thoroughly bewildered.

'We were due to overtake CX1 several hours ago, meaning that it should actually be behind us, not in front of us. So, we've reversed course and are travelling back in the direction of Rigil Kentaurus. To answer your question Jess, I would say that by the apparent size of Proxima we're travelling relatively slowly. We've probably decelerated rather than accelerated.' Mitch's mind was racing, trying to garner fact from very little. He thought that was the case, but wasn't totally sure.

'How long till we come near that thing again?' Jessy groaned, not really wanting to know the answer. Like the others, she'd grown to detest the red star.

'Maybe within the hour but I'm sure they know the dangers in getting too close. Considering the likely technology of this ship I'm sure they've been spacefaring for a hell of a lot longer than us. So, I think we can relax and assume that they know what they're doing.' Mitch returned to his seat and pondered the view of Proxima that was now oddly centre screen.

Jessy found her mind filling with thoughts and images she could have done without. And what about their craft and their intended return to Earth? Would the shipbuilders show themselves or would they remain permanently hidden, if they were here at all? And more importantly, did they know about our life support needs?

Yes, they must, she thought, thinking of the atmosphere and the temperature, but perhaps they only knew part of the story and were oblivious to their hour to hour necessities. The Finer details. She was thirsty, hungry and needed to go to the toilet. Desperately.

'But surely, they've done this before, just not with humans, right? So, they would know...y'know trial and error.' She looked terrified. Her eyes were glazed.

'Who knows, but it makes sense.' Mitch said. He almost laughed out loud. Of course, they knew, he thought, grinning slightly.

Jessy sat back and took everything in, and almost cried out loud as she considered her situation. Looking through some multiphase metal, she was reclining in an alien spacecraft light-months from Earth with a full bladder. Going who knew where in what sort of time frame. All with the knowledge that Earth was likely to be swallowed by some bizarre nemesis in the near future. Sweet shit! Jessy thought to herself. Narcotic delusion had somehow been sparked into real life.

Assuming no velocity changes, Mitch reckoned they'd be making a close pass by Proxima in about fifteen minutes. It would only be a close pass because thankfully it looked as though the craft was going to miss the red star comfortably. Assumptions made in an unknown vessel were always going to be tenuous though, because they'd all started to feel the effects of a further reduction in speed. The increase in gees was only mild though...but why was it slowing? Surely it should be speeding up if it was returning from whence it came. Rendezvous was Jessy's best guess, maybe they were slowing down to dock with another craft. To pick up passengers. She tried to block the thought but couldn't. Pick up more of them. Soon, it might be standing room only in here.

While they were considering the question of why, they didn't notice the bottom centimeters of the door eat outward from the centre behind them and disappear. Sean heard the strange sucking noise and knew what it meant even before he turned his head to look. He didn't know what was coming through though.

Mitch jumped out of his seat and stood behind it, agape at the sight of the thing that had shunted through the hole and into their chamber. Jessy's eyes followed Mitch's and they stopped dead, immobile and fixed on the thing in front of her. Sean was the only one to speak. The only one who could speak.

'Well, our friends have finally decided to pay us a visit, not in, er...person I would suggest but it's better than nothing.' Sean inched forward, wondering what the hell it was.

'What the fuck...' Jessy's voice broke and she swallowed hard, 'W-What the hell is it?' Her face was rigid like hardened jelly as she back-pedalled toward the wall.

Sitting on the floor about five metres from where they stood and immediately in front of the reformed wall was a small and apparently robotic something.

'...what does it want?' Jessy asked anyone who was listening. Silence. No one spoke but it was coming. She kept moving away from it, inching slowly with her back against the wall.

Eventually Mitch said. 'We'll have to wait and see, but so far it hasn't moved...it, er...um, doesn't look dangerous though.'

Jessy's eyes were like donuts as she looked on, still edging back. Sean padded closer to it, despite her grunting protests. He moved forward and Jessy edged further back.

The creature was shaped not unlike a turtle and was, outwardly at least, composed of the same familiar softish metal substance. 'What the hell is it?' Jessy's first words were predictable.

The smooth hemispherical shell of the thing seemed to sit flush with the ground so its means of locomotion, if it had any, which presumably it did, were totally hidden from view. At the end of the shell facing them, perhaps it was the front, were the familiar parallel lines that they'd seen in the walls and the door. Extending from them were about ten or fifteen stubby, thimble-like projections that resembled thick black cat whiskers.

123

'If a turtle's head pops out, I'm going to scream and I won't be able to stop, ever,' Jessy said, without a smile but with huge, unblinking, frozen eyes. Mitch reckoned she had eyes like his cat, Kodi, when the vacuum cleaner was dragged out. Sheer, unadulterated, wide eyed terror.

'I think you're safe Jess,' he offered, smiling gently at her. She looked petrified. Mitch felt for her, peering at her huge eyes…she looked truly horrified.

Mitch approached and stood next to Sean who was gawking freely. He jumped when the turtle started motoring toward the console. Jessy was frozen to the spot, both arms fixed rigidly by her sides, as it loomed, not straight toward her, but in her general direction. It didn't even slow down when it struck the ninety-degree angle the floor made with the panel. As soon as the nose of the turtle hit the wall it instantly recast itself so its shape remained the same but its bristles were facing upward.

'Unbelievable,' Sean said, 'Like a special effect.' He stared at the turtle, brows riding high.

Ending up on top of the console, it stopped dead, again without slowing down. Then it melted downward, disappearing entirely beneath the surface, only a metre away from Jessy.

'I trust you all saw that,' Mitch said as he inspected the area where the turtle had submerged. Sean's face was crammed with trepidation and wonderment, '...like sorcery, the technology must be awesome', he spluttered. 'We're lucky to be here you know.' Sean looked expectantly at Mitch and Jessy, his brows now forming massive halfmoons.

'That makes two of you,' Jessy whimpered, hinting at her lack of enthusiasm for their plight. She didn't feel lucky at all. Scared for Josh and herself yes, lucky, no. Motherhood had changed her, from worrying about Earth, Sean and Mitch, she now worried mainly about Josh, and his future. Go figure, she thought ruefully.

Having disappeared within the console, they assumed the turtle was running amok amongst whatever gadgetry or unimaginable servo-technology existed in there.

'Maybe it's a mobile mechanic,' Sean suggested. 'Perhaps there's a whole fleet of them running around, fixing anything that happens to go awry.'

Mitch nodded but he doubted that much would ever go wrong with a craft such as this. He watched Jessy as she climbed back into the oversized chair.

She looked like a tiny child with a petulant frown sitting in a grownup's chair, arms crossed and eyes fixed straight ahead. He felt like clapping his hands or snapping his fingers to break her stare, just managing to resist.

After an hour of contemplation, it became apparent that something had changed. The light seemed brighter somehow. They all turned around almost as one, a subtle radiance was bleeding from a set of parallel lines that had appeared on the wall directly opposite where they sat.

The lines were identical to those that had delineated the doorway which led them into what they referred to, for want of any better term, as the command room.

'I wonder, did the turtle organize those lines, and did it organize them for us?' Mitch pondered out loud.

'What do they mean, the lines?' she asked, nervously.

'It must be a door Jessy, it's got to be a door, and it probably works the same way as the one that led in here.' It seemed a fair assumption. It will probably eat itself away, under stimulation, but just what that stimulation is or was, who knows, Sean thought, looking at the lines intensely.

The newly appeared pattern was gently pulsing in colours of gold and crimson, as though it were a computer drive working on a complex problem. It seemed to beckon them toward it.

Before their eyes this time, the disintegration of the door started. A minute puncture ate itself rimward in a phosphorescent lather, gathering speed as it went, and in under three seconds, there was a manicured void that led to another small chamber.

Tentatively peering in, they tried to make out any detail within. They couldn't have been more surprised, wouldn't have been more shocked if they'd looked in and seen Whistler's Mother knitting a pair of socks.

'...mother of God.' Mitch murmured, unblinking. 'They must've read our bloody minds.'

124

'...not before fucking time,' Jessy added. She couldn't believe her eyes. Blinking several times though, the image remained. It was real. It was definitely real. She walked slowly forward, taking it all in.

Sean's eyes were massive. 'How can they know this? How can they know all this? It looks so perfect...so patently perfect...'

'Television Sean,' Mitch said softly, 'Fucking television...they've been monitoring our TV signals, no doubt about it. But as to how they actually engineered all this, well that's another question, because it surely wasn't here before. It looks as though they've spontaneously generated all this from scratch.' Mitch was blinking rapidly in time with his speech.

In front of them was a tiny piece of Earth. The room was about four metres square and had a single, apparently wooden or at least wooden-looking table to one side. On the other side was a stock standard European toilet complete with toilet paper on a wall mounted spindle. Next to the toilet was a white basin with a very Earthly faucet and on the table were four small glasses full to the brim with clear liquid. Water? Next to the glasses were several pieces of brownish looking material of unknown nature. The crescent shaped items were the only unfamiliar sights. The rest of it was Earth. Pure Earth. If they were trying to put them at ease, it was an excellent first step.

'Christ...all the modern conveniences,' Jessy murmured as they stepped into the room and picked up the glasses, convinced that whatever it was would be safe to consume. Why would they off them now? Because they can, came the immediate answer. She wished she hadn't thought of that.

'Tastes like water,' Sean offered as he gulped down the contents of the glass and filled it again from the tap. '...plumbing seems okay too,' he chirped, grinning widely enough to expose a bottom row of shining teeth.

Jessy fingered the crescents, 'I hope this brown stuff is edible because Joshy's food is gone and if he doesn't eat soon, he's going to put on a show like nothing you've ever seen.' She was looking at Josh and nodding, but still looking tense and a little dejected.

Mitch brought a piece of the brown rind to his nose and noticed with interest that it lacked any odour at all. He took a small bite and his features lightened. It was brown and ultrafine grained, as though it were previously molten.

'Not bad, it's really not bad. I can't even guess what it's made from but it actually tastes okay. Sort of like meat, a whitish meat, perhaps veal but with a slightly sweet, almost fruity flavor.' Fruit-meat, he thought, turning it over and inspecting it closely.

Jessy quickly collected some and with a glass of water padded over to a still sleeping Joshua. He was on his back and fast asleep.

After thirty minutes they were all satisfied, having eaten, drunk deeply and perhaps best of all, relieved themselves. Now, back in their seats, they gazed at the view of the Galaxy. CX1 was now adjacent and once again very central to their apparent motion through space. In fact, Proxima was huge before them, its bloated and misshapen physique now smothering their forward horizon.

Despite its nearness, the glare they noticed, had been progressively dulled...presumably by the strange material they were looking through. The deformed star was now in perfect focus, they could gaze at it without squinting and could see every one of its disturbing surface features.

Mitch guessed that the star was only a few million kilometres away and he felt as though they'd now come to an almost complete stop in space. But why? He couldn't fathom it. What were they waiting for...when was it, whatever it was, going to happen?

Inertia. There was abrupt movement.

Having reduced speed to a crawl, the massive vessel started to pivot through a half circle and ended up facing directly away from Proxima Centauri and back toward solar space. They looked back toward Sol which they could see, yellow and beautiful, as easily the brightest star in their new view of the Galaxy.

What now? Jessy asked herself with a shudder. She didn't want to imagine. Are they giving us a last view of our home star...for posterity? No one had a clue what was to follow but the next movement they thought would be an important one. They all agreed they really didn't have a clue. Sean and Mitch had nothing. Jessy had some ideas, all bad, so she held onto them.

It might spell out their fate and give them some clue to their destination. What Godforsaken star did these beings call home? Tau Ceti, Barnards, Wolf, 51 Pegasi? The possibilities were illimitable, but none of them wanted to spend their entire lives venturing to an impossibly distant destination. Even if they did travel at light speed, it was a vast, billions of light years, Universe.

The turtle emerged from the console and did in reverse what it had done on the way in. In a few seconds it was through the wall and gone.

'Do you think it engineered that room?' Jessy asked, glancing in the direction of the bathroom. Of course, it did, she thought, angry with herself for even doubting it.

'Undoubtedly,' Sean answered. 'I don't know how it did it, but I'm sure it did it. God, how I'd like to catch it and see how it works. Mind you I'd probably have no conception of its operation. Who knows, maybe it wasn't a robot, maybe it was a natural organism, an intelligence in its own right.' He hesitated and shook his head, frustrated by his inability to gather any insights into the tantalizing creature. Sean's ramblings were stalled by another lurching sensation. The next move by the craft, whatever it would be, was upon them. Changing its attitude in space, this time it was accelerating. The viewport showed that Proxima, which had been behind them, had quickly moved slightly to the right of exact centre in front of them. They were forced back in their seats and were struggling to vocalize as the gee's grew. After a few minutes the inertial pain largely subsided. They were heading directly toward CX1. Directly! They watched in horrified disbelief, staring as the star got fatter and brighter in front of them.

'What are they doing?' Jessy screamed, looking at Mitch who was frantically searching for an answer. Any answer. He had nothing. Jessy looked at Josh and prayed. Jessy looked straight ahead, stiff, with even her toes clenched.

Mitch's voice was confused, 'I don't know what they're doing...maybe stressing us to see how we react.' He could see Proxima continuing to swell as he watched, slowly growing more detailed as he stared at it. Mitch could now see brilliant plumes of fire arcing and jumping from its twisted outer torso. The detail was paralysingly vivid. Star. Right there in front of them.

'We're heading straight for it! What the hell are they doing?' Jessy pleaded, clenching her jaw so hard her teeth were almost cracking. She was still staring at him. Josh started to cry and wave his arms around. 'Not now Joshy, Jesus...not now!'

Staring rigidly forward Mitch said, 'Maybe the craft needs a gravity assist to get home, although it's hard to believe it'd be necessary.' He scratched his chin.' Maybe they're heavily into energy conservation.'

Not, Jessy felt like screaming.

'I wouldn't get too concerned about guessing,' Mitch continued, '...we've got about five minutes before we either fry, get pulled into a ribbon, or make an exit around the edge of that thing.' It was getting very close. Mitch watched as the wheel of matter got huge in front of him

'Option three,' Jessy said without a smile, unable to shift her gaze from the beast that was now so close she could almost smell its harsh metallic scent.

The pliable ship shone like molten iron in the rays from the very adjacent star. The gas being wrenched from Proxima was everywhere, a maelstrom of surging star stuff that girdled the black hole in a pinwheel of dazzling symmetry and beauty. The ferocious tempest completely dominated their forward horizon. They were all seated, silent and rigid like waxwork dummies, watching the twin horrors loom. It was magnificent and appalling.

What was their plan...and why? They must know what they're doing Mitch kept countering. This can't be what they have in mind. But what then? Maybe something's wrong with the craft. If there was then they were doomed without hope of reprieve. He looked around, shifting his head left, then right. He peered at Sean and then at Jessy. They were both clearly terrified by the sight of CX1.

'I hope this vessel can tolerate some pretty extreme conditions,' Mitch blurted hopefully, leering at the star, knowing in himself that their only hope for survival was a lastminute deviation.

126

He could see that they were headed almost directly for the mote of blackness, the rotating black edge that was visibly quaffing the tornado of star gas.

As they entered the last minute or so of their journey, and they thought, of their lives, the three of them sat and stared, breathing in the extraordinary vista, wondering what sort of twisted fate had dragged them here. Wondering how they'd inherited such a crazy destiny. Jessy thought it might have been better if the water had been lethally tainted. At least they'd know, she reckoned. Better off black and white rather than a pale shade of either, she was sure. None of them moved or spoke as they watched straight ahead.

The starlight throbbed in Jessy's eyes as she pondered her life. Sean still had the same look of wonder on his face that he'd had since entering the craft. She still felt like slapping him. Mitch, brow furrowed, was trying to find reason and understand why they were placing them in such a monstrous situation. He found it unfathomable as to why they would go to the trouble of getting them aboard just to have them fry, or die in a black hole. Why?

As the seconds washed away, Proxima became a hideous flaring horror before them. It was obvious to Mitch that they were going to spiral straight into the gob of the feeding black hole. They would experience it all in real time but outside they would look alive and stuck eternally within the event horizon somewhere. As the final seconds ticked nearer, Mitch was overcome by a flood of memory from his past. It came back to him like a baseball thumping into his temple, an experience he'd had as a youngster, that left him dead for longer than he cared to remember. His pupils imploded into ebony points, 'Oh shit, wait…of course…of course, that must be it!' Mitch bellowed, trying to recall old memories.

Jessy turned her head and looked at him with tired, bloodshot eyes. Mitch was screaming, 'They've mastered wormhole travel…Einsteinian stargates, well, I hope that's it. That must be the reason this craft is out here so far from anywhere. It must have arrived through…well, through…um…though Lorentzian hyperspace…you know, an Einstein-Rosen thingy. And that's why the sensors aboard Cygnus didn't detect it, because it appeared so close to the ship and didn't approach on a normalized trajectory.' Mitch continued to stare at them unblinking, wondering if it could be true. Willing it to be true. Safe travel through a uh…wormhole?

'Is it possible?' Jessy asked, looking desperately at Sean and squirming in her chair.

'That theory was canned years ago…physics told us they were too unstable, too short lived to be traversed, their mathematical structure was all wrong. But maybe they somehow got it right, unriddled it, perfected it.' Wormhole travel, she hoped like hell that's what was happening.

'Anyway, right or wrong, we're about to find out, and if we're wrong, well who knows what they've got in mind.' Mitch watched as they hit the pinwheel. As the craft hit the first colours. Space in front of the probe suddenly flared and exploded into blinding color. They were closing on the beast. Space became fantastic brightness and in front of them surged a brilliantly tinted storm flashing outward and around them, smothering the viewscreen in a stunning all-spectrum rainbow.

Crossing the torus of captured gas, they were riding the gravity wave into the very crotch of the spinning particle disk. The firestorm brightened a notch as they transected the gas plane, cut across it and through it, their destination obvious as they headed directly for the anthracitic vortex that lay ahead like an open drain. Where spacetime lay sliced and naked, where it was throttled and hacked to nothing by a stupendous graviton sabre. They could see it, blacker than the blackest space.

An edge to the Universe was staring at them, a frightening black well, where space itself was circularised, beckoning beyond the viewscreen, where apparently a wormhole resided. Jessy's childhood memories rose into her mind. She firmly believed that death was at hand. Dead, she mouthed silently, strangely calm. Blackness.

Rumbling and bucking like an old Moon rover, the craft threw them around in their soft metal seats, but after a minute or so the storm gradually abated and in a heartbeat was gone. They'd swept into a region of space where the untarnished blackness had returned, but in the blink of an eye it was drowned by a blinding, twisting nebulosity that arced outward and engulfed them. Suddenly, it was fantastic crimson space for as far as they could see.

They were inside the spinning black hole, gliding amid the gore of screaming photons, presumably closing on the singularity which was similarly rotating. It was a white-knuckle ride that lasted about twenty seconds, followed like before, by the vessel returning to its former smooth disposition. They continued to course through a soupy redness that ebbed and flowed like a monumental Martian dust storm. Redness then instantly gave way to a mindbogglingly vivid blue. There was no gradation, stark red became stark blue. The contrast was immediate and complete.

Directly in front of them...they all saw it. Nature's impossible paradigm. They watched in awe through the crystalline bow of the ship.

Ahead of them was a gaping, swaying something. A splayed tubescence was belching a flood of brilliantly shimmering particles that floated gently through the sapphire swirl around them. The glowing particles were slicing a uniform swath through the blueness directly toward them. Then they were upon it. In it. Within the gizzard of Mother's most unlikely offspring. Swallowed by the fantastic maw, they continued to move at undiminished speed, gliding like a subway train through the glowing conduit. It was something Einstein and Rosen would have been very interested in seeing, Mitch thought, gaping at the scene outside.

'Good God almighty,' Jessy muttered, watching with huge eyes and a hard facial twitch that made her look like a mad woman. She found it hard to believe the madness she was seeing. Through the transparent hull of the craft there was an apparently endless throat, slightly wider than the craft and consisting of what? Her mind did backflips at the thought. She gazed in stunned wonderment, the feeling of mental congestion getting worse with each breath.

Negative pressure from negative gravity, but where...how? Mitch wondered and continued looking left and right. He wasn't sure where to look. Sean just watched the whole scene, overwhelmed, holding his head at a strange angle, staring with red-rimmed eyes at, what he considered to be, impossible technology.

The uniformly rippled structure continued to whiz by, seemingly only arms-length away. Gut wrenching questions flooded into Jessy's mind. Where the hell was it taking them...what would they find at the other end? That was the main question. The other million would have to wait. Another time perhaps, another place certainly. A different galaxy, another universe? The possibilities daunting and endless, stabbed Jessy's already tormented mind. The sound of her heartbeat thrashed in her ears.

Rigid and expressionless in their seats, 'fuck' was all Sean could come up with as he stared at the scene in front of him, eyes deadlocked and head braced.

'Sweet baby Jesus,' Mitch exhaled, 'we were right...although I think at the last minute, we knew that. But to think that they've ironed out the theory...the instabilities, the hazards...it's incredible. How in God's name do they keep the fucker open?'

Sean hoped like hell the question was rhetorical because, well...fucked if he knew. Fucked if humanity knew. It was amazing. Negative mass he assumed...but where, how?

Mitch looked at Sean deliberately, his eyes brimming with realization. His voice was hushed, he looked everywhere, 'we're in...hyperspace!' They gazed silently at each other. No words were necessary. It was genuinely beyond imagining. They all knew what he meant.

'There's no doubt this is actually a wormhole is there?' Sean was watching the glowing throat as he spoke, wondering what sort of stuff he was looking at.

'No doubt at all,' Mitch responded immediately, nodding. There could be no mistaking what had swallowed them. It had to be the only solution to what they were seeing.

'...and we are going where?' Jessy proffered the obvious, unanswerable question that they'd all been chewing on. Where would they pop out? She hoped they would at least exit this place. If they stayed here...well, she preferred not to think about that.

'I think we're being taken home to meet the makers of this vessel,' Mitch guessed. '...they know we're here, so what other destination could there be?'

'I hope they've got some pretty serious radiation barricades on this ship or we are in very deep trouble,' Jessy said quietly. She had developed great confidence in the craft, so she was sure it was okay. She hoped.

128

They all focused on the throbbing vista outside, staring at the mildly reflective surface of the wormhole in absolute silence. After ten minutes they saw a sudden, blinding whiteness.

'Am I dying, Mitch?' Jessy heaved. He looked up and saw a brilliant white pyre dancing in her eyes.

'What the fuck?' Mitch turned to look at the source of the light and he knew immediately what she was implying. His first thought was star.

Ahead of them was a piercing light that was growing in size and intensity. Mitch was transfixed. NDE jumped to mind. Near death experience...he knew what it meant. The compelling aura that preceded death. Mitch had never believed it, but the sight of the light ahead, he grudgingly admitted, was somehow spiritual. It evoked a pit of the stomach emotion, a strange gut sensation he found difficult to define. Mingled despair and reverence perhaps. He wasn't sure. Jessy thought it looked like the near death and astral projection drawings she'd seen in Legacy magazine.

The brilliance suddenly started to ebb and flow, pulsing and throbbing like a rapidly variable sun. Were they near death? Jessy wondered. What sort of a gateway was it? Her mind filled with flickering images of fiery hell and eternal pain. Wormhole, she reminded herself, looking at the unimaginable scene laid out...outside.

'Mitch?' she asked, hoping for a rational explanation as to what it was, as if rational still applied in this most deranged of places. Jessy's eyes were feverish.

'...must be our way out...where it ends and hopefully where normal space kicks in again.' Mitch spoke through clenched teeth. He hoped he was right. Just how normal it would be though, he had no idea. Jessy seemed satisfied with the explanation and sat back, watching the "star" grow huge in front of her. It was many times brighter than Proxima, and was pure unadulterated white that even the "light shields" on the craft didn't appear to be coping with. She could barely look at it, it was sunlike in intensity although they felt no heat from it whatsoever which seemed wrong.

As the ship touched its periphery the buffeting they experienced before began again, lasted for a few seconds, then stopped abruptly. They looked at the viewport and saw only blackness, no wild color this time, just the familiar blackness of space. And millions upon millions of stars. Cosmos.

They had popped back into normal space, that was clear, but where in normal space were they? Jessy's mind ached as she contemplated exactly that. Where could they be? Nothing looked familiar, not stars, not star groups, nothing. Absolutely nothing looked familiar.

'Check it out,' Sean said, pointing with a gloved hand that was shaking slightly. He looked back toward their point of exit still sitting in the far left hand corner of the viewport. Their point of egress was a fantastically bright, rotating doughnut of light that was rapidly dimming. Within seconds it diminished to nothing and soon winked out. Gone. They were alone in space. But what space?

'I'm almost beyond being astounded,' Mitch said, gazing at the spot in space from where they'd been hawked. Instead of blinding light there was now a depthless ebony smudge, much darker than even the blackness of space around it.

Sean stood up and leaned against the console, looking out at their new neighborhood. It was totally overwhelming. The question gripped him again. 'Do you see anything familiar, because I don't. Not that I would expect to I suppose...we could be anywhere, literally anywhere...and in any time.' Sean swallowed loudly, making a sound like a single drumbeat, gaping at the alien universe.

The feeling of desolation and detachment was overwhelming. Jessy tried to digest the idea they might be a million or a billion lightyears from home. Or in a different Universe, or in a different time. It was terrifying. The concept of *anywhere* and *anywhen* suddenly gained a horrible new dimension. They could actually be *anywhen*. Jesus, Jessy thought grimly....so far from home, she brooded silently, feeling lightheaded. The spiralling distances were too much. How far away was their planet...the blue skies, the cities of people, how far away was Cygnus? Even if they were in the same time. Jessy gulped the suddenly leaden atmosphere. Her feeling of estrangement was almost complete and was threatening to turn into raw panic. Diogenes had nothing on them, she thought ruefully, trying to shut off the terrible line of thought. She knew madness lay that way. Jessy was trembling.

129

Having been belched from what they assumed was a wormhole, the probe had seemingly stopped in space. Was it waiting for something, for someone? Sean's brain sprinted again. He was hyperventilating, so he reeled his thoughts in. The ringing in his ears and tunnel vision told him to stop imagining and try and relax. A forlorn thought, but he had to try.

In front of them was a planet, a distinctly Venusian world that was choking on a massive blanket of clouds. A thick brown atmosphere totally smothered the disk and although it was difficult to tell, Sean thought he could see a ring of sorts extending around the planet's smoky midriff. Strangely though, it didn't seem to go all the way around. It also had three small moons further out, all of them reflecting brilliant sunlight. It was fairly clear the star to which this family belonged was almost directly at the back of them.

Jessy's eyes narrowed. 'Is that where they come from?' she whispered, looking at the pseudo Venus that hung in front of them, so familiar yet so palpably alien.

'...doubt it. The surface looks wrong, but nothing can be ruled out. Hell, they may even live in the clouds, we've seen what these beings can do so anything should be treated as possible until, or if, we find out some truths to the contrary. Who's to say they're even based on carbon?

They might live in places we assume are uninhabitable. We're biased Jessy, we naturally think they'll be like us but they might be based on any other suitably abundant element, solvent combination. Fluorine, methane, silicon, anything's possible. We shouldn't prejudge but it's likely that they're fluidy carbonites like us.'

They all wondered though. Form and composition, they knew, were probably as arbitrary and trackless as human evolution. Jessy's thoughts were sparking and fizzing. Radioactive uranoforms, she fantasized. Imagine, Jessy thought, degenerative beings that live their life decaying into radiogenic lead...anything's possible. She had to remember that. Not just what was logical to their own small minds.

'As you say,' Sean began, 'who's to know, we'll have to wait and see. Hell, maybe they won't show themselves. Maybe they're introverts and shy away from direct contact. Perhaps they're just keen to display their technical abilities, to boast to the new kids on the block about their wondrous grip on science...their magical abilities.'

'That's all very well, but I wonder what they look like?' Jessy whimpered, grinding her teeth, revealing her innermost nightmare-inspired anxiety. Her haunted expression was vividly hewn on her soft skin.

She knew her nightmares were simply out-workings of an overly elastic imagination but they flatly refused to be dislodged or even diminished by logic, no matter how hard she tried. Her heart skipped a beat as she considered what they might look like...what they could look like. Even if they were carbon based there were still as many permutations of form as there were atoms in the Universe...

9

Virija

'Absence of evidence is not evidence of absence.' ~ *Carl Sagan*

The equatorial spines grew to erection and gently drifted in the vacuum of space, swaying to and fro as though the stellar wind had somehow obtained the power of a terrestrial storm. The two states of matter that filled the bowels of the vessel stirred themselves for action. The Scout was home, back in its own star system and it carried with it the rarest cargo of all, a family of curious Minds, the stuff of ruptured stars grown to self-awareness. Alien to their planets.

They all felt the rumbling of the craft beneath their feet which they knew signalled a pending manoeuvre, either acceleration or deceleration. Inertia. The second law of motion. $F = MA$, a law which existed throughout the Universe.

Jessy grabbed Josh who was crawling around on the floor, idly sucking on a brown crescent. Dashing back to her seat, the alien food fell and broke on the polished surface, disintegrating like crushed glass. Josh looked at it and raised an arm. He thought about crying but didn't, banging his arm harder and quicker on his Mum, while staring with intent at the disintegrated crescent.

Rather than accelerating, the craft felt to Jessy like it was pivoting again, rotating on its axis without any movement fore or aft. And the viewport confirmed it, showing the shifting starscape as they turned through almost a hundred and eighty degrees. A new and more extraordinary scene locked into place in front of them. Releasing expletives almost in unison, they looked at what had previously been hidden behind them.

In front of them now was a craft that resembled a stupendous version of the ruined spider craft they'd observed some months ago on Cygnus. And there wasn't just one of them either, they were lined up for as far as they could see, several hundred kilometres apart. There was at least thirty or forty that they could see and who knew how many more they couldn't see. It was an amazing scene. Jessy couldn't breathe and tingled all over. She was so lightheaded, she thought she might pass out, which would be a great look, she reckoned.

A blinding flash came from somewhere along the titanic line, and they watched as a pseudo-sun coughed out a soft-contoured vessel that sped away at fantastic, instantaneous velocity. Something humans definitely couldn't' do.

'...this must be a node of some sort,' Sean said brokenly, trying to reconcile the impossible vista. They looked in awe at the incomprehensible. Nexus, Jessy thought. Like a railway station back home, except this one was for much larger transports and way more arrivals and departures.

'The scale of this is, er...unbelievable,' Mitch eventually added, licking his lips and blinking rapidly. 'Those craft must be tens of kilometres in diameter and they're everywhere, they must control the uh, wormholes...like the one we jumped out of.'

Mitch stopped talking and followed Sean's gaze which had settled on a different scene to his right. They'd been so busy watching the vessels pop in and out of what they assumed was Lorentzian space that they hadn't even noticed it

Mostly hidden by the edge of the clear zone was the parent star, bright and slightly orange, a ball of gas so much like home, lighting and nourishing this vibrant parcel of space. It gave them a real sense of deja-vu, it was so sunlike even in spite of its slightly odd color. But even this wasn't what Sean had been gaping at. To one side of the star was a coupling of two stunningly kaleidoscopic worlds that were bathing in the luxurious warmth of its parent. The planets were in tight orbit, one fractionally larger than the other, but both were unquestionably and unambiguously alive, blue and white with the facade of home. And by the look of them, probably with the gasses of home as well.

The twins looked so much like Earth that they all felt the emotional tug of their distant world reach out and sting them almost physically. This reality visual drove home what they would lose when Nemesis crashed into their planet. Not just a rock but a living, breathing world. A cradle, their cradle, rare and gorgeous beyond description.

Jessy couldn't stop the tears flowing down her cheek, falling onto the surface of the alien chair, forming tiny pools of glistening human moisture. 'They're just like Earth,' she sniffled, 'So much like home.' She watched in awe as the color drenched worlds expanded before her eyes.

After a few minutes, the planets and their sparkling ring systems filled their forward view, and it was clear they were not as they originally thought, not at all! They weren't natural loops of jostling planetesimals but instead were mindboggling engineering constructs manufactured, they reasoned, by the creatures, the beings, that had brought them here. By the people of the twin rings. They stared on, aghast at the full or bit space cities, stunned into wide eyed silence.

Sean was looking at the wondrous panorama, stiff and unblinking, staring like a concrete parody at what his mind construed to be impossible technology. They continued to gaze in total silence. Jessy watched the scene unfold, eyes blinking uncomprehendingly as the rings got close.

'Come on Sean,' Mitch eventually prodded, 'Their space habs are like ours, just a whole lot bigger and yes, a little fancier.' He was goading Sean, for he too, like Jessy, was astonished by the colossal rings that were now dauntingly close. 'Jesus, look at them,' Mitch said. He wasn't sure he could take more. He knew he had no choice, it would all unravel before him, like it or not.

'...a lot bigger and a bit fancier,' Sean repeated distantly without breaking his stare. 'They're millions of times bigger than anything we've built...than anything we've ever thought of. They're massive on a planetary scale, and there's three of them for God's sake. They probably hold as many people as a continent on Earth, maybe more, can you imagine that Mitch...can you? We think a thousand people is a lot. How about millions.'

'Settle Sean, it's incredible, but keep your head. Who knows what's ahead of us? Expect anything.' He was all talk, he knew that. He was talking more to himself than Sean.

'Easier said than done,' Sean whispered softly.

The vessel drifted on the cosmic current, a few kilometres from the rings that hung before them like glorious cosmic ornaments, crowning monuments to the lavishly painted planets below.

Because the equatorial ring city was geostationary, rotating at the same speed as the planet, it never moved relative to the surface. Each part of the globe below was always beneath the same portion of the orbiting domain. The polar ring was a completely different story, it changed its position continually as it rotated at right angles to the spin of the planet.

They were gliding toward a huge dim throat that dominated a mammoth supertecture with slightly convex sides. On what was a massive artificial satellite, their apparent destination was a tremendous individual structure that dwarfed the rest of the perturbations on its slick, pliable surface.

Jessy hadn't uttered a recognisable sound for a long time. She sat with Josh and gazed at the irresistible spacescape as it materialized piece by piece before her, trying to reconcile herself with the alien painting that filled their horizons. Her jaw was clenched and her eyes narrowed and focussed as she looked at the incredible scene. It was becoming increasingly difficult to accept that she was really here in person. She felt detached, as though she were watching a movie from the inside...a film into which she'd been manually inserted, like a virtual reality character. The image of the two planets, so Earthlike and yet so tormentingly alien, burnt deeply into her hypothalamus. All the craziness of the past year, CX1, Cygnus, Josh and now this, were becoming difficult to slot away as real memory. Her recollections felt dreamy and soft, gossamer-like, hard to conceive of as genuine experiences. All her life she'd been terrified of going crazy, of losing her grip and drifting off into some real life nightmare where any memory of what, when or who was simply gone. Erased or blocked by an impenetrable haze.

The last few weeks had re-awakened her fear of losing it. She could feel it clawing upward, getting ready to condense into something heavy and physical. Jessy closed her eyes and pleaded with herself as she tried to maintain her focus and loosen the icy digits that were kneading her mind. Like the rest of them, she wondered what their fate would be in this place. What were their intentions? Her mind squirmed and her heart dropped like a Cherokee in windshear. Would they be the subject of grizzly experiments the like of which Sapiens inflicted on lower animals…in the name of science? Or would they be lavished with a cerebral awakening such as none of them could possibly imagine? Logic dictated the latter or at least not the former, but her ability to reason logically was waning. She could feel her mind running down like an old clock. Her feeble grip on what was normal and reasonable was slipping. She felt herself being pushed closer to a pit of hopeless mental disarray.

Jessy's wits had been dancing a hellish ballet for twenty minutes but still she hadn't reached any comforting conclusions or convinced herself of anything, good or bad. She felt no better, and in fact was tempted to tightly grasp her skull to make sure her hold, such as it was, stayed put. That it didn't come careening out of her ears like friable gray sawdust. She knew her emotions were totally involuntary, pure hardwired instinct beyond her control, but it still frustrated her to tears.

Mitch gawked, like Sean and the almost catatonic Jessy, as they came within a few hundred metres of the gargantuan floating world. Aligning itself with the throat, the ship drifted slowly onward with its spines slowly descending into its body, deflating like a snail's antennae. The tumescent appendages shrunk and slid beneath the external gristle of the probe, leaving its skin unmarked and mirror-smooth, like the flesh of a newborn dolphin. Jessy stared at what was ahead, and unconsciously, her brow furrowed.

'Where the hell were we being taken,' she muttered?

They watched, all of them stupefied as their amblings through space shifted the relative positions of all that surrounded them. The smaller planet rolled into the path of the star, giving them a gradual and beautiful stellar eclipse, the planet eventually hiding all but the fiery stellar corona. 'Damn…will everything be so familiar I wonder?' Jessy mewed, stunned by the similarities with their own solar eclipse. Then she thought of how far away home might be and her mind sprinted again. 'Shit,' she thought, thinking of Earth and feeling totally disconnected. Breathing deeply, she focused on the vista in front of her. Bile bled into her mouth as she stared at the bewildering spectacle.

'Here we go,' Mitch whispered to Jessy as the craft slid into the mammoth bay, the mouth to which was perhaps a kilometre in each direction. It was huge. He was flabbergasted at the size of the opening which hadn't looked quite so massive from further away. Then he remembered the girth of some of the craft he'd seen and his surprise dwindled.

'Size demands', Sean mused, nodding his head, they simply had to be that big.

The last view Mitch had as they slipped inside was a glimpse of its curving white margin, onto which tens of thousands of tiny bubble-like structures were geometrically affixed. His view was quickly replaced by a massive sheer wall inside. 'Seems about right,' Mitch said quietly. 'Fuck' he said louder as he turned his head and glanced back at the view. They must be amazing, certainly in technology, Mitch reckoned, biting his lip and wondering.

Mitch and Jessy locked eyes as the realization of where they were hit them with a dizzying punch. Sean was like a child in an amusement park, his anticipation and impatience to find answers reflected like pyres in his eyes. He was seated but looked ready to bound upright at any time as his eyes visibly strained in their sockets.

'You've got to be kidding,' Jessy stuttered, '…how big is this thing. I'm not sure I can even see the other end…is that a wall in the distance?'

'Son of a bitch.' Mitch muttered, 'If this is a docking bay, how many craft use it, and how big are they? It's bigger than a goddamn city back on Earth.' He scanned the near distance for any sign of them. It was truly ginormous.

'…totally empty,' Jessy added, 'Not an irregularity or even the smallest contrast in sight. It's so bland I can't see where the floor stops and the walls start…like a massive Alpine whiteout.'

The probe travelled several kilometres into the bay and settled down on the surface without even the slightest suggestion of a bump.

'Soft as a baby's kiss,' Jess said. 'Like we landed on marshmallow...'

Sean's ears were almost twitching as he strained to catch any noise within the craft. 'And what about the propulsion system?' he said. 'I didn't hear anything turn off, turn on or power down as we entered the bay.'

'Whatever it means I think we can assume that this thing doesn't operate on standard chemical power.' Mitch grinned and looked away, realizing he was stating the bleeding obvious.

'Der,' Jessy blurted, to emphasise the point, watching for any movement outside.

As they watched, the gigantic throat started closing off behind them, reforming and sealing itself off from the vacuum beyond. Molecules were returning in their centillions to fill in the space that was diminishing in size from the outside in.

Within a few seconds there was only a tiny circle of space left in the bull's eye of what had been the ponderous yawn, and then it too was gone. The kilometric doorway had vanished, replaced by an unbroken slab of featureless alien supertecture. It was like magic...here, gone.

Despite the colossal volume of empty space that surrounded them, the feeling of imprisonment was immediate and intense. It was an instinctive reaction because they all knew that escape was hardly an option, with or without an exit to space. Nonetheless, the anxiety for Jessy was paralysing. No way out! They were stuck in what was a very large space.

Jessy looked upward and pointed at the ceiling and shrieked. Mitch followed her gaze and saw tendrils of pale gas spewing like steam from the ceiling, and also from numerous points underfoot. They had nowhere to go. The strange miasma was everywhere in seconds, enveloping them while Mitch was trying to decide what to do. Jessy was trying not to breath but eventually gave in to the pain. It smelled sweet. Her eyes bulged with terror as she sucked in the vapor, fully expecting some exquisitely painful fate. Death certainly.

'...seems okay,' Sean said, having already gulped it in. He wasn't sure either. The emission stopped abruptly and rapidly dissipated.

'What the hell was that?' Mitch coughed and breathed deeply after having held his breath for as long as he could.

'I think we've been deloused,' Sean guessed. 'Maybe they don't want any primitive germs, although it's difficult to believe they wouldn't be able to deal with them.' He smiled at Jessy who didn't return it. She looked away in disgust. His calmness and clarity of mind under stress was starting to get to her. Piss her off, she meant, looking at the stupid gleam in his eyes.

'Couldn't they have given us some warning first?' Jessy questioned through grinding teeth. 'Surely, they're advanced enough to make the process a little less traumatic, assuming that's what it was of course. Christ, it could've been anything...maybe it was a mutagen of some sort.'

'If you grow another leg in your sleep Jess, then I guess we'll know for sure,' Sean offered with a bombastic grin that was only centimetres away from her nose.

'Back off,' she snapped. Jessy meant it. He was really getting to her. Pushing Mitch and his annoying platitudes away, she walked over to the viewport and looked out at the expanse of vacuous whiteness beyond the ship. She physically shuddered at the thought of being the only woman for what...a million light years? Jessy couldn't help but wonder what problems the mismatch of sexes might lead to, especially if they ended up here for years. It was already a problem for her as much as it probably was for them. Jesus Christ, life imprisonment surrounded by misogynists. Fuck, she thought, expelling a grunt. And it would no doubt get worse. Jessy felt horribly alone, stranded and isolated in terror town. Years, perhaps forever. She gulped thickly and looked around. Everything and everyone seemed a little closer and a little unfriendlier. It was also way too bright.

Jessy put Joshua in his backpack and the little darkhaired child proceeded to watch his mother with considerable interest. She was pacing around the room looking decidedly ill at ease and Josh's eyes followed her every step, his arm started banging up and down, meaning he wanted to play.

'I want out of this place Mitch, I've got a bad feeling,' she murmured without taking her eyes off the blandness outside. 'What're they going to do next, drop us in nitro to test our skin...or maybe they'll just eat us and be done with it, hell, maybe humans appeal to their sweet tooth. They just send out a ship and we hop in...like gudgeons to a worm.'

'Shut up Jess,' Mitch snapped. 'Settle down for God's sake, I don't think we're in danger and I don't think even you believe we are. You're a scientist and a physicist, not a xenophobe, so snap the fuck out of it.' Mitch looked away sharply. 'Grow up,' he added.

'Here, here,' Sean chimed in, adding unnecessary agreement. Jessy sat down and pouted. It was starting, she thought. Gang warfare. Males versus female.

Hormones, Mitch assumed, gazing at Jessy, her body was probably still trying to normalize itself after Joshua. Her growing bouts of irrational behaviour were becoming more pronounced though, although given the crazy circumstances it was probably a normal reaction for someone of Jessy's unusual psyche. He hoped her moods would eventually even out but he wouldn't bet on it.

For the next ten minutes they sat in silence in the empty cargo bay or space dock they'd been deposited in. Nothing moved. Just monochromatic brightness for as far as they could see.

'Where's the welcoming committee?' Jessy asked loudly. '...if your aliens are so intent on making friends, shouldn't they be here by now?' She scrutinized Sean closely, screwing up her eyes up and turning her head sideways.

As Jessy spoke, Sean saw a minute image moving toward them and gradually start to grow larger. It was in the far distance. Mitch saw it too but Jessy kept babbling.

'Quiet Jess, take a look.' He thrust his arm out and pointed at the growing figure. Her eyes turned from Sean and looked toward the gleaming entity making its way toward them.

'Is it one of...them?' she asked tentatively, studying it and trying hard to focus. It didn't look like it, but then again who knew what form they might take? Jessy edged closer to Mitch.

'It looks more like a vehicle of sorts,' Mitch suggested, and Sean noddingly agreed.

'Definitely a vehicle I would say and it looks like it's got some business with this ship if its direction of travel is any indication.'

Jessy felt the panic rise as she watched the smudge start to gather symmetry and form. 'It's coming straight for us,' she bleated. Stay calm she silently pleaded, clenching her toes, feeling her heart start pounding on her ribs like a wooden mallet. She was breathing raspily, waiting for it to arrive. She couldn't tell what was approaching. Like the turtle there was no distinction between the base of the object and the surface it scooted across. For all intents and purposes it was entirely flush with the ground and part of its roof seemed to be swaddled with minute bristles.

On the triangular faces there were myriads of parallel grooves that reminded Mitch of the multiple growth shown by certain mineral crystals on Earth. In fact, the similarity was extraordinary, it looked to Mitch like one of the "stepped" salt crystals from his own private mineral collection. It made him wonder if the object had crystallized from some sort of aqueous solution. The buggy reflected so much light its skin dazzled like a main sequence star. It was about fifty metres distant and closing rapidly in a direct line with their craft. It was clear that it had business with their ship.

Sean watched as the thing slowed and halted about twenty metres from where they stood, directly in front of the clear zone. They all looked straight at it, trying to make sense of its shape, wondering what the hell it was and more importantly, what it wanted?

'Do you think there's something in it?' Jessy muttered, peering deliberately at Mitch, pondering what sort of horror might be making preparations to get out.

'It's totally opaque so if there is, we won't know until it comes out, but I would expect that it's robotic.' Mitch glanced at Sean and shrugged, trying to smile, about to prod him for an opinion, but he quickly decided to save his breath.

Sean's gaze was inviolably rooted on the vitreous vessel that sat motionless in front of them. He was the first to see the change. 'Jesus Christ,' he blurted, 'I can see inside. Look! It happened so quickly, I was looking straight at it when it changed color...er, I mean when it became clear.' The buggy had indeed become completely unreflective, transforming it instantly from opaque

135

and vitreous to absolutely transparent in the blink of an eye. Only a twenty centimetre strip around its base retained the inclarity.

That and the bristles which could now be seen for what they were, short cylindrical stumps perhaps five centimeters long which formed a knobby carpet along and partly around the apex of the roof. It was like a close mown coral reef, Sean thought, gazing at the thing in unfettered awe. He was speechless and was having trouble just thinking…what was his name?

Jessy's eyes settled back into their sockets, '…empty,' she whispered, exhaling loudly and unfurling fists that had been tightly clenched by her sides.

Sean grunted. It was apparent that there was nothing aboard that remotely resembled a being, at least as they would define it. Jessy deflated like a stuck balloon. All they could see were numerous metallic chairs, very similar to those on the probe. There was absolutely nothing else in the belly of the buggy, not even a control panel, or again, none that they could see or recognize.

Sean said, 'eight seats and no controls ... I wonder how it operates?' He spoke softly pondering his questions as he went. 'I mean you'd think there'd be some facility for manual motoring.'

'There probably is,' Mitch added, raising his eyebrows. 'We just can't see it, right?'

Sean was straining at the lenticular panel within the ship, bending over it so his face was only a few centimeters from the clear surface. 'I get the impression that this has been sent to collect us. It's clearly here for a reason and given that it's empty, that reason must be to take us somewhere.' He gazed at Mitch and Jessy with an uncertain grin on his face.

'That's fine,' Mitch said, 'but how do we get out of this ship, and into the buggy? If they want us to do something, they're going to have to lead us in the right direction. They must know we're not bloody mind readers.' They probably know more about us than we do, Mitch thought. having no idea where they were being taken. Maybe for a meeting, maybe not. Maybe for something less pleasant than a meeting. Defining "less pleasant" was something he preferred not to do.

Mitch smiled at Jessy as he went to sit down, but just as he made contact with the soft seat, one of the trihedral panels on the buggy's exterior opened. The middle of the panel dimpled, pocked, then ate outward and disappeared, all in front of Sean's eyes.

'Christ, shit, it's like they're listening to us,' Jessy gurgled. 'I mean as soon as you said we needed direction, bam…it happened. We got direction. You don't suppose they're still watching us do you...monitoring us.' Jessy's head bobbed around like a pigeon looking for a hidden camera.

'I'd be surprised if they weren't,' Sean answered casually, 'but I doubt that they'd be doing it with something we'd recognize as a camera. If they're doing it, we'll never know.'

'Shit,' Jessy sobbed. '...watched by aliens, I'm not sure I like that Mitch.' She looked visibly aghast at the idea. She cringed a bit and felt sweat break out everywhere.

'Take it easy Jess, there's…'

'What the hell?' Sean geysered, pointing at something else inside the ship.

Mitch spun around and immediately saw. In the wall adjacent to the bathroom, in what was presumably the outer hull of the ship, a sphincterish cavity had opened about two metres across. Jessy wasn't sure whether to be relieved or scared. It was a way out certainly, but a way out to what? No thank you, she thought, looking aghast at Mitch. She was happy where she was. They could come right here and meet them, instead of this annoying and chilling game of follow the leader.

Mitch noticed that there wasn't the slightest indication of pressure loss. And given that they could still breathe okay, he assumed whatever atmosphere and pressure was outside was precisely the same as inside. Surely, the atmosphere wasn't just for us to breathe, was it?

Sean walked deliberately over to the cavity and peered out, staring like a wide-eyed child into the stunning white emptiness. He noticed with growing excitement and anxiety that a metre wide ramp led to the ground level of the alien super chamber. It was pulsing and arcing with a strange sulfurous light as though it were beset with some static electrical buildup. It looked like the answer to the first of their questions...how to get out. Simply walk was the reply.

Jessy looked at it and wondered whether it was safe to walk on, or whether they would be roasted from the feet upwards...broiled like prawns on the soft metal griddle that lay before them.

But they'd come this far unharmed, it should be okay, shouldn't it? Jessy's mind was waxing and waning between positive and negative outcomes. If they'd wanted to do away with them, they'd had plenty of opportunities before. But why in God's name would they want to kill them?

They exited the craft after Sean toed the rampway and assured them it would support their weight. Mitch and Sean felt an all-consuming confidence in the technology of the ring builders. After all, they'd travelled through a black hole and survived., That was damn good advertising.

The slope was steep and if not for its amazing adhesion they would surely have slipped and fallen most of the way down. As it was, their feet partially penetrated the surface, giving them extraordinary footholds while amazingly, still allowing easy movement. Descending slowly and cautiously to ground level, they sucked in lung-fuls of the vibrantly oxygenated atmosphere.

'They must have some mighty atmosphere processors,' Sean whispered. '...this area was open to vacuum about thirty minutes ago...meaning they've fully pressurized this colossal space in that time. That's a hell of a feat, and we've got near normal gravity too. I wonder if that's for us or whether it's the norm for them.' They looked around and wondered. Nothing seemed to be rotating, so the source of the gravity was unknown.

Sean considered his own question. 'By the look of their planets I'd say it's probably their gravity not ours. Mind you, if we were cloud dwellers from Uranus and needed high gravity to survive, I'm sure they could've accommodated that as well.' These guys were techno magicians, although his use of the term "guys" might be wrong. They could be damn near anything.

'...what if we decide not to leave?' Jessy asked suddenly, staring at Mitch, examining him carefully. 'What if we just stay here and ignore their little vehicle and refuse to budge? Why should we cooperate when we have no idea what they've got in store for us? I think we should stay put until we get more information.'

Sean looked at her and shook his head slowly. Information ? God, was she serious, he wondered? She's a fruit loop for sure, a dead-set nutter if she reckons that's what's going to happen. There was clearly a plan in place and they had zero input into it.

'I don't think we're in a position of strength here,' Mitch said, 'and I for one don't want to upset them. Not that I think they'll harm us but because I think we should cooperate. We're on their turf and ultimately what they want, they'll get, whether we cooperate or not. So, let's do what they are very clearly suggesting we do. Let's get in their little buggy. It'll be an amazing adventure Jess...count on it.' He winked at her, trying his best to appear relaxed.

As they thought, there were eight seats inside in two rows of four, all of which faced in the same direction, presumably forward.

'A remote controlled envoy perhaps?' Sean offered. 'Wonder why they didn't meet us in person?' He said it with bulging eyes, looking around, pondering.

Mitch replied softly, 'maybe they're hideous and don't want to scare us.' He was grinning but he quickly lost it in favor of a more thoughtful expression.

'You could be right,' Sean said, echoing Mitch's thoughts. 'They may meet a lot of primitives like us and well...if they are really different then it could be a big problem. Of course, they wouldn't think they were ugly but maybe enough civilizations have told them so, and they've come to realise it. Hell, maybe humans are repulsive on the absolute scale of cosmic beauty.'

Jess looked up quickly, grinning, 'you perhaps Sean, but the rest of us I think are probably okay.' Jessy smirked. One for me, she thought. About time, she reckoned. Licking her finger and painting a one in the air was probably taking it too far, she supposed.

'Funny,' Sean returned, rolling his eyes and pretending to look hurt. He was shocked by her attempt at humor and wondered if she was finally coming around. Doubt it, he thought after a moment. She was all work, no play.

The floor of the buggy was, to their eyes, at the same level as the surrounding surface that spread out for kilometres in every direction. The feeling of open space, of vast, unrestricted emptiness was overpowering and unsettling. Mitch was suddenly hammered by disturbing memories of Tharsis, when he'd strode away from his Sojourner near the middle of the Great Golden Plane on Mars. Three hundred and sixty degrees of freezing ochreous nothingness had left him haunted and paranoid, a feeling he hadn't been able to shake for hours afterward. He was the only person on Mars, but he felt sure he was being watched.

He was equally uneasy here, feeling totally at the whim of whatever strangeness might be milling at the periphery of their vision. Were they there? They were disturbing thoughts, swollen by earthly prejudices and fear, but none of them could avoid it, simply because … they were human.

Hunched over, they trooped into the buggy and sat on the seats at what they thought was the front, based on its attitude of approach earlier. As expected, the entire superstructure of the vehicle appeared to be made of soft metal, the seats, even the floor and the clear bubble top which, like the viewscreen, developed glowing green finger lines when touched, but otherwise was totally invisible.

The seats were large and had no arm rests but had solid and very high back supports. Again, they looked to be made for significantly larger beings. The base of the chairs consisted of arrow-thin cylinders of material that disappeared into the floor.

'Very unimpressive,' Sean said as his eyes roved the interior of the buggy, taking in every detail. It appeared very modern, and very minimalist.

Some minutes after they entered, the trihedral yawn dropped inward from all sides and they were locked in. Without a noise or even a jerk, the buggy started forward, turning in a wide arc and apparently sledding back from whence it came.

The womb of the vehicle was now glistening stainless steel with only a small circular zone at the very front remaining clear. It looked something like a ship's porthole, beyond which they could see the whiteness stretching outward like a pale ocean. Jessy sat there frowning, feeling like she was being shuttled to her own execution, she knew it was silly, but she couldn't shake it. Mitch had little doubt that the buggy would've regained its reflective dazzle, such that they'd seen when it approached. Sean stared rigidly at the nothingness beyond. Endless white. Expectant human statues, waiting for the moment that was coming. They all assumed they were being taken to meet *'them'*.

The minutes passed slowly. No one spoke. They all silently mulled over the end of their strange vehicular journey. Who or what would they meet, and were they equipped to cope with a meeting should one occur? The answer was exclusively no, even Sean doubted he was ready. Of course, they would have to do it, but they would never be ready for it.

Would there even be a meeting, or would they be poked and prodded by some malleable metal robots and then returned to Cygnus with absolutely no answers? With absolutely nothing to show for their fantastic encounter? Sean found that thought repugnant. Would they even survive a meeting? Jessy asked herself. She couldn't avoid feelings of dread, fed and fattened by her vivid nightmares. And there was all the ridiculous stuff on TV and DVD. None of it had helped.

It appeared they were making no progress at all toward the towering cliff on the horizon but now it started to approach at speed. All of them watched intently as their destination became obvious. But where the hell were they going? No one really knew, although they suspected.

They were sliding toward a featureless and sheer wall that stretched upward to an impossibly high roof that was suspended at least several kilometres above them. Sean was certain that a gap or a hole would appear in the wall, but as they came close enough to see the pattern of parallel lines, he was losing faith. Surely, they hadn't come this far to die in a vehicle accident.

Jessy and Sean held their breath. With maybe fifty metres to go, they started breathing again as a dimple rapidly blew into a bigger than buggy-sized opening. The vehicle slammed through the opening without slowing. Josh remained quietly sleeping. Thank God.

They motored into a dimly lit tunnel that was flat on the surface they were travelling along but cylindrical and mirror-smooth everywhere else. After a few minutes they slowed and eventually stopped in a part of the structure that looked no different from the rest. Mitch had the overwhelming impression that it had simply run out of fuel and coasted to an unpowered stop.

Stopped? Jessy wondered. Why…was it time? She looked around with eyes that couldn't go any rounder. It wouldn't happen here…surely.

138

Jessy looked through the porthole and peered ahead where she could see the tube stretch endlessly in front of her. It finished as far she could tell, in a curved horizon hundreds of kilometres ahead where the gradual curve of the ring took it out of view. It looked fantastically vast. The nether reaches of the tunnel were shrouded in a haze of distance. It looked like something was up ahead in the distance, but that may have been a mirage. None of them had any idea.

Although there were no apparent accessways in or out, she knew they'd entered through a mouth that had appeared suddenly and would probably disappear just as quickly. That answered that question, but how many of these tunnels were there? This one only had room for one vessel, so she reasoned there must be a lot of them, but maybe this wasn't the major means of transport? But if it wasn't then what was, and where was it? Where were they? Everything was so empty and quiet. Were they watching? Her mind shuddered and gurgled, burning with the hunt for answers to this rather enigmatic, strangely empty floating world.

They watched in awe as the vehicle's chassis became crystal clear, followed by a section of it sloughing away to allow them easy access to whatever was outside. Jessy's breathing came in rapid spurts as she contemplated the next step of their journey.

Sean stepped straight out and beckoned to the rest of them to follow. 'Come on,' he shouted, it's fine.' He demonstrated it by taking a huge breath. 'Smells and tastes fine,' he said. Of course, it could kill him in short order, he reckoned, but at this stage it seemed fine.

Standing next to the buggy they were nearly mown down when it found new life and silently wheeled away, leaving its human cargo in the midst of the barren alien throughway. It rapidly fled into the depths of the tunnel and vanished. It was clear the aliens had an agenda but just what it entailed they could only guess at. Jessy tried not to ponder the question too deeply. Presumably, this was a link in the chain, on the way to meet them.

'So…what now?' Jessy asked the obvious question, looking hopefully at Mitch, trying to keep her heart and her breathing under control. She felt very exposed.

'We wait is what,' he said abruptly.

'Wait for what?' Jessy asked, searching around for something and seeing only whiteness for kilometres in every direction. She shrugged and kept looking, moving her head left and right. She couldn't see a thing, there was nothing to see in any direction. The massive expanse, was empty.

They didn't have long to wait though, as a new cavity sparked its way silently into the tunnel wall only a few arm's lengths away. Through the chasm they spied another craft, a smaller more slipstreamed vessel encased in a cavity seemingly little bigger than it was. Jessy thought it looked like a shining silver bullet in the chamber of a gun. For a full minute they stared in silence.

'Well? Jessy whispered, trying to manage her volume to keep the echo under control.

Even Sean seemed strangely reticent. What to do? Get in, don't get in? Its appearance seemed to be concrete confirmation they were part of a plan, a blueprint designed specifically for them. To lead them somewhere…to something or to someone. He felt undeniably proud they had gone to all this trouble for their kind. People from Earth, a clearly inferior race, in technology at least.

Mitch asked himself, what did they want? Simply contact…or something more? He thought back to Jessy's comment a few minutes ago, *what if we refused to follow their directions*? Refused to budge. Would it flush them out, or would it lead to something else … something less palatable? No one had an answer to that one. They'd have to place a toe in to see, nothing else would work, otherwise it was logic and guesswork they had to rely on. Back on Earth it might be enough but here…well…who knew?

'I guess it's an invitation to board,' Mitch said, stating the obvious. 'It looks like a rapid transit vessel of some kind, so wherever we're destined to go, I suppose this is the means of getting there.' Mitch bent down and hopped aboard, looking at them, urging them to do the same thing.

On entering, Sean noticed instead of individual chairs this time, there were two solid strips of soft metal about two metres high and a similar distance long. Set into each of the two strips were three concave depressions angled slightly backward. Park benches, was Jessy's immediate thought. To Sean at least it was fairly clear what they were.

'Follow me,' he said as he walked over to the metal plates and placed his back and backside into one of the imprints. 'This is incredible, so soft and...stabilizing.'

Sean was immersed in the metal surface so that about half of his back and rear end were encased in the warm, gripping seat. From the look on Sean's face, and the 'aarrr' noise, it was clearly a pleasant experience. What the hell sort of material is this he wondered as it rubbed and throbbed against his flexisuit as though he was bathing in a bubbling volcanic spring. 'I don't know how fast this thing goes, but to need support like this it must be the ultimate bullet train.'

The rest of them copied Sean's partially supine repose and were amazed at the consistency of the material that so much resembled regular saucepan metal. To press your finger in and see it penetrate the substance and feel it encase your digit was a uniquely strange experience.

Jessy likened the feeling to pushing at a railway track only to find it was made of jellyfish protoplasm, gooey glue that only had the shape and the look of railway metal. It was a tingling and unworldly feeling, seeing the sense of touch so blatantly defy the expectations of sight.

Jessy was immersed in the substance and could feel its inner warmth as the strange marrow stroked and caressed her. In spite of the situation, she started to feel aroused. She had to consciously divert her thoughts to avoid the compelling feeling. God, how strange and yes, comical, she thought. Here she was in a gluepot of gyrating alien metal on a massive space city in another galaxy and she was feeling, well...amorous. While Jessy was fighting her own flesh, the pod had sealed itself and started moving. She could see the tunnel ahead through a clear lenticular zone in the bow of the vehicle and noticed it was quite dark outside, lit only by a faint glow from the narrow throat itself.

By the growing g-forces she knew they probably weren't far from wherever they were being taken. They were going fast. She gulped at the prospect of reaching their final destination. Jessy focused on Josh who was thankfully still asleep. Christmas trees...

Sean's voice abruptly filled the pod, 'Fork in the track, er...tube ahead,' he barked without shifting his eyes from the looming Y-junction. Approaching the crossing, it zipped up the left hand side and continued its journey undisturbed by the momentary change in direction. They were all forced sideways in their slabs a little but felt no discomfort at all. Rapidly coming to a halt, they sat and watched in total silence.

Sean was impatient and restless, desperate for whatever might be next. Mitch was pumped with hope and expectation as he nervously pondered their barren surrounds. Jessy's whole demeanor bespoke anxiety and terror, despite her efforts to cast out the demons kindled by her incessant dreams. Josh was still sleeping peacefully, oblivious and totally at ease. Four humans, four contrasts.

'...here we go again,' Jessy whimpered as an opening melted into the curved rampart of the pod. She was about to add that there was no room to exit the craft because of the narrowness of the tube outside. But before she could speak, a mote of unalloyed whiteness arced onto Sean's forehead from outside the tubeway.

The pinpoint of light quickly diffused into a blinding curtain as the hole in the tunnel grew to mirror the mansized doorway in the pod. Through the matching voids they could see nothing but billowing, almost phosphorescent light that flowed through the opening and drowned them in a brilliant, twisting aura.

Jessy's eyes were buried in Mitch, her feelings vividly written. The prospect of entering the eerily lit space was not high on Jessy's list of wants. The tremor in her voice painted her feelings perfectly. Jessy closed her eyes and took a calming breath. It felt different. She didn't like it.

'I don't know about this Mitch, that light seems odd, uh...disturbing...like nothing we've seen before. Are they in there?' she asked softly, almost whimpering at the prospect.

'It's a possibility,' Mitch said casually. There was no use lying to her. Jessy could barely move anyway, she was paralysed with fear. It couldn't get much worse.

Sean said loudly, 'we have to enter, so let's get about doing it.' He spoke the words as he stepped from the pod and was immediately engulfed by the shield of light, and disappeared.

Jessy watched, still frozen, as he dissolved into a formless smudge, holding her breath as he stepped through the passageway and vanished entirely. A minute passed and he didn't reappear.

'Shit,' Jessy whispered, for a long moment staring bug-eyed at Mitch and then back at the whiteness, waiting for Sean to return. Mitch and Jessy could only stare at the apron of light, straining their eyes to discern any movement within. It was as though he'd been swallowed by a dazzling white well that had slammed shut as soon as he'd entered. He'd quite simply disappeared, descending into the light like a rock beneath a muddy stream.

'Sean?' Mitch eventually said. No reply. He tried again louder, same result. The only thing that was coming back was his own voice, bouncing, echoing off whatever manner of stuff was inside.

There was no sound from Sean at all. If he was inside, he was totally silent, which was strange in itself, unsettling certainly. Something had obviously captured his interest in a big way. Jessy tried to discern form within, but couldn't, it was too bright or the space was empty.

They turned and looked deliberately at each other, knowing that Sean's impatience to enter had forced their own hands, although they well realized that the next step was inevitable anyway. They had nowhere else to go. Forward was the only direction possible, retracing their steps not an option. It was either go forward or refuse to budge. The latter didn't appeal to anyone, not even Jessy at this point. She and they, didn't want to piss them off.

The buggy had delivered them here for a purpose and they knew what that purpose was, to enter that which lay open before them. Still, inevitable or not, it didn't make the prospect of penetrating the light any less terrifying. One look at Jessy told the story. She didn't want to move.

They inched their way into the maelstrom of dizzy brightness, adding three drumming hearts to the vascular pumping that was already deeply in residence.

As soon as they entered, Jessy felt disoriented and nauseous and actually thought she might vomit. Her head was spinning, and she could see that Mitch was suffering the same unpleasant sensation. Whiteout to the max. It was so unbelievably bright that she had to shield her eyes, and even that didn't help much. The light seemed to be inside them, as though their insides had suddenly started radiating starlight. The room felt small but as usual she couldn't make any distinction between roof, floor and walls. All the detail, if there was any, was simply washed out by the light that seemed to be constant in every direction, including down.

'I feel dizzy Mitch,' Jessy said through hands that were plastered over her face. She held both arms straight out trying to get her balance.

He glanced at her and narrowed his eyes to slits, 'I think there's less oxygen in here for some reason.' He looked confused, '...unless it's the light, bear with it, whatever it is, hopefully it'll pass.' Mitch looked around, left, right, up and down...searching. 'Where the hell is Sean?' He couldn't see him anywhere, if he was in the room, he was well and truly shrouded by the glare.

'Oh God,' Jessy whined. Her mind thickened and her thoughts slowed to treacle. The approaching figure made her bleat with terror.

'Jesus!' Mitch whispered with force as the figure grew in size and strode confidently toward them. He quickly realized it was Sean. 'Where the fuck have you been,' he yelled, his voice cracking with venom. 'You scared the shit out of me, not to mention Jessy.' He glanced at her and saw the terror and the dread flickering behind her eyes.

'Shit, fuck,' she cried, ready to run. She may as well have had her feet in starters blocks.

'Just been checking out this room,' Sean soothed, 'You must've lost me in the light. What'd you think, that I'd been abducted?' His smile stretched almost ear to ear and was only centimeters in front of Mitch's nose.

Mitch ignored the question, 'so...um, what did you find?'

'We're in a small rectangular cell about twenty metres by thirty metres, and about ten metres high. There's no detail on any of the walls or the floor. It's all stark, barren and white, and surprise, surprise, it seems to be made of the same stuff that appears to be so common in their world. As for the light, I don't know where it's coming from, but I suspect like before that it's bleeding from this substance around us.

141

'You'll also notice that the doorway we entered through has now gone.' Sean's smile disappeared, in favour of tense facial muscles and grinding teeth. He looked at Jessy whose head was bowed, jaw and fists clenched. She wanted out, that was clear to all.

Mitch and Jessy turned around and saw that the puncture had indeed vanished in favor of its former solidity, as though it had undergone a process of accelerated healing.

'So, we're stuck in here until someone lets us out, because I've looked and there's no other way out.' Sean's eyes were glazed and bulging. 'I think this may be where we meet them. This would seem the destination we've been heading for, since we stepped foot on their ship,' he said quietly.

'Let's just wait here…that is don't move,' Jessy said. She emphasised it by banging her foot down. She was tired of acquiescing to everything so easily. 'Let them come and get us,' she said, not sure if she believed what she was saying or not.

Mitch looked around and wondered, what they were supposed to do? What could they do but sit and wait...but wait for what? He felt his mind tilt at the prospect of what could happen. The possibilities were endless and not all of them were pleasant. But they were only possibilities.

There was nothing in the room that resembled chairs so they had little choice but to do their waiting either standing or sitting on the floor. There'd been no attempt to make them feel comfortable, which was worrying in itself, it was just a room, an empty bright room, prosaic and unsettling.

Sean was still nosing the walls, hunting for some sign of imperfection or anything that might indicate a blemish or a deformity, or suggest something different. Something apart from boring sameness. The basis of their technology: boring sameness. There wasn't a flaw or a bump anywhere.

Always the inquiring mind, no matter what the circumstances. Mitch was glad Sean was here, for he could be relied on to keep a level head, and more than anyone else would refuse to be overawed by the extraordinary. If there was to be an encounter, a profound encounter, it was Jessy he was worried about. She was a goddamn space cadet, as fragile as they came. He was surprised how delicate she was. He'd learned a lot on this mission, about himself, and more particularly, about others. Others meant Jessy.

Time. An hour passed and nothing happened. No noise, no movement, nothing. Just the light and the distant thunder of their own heartbeats. They all suffered the gnawing effects of the anodyne enclosure. Maybe nothing was going to happen but that didn't make sense. Why were they here? Jessy thought she heard something, but it only turned out to be Sean humming some fucking inane tune. Christ, he could be annoying.

Instinctive fear was gradually congealing into something sinister and mind altering, into frenzied visions of something rearing up at them from the blanket of bright whiteness, something impossibly grotesque. Logical thought was dissolving as time passed, strangled by the jagged uncertainty of their plight, fed by too much time spent in the featureless white expanse.

Too much time to think. They simply had too much time to ponder and speculate, and from Jessy's point of view, to fantasize in a vivid rainbow of bizarre imaginings.

How long? Sean kept asking himself. Twenty minutes earlier, the wall adjacent to where they were standing had sphinctered and broken like a limestone sinkhole.

Looking through with breathless expectation, they saw an exact replica of the bathroom that had appeared on the alien vessel, complete with glasses and water and everything else they'd seen. Every detail was exactly as it had been before. Sean was desperately worried that they were in for a long wait. They'd expected the profound and got a bathroom. Again.

While Sean was deep in thought about that very idea, a bright and distinctly yellow point of light ignited from nowhere almost directly above his head. The light in the room changed immediately to a more sedate pale yellow, the source of which was hovering above them like a luminous primrose sun.

Sean's face imploded. 'Thank God,' he enthused before he even knew what had happened. Something, Sean enthused. Jessy shuddered and stiffened, her frozen eyes straining upward at the imperious light. 'What in God's name is it?' Jessy said rigidly. It's not them, that was the main takeaway. Some five metres above the floor, a bright dot, perhaps only a centimetre across, grew slowly and steadily until it reached the size of a basketball. It was a perfect sphere that simply hung there motionless, very much starlike in appearance although clearly not radiating any heat.

The swelling disk suddenly shattered and jumped outward slightly, becoming fuzzy and blurred as though it was a star and had just turned on...somehow achieving nuclear burning.

Sean watched the miniature flares and galloping swirls as they ebbed and flowed on the surface of the thing. It confirmed what was sprinting through his mind. Visually at least, it was a star.

'What the...?' Mitch said as he stumbled from underneath the object to get a better look. Jessy was terrified, she knew it was starting. Her eyes were enormous as she looked not at the light source, but around, expecting anything...anywhere.

Several other objects started to accrete from millions of spinning pinpoints, giving birth to spheres that immediately started rotating on their axes. After a minute or so the lesser orbs started dancing around the "star" in circular patterns and it became quickly obvious what it was. They were looking at a scale representation of what was almost certainly their own solar system. Jessy peered at her feet, she didn't want to look up.

The third globe from the "star" suddenly inflated until it was fully a metre through the middle, growing at the expense of the others which shrivelled and dimmed then quickly shattered and vanished to leave only the vivid representation of number three, of blue Earth, hanging totally still almost directly in front of them. It was their world alright. Jessy could see the familiar continents, the swirling clouds and an orbiting Moon with all the larger craters, as far as she could tell, in the right place. It's perfect she thought, finally looking closely, feeling gut wrenchingly nervous.

Sean rubbed his chin with the point of his thumb. 'They're telling us they know where we come from,' he said quietly.

'But how can they know that?' Jessy asked, 'How can they know so much and be so precise about Earth. Are they saying they've been there, is that what they're telling us?' Jessy looked horrified. Maybe some of the stories are true, she thought.

'Maybe,' Sean said, 'but it's more likely they've observed us from a distance, intercepting our transmissions. Remember how close the probe was to Earth when we first saw it. Less than a light year. No doubt it had the ability to intercept our radiation. It had uncountable protuberances, any of which might act as microwave sensors, probably with unimaginable sensitivity. So, they've been spying on us,' Sean said, more as a statement than a question.

'It's the most reasonable explanation,' Mitch offered as he stretched his arm up and almost managed to touch the large blue spheroid, only failing by a few centimeters. As his hand was in the motion of reaching upward, the "Earth" fragmented, dissolving into a billion shimmering flecks and disappearing like a dying magnesium flare.

'...did I do that?' Mitch gasped, looking closely at his hand, expecting to see so much burnt skin and exposed gristle.

'I doubt it,' Sean exclaimed quickly. 'I don't think it matters what we do, we're part of some masterplan that is pretty much beyond our control. All we can do is wait for their next move.' Reveal yourselves, he emplored. For fuck's sake do it, he implored silently, reckoning it was time.

'Masterplan, yes I think that's right,' Jessy agreed, nodding her head vigorously. She continued to look around, still expecting anything to pop up from anywhere.

The show had apparently finished, terminating with another increase in light levels. Their prison was once again devoid of anything but consuming whiteness.

'So, they know where we come from,' she said softly. 'Big deal.' The sarcasm and the frustration painted over a dark dread. 'Surely they could have...' she paused in midsentence as the light dimmed and levelled off at a more bearable glow.

'Look...' Sean yelled, pointing briefly upward, 'it's starting again.'

A new light, a new star had begun to congeal above their heads like a ball of clotting amber. It was noticeably orange this time and was slightly more rotund than the Sun had been. Again, several other lesser dollops accreted and formed rotating pseudo planets that swarmed around the parent sphere. It was a depiction of another star system, not the solar system this time. 'That was this…er, their star, right?' Jessy had an empty feeling in the pit of her stomach.

The inner two rocks were pale and barren with heavily cratered faces. The third was a Venusian world, obscured by what appeared to be impermeable vapor that they could see swirling and eddying around the globe. The detail and clarity of the mockups was astounding. It was as though these worlds were real, only an arm's length away.

The smoggy planet was clearly the one they'd seen near the exit of the wormhole, with its partial ring system and moons that orbited far away. There was no doubt that it was the same one. To put it beyond doubt, the fourth and fifth planets were those that occupied space below them, both blue and white and uncannily Earthlike.

'That's this system, right?' Jessy stated more than asked. 'They're showing us where we come from, and er…now where we are, where they come from.'

'No doubt,' Mitch responded, glued to the beauty and the perfect choreography of the multidimensional display. It had a symmetry and synergy that made it look profoundly different…more profoundly real than anything he'd ever seen before.

Before Jessy could continue, the star and most of the planets dissolved, leaving only the double planets that like Earth before, inflated to an impressive size. The twin planets started to revolve around each other and the artificial rings grew slowly by degree, extending rhythmically around each of the globes. Then they started rotating on steeply inclined axes. The sight was magnificent, Jessy conceded. Washed with white light, the colorful planetary vista possessed a supernatural beauty and coordination. Not to mention detail.

Mitch peered spellbound as the image of the two vibrant worlds diminished in size by about half, and rose to within a metre or so of the ceiling. Underneath them, an image or more accurately a three dimensional and extraordinarily defined hologram appeared from nowhere.

Mitch felt his breath ripped from his lungs. 'Sweet...' he croaked, running out of breath, looking fixedly at the new image that hovered above them. The new likeness that appeared wasn't so much unbelievable as totally unexpected. Being the only one fluent in chemistry, Mitch was the first to recognize the simple atomic configuration being portrayed above them.

'Holy shit,' he stuttered. An atom...a carbon atom...are they telling us that they're made from the same stuff we are...that they're carbon based?'

Sean nodded slowly, his eyes fixed on the floating figure. That has to be it, He reckoned, clearing his throat loudly. 'Revelation at last,' Sean hoped, holding the back of his neck while he gawked up. He was completely dazed. Keep it going, he implored.

'Dear sweet Jesus,' Jessy groaned, feeling a fine layer of sweat ooze from her pores and coat her body with a fine patina of ice water. What do you look like? She said to herself, with eyes staring as though she were in a trance.

The image of the carbon atom shrunk to the size of the planets, and like the others, retreated upward toward the ceiling. It was replaced by what appeared to be an impossibly complicated and disorganized knot of unmeaning. Floating icons showed chains and loops of gibberish molecules. She understood some of it but certainly not all of it. The whole midair region of the room was crammed with odd looking images.

'Chemistry was never my strong point at ANU,' Jessy grunted, straining at the organic soup that filled the room like a lecturer's blackboard in 3D. 'Remember, life is just chemistry', she said still feeling fluttery in the stomach. She wondered again what the hell she was doing here.

'It's more than just chemistry,' Mitch returned. 'I think they're trying to indicate their similarities...indicate their origins...trying to make us feel more comfortable. More at ease perhaps.' Hallelujah to that, she thought. Seriously, hallelujah to that.

Mitch stared at the images, trying to recall his organic chemistry when another image appeared. Drinking in its detail, his throat almost closed as he tried to get his voice out. He felt like he'd swallowed a river rat that was struggling in his throat.

144

'...that's uh, that's RNA,' he wheezed brokenly, 'It must be, look at it, single thread, twisted, studded with what I suppose is, uh...uracil and ribose.' He patted his chin and remained staring rigidly upward. Are these alien genetics? He pondered, astounded by the familiarity of what he was seeing.

Next to the image a new form gradually condensed, borrowing bits and pieces from the chemical muddle that shuffled around it. Eventually, a deep green and stunningly defined form was born, and it contrasted brilliantly with the pure whiteness behind it. They all knew what it was, but to Mitch at least, it looked a bit odd. Jessy knew it was odd as well, RNA definitely, but it had extra bits, Jessy could see, well...she thought she could see.

Sean could almost feel his mind burn through his scalp as the story of them gained impetus and started unfolding above him. He thought he knew what the plot was, but more importantly, he wondered about the conclusion, he wondered how the story would finish. Where was all this leading? To what? Or to whom, his brain filled with thick fog.

Mitch's head was still twisted upward at a strange angle, as though he'd been involved in some tragic accident, '...and who would've doubted the next installment. DNA, absolutely no doubt,' he said, tapping his lips with a fist. His neck started to hurt as he continued to look upward.
There was something odd about it though. Mitch frowned as he scanned the image. He could see that it was somehow too complicated...and its orientation didn't look right either, but still there was no doubting what it was.

'That's DNA but, er....' He looked again, straining upward and he saw the problem, rubbing the back of his neck hard to try and loosen it. There were definite differences, very basic variations that he should have seen immediately. 'It's lefthanded,' he blurted. 'Our DNA is wound in a righthanded way but this goes in the other direction, uh...to the left. It's a mirror image of Earth.' Southpaw DNA, he mused, pursing his mouth to continue, '...there's three chains of nukes instead of two, which is why it looks so complicated...the helix is blurred by an extra chain. DNA with differences.' The stuff of the Universe', he exclaimed. Jessy just gawked, couldn't understand a thing.

Mitch thought about it and was thunderstruck, not by the differences this time, but by the dazzling grains of parallel development he could see. It was a double helix, blurred by a higher complexity, but it was still there. Quite distinctly. It was probably chemically the same, but physically Mitch could see its endoskeleton was very different. A pseudomorph, he reckoned, or maybe artificially extended ..., or just different.

He continued babbling and pointing at the image like some manic street corner prophet. If these were alien genetics, then the parallels were nothing less than stunning, but deep down he knew he shouldn't be surprised. Not surprised at all. The odds were always stacked in favor of others being similarly protein based. After all, it had happened once before...on Earth. DNA was a proven life carrier. Although it was profoundly conceited to make assumptions, what other evidence was there?

Despite all that, he was still stupefied by the probable confirmation of such poorly founded Earthly theorems. He also realized that the actual form of those that had brought them here, their physical appearance, could be anything. Literally anything. What did the differences in the DNA structure really mean? The DNA of chickens, mice and dogs looked pretty much the same, and they were almost indistinguishable from humans.

What implications did the clear differences hold for physical form? He pondered the question briefly, suddenly blinded by the light that turned on near the centre of his brain. He swallowed heavily and shook his head, thinking it was time.

Jessy took a final look at the genetics above and fought rising panic, pretty much knowing what was coming next. After all, what was left? The figure rotated and slid upward, diminishing in size as it went.

Sean had always wondered just how unique DNA was. Was it some unimaginable fluke...an unrepeatable miracle, or was it simply geochemistry becoming biochemistry? Was it the outworking of some natural evolutionary inertia that was built into the heart of the Universe? And now he knew, it wasn't a fluke at all. Despite the differences, it was still DNA. If they were reading it right, the planets below and the rings around them were filled with creatures that had a similar genetic substratum as they did. It was just a tad different. He watched, the helices above him unwind and separate after being briefly consumed by a foggy haze. Two copies of the unwound strands appeared, now there were six strands dancing above them.

'Reproduction,' Sean whispered, staring wide eyed at the image above, at what was happening around and to it.

'The Editor,' Mitch said distantly, knowing precisely what had just happened. 'The polymerase makes sure that everything is copied just so and if it's not, it cuts and splices it back together like it should be. It's Earth...it's just like bloody home Sean,' Mitch said quietly, pumping a fist at Sean who was smiling broadly.

'They're trying to put us at ease ... as far as they can.' Jessy said, repeating Mitch's earlier contention. She hoped that's what they were doing. If they were, it was a good sign.

Sean eyeballed Mitch. 'So much for the alternate life theory,' he whispered.

'Oh, I think they're alternate alright,' Mitch said, '...just not made from silicon or sulfur with an ammonium solvent, and that's no surprise to me and it wouldn't be a surprise to any of the scientific bods on Earth either.'

'But I wouldn't expect them to look like you or I.' Jessy glanced up apprehensively.

'Do you know how many physical permutations the carbon atom can provide?' Mitch prodded,... 'think of all the animals back home...there's more than a million species you know. Trillions of permutations, legs, arms, heads, eyes, we should rid ourselves of any preconceptions or expectations of form. Christ, they might be plantlike, you know flora-forms. Anything's possible. Our DNA looks pretty much the same as bananas and chickens, best we all remember that.'

The entire group of images vanished and was replaced by the image of Earth and its solar system. Underneath were human images. A man and a woman, finely detailed, showing muscular and skeletal configurations together with major organs, minor organs and a whole lot more besides.

'And they got this detail from television?' Jessy asked softly, believing her every word was being listened to and scrutinized. 'Surely not from TV...the detail,' she whispered. 'Or is it from us?'

'It's the only way, apart from direct involvement, er...that is, dissection or imaging,' Mitch said, making zero eye contact. He didn't want to set her off or worse, Sean. They all looked at each other, realizing the implications of the statement. Sean looked at Jessy and was about to speak, but Mitch beat him.

'No, I don't think they've visited Earth and cut people up! I've never believed the stories and still don't...although it is interesting.' Mitch looked at Jessy and scratched his chin thoughtfully. They probably got the information from us since we entered their craft.'

Sean nodded. Jessy felt queasy thinking about the analyses and the scrutiny that might have happened, might still be happening, without their knowledge.

The images and holograms vanished same as before and the room was again totally empty save for the white light that continued to fill the enclosure. After ten minutes of sitting and waiting, mostly in silent contemplation, Jessy toed carefully over to the wall nearest her and tentatively poked at it with an index finger.

Although strangely drawn to the cadaverous surface, she'd only just summoned the courage to approach it, and as she expected, it was soft and rubbery. Up close she saw it was minutely pocked with what could have been tiny pinholes, in contrast to the parallel linear textures they'd all previously seen. It was also sticky, somehow gluey and adhesive, perhaps even biomagnetic, seeming to grab her finger as she tried to withdraw it. It seemed to have its own magnetic field. What the hell is this stuff? Her brain was doing cartwheels trying to extract answers from nothing. She had no idea, it was so alien to Earth.

Jessy was about to call Mitch when the striking image of the twin planets returned near the centre of the room. As it appeared, the lights reduced in intensity again, but only slightly this time.

Like dying stars, the dual worlds ate themselves outward, swelling and dimming, proceeding to dance and wheel several metres above the floor. Mitch focussed up and rubbed his eyes roughly.

Sean's heart was pumping like a windmill in a tornado. His mind had done the sums, and come to an irrefutable conclusion. They all knew it was time. Jessy pushed her arms out to stop falling to the floor. She was lightheaded and felt bilious.

'...what now?' Jessy shrilled, wondering what the sudden reappearance meant. She didn't have to wait long for the mind bending answer which she knew was coming. A figure sculpted itself from nothing, and it was more vivid and more stunningly eurhythmic in form than the most exquisitely hewn Tsumeb azurite.

The figure thrust them into earsplitting silence, swamping their senses with a dizzyingly traumatic rush of disbelief. It loosened their reason, sending it crashing against the bony cages of their struggling minds. In a millisecond their expressions were hammered into masks of repulsion and shock, to the point where they were unable to immediately comprehend where they were or what they were looking at. Jessy was tingling all over, breathless and shuffling back a step, overwhelmed by a racing heart, to the point she was certain she was dying. Who was she? She had no idea. What was above her was totally unexpected. Everything she thought they might be, they weren't. Their minds were consumed by what they were seeing, bleeding every conceivable emotion in a pluvial downpour of confusion and dread.

They knew what it was but they couldn't think or see through the haze of disbelief that was being coughed up like cognitive lapilli by their faltering brains. They were expecting revelation, but they weren't ready for it ... probably would never have been ready for it. The image. Jessy's bowels felt loose and her legs were like day old Jello beneath her. Sean stumbled closer for a better look, but Mitch could only stand there, glued to the spot, staring through massive eyes that incredibly, were getting larger and rounder. He thought of himself as a young boy, reading Carl Sagan, wishing...hoping. And here he was.

Jessy swayed visibly, catching onto Mitch's arm at the last second to stop herself crumpling to the floor like a boneless fish. Sean cried instinctive tears of joy, overcome by unequivocal wonder and total, thorough, complete astonishment. Others. This is what they looked like. Finally.

Dancing in front of them was a single image of a manifestly alien life form. A life form they all assumed was a facsimile of those that had brought them here and which inhabited the worlds below them, and probably the rooms around them. The rooms around them...

There was only silence and stillness as the three stared at the motionless image. They all believed that something was going to be revealed to them in the white room, but the revelation of physical form shocked them to the marrow.

Silence persisted as Sean searched for his voice. Others. He couldn't get past it. Expected, but totally, utterly unexpected. What did they expect, fuck knew? Not this.

Jessy finally managed to mutter a broken sentence as she continued staring at it, '...so...that's them, that's what they look like...they've got three arms...three fucking arms,' she repeated hoarsely. Triformers, Mitch thought. Amazing. He expected no less.

'Incredible,' Sean finally murmured, '...look at the head and the fingers, there's five on two hands and, er... four on the um...middle thing. Hell, that's fourteen in all, and the head. I would never have pictured them like this, but then, I'm not sure how I pictured them. Smaller, I think, thanks to Hollywood. They look solid and they're probably tall as well, though it's hard to tell.' Sean ambled closer and edged around the hologram, breathing it all in.

'They're ugly,' Jessy muttered, drawing in a shaky breath, still trembling inside. 'The skin, the hair...the carbuncled head...Jesus. I wonder what they think of us? They probably reckon we look primitive, and hell, maybe even hideous...although perhaps they've had experience with others such that physical form is of no consequence. They're probably unshockable. But why don't they come out in person, why the hologram?' Jessy asked huskily, staring from underneath the image.

'To reduce the shock,' Mitch suggested. By revealing their form, they've reduced it, although by how much it's hard to say. Imagine if they'd just sauntered out and walked up to you.'

Jessy thought about it and was mortified, '...you're right. Christ...you're absolutely right.' She glanced back at the image and shuddered, her shoulders sagging under the weight of what was hanging so casually in midair. Jessy felt stiff and found it difficult to move as she continued to stare at the image. Her legs were heavy, her mind a bit fuzzy and she flinched when Mitch touched her.

'So that's them, Jesus,' Mitch said, looking at the image, wondering how evolution worked on their world, wondering how the hell it ended up with that.

'We should prepare ourselves,' Sean said slowly. 'Their preparations must be about complete. Bar coming out in person I can't see what else they can do.' They've laid the groundwork, now it was time surely. Sean was choking on a tingling, almost hallucinatory expectation at the possibility of contact. It still seemed like a dream, a dazzling fantasy born of impossible desires and juvenile imagination. Intelligent aliens. He really couldn't believe he was here.

'They must be coming out in person,' Mitch agreed, pointing fleetingly at the airborne figure. Surely this won't be the only contact we have with them.' He glanced at Sean who was staring back at him, like a snowman with golf ball eyes.

'If they don't come out, I'll go looking for them,' Sean grinned quickly at Mitch.

Mitch knew Sean would eventually start hammering on the walls if that's what it took to coax them out. *"Hello out there...come in for God's sake. There's Earthlings to meet!"*

The images disappeared abruptly and the light resumed its painful intensity. Standing in the middle of the room, they shielded their eyes and again they waited. Sean scanned the room for movement. Jessy was sure she'd fall down if she tried to take a step. *Timber.*

Sean was sure the moment he'd been waiting for was near, unless he was reading the signs wrong. Yes, they were ugly, but they were other life.

The emptiness of the room left them all feeling more exposed than ever. Mitch didn't reckon they were in danger but even a chair or anything to break up the stark empty whiteness would have been comforting.

Sslluuuurrrppp. A faint noise began off to their left. Something was happening at the far end of the cell, and they all knew what that something might be. They were too far away to see exactly what had made the noise but there was a sudden contrast, a dark smudge against the encompassing milkiness, and it was growing.

Something was clearly looming. Approaching. Sean couldn't tell what it was, but he could tell it was big. They were all gaping as one toward the far wall, the focused eye of humanity, watching and waiting, hearts drumming almost as a single organ. It was a smudge, that's all they could tell. Jessy felt like closing her eyes and rolling into a ball. All of this was way beyond her pay grade.

As the darkness grew, its form solidified and its identity became quickly obvious to everyone except Jessy. She grabbed at Mitch as she slid slowly to the floor in a dead faint. He picked her up and brought her slowly, groggily back. '

Starting off as a cleft in the white fabric, the darkness quickly grew through a predefined pattern, from a quantum sized rip to a metric doorway. An entry that led into a dim chamber. She was sure the chamber was still bright but not as bright as the room they were standing in, like a sunspot. Although it was many metres away, they could see it and recognize it for what it was.

'...my God,' was Jessy's whispered cry,. 'They're going to emerge through there aren't they?' She felt physically sick with the enormity of their plight. Run, was her brain scream. But run to where? Quite simply, there was nowhere to go...no way out.

'Hopefully,' Sean answered before Mitch could open his mouth. 'Of course, it's just as likely that we'll meet a robot or a synthetic something, as one of them, although the holograms would suggest that they'll come out in person. Perhaps it'll be some sort of variation on the turtle we saw before...remember anything's possible.' Sean gave Jessy a salute, although he felt like throwing up.

Mitch's eyes glazed slightly contemplating what they were on the verge of. He was a part of what might prove to be a standout moment in Man's three million year narrative.

In the thousands of millennia since H habilis had strutted the planet, humans had come far. Achieved a complex technology, forged a global society, and even built ferries to other worlds...but today he thought, right now, we may well, truly come of age.

Our juvenile philosophy would expand like the most extravagant supernova. And he, Mitch Taylor was here, would be part of it. He savoured the thought and compared it with his own conquest of Mars. He could almost taste the same throbbing emotions taking root in his heart. The same ones that gripped him when his left and then his right boot sunk into the red and orange ferri-dust for the first time. When he looked behind himself to see a single ribbed boot print hewn in the belly of Mars. His footprint. He realised how full of it he was being, but he reckoned he couldn't help it.

Jessy was crying. Tears were running down her cheeks. She couldn't stop it although she tried. Staying calm and unemotional wasn't an option, and despite digging fingernails into her thighs, the glistening rivers continued. Until she looked down at Josh, she'd been okay...but what a future he had, or didn't have, she wondered. The future was right now. She wasn't crying at the profundity of the moment, she was crying for Josh. The probability of Earth destroyed and them fated to live who knew what sort of existence in space aboard Cygnus or perhaps here on these unfamiliar alien rocks. She looked at Joshua and cried, for his future and for their future and she was still crying when the blackness of the adjoining room changed color. They all detected other motion in the room.

They stared, unable to draw breath as the two creatures walked slowly, almost casually toward them. Even at distance and with no objects in the room, they could tell that they were tall. Monumentally so. Big and very tall.

None of the three breathed for a long time. Sean gulped and almost choked but finally cleared his airway with several piercing coughs. Mitch simply stared without expression, disbelief written in his slack, open mouth and wide, bulging eyes. Jessy wanted to run, to hide, to put some distance between them and the approaching...whatever they were. Jessy still had little feeling in her legs and was sure she would topple over if she tried to move. The hair stood up on her skin and as they came closer, a strange pressure built in her throat and between her ears. It felt like she was a long way underwater. She suddenly couldn't hear a thing.

'...shit,' Jessy wheezed under her breath, staring at the floor.

'Steady,' Mitch soothed, not breaking his stare, unable to break his stare.

'Jesus...they're incredible,' Sean hissed, intoxication dripping from every word.

The two xenoforms padded to within a few metres of the three and stopped abruptly without slowing down. They had faces certainly, but no expression, or none they could read anyway. Just blankness that looked almost like disinterest. Surely that couldn't be right, could it? Mitch wondered, staring wide-eyed at the two aliens. Both had knots of callused flesh on the right sides of their craniums, proximate to where their temples might have been. Sean watched in awe as it quivered and vibrated at rapidly altering speeds.

It would vibrate rapidly, slow down, stop, fast again, stop. Jessy could taste bile in her mouth. Jessy reckoned the squirming flesh looked like a pulsating heart. Like some sort of goitrous external heart. Fuck, she thought and averted her eyes. She couldn't look at it, not yet.

'They're crying for God's sake,' Jessy said under her breath, not really having a clue what they were doing. Both creatures had what looked like tears emanating from shallow set eyes that looked disturbingly feline. None of the emotions that went with crying, if that's what they were doing, were evident on their faces. They still appeared thoroughly disinterested. Perhaps their eyes were naturally fluid filled.

The two suddenly extended their middle appendages and held their four digits out, clearly searching for something to grasp. 'What the...' Mitch gasped, and stepped backward.

Sean was standing at the front of the earthly group. 'They want to shake hands I think...I guess they want to greet us. TV', he reminded himself.

'Shit, of course,' Sean said, 'TV...they want to shake hands.'

He took the hand of the leading being with little hesitation. His tiny primate hand was lost in the bulk of the four fingered thing. He shook the paw and the shaking was immediately returned. Did they get that from our carrier waves? he wondered as he watched the expressionless creature probe him with eyes that were barely half open and very moist.

Jessy stared at them and looked disgusted. She may as well have had her tongue hanging out of her mouth. As it was, she almost had her eyes closed and her nose crinkled and twitching with distaste. It was hardly the ideal hello.

Sean felt like he was drowning in a dreamlike aura that made him tingle and tremble from head to toe. Should he attempt to say something? He wasn't sure. If so, what? His mind was blank. Perhaps he should've put more thought into it .

'Uh...Sean,' he eventually croaked, pointing to himself and making what he assumed would be a fruitless effort to communicate. He felt he had to try though, what else could he do? Stand there and stare in silence like a dummy? There was no response apart from a sustained vibration of the knotted head flesh. He was starting to feel self-conscious, glancing from Sean to Jessy and to the creatures. He wasn't sure what he should do, sure as hell they weren't doing anything.

Jessy was still staring, not moving, looking like an owl, scanning their faces closely while remaining at a decent distance.

Mitch forced himself forward and took the other's hand and repeated the arcane gesture. Jessy remained totally immobile, still unable to move, still unable to breathe properly. Her eyes had opened and were almost sitting on her cheeks.

'Their skin is warm,' Sean murmured as he moved back to where Jessy was standing. 'Slightly sticky...much, much hotter than ours, almost like warm bread...not quite cooked.' Alien damper, he thought instantly.

The details weren't helping Jessy, who still looked drop-dead scared. Her eyes were huge and she was swallowing hard. Jessy was numbed by their unearthly flesh and the gristly dark arteries that were easily visible through the pasty and partly transparent skin. Her eyes were bugging out as she gaped at them. The veins in their foreheads and temples were at least half a centimeter thick and she could see them branching and interconnecting and pulsing with fluid...throbbing and twisting with alien blood that was dark but didn't look red. Maybe they had black blood. Shit, Jessy swore, silently appalled. Who...what were these things? Evolution, she had to keep reminding herself.

The sight in front of them was indescribably bizarre. The yellow-centered eyes, the throbbing veins, the pallid flesh, and the three upper limbs all clotted in Jessy's mind like heavily floured soup. She tried to fight the lightheadedness and tried not to look too closely, but it was hard...it was impossible, despite their grotesqueness. Their oddness demanded to be looked at, to be stared at like some hideous circus freak. She equated it with looking at a car crash. There was no way she could touch these creatures, not yet. The quiet urging of Mitch and Sean was ignored and she remained immobile and safely out of reach. At the moment. She knew she'd have to give in eventually. The last thing she wanted to be was rude. She was on their turf after all.

Jessy squirmed when Sean shook its hand and she saw the pendulous grippers reach a quarter of the way to his elbow. And it was starting to smile when it touched him. Its nearly human mouth was flicking upward at the edges, giving at least the appearance of a smile, but it could have been some other Godforsaken response or emotion with which they were totally unfamiliar.

No ears?' Jessy whispered, 'There's no holes where ears should be. Do they hear?'

'Why don't you ask them, because it's the only way we'll know., They might hear through their nostrils,' Mitch whispered, grinning at Jessy who still looked terrified.

The two aliens stepped backward and stood appraising their guests for several minutes, not moving, certainly not saying anything. Sean, Mitch and Jessy did the same, with Sean standing at the front and Mitch and Jessy a metre or so behind. It looked like a bizarre Mexican standoff...a celestial modus vivendi.

'The clothing they're wearing,' Jessy began, 'they both look fairly much identical.'

'I think so,' Sean said, 'But I doubt they're made from cotton or Rayon. Look at the way it flows when they move...it doesn't crease or buckle.'

'The ultimate in comfortable office wear', Mitch said, still staring at it.

'Yeah, good one...idiot.' Sean said, smiling widely at him. That's good, Mitch thought, smiling back at, Sean's relaxing a bit.

150

Stepping slowly and deliberately around Sean, the two beings made their way toward Mitch and Jessy. She saw them coming and the gut-wrenching fear returned in an avalanche. Her pulse surged and her head crawled with a terrifying white light that throbbed in time with her heartbeat. At Mitch's insistence she remained completely still, stiff and inert, like set concrete. It wasn't hard, Jessy was frozen to the spot, not thinking, drawing in quick and painful breaths.

'Hold your ground Jessy...breathe and stay calm.'

'I couldn't move if I wanted to.' She murmured. The words dribbled through the almost lipless line of her mouth. All blood had been expelled.

'They just want to say hello, don't move Jess.' The knot in her throat pinched tighter and her eyes swelled with fluid as they approached. Sean stared fascinated as the two squared off with Mitch and Jessy, standing and facing them from only a metre away. Jessy's eyes told the story. She wanted out. Stay put, Sean pleaded silently. He knew first impressions could be important.

Raising their compound arms, the creatures unexpectedly placed them over the two. Jessy cried out and swayed backward, an involuntary reflex, totally instinctive. She backed away from the two and moved toward the wall.

'Jessy,' Mitch implored, 'Come back...' She was over by the wall and didn't want to come back. She didn't want to be touched. Or for that matter, do anything that involved getting closer to the two creatures. They felt warm and sticky and their skin squirmed with horrible venal life, but equally she knew there was little choice. They would get her in the end. Slowly, Jessy edged her way forward until she again stood beside Mitch, glancing nervously up at him with vision that was beginning to blur. They immediately returned their arms to her, like a squid embracing its prey. Mitch and a still sleeping Joshua had already been touched all over by the creature to the left of her. Now it was her turn.

'Perhaps this is their idea of a friendly greeting,' Mitch whispered, as the arms released him.

A bit...too friendly.' Jessy squealed and closed her eyes. She could actually feel the pain from her straining heart and looked down, fully expecting to see it drumming like an African bongo through her flexisuit. Starting on top of her head, the arms moved in a patting motion as they touched every square centimetre of that part of her body that was facing them. Its middle limb moved over her breasts and circled down to her stomach. It remained totally expressionless. Just moist eyes and pulsing. Jessy was nearly crying with fear, and nausea was smothering her but she didn't move, trembled and shook, but didn't move. Mitch held her hand tightly. Its clasper moved down from her stomach and moved over her pelvis and lingered there. She held her breath. The paw inched downward along her thighs to her feet and was eventually off her. The creatures retreated backward a couple of steps and stopped, still facing them.

Mitch saw the twisted goitre on the creature nearest him swell slightly and start to beat like a drum, more rapidly than it had before. He felt a tight tingling sensation beneath his temple and was struck by the realization that he could hear and comprehend words, English words that weren't coming from any of the others. Sean gestured with his arms to say "it ain't us".

He was being welcomed to something that sounded like Eljit. Mitch turned around and confirmed that Sean and Jessy were obviously hearing the same thing.

'What the hell...?' Sean mumbled, looking around, searching for the source of the sudden noise. Jessy was staring at Mitch, her unblinking eyes boring into him as she focused on the echoing syntax in her head.

Sean realized what was happening and he was stunned, but after considering it, not really all that surprised. He heard a thump behind him and turned to see Jessy in a heap on the ground. She obviously found the sound rather surprising.

'What the...again?' Mitch time kneeled down to help her and quickly dragged her back to her feet. 'We'll have to watch her, if she keeps fainting, she might end up breaking something.'

'That voice...was inside my head,' Jessy wheezed, breathing hard, looking at Mitch.

'They're talking to us,' Mitch said as he eyed them, 'not talking as in talking...they're inserting their speech...their words...directly into us.'

151

Jessy shook her head and rubbed her eyes. 'How can they know our language, I know they've seen our TV, but without any real perspective how could they decipher it to the point of being fluent...how?' She peered up at Mitch with cow eyes.

'Who knows,' Mitch admitted, 'But they've either done it or developed some sort of communication that overcomes that sort of difficulty, that transcends the phonemic difficulties of individual syntax. Sounds impossible but maybe we've just heard the proof.'

'It can't be...can it? Jessy said, trying desperately to understand, not the words, but how they imparted their language, how they got it directly in our heads? No doubt they did it all the time but that didn't reduce its impact on them. They all gaped at each another, dazzled by what was rattling around in their brains.

The two stunning creatures introduced themselves as Renchjiok IV ("Renchock") and Zamindar IX. In a tight voice, Mitch presented himself and the three others and wondered if he'd receive a response. He knew they could transmit, but without ears as they would define them, could they hear? Surely, they must be able to, he decided. But then again, who the fuck knew?

The answer was swift. Zamindar responded by welcoming them to their home planets in perfect English. It was eloquent and without accent or inflection. He told them they had been searching for cognitive creatures for eons. Sean was stunned by the knowledge that this was their first encounter. They'd looked for that long, and we were the first, Sean thought, stunned by the realization. 'The first,' Sean repeated. Jesus, he thought.

They instantly realized, with undeniable pride, that just by being, they had fulfilled the overriding aim of this ancient race. Zamindar continued the articulate welcome and while he toned, neither of the Virijians shifted their magnetic gaze from their guests. No emotion, that they could see, but plenty of iron gaze.

'My God...you've been looking for that long...and we're the first!' Sean exclaimed, truly taken aback. Maybe DNA is as rare as some say, he said silently. Even DNA with differences. Zamindar's response was immediate.

'Intelligence is a rare thing as is life on even the simplest level. You are very special indeed.' He stopped toning abruptly.

Jessy glanced up and finally found the power to push some air through her voice box. 'How do you know our language?' she asked timidly, glancing from Mitch to Zamindar, then quickly averting her eyes to the floor, unable to hold their gaze quite yet.

'You have already answered that,' came the reply. 'We have monitored your radiation and have learnt from it.'

Mitch shuddered as he considered all the crap that must be drifting through space, the porno channels, the violence, the death, the trash and the dribble. What must they think of us? They're not judgmental though, he could tell that already. They were as fascinated by us as we are by them, probably more so, given the amount of time they'd been looking.

They'd been searching for intelligence for tens of thousands of years. We'd only been doing it properly for fifty years. The difference in timescales was incomprehensible, yet still, this was their first contact. And to think that some scientific "scholars" on Earth were already starting to consider that humans might actually be alone in the Universe...already. How would they feel after looking for a thousand or ten thousand years without success? Fucking incredible, Mitch thought.

The two from Virija had been toning to one another for several minutes, leaving Mitch, Jessy and Sean none the wiser. Finally looking up, Renchjiok "spoke" to them, with his closely set, fluid filled eyes flicking over each of them first. They could apparently speak to whom they decided.

'We wish to document certain of your anatomical processes,' he said tonelessly. His unblinking gaze remained fixed, like twin lasers. They bored into her, waiting on a response.

'Oh shit, Jessy said quietly, 'Shit...shit!' she repeated louder. Her nightmares were crystallizing in a hideously detailed rush. 'And here it starts,' she cried. She opened her eyes wider looked at Mitch and then Sean, closing them again in terror, shaking her head and breathing loudly.

Mitch stepped in and spoke firmly, 'What do you mean "document"?'

152

'No way, no fucking way,' Jessy whispered with all the strength she could muster. 'No way they're touching me Mitch.' She looked directly at him, hoping he'd back her up.

'Your health will not be compromised. We only wish to collect some fluids, take some internal images and harvest some cells from specific areas of your biology. I understand your reservations but we wish to learn everything about you. We are familiar with your gross anatomy and know much about your internal structure and biochemistry. But we wish to know everything before we visit your planet.'

'Before you what?' Mitch asked, having heard very clearly. They were all gawking at Zamindar now.

'We planned to shift to a position inside your star's heliosphere, and from there make the short transit to your planet.'

'Earth is going to be destroyed,' Sean barked, ogling the sight of the two creatures.

'It will not be destroyed.' he said quickly. 'We are aware of the unique problem that has arisen with our transport and will remedy it when we return through the repaired GraviTunnel.'

Jessy looked at the creature, realizing what he was saying. '...you mean you are responsible for that mess out there. I mean, are you saying that your black hole picked up the star along the way?'

'Yes...it is regrettable.' Zamindar toned without any hint of emotion, making use of the adjective questionable. It seemed like he didn't give a toss.

'...regrettable?' Jessy asked incredulously, 'That's the reason we were out there in space. We were trying to save our planet, trying to correct the mess you created.'

'We would not have let it destroy your planet,' Renchjiok assured her.

'And how were we to know that? How in the name of good fuck were we to know that? She said, almost looking directly at Zamindar. She was looking at his neck. That was the best she could do so far. Looking at his face was, as yet, a bridge too far.

'It was unforeseen, impossible we believed. Unfortunately, not everyone was in favour of us making contact with you. There was an unexpected event, that caused one of our tugs to lose its way and, it is apparent that you know the rest of the story.'

Sean looked agitated and was glancing back and forth at the two Virijians like a reptile about to lunch on a flying insect. As soon as there was a break in the toning, he jumped in.

'...there's so much I need to know, your use of curved space, your propulsion systems, the composition of your spacecraft, your energy sources.' Sean looked at them pleadingly, praying for something...anything. His desire to learn about them was killing him, death by a thousand cuts.

'We will answer some of your questions later, but before we do, we would like an answer to our request.'

Sean looked at Mitch and they both indicated their willingness. Jessy grimaced and looked away. 'It's the only way Jess,' Sean pleaded. 'If we say no, they may refuse to cooperate with us and who can blame them, this needs to be a two-way deal. Look, they could march in here and take us by force but they clearly don't want to do that.

If we refuse, they'd probably do what they need to and we'd never know, so I think we should agree as a sign of good faith.' They both looked at Jessy, hoping she'd see sense.

'C'mon Jess,' Mitch prompted. After a minute she eventually nodded, having worked through the pro's and con's, she slowly and reluctantly nodded her head. Jessy's eyes could never lie though, Mitch and Sean could see the terror roughcast in her trembling expression. She knew she had to do it, but didn't want to. No way, she thought, looking at them. She didn't want to acquiesce, period. Mitch could go on and on and on all he liked, but she would never agree.

Sean turned to look at Zamindar and was shocked to see him smiling. At least that's what he thought he was doing. His thin bluish lips were pulled upward at the outside but in the middle, they were slack, as though they'd fallen downward from the effort of keeping the outsides up. Somehow the expression didn't look right, as if it was being forced, like a grotesque half smile, half grimace from an apoplectic face, one in the more untidy stages of leprositic attack.

Jessy looked at Zamindar and shuddered, feeling like dry retching, but realised she had little power to say no. Again, she felt like running.

'Okay we'll do it.' Jessy exhaled loudly behind him. The dread swept through her in torturous waves. Her shoulders slumped and she started trembling. With that, the Virijians moved swiftly through the puncture from where they'd emerged only minutes before. The chasm in the wall rapidly healed and they were gone as though they'd never been.

After a while Jessy spoke, 'did that really just happen?' She mewed, still trembling, gasping a bit for breath. Sean and Mitch smiled weakly. The Meeting had come and gone. Contact. Others. First communion. Call it what you like. It had actually happened. And now they were gone with nothing to show that they'd ever been.

They knew what had happened but the empty room and the lack of evidence made it already seem like a dream. A crazy delusion. Equally though, they knew it was only a ruse thrown up by their struggling minds. The experience was already being packed away and catalogued as a dream. Couldn't be real. But it was. It actually had happened.

Joshua only now woke up from what had been a long sleep and started to cry in increasingly vociferous bursts and both his arms were getting a good workout, banging on the back of the soft metal chair over which Joshpack was draped.

'Oh God,' she moaned, knowing what was in front of them. Inspections. What the hell did it really mean? She clenched her teeth and balled her fists, shaking her head as she considered her own question. 'How do we know what they're going to do while we're asleep? Who knows what their aims are, I don't like it, I've agreed to it but I feel really uncomfortable about it. We don't know a bloody thing about them...their intentions...nothing.' Jessy's mouth had fallen open and she felt like time had somehow slowed down.

'...a natural reaction,' Mitch soothed, 'But we're all in it together.' He held his arms out in a supplicating move. It didn't do much.

She blinked slowly, '...that's not very reassuring.'

'That's the best I can do Jess. We're all in it together.'

After a couple of minutes, a hole, smaller than the last, yawned on the opposite side of the room like a newly opened coal stope.

'I guess that's for us.' Sean was already walking toward it as he spoke, and inside he could see beds. There were four of them, three normal sized and one tiny and crib-like with inward curving metallic walls.

'You mean they're going to inspect Josh as well?' Jessy said in disbelief. '...and you're okay with that?' she added, glaring suspiciously at Mitch. She tried to understand him but couldn't.

'I'm sure it'll work out okay.' It was just lip service Mitch knew, but they had to try and remain positive because the next step was no longer optional, was probably never optional.

'Always the optimist.' Jessy spat, terrified at the prospect of *"inspections"*, her body was cold with dread, she rubbed her necklace and crossed herself. She doubted it would help but she did it anyway.

After much coaxing, she gently placed Josh on his side in the crib-thing and moved over and took her place on one of the very normal looking white linen and wood framed beds. They looked at them, all wondering the same thing.

Was it really wood and linen? Their structure was clearly based on intercepted data from Earth so whilst it looked right, they couldn't help but wonder what exotic substance they were really made from. Something incredible maybe, or perhaps they were composed of the real thing. The doubts and the fear of what might lie ahead was swelling in their minds like festering tumours.

The next step was fairly clear. They padded over and lay on the beds, and in under a minute fatigue grew into full-blown sleep, or more accurately, into a state closer to death than life. All three were on their backs, eyes closed, dead to the world. Josh, comfortably curled up, was also fast asleep.

Jessy could feel herself waking and despite her eyes being closed she sensed movement around her, and there was pain. Trying to scream she found no vocal power at all. Quadriplegic was her horror thickened thought. Bar some movement in her neck, Jessy had no voluntary muscle power at all and despite trying, she could only remain totally still, and silent. Jessy instantly recalled the images of her poor cousin, totally paralyzed, unable to walk, talk or even breathe on her own. Bedridden and useless, she could only communicate by blinking. Locked in syndrome. She felt her sanity slipping like a straining fault line, on the verge of yielding to an apocalyptic earthquake.

After what seemed like only minutes, but which was actually almost an hour, they awoke, all apparently none the worse for wear.

'...everyone okay?' Mitch enquired, looking first at himself and then at the others.

'Yeah...fine,' Sean eventually said, looking himself up and down, then over at Jessy. 'All good,' he reported.

Jessy didn't report her experience, maybe it was only a dream. She knew it wasn't though, the dull ache in her lower abdomen had come from somewhere real. That wasn't imagined, how the hell could a dream inflict pain? She shuddered at the thought of what had happened while they were asleep. They'd agreed to biological rape, she knew that now, and Sean and Mitch had forced her into it. Two onto one. It had happened again.

'I'm okay Mitch, I think,' Jessy offered quietly. Josh was standing up in his crib, balancing against one of the walls, banging on one of the bars. He seemed happy enough.

'Well, well,' Sean said, pointing to a passage that had appeared while they were asleep.

'How unsurprising,' Jessy said, noticing another bathroom that no doubt housed the same human essentials as the others. She was glad though, mainly for Josh because he actually seemed to like the alien fruitmeat, and there was no doubting his current hunger. She couldn't help but wish they'd show some imagination though, Pizza maybe, although the topping would probably be some sort of fruitmeat, Jessy was sure. Surely, they had intercepted pizza commercials. Christ, near space must be humming with them. She considered the traffic jam of juvenile images that must be out there, the brief portraits that would convey the at times embarrassing state of the human race.

After waiting for almost an hour, they were shaken from their mental chewings by yet another void penetrating the skin of the chamber like a birth canal readying itself for action. Peering through, they could see the familiar form of the vehicle that had sped them to their current locale. A polygonal breach in the cabin led directly to the bowels of the craft and inside they could see Zamindar. They didn't need to be told, Mitch grabbed Josh and they filed through the wall and into the pod, taking their positions in the cushioning plasma.

'Where are we going?' Mitch asked of the imposing driver who shrouded their view ahead. The noise in their heads was immediate and loud .. headache loud.

'To see some of our world, a tour if you will. Time is precious so it will be brief, no doubt too brief for you Sean but it is the best we can offer at this time.' The vessel accelerated and they were thrust gently backward in the supporting metal soup around them.

Sean murmured incoherently. He idly wondered how the pod overcame friction with the atmosphere...but the answer came before he took his next breath.

'It is powered by electromagnetics and runs in a vacuum, its velocity could be considerably greater but it is not needed.' Zamindar's toning was brief and ended abruptly.

The pod slowed and stopped, and after a few seconds an atmosphere crystallized in the narrow tube around them. They trailed Zamindar into another room, a featureless white cell, save for what appeared to be a bench of isometric controls, similar to those in the craft that had run the gauntlet of the black hole.

It was similarly encrusted with the same cytoplasmic substance, which to the human eye gave it the impression of being a million years old. Moving through the room to the far wall, Zamindar stood facing it. The mound of dough flesh that sat near his temple suddenly spasmed and a dimple ripped into the wall, deepening and widening until it was a metre or so across.

Mitch saw the emptiness of space through the swelling mouth and despite himself he gasped and stiffened, waiting for the thunder of explosive decompression, which, thinking about it, made no sense at all. He heard their horrified screams and saw them skyrocketed into the vacuum

155

beyond. It didn't happen of course, but by Jessy's expression it was clear that she had expected the same fate. It was totally against the human experience.

Mitch's surprise deepened as Zamindar ambled straight through the cavity and out into space as it were. With the creature out of his line of sight, Mitch could see a minute upright panel which he assumed was protected by a clear membrane of some sort, or at least by something that was holding the cosmos at bay.

'This is Ajiron,' Zamindar offered, 'A personal vehicle, one of billions that exist here and in the Virijian colonies.' Sean looked up quickly. Jessy looked at Sean, expecting a reaction.

'...colonies...you exist on more than these two worlds?' Sean already knew they must, their technology demanded it.

'We exist on many worlds. There are slightly less than four thousand planets that we have bioformed or directly annexed within a sphere of four hundred million light years.'

'Sweet Mother...' Sean said slowly. '...this has been accomplished by using, um, hyperspace?' Sean was reasonably sure that term would mean something to him. Non "flat" Lorentzian space he really meant. He or they were students of human language apparently, so that should mean something to him.

'You will understand and see its importance to our social organization later.'

Mitch realized that the shining bubbles he'd seen before they entered the space hub were these same craft. Thousands of them, stuck like barnacles to its skin, waiting for someone to hop in and arc away on some fantastic Lorentzian journey. He was stunned, flooded with awe by the first clues to the nature of these others.

They waited and watched as the vista was laid out before them in every direction, encompassed as they were in a totally transparent cocoon. Their view of the cosmos was mind boggling in its clarity, in its three hundred and sixty degree completeness. No human had ever been lavished with such a magnificently unimpeded perspective. It was emotional and humbling beyond words. Jessy looked at the view with one hand covering both eyes with fingers spread.

Mitch watched a massive storm slowly rotate below him, inching across a huge alien continent on the stunningly blue world, its depth of color, he thought, surpassing even that of Earth from space. His awed, staring observations were interrupted by Zamindar's sound.

'...will travel around some of the structure that is Eljipt and into the atmosphere of the planet below, although we cannot permit you to set foot on Virija at this time nor will we be visiting Trijicyon or Sjern.'

Sean looked confused. 'Why?' he asked impatiently. There was no response so he repeated the words and again there was nothing, except silence. So, he left it. He doesn't want to answer, fine.

'Leave it alone Sean,' Mitch suggested. Sean nodded, the dimple in the exoskin closed while Zamindar dexterously moved four digits over the simplistic and very nearly featureless console that lay tiny and insubstantial in front of him.

The bubble slid away from what they could now see was a sheer wall in space, a massive floating visage kilometres in depth that was lit by a dull glow that permeated most of its pliant surface. Ajiron commenced a gentle flight around the girdling ring city, and in the distance, perhaps five hundred kilometres away they could see the other polar ring where the two fabulous structures rotated past one another. The whole scene was incredible.

Sean's nose was plastered to the invisible soft skin of the craft as he fought to take everything in. They were totally surrounded by transparency, including beneath them. Surrounded by nothing as it were. The controls had gradually faded before their eyes and then abruptly winked out, vanishing totally soon after they departed. They were now motoring through space with no visible means of life support. A clear bubble took on a new meaning.

Sean felt part of the cosmos, intimate with the void in a way he'd never felt before. He felt less of a passenger and more of a denizen. A human baryon as it were, floating unimpeded on the ebb and flow of the cosmic zephyr. It was an astonishing feeling, sort of scary, made especially so by their proximity to the spectacular space city and the ponderous blue world that languished below them. They all felt something akin to vertigo when they first jumped in Ajiron, light millennia of space on either side of a craft that existed of almost nothing, the canopy disappearing soon after flight began. Jessy folded her arms across her stomach, laughing nervously at Sean, who couldn't hear her.

With unrelenting clarity, Sean could see that the sheer wall they'd just moved away from was pocked with thousands of craft identical or at least very similar to the one they were in. He gazed at the starlight glinting from the bubbles as they made their transit past them. Each was attached to the wall in tightly grouped, crossing and recrossing linear patterns. It was truly a sight to behold. Groups of Ajiron attached to a gigantic wall, glinting in the light, with their star behind them and beautiful Virija in the immediate background.

Something caught Sean's eye and he looked up. 'Check...it...out,' he rejoiced slowly, pointing over Jessy's left shoulder. She turned and she saw it.

Mitch also looked and saw that the sister world had just slipped into view from behind Virija, its ringing girdle now clearly visible as a dazzling circumferential sprawl. Virija's sun was immediately behind them and it lit the entire fabulous scene with brilliant starshine.

'That is Trijicyon,' Zamindar advised them, '...their external habitat is identical to that which you see here.' His middle arm and two graspers pointed fleetingly at the floating platform only a few kilometres away.

Even though Jessy was unnerved at being surrounded by space on all sides, she too was totally moved by the sight. Looking at the scene, Sean felt a tightness growing between his ears as though he were deep underwater. Everything was happening too quickly. He would've killed for his Pentax K3 or his phone.

'God, it's unbelievable,' Jessy marvelled, looking from the view to Mitch and back again. Zamindar pointed forward with his left hand extending his third finger and motioned toward Eljipt.

'We are approaching Space Axis, the focus for all our craft,' Zamindar said. Sean glanced up at the looming structure. 'Look at the size of that thing,' he said thickly, clearing his throat. To their left was the space bay, or Space Axis, the only geometric mismatch on Eljipt. Amid the symmetrical sameness of the ring, Space Axis was a colossal almost cube, the place where they'd first entered the ring city. The size of the bay dwarfed the other individual structures. It was literally hundreds of kilometres in all directions, truly colossal.

'Makes our Shuttle hangars look rather meagre,' Sean whispered, staring unblinkingly forward. Jessy was still frozen, just watching the view, momentarily forgetting everything else. Zamindar placed his middle appendage over the now invisible console and Ajiron accelerated around the curve of the ring. It then decelerated and rather than following the arc of Eljipt, it broke away and under the floating paling, heading slowly, deliberately, toward the earthly planet below.

'Welcome to our cradle,' he toned without turning toward them.

The dancing callus was all they could see, and it was still intensely unsettling to the four who were crowded behind him. It, more than anything else looked truly xenomorphic, especially to Jessy who was so close to it she had to consciously avert her eyes. She couldn't bear looking at it. She shuddered every time she was forced to look at it. She tried to avoid it wherever possible. It was like a shivering loaf of uncooked dough, pasty, pale and criss-crossed by shallow livid veins. All of it was constantly in motion, undulating and rippling like a poorly assembled pie.

She couldn't help but wonder what genetic marvels were wrapped inside it, despite its primeval appearance. Neurons, dendrites, axons? Synapses and vesicles maybe, or was it something totally different and perhaps even artificial? An add-on, maybe it was a synthetic extra, a cognitive accessory? She doubted it but who knew? Well, he would of course (was he a he, she suddenly thought). Would he answer her question if she found the strength to ask it? Jessy remained quiet. Perhaps later.

Zamindar resumed toning, 'normally this area of space would be teeming with local and nonlocal craft of all types, but there is an exclusion zone that corresponds with our course to Virija and around Eljipt. Had we not insisted on this, we would be engulfed by curious sightseers in personal craft. You have created a unique wave of interest you know. Your presence here is considered to be the greatest happening, the greatest and most meaningful breakthrough in the history of our kind. There has been many, but this is considered to be the greatest. There has been huge demand for information about you, both from our local area and from our regional and transgalactic colonies. You can understand that if we allowed you to mix with the population or even to land on our planets, there would be pandemonium that would be difficult to control. We are a highly structured and ordered society but overriding that is a fundamental curiosity, and the combination of that and you have piqued that curiosity like nothing before. With a chance to observe you or even to touch you at stake, our people would likely reveal qualities that have been dormant for thousands of years. So, you can understand why we must be careful, for your sake as well as for ours.'

Jessy was still overwhelmed by the creature's ability to tone in articulate, eloquent English. There was no hesitation or uncertainty...only natural, fluent human speech minus any real intonation or identifiable accent. It was a little like listening to a computer generated voice, except it wasn't.

So much for the irresolvable communication problems, she thought. It did make her wonder though, what was their natural language? Did they have one? Maybe they didn't. Did they simply rely on direct impulse exchange? Surely it started with language, a long time ago? It had to, but perhaps they evolved that way? Who the fuck knew?

Maybe there was no phonemic content at all. She realized that this must be how they were communicating with them. The Virijians were inserting impulses directly into them ... into their Wernicke's brain which was able to interpret them as words and language, but which in reality weren't words at all, just configured electricity. Like a telephone, she reasoned, electricity into words. Apple would pay a fortune to understand it. They'd pay another truckload of cash to be able to use it, or at least muck around with it.

They all jumped when the pod turned from totally transparent to dark and opaque in a heartbeat. They could now see nothing except a narrow strip as well as the vitreous womb of the now dim vessel. The control console, looking something like a toy, was now clearly visible as it had been when they'd first entered. 'Oh, you must be joking,' Sean said, shaking his head, looking at the controls, chuckling.

'We're entering the exosphere,' Sean said, stating what was obvious to all. He watched as they thundered planetward at what seemed like breakneck speed. Jessy gaped at the roiling clouds that suddenly swallowed them. Her voice fell out in a sudden wheeze, '...can we breathe your air?'

The atmosphere looked friendly enough, she considered, but Mitch's gasping account of Mars suddenly flashed back at her. He'd settled to the surface in the midst of a stunning Martian afternoon, perfectly still and almost zero centigrade. He'd peered beyond the vacuplate of his MEX and was overwhelmed by the very real feeling that he could simply stroll into the duned landscape and take deep guttural breaths as he went. Of course, he would've swelled and exploded like an overripe melon if he had. Looks could be very deceiving.

There was a long silence. Just when Jessy thought she'd asked an inappropriate question, he replied.

'You can breathe the atmosphere. Whilst you will not be provided an opportunity to do so, you would be quite at home in our air. It is slightly poorer in oxygen, and methane substitutes for your argon, but otherwise it is very similar to your biosphere on Earth.'

A faint red glow appeared, rapidly diminished and disappeared after a few seconds. Sean had been dying to ask Zamindar about the nature of the stuff that seemed to be so ubiquitous around them, that seemed to be at the very soul of their space technology. He felt like he'd burst if he didn't ask. He needed to vent some pressure from his bulging mind, a feeling getting worse by the second, as he looked around to take in the unfamiliar.

'...what is this flexible material that seems to form just about everything seen. We've called it soft metal, are we close, is it metal?' Sean ran his hand over the now visible skeleton of the tiny ship, wondering what manner of stuff it really was.

Zamindar eventually looked down and opened his eyes wider than they'd seen before, exposing brilliant yellow margins to his grey eyeballs. They looked like glowing boundary lines, the

158

same disturbing color as his feline pupils. 'I see your reasoning,' he toned, 'but to explain it in purely physical terms would be meaningless to you. None of the technology exists on your planet, in even its most basic form. I can tell you that it is a tetramer, that it is organic and colloidal and a metal. You would call it a three in one perhaps, a living tribrid plasma that has inorganic qualities and genetic capabilities. Self replication, self repair, integrity maintenance and memory.'

Zamindar stopped toning and looked at each of them quite deliberately through half closed eyes, summing up their reactions. Building the suspense Sean thought. Jessy reckoned it all sounded rather implausible. Living, yeah right.

'It has the ability to grow and to recoil ... to alter form in various atomically defined ways under stimulation from the quantum receptors that are embedded in the structure of the substance. As there is no parallel on your world, I cannot give it a name, but soft and perhaps intelligent metal is a good one, although it is something more than just a metal.'

They watched the swollen back of Zamindar's head as he continued to pilot the pod through thick gray clouds with little view of what was in front of him. They thought he'd finished when he abruptly proceeded with a monotone.

'... its structure is mainly crystallized carbon platelets that super rotate within a sealed neutron plasma. The outer membrane, that which you found so interesting to the touch Sean, is an organic monomer only a few microns thick. This layer of skin controls the amount of heat and light delivered from the inside to the outside.'

The voice inside their skulls abruptly ceased. Sean was hanging on every word and wanted more, but despite his prompting Zamindar remained silent.

'Let him be,' Mitch said, 'don't push him, just relax.'

'Relax? Tell me you're kidding?' Sean pursed his mouth sourly. 'Dickhead,' he thought, suppressing a chuckle.

Mitch turned away in frustration and as he did, he saw the skin of the pod lighten and then clear. Opaque metal abruptly became diamond clarity. Jesus. His mind seized. Almost instantaneously, the verdant kaleidoscape of Virija crystallized beneath them, lavish and drenched with color like a surrealist's palette. It was a vibrant, tessellated panorama which, despite its alienness, looked so very familiar. They broke through the lowermost layer of clinging gray fluff and flew into the clear air of the vividly living planet. It was alive in every sense.

Earth. That was Jessy's first thunderous thought. Just like Earth. Sean and Mitch had the same thoughts. Blue skies and swirling clouds, but on closer inspection this was not their planet. Earth was a slightly different colour from space.

Off to their right was an alien star, the same size as the Sun, but unlike their familiar orb this one had a noticeable orange tinge to it. To the Earthly eye it carried the suggestion that it was about to set, although it was still high in the sky. Still powering a middle-aged day. Still, it looked like good old Sol. It looked so very familiar, apart from the colour. So both were a slightly different colour – the star and the planet.

Beneath them and for as far as they could see was a stupendous megacity that was bathing naked in the peculiar light.

'This is Cjaript, one of fifty cities around the planet, this one is home to a million Virijians.'

'God, it's massive,' Jessy said as she ogled the tremendous construct, 'On Earth we'd squeeze fifty million people into a city this size, probably more.'

'Overpopulation is a problem you will learn to handle if you are to survive long term,' Zamindar declared without breaking his forward stare. It was a clear and precise statement which required zero response.

Mitch looked at the sprawling city and was amazed at its homogenous appearance. There were maybe ten or twenty thousand structures he could see and all were similarly pentagonal in section, and all seemed to be reasonably low-rise although they probably extended far underground, he thought. He didn't ask about their system of Government, but he did wonder.

'You are correct, they extend far below the surface.'

159

Mitch spun around to look at the back of the Virijians head as it pulsed and squirmed. 'You can scan our thoughts?' He looked incredulously at him, already knowing the answer to his question. 'If we choose to, yes.'

Mitch was stunned. After a second, the shock dissipated. He thought to himself, why should he be surprised? Despite the fact that it seemed impossible, anything was possible. This was definitely possible. They'd already shown their capacity to tone, the sky was the limit. The consistently five-sided structures below looked vaguely like some of the modern ArchoTek buildings on Earth. What were these pentagons? He knew closer up their composition and appearance would be most unfamiliar. Sean was about to ask Zamindar to explain their origin when the Virijian filled his mind.

'They are organic structures, grown from synthetic amino based proteins and cellulose fortified with colloids and polymers and low weight metal fibres.'

'You grow buildings?' Jessy asked disbelievingly. It sounded ridiculous.

'We grow buildings,' Zamindar replied matter of factly.

Sean could just see his small mouth turning upward at the ends. 'Son of a bitch,' he muttered, considering the idea of growing a house or a building. It was crazy, comical...preposterous. Trees, flowers, okay...but buildings? Fuck he thought. There was so much to learn about them. Sean looked totally dumbstruck as he glanced from Mitch to the buildings and back again.

The city that had been spread out beneath them suddenly ended. There was no thinning of the built up area of pentagons, it simply stopped without any transition at all. A distinct line which they had failed to see from a distance marked the edge of the zone of buildings and they were now skimming over what looked like virgin country. It looked like nothing had ever touched it. They were low enough at about a thousand metres so they could see some of them. Where the city had stopped there was luxurious emerald and aquamarine vegetation, although she couldn't make out individual trees if that's what was down there, it was like looking down on an unbroken carpet of lustrous color. The familiar greens were broken here and there by brilliant tracts of blue vegetation, as though tendrils of Arctic meltwater were intruding into a tremendous rainforest. In places though, Jessy could see what looked like thick twisted vines and pendulously leaved palms. But they were blue. No wonder the planet was a different colour from space.

Jessy wondered if the climate outside was tropical because, despite the colour, the vegetation sure looked tropical. There were kilometres of paths, cleared areas between the vegetation and it was on these that she saw them, the Virijians, the aliens. They were walking in pairs and in groups and seemed to be looking upward, they were definitely looking upward and some of them were pointing with their middle arms, they were all pointing at them. They were the aliens, to them.

'They know we're in here,' Jessy said softly, staring through eyes that were wide with dread. 'Fuck,' she uttered, they know all right.' She felt cold, holding a shaking1 hand to her forehead.

Sean spoke without taking his eyes off the vista below, 'It wouldn't be too hard to guess, given that we seem to be the only craft in the sky. I can't see a single anything, anywhere.'

The vivid landscape went on for hundreds of kilometres, but in the distance, Mitch could see the beginnings of another city and it looked the same or very similar to the one behind them. Uniformity was a constant theme in everything they'd seen since entering the cosmic landscape of Virija. Sean wondered whether they would end up like that. Was it a natural outworking of intelligence, that the peaks and troughs in society gradually dissolve? That the disparities and differences between people and places fade to nothing? Very probably, he concluded. It seemed logical enough. Jessy was still feeling the tingling in her chest and was having trouble breathing as she stared at the sights. Sean had been listening for any signs of noise from the craft they were travelling in, but as far as he could tell there was absolutely none, although when it decelerated, as opposed to when it accelerated, he'd noticed a very slight rumbling. Not beneath him, but all around him. Sean suddenly took his eyes off the scene below and looked up at Zamindar, unable to hold himself back any longer.

'How does this vessel move, er...propel itself, it seems to be incredibly mobile and can travel atmospherically at any speed without any aerodynamic means of holding itself up.' Nice

160

statement, Sean reckoned, grinning at the Virijian, getting nothing back. Nothing but what looked like indifference. He felt like clapping to bring him back to the here and now, but didn't.

He waited, hoping he hadn't overstepped the mark. There was a long silence and he began to wonder if maybe he had. Zamindar's callused whatever it was pulsed back to life but none of them were blessed with an explanation. After a minute of silence, it came, like a buzzing earache.

'Our most prevalent mode of propulsion is common in slightly less than ninety percent of our craft. The first, and that which gives Ajiron its abilities, is a domestic system called gravity sponging. Running around the rim of this vessel, hidden within its carbon membrane, are billions of nanometric conduits that emit packets of energy at intensities that are continuously trimmed by the craft's pad. The energy comes from a superluminal particle with which you are not yet familiar. Its most unique feature is its ability to absorb gravitons or if you like, modify gravity. By manipulating the degree of cancelling at different sites along the pod we not only effectively neutralize gravity but can induce forward thrust, deceleration and nimble navigation. In effect we are now floating as freely as we would be in deep space. Gravity is not affecting the craft but it still affects us, the occupants of the craft. Of course, the technique is only useful where there is a strong gravitational source. In the absence of that there can be no propulsive movement.' Zamindar fell quiet once again.

The pod arced away from the planet's surface and they were soon speeding back toward the glowing megapolis that hung above them like a magnificent Saturnian ring. Sean watched the Virijian massage the controls of the craft by waving his hand over the spot where the console used to be, before it disappeared. During normal flight the controls simply vanished. The apparent ease with which he piloted the ship was almost absurd, leading Sean to the conclusion that there had to be more to what he was doing than there seemed.

'Much more,' Zamindar toned. Sean jumped at the sudden incursion, almost banging his head on the clear dome above. He looked up, half expecting to see green lines of friction. The small bubble slid in close to the sheer wall and with no clunk or bump, it kissed the flaccid dermis. About twenty metres above and below them were other identical craft that lay similarly attached. They seemed to be magnetized or somehow pressure welded to the wall.

Sean hoped for an answer to his mental query but this time none was forthcoming. Both the wall and the pod seemed mutually elastic and perhaps mutually attracting as well. He shook his head. Everything looked so easy. Simplism. Nothing looked complicated. He was sure it was though.

Matching dimples opened in the wall stuff of the circumcity and Ajiron. No one was shocked when inside they spied a featureless white room, homogenous boring architecture.

'Shit, not again,' Jessy cursed on seeing the room. Surprised there's no bathroom although I'm sure it will come later, she thought.

Zamindar turned and looked at them deliberately. Jessy couldn't help an involuntary wince. She was still finding it difficult coming to terms with his looks. The throbbing contours and the spidery pumping summed to a form that still sent Jessy's pulse racing. Christ, you are ugly she thought, also suspecting he could hear their thoughts anyway.

Zamindar looked at Jessy, seemingly confirming it. 'Sean?' Zamindar waited until Sean looked at him. 'Yourself and the child will remain with me. Mitch and Jessy, you will enter through there.' He pointed with his four pronged grasper to the white room.

'Why are you separating us?' Mitch demanded, knowing that Jessy would panic at the idea of leaving Josh. One look at her terrified expression and he knew he was right. Jessy was mortified.

'I want Josh with me,' she said quickly, 'I'm his mother, I know you understand.'

'I do understand but your separation will be brief and no one will be harmed.'

Mitch looked at her quizzically and shrugged his shoulders. She suddenly felt dizzy and pressed a hand to her forehead. Only after several minutes of animated persuasion did she reluctantly acquiesce. Sean didn't ask what was in store for him. He was grateful to be staying with Zamindar in case he managed to pry out something else about the workings of their technology.

Jessy kissed and hugged Josh who was still strapped tightly in his own chair. She and Mitch stepped reluctantly through the opening, hearing the dimple close with a quiet slooshing. Jessy realized she was now totally separated from her son, although she took solace in the fact that Sean was with him. And despite her intense misgivings about the way Zamindar looked, she did trust him.

'So, what now?' Jessy asked distractedly, wondering what was waiting for them in the painfully featureless cell.

'I guess we're about to find out why we're not with Sean.' Mitch pointed briefly to the far wall as a section of it fell away to reveal a dim, and in fact almost totally dark room.

'I suppose we're expected to enter,' Jessy muttered, looking from the cavity to Mitch.

They both padded quietly up to the doorway and stood at the edge, peering in like two wide-eyed children. They immediately turned back to each other, staring in disbelief. Looking inside, they struggled to come to terms with what was there. It was dark but they could easily make out the strange contents of the little room.

'What the hell is going on?' Jessy spluttered.

'In the name of God...,' Mitch trailed off.

'Not very subtle...'

'More inspections I think.'

Inside the room was a large circular bed, made up with red satin sheets and similarly endowed pillows. On the bedside table, which looked to be made from a rich polished wood was an open bottle of Penfolds wine and two pendulously stemmed glasses. Through another door they could see a bathroom but this time it came complete with a shower and gold tapware.

As Jessy inched up to the bed, she saw what had initially looked like a torch was actually a sexual aid, next to which was a sealed jar of clear jelly. She gulped and wondered again, what the hell was going on here?

'They've got to be kidding,' Jessy scoffed. 'For an advanced community they certainly lack something in the area of subtlety.' Jessy smiled but she was starting to feel distinctly uncomfortable. What do they want from us? She took in the whole bewildering scene.

'I bet they intercepted an Xchannel. That must be it, where else would they get this from, I mean, check it out!'

Despite their lack of subtlety Jessy found it difficult to feel angry. Just a bit annoyed.

'They want to watch us make love.'

'You mean they want to observe and assess and analyze,' she said without malice.

'They won't force us, you know that as well as I do. They're inviting us to do something we probably want to do anyway.' Mitch looked at her wondering, hoping it was true. 'Only the circumstances are different.'

'Circumstances are Different?' Jessy repeated... 'the whole thing is totally fucking bizarre you mean.' Her eyes were almost popping out on their stalks.

'They won't be looking over our shoulder you know, I bet we wouldn't even see them. I'm quite sure its pure scientific interest only, like taking data on two animals rutting.'

'Thank you very much Mitch.'

'You know what I mean.'

'I know what you mean,' she murmured, gawking at the luxurious cushions.

In spite of her suspicion, the surroundings, be them synthetic or even totally hallucinatory, made her unwilling to refuse the rather forward invitation. The wine, the bed, the shower and Mitch, she had to admit it all looked quite inviting. They glanced at each other and without a word understood that they would comply with what they assumed were the aliens' wishes. Like their new friends, the two from Earth also had the ability, on occasion, to communicate silently and effectively. Mitch took Jessy's hand and led her to what appeared to be a brand new gold embossed shower.

'I hope they know we like hot water with our showers,' Jessy mewed.

'Well there's a tap with an 'H' on it, that's a good start.'

Mitch slowly undressed Jessy. God how he loved the look of her, especially when she was naked. Mitch's excitement was all too obvious to a watchful Jessy who reached out and grabbed him, pulling him into the surging flow of strangely effervescent water.

They washed each other and Jessy fairly purred with the delight of a much missed luxury. The water was beautiful. The scenario was insane.

Mitch carried a naked Jessy the few paces to the bed and placed her gently in the middle of the finely clothed circle. She languished on her back, curling up amid the extravagance of the alien satin. Smiling, she looked up at Mitch who was watching her intently.

'Oh no,' she moaned suddenly. Mitch looked up, following her pointed finger.

'A bloody mirror,' he trumpeted. 'I was right about that porno channel. I don't know whether we should be embarrassed for Earth or grateful to the Virijians for their attention to detail.'

On the ceiling was a massive mirror, at least three square metres in size, swamping the ceiling entirely and reflecting Jessy's prone form, and it was a sight to see. Beautiful femininity ensconced in a billowing ocean of satin. Looking at the mirrored vista, Mitch switched to autopilot.

'Enjoy the show Renchjiok,' he offered quietly.

When it was over Jessy muttered to Mitch as her breath slowly returned to normal, 'Hope their recording levels were okay,'. They both eventually rolled off the bed. Mitch poured some wine and picked up the vibrator, shooting Jessy a lurid look.

'Oh, give me a break,' she screamed, grinning and laughing. 'Put it down...put it down!'

They laughed and drank deeply, and talked incessantly for over an hour. The wine was so unbelievably dry it made them wince, but it was wine although nothing that the famous winemaker on the label would ever lay claim to. In fact, wine had never tasted so good and after finishing the bottle they slipped into a deep and undisturbed sleep.

Mitch woke first. He had no idea how long they'd slept but he felt groggy which normally meant that he'd slept too long. Looking at Jessy, he smiled to himself. It didn't matter what position she lay in or how she was dressed, or even if she was dressed, Jessy was a beautiful woman, Mitch thought. Vulnerable and emotionally frail at times but beautiful in every sense of the word.

He nudged her and she groaned as she began the slow climb to consciousness. They both showered individually and dressed, and waited for something to happen.

10

Mars

'Nothing disturbs me more than the glorification of stupidity.' ~ *Carl Sagan*

Sitting in space a light year from Earth and in a line between that planet and Alpha Centauri, an observer, should there have been one, would have witnessed the passing of a patently furious star. It would flash past as it violently swung around its dark attractor in a few days. Its gas would be visibly boiling away from its tear-shaped torso, arrowing into a roiling plasma ring which surrounded its dark partner. The bizarre couple would arc past and instantaneously vanish amongst the background of stars. Little would the observer realize that the rabid pair was on a course toward a living star system. To snuff out the life that had persisted there for billions of years...in an instant of unimaginable apocalypse. The observer would go on his way, little the wiser, but thankful for whatever luck had allowed him to remain an observer and not a victim of its passing.

Ben White was sweating profusely. The perspiration stains on his flannel T-shirt, emblazoned with Sydney Swans F.C., were adequate evidence of his exertions.

'I truly hate this,' he grunted through gritted teeth. Ben was jogging along AASSA's enclosed sports field at Woomera. It was a morning ritual that started soon after the news had been broken to the disbelieving masses on the planet. Coming to a halt near the main seating area, he bent over and held his hips, puffing vigorously. 'Too goddamn hard,' he gasped breathlessly. He wondered why in God's name he put himself through it.

Ben staggered off the track and walked through the open gate between the two small grandstands. Shower, he thought to himself as he wandered back to the ten-storey block that skirted the main facility. Walking into his room he headed straight for the bathroom.

'You okay?' came a voice from a figure lying on the bed.

'Buggered actually...' he panted. The figure on the bed turned over to look at him through the open bathroom door.

'Wanna come play?'

Ben looked in at the bed, 'You're kidding, take a look at me, I smell like a K4!' Disrobing, he stepped into the steaming shower, grunting with pleasure.

'Okay...it's you're call.'

Amy Hudson was a talented radio astronomer and had interests and desires that complemented Ben's. Their sex was great, but their other intercourse was just as good as far as he was concerned. In these times of tenuous longevity, he was ecstatic to have found a soulmate.

There were now only twenty-six people left at the AASSA spaceport. The rest had left soon after the news was broken and others had gradually drifted off in the following months, simply driving away or "borrowing" one of the light aircraft from the neighbouring airfield. Those that had stayed were like an extended family, all of them occupying the ground floor of the accommodation wing. The other three hundred rooms were empty. They were a huddled remnant of the good times.

'Miss Hudson, would you come here please,' Ben commanded.

Climbing off the bed and wearing only a loose shirt, she padded over to the shower. One hand and then another sprang out from behind the curtain and grabbed her, removing the shirt in a flash and pulling her naked form into the shower. The giggling and laughing was gradually replaced by a softer emanation that bounced off the walls and didn't escape the room.

Within an hour Ben and Amy and several other of the team were in the Comtower, pawing through the latest Solarnet media reports.

'It's weird to think that the fate of the world has been decided and we don't know which way it's gone...for or against.' Amy looked at Ben who was hunched in front of the computer terminal. They had already had this conversation several times before.

'The decision is out there, assuming that Cygnus actually made the rendezvous site. Shit, so many things could've gone wrong with it. Literally hundreds of unforeseen problems might've occurred, with any part of the propulsion system, the weapons, the deployment pod or life support. There was so much untried technology, it's likely they didn't even make it to rendezvous.'

'Christ, you sound more negative than usual,' Amy muttered, shaking her head.

'Realistic is all. You know as well as I do, they're probably dead or floating aimlessly through the void without power. Not a pretty thought, but hell, get real would you.'

She looked at Ben with massive eyes and wondered what the hell had gotten into him. She knew he was a realist but they needed something to hang on to. God, at least let them hope, but he was even taking that away. She continued staring at him. What an idiot, Amy thought.

Earth had rebounded somewhat from the dark days that followed the news. The world economy was still in tatters but the Stock Exchange Central had finally reopened. The social structure of the planet had been redeemed slightly, but certainly not resurrected. Crime on a massive scale had generally ceased but in a few areas, gangs and civilian armies continued to remain in control.

It was here that the darkest side of the human reaction to the news became appallingly obvious. Local militaries and the UN International Guard were fighting battles on several fronts in twelve countries.

In some areas they were confronted with frighteningly organized and heavily weaponed urban armies that fought and killed without conscience. They were highly motivated and as they saw it, had little to lose, fully believing that Nemesis was at hand, which seemed about right.

The heady rhetoric of Armageddon and Revenge had been thrust down their throats by their leaders. Most attempts to absolve these areas by the regular army had been abandoned after daily routs and truly terrible death counts. The urban battlefields were evacuated and surrounded by the Guard, and monitored at a distance. Their spread was the only thing they could hope to contain. The United Nations had designated eleven areas of the globe as No Mans Land, neighbourhoods that were fringed by kilometres of razor wire and soldiers, written off until the hordes ran out of food and ammunition. So far, their spread was being checked, but not their existence.

In most areas though, life wasn't that much different from before. A quarter of the population had given up working, but the remainder stayed on and still managed a reasonable standard of living. Reasonable as it was though, the big picture for Earth had been swallowed whole. The vibrance had been removed from society, the happiness and the optimism and the fun, not to mention the motivation that money can bring was gone. All that had vanished from the planet, and had done so almost overnight. It was as rapid as it was complete.

Life on Earth had devolved into a shallow facsimile of what it had been before. Sporting events and movie production houses, even stage productions and places of higher learning, commerce and primary production, anything that looked more than a few months down the track was fairly much lost on the populace. Money and future had suddenly lost their appeal. Career and security and wealth became distant, irrelevant concepts. After all, what was the point of all that without life, without incentive. Without a goddamn planet?

From a distance, life looked okay. In places it looked almost normal, but hidden beneath the facade was the cancerous apathy of a doomed society whose fate had been dragged from the dark place and thrust into the light of day to eyeball the masses, naked and horrible. Black and dead.

Constant media bombardment by the UN and nearly every Government on Earth had told the globe that Earthshield would succeed. Positive commentaries had saturated the planet for months, gradually diluting the apocalyptic view of the first few weeks. Much of the population had decided that they would either be saved or be destroyed, but realized that the result was beyond their control.

165

Way, way beyond. Many had simply come to terms with it, trying not to look too far ahead. Time was the enemy.

Ben had feared the planet would self-destruct even before they got the news from Cygnus, if, in fact that news ever came. He was horrified by the consequences of the signal bringing bad news, that Earthshield had failed.. He, Ben White, would get that message first. It would be received only in the southern sky and the AASSA facility was the only base that had the "gigakey" to the complex and deep code it would be encrypted with.

Eight of the twelve Deep Space Network facilities had been destroyed during The Chaos which meant that NASA would rely on Ben to electronically landline the message after it was received. NASA trusted Ben.

He was reasonably confident that the planet and its people would survive intact, at least until the message came. The question of whether or not the message came at all weighed heavily on him but if it did arrive, what the hell would it say? He still believed they should pass on only good news, irrespective of the message's content. What possible good would it do to tell the people of Earth that they would all die in less than six months? Most of them believed the worst anyway, but he shuddered at the consequences of confirmation.

If the world's Governments thought the pandemonium after the news was bad, they would barely be able to conceive of the global chaos that would follow hot on the heels of any truly apocalyptic news. It wasn't his decision though, and for that he was very grateful indeed. He was simply an intermediary. What NASA chose to do with it was their business. If it was bad news, it was up to NASA what they did. Pass it on filtered or unfiltered, he didn't care.

Ben looked through the massive glass aperture and out to the launching gantries that filled his vision wherever he looked. The metallic scene in the foreground was flanked by the red desert that eddied and shimmered to the horizon. He knew the Sun and the elements had scorched the archaic hellscape for hundreds of millions of years almost uninterrupted. He rubbed his chin and gasped, could it be that this dazzling stretch of time would have its curtain call in only a year or so, it sounded inconceivable. It simply couldn't be.

'...you okay Ben?' Amy questioned. He hadn't moved or spoken in several minutes and was still hunched uncomfortably over the terminal. Hearing a faint voice, he realized it was Amy.

'Er...I'm fine...thanks, deep in thought is all.'

'I thought you'd fallen sleep.' She grinned, hoping to elicit a similar response.

'Tired, yes, sleep, no.' No grin. Ben punched the keyboard in front of him to cycle up the morning's media reports. The front page of the Washington Post appeared before them. Staring at the headline, the words struck them like a fist, the bold black letters penetrating their minds.

'Oh fuck,' Amy screamed, '...not this, not now.'

Ben was silent. He knew immediately what the consequences would be. It would be bad. 'Shit,' he finally whispered. Other people were walking in their direction, realizing that something was afoot. 'Shit, fuck, damn!' Ben put his head in his hands, contemplating the nightmare that had been abruptly thrust on them. There was a group of at least ten people around the terminal now, all looking at the glowing screen...scanning the headline and all murmuring incoherently.

PRESIDENT YORKE ASSASSINATED

'Not him, please not him,' came a voice. Anyone but him. United States President Sam Yorke, the first black President had been a unifying force, a profoundly calming voice, not only in America, but throughout the world. He was the closest thing they had to a saviour, and now he'd been erased. Murdered by some insane fucking zealot.

'What the hell are we going to do now?' Amy asked, crying freely.

'Who's going to replace him?' Ben muttered, 'there's no one capable...if that idiot Ramone takes over, we can really kiss our asses goodbye. Stupid orange idiot.' It was a reference to his love of the artificial tanning product.

166

'Look at the way he was taken out.' Amy continued to scan the page. They didn't leave much to chance, a French petite nuke atomized a thousand people including the President, destroyed everything within half a kilometre. Three thousand dead in total, lucky it wasn't more, they say.'

"Lucky it wasn't more"? Lucky? Ben pondered. Not at all. The President was dead for Christ's sake. Luck didn't come any worse than that. He shook his head and lowered it into his hands as the realization set in of a nuke being detonated in Chicago, to murder a President no less. 'We were just starting to get a grip on the situation and now this. It'll fuck everything up.' He dropped his head back in to his hands, ruffling his hair as he pushed his hands through it.

They flicked through all the other major dailies and they were flooded with the same story. There were various claims as to who might have been responsible but no one had any real idea. How could they? The "delivery boy" was turned to dust and ash by the blast, and with very few major countries not having a nuclear arsenal, pointing the finger with any certainty was impossible.

Ben was still shaking his head as he pondered the final straw that stared at him from his online terminal. Ben widened his eyes as he considered the implications.

'I really thought we were going to make it through you know, from the disorder of the first few months we'd sort of come to terms with it...mostly. But now what? There's other leaders but it was Yorke who really convinced the world that it could survive. But with him gone, well, maybe someone'll take up his mantle but I honestly doubt it. As a black President and as the man he was, he had the appeal and conviction to do what was needed.' He looked at Amy who was doing a poor job of hiding her tears. The room was full of tears. 'I'm worried Amy, now I'm really fucking worried.'

***

Fantasy Land. Sean was spellbound, staring through the transparent skin of Ajiron as the red and yellow worldlet zoomed up on them. It was obvious that the rock's pigments were born not from its atmosphere but from its ancient and heavily eroded crust.

As they decelerated, they flashed past a strangely oblong moon that hurtled eccentrically around its midriff like a discarded box. Sean stared at the planet in front of him, looking over Zamindar's shoulder, seeing that it had at least some atmosphere. Maybe it was the desecrated leftovers from a rich and vibrant biosphere, or perhaps it was the first stirrings of an atmosphere that would grow to support intelligence and life. He saw thin Cirrus clouds floating and wafting, shrouding parts of the color ridden surface. At one pole he could see a ragged bluish icecap, perhaps frozen water, but at the other end there was nothing but the unbroken hues that characterized the rest of the profusely scarred world.

Since he'd left Mitch and Jessy on Eljipt, Sean had been on a cosmic joyride in a craft that, visibly anyway, had no superstructure whatsoever. Sean was flown into a black hole and through Einstein-Rosen space to a spot which, according to Zamindar, was twenty-three million light years from Virija. Sean took it all with his eyes wide open. He was terrified and enthralled in equal measure. In a suburb of space that had only been recently accessed, he watched, disbelievingly as he sliced straight through the black hole in a transparent ship no less. Through the red, through the blue and straight through its cyclonically spinning heart. Sean's eyes peeled open, looking at what he considered to be impossible.

To pass through one in an enclosed vessel is one thing, but to do it in a tiny nothing ship where vision was wholly unimpeded, was almost too much to cope with. Sitting in the bubble he waited for the billions of g-forces to reach out and knead him into a human spindle, but he felt nothing and saw everything from a stunning viewpoint. Sean's heart froze then started pounding like a drum as he continued to watch the show.

They had dropped into the vicinity of a brilliant primrose star whose rocky family, or at least a few of them, were parading only a stone's throw away.

'We've chosen a couple of things to show you Sean, to keep you busy while Mitch and Jessy help us out,' Zamindar boomed into his skull.

167

'Help you out?' Sean repeated, 'you said nothing of this.'

'Nothing that will cause harm.'

Sean proceeded to pelt questions at Zamindar but there was no response as he waved his axial grasper over the area where the control console would have been. The familiar voice, toneless, slightly metallic, permeated his mind and erased any thoughts he might have had for Mitch and Jessy. Sean's eyes were so wide they looked like they were about to drop out of his skull and onto his lap.

'The basis of our space technology is to locate, pinpoint, map, classify, transport, assess, bio form and colonize. But overriding these aims has always been the search for other minds. Until now, colonization has always been the final result of our endeavours. It was hoped of course that the further we went in space the better our chances would be for contact, so we believed that one would ultimately lead to the other. After long millennia it proved to be correct, so you can understand just how important you are to us.'

He wanted to ask more questions of this majestic being but with all the magic he'd seen, his throat had swelled and his voice simply wouldn't work. He thought questions but Zamindar either didn't pick them up or chose not to answer. For Zamindar, it was the latter. He chose not to answer.

He wanted to know how they got out, but to no avail. If the smallest of particles couldn't get out, how could they? He understood Hawking radiation, but that didn't answer the question.

Ajiron morphed and Sean could no longer see anything but the silvery gizzard of the small vessel. They were piercing the atmosphere of this far away world, but this time he didn't see any red glow. Maybe the atmosphere was too thin, he thought, when in an instant the bubble cleared and a fantastic panorama, a pseudo Mars crystallized before him. There were no oceans or rivers that he could see but the landscape was intricately sculpted. It had been gouged and scored by long gone fluvial systems that had carved their watery signatures deeply into the red and yellow hemisphere. Sean's head jerked from side to side as he tried to absorb everything he could of the planet that sat before him like a spectacular sculpture. Something odd on the surface caught his eye. Something pipelike, cylindrical…or tubular.

'What are those things?' Sean stuttered, eyes almost hanging out, spying the numerous, obviously artificial structures that pimpled the surface, and also hung motionless in the atmosphere.

The ones in the air were simply floating there, not moving and with no apparent means of support or propulsion. They were just there, seemingly stitched in place, and girdled by slightly luminescent envelopes of air that looked something like a heat haze.

Sean could see that the stout prismatically terminated cylinders were expanding and contracting at regular intervals. Drifting toward one of the "floaters", it looked like it was breathing. When it swelled, its color seemed to bleach away, from gunmetal gray to a quite stunning snow white and then back to grey when it contracted. Expansion was accompanied by a "heat haze" extending for kilometres in every direction, swaddling the breathers in a misty aura. Sean gazed at Zamindar deliberately, his curiosity bristling, his questions chiseled like coarse carvings on a granite face.

'They are atmosphere conditioners, bio-animators, we have five hundred of them spread across the belly of the planet. Within two hundred years they will modify the molecular componentry of the atmosphere. These have been operating for fifty years.'

Wow, there was a long way to go, Sean thought, but then he remembered how long they'd been looking for us. Clearly, their space research was predicated on longer time frames than ours.

The scene before him was totally surreal, a dead dusty wasteland being rapidly transformed, being brought to life by an alien society to make it livable. He was familiar with the concept of terraforming, but this was on such a magnificent scale. And it was happening right in front of him, around him. Science fiction, he couldn't help thinking.

'Fact,' Zamindar corrected. 'Those vessels you can see each grew from a single seed.'

'Grew, as in biologically grew…reproduction? Like your genetic buildings you mean?' Sean's voice diminished as another knot developed above his larynx. He couldn't talk, or even make a sound.

'We send one of our processing units through to a targeted world, and yes they reproduce biologically and are in essence alive in a primitive sense. The cylinders are totally organic protein based lifeforms that have the ability to reproduce. They can do so only once though, cloning precise copies of themselves and spitting them out complete with their own task specific ganglia.

'They breathe in the unbreathables, in this case ammonia, acetylene and sulfur, and breathe out the new breathables which they manufacture by intense thermal processes. Other similar units are located in natural basins and extinct fluvial systems to build oceans and rivers, and where such geomorphic features do not exist, they are excavated and created. The units can also do the opposite, converting water to gaseous hydrogen and oxygen and effectively bio forming water worlds. 'We have a host of planetary processors Sean, I knew you would be interested in seeing them, if only briefly.'

'Interested is an unholy understatement.' Sean stared at the fantastic organic Chameleons, that defied gravity around him.

Zamindar traversed the Earth sized globe and detailed the various aspects of their plans for this distant rock. It would eventually form a critical stepping stone in the Virijian push to deeper space in this direction.

On the other side of the planet Sean saw close hand a gargantuan floating water processor as it spewed its watery excreta into an already huge ocean that only partially filled a Mediterranean like basin. Like much of everything else he'd seen, the scale of the operation was positively daunting. It was massively massive. Sean sat back and stared unseeingly at the incredible vista before him. He was nearly arrhythmic with unalloyed wonder. He held his chest as he watched, feeling his brain swell and threaten to break free of its bony cage.

'There will be one final excursion before we return to Virija.'

Sean almost cringed. How much can a person bear, he literally didn't know if his swimming mind could handle more bewilderment right at the moment.

'Are you interested?' Zamindar looked unconcerned with his response.

In spite of himself, Sean answered with a resounding yes, despite Zamindar's seeming disinterest. He really did want to see more, knowing it was a truly unrepeatable opportunity.

Sean felt Ajiron change direction abruptly. They left the anaemic atmosphere of the future Virijian colony, and Sean pondered what he would see if he returned in a thousand years. A lavendulan paradise with clouds and oceans and vegetation...and people...Virijians?

Within a few minutes they were back inside the GraviTunnel. Before Sean could recover from the sights, he'd just seen he was back through the ivory curtain, gliding through the void of normal space in suburban Virija.

Zamindar's voice boomed inside Sean's skull which was starting to pound from his repeated incursions. 'We will travel to something only recently uncovered and only more recently stabilized and made navigable to our craft.'

Sean's enthusiasm was rapidly returning. What now? he exulted silently as he watched the bubble race down the imposing line made by the sentinels Zamindar called Rou. They were skimming past the stupendous vessels, seemingly only arm's length from the tubercles that looked like colossal spokes from some gigantic, dismantled wheel. Slowing, the pod altered direction, sliding between two of the tugs and exploding toward a spinning chasm whose proportions were dimly lit by the particles that were being rained into it. Within seconds they were inside.

'This connects our region of spacetime with its distant past.'

Sean's head snapped up. Surely not, he thought. It's distant past, Sean echoed, silently dazzled by the implication. Ever since Frank Tipler had penned his famous paper, the concept of tinkering with time had occupied a special niche in the index of his mind.

Facing each other, Sean marvelled at the soulful eyes of his new friend. He no longer saw Zamindar as ugly or even for that matter as alien, he'd gradually assumed the form of a friend and a benefactor, a being to be respected, and after what he'd seen, revered. The time platform, it turned

169

out, was buried within a black hole that wasn't. The Virijians had located a bright radiation source when it "turned on" in their skies less than eighty thousand years ago.

They knew what it was well before they inspected it and hauled it closer to home. It was the sausage shaped core of a black hole that had shed its envelope of blackness, that which normally clothed it. The Black hole had become naked singularity in a heartbeat.

Zamindar toned, '...within it was a strangely twisted stargate that led us to a region of space that for some time remained a mystery. The probe's pad eventually gave us the answer, that it had exited in exactly the same cubic metre of space as it had entered. Its spatial position was entirely the same despite the voyage through the GraviTunnel. Instead of a three dimensional jump in space, our vessel had suffered a vast fourth dimensional dislocation. Motion without motion as it were.

Spacetime has somehow come apart inside this most extraordinary collapsed star, unravelling and then recrystallizing as a fifth dimensional timescape. The probe was actually sitting in the same place as far as location was concerned, but temporally it was eight billion years away.'

Eight billion. Sean struggled with the concept, hearing the words but lacking the mental power to digest them. Fuck, he thought, aghast at the scope of the idea. A hundred years maybe, but eight billion? Jesus, it was too much to accept, couldn't be true. Sean was bending forward a bit, watching and almost hyperventilating at what was in front of him.

Zamindar paused, then continued. 'It is apparent that some transitional disconformity, an embryonic tangle in spacetime has manifested itself as this bridge to the far earlier Universe.'

All of a sudden Ajiron exited the first tunnel and entered a blinding inferno of white light. He could see it dominating space ahead. Sean stared at the rotating sphincter of light and was astonished when it suddenly turned blood red as they approached.

'Christ, the gateway to hell.' His eyes were bulging with wonder-terror.

Ajiron arced around to one side of the object and then flashed forward and into the maelstrom of twisting light. Sean pressed his hands over his eyes and prayed.

Spreading his fingers, he was blinded by the glare that was all around him above, below and to every side. Naked singularity. He knew what it was.

'Just relax Sean, we will be exiting in two minutes.'

A small sound of wonder came from Sean's throat. He nodded uneasily. The light suddenly diminished, leaving him with the impression that Zamindar had turned up the "tinting" on the vessel. He could now see knobby protuberances on the dirty surface of the GraviTunnel as they flashed along its curving tubescence.

'You mean we're going to pop into a Universe which is only half the age it was when we entered a few minutes ago?' His face was like a coarsely sculpted diamond, hard-edged and furrowed. His eyes widened as he gandered over Zamindar's shoulder.

'Every minute removes a billion years from the cosmic clock. Every minute in the tunnel sees large stars born, live their lives and die. Five minutes sees whole solar systems complete their lifecycles. In eight minutes, you will have lived longer than all but the most stable stars in the Universe.' Zamindar smiled at his awed guest, taking pleasure in his ability to completely stun him with super-understanding.

'Holy sweet mother of God,' Sean whispered hoarsely. The reflections in his moist eyes were white and then colored, a rainbow of brilliant effulgence. They exited through a dizzyingly white hole into brilliantly painted space. Sean felt as though they'd popped into the centre of a massive nebula of crimsons and turquoises and greens. Further away he could see bluish stars, some dim and some blindingly bright, but the overwhelming image was of space brim full of brilliant, turbulent gasses.

Eight billion years, Sean thought again, as he tried to deal with the impossible wonderland that stretched around him like someone's freakish cocaine fantasy.

'No Sun, no Earth...no solar system,' Sean gagged to himself. The contradiction, the crazy paradox, was staggering. He felt like he was choking on his own blistering thoughts.

'That central bulge of gas,' Zamindar said, pointing with his left limb and long third finger, 'is that from which our star Valtrioj will ultimately form. You can understand our disbelief when we realized what we had uncovered here. That we should discover a means of observing the birth of our own star and eventually of ourselves is unimaginable. If we return a few million years hence we will see Valtrioj blazing and our twin planets as still nothing more than a condensing ring of particles. This is why the time facility is known only to the ruling Morij. We have recently observed an episode of sabotage, which was involved in translocating the Neptune slip. We were unprepared for this simply because crime has been all but unknown in space. Imagine the implications of a destructive raid on the gas cloud from which we all originated. We cannot conceive of such a mission but equally we cannot take a chance.' Zamindar fell quiet and appeared to be pondering what he had just said.

'A raid on the cloud of gas from which you all originated,' Sean echoed slowly. Maybe that GraviTunnel was truncated and hidden for a reason, he thought. Perhaps they've damned themselves to instantaneous dissolution sometime in the future.

'You are probably right,' Zamindar said, responding to Sean's thoughts. 'Curiosity can be a dangerous thing but once you come to know us you will realize it is part of our genetic fabric. It may be better if we close the portal but we will not or more accurately we cannot, because it is simply too much of a scientific opportunity, and science is a fundamental priority.'

Sounds like a very human problem, Sean brooded, scratching his nose, thinking. Curiosity and science versus morals and logic. 'Always a difficult choice,' he muttered audibly, realizing the Virijian could hear his thoughts anyway. Sean's brain snapped back to what was outside, and started ticking over the insane puzzle, hunting for logic. Eight billion years ago Sean's mind was somersaulting in a far distant moiety of a juvenile Universe.

What was he doing here in this most unnatural of locales? A collection of atoms hewn into a thinking being, spawned from heavy atoms that were still very rare in this baby cosmos. The stars that cooked his atoms from hydrogen and helium hadn't even been born, let alone blown their tops and spread themselves around.

Yet, in spite of the mind bending paradox, he gazed down at himself and yes, he was here, living, breathing and observing, the only human being in the Universe. And one without a home. Without a home because it hadn't formed yet.

His mind was struggling to keep up, stripping its gears as it ran up an ever-steepening logistical ravine. How was it possible...how could it be possible, surely there must be laws that prevented this? But he knew there wasn't. Just look around yourself, he said.

Of course, there weren't any laws that forbade it, there should be, but there weren't. Relativity provided for what he was seeing, demanded it even. It was built into the physical fibre of the Universe. He knew if it could happen, then quantum theory would demand that it did happen, somewhere, with only the laws of probability holding it back. He knew that everyday things, gravity and mass, had conspired to gouge out this crazy conduit to somewhen else. Glancing around, he realized with a sudden richness what a bizarre place the Universe was. What was natural or normal anyway? The thought would come back to haunt him.

'I think I'd like to return,' Sean said weakly, bereft of strength and reason. He was truly befuddled. His mind was mash.

'It is time anyway. I sense your distress but you are in no danger and you will be reunited with the others in a short time.'

'Thank you.' He meant it. The bubble pivoted and returned along the identical path it had arrived on, back through the naked divide. 'So long,' he said out loud, pondering the brief multibillion year journey that stretched ahead of him.

'You must sleep now,' Zamindar toned. Although Sean didn't feel much like sleeping and despite the adrenaline that was flowing through him, he was almost immediately fast asleep.

Sean continued to tumble away from the pod, sprawling toward a distant yellow sun. He was trillions of kilometres from nowhere. Trying his roto-thrusters, he realized he didn't have any. They were missing! No air, no thrusters, no help. He was powerless and helpless in the midst of the chalcocitic void. Sean felt the panic now, the wrenching horror of certain death. The understanding pricked him with a thousand hot pokers. The soul whipping realization that you were going to die...without any hope of reprieve. The absolute certainty of death. He could hear screaming...his own tortured voice filled his ears.

Seventy five seconds. The atmosphere thickened and he heard his own desperate gasps, resonating in his helmet as the nitrogen and oxygen dwindled to single digit pressures. Die he thought to himself, just die. The pressure was building in his brain. Backpressure. He tried to draw breath...but it felt like he was sucking through a sponge. The inability to do what he'd done since he was born, to breathe, was unbearable. The strobing greenness lost focus and he saw the numerals cycle downward passed twenty seconds...past ten seconds. The pressure in his throat was agonizing, the pain was murderous, no air, trying to breath, gasping...then there was nothing at all. Minus pressure.

The last puff in his lungs was ripped outward, splashing blood and his final misty breath over the visor in front of his eyes. His eyes popped from his skull and as his shimmering ocular stems bloodied his cheeks Sean finally lost consciousness and knew he was dead. Could feel himself dead. The joy of death.

Sean opened his eyes and dream flooded his mind. He could feel his heart thudding near the back of his throat, hard enough to make his head pound. He was alive. No pain. He silently thanked God. Just a dream, he puffed and thanked God a second time. For an atheist, thanking God twice in under a minute was a very good effort. What a dream though, it was vivid and real beyond reckoning. He swore again, stunned by the explicit reality of the frightmare. He was looking at a sheer wall in front of him. Ajiron had already joined with Eljipt and as he watched, still dazed from the dream, both surfaces parted. Moses, was his sleep thickened thought.

'You should join the others Sean,' he said pointing through the opening with his grasper.

'They're in there?' he asked. No answer. The finger simply remained pointing doorward. Sean padded through and immediately saw movement in a dim space that led through to another room. Sean hurried in and then stopped on a dime, staring. He couldn't believe the sight. If he'd seen his own father darning a pair of his footy socks, he'd have been less surprised.

'What the hell...?' He was dumbfounded at the scene that was layed out in front of him, noticing with gushing relief that Josh was asleep in his cot. How did he get there, he wondered? Sean knew Josh was with him when they left in the pod, but after that he hadn't given him another thought. His gaze was drawn back to Jessy and Mitch who were seated next to the bed, both smiling.

'We cooperated in a little experiment,' Jessy said, grinning first at Mitch and then at Sean. He knew exactly what she meant. The smile was unmistakable.

'You mean...you had sex in front of them...Christ, I'm right aren't I?' Sean looked perplexed and not a little embarrassed. 'I mean I don't personally have a problem with that, if you don't.' He thought about it for a second. 'But wasn't it a bit uncomfortable...demeaning?' His blush was obvious, a scarlet punctuation to his strangely pious face.

Jessy was taken aback, not expecting Sean to act so righteously. At home she would expect major A-grade shock, but here in crazyland where anything was possible, she wasn't expecting it.

'Actually, we didn't feel embarrassed, and it wasn't in front of them although I have no doubt that they were watching, or taking notes or doing something.'

'I don't think they're a race of perverts Sean,' Mitch said casually, looking at Sean.

'I wasn't suggesting that, all I meant was...hell I don't know what I meant really. With everything that's happened, I don't know why I'm shocked or surprised.' Sean slumped into a chair.

'They put all this on for us Sean,' Jessy said, waving her hand in the direction of the bed and the shower. 'It was a fairly natural response on my part and from what I saw they didn't have to coax Mitch much either.'

Sean's expression finally yielded, losing itself in a broad smile. 'Jesus,' he said, nodding his head and making incomprehensible noises.

He recounted his adventures to them over a glass of water and his revelations left them in wide-eyed disbelief. Hearing his own voice, Sean wondered if they even believed him. He wasn't sure that he would, in the same situation, after all who could believe it. Living, breathing bio animators, and a time bridge that had sent him backward in time billions of years. They believed him though, unequivocally, he could see it in their eyes. What a story for the grandkids.

Jessy caught a movement in the corner of her eye and turned to see Renchjiok and Zamindar standing motionless in the doorway. They all tensed in anticipation of the booming cranial resonance. 'It is time to leave,' Renchjiok said, 'follow us to Ajiron.' Jessy noted there was no wasted language, no extra nouns or verbs that might act to confuse or obscure anything. Just to the point and precisely germane. Nothing else.

'Where are we going?' Jessy asked nervously, hoping all the "inspections" had finished. 'We are ready to return you to Earth, all arrangements have been finalized so there is nothing to delay our immediate departure.'

'What are your plans for Earth?' Mitch quizzed. No one moved, they were all aware that without the intervention of the Virijians, Earth was likely doomed. The question was really only one of curiosity, and hope was in there somewhere.

'We wish simply to make contact with your planet and its people, visit and observe, and be observed. We seek nothing tangible. It was unshakable destiny that our two cultures should meet. If it was not today it would have been tomorrow or perhaps the next day. Our cosmic spread ensured its inevitability. We are simply too close on a cosmic scale not to have crossed paths or to have detected the others presence one day. This is an historical moment, an event without precedence, and as far as we are concerned this is the first meeting between two transgalactic cultures since the Universe began. We consider that your society is mature enough to cope with controlled contact, but we must exercise great care. It is conceivable that we will provide you with the tools to destroy yourselves, in a literal sense as well as a social and cultural sense. If not handled properly, the shock of contact could destroy your planetary framework, and set in place a terminal necrosis.' Renchjiok walked closer, moving all three arms in a ballet of emphasis.

'It is still likely you will devastate your planet with nuclear weapons. You seem to believe the risk of atomic conflict has all but passed. Your confidence that the days of potential destruction are over is growing to the point where you are overconfident. A natural reaction and an expected and predictable one. There is considerable global cooperation and nuclear stores have been significantly reduced, and despite the global pandemic, all of it has caused complacency, a nuclear apathy that will gradually snowball into almost complete indifference. We consider that you will not be safe for at least four hundred years. This is based on our experience.' Renchjiok paused momentarily.

'What do you mean our experience?' Sean asked. Not them...surely. Nuclear war?

'Virija was scoured by these weapons several thousand centuries ago,' Renchjiok monotoned.

'Nuclear war.' Jessy whispered, confirming it, not that it was needed.

'Global nuclear war...chain link fusion weapons,' Zamindar boomed. 'Before we bioformed Trijicyon there were divisions on our planet similar to Earth. Not overtly warring factions, but factions divided by ideology, politics and socioreligious beliefs. We too felt that we had outgrown the phase of potential self-destruction. And I guess in a sense we had because only two-thirds of the population of six billion were killed.

'Four billion deaths,' Mitch whispered, 'God...four billion,' he repeated. They looked at each other in silence, stunned by the appalling devastation and death count. Zamindar and Renchjiok looked very matter of fact about it, as expected. Looking emotional was definitely not their thing.

'This could happen to you,' Renchjiok continued, 'but we are hopeful that we can strengthen your resolve. If we can convince your people, your leaders, to look longer term and wider scale. And to appreciate your indescribably important place in the order of this part of the cosmos. It will be put to your people that sentience and mind are rarities on an unimaginable scale. We live in a cognitive wasteland and you should be aware of the implicit responsibility that such a realization carries. You have an obligation to survive. If your society simply continues to endure it will obtain a technology the equal and eventually superior to ours, of that you can be absolutely certain. The certainty is

173

ingrained in your self-evolving genes, embedded in the base pairs and bonds of your DNA. You simply must continue to survive, avoid extinction to achieve your cerebral and technological destiny.'

As Ajiron broke away from Eljipt, Sean wondered whether they would ever return to this dazzling place where super technology had carved out a stunning celestial Disneyland. He couldn't decide on an answer but he thought probably not, but then he thought well why not, because once the gravity link was established near Neptune, the hop to Virija would be a short one. In interstellar terms it would be very short, so it would be possible. He prayed that he might be allowed to return and have the chance to take stride on their planets or perhaps visit a distant colonized world.

His superficial brush with their almighty abilities made him hungry for more. Ravenous for detail. And he knew the craving would burn hotter with each light year they put between themselves and Virija.

The bubble flashed outward toward the hypernode, but between them and their destination, a strange shape, a new shape began to loom. It was a craft of sorts, different from any they had seen before and it clawed its way from hyperspace and was growing larger as they watched.

'This will take us to your planet,' Renchjiok told them, referring to the odd beast that had materialized before them, massive and geometric, but unfamiliar.

It was perhaps four hundred metres in length and a similar distance high but was quite narrow in depth and shaped distinctly like a shark's fin. The base of the vessel was considerably sturdier than the upper tip which terminated in a prominent tetragonal point. Its orientation relative to them was like an upright fin moving through space. A cosmic dorsal fin, Mitch thought with an audible grunt. Deep gray in color with splashes and blotches of white it was as bizarre as anything they had seen, but there were no appendages or surface convolutions at all.

In fact, nothing ruined the aerodynamic look of the craft, in stark contrast to the other spiny and spiky vessels that seemed to be so characteristic of Virijian spaceware.

'...a pleasure cruiser,' Jessy quipped as she watched the Fin hanging in space, apparently waiting for Ajiron to run it down.

They all saw the ringed and smoggy planet that had greeted them when they first popped into Virijian space, hidden partly behind the line of massive Rou. Ajiron approached the Fin and without slowing, hit it with no inertial impact at all, sticking fast to its surface like a zirconian oyster. '...suction pad,' Jessy offered, gripping the seat tightly, or at least trying to.

Six figures moved through the open dimple and into a narrow and bright corridor within the Fin, for the journey. A journey home for three of them, a journey to a new home for one of them and a journey of profound discovery and unbridled expectation for two of them.

Inside the Fin now, Sean rubbed his hand against the coarse surface of the wall to which he was closest. "Cats tongue" was the thought that came to him, one way it was coarse but the other way it was like oiled glass. He'd never felt that texture before and he wondered what it meant.

The tense humans moved slowly down the corridor, taking mincing steps toward what they didn't know. There appeared to be nothing at the other end. They followed the two Virijians who were edging toward the slightly darkened end of the corridor that seemed to terminate in a solid wall. With the dimple to Ajiron now closed they were totally enclosed. There were no doorways at all. No way out. He was sure there must be hidden rooms behind the walls, evidenced he thought by the familiar patterning of parallel lines, but he couldn't be sure.

In the confining space of the dimming alien corridor Jessy started feeling her claustrophobia getting worse. A feeling of dread started gnawing away at her insides. She could now feel the sparks of panic, a growing urge to flee. But flee to where? She had her hand under her chin supporting her head. Jessy looked around and knew there was no escape, "no escape", the tide of feral panic inched upward in her throat, stifling her breathing as it went. She held her breath and hoped. They were stuck on the spacecraft, she knew that and accepted it, but she couldn't cope with being stuck in here, in this stifling rectangular space...no way.

Renchjiok strode forward toward the "dead-end", and the surface collapsed, a needle, point quickly ceding to a comfortable entry space. Without breaking stride, the two Virijians ambled through with the others close behind them. 'Thank God,' Jessy said to anyone listening. She was far away from taking Virijian spaceware for granted as they did.

In front of the far wall, which Sean knew would become transparent during flight, were five seats and a crib-like cell, complete with blankets and a pillow. There was a table full of edible crescents and several pitchers of water. Everything was the same as before. Nothing fancy, just functional to the last detail.

'No expense spared,' Mitch said lightly, looking around, seeing the familiar alien buffet.

Renchjiok and Zamindar moved to the two seats that sat in front of what looked to be a large circular dinner plate made of mildly smoked silica. About thirty centimeters thick and a metre in diameter, supported by three hair-thin legs that disappeared into the vitreous shine of the floor.

There were no visible controls or textures, not even the console full of millimetric holes that interfaced with some of the controls on the other craft. It was totally flat and entirely featureless.

Mitch and Jessy offered Josh some mashed crescent food which to their continued surprise he ate, and if his face was any guide, he actually seemed to enjoy. Sean walked over and took a closer look at the glass plate which had suddenly started belching brilliant plumes of light. Monstrous shadows were cast on the walls and ceiling around them. As he looked down, he could see motion within, gyrations and eddies, as though two viscous fluids were in mortal combat, both trying to penetrate and overwhelm the other. Every now and then there was a piercing flash of blue that lit the entire structure. He could also see what looked like millions of white and turquoise pinpoints appearing and disappearing, their distribution and patterns of illumination different each time.

'Take your seats,' Zamindar boomed from his seat.

Within a minute they were all securely fastened, and immediately felt the gentle pressure of acceleration. They saw that they'd almost immediately pierced the line of Rou and watched as space in front of them shimmered. shuddered, as though beset with a tremendous heat haze. The massive vessel near them was doing its job, exciting, inflating and stabilizing the Orion wormhole.

Sean couldn't hold himself back any longer, '...er, um...how is this craft controlled?' he asked, directing his gaze toward Zamindar. 'I assume...via this here.' He pointed to the glassy plate with slightly shaking fingers. Just when he thought he'd been ignored, the response came.

'...as you say, we instruct it via this which sits before you. We communicate directly with it. It is the brain of the ship and it manages every function down to the finest level of detail. It is a sophisticated version of the controller you have aboard your vessel.'

'But that's a computer...you're telling us this is a brain, that's quite a difference,' Sean said quite certainly. He was sweating, confused.

'A brain is an organic computer, no more, no less. They are functionally identical.'

'So that's a computer?' Jessy was pointing at the pad.

'Yes and no. To us there is no distinction between your two terms, for you there is a large distinction, but the difference is simply in technology. This plate as you call it, is a compressed cognitive network, it is conscious but its neural facility allows it a task specific consciousness only.'

'It can think?' Mitch asked in astonishment.

'It can think, most definitely, it can analyze, assess, guess, formulate and do everything we can do, but only along the lines of the operation and performance of this craft. It is totally in charge of all its systems, macro and micro, just as you are in charge of the biosystems in your own bodies.'

Sean touched its surface, it was soft and gooey, vaguely like the monitor of a laptop.

'What's it made of?' I mean...is it organic or inorganic?'

Zamindar's lips moved upward at each end, and Sean thought he saw a fleeting twinkle in his brooding eyes.

'It is totally organic and alive in a literal sense, but it was constructed by us, not grown, but manufactured, assembled in our neuron mill on Sjern. We engineer organic, long living neural dendrites that form the basis of what you would call our computer industry. Our cybernauts, flatdrones, our ersatztribots and protocomps. This plate in front of you has as many neurons as you possess and almost twice as many axons and dendrites, which as you can understand gives it a large

175

cognitive potential. I can assure you that your medical people, would believe it was entirely natural, and to a certain extent of course it is. There are billions of these living in every region of Virijian space. Our purpose built brains run virtually all aspects of our technology, freeing us from the purely mundane. Liberating us from tedium, allowing us to explore the cosmos, and to expand every field of Virijian endeavor...to research, to discover, to wonder. One day you will achieve a similar stress free society. You just need to survive.'

While they were listening to Zamindar, Jessy noticed that they had dived into hyperspace. She was hypnotized by the carbuncled skin of the GraviTunnel only metres away. Although she couldn't see it, Rou had followed them into the portal and was only a hundred or so kilometres behind them, arms fully retracted. It was like a massive gray bowling ball rolling through an only slighter larger tube, bearing down on the tiny Fin ahead of it.

After half an hour they pierced the "birth light" and popped out into a crazy, furious maelstrom. The Fin and Rou slid away and took up distant orbits around the hellish stars they knew so well. Sean looked at the star and the spinning disk of stolen gas and knew they were back.

Rou was right in front of the Fin, giving its occupants a magnificent view of thousands of pendulous spokes expanding into space in front of them, orienting themselves so their terminal bulges were staring fixedly at Proxima. Sean watched as its skin lost color and became distinctly pale, ending up almost white. Flocculi of brilliant pink energy streamed from the bulges and arced toward the red star, hitting it in a pinpoint on its lopsided equator.

'Insulated antiparticles,' Zamindar toned, guessing Sean's question. 'The pink tube of configured neutrinos prevents these particular antiparticles from annihilating themselves before they acquire their target.'

As they gazed into space, there was a fantastic explosion that ripped forward and sliced away a massive chunk of the stellar disc, hurling it away at fantastic velocity. There was very little explosion of matter in their direction, most of the innards of the star were shot backwards in a spectacular detonation. Jessy was frozen in terror as the star fragmented before her eyes, turning into a sea of glowing starlets that blew away at a good percentage of light speed.

'Fuck,' Mitch said, '...makes our attempt to move it look rather pathetic doesn't it?' He watched through bloated eyes, stunned by the power of their weaponry. The colossal arms realigned themselves as the black hole continued to chew on the ring of gas that still hung around its neck, even though its source, V645, was no more.

Mitch thought about it and smiled wryly. 'Who the hell would have thought, saved by the grace of an alien technology.'

'...inconceivable,' Sean agreed, as he watched the remains of Proxima arc away into space. The difference in technologies was never better highlighted.

'It's only fair they fixed what they caused,' Jessy said loudly, grinning at Renchjiok who returned her gaze blankly, quite aware of the implication of her words.

'We have apologized and we have remedied the problem...this is all we can do.'

'You are forgiven,' Sean assured him, speaking for all of them, watching Mitch carefully. He watched space outside shimmer and flare as Rou grabbed the black hole with a deft flick of its gravitational lenses. Zamindar turned back to Mitch and hesitated before his callus broke into an animated ripple.

'We feel, as I know you do, that we should try and reach your planet as soon after your message arrives as possible, to minimize the impact of mission failure.'

They looked at each other briefly, Jessy looking from Mitch to the ceiling. She looked a bit ill. Jessy's mind was reeling at the likely impact of the bad news, which she hadn't really even contemplated. How would Earth react when it received their coded message in eleven months' time? God, it was beyond imagining.

It would be pandemonium on a massive scale, the worst possible scenario for meaningful and effective contact with their new friends.

'Given that we travel at close to Luminal speed we should arrive close enough to Earth to send an effective counter in short order?' Jessy framed it as a question to the massive Virijian.

'It depends on your definition of short,' Zamindar toned.

'I don't suppose you can travel faster than light,' Jessy asked with a wry smile.

'Sorry,' Renchjiok said, 'Mass is an unforgiving factor, the shatterer of dreams I am afraid.'

Jessy smiled again. 'In that case I hope you've got some sort of suspended animation because if I have to spend a year sitting in this chair in this room, I will arrive on Earth totally mad, one hundred percent certifiably insane.'

'...situation normal,' Mitch said chuckling.

'Bastard,' she quipped. They all laughed.

The Virijians watched their guests intently, understanding what they were doing but not really having a feeling for why they were doing it. Jessy noticed that the Virijians seemed to be smiling back, but were they really? She knew what looked like a smile could be a grimace or another incomprehensible emotion. One day we'll know, she thought. One day we'll know everything.

'We have something considerably more efficient than suspended animation Jessy,' Renchjiok said. 'Over the last hour we have gradually accelerated, although you have not noticed it, and are now travelling at seventy percent Luminal. The inner biozone of this vessel floats on a compressed plasma stream that runs between the outer skin and the rotating inner surrounding walls. This absorbs the gravity induced by acceleration and deceleration. Accomplished gradually, the shift to virtual light speed is not noticeable.'

'Rou hasn't shifted,' Jessy said loudly, 'It's still in the same position, in fact it looks to be in exactly the same position.'

'It too is travelling at the same speed, the pads aboard both craft communicate continually and have accelerated simultaneously along precisely the same course. Symbiotic navigationf you like.' Zamindar swivelled his bearish shoulders and faced Jessy. 'Our work here is finished. It is time to take up positions in Ajiron. Jessy, this is what I was alluding to, you will be happy to know that you will not be sitting here for eleven months.'

She surprised everyone, including herself, by smiling warmly at the imposing pilot. Thank God, she thought but then she wondered with sudden anxiety what he actually had in mind.

Unfolding themselves from their seats, the Virijians walked to the same spot through which they had entered the Fin some hours earlier.

'We will be travelling toward the black hole,' Zamindar said pointing into space, 'and will make a gradual revolution about it, not far from its photon rim. We will counter its attraction as we go, but will slowly allow it to take hold of Ajiron and pull us around and out the other side and off into regular spacetime. In short, we will get a gravity assist and use it to first descend into its gravity well and then climb out of it. The photon stretching we will experience during the descent will mean that in fractionally over twelve minutes by our onboard time, eleven point one nine eight Earth months will elapse in normal space.'

Jessy's mouth fell open and her eyes bulged. Mitch and Sean looked at each other like dumbstruck children.

'Time travel,' she whispered.

'Not really,' Zamindar countered, 'but time distortion definitely.'

'...what a way to avoid aging,' she muttered excitedly.

'It's all relative Jessy,' Mitch said, 'only someone outside would notice it, for you twelve minutes is still twelve minutes, aging occurs at the same rate.'

Zamindar turned toward the rest of them. 'After twelve minutes we will re-enter normal space and be within view of your outer worlds, Pluto and Charon.'

Ten minutes in and none of them had felt any pull or squeeze from the horrendous forces that lay so close to them. Sean could barely conceive of the technology involved in obtaining such a shield, for they were within a few heartbeats of the most powerful nothingness in the Universe. And yet they were feeling absolutely no effects. It was like a day at the park.

Although the craft was totally opaque Sean could imagine the sight that would greet him if he could see through its hull. He'd seen it before. Brilliant light, severely reddened near the "sky" and blue near the core. But he couldn't see a thing.

They all tried to picture the image of time whizzing by on Earth in the few minutes that they sat huddled in the pod. For every minute that passed to Jessy, a month passed on Earth. God, imagine it she thought, an entire month gone in a minute, the lifetime of a loved one would pass on Earth in about fourteen hours up here. She shuddered and placed her hands over her face. Nausea and a consuming numbness hit her body. The whole concept was inconceivable.

***

Ben White had been pondering and brooding for hours. Woken by thunder at 3am. he couldn't get back to sleep. He tried but failed. the first vestiges of light were creeping under the flimsy rattan blind in his room, illuminating Becky, naked under the sheet that only partly covered her.

He looked at her body, her breasts, her waist, the copper spikes and the rest of her, but couldn't muster any enthusiasm. He realized, all going well, he would be receiving The Message in a few hours. Assuming it was sent as scheduled, or at all. Nothing would surprise him. He'd mulled over the possibilities a million times and was sick to death of thinking about it, but he couldn't help it. Cygnus was implanted in his brain like a surgically implanted pin. A jagged one that was permanently moving, slicing up and down like a steel edged razor.

A beeper was attached to his belt which would be activated automatically on detection of a Tristack code. He was simply biding his time and waiting for it to beep. Having weighed up the pros and cons, he finally decided he didn't have a bloody clue what the message would say.
Becky opened her eyes and saw Ben staring back.

'Something you want?' she murmured, stretching like a cat across the bed which tore the sheet away completely.

The sight of her stirred something in him. He loved her thighs, tight and sexy and between them, well that was okay too.

'Just thinking Becky,' he said quietly.

'Not about me though, right? About that goddamn message.' She said it without any real malice but as though firmly stating a fact.

Ben grabbed her shoulders and pulled her over to him, kissing her firmly. His enthusiasm returned in a rush, but as she brought her legs up beneath him, they both heard the ear rattling tone of Ben's beeper.

Along with his clothes it sat untidily at the foot of the bed, pulsing and screaming like a winged seagull. Hearing the sound and knowing what it meant he flew off the bed, grabbing the pocket sized instrument as he went. Becky hadn't moved.

'Oh, come on, it can wait a few minutes can't it...please!' she begged.

Without saying a word Ben dressed and ran from the room to the Comtower. Jess was still on the bed, naked, ready and unsatisfied. 'Fuck it!' she shrieked, and almost cried.

Ben was bending over the main instrument and control bank in the AASSA Comtower scrutinizing the data readout coming from the primary deep space receiver via the Detente satellite.

The gibberish of the Tristacked code fairly leapt out and punched him. He was ecstatic to know they actually made it to rendezvous. A light year. Goddamn it.

'After so long in space you're finally here,' he scowled. 'You little fucker!'

He punched his nine digit password into the DSR mainframe. All the doors around him locked with a loud clunk and the scanners loudly announced that there was only one person in lockdown. As such, the decoding protocol unravelled itself and would proceed automatically unless manually overridden within sixty seconds. The software in the AASSA computer was unique and designed specifically to decrypt the Tristacked gigadribble. It existed in three places in the world, at Woomera, NASA headquarters in Washington, and at the USPA Tower in New York City.

The code was guaranteed "unbreakable" and so far, all tests and independent attempts to crack it had supported the claim. Ben felt confident that the rain of nonsensical microwaves falling onto detectors in the southern hemisphere would remain just that, except here in this room.

The symbols and dots and numbers on the screen stopped dancing. They transformed slowly into meaning, into alphabetical letters, into a readable message. A halo of dizziness settled around his brain, blanketing his thoughts as he looked at the screen. Shards of light rifled from nowhere and everywhere, igniting his mind's eye. He wobbled and thought he might actually faint but he fought it and concentrated on the blurred monitor in front of him.

He regained control and read the fatal letter to Earth, first it identified itself, then it got serious. The monitor danced and glowed in luminescent green, with words of doom.

Decoding Paradigm 17.10.20X
UN Disclosure AAtiA
Message: Scheduled Earthshield Mission Response   CX1 Intercept
Mission status negative. Rhys dead. CX1 traj unchanged. Totality 97% assured. Cygnus returning to Earth. Arrive ~12 Dec 2023. CX1 impact approx 2 weeks hence. Rendezvous successful, nuclear phalanx unsuccessful. Recommend care in distributing data. Good luck. End.

'Holy fuck. "good luck", what the hell does that mean. Shit...fuck shit.' Ben proceeded to rant to himself, imprisoned and alone in the Comtower. 'I thought they'd actually do it...despite the odds. What the hell do I do now? Send it to NASA, to the UN? To the fucking eggheads at USPA? "End", seems about right.'

Ben paced the floor, his mind reeling, his thoughts confused and his emotions brawling.

'My worst fucking nightmare,' he said loudly to himself, hitting himself repeatedly with a clenched fist to the forehead. He logged out of the system and the doors unlocked. Mission status negative, he mused. He knew he had to transmit the message and transmit it in unabridged form. There was no choice. He had to supply the original message which they would decode themselves. "Just a matter of policy" NASA had said and he couldn't say he blamed them given the thoughts that were rattling around in his head. NASA was pissed because their Deep Space Network was inoperative and they couldn't get the message for themselves as soon as it arrived.

Ben shuddered, not only at the prospect of having to advise the Secretary General on the Secureline, but also at telling his friends here at Woomera. I'm passing on a terminal judgement to every occupant of this planet, that's a fuck of a responsibility, he thought glumly. 'What else can I do?' he muttered almost silently as he searched for options. He knew he'd be found out if he tried to cook the message. They had too many checks and balances in place.

Ben toed over to the separate corner console that housed the triple destination Secureline videofax that could simultaneously deliver a message to the UN, USPA and to NASA. That was the protocol that was in place and they would be expecting his communiqué, of that he was also sure.

The President of the United States and other world leaders would be waiting to be briefed. There was no time to think, only time to do. He entered his password again and the videofax dialled the numbers. Let them worry about how to disseminate the fucking news, he thought. He was sick and tired of contemplating the issue.

***

The diminutive ship moved in a tight arc away from the rotating beast, away from the photon stretcher, and headed slowly toward the pendulous vessel that tugged the black hole forward.

Rou had been decelerating for some time and was now totally stationary in space. The Fin was adjacent to Rou and it was there that the bubble was headed. The pod fizzed and cleared, not slowly, but instantaneously in front of the eyes of the six occupants.

'Jesus...mother. We're home,' Jessy barked as she drank in the spectacular view of the two icy rocks hanging in front of them.

'Pluto...Charon, we're almost there,' Mitch murmured '...we've travelled a light year in twelve minutes. Holy God on Earth, it can't be.' But he knew it was. This was time dilation. A light year in a few minutes. Gravity could do damn near anything.

The frozen worlds looked beautiful, especially to Jessy because it meant that home was so very near. She stared at her little friends, taking in every wonderful detail, purring over Pluto's blindingly white poles and its lovely orange torso that was pocked here and there with colorful chemical splashes, that ranged from black to dark blue to snow white.

Little Charon was like an icy blue snowball, a little dirty in places and a bit pinkish near one pole but to Jessy it was basically just blue and stunning. Renchjiok swivelled his massive head and looked at them deliberately.

'We will remain here for several hours. You can transmit your message advising that the threat is over and that you will be returning to Earth...with two guests.'

Zamindar glanced fleetingly at Renchjiok. 'We will then travel to Earth, arriving some ten hours after that message is received.' They were all silent. The three humans looked at each other and nodded, slowly and distractedly.

...with two guests, Mitch considered plaintively. God almighty! 'Thank you Renchjiok...by what means will we transmit the message?'

Zamindar handed Mitch a piece of white paperish material. It felt silky to the touch but was otherwise just paper. The pen had the appearance of a normal throw away type from Earth. Jessy looked at it fully expecting to see a brand name emblazoned on it.

'Simply compose your message and hand it to me when it is complete and I will communicate it to the pad. It will be sent in identical code to that of the previous message.'

'Compose a message?' Jessy queried, 'what the hell are we going to say? That we're coming home four months ahead of schedule, and that we have guests, oh...and by the way they're aliens...extraterrestrials! Fuck me, it's going to blow Ben's mind, that is if the first message didn't do the job. They'll think it's a hoax, I know they will.'

'No, they won't,' Sean argued, 'how can they explain receiving a message from here four months before we should have been able to get there at sixty percent Luminal. They know Cygnus can't go any faster, that can't be fudged and you know it! They will know reasonably closely just where this new message should be coming from. And believe me, a message from this close would not be expected. There's no way we could be as close as that.'

'He's right,' Mitch agreed. Jessy nodded her head in agreement. 'Yup,' she said.

'Okay, so what're we going to say?' He looked directly at Sean.

Jessy gave up, she was outnumbered by male voices.

'Keep it simple and short,' Sean said, 'that's all that's required, get the message across and leave it at that. ' Yeah, right, Jessy thought, thinking about Ben's reaction when he read it.

For the next hour, while the Fin ambled through space toward Jupiter, they constructed the message, and just as the fabulous Jovian disc threatened to jump out and hit them, they finished. As they passed what they thought was perilously close to Europa they handed the note to Zamindar.

Zamindar scanned the message and almost seemed to frown as he took in its detail. His rippling callus suggested that he was sending the message to the pad which would hawk their poignant verse in the direction of Earth. Transmission was instantaneous. In slightly under three hours, two hours after the message arrived, the Fin would commence a leisurely journey to Earth. It would allow the Virijians time to enjoy some of the sights along the way, sights that belonged to the neighborhood of those that they had, for so long, sought.

180

11

Enemy

'The cure for a fallacious argument is a better argument, not the suppression of ideas.'
~ *Carl Sagan*

The Fin cut within a kilometre of Jupiter's southernmost icicle ring, skimming low and slow over the freezing phosphorus storm for the last time. As the craft dipped from orbit, Sean mouthed a silent farewell to the planet sized hurricane below. He stared at the Great Rotation, the storm that inched along high above the ordinary cloud tops, so rich and intricate, exquisitely stippled with a hundred shades of crimson and pink. They departed the titan's gravity well effortlessly and slid into space, arcing toward Earth at a leisurely ten million kilometres per hour. Not far behind them, near the snowfields of Pluto and Charon, space was once again breaching to reveal its most private appendage.

The black hole inflated, briefly lighting space and allowing passage to a tiny invader that jumped into the darkness of solar space. The tiny vessel didn't falter. Free of the vortex it accelerated to near Luminal speed and vanished, expediting a course toward Mars which happened to be almost precisely in a direct line with Earth and the Sun.

Earth though was sitting at the extremity of its ambit on the far side of Sol.

'I've never seen Mars so close, God it's beautiful, so orange and so peaceful.' Jessy almost purred as gibbous Mars grew larger through the clear hull in front of her. Jessy's eyes were sparkling and gleaming as she took it all in. The spectacle was glorious.

'It's normally anything but calm,' Mitch returned. 'It might look okay now but they get a fair dust storm down there, months on end, blizzards that would eat Cheops whole in a week.' Mitch knew that was an overstatement because of the lack of air pressure, but still, the point was made.

'How close will we come to Mars?' Sean asked of the stooped Virijian.

Zamindar responded with melancholy silence. The wrinkled mound of flesh near his temple looked like a twitching pseudo podium. His small mouth was tightly drawn and his eyes firmly closed as though he were desperately trying to concentrate. Greasy wrinkles had formed where they had never seen them before.

'... a problem?' Mitch quizzed. No response. He repeated the question. Nothing.

Jessy and Sean returned their gaze to the belly of Mars as it grew slowly before them, a congealing drop of the ruddiest planetary blood. They approached Mars as though viewing it through a tremendous telescope that was changing rapidly to higher and higher magnification.

Zamindar finally opened his eyes and disengaged himself from the pad. The wrinkles disappeared like a crumpled bedsheet suddenly pulled taut. 'We have company in the form of an unidentified craft, an Ajiron is decelerating rapidly behind us, forty million kilometres away.'

They spun around to the Virijian almost as one. 'Why is it here?' Sean spouted. It was a question but Sean could taste the answer, could feel the dread that was veiled in the Virijian's simple, toneless statement. Jessy was whimpering, she couldn't help it, she clamped a hand over her mouth.

'Totally unexpected,' he toned, 'and there has been no communication from it as to its purpose. It is not an authorized visitor to this part of space. I am afraid it is hostile.'

'Oh shit,' Jessy blurted.

Sean's heartbeat jumped a notch in the back of his throat. Surely not, he thought...pacifist, peaceful, nonaggressive, super intelligent. 'Are we in danger?' Couldn't be, he thought. But he already knew they were. Clearly, they must be fundamentally different to the ordinary Virijian.

'We are in danger,' came the emotionless reply. There was no panic, no change to his patrician tone. 'No Virijian vessels carry weapons such as this, and have not done for millennia. This Ajiron carries relics of the interplanetary war which terminated eons ago.'

Zamindar eyeballed Renchjiok from only a metre away and Mitch noticed his axial clasper quiver slightly and deepen in colour as he started to tone. This was brand new, He was like a chameleon. 'An act of sabotage was carried out against Rou. It is clear that this was the craft responsible. How it gained access to the GraviTunnel we cannot determine and since security has never been a problem, we cannot explain it.' There was a long pause. 'We have no answer,' Zamindar finished on.

'Why would they want to harm us?' Jessy croaked feebly, feeling a rush of panic in her stomach. 'You said your people are not warlike, not aggressive, so why?' She was getting worked up now. Fear was gripping her throat, winding her up like an oversprung clock. Being flung into space didn't appeal to her in the least.

'There are some who feel that Earth itself poses a risk to them.'

Mitch looked like he'd been hit by a knuckled fist. 'How can that be?' he snapped wildly, flashing his eyes at Zamindar. 'I mean the way you flicked that star aside, you have command of destructive forces that are thousands of years beyond us. How in God's name could we pose a threat to you?' It isn't possible, he silently screamed, feeling compelled to grab the Virijian and shake him back to reality. He seemed so damn calm and unperturbed.

'We have the capability for mass destruction and it is their belief that we will be too giving with the secrets of our technology. They say we will quickly convey the power to control these forces to yourselves. They fear that you will use them on us, not now perhaps, but sometime in the future. Given the opportunity and the technology, they feel you will turn to invasive imperialism in space. They know your history and they believe you are several thousand years away from being able to cope with what many of your people would view as entirely supernatural powers.'

'So, they're here to kill us and destroy Earth?' Jessy exploded, her eyes searching the room. 'Surely they can't...

'...we know they wish to avoid contact, to allow your planet to develop naturally, to let you recover from the growing pains of atomic technology. If you endure another thousand years, they believe you will have digested the cultural lessons that would allow you to safely employ some of our technologies. Then and only then will they favor contact. They would prefer to forego the benefits and the exultation that would come with the meeting of our two cultures, a jubilation that we believe would be undiminished by our asymmetric technologies.'

Joshua stirred and started to gurgle softly, moving both arms up and down like he always did. Renchjiok moved his left hand over the pad in a jerky but clearly precise fashion. The baby fell back to sleep almost immediately.

Despite their situation, Sean couldn't help a wry smile. The ultimate parenthood tool, he mused, pondering the market that would swallow it whole on Earth. Put your bub to sleep guaranteed. He was sure Earth would love it.

'Their basic philosophy has some merit,' Renchjiok agreed, 'but we have no intention of revealing ourselves too fully. Unfortunately, they refuse to be comforted by our undertakings. They are certain that our curiosity is an overriding emotion that will in a short time see us empower you with the forces of Armageddon.'

Jessy felt the craft accelerate and take up a more direct ambit toward Mars which was now dead centre ahead of them. The rusty bulls-eye was again growing rapidly before her eyes and in a few heartbeats the tortured landscape totally smothered their forward horizon. The image was overwhelming, as though space had suddenly exploded in a fireball of honey and bronze. They entered a low orbit and were edging gingerly toward the heavily cratered southern hemisphere.

'God it's so clear,' Sean exclaimed, his head touching the clear viewport and leaving bright green headprints. '...no dust, none at all...' He cleared his throat and blew out breath with an emphatic wheeze.

'The pod is not responding to our requests,' Renchjiok said. Zamindar moved his hand quickly, three of his tapering fingers actually penetrating the gluey surface of the pad. Something outside abruptly changed.

'Plasma sphere,' The toning was pure ice. No panic, just advice.

Zamindar glanced calmly at Renchjiok with eyes that all of a sudden changed to a mahogany brown color that was only stippled with their original tones. Both sets of alien eyes seemed to morph in symphony with the other, like silver crystals suddenly exposed to the noonday sun.

'They're firing on us? Jessy yelped, '...do something!' She looked desperately at the Virijian pilot, hoping to see some sort of intensity written in his chocolate eyes. A vain hope she knew. He looked as nonchalant as ever, at least in facial expression.

Were they to die here, when Earth was now so close? A sense of impotency rushed her senses. She contemplated their fate resting solely with these passive, melancholy creatures. They could do only sit and wait. And hope they were more interested in saving them than they appeared.

'We are unable to do anything, we cannot avoid a magnetic sphere.

Jessy looked terrified, she was white and going whiter.

'So, we just sit and wait to die?' Mitch asked incredulously, 'Surely there must be...'

Mitch's voice was drowned out by a horrendous thud that shook the entire ship as though a tremendous creature had seized it and was trying to break it into bite sized pieces. Space outside ignited into brilliant color...green, then yellow and eventually to black again. The shaking stopped and was replaced by a faint thumping, followed by a higher pitched whine and then all was still and quiet. Jessy grabbed Mitch's hand. She was convinced death was at hand.

Alive, she thought, as she loosened her grip on Mitch. The stars outside the viewport returned. Zamindar deftly fingered the pad.

'We're still here,' Sean uttered breathlessly, '...what the hell happened, shouldn't we be dead?' She was readying herself for the caress of space, for the horror of the pressure less vacuum. Sean knew their weapons carried the power to shift stars. Surely it wouldn't have had any trouble vaporizing their ship.

Renchjiok looked down at Sean, 'It is not that type of weapon...not designed to do physical damage. It is more subtle but quite effective in achieving a certain goal.'

Mitch glanced around again, '...what the hell is the goal?' He looked intently at Zamindar, waiting for an answer.

'The goal is to disable the pad , to interrupt its flow of electrons and prevent the proper operation of the ship, which would enable them to board the craft and take control with portable weapons.' Zamindar continued caressing the pad. 'Fortunately, we avoided a central contact. The pellet struck near the apex and in fact almost missed us entirely. We still have control of the ship but the pad is damaged, less than seventy percent functional, and will require a short time to heal. It has the ability to rapidly synthesize new nerve fibres but it will take more than an hour. It is clear that whoever is navigating the other vessel is not experienced, and with that in mind, whoever it is may think the craft is totally disabled.'

The Fin continued to chew up the weather-beaten disk, skimming over the fantastic hole in Mars, the six kilometre deep gouge of Hellas Planitia. The crash print of the life destroying snowball that rammed the planet a billion years ago.

Suddenly they pivoted in space, turning through a full hundred and eighty degrees, putting them in a position where they could front their attacker which was following closely behind, just below the bright sunward horizon of Mars. Sean watched as the red vista before him shifted. The pod completed its manoeuvre and the stupendous mega crater fell into view again. He fully expected to see a weapon laden horror approaching, but space in front of them was empty.

All he could see were the bright pair of eyes that were Venus and Earth, dancing in front of the distant glow from Andromeda. Mars space was a hard vacuum, black and empty.

Zamindar and Renchjiok were massaging the pad, silently communicating, their long fingers sliding over its pliant surface almost impossibly quickly. Expressions were calm but their actions looked panicky although he doubted that in reality they were. Jessy was the first to see the tiny glistening bubble slide over the horizon and continue on a bearing directly toward them.

'There it is,' she shrieked, looking directly at the two Virijians, waiting, praying for positive action. Sean and Mitch also spun their heads toward them. But the Virijians showed no interest, remaining transfixed by the pad even though the little craft was growing larger and more detailed as they watched. There was just silence and thankfully, abundant hand movement. She felt like banging their heads together to elicit something. But thankfully there was motion.

A narrow beam of light arced from Fin at the same time as a blob of shimmering material loped from Ajiron. An instant later the small craft ignited in front of them, detonating and vanishing like a dying flare.

Mitch watched as the football like mass of glittering glue loomed toward them. It was on them in seconds and seemed to hit almost directly over the viewport. The ship lurched and again they were drowned in a blinding flash of green, then red, then black, no stars. It was much brighter and lasted much longer this time, which they knew was bad. Had to be bad.

They were lost in darkness, there was only a faint glow from the soft metal, and only after several minutes did the stars finally return.

Renchjiok looked up and removed his paw from the glutinous belly. His toning was considerably more rapid than they were used to, 'we have sustained a neutron flux. The pad is damaged and will require hours to heal, but we have removed the problem, assuming that this was the only vessel involved.'

'You mean there might be more?' Jessy whined, feeling the terror seep into her system like molten rheum. She'd had had enough of this, so much for pacifist and nonaggressive, she thought.

'Christ, we're sitting ducks up here, and there's nothing you can do?' Mitch asked, totally bewildered at their apparent disinterest.

As Zamindar started toning, his anaemic lips began thickening and changing color, as though engorging with some murky fluid. And if that wasn't strange enough, they were suddenly alive with hordes of silver rimmed pinholes, arranged in a strange geometric pattern, as though a lawn corer had run over their surface. 'We have little power,' he said, while engaging with the pad.

'You must understand that the plasma pellet is designed to destroy the ship's neuro fibres by sending a wave of heavy neutrinos through the hull of the ship and into the pad, which is the only substance that will halt their progress. Although these particles travel through the skin of the ship and through us totally unimpeded, they rattle and bump around inside the pad and all but destroy it. It will heal but it will take time. We cannot go anywhere that our current momentum will not take us, meaning we are confined to Mars orbit until recovery reaches sixty percent.'

Zamindar's response was immediate. 'You will not be sitting here for fifty hours. You will leave Fin and make transit to the planet below, we know of your base on Mars and it is here that you will spend the recovery time. We are keen to observe your technology.'

Sean groaned. 'You will be very disappointed. The structure is our first effort at building a self-sustained colony on the planet, one we'd hoped to build on as a base for future interplanetary departures. Don't expect too much.'

Don't expect anything. Mitch echoed silently. Jesus Christ, it's a dump, he knew.

'You do not understand,' Zamindar replied, 'we simply wish to see, and have no doubt, we will be fascinated. You are a totally independent intelligence. Feelings of inadequacy are not required.' He looked directly at Jessy, looking disinterested, belying the words he'd just spoken.

She was terrified by the "other vessels", feeling anxious and blinking more rapidly than before. Were they to be killed while on the verge of something so special? Jessy's blinking continued as she considered it. Surely not.

They gazed at the alien creature in front of them, and it was obvious that he was agog at the prospect of observing anything that was not of them. Anything that was a product of someone else...an alternate mind, irrespective of its technical nature, irrespective of its nature, period.

Zamindar's brooding eyes reflected the spectacular desert world that filled space beneath them. Jessy found herself wondering what thoughts and feelings lay bubbling beneath the colorful gristle of those staring eyes. Every hair on her body suddenly bristled with the terror of not knowing.

The inner dermis of Fin breached as they approached, revealing the bubble craft that lay like a suspended cocoon between them and space. They were now only five hundred kilometres from being directly above that part of Tharsis where Mars Hab 1 lay.

Sean padded through the cavity and watched transfixed as beneath his feet he spied stupendous Olympus Mons. The fantastic volcano that he knew was as high as two and a half Everest's with cratered flanks the size of a country on Earth.

He could see its dusty fringes career in massive kilometric cliffs to the silt of the dusty regolith below. The vista was so breathtakingly vivid it sucked the air from his lungs and the voice from his throat. Never before had anyone had such a nakedly explicit view of Mars, or for that matter of any of the solar kin as they had at this very moment.

Ajiron detached, broke orbit and skimmed Marsward carrying with it the goggle-eyed humans and the Virijian, all clearly visible through the nothingness of the carbon membrane.

Moving slowly toward the plateau, the pod slid over tumorous volcanoes and flatbottomed craters as it went. The meandering ghosts of long gone waterways lay intricately sculpted below them, dusty reminders of a bygone age of richness and life. Only one final ridge of mountains, composed of dozens of immense volcanic cones, separated them from Tharsis and Mars Hab. The little settlement was almost four hundred kilometres from the final volcanic spine just beyond the perimeter of the primary lava plain. Three of the cones dwarfed the rest, and they were dead ahead.

Jessy stared at the Montes of Ascraeus, Pavonis and Arsia which were truly monumental, even for Mars, and watched, trying desperately to concentrate, as they seemed to reach out like angry Protectors of the hallowed plain beyond. She knew it only seemed that way.

She was sure their frightening proximity was due to Zamindar's innate curiosity, he clearly wanted to check out the little dust bowl that was Mars. Was he thinking bio-animation, she wondered? Jessy was sure Mars would fit any criteria they might have for such planetary surgery. Given a push, she was sure it could be brought back to life. Back from the dead.

Passing within a few thousand feet of Pavonia, Mars base literally dropped into view, observable as a silver something on the mangled horizon of red and pink. Accelerating, Zamindar brought them to the rickety human outpost within a minute.

The flimsy appearance of the dwelling became more obvious as they drew nearer. A vague shimmering contrast grew rapidly into a tiny fragile refuge, a tumbledown shelter that sat naked in the middle of the freezing tundra.

Mitch found it strangely embarrassing despite the assurances of the Virijians, it was minute, ramshackle and dark, there were no lights at all. In fact, there was no sign of habitation whatsoever. It looked as though some ponderous black insect had been squashed and dropped onto Tharsis and was now well into the terminal stages of decomposition.

The three MTV's, the stub winged Martian Transfer Vehicles that should have been visible were nowhere to be seen. There was only one they could see and it clearly wasn't in good health. It was a dust obscured wreck that sat untidily on the lesser Tharsis plain a few hundred metres away.

'Where the hell is everyone?' Jessy asked quietly, her eyes scrutinizing every part of the apparently lifeless structure below. They were all pondering the same thing but no one bothered to respond. The answer was fairly clear, in fact it was obvious.

Ajiron touched the plateau, and as it did so its clear carcass melted, liquefying and altering symmetry to square itself on the coarsely pebbled surface. They had landed in the midst of a ferocious windstorm that had gathered itself from nothing in the blink of an eye. In fact, it had empowered itself as they were descending from orbit, literally in a heartbeat. Half an hour ago the weather had been fine and still, virtually dust free and a temperate two degrees centigrade. A glorious Martian afternoon, pink skies and unimpeded vision all the way to the close horizons. Now they were swamped by a freezing blizzard of dust, a cyclonic orange soup with visibility close to zero.

They'd seen it coming only as it swallowed them, it was so quick. Quicker than they'd been told. Jessy watched, terrified as the colours of Mars were whipping against the skeleton of the craft. Whizzing, swirling sand was stopping dead in its tracks only a centimeter in front of her nose, halted by an invisible hull. She couldn't help but flinch as the broken duricrust was flung toward her. The air pressure was low, but still, it flung the sand at the vessel.

'Quite rare to have such winds here,' Mitch said, '...one of the reasons the base was relocated to the eastern flanks of Tharsis, for a flat area, it generally has moderate winds and few dust storms.' He glanced out at the ochreous swill, 'Although it clearly does have its moments...'

His old friend hadn't changed a bit, he mused. Still a bloody Schizo. A land of a thousand faces and moods. Most of them bad. He reckoned they were all bad, it was so incredibly cold. Mars put the Arctic and even Antarctica to shame.

'The base definitely looks deserted,' Jessy offered, watching Mitch who was desperately searching for some sign of life. There has to be someone here, he thought, as he scanned the area. They didn't all leave, he knew that. Well, he thought he knew that.

Descending toward the base, Mitch and Jessy's surprise at its almost wobbly appearance deepened. From the air it looked like a dozen fly eyes loosely strung together and assembled in a Lego like group. It was more embarrassing than he remembered.

Black hexagonal domes huddling together, a single dark oddity in a vast orange wilderness of dirt and ferrous pebbles, punctuated here and there by the occasional dark outcrop. With the wind driving tons of sand over and against it, and with no one left to manually restrain it, Mars Hab looked abandoned and forgotten, and on the verge of being swallowed by the advancing dunes.

The sight of Man's "best effort" on Mars left Mitch cold and depressed. In the decade since he'd left the first boot print they'd gotten absolutely nowhere. The dreams of the First Thousand and Mars town remained just that. Dreams. The "town" part of it was a fucking joke. An utter travesty. There were, apparently, better things on Earth to spend the green on. Jessy looked at Mars base and she felt sad, taking deep breaths, wondering what the hell happened to it? She had trouble believing this was our number one effort on Mars.

The entrance to Mars Hab was via a tiny ceramo-carbide pressure hatch that was attached to the first and largest of the fly eyes. This outer chamber had, during the good times, formed the living quarters for a dozen men and women, but now it was just dark and dead.

Zamindar caressed the pad. The bubble moved sideways across the corrugated surface without a hint of unsteadiness until it was a metre and a half from the dust and rust encrusted entrance.

'Now what?' Jessy muttered uneasily. 'I for one am not making a dash for that airlock. You do realize what the environment is like out there don't you?' She looked at Zamindar, instantly realizing the question was unnecessary. Still, it made her breathe easier having asked it. Mitch glanced at Jessy rolling his eyes. Of course, he does, he thought, a little embarrassed by the question.

'To the finest level of detail,' Zamindar toned as he fidgeted with the pad. His understanding of physical Mars was already far beyond theirs. Mars, as it turned out, was a fairly common species of near star rocks, color ridden worlds that fairly ran over with the fossils and the furrows of a more vigorous, vibrant age.

Dead worlds to be sure, but those that still maintained the minutest pulse, that with a kickstart and a few discretely injected chemicals could be brought humming back to life. Of all the rocks in all the galaxies, Mars and those like it literally the insects of the planetary world. Colorful testaments to better times. Not gas giants like we thought. Humans were wrong.

The protective bubble became opaque in one small region nearest the airlock. It stayed opaque for several seconds and then abruptly declouded. During its inclarity the bubble had been very busy, altering its contours and without ever opening its womb to the thinness outside, forming an airtight yoke around the exterior canopy of Mars Hab.

They now had airtight access to both the airlock and to its dusty controls, and to Mars Hab.

Mitch looked deliberately at Jessy and offered her a winning smile, 'the answer to your question,' he taunted. Mitch stared at the partly buried cover that had fallen off the airlock controls, exposing the inner mechanisms to the abrasive atmosphere. 'Hope it still works,' he said, pretty sure it would, after all, it was made for Mars. Fine dust was its thing, as were most things manufactured for the red planet.

Josh started crying loudly...louder. He'd slept for the past hour but was now most definitely awake. His arm was tapping a rapid beat on Jessy's shoulder. Sean gently retrieved him from Joshpack and made efforts to sooth him, which, as Jessy expected, he did so in short time. Even the arm stopped. She'd watched Sean become a wonderful paternal figure to her son, having developed quite amazing powers to entrance him and pacify him. And doing it when everyone else and everything else had failed. Would she have coped without him? She doubted it. Jessy watched him take Josh and his flailing arm stopped almost immediately. Josh looked directly at Sean, with large chestnut eyes following his every move.

After much massaging of the stiff numerical panel, the outer hatch eventually yielded, cycling open and venting a foul sulfurous parcel of air into the pod. They could see the inside of the airlock, carpeted with a thick layer of coarse dust.

Sean pushed his boot through it as he spoke, revealing the ceramic base of the airlock. 'They must've left the hatch open for a long time,' he said, '...check it out.' The airlock floor looked like a tiny chunk of Mars, red and orange and replete with perfect micro dunes.

Mitch ambled into the airlock and checked the internal pressure display. It showed that the atmosphere beyond was intact, as he'd more or less expected. With the rest of the crew assembled beside him, he cycled the outer door, more from habit than necessity knowing with Ajiron in position the integrity of the atmosphere was assured. Decompression wouldn't happen in that direction.

Mitch punched the int hatch open toggle and as he did so he felt a sudden pang of fear, maybe the pressure gauge had stuck on normal, wasn't really normal, and they were opening the hatch into anorexic Martian air. With a dull hiss the inner door crackled back into its grit choked cavity. No death screams. His eyes settled back into their sockets as he realized they weren't being sucked into the next room.

In fact, the pressure inside the chamber was marginally higher than the airlock, causing a rapid inward pulse of air. It thrust much of the silty carpet upward, covering them with eye reddening dust and shrouding their view completely for almost a minute. After it settled, the interior was revealed. Dim but not totally dark. A faint secondary light had remained on and allowed them to see most of the living quarters where they now stood. The place looked like a wreck.

Mitch turned toward the Virijian, 'Welcome to Mars Hab 1...such as it is.'

Zamindar paused, just as he was about to tone. A padding and scratching noise caught their attention, coming from behind them, from the second hexagon, the hatch to which was partly ajar. Something was inside. They looked at each other, silently noting they were all accounted for. Their eyes widened as they pondered the unexpected sound.

'...who's there?' Mitch asked tentatively. Silence. Jessy sucked in a deep lungful of air. More silence. Mitch held a finger to his lips, asking for quiet, wondering if there'd be more. A voice eventually echoed from the darkness of the second chamber.

'Mitch...Mitch Taylor, is that, can, um...that be you?'

'Jesus Christ,' Mitch said under his breath. 'Yes, this is he. Come out and show yourself.' He thought he recognized the voice but he couldn't place it. He looked at Jessy with a furrowed brow. More padding, and then two indistinct figures made their way through the open hatch and into the light. One man, one woman, both terrified.

Mitch was dumbfounded. 'Stella...Todd! We thought this place was deserted, what the hell are you still doing here? Why didn't you leave with the others?' He held his arms out. No response, only total catatonia, both were almost comatose but definitely awake.

Stella De Lint and Todd Bouvay were environmental engineers and aerographers, short termers who'd been stationed at Mars Hab for six months. They were standing like mannequins, frozen, staring at Zamindar whose macabre features were easily recognizable, despite the dim light. Todd jimmied his gaze over to Mitch, then immediately looked back at the Virijian. Stella simply

187

stared at Zamindar, eyes froglike with uncomprehending horror. She was totally unable to shift her gaze. She was holding back a scream, heart pounding, totally and utterly confused.

Todd's voice erupted without warning, '....what the hell is going on? Who is that? Is it, er..is he, friendly? Shit Mitch, speak to me, what's going on here?' Todd's brain was throbbing and his eyes were like headlights. Stella was no longer motionless, she was visibly wobbling on disbelief weakened legs. It couldn't be. Blackness filled her mind, the precursor to a dead faint.

Todd's mouth dropped open, the disbelief colouring his voice. '...an alien right...Christ, an alien...an alien! You made contact? How, where...' His eyes were everywhere at once, looking for explanations. Todd glanced at them all, waiting for someone to say something.

'Relax Todd, all will be revealed in time but yes, he is definitely friendly, in fact more than friendly. Come and I will introduce you.'

'...you'll what?' 'You're fucking joking, right?'

'Introduce you I said, now get over here, you too Stella.' Still no movement, just terrified, glacial stares.

Todd and Stella approached, looking at Mitch for direction, and for the strength to keep moving. They both felt the touch of his clammy paw. As with the others they were profoundly moved by their meeting with the triformer, so bizarre, so positively, stunningly unearthly. A mind blowing experience for the unprepared. A mind blowing experience even for the prepared. Mitch wondered if this was an insight into what would happen on Earth. Probably, he thought, it made sense.

Their brains were a hive of struggling emotions...terror, repulsion, curiosity and breathless, desperate fascination. The human passions from Todd and Stella filled the room like a gelid smog. The encounter carried a fuzzy dreamlike quality, pervading them with a dizzy feeling that they were experiencing something shattering, not from theirs, but from another's perspective. The very fibre of their bodies, the inner corridor of their brains where mind and awareness resided, told them that it simply wasn't possible...that personal contact should happen for them, here and now on Mars. In spartan little Mars Hab.

After an hour and a half, they had regained their grip, and decided that what they were looking at actually was real...did exist. They were overjoyed by the news that CX1 had been neutralized and were totally befuddled by Mitch's story of how it happened.

Todd finally pulled his head up and looked at Mitch. 'When we picked up your ship and swung the scope onto it, we knew something extraordinary was afoot. That crazy craft in orbit and then the tiny EM you arrived in, we fairly much knew that nothing on Earth could be responsible for it. When you landed right next to us, you have no idea what we thought. And then to come out and see Zamindar here, well that capped it off nicely, it really has been quite a day.'

'Ben, this is Mitch Taylor from MH1...can you hear me?

Static.

'Just static Todd, is the uplink okay?'

'Okay and secure,' he replied quizzically.

You sound surprised Mitch, you're forgetting something rather obvious, although having been where you've been, I shouldn't be surprise I suppose. It'll take your utterings more than twenty minutes to reach Earth from here, so nothing is all you'll get for at least forty minutes. Remember the speed of light Mitch?' Todd smiled as he waited for the realization to clobber him. Mitch grinned widely, wholly taken aback by his sudden loss of mind.

He activated the AASSA line and eventually heard it engage, a green light glowing to signal that he could speak. The speed of light isn't quick enough, he thought. Mitch finished speaking. The line was cut. He was brief but he was sure his words would be almost as astonishing as their near Jovian message that told Ben about their guests. That first message, though succinct and clinical, and without emphasis or detail, Mitch knew, would have blown Ben's mind.

Seated in the dusty living quarters and nursing cups of Mars dried coffee, they were all ensconced in animated discussion with Zamindar. Besieged with questions, he was doing his best to field them while being careful to broach his responses in terms that they could understand. He gave

188

only rudimentary details, enough to satisfy immediate curiosities. The Virijian seemed to be enjoying himself though, toning in a manner that appeared almost boastful but probably wasn't. Zamindar's tonings were drowned out by a stupendous thundering thump. An explosion, followed by a dull but intense howl that they could feel more than hear. The vibration was painful, penetrating Mars Hab and their bodies. The whole structure around them was vibrating and shaking as though they were thundering through the atmosphere of some ponderously clouded world.

Everyone except Zamindar instinctively looked upward, toward the apparent source of the body rending cacophony. Outside, Marscape was as it had always been. Red, barren and desolate, the almost featureless plain of Tharsis curving untouched beyond the Duriplast window, ending in a brilliant pink horizon.

Zamindar pulled himself up to his full height and moved deliberately to the window while everyone else remained rigidly seated, waiting for what seemed to be an inevitable, life destroying impact. The horrendous dissonance increased a notch and became earsplitting, adding pain and disorientation to their terror. Something was looming. Something big.

'It's them isn't it?' Jessy screamed, 'They've found us, haven't they?' Her eyes were like massive snowcaps, the terror stuck in her throat like a sharpened stick.

'Probably,' came Zamindar's calm reply. Probably? Jessy glanced at him and couldn't believe it. Jesus Christ, she said to herself, show some intensity for God's sake.

The thundering noise gradually started to change pitch. The jarring vibration was lost in favour of a gradually lower Doppler pitch that was instantly more bearable. They all waited for the explosive decompression that would suck them violently into the thinness outside. Jessy saw herself sail through the shredded shell of the base, swelling and exploding like a ripe melon somewhere in the freezing desert beyond. They waited and listened, unable to move, five humans, frozen like Howdy Doody puppets in what they thought of as the moments before death.

Looking up, Zamindar saw the Fin, already a ruined wreck, plummeting through the air. It struck the plateau at over two thousand kilometres an hour and detonated in a meteoric explosion of alien materials and red dirt, digging a crater five kilometres wide and two hundred metres deep. It all happened only three hundred kilometres from the base. Dust and boulders and chunks of ferri crust were hurled into the darkening sky, swamping the horizon for hundreds of kilometres.

They were thrown from their chairs as the sandscape rocked and rolled around them, lost in swimming tones of orange and gray. Everything quickly became still. No one spoke as they clambered back to the window to view the dusty devastation beyond. The flexible structure of Mars hab was thankfully still intact, surrounded by cubic kilometres of dust.

'Renchjiok is gone,' Zamindar toned without detectable emotion. He scanned the landscape and could see nothing but swirling regolith, grays and browns, the colours of Mars freed by the colossal impact.

Everyone saw the Fin as it passed over them before impact, the ruined dermis evident even from their distance. What had been a perfect fin shape had become a squashed pseudo rectangle with the triangular termination either sheared off entirely or crushed. The Fin hit Mars and they hit the floor as it leapt violently up at them.

Some minutes after the impact, Jessy found the mind to ponder her new situation. 'What now?' she asked loudly, 'What the hell are we going to do now? They're going to come for us, now aren't they?' Jessy could taste her own demise. She felt empty and gave a halfhearted shrug.

'They probably thought we were still aboard...,' Mitch hoped, looking at Zamindar, who appeared indifferent, as usual.

'They would have known that Ajiron had already departed before destroying Fin, so they would equally know that either Renchjiok or myself or both had left and very likely left with yourselves. So, they will come looking for us, for our Ajiron. They won't leave your system without confirming their suspicions, that is that they destroyed an empty ship. Their plan is to capture or kill us, it does not particularly matter which. But only after they have permanently disabled the black hole, which they also have the power to do I am afraid. They want to prevent all contact, and they will do whatever is necessary to achieve that end. They will stop at nothing to complete their mission. They have...'

Sean bounded up from his chair and sprinted to the window. He was looking almost directly upward, through the very top of the curving dome. He pointed toward the dim sky, 'What the fuck are they?' Holy shit, he mouthed silently. They were huge.

Almost directly above them where the sky was momentarily free of the swirling dust, two craft, patently massive even from their distance, skimmed across the sky in perfect formation.

'They're looking for us,' Sean said resignedly. 'Just a matter of time,' he was sure.

'I do not think so,' Zamindar replied, 'If they were, they would have found us, it would not be difficult for them. They have assumed, incorrectly, that we headed for Earth. You must remember that whilst Ajiron is small it has the capacity for almost Luminal speed. We could have gotten to Earth in minutes had we decided.'

They watched, all pressed to the window, as the two craft broke from their slow ascent and arced from the atmosphere, quickly becoming lost in the lower latitude swirl of obscuring dust.

Todd took a deep breath, then spoke to Stella. 'Can you lock on to them and check their heading?' Confirm their heading, he really meant because it was pretty clear where they were going. Earth was their destination.

She moved quickly to the adjacent chamber and fingered the keyboard in front of the small bank of cryo units that stood untidily in the corner. After several minutes she swept back into the main quarters, feeling the heat from several sets of staring eyes.

She wasn't sure what to say, so she just went for it. 'Those ships are each about six kilometres long,' she croaked, still dumbfounded by what Prox had spat at her. 'They're heading toward Earth and they are travelling. I can't get an accurate figure but they're going thousands of k's per second. They shot out of range in under five seconds, I just managed to get a fix and then bam, gone, straight off the screen and straight through the scope's perimeter. They definitely seem to be heading toward Earth and assuming their traj or their speed doesn't change which it conceivably will, they'll be there in a very short time.'

Jessy stuttered. 'So, what now, they destroy Earth to make sure they get us. First CX1 almost ended us and now this, which will probably do the job properly. For an advanced and peaceful race, your words Zamindar, you're incredibly prone to brutal outcomes, can you do anything to stop them?' She stood there with hands on hips, eyes narrowing to slits and mouth pursed in a scowl that was patently accusing. Fucking aliens, she thought, first they fuck up the neighborhood and promise death, then they just promise death...to eight billion residents of Earth.

Mitch took hold of Jessy and pulled her away by the shoulders. Zamindar swivelled his bearish head and looked squarely at the retreating woman.

'They would not harm Earth. They will threaten to but you can be assured that they would not destroy or impose physical harm on your race. You must, however, advise your planet of their imminent arrival and be sure they do not conceal our location. If asked they should be forthcoming. I will advise the Pylon via the pad on Ajiron and request assistance from the Morij. We are not beyond help but we must act quickly.

This'll be good, Jessy reckoned, the Virijians moving fast. She couldn't wait to see that.

Zamindar moved to the outer airlock and moved through to the pod. Mitch jogged over to the Earth relay and without thinking, started typing. He couldn't speak this time. His mind was spinning too wildly for that. Mitch had three choices, he punched in the code for AASSA. Ben White would receive the data personally.

Mitch hit the transmit button. Reaching the Vikmar 4 satellite in a millisecond, the microwaves were scrambled, boosted, and sent on their way to the faint blue light in the sky. Travelling at the speed of light, the message would not overtake the Virijian vessels.

Zamindar loped back into the chamber, with minimal urgency. The airlock hissed partly closed behind him but faltered halfway and stopped. No one looked twice or cared. The sudden brain racket made them jump with fright. 'The command has been issued, help has been summoned.'

190

Jessy glanced up at him and was mesmerized by the sudden pumping of his veins...naked bioactivity that was barely veiled by his moist cellophane skin. It was hard to come to terms with. Impossible to get used to. He was the epitome of ugly. A living, fucking nightmare she shuddered silently to herself. Her emotions were moving again, rippling in her chest and swelling behind her eyes, she could feel it. She was coming apart and she knew it.

The two craft which smashed the Fin had reached Earth fifteen minutes after breaking from Mars. They were now staring at the planet, orbiting at twenty-two thousand kilometres per hour, unmoving and seemingly fixed in space, above North Africa. Two immense alien machines looking something like grotesque gray brier fish were ready to make contact with the chaotic globe below.

Ben White knew they were there soon after they jumped into geosynchronous orbit. NASA and USPA had also detected their presence as no doubt had other bodies and individuals with access to the sky. The entire planet would soon know. This couldn't be kept quiet, Ben knew. He shuddered to think what sort of new panic it might lead to. NASA knew they were coming just before they arrived. They initially thought asteroid but it was travelling too fast, then it started slowing down...well that just about did it.

'I hope to God they're friendly,' he said to no one. From what Mitch had told him, he knew they were anything but.

The pad of the slightly larger of the two vessels was being caressed by long, pale fingers that moved deliberately over its translucent and pliant body. The craft was sensitizing its weaponry in the direction of the busy world below.

It had the power to atomize the planet. If they chose to, they could reduce it to a dimly colored nebula. A band of planet and people particles that would drift on the solar wind in the new void between Venus and Mars. Earth and Mankind's destiny had suddenly come to rest with the simple choice of an alien society. Yes or no. Life or death. Civilisation continues or not.

An intense beam of spango lite blue bounced from the ship and pierced the outer atmosphere, punching through the planet's dense life belt, the troposphere, on its plundering journey to the surface.

The rod of energy forged a narrow vacuum for itself, like lightning, from the craft all the way to the world's crust. The cloaked antiparticles struck the ground and dug four hundred metres into the sandy landscape, throwing up millions of tons of debris and leaving a crater three kilometres through the middle. The concussion from the annihilation knocked the landscape around the crater flat, leaving not a single surface perturbation for fifty kilometres in any direction. The stupendous clap of thunder from the air falling back into the vacuumed void killed thirty thousand birds. And could be heard two thousand kilometres away. The detonation was like nothing Earth had seen for millions of years.

The two warships had departed Mars almost an hour before and Mitch had sent his warning to Ben almost fifty minutes ago. On Mars Hab there was only silence. No one cared to speak, to be heard, or to listen while they waited for news from Earth. They were all engrossed in their own private nightmares. Had their planet been destroyed, why hadn't they responded to the message? Were they now alone in the solar system...in the Universe? Had what CX1 promised to do now been accomplished? Zamindar's assurances left them cold. No one believed him anymore.

Mitch was readying himself to send a message when the yellow strobe started flashing in the corner of the dim room, signalling incoming telemetry. He dashed to the small control chamber and punched print on the keyboard. The yellow light and dull klaxon stopped and the printer jumped to life. It was brief.

'Holy shit,' Mitch muttered as he scanned the message. 'They've fired on Earth, they've actually deployed a weapon, destroyed hundreds of square kilometres for God's sake. Your guarantees don't seem to be worth much Zamindar. They've pre-empted dialogue by discharging some sort of...some sort of bloody doomsday device.'

Jessy watched it all from the background and with eyes focussed on Zamindar, found it hard to believe she was still alive. She hoped like hell that Earth remained in one piece.

After a few minutes the klaxon and strobes interrupted Mitch's frustration with the emotionless and silent Virijian. Jessy took the lead and strode to the com chamber. She literally punched the laser printer. It had only been a few minutes since Ben's last communication yet there was another message on the tail of the first.

'...maybe our friends have started talking,' Sean muttered, with eyes that were downcast.

Mitch, Jessy, Sean and the two engineers from Mars base were clustered around the instrument panel while Josh crawled happily around the small adjacent chamber. Zamindar remained seated in the living quarters near the Duri window, looking out on the rapidly darkening desert.

Was he reflecting? Jessy wondered, debating whether he had the capacity to do any such thing. The laser printer stopped its staccato chatter seconds after it started. The message lay before them in bold type. Jessy looked away and shook her head. Todd and Stella bustled for position.

'Pacifists...mmm...either Zamindar was lying or this group of, what did he call them, contact opponents, really are out of the box, somehow different from your normal Virijian,' Mitch whispered, with an icy stare, toward Zamindar.

'More likely the latter,' Sean said. 'Zamindar wasn't lying, I'm sure of it.' They all nodded. Jessy wasn't sure but she nodded anyway, with no conviction whatsoever.

Mitch picked up the print. For Stella and Todd's benefit, he outlined the contents of Ben's message. 'They've put out an uncoded message in English and Mandarin on every data receival unit, using every satellite in Earth orbit, all the Comstars, Intelsats and Satcoms. They want our precise whereabouts to be issued through the Millennium broadcast satellite where they will monitor... '

'And if Earth doesn't comply?' Stella squawked, clearly horrified by what she thought might be coming. Dark images occupied her mind, but they were just her imagination, weren't they?

'That's the best bit. If Earth doesn't comply, doesn't provide the information within thirty minutes, they've threatened to remove the Pacific Ocean.'

'Remove the Ocean...what, evaporate it?' Jessy croaked, Surely not, she thought.

'Leaving only so much steam and boiled fish I'd imagine.'

'Fuck,' she said, thinking about all the creatures, the fish, sharks...whales. Jesus.

Mitch looked briefly at the message and continued, 'And if that doesn't stimulate a positive response, they will continue to remove oceans and then start on the continents and then the mantle of the planet itself. They're warning us that with their people's security and future at stake, which is how they see it, they absolutely require the information. If it isn't forthcoming, the planet will be destroyed. No apologies.'

'We've already directed Earth to give them our location,' Sean said quickly, staring at the comms unit.

'That's the final portion of Ben's message. They will broadcast our position to the Virijians at 2150 hours CST, five minutes inside the deadline and thirteen minutes from now. Once they have the information, we can expect the quickest possible transit of these craft to Mars, to obliterate us.' Zamindar moved back into their small chamber. 'I'm afraid it is a little worse than that,' he toned with a mild vibration of his callus.

'Worse... how is that possible?' Jessy stammered, staring fixedly up at the Virijian. 'What's worse than obliteration for Christ's sake?'

'Equipped with the information they seek, no chances will be provided. There will be no search, they will simply destroy Mars. They have the weapons to reduce it to vapour and they will use them to their fullest. As you have rightly surmised, these individuals are serious in their endeavours. They are even more serious than we believed.'

'We have to get the hell out of here,' Todd yelled, echoing the sentiments of all.

'Immediately,' Zamindar confirmed, looking at each of them in turn. 'There is one problem however, which I know you will find unpleasant but which I am afraid there is no avoiding, given the circumstances.' Mitch instantly had an inkling of the problem and his mind reeled. Oh fuck, he thought. The realization of what Zamindar was about to say pricked his brain like a chemically sharpened needle.

Zamindar gazed at them blankly, as usual. 'The only means of escape is Ajiron. None of your craft that remain are serviceable.' Todd and Stella nodded. 'The pod can only hold four of us plus the child. Any more and it will not operate as we will require it to if we are to evade these craft. You now understand the dilemma, two of you must remain.'

'Oh God,' Jessy muttered, looking suddenly nauseous, feeling the horror of the idea prod the pain centres deep inside her brain. 'Are you absolutely sure?' she begged, already knowing what Zamindar's toneless and emotionless response would be. The rest of them looked equally mortified at the prospect of leaving two of their own behind to meet their death, to be vaporized along with the precious marrow of the red planet. And Jessy was sure that Zamindar couldn't care less, at least that's how it looked and sounded. Not a good look for a newly befriended race.

Zamindar turned and squared himself deliberately toward Todd and Stella. They looked at him and then at each other. They knew. They were the ones.

'Last on, er…first off,' Todd said slowly, guessing their fate, feeling sick.

Stella stared at him unseeingly, contemplating her imminent, unavoidable demise. Zamindar had laid it out like a macabre tapestry right there in front of her. She suddenly had an overwhelming feeling of desperation and despair. '...dear God,' she said and looked away, feeling the anguished scream welling in the back of her throat.

'Where will we go?' Mitch asked, 'surely they'll find us and destroy us, is there any point of leaving at all? Maybe we should all stay.' Jessy spun around and her mouth dropped open, but Zamindar beat her.

'We must buy time', he toned, 'Help is on its way and when it arrives, we will be safe. All we need do is avoid them for a short time. The pod can match the larger craft in velocity within only a few percent, which may or may not prove to be the difference. We cannot match it in weaponry or sensing. We must try and conceal ourselves somewhere within your system until our rescue is assured.' Good luck with that Jessy said to herself. Where, for God's sake?

Zamindar directed everyone except Stella and Todd to Ajiron. Jessy picked up Josh who broke into a cry, and carried him to the conjoined ship. Within minutes they were seated and looking at the rim hatch cycling closed, revealing its clinging patina of Martian crumbs. Jessy had a last look at Stella whose terrified eyes could be seen clearly as she fumbled with the faulty inner door, her sallow features on show as she gaped through the window at her only hope of salvation.

Stella watched unblinkingly as the door to her freedom and in fact to any life at all wound shut in her face with a dull thud. They had all exchanged emotional farewells. The belief that perhaps they would not destroy Mars was only marginally comforting to the two despairing castaways. Zamindar's firm belief in Mars destruction stung them. He knew and so did they. The knowledge of certain death bit deeply and raggedly.

The distended bubble that tethered them to Mars Hab retracted, immediately regaining its clarity and its precisely curved morphometry. They were ready to leave.

***

The gargantuan vessels pivoted and retreated from the vividly painted world, their course being monitored directly and at close quarters by USPA's floating hardware. Suddenly, the lumbering vessels vanished, disappearing in a millisecond, already out of view to the orbiting watchers. Negative protons annihilated with positive protons deep inside their gizzards and thumped the craft toward the distant but rapidly swelling face of Mars.

The satisfaction aboard the larger of the two ships was deeply felt if not apparent. They had obtained what they sought and if the information was incorrect, they would return and if necessary, carry out their final threat. The mission objective was of greater significance than the conservation of a planet, even one with indigenous, sentient life. Their attitude put them in total opposition to most of the rest of the Virijian race. They were truly rebels.

***

Stella and Todd glanced briefly at each other as they sat down, the resignation and the despair splashed thickly in their eyes. Zamindar told them that the craft would reach Mars vicinity within fifteen minutes.

They contemplated an escape but there was none. The only vessel was a broken down Beetlebug, cannibalized to feed other breakdowns when service calls, or any calls for that matter, were suspended. The MTV Valmar had no means of propulsion, or any atmosphere generators. Hardly a solution to their problem. They had no vehicle that was ready to go now. So, they sat and waited, peering silently at equally doomed Olympus Mons which lay partially consumed by a haze of orographic clouds. Stella envied its lack of mind. For Olympus Mons, what would be, would be.

The hostiles were six million kilometres away, approaching at seventeen million kilometres an hour and decelerating rapidly. They would be close to Mars in less than a few minutes.

Stella and Todd took turns in composing messages to Earth, to be passed on to their family, friends and loved ones. They would be killed, of that they were now convinced, but their messages would still reach Earth, even after their demise had become fact.

Ajiron drifted slowly from the planet without disturbing any of the orange talcum that ringed Mars base in a deep plot of aeolian rust. Jessy watched as they rose gently and silently above Tharsis, deeply saddened to leave Stella and Todd and abandon them to their fate. She couldn't help wonder if there was another way. Jessy could see them embracing through the window of Mars Hab.

The rhodonite plain grew slowly in dimension, its desolate flatness emphasized by the towering volcanic ridge that tiptoed on its boundary. As they loomed closer, Sean watched the southernmost cone belching intricate filigrees of soot into the dim Martian sky. The cloud of soot hid tiny Phobos, the bantam moon he'd just seen as it whipped over the horizon on its equatorial passage.

Within five minutes they were in orbit on the opposite side to Earth, looking down on a darkened coin. Zamindar fingered the pad and they all felt the inertial change as the pod accelerated, gradually at first. In three minutes, they were half a million kilometres from Mars, which Jessy saw dwindling rapidly to nothing behind her. The sands of time, she pondered, sadly.

Todd and Stella couldn't help but watch the two craft as they approached Mars. Their old version of Prox showed that one of the vessels had stopped a few million kilometres from the planet. The other had maintained its course and continued on toward them. They abandoned the small control chamber and moved over to the window in the spartan living quarters. All lights, even the dim secondaries, had been doused. It wouldn't help but they had to try. They had to do something positive, pitiable as it was. And it was pitiable.

The human occupants of Ajiron were exhausted. Despite what was happening around them, Mitch saw Jessy and Sean had fallen asleep. Their heads rested limply against the invisible hull of the ship, resting against the cosmos as it were. There was no green headprints because there was no friction. They were asleep in a welcome slumber.

Mitch couldn't believe they could fall asleep, but he too felt an overwhelming weariness suddenly wash through him. His eyes felt sore and his brain tingled oddly, almost pleasurably. His last thought before he slipped away was whether Zamindar had anything to do with it, whether he was somehow inducing sleep. He had no doubt he could do it if he chose to. As he lost consciousness, he had a final dim thought of Mars, his Mars annihilated, then abrupt sadness. Then he was asleep. They were all fast asleep, except Zamindar who continued to pilot the craft away from the shrinking, terminal red world.

Neurons and electrochemical impulses began firing and sparking within the pod, but the sudden surge of cognitive energy had nothing to do with the pad. This time it was human energy.

Everything was red, red and touched with tiny bits of orange and brown and white. But it was mainly vivid red, like a gargantuan garnet dropsheet. Mitch was looking down at the surface from somewhere above. The horizon was much closer than Earth. He remembered thinking that the pictures of Mars really did not do it justice.

He could see the remnants of Viking and he could hear it. It was screaming...an inhuman cry of agony and torture, and it was earsplitting. Viking 1, or what remained of it, was visibly convulsing, moving, alive, writhing in pain. Mitch could feel the panic and the hopeless sorrow rise in his knotted throat and he could hear another noise, another scream, his own scream. He was crying anguished tears for what was an impossible happening, but he knew it was real. It was happening.

Mitch opened his eyes and tensed. 'Fuck me,' he said to himself. 'What a goddamn trip that was.' Looking around, he saw only the interior of Ajiron. A dream he said, and repeated it several times to himself. His heart was pounding like a speedboat on choppy water. Holy shit, was his first thought. Mitch instantly thought how pleasurable it was to relive his finest moment, but what in God's name had prompted the grotesque ending?

He puzzled over it for minutes while his breathing slowed. Then it hit him. They would be responsible for killing Mars and for killing the little lander, they from Earth, him particularly. Strangely though he felt sadder for the pending destruction of the little Mars lander than for anything else, his intimate friend of so many years.

***

Waiting in the dark they gazed at the landscape outside. They didn't want to die, especially like this and they couldn't help but hate the creature who had so easily and unemotionally passed sentence on them. 'Piece of shit,' he said to Stella, shaking his head, he couldn't believe it was happening to him.

Within minutes they saw the light from the nearest hulk somewhere beyond the orbit of Deimos. Prox showed it up as a slowly moving gamma source two hundred thousand kilometres away. 'Here it comes,' Stella said sadly.

Todd was watching the single light from the craft when it started to vary in intensity, from dull to brighter to quite bright and then back to dull again, all within a second or two.

'Not long now...' he muttered tonelessly. Stella was gazing at the dim silhouette of Olympus Mons that towered above the horizon like a tremendous sentinel. She looked haunted and hopeless, a refugee from the next planet down, doomed by the worst luck imaginable. Todd moved his eye back to the scope. The klaxon started wailing and the red strobe started spewing staccato light. The craft had breached the outer limits of Prox's line of sight. The light kept brightening by degrees until it formed a blinding pinpoint of pure white brilliance. So bright that it hid the stars for several degrees of arc around it.

'Oh shit,' he growled. Whatever it was, was about to be wrought. For Mars and for them the moment had come. He left the scope and slid over to Stella who was predictably crying. She was sobbing quietly, tears of terror mixing with tears of unqualified sadness. Stella felt like a character in a nightmarish play. She couldn't deal with the fact that initial contact had somehow spelt out their own death, and that they would miss out on being part of Earth's brand new future. It was the cruelest, most horrible irony of all, it was hell, pure and simple.

All of a sudden, the pinpoint of light shed its focus and noiselessly exploded, inflating to become a brilliantly glowing cloud. It illuminated the Martian sky in a brilliant Earthly blueness, the likes of which the planet hadn't seen for three and a half billion years. This time though, the blueness didn't indicate life, this time it spelt out extinction and annihilation. Goodnight.

Stella squinted at the razor sharp shadow of Mars base, cast against the new brightness of the plateau beyond. They watched the desert continue to brighten until the whole scene was washed out by an almost perfect laser blueness. They realized that something fantastically bright was approaching.

In fact, the light had not lost focus at all, it was simply speeding toward them, getting closer and larger. Through the brilliance outside, a cylinder of distinctly deeper blue, several hundred metres across punched through the atmosphere. It hit the fluted surface of Mars somewhere near Kassei Vallis. Stella clung vicelike to Todd, drawing blood with her fingernails and crying uncontrollably. Watching in terror, she saw the azure wall of insulated antiparticles hit the dunes. It was only a fleeting glimpse though.

195

Mars was struck a fatal blow. The cylinder sliced through the crust of the planet and annihilated sand, boulders and bedrock in a distinctly geometric pattern. It blew through the iron and nickel core in a second and then cut laterally in all directions, cracking the fabric of the planet and creating a dozen separate planetoids. The red world fractured and refractured and dissolved into tiny particles and planetesimals, repeating the five billion year old birthing process, only in reverse.

The Virijians had done what Marineris looked like it was threatening to do from space, to crack right through the planet and split it asunder. They had in fact done a singularly better job than that. Mars was dead. Not only dead, for it had been dead for billions of years but ... it was gone.

Mitch was still trying to shake off the nightmare. His mind was throbbing uncomfortably in its afterglow. The Viking lander becoming a writhing, tortured soul had left him harrowed and confused. Staring forward, he tried to put it aside, tried to concentrate on the vista before him but he couldn't shake the terrifying image and worse, the terrifying sound. And then there was Mars...

Mitch rarely dreamt but when he did, he did so in enormous detail and with torturous clarity. This one had been no exception at all. He knew now what Jessy had been going through.

Jessy suddenly awoke, and looking up she saw the front of the craft immersed in a dancing white light. It took her no time to realize that something was illuminating them from behind. She gulped thickly at the implications of the rearward fireball. The three of them spun around almost in unison to look behind. A starlike sphere of light had exploded in space, growing and brightening until it was blinding. The Sun and stars paled to nothing.

'My God,' Mitch said slowly, staring at what was once the familiar red planet...what was once one of the family. The fireball was pregnant with horrible meaning.

Jessy's voice was barely a rattle in the back of her throat, 'Mars, Phobos...little Deimos...Stella, Todd, Mars Hab, all the probes and equipment, the history, the canali, everything, gone! Those bastards...' Jessy muttered venomously.

'Do not judge us all on what these individuals have done,' Zamindar toned. 'This is not our way. It is pure disaster that this has happened on the dawn of our first meeting, but we will remove them and to do this we must continue to evade them.'

'Those bastards!' Jessy repeated, her eyes angry and her voice furious and low.

Mitch couldn't speak. Viking was most definitely gone now and he felt like part of his heart had been gouged out. It was a grievous, empty feeling. He felt like shit.

Behind them the brightness dimmed and was now all but swallowed by the vacuum of space. Ajiron arced beyond Jupiter, skimming very close to its tiny rocky moon Ananke which Sean thought was a spitting image of little Phobos. It was a distressing reminder so soon after the demise of Mars. They were beyond the moons in seconds, accelerating gradually past forty percent Luminal.

'Where are you taking us?' Mitch asked, struggling to conceal the rage he felt toward Zamindar's piratical kin.

Zamindar was still connected to the pad, his middle limb sticking into its glutinous surface. He didn't look up or change what was apparently a sombre expression.

'We are heading to Titan, sixth moon of your Saturn. The Pylon has already been informed of our course.'

Titan? Jessy frowned. 'Why Titan?' she snapped. 'Shouldn't we just keep going and try to stay ahead of them, try for the wormhole or just keep going, out of the solar system?' Jessy looked directly at Zamindar, almost tapping her foot, waiting for a response.

'They would catch us before we reached the black hole, as they would if we maintained a course into unprotected space. I said our pod can almost match them for speed, unfortunately there is a seven percent deficiency which would fairly quickly bring us into their range.

Titan is simply somewhere I consider they would not initially start looking for us, no better than a host of other places but certainly better than some and no worse than many. During our passage to Mars it demonstrated a few interesting characteristics, some that may be helpful to our cause, so Titan is where we are heading.' He sounded like he'd made up his mind.

196

'It's hardly time for a field trip to satisfy your curiosity,' Jessy muttered, feeling her throat tighten and rage swell. She was starting to feel pissed off with the Virijians. Both of them.

'You need to be more lateral in your thinking,' he returned. 'Why not choose Titan if we can accomplish more than one goal, and remember Jessy, I said there is something there that will help us.'

'Christ, you're unbelievable,' she spat quietly. Zamindar looked up at Jessy and removed his fingers from the pad.

'No Jessy, you're unbelievable.'

The vista was exquisite beyond imagination, a dazzling rainbow of kaleidoscopic symmetry. Color and harmony were Sean's irresistible first impressions. The vista was so stunning that it hit them with a dizzy feeling of almost supernatural disbelief. It was like a tremendous floodlit Faberge egg surrounded by blackness. The endless ring plane was all they could see as they closed on the gigantic, super rotating world. Several of Saturn's family were also visible, shining like faceted diamonds against the background of space. They all felt the deceleration. Sean felt like he was coming to a complete stop in space. They slid past the oblate giant only a thousand kilometres from its outermost ring, a fabulous pink water ice paling that rubbed against a finer ring of silver and snow. They all saw the tremendous Auroras covering both poles of Saturn as they shot past.

They left Saturn behind and loped out toward the distant moon that was already distinguishable by its size, and by its incredibly striking color..

'God...it looks like Mars from here,' Sean whispered, stunned by the beauty of the red orange moon. Jessy looked closer, studying the world before them, a colossal jewel bathing in the almost fluorescent arclight reflected by Saturn's girdles. 'A cross between Mars and Venus really, although it's a lot colder,' she breathed raspily. 'It's the only place with liquid anything on its surface, well, apart from Earth of course, and in this case its ammonia,' Jessy said. 'What a place huh?

Setting it apart, Sean noticed, was the vivid tail of what he knew was escaping hydrogen, an element too light to mix it with the heavier atmospheric soup. It was being thrust away into space and they could see it as a fantastic trailing nebula, lit up by the rays from an anaemic Sun.

Jessy spied something she didn't expect to see. 'Is that a ring plane around its equator?' She could see something. It was fuzzy and sparse, but something was certainly there and it was moving...rotating, about its midriff.

'That is the reason we are here, it is an unusual planetary ring composed of boulders rather than lesser particles. More unusual though is its age, this ring is strangely juvenile.'

Jessy got the picture. 'We're going to hide in the boulder belt? Are you saying they won't be able to detect us in there?'

'Yes and yes Jessy. They will not distinguish us from anything less than a few million kilometres away unless they are really searching in this area. This craft does not produce a trackable signature.'

'Sure Zamindar, I've heard your statements of fact before.'

He looked directly at her and said nothing.

They watched as Ajiron drew up on the strange smog obscured moon planet. As they approached, it was apparent that the little world was not much smaller than Mars had been, and had a thick roiling atmosphere, white and slightly grayish clouds on occasion interrupting the purely rusty red and in parts, black disk. Its status as the second largest moon in the solar system wasn't surprising. It looked like a planet, and the atmosphere added to it.

Jessy watched the narrow ring of boulders grow larger in front of her, quickly hiding the moon's northern pole behind a rotating rocky panorama. Below the arc of shattered moonrock she could see an almost perfectly straight equatorial line divide a darker northern hemisphere from a distinctly lighter south.

Up close she couldn't believe how sharp and obvious the divide was. Was it simply a cloud feature, and if it was, what did it mean? She wondered, scratching her chin hard and looking at Titan intently. Jessy's fear was still pulsing inside mainly because of Ajiron's clarity and their unsurpassed view of Titan, but also the boulders she could see were big, and some so angular as to look sharp.

Within seconds they were upon the ring plane. The pod slid alongside and maneuvered itself so it was moving in perfect synch with the orbiting debris. In a turn of blinding speed and agility they slipped inside the ring and were effectively stationary within it, surrounded on all sides by tumbling gray and brown boulders.

'...contact. They are in range,' Zamindar advised. 'The vessels are within sixty million kilometres, course still Neptune bearing, velocity ninety nine percent Luminal. They will quickly realize that we are elsewhere, and will search until they find us. They will not give up. Ever.'

Jessy looked uncomfortably at the rectangular pseudo potatoes tumbling around her, above, below and to each side. 'I don't fucking like this,' she groaned softly, overwhelmed by their closeness to what was so casually dancing around them. And them in a craft which visually offered no respite from the view.

Despite their proximity, Zamindar stressed that they were safe, something to do with "charge repellers" that kept the ship at a constant distance from their monolithic escorts.

'They are out of range,' came the slightly metallic toning.

Travelling at the best part of light speed, the two vessels flashed into range and just as rapidly moved out of it. Ajiron was safe, albeit temporarily. Zamindar turned slowly to face his human cargo. His next tonings took the air from their lungs as though they'd been suddenly thrust into the emptiness outside.

'Are you aware that there is life on this moon?'

Their expressions of surprise were instantaneous and vividly chiseled, concern wiped away by astonishment.

'Wh...are you sure?' Sean spluttered, after finally finding his voice, looking squarely at Zamindar. 'Actual life?' The question was unnecessary. Jessy looked Zamindar up and down critically, stunned and taken aback.

All eyes were plastered on the Virijian. They were well aware that the possibility existed, perhaps more so here than on any other of the minor or even major worlds of the local family, but they hadn't given it a second thought.

None of the Earthly probes had detected much at all. NASA's Odysseus lander found nothing but a harsh chemical broth, a fully loaded cocktail of hydrocarbons, acids and raw elements. The precursors for life certainly, but life itself, there was no sign of that. Mitch stared at Zamindar with a mouth that was literally hanging open.

Jessy's mind flailed with the idea of life in such a savage environment. She knew there were Earthly swimmers that lived and loved in boiling mid oceanic vents...tiny crawlers on frigid Arctic tundras...but Jesus, Titan made those places look like an ambrosia. '...what sort of life?' she finally stuttered. That's three examples of life in our system, Sean said to himself, counting on his fingers, can't be a miracle, no fucking way. 'Three life events,' he whispered to himself. He kept repeating ''three''. Miracle forgotten. Life must be everywhere. Everywhere conditions allow, everywhere there's liquid water – there is life. Geochemistry naturally becomes biochemistry, now they knew for sure!

'Difficult to say from here. It is a rather remarkable world, like none other in your group and is in fact unique in my experience of many thousands of star systems. It is far away from your star's lifebelt yet it has acquired, by other fortuitous means, a small and easily missed surface zone that is thermally habitable, as you would define it.'

Sean was staring fixedly at the Virijian. 'We're the best part of a billion and a half kilometres from the Sun, how...

'Your Titan is shrouded by thick aerosol clouds that do not extend right to the surface. There is an ecosphere right at the surface that is fairly much clear of the dense mat of photo substances. It extends upward from the surface only a thousand metres or so. This mat acts as a thermal blanket and has kept the surface, not warm, but also not as cold as it otherwise would be.

Surface temperature is of liquid methane.' Zamindar's use of the words "your Titan" made Sean feel good, and in a sense, he was right. It was theirs, as the only intelligence in the system, it was theirs.

'And there's life in that cold?' Jessy questioned in disbelief. She tried to imagine what creatures they might be, what they would look like as they groped blindly through the murky depths of a frigid methane sea. Holy shit, we were actually right in predicting life, Jessy thought proudly. She didn't know what sort of life yet.

'No there is not life in that cold, but I did say average temperature. There is a small equatorial zone of subterranean vulcanism that is both surrounded and criss-crossed by shallow magmatic veins. This heats one tiny part of the planet to more than zero degrees centigrade. The warmth is efficiently held in by the greenhouse atmosphere in that area but it is quickly dissipated by winds. The critical factor is that it is continuously replenished from beneath. The long term vulcanism, there is no crustal movement, has allowed lakes of water to remain liquid in this area for as much as half a billion years which is...

'What about the life?' Sean interrupted. 'Forget the planetary lesson.' Magnesium spires were dancing in front of his eyes as he contemplated what Zamindar had just told them.

'Carbon based, RNA/DNA multicellular, liquid water dwelling, you would call them cold blooded fish, more or less. There are also varieties of highly efficient sea plants. Food chains exist that have been there for millions of years.'

'You mean there are proper oceans down there?' Mitch asked softly, finding it difficult to believe what he was hearing. Jessy's eyes were almost popping as she waited for more information.

'Not oceans, shallow pure water lakes kept liquid in that one small area. Remember, almost the entire planet is freezing and volcanoes on the surface are of the cryo type, nearly all the lakes and seas are filled with nitrogen or ammonia or methane, not water.'

'What about on the land?' Sean asked. 'Any life?' His heartbeat pummeled his ribs waiting for the answer. Jessy's face was ashen. She didn't care as much about life on Titan as staying alive.

'Evidence of small land plants similar to your lichens, highly resistant to chemical attack and intense cold. And able to rapidly consume raw hydrocarbons, acetylene, cyanogen and the like, and respire oxygen. No mobile life… Do you wish to visit the surface of Titan?' the Virijian asked, twisting his middle elbow and moving his paw back to the pad. 'We have twenty-four minutes before they can get back within range. Travel time to the surface is two minutes thirty seconds. We can make a round trip in that time. I can monitor their location from the pod, remember their craft are a thousand times larger than ours, I can see them but they cannot see us from this distance.'

'Let's do it,' Sean urged. His eyes said "yes".

'No, it's not worth the chance,' Jessy pleaded, 'Something will go wrong.' She shook her head and looked to Mitch for support. 'For God's sake,' Jessy yelled, seeing the course they were on.

'Can anything go wrong Zamindar?' Mitch asked firmly.

'No.' He toned immediately. Yeah right, Jessy thought. The threat of catastrophe gripped her throat like a hungry lion.

'It beats the hell out of sitting here, imagine passing it up!' No way, Sean thought.

Jessy looked at Mitch and knew his mind was set, not to mention Sean who would've jetted to the surface in his astrosuit given the chance.

'Okay, let's do it…if it's no risk, why not?' Mitch sat back and waited. Jessy groaned quietly. Outvoted yet again.

Zamindar was at the pad, not touching it, but clearly investing it with, what was to them, silent instructions. The tiny craft farewelled its potato shaped sentinels and departed their protective veil, arcing straight into the swirling atmospheric soup.

Like a bullet through a sandbag, it punched a short lived hole in the outermost layer.

A blanket of boiling orange and brown clouds engulfed them instantly, giving them the uncanny impression that they'd just dived into a tub of raw sewage. Vision was nil. Billions of supercooled crystals, methane and dirty hydrocarbons, thumped and thudded against the bubble, making a tremendous noise, a pounding unmelodic resonance that was earsplitting.

Zamindar appeared to nullify the racket by caressing the pad with what looked like a deft two finger tickle. Cacophony became encompassing silence and Jessy noticed that she could still see Saturn despite the growing haze around them.

They followed her gaze and saw the fabulous pinwheels hanging above them like a huge and surreal mobile, a breathtaking sight with little Rhea silhouetted in front of Saturn's squashed southern pole. The whole picture was quickly swallowed by the swirling chemical slush above them. Then it was gone, only ochreous haze remained, everywhere.

In places, the pod fell through clots of brown ooze that hung and drifted in the twisting zephyr, momentarily engulfing and sticking to Ajiron. It was an oily, greasy ride, like a rapid transit through partially congealed pumpkin soup. Then they were through and into clean atmosphere. Colorful opaqueness rapidly became striking crystal clarity. The ground loomed up at them.

'Shit! Mitch barked. Sean and Jessy squawked similar sentiments as the surface punched up at them like a gloved fist. Vertigo. Jessy's heart started racing as she looked across at Mitch wordlessly with eyes that bespoke terror.

The pod broke into a dim, thinly oxygenated world of pale primrose mist through which the ground could easily be seen. They stared at the fluidscape of Titan, now at close quarters. The bubble was flying at eight hundred metres and below them was Saturn's most corpulent offspring, laid out naked, the second largest moon in the solar system, a wonderland of astonishing diversity.

'My God...who would've thought,' Sean trumpeted slowly as his eyes digested the unexpected scene. It was light and dark, black and ochre. Titan was amazing.

'We are directly above the equator.' Zamindar touched the pad briefly, more of a fondle than a real touch. Jessy watched with eyes that were looking nervously ahead.

Below them was a tremendous ridge of deeply eroded mountains, intensely furrowed and wrinkled, brimming with the open wounds of profuse fluid attack. The tops of the alien plateau easily penetrated the base of the swirling orange clouds which Sean noticed had a spirit level flatness. It was a stunning sight.

The volcanic spur beneath them formed an almost perfect rectangle, a geometric crucible within which were the scattered nests of bio lakes Zamindar had referred to as the receptacles of life on Titan. Volcanic warmth was everywhere, swaddling everything, boiling steam venting from at least a thousand cracks and fissures. In the distance, Mitch could see the cryovolcanoes spewing methane and ammonia and some water into the atmosphere which quickly settled onto the landscape.

The warmth trapped beneath the lakes must have been enormous, a fact evident to all of them as they gazed at the tiny percentage of it that was finding its way to the surface. Jessy wondered what sort of unimaginable pressures were building up beneath them, hoping what was being released was enough to derail an apocalyptic blow through.

Trapped within the hundred square kilometres nestled between the cradling mountains was a series of lakes, interconnected and some isolated but all of them brim full of liquid. Water as it turned out, which appeared to be a vivid orange, born from the reflection of the colorful muck above.

The land in between the lakes and beyond the mountains was uniformly flat with only a few isolated undulations here and there. All of it was carpeted in foreboding darkness for as far as they could see to the almost arm's length horizon.

'The landscape...the browns, the blacks, it looks so smooth. What the hell is it?' Sean asked, having a fair idea of the answer. Peatbog, he thought. He was wrong.

'It is chlorophyllin vegetation, similar though chemically and functionally different to your algae on Earth. It drinks the raw organic solvents which flood from the atmosphere and breathes oxygen into this narrow under cloud region, a most fortuitous adaptation. If it were not for this aggressive flora, the whole area would be drowning under masses of ooze and slime. With the vulcanism and the blanket of fog providing the warmth, the cyano-compounds in this slime have built the blueprint for life.'

Zamindar's almost instantaneous understanding of the moon's character was testament to the profound wisdom and biological perspective of his species.

The tiny pod descended gingerly toward one of the smaller orange lakes near the bull's eye of the rectangle. As they edged closer, immense ebony mountains penetrated the clouds. There appeared to be an impenetrable coalface, a barrier of inviolable rock.

The ominous vista was more overtly alien than any other Jessy had seen on this crazy voyage. She felt trapped by the towering three hundred and sixty degree horizon of unbroken blackness. With the haze crushing down on them, it seemed like there was no escape.

Scooting inward, the pod stopped three metres above the ground and gradually descended to touch down only a metre or so from the water's edge. It sunk only slightly into the ubiquitously coarse and metres thick pseudo algae.

'No wind,' Jessy remarked, gaping at the glasslike surface of the lake which perfectly mirrored the twisting alien sky above.

'This moon is odd in many ways,' Zamindar replied. 'Wind is apparently either here or it is not. There is little halfway.' He connected with the pad momentarily and the lake closest to them became almost totally clear if not a little brown. 'The light is being filtered through the nano prisms in the skin, to allow you to see what we came to see. That which is underneath.'

They all looked and immediately they saw. It was incredible.

'Mother of God,' Sean said through a mouth that stayed open long after the words had escaped. He made some sort of noise, totally incomprehensible. Jessy's heartbeat shot to the roof.

'What the hell...' Mitch blurted. Sean stared. Jessy stared. Milling around only a few metres away and not far under the surface were absolutely snow white cylindrical things, watery creatures that tapered only slightly from their mouths to their short-paired tails. Alien swimmers, like delicately hewn ivory sculptures, wallowing and wheeling right there in front of them.

'...God,' Jessy murmured, looking aghast. at the odd tubular things that seemed to grow from their "snouts" and run all the way down their spines and past their tails. They looked like saffron streamers blowing in the wind, she thought, blinking at them uncomprehendingly.

'Fish,' Sean grunted, 'Like catfish...sort of.' Sean was thrusting his head forward, peering at the odd denizens of this moon.

Jessy and Mitch elbowed one another to get a better look. Their noses were almost hard up against the invisible membrane of the craft as they strained to see. 'Cylindrical fish,' Sean croaked, not really believing what he was seeing,'...with whiskers and sharp looking horns,' he was pointing.

There were other swimmy things too. Spherical white ones, like polished cue balls with huge backward arching ventral fins. Floating between the "cue balls" were pairs of partially transparent tubular creatures that seemed to move by opening and closing their sleek purple duckbills.

And there were others that looked like gyrating football bladders, translucent and full of something that looked like bubbling hair gel. Their bodies looked slippery smooth and terminated with staring eyes that sat on the end of long golden filaments.

Jessy could see swarms of squashed ones too, totally flat circular things with no apparent means of locomotion, looking like spinning blue sanding disks.

Sean looked and could make out the squirming internal organs of several batches of crawling things that were one hundred percent, transparent. He could see the weeds and the other creatures directly behind them by looking through them. Some of the transparent ones, he could see, were internally fired by some sort of colorful electrochemical discharge which episodically lit them into brilliantly glowing pyres. Just like Earth, he mused in awe, staring as if in a trance. But they were deep sea creatures on Earth, here they were near the surface. Go figure. Evolution, he assumed.

The vista was ineffably strange. 'They're everywhere,' Sean exploded. His head was bobbing from side to side like a hungry barn owl. He saw tongue-like swimmers that wormed along the shallow lake floor, alternately clear and yellow almost squid and long snouted pink tubes with colorful tumorous excrescences. There were oozing ovular pods, spherical filamentous pseudo anemones and brilliant crimson sponges that throbbed and shivered like blobs of barely set jelly. Stuck to the floor nearest them were luminescent beds of whiskery green ferns, ebbing and flowing in the Herculean tide imposed on Titan by its corpulent parent.

Jessy brought a shaky hand to her now moist forehead. Mitch felt like he could've reached out and grabbed any one of them. It was a biological Eden in the midst of unthinkable harshness.

All this on Titan...in our own solar system, Sean pondered dizzily. 'To think we were so excited by the fossils on Mars, the tiny imprints, the three and a half billion year old pseudomorphs. This makes them look almost inconsequential. And now this. Fantastic, dazzling complexity in the flimsiest of microcosms. Holy shit!' He looked again at the watery abode outside and wondered how much like ancient Earth this place might be.

Most of the creatures they could see were a variation on the same odd cylindrical shape. They were like obese fish, Mitch mused idly, trying to compare the Titanian creatures to their own version on Earth. 'Cylindrical fish,' he blurted. 'What happened to natural selection? Surely a more slipstreamed shape would...'

'Mitch, you told us not to apply our own logic to the unknown,' Jessy said. 'Cylifish! Darwin was an Earthling you know, he'd never been to Titan.' She looked quizzically at Mitch.

'Why silly? he asked.

Jessy raised her eyebrows and offered him a smile. Dummy, she thought.

'Oh...cyli. Yeah right. I knew that,' Mitch grinned. He had no idea. Mitch's head was everywhere. A large black blade darted close to shore and swallowed a cylifish, retreating out again before they could get a good look at it. It was more of a shadow than a real form.

'Jesus Christ,' Mitch yelled, 'What the hell was that?' Predator, he knew that much. Thinking about it, he was stunned and almost unbelieving, but it made some sort of sense. Food chains...lithium chlorophyll...Titan. And to think they never knew! Never had a clue.

Jessy looked totally bewildered, all wide eyes and furrowed brow.

They were everywhere, the lakes in this small restricted zone of an otherwise deep frozen moon were literally teeming with life, brim full of plants and strange xenothings, swimming, crawling, jumping, whirling, hopping, spinning, gyrating or just sitting motionless. Overpopulation seemed to be the only looming problem. Apart from the breakdown of their warm environment that is. That would mean a quick death in this Sun distant place. Its proximity to Saturn would help, but it wouldn't be enough. Tidal heating alone wouldn't be enough to keep all this going.

Sean was sitting back and trying his best to take it all in. Compared to the transgalactic wonders he'd seen, this was very mild in comparison. But this was in their own solar system, their own backyard, and it was so incredibly unexpected. Life on Titan had been mooted before but life as advanced as this in such an unusual and unique environment, that was not, *absolutely not*, expected.

The surface of the water suddenly broke into life. Millions of huge splashes ruined the perfect glassy surface. Sean's first thought was that some fantastic alien beast was rising from the depths of the lake.

'It's raining!' Jessy said, stating what was obvious to all. 'But what rain!'

The bubble was being pelted with pendulous drops of oily black rain that struck the pod and ran rapidly down its slick dermis.

Jesus...Exxon heaven, Jessy mused, looking at the greasy hail of hydrocarbons.

'...cauldrons of hell,' Mitch whispered, gazing at the suddenly violent sky.

Sean just stared, at Mitch mostly, seemingly watching his reaction.

Massive laceworks of fork lightning were exploding in the distance and the sound of the thunder was so unbelievably loud that Jessy thought her eardrums would burst. She had visions of the bubble cracking and shattering, allowing the thick nitrous poisons from without to bleed in and turn them instantly frog green.

Zamindar suddenly reconnected with the pad with a speed and an intensity they had rarely seen before. Never seen, actually, Mitch mused to himself. His movements were normally slow and deliberate, but now they were at the very least hasty.

His expression was different too, somehow harder, any facial expression was rare and this one was brand new to them. Jessy gulped as she looked at Zamindar, something was clearly wrong. There was only one thing it could be.

202

'They are back within range,' he said simply. '...are heading toward Titan.'

Mitch turned and looked at him wildly. 'You said we had time to burn, how could you be so wrong? I asked if you were certain and you said you were, without hesitation. What happened to no risk?' He was only inches away from the pallid flesh of his cranium.

'I was not wrong. They somehow misled the pad, it appears to be the only explanation. There is only one craft heading this way, meaning there might have been a third vessel travelling behind the first two which it did not detect. It is likely this is the third vessel. You have to remember that our technology is not designed for warfare, for locating hostile craft or for anything related to aggressive behaviour. Our whole society is oriented differently to yours, as yours eventually will be. It is structured along technological munificence...and that has been part of our undoing here.'

'Fuck,' Jessy swore, shaking her head and looking at Mitch, aghast at Zamindar's ill founded bullshit, his stupid decision was probably going to kill them and Earth.

'It seems that they have a precise fix on our location and will be able to track us wherever we go. Their craft is considerably superior to our personal vessel. It will take us a minimum of two minutes to exit the atmosphere and by then there will be insufficient time to escape.

'So, what are you saying, we just sit here and wait, to be destroyed, to be killed?'

'They will destroy Titan if we stay here. We must at least depart this world and make endeavor to reach deeper space, for the sake of the life that is successful here.' The Virijian looked straight ahead, not making eye contact with anyone.

Jessy tuned out and focused on her young son. She thought of future opportunities gone, for Josh, for her, for her and Mitch, for Earth. Fuck it, she thought and felt like crying.

Ajiron shot away from the lakes with an inertial urgency they hadn't felt before and they were spearing through the carrot soup in seconds. The glutinous rain continued to pummel and darken the bubble as they rose rapidly from the moon's gravity well. In two minutes, they would be back into Saturnian space to an uncertain, but apparently violent reception.

Jessy again saw Saturn fall vaguely into view, first one pole, then part of the rings, then the other pole poked through the thinning, swirling overcoat. Then it was there in all its unimpeded magnificence. But this time the view wasn't nearly as uplifting. This time it meant goodbye.

By the time Ajiron hit the tenuous rim of Titan's soupy atmosphere the third vessel was only a quarter of a million kilometres away. Almost on top of them. It was readying its weaponry.

The tiny pod extricated itself from the last swirlings of the tenacious atmosphere and was all of a sudden staring at clear black space, Saturn on one side, other moons in the distance and Titan beneath their feet, orange and roiling like a bloody axe wound.

***

Charijiok caressed the pad and instructed it to act.

***

They all saw the beast a short distance away in space, sitting like a massive barnacle just below the shining eye that was Rhea. The vessel was stationary and rapidly pivoting to face their pod head on, although it probably could have destroyed them without turning at all.

'Oh God!' Jessy croaked, 'Go, get out of here, now!'

'It will do us no good...'

Their vision exploded in shards of dazzling blue, a blurring, fiery detonation blinding them. Tentacles of glimmering material hurtled past, some of it hitting and rocking their tiny ship. In front of them the rebel ship was a supernova, bright with the light of its own destruction. It quickly faded and went out and then ... nothing. Everything it had been had sped past them in small fluid pieces.

Nine immense Pylon craft approached slowly and stopped in front of them, suspended and silhouetted in front of the fabulous ringed orb. Zamindar joined with the pad. He communicated with Charijiok. They had intervened with a few seconds to go.

Jessy had been fully prepared to die, at the last moment had expected to die. Now they'd been given a reprieve by the same race that had twice promised them death. She was overwhelmed with emotion, sobbing quietly, clutching Joshua tightly to her chest.

Despite her lingering terror she couldn't help but wonder whether they felt emotion. Jessy knew that Zamindar hadn't shown anything remotely akin to emotion, even in the final moments when death was staring at them from space. Maybe they felt, but the passions and emotions simply ran their course independently of expression. Perhaps feelings or expression were outgrown over time, discarded like a worn out boot in the rush to super cognition. Jessy was dragging in air like she was drowning but was starting to calm down. Alive, she thought, shaking her head, closing her eyes.

Zamindar finally removed his paw from the pad and as he spoke, he pointed, using the inner thumb on his axial grasper.

'We will take Ajiron aboard the first of the craft but before we do there is something the pad has found in the boulder belt. I have advised Charijiok and he agrees that we should investigate while we are here, so with your consent I will... '

'Does your curiosity know no bounds Zamindar?' Jessy moaned. 'We were almost wiped out because you wanted to see Titan, but that doesn't seem to have fazed you at all. I thought we were curious but if you are typical of your kind then we're not even in your league...not even close. It seems that you'll give up all else in the name of discovery.' She shook her head and looked away, knowing she might as well be trying to convince Saturn to shed its rings.

'Our curiosity knows no bounds, you are correct but the danger has passed so there will be no peril in a short voyage out to the ring.'

Jessy rubbed the back of her neck and made a noise like a deflating balloon. She didn't believe him and she didn't like it. The idea of doing anything but returning to Earth was an abhorrence, to her at least.

'What has your pad detected?' Sean asked, feeling the first twinges of excitement tickling his cortex. He could see Jessy wasn't happy. She wanted to go home...now.

'Something curious,' Zamindar replied. It has distinguished an object that is clearly not the same as the rest. It is within the ring but appears to be not of the ring. Its spin is more rapid and it shows almost no reflective variations. It has no light curve, meaning its surface is very uniform. Objects with uniform morphometry are unlikely to be natural. And it is by definition, totally unlike the other billion or so objects that tenant the ring, which is very interesting. Your kind have never been to Titan before?' He knew the answer.

'Never in person,' Sean replied. 'Are you saying it's artificial, that it's not a boulder?'

'It is a reasonable conclusion.'

'In God's name!' Jessy uttered in desperation. 'What now? I think we should make Earth a priority, I'm not so sure that we... '

'Quiet Jess,' Sean said loudly. 'Where's your sense of adventure? We're pioneers you know.' He glared directly at Jessy. 'Maybe it's nothing, but maybe it's something.' His eyes were fired by the adrenaline that bled into his veins like a warm amphetamine.

'We were nearly all killed, we were only seconds from death,' Jessy implored. Haven't there been enough firsts on this mission already, for God's sake, think of Josh!' She looked down at their precious child, trying to stifle the scream that was again welling in her throat, three-quarters of the way up. She glared at Sean and narrowed her eyes scornfully.

'I'm not forgetting Josh, but Zamindar will do this anyway, you know that, so why not just relax and enjoy what might be an interesting pit stop on the way back home. We're almost home Jess so let's do this one last thing before we get there, anyway I know you're interested in seeing what this object is.'

Jessy eyed Sean angrily and didn't respond. She hated it when he seemed to know her better than she did. She did want to find out, but not at the expense of Josh, or anyone.

Bastard, she thought without malice. Goddamn him.

12

Prophecy

'The universe seems neither benign nor hostile, merely indifferent.' ~ *Carl Sagan*

Zamindar piloted Ajiron to the band of rotating rectangles that skimmed only fifty thousand kilometres above the boiling cloud tops. Mitch watched as the boulders increased in size before him. Sliding to within a few hundred metres of the ringlet, the craft changed its path to follow the curve of the shattered cometary nucleus, like a rollercoaster hugging its track. The pad had acquired its target. Sean's imagination fired and his heart pounded as the passage of the boulders slowed beneath him. Ajiron slowed.

They were closing on their prey. Emerging over the horizon was something clearly different, a single eurythmic form lurking amongst a sea of asperous pseudo potatoes. It already looked profoundly out of place.

Almost as black as space itself, the background of Titan's carrot soup allowed them to see it, silhouetted and vivid and now only metres in front of them. Up close it wasn't black at all, it was grey, like the hull of a naval warship. If someone was trying to hide it, they had done a singularly bad job. It was, as Zamindar pointed out, overtly not of the ring. An entirely lusterless and very precise sphere orbiting where it should not have been. Looking at it, Jessy felt her heartbeat start to rise. She didn't like the look of it, at all. Up close, it looked as though it were purposefully designed to stand out from the jostling boulders that surged around it. A celestial black sheep, skating on the gravity well of the great moon, inside an almost solid wall of rock forged by its less geometric kin.

'What the hell is it?' Sean's whispered first words were predictable. 'Obviously artificial, but how, when, and most importantly who?' He hunched forward and examined it as closely as he could. 'How, when and who?' Sean muttered.

'That'd be right,' Mitch muttered, looking at no one, thinking they were asking a tad too much, if they wanted answers to each one. Fuck me, he thought and shook his head.

Sean stared unblinkingly forward, mesmerized by the dancing object which was only metres away. He was struck by its indefinable grace, watching it move as though it were being driven by an impossibly deft hand. There was, no doubt that it wasn't just orbiting, it was wobbling in every direction, seemingly dodging what was so close around it. But dodging how? He wondered, feeling a touch more uncomfortable than he had before.

Jessy looked at it and was struck by the sinister air it presented. It looked menacing, she reckoned, as she followed it with owlish eyes, studying grimly. She definitely didn't like the look of it. It looked threatening, even though it was just a sphere.

Sean finally broke his stare, and glanced at Zamindar, 'was there something on Titan we missed, an intelligence capable of putting this thing in orbit?'

'Absolutely not,' came Zamindar's immediate reply. 'The creatures you called cylifish are the most advanced denizens of that moon. Something else from somewhere else must have placed it, but until we can inspect it, I can tell you no more. The pad cannot penetrate the walls of the sphere which in itself is unexplainable.' As he delivered the last few words, his cranial flesh rippled a bit, as though an icy breeze had just washed the surface of his finely bristled scalp.

'Could it be something from Earth gone astray?' Jessy asked casually, not believing it for a second. Despite being a familiar earthly shape, sort of like a brand new wrecking ball, everything about it struck her mind as alien, not like the Virijians, but genuinely alien. As positively unearthly. In this case she was sure that appearance would prove to mean absolutely naught. After all, she considered, the shape of the object was the most common and mathematically pure in the Universe. So, why the terror she felt? It was like coming face to face with an ancient human bungalow on Mars.

'There's only been a few craft sent in this direction that were lost,' Mitch said, '...but no way it's any of those.' He craned his head up at Jessy who was standing above him, '...the Brahma went offline somewhere around Saturn, Huygens ran out of power on the surface and Cassini dove into Saturn's atmosphere...so no way it's something we sent.'.

If it's not ours, or the Virijians...whose? Who the hell put it there? The unasked question hung in the air like a second atmosphere, crushingly in need of answer. None of them had a clue about the sphere. Sean gawked at Mitch and shrugged. He had no idea what it was.

Sean gazed at the Sphere, feeling a surge of wonder run the entire length of his body, edged with something he couldn't quite define. Something that was beating in the pit of his stomach. He felt like he was strapped in an aircraft that was dropping from the sky...the same feeling he'd experienced as a boy in a freefalling elevator. It was the unpleasant sensation that your stomach had come apart from your body and was fighting a losing battle to catch up. He remembered the feeling well and didn't like it one bit.

The thing was about three metres through the middle and had three indistinct markings (grooves maybe) near one of its poles which showed that it was spinning rapidly. Why did it have angular momentum at all, something to do with the ring of boulders it was orbiting with, maybe?

Jessy clenched her fists and toes, and said nothing, thinking how obscene and sinister it looked. She was suddenly consumed by an irrational dread, by visions of a malignant cell in the last seconds before rampant propagation. Or a neutron remnant, , the horrible gray guts of a suicided star. But it was just a ball, that was the reality, they had hooked onto a featureless grey sphere. The rest was just, the irrational, illogical fear of the unknown. Even the Virijians seemed oddly reticent.

Sean's brain had been spinning along for ten minutes now, wrestling with that likelihood. He took deep breath before speaking, 'Could this be an artifact, the so called "calling card" we've talked about? You know,' he looked knowingly at Mitch, 'left by someone for us to find in a place that would guarantee we'd evolved to a certain level of sophistication, worth talking too, so to speak. Wouldn't it be funny,' he said chuckling, 'If it's true then we've really ruined their plans. We wouldn't have found this thing for hundreds or maybe thousands of years even if we did manage to get a manned mission up here sooner. If this thing was orbiting Mars or even Luna, we probably wouldn't know about it. To find it we'd have to be right on top of it. It must have an albedo close to zero and remember, we've already sent three probes out here and didn't come close to finding it. I mean, to find this thing would be like stumbling on the proverbial needle. But I can't understand why we didn't know about these boulders.' He looked around, focussing on the field of rocks.

Jessy scratched her head, she had no idea, and by the bewildered look on Mitch's face, nor did he. For a long moment Jessy and Mitch stared at each other, pondering the likelihood.

Sean paused and briefly rubbed his forehead, brooding over what he'd just said. 'Our last probe found nothing but a freezing planet, no ringlet and certainly no life. Only the chemical foundations for life, same as the others. They uncovered some stunning information but nothing like what we found. Not even close. Christ, imagine if Hugyens had dropped into one of those lakes. Could you imagine the reaction back on Earth? Pandemonium! It would've sparked the quickest manned mission response in the...'

'That aside,' Mitch interrupted, 'I'd say we're at least five hundred years away from detecting something this small and this far away.'

'A probable theory,' the Virijian toned as he dropped his axial limb so it rested near his groin. Zamindar's exocranial knot shivered as he moved, looking like some horrendous tumour full of a million tussling may-flies.

Jessy looked nauseated, averting her eyes and unconsciously putting a hand to her nose. It was instinctive, she couldn't help it. 'Shit,' Jessy whispered. She knew she should look, get used to it, but it was hard to look at. It was ugly. Too ugly to look at, now or maybe ever, she reasoned, forcing herself with a lot of self-inertia, to look.

206

Mitch glanced at Sean, full to bursting with questions, 'Jesus, if it's true,' he blurted, staring at Sean with unblinking eyes, '...wouldn't they be stunned to know we found their capsule by hitching a ride with another civilization.' It was crazier than fiction, he reckoned. It was totally bloody insane.

'How old is the ring?' Sean asked, with huge eyes. 'Are you able to tell?' He looked squarely at Zamindar, waiting for the answer he was sure he had. Please have the answer.

'The pad is telling me that it is only fifteen years old. The comet that died here did so virtually yesterday. Any artifact as you call it, would, by definition, be thousands or millions of years old. So, what is the answer? If you are correct and we believe you are, then the Sphere has been freefalling around Titan for at least several thousand years. And was attracted to the juvenile ring, for reasons we can only guess at.'

'It was attracted by the veiling qualities the ring provided,' Sean deduced hesitantly, not really having a clue. It sounded good though.

Jessy looked at the Sphere, feeling sweat ooze onto her skin like lava. 'God, I hope it's not a bomb...it looks like a bomb,' she croaked, swallowing hard and wiping the moisture from her brow with the back of her hand. She was scared of this thing, although she didn't know why? It hadn't shown anything close to aggression. It hadn't shown anything, period.

But still, she wanted to leave it alone. She felt like screaming. The path they were on was set in carbon mortar, she realised that, so she stayed quiet, staring at the orb and Mitch through massive eyes. The irrevocability of knowing was almost too much, even though she had no idea what the knowing might bring. It could be anything. It might be nothing but it could also be something. Maybe the Virijians couldn't extract anything from it, perhaps there was nothing to extract? She guessed they wouldn't know either way unless they tried to open it. Jessy's gaze returned to the orb.

With no noticeable resistance, Ajiron plucked the thing from the orbit it had been following since whomever or whatever had put it there must be long gone. The strange ashen object was theirs now, the property of the new celestial alliance.

Forty years or forty million? Sean grunted silently. How bloody long have you been waiting? The thought gripped his heart and expelled every scrap of air from his lungs. Why, he wondered...why was it there? Jessy watched, rubbing her brow as the orb approached them. It was a sight almost defying description, a group of unsuited beings in a totally transparent vehicle, seemingly open to the emptiness of space, hauling a minute sphere toward an overwhelmingly massive hulk. The girth of the other vessel became more apparent as they approached. On one side was stunning Saturn, and on the other the palpably alien monstrosity. The contrast was complete.

They and their snared Titanian booty were inside the darkness of the vessel within minutes, feeling like they'd just sailed into a stupendous coal stope. The sphinctered hull pinched off and pure whiteness drenched them in a heartbeat, indicating, Sean believed, that an atmosphere had condensed around them. Only seconds later, a dimple sucked open in the wall stuff nearest Ajiron and a huge, unfamiliar Virijian ambled through. Belying his bulk, he moved nimbly up to the craft, slightly bent over, staring in turn at Jessy and then Sean, then at Mitch, without the slightest hint of expression. He was huge. A Giant in the true meaning of the word.

Jessica smiled weakly but Charijiok's gaze never wavered, staying level and frozen as he scrutinized the strange cargo of the tiny sailing ship. It was almost as though he couldn't believe what was inside, although that was probably an added Earthly emotion because his face was frozen. Like a whopping Halloween mask, his face was rigid and staring and slightly blue, as though chiseled from the deepest pack ice. He looked for a long time at Jessy, seemingly wondering what the hell she was. Was she ugly to them, Jessy wondered?

A whole section of the bubble dissolved and Zamindar, who appeared short when compared to this guy, slid out and stood next to the newcomer, immediately joining him in a coarse vascular rhythm that had both their bristled craniums squirming in fluid harmony.

Sean had Josh and with the rest of them, they descended onto the white glacier that was the illimitable docking chamber.

Jessy eyed Charijiok, watching him closely as he went from one to the other in the pod, just gazing, at what to him must have been three very strange beings.

Charijiok was grizzly bear huge, perhaps ten centimeters taller than Zamindar, who himself towered over the humans. God, maybe Zamindar was short for a Virijian, but then Sean remembered Renchiok, and reckoned, perhaps not. He introduced himself to each of them in turn, placing his left limb on each's shoulder as he did, and they couldn't help but sway under the weight of his ponderous paw. Jessy fixed her eyes on Charijiok and regarded him with the strangest unreadable expression. She found it hard to believe what she was looking at. Charijiok no doubt thought the same.

Zamindar turned and motioned to them, using all three arms and rotating his twin outer elbows through a full three hundred and sixty degrees. He looked first at Mitch. The resonance almost K.O.'d him as it thudded into his Wernicke's brain like a serious migraine.

'We would like to help you explore the object.' The giant creature peered downward, speaking as his long neck articulated just above his shoulders. 'If you are agreeable.'

Where the hell would we start anyway? Mitch thought. They all wondered, staring at the slick object that looked like it was cut whole from some impossibly hard alloy.

Sean knew how deceiving looks could be though. Soft metal, he hadn't forgotten what was so abundant around them, so hard looking, yet so perversely malleable and yielding.

Zamindar glanced at Charijiok, seemingly filling, investing him with silent instruction. Standing tall, with pseudo podiums throbbing in step, they moved toward the extraordinary ball which even despite the bright light, remained dull and lustreless.

The thing was entirely unreflective, almost supernaturally dark and foreboding. It looked like tarnished cannon fodder from some ancient Titanian war, a gun powder driven missile that had missed its target a million centuries years ago.

But what was its purpose? That was the burning question. And what the hell was it doing here, only a stone's throw from their own planet? They all had their theories, but the questions and the anxiety were suffocating, filling the chamber like a gradually condensing fog. The unease was frozen in the expressions of the two armers, and similarly cast in the vascular quickening of the triformers. Their fattening veins were swollen by the same wondrous ponderings. Who? Why?

Jessy's mind was wrestling with the possibilities, none of which she particularly liked. She knew there were potential positives in what lay before them, there had to be, but all her mind could find was trepidation and fear. Sean was almost the exact opposite. He was like a dog with several bones. And he wanted all of them.

Moving toward the Sphere, Sean took the lead and walked straight up to it. After briefly assessing its surface from close range, he reached out to touch it.

'No!' Zamindar barked. It was like a well timed punch. Sean reeled and swayed backward as if he'd just been struck with a sharp left, right combination.

'What?' he shot back, feeling slightly groggy. 'Jesus,' he snapped, rubbing his temples. It felt like Zamindar had reached in with his grasper and given his parietal lobe a tweak.

'This has lived its life in a pure vacuum,' he toned, 'its superstructure could be close to absolute zero or be the temperature of molten metal. You could lose your fingers with a single touch. Just because it does not feel cold or hot at close quarters means nothing, remember, we know nothing of its composition.'

Sean stared at Zamindar frozen, with his heart in his mouth, eventually shoe-horning his gaze back to the Sphere. Jesus fuck, he thought, still giddy from the sudden incursion. Charijiok tossed a small fingernail sized object at the orb.

It kissed it for a second or two and then fell, hitting the floor with a dull chonk. The Virijian retrieved the device and held it tightly in his pale fist, tousling it dexterously, pondering the information it was silently investing him with. It was lost in his mighty paw when he held it.

'Surface temperature is twenty degrees Centigrade. It has almost immediately assumed the ambient temperature of the bay, and it is at least partially hollow.'

208

The word struck her like a hammer blow. Hollow. Bile seeped into Jessy's throat and her eyes were wild as she silently chewed on the word. Christ, if it was hollow, then there was an inside. What the hell was inside…what could be inside? Her mind backflipped. Was it some bizarre egg, a metal casing that hid some horrendous organic sac?

She looked above the orb and out at the endless whiteness, trying to forcibly slacken her mind. 'Dear sweet Jesus,' she murmured, trying to drag her mind from the terror of unchecked fantasy. 'Fuck,' she finished on, staring deeply at the ashen relic.

Sean ambled back to the Sphere and this time didn't hesitate. He touched it, caressed it, nudged it, and then tried to push it, eventually putting all his weight into it. He was grunting with effort, trying to force it, to move it as though it were a stalled car with the handbrake firmly engaged. No movement at all. It just sat there totally motionless. '...it looks as though it should roll away or at least wobble a bit, after all it's a perfect sphere and this surface is reasonably firm. But it's stuck fast, sort of like it's adhering or is magnetized to the floor.' He had a sudden vision of a metallic taproot extending from the base of the thing right through the hull of the vessel and out into space. Sean shook his head to get rid of the vision.

He immediately knew where the idea came from. Despite it looking like an everyday object, the thing somehow struck him as being alive, as having the power to think and to do. It was ludicrous, but still he couldn't escape the distressing idea of animacy and certainly, intelligence. Sean stared at the orb, puzzling over it. Who left it and why? Sean gave up trying to push it. It wasn't going anywhere, that was clear if nothing else. It was part of the ship now.

Mitch walked up and touched it with an outstretched finger. It felt like regular metal.

Jessy dragged her hands through her hair several times. She was at a loss for words as she peered at Mitch with lips parting. She was going to pose an inane, unanswerable question, but closed her mouth instead.

'Maybe it's designed that way to make its inspection easier.' Mitch said, bringing his face close to its surface. It was totally, unremittingly smooth, mirror perfect but dull. So dull that its shape was somehow indistinct even with the stark whiteness of its surrounds. The background should have made it stick out like a lunar mare, but it didn't. Was it trying to hide itself? It was almost as though it were making a deliberate attempt to camouflage itself.

Sean knocked on it. No noise. None at all. He tried again, this time a little harder. No noise. He thumped it with the base of his palm but it seemed to absorb all his energy. Totally, thoroughly non acoustic, he decided.

'If this is partly hollow, as you've said Char, why isn't there any noise? It's like I'm knocking on rubber, except the skin is totally unyielding and it feels like metal. What the hell is this stuff?' He looked at the Virijian who was looking down at his paw. He was a fat lot of good.

Zamindar was holding the fingernail sized device and staring intently at it. He looked at the object and said, 'its composition...' he faltered, for the first time, '...I am unable to tell you what it is made of.' He paused and continued staring at the small object. 'I can tell you that it is crystalline and made from a single molecule, two atoms in a vaguely triclinic arrangement, but while we can differentiate the single molecule that forms its basis, we cannot...' Zamindar abruptly stopped toning and closed his eyes, unfurling heavily wrinkled eyelids. He hesitated, looked down and then just as suddenly opened his eyes and resumed toning. '… both the atoms, one light and one relatively heavy, are,' he paused briefly, 'not definable.'

He emphasized the last two words which seemed very odd. It was the first time they'd detected any real emphasis or inflection from the Virijians. They knew it had to mean something, something important probably. Was it a hint of their emotional selves, Sean wondered? Perhaps it was a glimpse of some ancient emotional kernel that was buried beneath the gristle of their highly evolved frames. An archaic splinter that had been eroded almost to nothing by the climb to true physical understanding. Of course, this was their first attempt to use English which led naturally to the question of what their real language was, if they had one, which they presumably did. Possibly, there were many languages like Earth, or maybe each planet they'd seen had their own language. Maybe there was only a single language. Who the hell knew?

'It is apparent that the subatomic structure of this material is different from that with which we are familiar.' Zamindar toned.

Confusion coloured the expressions of the humans. What? Different...how? What do you mean, they all wondered? Mitch felt like yelling at Zamindar to give them an answer. It sounded like bullshit. No one could make their own matter, could they?

Sean narrowed his eyes, 'what are you saying?' he whispered. He felt his heartbeat start to rise in his throat as he waited for the jarring response. 'You mean like Dark Matter?'

He ignored Sean. 'It would seem the Sphere is composed not of a decay product but of atoms that are different from those around us.' He stopped and looked at Char, then resumed, louder this time. 'The Sphere is made from particles that seem to contrast with everything we have ever encountered in the Universe. It seems impossible but there it is sitting in front of us, real, but in a sense not real. 'They are quite simply not our atoms.'

The last few words struck them like a cerebral Chinese burn. "Not our atoms". What the fuck did that mean? If not ours...whose atoms were they? They looked up at Zamindar and their ponderings changed direction slightly. He definitely seemed to be behaving differently, displaying something like emotion.

They weren't completely sure but something about him was odd. There was more emphasis in his toning, more animation in his movement. After another brief faltering, he went on, shaking both elbows on both outer arms in some sort of restless sympathy. He also seemed to be changing colour slightly. Yellowing a bit.

'While we can resolve the two atoms, their weights and configuration are different from any of our elements. They are clearly not antiparticles, but the nucleons and the electrons are all about the same size. Oddly though, the much larger electron still has a minute mass, like ours. But the orbital shells they move in are smaller, they are much closer to the nucleus. So rather than a tenuous haze, the electrons offer something far more substantial without adding too much more mass to the atom as a whole.'

Sean was suddenly blinded by a stupefying light in his head that grew from nothing to a supernova in seconds. Larger electrons without larger mass, it sounded preposterous but it clearly wasn't. How could it be though? It couldn't be, based on what we know about particle physics. But there it was, right in front of them. He pondered the point briefly. Were these fundamental particles hollow somehow...or made up of something else...other than quarks? Maybe they weren't fermions, they were made of something else. But made of what, he wondered? Christ, it was absurd. No, he thought firmly, it was impossible. These atoms should have been unstable but they clearly weren't. They were the opposite of that, they were very stable indeed.

'The Sphere atoms are many times more compact than those we are familiar with. The only consistency with ours are the electrical charges. The one thing you would perhaps expect to be different is the same. Morphometry, that which you would expect to be the same, is different.' Zamindar seemed to show some agitation. Perhaps worry?

Sean tickled the Sphere's surface with a single finger. It sure felt like regular metal, like the dull gray surface of a Teflon wok, but it apparently wasn't, and according to Zamindar it was something unimaginably exotic. Metal no doubt. But...where, why, who? The questions flooded through him like an obscuring tide, drowning everything but his thirst for that which sat before him. What the fuck was this thing?

'So, er...this comes from somewhere else...somewhere that has a different table of elements, er...that has different building blocks?' Mitch suggested weakly, knowing that stability would surely be an issue.

'Perhaps,' Zamindar returned, 'or maybe these are additions to what we would consider the regular palate of matter and energy. Without doubt though it is an extraordinary material, clearly very stable.'

210

'Jesus,' Sean muttered. The ability to make stable matter...energy can't be created...only transformed, he knew that. The fundamental law of energy, like all the others, was tattooed on his mind by his early mentors in scientific philosophy. Still, Sean's eyes burnt with the wonder of impossibility. Where the hell was all this leading? he asked himself, bathing in the scope of his own question. Sean's eyes were slowly widening as he contemplated the possibilities.

'What could it be made from?' Jessy quizzed from behind them. It had taken all this time for her to pluck up the courage to ask a question.

'The individual atoms, we'll call them Spheratoms, are boron-like and platinum-like in mass but they are not those elements, most definitely not.'

'How were these molecules synthesised to avoid becoming one of our molecules?' Sean said. Then he remembered the larger electrons and his mind surged. Where did this thing come from?

Jessy watched all this from the background with Josh. She found it all quite implausible. It must surely be due to something else. 'There must be another explanation,' she suggested meekly. '...have you considered this might be a bomb or some other servo device that will create catastrophe? As you said Zamindar, almost anything is possible. We know absolutely naught about it, not even what it's made of. So, we shouldn't rule anything out, and should proceed with caution...right? It could kill us all for Christ's sake! Maybe they're seeded through the Universe as a sort of population control, to keep the number of cognitive races in check. To limit the number that leave home and go pillaging through the cosmos. Damage control if you like. If you can't identify the atoms how do you know they aren't engineered for destruction, for annihilation on a galactic scale? You don't and you can't. I think we should put it back where we found it. Remember Troy Mitch? We're deeply into the unknown here.'

Take that, she thought, looking at them as aggressively as she could, given how she was feeling. She felt like curling up and lying down with eyes tightly closed. Her eyes were wide and gleaming like a pair of Chevy hubcaps, daring anyone to question her, which no one did. Of course, it was a possibility. Anything was.

Not even the Virijians wanted to provoke Jessy into more of her morbidly fatalistic explications. It was clear to everyone that she was hanging on by a thread, looking down at the floor, shaking like a horse getting rid of blow flies.

'Up Joshy,' she called to her son as he crawled around like a curious puppy on the warm surface. Gently picking him up, she carried him over to the towering wall nearest them and sat down with her back against the wall. Jessy proceeded to stare at them all, wondering who the hell put them in charge. Josh was banging his arm on Jessy's shoulder, quite happy with what was happening. He thought it was a hoot, nary a problem with the huge, odd looking Virijians. He looked at them like any father figure. A good lesson for everyone, Mitch thought, bemused by the reaction he could expect from adults back on Earth.

'We have to try to open it,' Mitch echoed after her. 'Using whatever logic we have, we have to assume it's benign...but you're right, we can't guarantee anything. But equally we can't just leave it. Surely as an astro-scientist you can see that.' He knew how painfully unscientific she could be at times. She was like tiny baby on occasion.

'Amen to that,' Sean said grinning. visibly sweating in the warm Virijian atmosphere.

Like Jessy, his eyes were swollen and bloodshot, not from fear though or even uncertainty, but with raw unalloyed wonder. He was pumped with a naked desire that was almost sexual in its strength, as he stared at the object wordlessly.

'We agree also,' the Virijians toned collectively. 'We do not believe it is dangerous. It would be wholly illogical to assume it is.'

'How pragmatic and rational,' Jessy whispered softly with more than the suggestion of angst. 'I've seen where your curiosity can lead, to death and destruction on a planetary scale.' Jessy spoke a bit louder with more acrimony. 'Perhaps you should try mixing it with a bit of forethought.' She spat the last sentence as though hawking up a swallowed fly. Jessy still had Josh on her hip banging her on the shoulder. Josh was studying his Mum closely.

She started to question whether these Virijians were as advanced as they'd all assumed. Advanced technologically, no one could doubt that, but in other ways they were so much like curious youngsters. Letting their untethered desires, their curiosity drown everything, to the detriment of even their own personal safety.

Not to mention ours...us, who they say they have searched for, for millions of years. Clearly in their case, she thought, supreme age and timeless evolution didn't require or even engender pure rational thought. Anything but. Curiosity was the lynch pin, the cognitive star, around which everything Virijian seemed to revolve. Jessy could see that and knew instantly that it would form a crucial basis for their mutual understanding, if, and it was a big if, they managed to survive that long. She returned her gaze to the orb and wondered why it was near Titan. Why was it near the enigmatic little moon called Titan, was it because it had a decent atmosphere, or were there other reasons, she pondered. She'd go with "other reasons", but had no idea what they might be. Atmosphere, life, maybe it was random. All she knew was it was a long way from Earth.

Zamindar moved deliberately forward now, only centimeters from the orb. Closer...contact. He placed three of his pendulous digits in the grooves that sat near the top of the Sphere just below his eye level. They were the only marks visible on its otherwise unblemished dermis. Jessy held her breath as the Virijian didn't hesitate and pressed his fingers deeply inward, into whatever was inside. For a long time, nothing happened.

After a minute the towering creature reclaimed his paw and padded backward, not moving his feline eyes from the grey ball. They hadn't seen a Virijian stare so intently, as he studied the object. It continued to remain totally motionless and unyielding in front of him.

How to open it? Sean pondered to himself, surveying it closely. Cracking it open seemed unrealistic. He had visions of cracking it like an egg. It wasn't going to happen.

'Perhaps it's broken,' Jessy offered. 'Maybe it's just a galactic marker that broke anchor.' She was relieved that all was still, and just hoped to God it stayed that way. Jessy looked down and found a smile that was instantly mirrored by the little star-child who continued his exploration. He was banging his arm on the ground, and having a good time doing it.

Then it happened, while Josh was banging his arm.

Like air from a punctured tyre, they heard it before they saw it. A shrieking hiss rose from inside the Sphere and a spreading black stain sliced the object into two precise hemispheres. A churning cloud sprayed in a vivid arc from its splitting midriff. For a few seconds it brandished a tenuous Uranian ring plane that was only broken where the Sphere sat on the chamber floor.

Oh God...atmosphere? The unexpected sight filled Jessy with an excruciating dread. What the fuck was going to clamber out? Her brain sprinted, full of grotesque dream inspired horrors, gnashing jaws, drooling gobs and carnal, devouring desires. No way, she pleaded, trying to concentrate on the blandness of the pale surface in front of her.. Relax, she told herself, clenching her toes, revelling in Josh's smiling, unconcerned face.

The vapour leaked away and wafted into the great openness, vanishing like hot breath in a vacuum. All of them instinctively swayed backward. The Virijians though remained still, watching expectantly, totally frozen, faces like set jelly. There was no fear in their expressions, not that they would have expected any. Just glacial stares and washed porcelain features, like two tremendous waxwork dummies. That was them. They were all starting to get used to it. No facial expressions whatsoever despite the astonishing goings on.

Without a sound the newly appeared division started to swell, slowly and smoothly revealing more and more of the dim interior. Jessy steeled her mind. Despite herself, she braced and waited for something mind-bendingly insane to unfold itself and scrabble from the split gizzard. She held her breath and balled her fists, looking a bit like a stiff prizefighter. Jessy wasn't ready to die, but she'd protect Josh, come what may.

The twin hemispheres slid further apart until they forged a wide V, the two east and west structures, two great circles, were now only joined by a narrow line of Sphere material.

Everyone but Jessy moved forward quickly to look. Sean almost tripped over his own feet in his haste, desperate to see what was hidden within. Watching him, Jessy was compelled to wonder whether he knew fear of the unknown. There was absolutely no doubt that the Virijians didn't. They apparently wanted it all.

Curiosity versus fear and logic, the thirst to know won every time. For Sean and the Virijians, it was a laydown misere as to which emotion won. For her, she reckoned it was more measured. Risk and reward were far more balanced, she was sure. She hoped.

The mucid cloud had disappeared and the inside of the Sphere was now spread like a foldout nursery book. Everyone looked, scrutinizing the interior of the sphere, but no one spoke. There was precious little to see and what could be seen predictably made little sense. Nothing was remotely recognizable, but equally there seemed to be very little to recognize. Nothing came scuttling out so Jessy was happy. She knew it was illogical to expect it...but still it was one of her fears.

It was all but empty. Jessy thanked God for the second time and pleaded with her heart to slow. Fucking empty, empty, she said to herself. That was it, done. Unfortunately, she knew she wasn't the one to make the decision on go or no go.

Mitch said, 'perhaps it wasn't meant for us. Maybe it did get to Titan by accident, fell off a starship maybe.' He didn't break his expression or shift his eyes. He knew that would make them speak because he knew it was bullshit. It was clear that nothing annoyed them like someone who was just plain wrong.

'No,' Charijiok toned, 'take a closer look.' His elbow rotation perfectly punctuated his toning, as though the two were intimately linked in the process of communication, even though he was speaking other than his native language. He was sure that the same would apply to whatever passed for their natural dialect, probably more so.

Mitch slid back to the splayed Sphere. One side looked like it was totally solid or at least where it had parted there was a solid unblemished face, the same or very similar to the external casing of the object. The other hemisphere was mostly hollow and empty. On the hollow side, the skin was only a centimeter thick but in what appeared to be its precise bullseye was a cube. A metallic block of isometric material that stretched outward from the middle of the vacuous space, making the hemisphere look something like a gray rendered satellite dish.

'What the fuck?' Jessy whispered, looking at the thing and thinking how familiar it looked. Well, some of it at least.

The cube had, on the face that was perpendicular to them, a series of deep grooves, identical to those that pocked the surface. Above and below the cube there was nothing but an empty compartment bounded by the gaunt spherical superstructure.

The five grooves seemed to literally beg inspection, beckoning to Sean like an irresistible cerebral bait. He felt like thrusting his hand into it, to see what happened, he felt sure it'd be okay.

With little hesitation, Zamindar did just that, placing five fingers in the grooves without waiting for the unavoidable debate with Jessy on the pros and cons of positive action. They were going to do what they needed to do to resolve the mystery, so why debate it? He mused. Especially with the inanities raised by the humans.

Again, nothing happened and after a few seconds the Virijian withdrew his digits, wondering what else they could do to stimulate the thing into some semblance of activity. Jessy was nervously pondering the coincidence behind the number of grooves.

She looked at her fingers and then back at the grooves. Coincidence? Her anxiety deepened again. She was sure they were for fingers...their fingers? She took an almighty swallow and glanced at Mitch who looked as unsure as she felt. A fat lot of help he'd be, be it personal emergency or confronting the unknown. Forget Mars, she reckoned. He looked like he'd collapse if called into any sort of action.

They were all staring at it when it happened. A piercing aura suddenly reached out and blinded them temporarily, dazzling them with a fiery burst like a strobe of newborn sunlight.

'…fuck's sake,' Mitch yelled, shielding his eyes with his hands. Sean looked on, just glad something was happening. He leant toward the orb, eager for whatever was next, to finally start.

The front and sides of the cube had broken into a cacophony of bright geometry. Myriads of tiny shapes appeared, oblique and right angle criss-crossing lines, parallel lines of varying thickness and length, and more than anything else, numerous, what looked like numbers, zeros and ones and twos, threes and so on.

Our numbers? Sean wondered, feeling the confusion building behind his eyes. They couldn't be, they surely had to be something else. They couldn't be ours. Surely not fucking ours, it didn't make a lick of sense. Our numbers were totally arbitrary. Not based on anything, except language, invention and maybe the human hand. They weren't even binary.

Once they appeared, the figures didn't cycle or change and they were vividly luminous against the grey of the Sphere's depthless penetralia. Jessy was tapping a fist against her lips, hoping this thing would just close, but knowing better.

Sean stared at the sudden animation, dumbfounded by what was dancing in front of his eyes. 'Holy shit, is that, er…writing of some sort?' he blurted, inching closer until his nose was almost touching the surface. He spoke in hushed tones, 'whoever they are, have apparently designed this thing to talk to its finders, to communicate with, er…us.' Sean moved closer, blinking furiously and rubbing both corneas with a swipe of his fingertips. At least that's what it looked like. Sean's eyes were wide and his eyebrows were about as high as they could go. He couldn't get the question of "who?" out of his mind. Who the hell left this, and why? What did they have to say? So many questions. Hopefully, at least some of their questions would be answered. Actually, he admitted reluctantly, he wasn't sure if he wanted anything answered. Except maybe dark matter and dark energy. No one had managed to get a handle on those two.

'But what does it say, we have to find out, we have to know. Zamindar…can you read it, come closer and look…' Sean was rambling and spluttering in his haste to garner any syntax that might be hiding within the marrow of the meaningless brightness that glowed in front of him.

To everyone's astonishment the shapes seemed to consist partly of familiar numerical forms, even though they were thoroughly oblivious to any deeper meaning they might have had. Sean knew there was something profound buried in them somewhere, there had to be, but how deeply was it buried and how cryptically was it written? All he knew was, it was deep. How in God's name do we read it, he puzzled? The thought of never knowing tore at his mind with serrated teeth. We have to know, was Sean's recurring thought but it was tempered with something he found difficult to define. He kept staring at Zamindar, who as usual looked nonchalant. He seemed so casual and disinterested, like he'd done this sort of thing hundreds of times. He almost expected him to yawn.

For ten minutes, the humans stood and watched as the Virijians inspected and silently debated the contents of the cube's forward facing surface.

Sean finally turned around and faced them from the other side of the Sphere. 'So, what does it all mean…it's nothing more than gibberish, right?' He paused, hoping for a positive response. After more painful, lengthy silence, he continued. He wondered when their "help" would start? 'But given that we've encountered this thing way too soon, then we've probably got no hope of deciphering it. Is there any indication of how to read it…how to interpret the lines and symbols? Assuming they actually mean something of course.' Sean continued, 'maybe you could…'

'It is a physical language,' Zamindar toned, stopping Sean in his tracks, who looked at the Virijian blankly.

'You mean you can read it…already?' It was impossible. Surely not already,

'Not quite,' Zamindar returned, 'but yes we will be able to understand what is written. As you said, this was probably aimed at yourselves finding it in the not too distant future. Clearly, we will have no trouble. Millennia ago, we put much thought into the method with which we would communicate information to another society, separated as we knew we probably would be by a vast ocean of space. The physical and mathematical language, one based on the laws of the cosmos, was logically going to be the most universally comprehended, especially by spacefaring species. This

214

Sphere language is premised on the constants that are forged into the fabric of spacetime, the laws that give the cosmos its special character. In this case it is based on what we have called hyper symmetry, a pivotal theory that still eludes your people, and will do for some time, based on what we have seen. It explains the physical nature of the Universe and provides a key to races separated by a vast transgalactic distance. It supplies complex directions that allow certain ciphers, lines and numerals to acquire particular meanings.' His toning stopped momentarily. Then it came back, the words coming marginally quicker, with a tad more urgency.

'Meanings are translated into words or entire precepts in a physical means of communication. The glyphs and their groupings, and the different appositions of recrossing lines can all be interpreted by the theoretical premises laid out in the full mathematical description of hyper symmetry, that is, quantum mechanics and gravity, or your Einstein, together. I will explain the intricacies later but I think at this stage we should proceed to read it.'

Sean nodded furiously, seemingly at the risk of slipping a disc. He was tripping on his own opiates, surfing on a wave of unimaginable discovery...of, uncovery. What will it say? He didn't have the slightest clue but he well realized the stupefying possibilities. Sean's mind continued to churn and bubble, his thoughts like rapids flowing roughly over the bedrock of his mind.

Charijiok bent down and, in a fluid motion, he moved his upper torso toward the Sphere and peered again at the first twenty or so lines. He remained totally motionless for more than thirty seconds, the carbuncled callus the only sign of life. Sean jumped when the inevitable toning finally came. Fuck, he thought, this had better be good. He stood in a state of sweating impatience behind the Virijian.

'The first data tells us what these figures relate to and what lies at their base, which by extension would have told us what they mean if we did not already know. But it does assume that the finder has a precise knowledge of the Universe. Without it, the Sphere cannot be accessed, it can be opened but not accessed. I am able to tell you that it was placed in your star system specifically for you, the sentient occupants of the third planet, the single intelligence in your galaxy, it says.'

Jessy snapped her head up. 'Jesus, fuck, they do know about us,' she stammered, feeling distinctly queasy in her stomach and chest. She felt like she'd swallowed a beehive and could feel the wings and the antennae buzzing and scratching at the soft lining of her throat.

'So, all the intergalactic exoplanets are dead, Mitch asked? He was totally taken aback, looking at Zamindar with enormous eyes and a concentrated stare.

'...so, it is an alien artifact,' Sean uttered softly. 'Sonofabitch, some suggested it, but most, even of those who suggested it I think, didn't seriously believe it was true. A possibility of course, but a reality, who would have seriously considered it?' He looked at everyone in the room, shaking his head. Sean truly couldn't believe it. 'Fuck me, it's a dream come true, an unbelievable, impossible dream.' Sean's eyes glowed with naked wonder as he chewed on the implications, on the million or so questions that suddenly flooded his brain. One question stood head and shoulders over the others though, how did they know we were the only intelligent species in the Galaxy?

'Let's wait and see what it says Sean,' Jessy offered, '...before we start calling it a dream come true. There's bad news and good news...nightmares and dreams.' She scowled at Sean but needn't have bothered, he was firmly staked in his own personal wonderworld, neither seeing nor hearing. Just thinking.

'Always the pragmatist Jessy,' Mitch said deliberately.

'Just a realist and maybe a pessimist, but like the psych's on Luna said, after my Recon, that's my nature and no one's gonna change it.' She folded her arms roughly across the front of her flexisuit and shot them a sour look. Fuckers, she thought without malice. They were still a team of two...which left her out in the cold. Certainly, not teamed with Zamindar or Charijiok, they were on their own team.

Zamindar swivelled his yellow centered eyes, moments before the resonance hit them. 'We have scanned the first cycle and can tell you that there are only forty others, which gives us about three hundred thousand bits of information. We expected considerably more but I am afraid that is all there is. It will not impart new technologies, that is clear, but rather it is more of an insight into yourselves, to give you an idea of your place within the order of the cosmos. And the place of others.'

Zamindar wore an expression Mitch hadn't seen before, something he likened to surprise, to emotion anyway. To less than nothing at least.

Sean spun around, his first word a rifle shot, 'Others, what others...you mean it talks of other people, other er, civilizations or just other life, non-sapient life?' He clenched his toes and held his breath. It was happening too fast.

'It is a little ambiguous but we believe it refers to other intelligences. We will have to wait until those cycles are reached.'

Zamindar motioned Mitch to approach with a double flourish of his middle limb. 'It is time you took an active role in this. Place all your fingers in the grooves and it will cycle forward.'

Mitch shifted his palm so it rested on the corner of the cube and then winced as he inched his fingers deep inside. His trembling digits were mirrored by his mind. There was something deeply disturbing about sticking parts of your body into something so explicitly unfamiliar. He had the ludicrous but unwavering feeling that something within would attack his fingers. That he'd remove them to find bloody stumps and so much ragged flesh. His flesh touched warm metal. There was a mild caressing sensation as though his fingers were stimulating or perhaps interrupting a mild power source. Maybe it was sort of like an Xray. The symbols on the cube changed instantly and this time there was more of them, much smaller in pitch than the previous page. The scrawl looked thoroughly meaningless to him. It looked like a crazy, foreign language of indecipherable scrawl. Total gibberish.

He stared at the sea of alien figures, feeling like an infant suddenly confronted by a sea of non Euclidean geometry. Christ! 'What does all that mean?' It looked like so much gobbledygook.

'Mitch, behind you!' Jessy yelled. 'The other hemisphere!' She stepped backward with Josh and held his head in her breast.

'What the hell...' Mitch turned sharply and saw that the hemisphere behind him had suddenly flooded with white light that was already starting to dissipate. The half sphere was seemingly returning to black...or was it?

'What is happening here?' Sean said slowly, not moving his eyes from the murky hemisphere in front of him. After hesitating, his voice came lower this time, disbelief and awe mingling in his muted breathing. 'My God,' he whispered. 'That's Earth, has to be Earth, right? There's America, but what is...' Sean gazed at the waning storm on the other hemisphere. Jessy gaped, slackening her mouth as she digested what was being shown. The brilliant radiance had quickly leaked away and sculpted itself into a crisp image of space. And dominating that space was Earth and a gibbous Moon that hung like a miscarried offspring in the far distance.

The image was from about thirty thousand kilometres above the cloud tops. Underneath were four distinct rows of minute figures, mainly parallel and oblique lines with dots of varying diameter studding their length. Some were solid, some only outlines and all of them were separated from one another by numerous stacked ones and zeros that were presumably binary. Some of the figures were cycling, the lines and other symbols changing once every few seconds. The rest of the figures remained fixed. Stable and boldly white. Swollen with meaning,' Sean thought, '...but what meaning? His scalp was burning from a mind in cerebral overdrive. What the hell were these figures, he pondered? They were something, he was sure. Thank God for Zamindar. If it was just them, they'd have no hope, they'd be left staring and very unimpressed, Sean thought. Very unimpressed with a Sphere they could open but not access. Sean was certain the sledgehammers and Phillips Heads would eventually come out.

Jessy watched, eyes darting from Zamindar to the orb. She felt hot and her thoughts were slow. She stayed as still as she could, staring at the Sphere, thinking and making occasional teeth sucking noises as she ogled the Sphere. She had no idea what to do or what to think.

The Virijians returned to the script while Mitch looked on, motionless and waiting, trying to quieten his breathing but failing. His thoughts had jaws that gnashed and crunched.

216

What was going to be revealed? The question kept clawing back to saturate his thinking. He silently pondered their situation, feeling giddy and profoundly uneasy, but wasn't really sure why. Actually, he was sure, but refused to concede the point, even to himself. He was frightened by the Sphere just like Jessy. And that surprised him because he'd already been privy to so much that was extraordinary, so much that to the ordinary person would sound like pure delusion. Since leaving Cygnus he'd been lavished with a celestial joyride truly without peer. Yet he was scared of this dark ball that sat before them. What would it say? That's what really scared him, but it was a Jekyll and Hyde emotion, because he was also gripped by a furious need to know. Like Sean, he wanted to know why the hell the orb was placed in orbit around Titan.

Warring emotions pushed him then tugged him back, like the sufferings of a schizophrenic.

He could feel part of himself back in Principal Sewell's office at Dover Primary, sweating and waiting for his wooden wrath to be meted. The reason for his recollection was obvious to him. Had the human race been good or bad...did they care, did they even know the answer? If they did then maybe he was right to worry, seriously worry. He tried to put it aside, but visions of Judgement Day kept elbowing their way back at him.

They were agog at the picture of Earth that was so beautifully laid out in front of them. It wasn't just a representation of Earth, it was Earth and they knew it, but something wasn't right with the way it looked. Sean saw it straight away. No way that was our Earth.

'The continents don't look right,' Mitch's eyes were locked onto Earth. '...is this a mock up or is it real? It looks real but something is wrong with that picture, it looks...um?' Mitch stopped talking and moved his head closer to the orb. 'This is...'

'It is not a mock up,' Zamindar intruded. 'They say that is your planet at 13.205 billion years after The Beginning.' He hesitated momentarily. 'That puts it, based on what we know and we know we are accurate, at Earth sixty-six million years ago.'

It hit them like a hammer blow.

'Million...sixty-six million years ago...an actual image?' Sean whimpered, struggling to draw breath to feed his voice. His anxiety was replaced by a blistering thirst. What was going on here, what was this Sphere?

'Are you sure of your timeline on Creation?' Mitch asked tentatively.

'Yes, completely.'

Sean's head spun around as though someone had landed a haymaker on his cheek.

'That's it,' he suddenly stuttered, 'look at the continents...that's why it doesn't look right. Africa and South America are in the right place but they're too close...the Atlantic is too skinny...and Australia's not even there, it's still part of Antarctica. Continental drift is still splitting the continents and shuffling them around.' He paused and savored what was racing around in his head. '...imagine Alf Wegener's reaction if he could see this.' He was stunned by the vision.

The ultimate proof, Mitch considered silently, as if he needed any, it was written in the rocks. The proof was literally under their feet.

Charijiok rapidly interpreted the last lines of cycle seven and turned, looking directly at Mitch with pupils that resembled planets. His toning came, more softly, almost a whisper. As the undertone gathered momentum, his pin-holed lips seemed to tremble slightly, as though they'd suddenly developed a heartbeat.

They all saw them and wondered what it meant, if anything. They were now pulsing freely as though connected to a pair of air bellows. With the squirming goitre that clung loosely to the side of his head, his pallid, greasy features were impossible to reconcile with the wisdom they knew he possessed. He looked a bit like Herman Munster, but far less pleasant.

Softly Char said, 'they are telling you that your kind played a role in your emergence on the planet, in your evolution, your ascent to intelligence.'

Confusion rolled through the space bay. Heavy breathing, searching eyes, frozen features. Still more silence. A role? What the hell did that mean? Jessy felt something crawl up her spine and flush her face with warm blood. She was quickly tingling all over.

217

'Wh...what?' Mitch eventually spluttered uncertainly. They all gaped at the Sphere. Six unblinking eyes stared at the vascular rapids in his rubbery cranium. This creature that stood before them was fucking incredible. Char went on.

'This was not the first time they visited your planet. They touched your world four times, necessitated they claim by the unusual features of your biology. Life on Earth apparently refused to grow along what they had come to consider as the normal pathways and the expected rates.' Without moving his head, Char shifted his gaze downward onto Mitch. His next toning came much louder.

'It claims that Earth was biologically retarded.'

Sean's world suddenly tilted a bit. Excuse me? He demanded silently, finding the suggestion deeply offensive, not to mention entirely unexpected. Retarded?

What a way to start, he thought. By insulting the entire bloody planet. His heartbeat jumped several notches. The statement seemed unsettlingly venomous, somehow too stark and upfront, even though he had absolutely no idea what he expected. Maybe politeness was a strictly human quality, who the hell knew? The bar was now set very high for direct, unabridged truth. Hold that thought, he mused, feeling slightly more uneasy than he had a minute ago. These fuckers might say anything. Not that it was the Virijians fault. What was written, was written, Sean supposed.

Char's entire skull vibrated like an old diesel engine suddenly sparked to life. They could literally see the nickel rich blood surge through the fat black vein that dominated his forehead. Wait for it, Mitch thought, tensing for the inevitable noise. And it came almost immediately, a torrent of mind shattering English.

'...their first time on Earth was more than half a billion years ago...'

Sean blew his lips out, 'Oh come on,' he exclaimed, and was shut down by Mitch before he could go any further. 'For fuck's sake,' Mitch said sharply from the background. 'No way they were around that long ago.' He thought different, but Mitch said it anyway. Jessy stared at Mitch, feeling the fear pulse through her, again she felt like running, going as far as inspecting the room, hoping to find an exit. Jessy saw nothing but a white wall. No chance of escape.

Char continued, '...when they realized that things were starting to go wrong. Life was failing to ripen as it had done elsewhere, on other planets in other galaxies. They say their input was essential and was demanded by the laziness of life on Earth. They keep repeating this point, lazy Earth. The biosphere seemingly needed a prod to save it from what they saw as a meaningless future, a totally noncognitive future where life would...'

'Half a billion?' Sean slobbered, he couldn't help but interject. 'These, er...creatures had the capacity for interstellar flight half a billion years ago? How can that be? It's possible I suppose, well of course it is, but Jesus, how advanced are they, um...now?' Sean hesitated and looked a bit wobbly on his feet. He was shifting his weight but it looked like he was staggering left and right like a drunk. The realization was a bit much even for him. Jessy and Mitch simply stared at the Virijian, wondering what the fuck was going on?

Revelation, she thought, knowing the word had suddenly grown another leg.

It was happening too quickly to get a grip on its meaning, certainly too fast for them to digest it properly, but Char continued anyway. The story...their story went on, steeping itself further into the absurd as it went.

'They knew more than fifty of their genesis pods had impacted Earth almost four billion years ago.'

Sean's head jerked sideways, toward the Sphere, then back at Char. His voice dribbled out like polar treacle, stiff and struggling to move. 'No way...four billion, they were around four billion years ago? Christ, this is insane! How freaking old are they...do they say? I mean how old can they be?'

This was rapidly getting ridiculous, Jessy thought, wondering what they were like...now. 'Jesus, they've been around that long?' Jessy blurted, feeling ice-cold and lightheaded. Was that possible, she pondered? Jessy shook her head and wrinkled her nose. She couldn't believe it.

218

Sean looked at Zamindar blankly, wholly stupefied. They were now talking about a very significant percentage of the age of the Universe. It was genuinely beyond thinking. Beyond the scope of what he realized was a very primitive, very juvenile earthly mind.

The two Virijians were as stunned as the humans, perhaps even more so, but outwardly as they toned, they appeared little different. Their nonchalant expressions betrayed little of their real surprise, unlike the uberous exhibitions of their friends, the transparent two armers who wore their emotions like garish masks. Zamindar's voiceless words drowned out their colorful ponderings.

'...they knew life would rise on your planet, they fairly much made sure of that. And it did, but for reasons beyond even them, the carbon molecules on Earth did not show the same desire to self-organize as they had elsewhere.' Lazy Earth. Again.

'Elsewhere?' Sean looked at Char curiously. The implication was obvious but the Virijian simply gazed back at him, blankly and without comment. Other planets, other galaxies, Sean assumed, seeing his question hang in the air unanswered. He felt like knocking on that great big head to get an answer.

Anyway, he thought, the answer was obvious, Earth wasn't their only conquest, Christ, of course it wasn't. Why would it be? Jessy looked at the orb. She wondered who these creatures were? How the fuck old were they? She would be happy to stop now, put it back where it came from, say thank you, and move on. But she equally knew that wasn't going to happen.

Why should we be the only ones? It was pathetically conceited to assume we were. As a player in the Grand Scheme, Sean had always felt that Earth was far less golden than most thought, but equally he knew there was a tiny sliver of Aristotle buried in everyone. Egocentrism.

'Again, they reinforce the idea that life on Earth was painfully sluggish and to them seemed content to remain as simple as possible for as long as possible. Progression was not something your planet's biochemistry seemed particularly interested in, despite the favourable conditions. For billions of years after their seeds gave rise to life, very little happened. They got a few primitive multicellular ocean crawlers. Single celled life, bacteria and algaes, were still overwhelmingly dominant. It was an extremely poor result. And one they had difficulty fathoming. Earth was lazy,' Zamindar toned, looking at the image of the planet and then at Mitch, then he lingered on Sean. Jessy wondered why he didn't look at her. Goddamn males of the species, she reckoned. Surely, they were old enough as a species to have outgrown such things.

Zamindar continued. 'They stress on every cycle so far, that, without their intrusion, life on Earth would have moved sideways into mass extinctions and would never have evolved forward into life that would present itself to be selected for complexity, or awareness. As far as they were concerned, Earth was incomprehensibly odd. Out of tune with the bigger picture of life in the cosmos.'

Jessy felt strangely lightheaded as she listened to the metallic throbbing in her head. Could it really be true? She debated, trying to wrestle through the dizziness. And what else was the ashen relic hiding...what other details lay squirming beneath its sombre grey casing? Could they cope with them? The answer to the last one was probably no. But the sphere didn't give a shit, still it went on. The Virijians went on. The scale, the nature of the information was so monstrous as to sound comical, the colorful trumpery of some atheist nutter. But Jessy knew that it wasn't. The source of the insanity demanded respect, because it clearly came from somewhere other than the quirky mindset of home. It clearly came from somewhere astonishingly, and stupefyingly old.

Char's shrill invasions returned. Jessy shrugged her shoulders at Mitch. She knew it was coming, there wasn't a thing anyone could do about it. Not while Char was drawing breath, anyway.

'Even after sufficient ozone was produced, life still continued to be strangely retarded.' Sean winced again at the mention of that word, it sounded like the planet was a shelter for idiots, but they would not let it rest. 'Your world had captured their interest, simply because it was different. Because it tested their ability to bring forth cleverness on a world that tangibly resisted the idea. To spawn something meaningful they personally visited Earth, trod the planet. Although how they got there, where they came from, and how they did what they did are not mentioned, not yet anyway.'

219

Why the fuck did they visit Earth, Sean wondered? Not why did they visit, more, what did they do while they were there? What godawful experiments did they conduct…and how? He nodded to himself while he rubbed his eyes, looking at the orb sideways.

Char said, 'they genetically altered some of the unicells that were heading for extinction, and impelled a global explosion of multi cells. Earth was handed a sudden diversity that for the first time gave it hope for what they term a useful future. By intention their spawn included the first backboned creatures, that you eventually grew from. The fundamental life design set here by them, carried the likelihood they believed, that something intelligent would ultimately come.'

Jessy felt the first stirrings of panic as she really contemplated what they were saying. Her skin was a hive of gooseflesh and the dread, she could feel it tapping on her ribs, trying to get to her heart. She felt like blocking her ears, wadding them with cottonwool, but she knew the noise would get her in the end. Ears had nothing to do with it. There was no way out, they would be privy to the whole story, whatever that was, like it or not. She breathed in shallow, quick bursts, feeling the breath burn in the back of her throat. What was the whole story, she wondered grimly? Jessy shuddered and looked at Josh who was banging one part of the floor with a fist, like he was trying to dig a hole.

'Their blueprint set over half a billion years ago was never changed and eventually, through billions of generations of creatures, it led to you. They made you, by specific intent, they made you the intelligent landlords of that planet.' Char held out his axial claw and pointed at the image of Earth so beautifully laid out before them. 'That was made your home.'

Sean's expression was like someone who'd been struck in the face with a heavy saucepan.

Mitch felt a pressure in his mind as he manfully tried to digest what Char was saying. He was thinking of Darwin and all those who'd followed him on the trail of evolution. Natural selection, natural, what a fucking joke, he thought. Evolution might have been real but it was apparently conducted on the shoulders of them.

He was visibly sagging, when into the field of view on the opposite hemisphere rocketed a visibly massive asteroid. An oblate chunk of vapor trailing rock appeared, grew smaller and seconds later penetrated the atmosphere in a fiery hail. It struck near the central Americas in a stupendous detonation of ocean and bedrock. They looked on, stunned by the unexpectedly graphic vision.

'Fuck,' Jessy couldn't help swearing. Her distended eyes were glued to the hemi vision, her mind struggling to believe what was being beamed to it. She knew exactly what she was looking at. All the details gelled immediately, it wasn't hard, the continents, the date, the death chunk from space, the area of impact. The knowing was stippled like broad brushstrokes in her eyes. She unconsciously furrowed her brow. 'God Almighty,' she muttered, while gawking at the orb.

'Chicxulub, Chicxulub, the ash, the radon…Jesus…the K/T boundary. Now we damn well know,' she murmured, 'Now we know for sure what killed the dinosaurs.'

Sean and Mitch looked at Jessy, then back at the Sphere. They had also made the connection. They all knew what Chicxulub and K/T meant. It was English for dinosaurs and global disaster. And extinction.

'How old are the beings that made this thing? Is "being" even the right word.' Sean repeated his question as he breath-stroked in an ocean of disbelief that was thickening around him. He tried to ponder these mind numbingly ancient creatures. His eyes were round and he was white as a bedsheet as he blinked quickly at the Earth so beautifully laid out for them.

It was nearly too much. Billions of years beyond Mankind. Maybe we aren't ready, he thought. The vision in front of him caught his eye.

They all watched, not really believing what they were seeing. The ripples in the ocean and the blinding fireball hurtling skyward from the impact site could be plainly seen from their deep orbital viewpoint. This must be a joke, Jessy reckoned. She was seemingly looking for a cord or a WiFi connection to the orb, but her probing eyes found nothing. She remained skeptical though, but watched on. Jessy remembered where the object was found and that screamed legitimate, she thought. Her face contorted with disbelief as she watched on.

The "ripples" they could see were death shells of titanic tsunamis several kilometres high that would hit and devastate the continents. The pall of dust, rock, crust and vaporized water kicked up by the impact could already be seen as a mighty sulfurous stain bleeding from the Americas. Volcanoes would soon turn on in a massive global reactivation and the crust of the planet thrust high into the stratosphere would return as an apocalyptic meteor blizzard. One that would turn the atmosphere red hot and set the world ablaze with a vicious thermal pulse. And they were looking at it, live on TV as it were. They were there, watching the death of the dinosaurs. And the start of the rise of the mammals.

Jessy's mouth tightened, muffling her words. 'You mean there's dinosaurs down there?' Her eyes were like marbles, her breathing rapid and shallow. She remembered being fascinated, obsessed even, by the lumbering creatures when she was young. And here she was looking at their world, watching and witnessing the end of their world. The idea of all this being somehow fake had evaporated. Jessy was a believer. This was real.

Her gaze was broken by the buzzing in her head. The toning was coming back. She gulped thickly for a second time. Like Sean, she felt the prodding pulse of adrenaline that was coupled with a numbing dread, a dread of the unknowable being made known, of crazy fiction being made fact and set in tempered steel. Like a fantastical caricature finding life and walking up to you in the street.

Char's trembling goitre was swelling. He continued to probe deeply into the cube, cycling its characters and decrypting the contents. Jessy cringed at the sound of his words, he was loud. She reckoned nothing could possibly live up to what they'd already learned. She was wrong.

'They say these dinosaurs would have dominated for a billion or more years without real cerebral evolution. They were only taking up room, preventing their so called "blueprint" from switching to the next level. Dinosauria was not destined to be truly successful but the other creatures, the mentally stagnant mammals, carried that potential. A deeply buried potential that they recognized, and chose to unlock. These beings of the Sphere are emphasizing what we have known for eons. That it is not certain that even unlimited time will ensure graduation to intelligence and Mind. It is a furiously delicate game of chance mutation and happenstance. Although they seemed to have superseded all that. They made sure.'

Imagine an intelligent shark, Jessy cringed. Most creatures weren't destined to be intelligent. For good reason. They were just essential to the ecosystem of the sea.

'They literally made their own luck and engineered their own happenstance. Absolutely no luck required, simply a stunning technology, a technology that allowed them to manipulate Nature as required. Magic, if you will.'

Silence pervaded the space bay as the Virijians words were digested. Jessy turned her face away from the orb and the Virijians. She was trying to understand why they were telling them. It seemed so perverse.

Sean stuck his chin out and spoke rapidly. 'So, they wiped out the dinosaurs to initiate a new beginning...I mean, raked over what was there, got rid of 'em, to try and extract something better...something with more potential?' But how, he thought, hoping Zamindar would pick up on the question.

'They took pains to eradicate them "naturally" by impelling a large asteroid close enough to Saturn to break it up, and then tapping a fragment on to Earth. One that would do the job they required. It was large enough to kill every animal weighing over twenty kilograms but not large enough to manifestly damage the planet itself or its orbit. They wanted no evidence of artificial intervention so they chose a masterful technique, a way of evicting the stagnant dominion on Earth. Without their impact, their contention was that mammals would never have prevailed.'

Jessy's mind slowed and her gaze loosened into a hazy stare. She started feeling questions she wasn't even sure she wanted to acknowledge, nebulous half thoughts that were chaffing like barbed wire near the root of her mind. How in God's name do you "tap" a fragment, she wondered? Her mind was spinning. "Tap a fragment on to Earth", she repeated in her head. How the hell do you do something like that, she fretted anxiously? What the fuck, was her final considered thought on the

221

matter. She had no idea whatsoever. Who the hell were these beings? Zamindar's words brought her crashing back.

'Earth was handed a hundred and fifty million years but they did nothing, achieving almost zero in evolutionary terms. Dinosaurs would still be the high tenants of your world and you would simply not have been, not as a race, not as a species. This is the first part of their message, they say they delivered your ancestors from what would have been eventual extinction from Earth.'

Extinction, Mitch thought...Jesus. Was it possible, gone before we even got going? How indebted are we to them? He continued to gawp at Jessy while he ruminated. Is that why they're telling us, he wondered, do they want payback? Some sort of recompense for services rendered in the ascent of our people, in the emergence of our species?

What was it that they wanted? Sean wondered, nothing or something? He stared down at his moist palms, he could feel them warm and wet as he considered the question. He fumbled for his voice, eventually forcing it over the gravel in his throat, '...how could they be so sure that mammals would rise to intelligence. As you said before, nothing is predictable, nothing is certain. They made room for us, okay, but how did they know our ancestors would make a go of it, given their history of evolutionary paralysis.' He stopped talking and waited for some sort of response, almost tasting history in the air, a bittersweet sensation that seemed to imbue every pore of his body. The ponderous silence went on. They waited...and waited. And waited.

Char didn't even acknowledge Sean's question, instead delivering two huge fingers to the grooves and cycling the data. The figures and this time the vision changed. 'Fuck me,' Sean blurted, overwhelmed by everything...the slightest movement or sound made him cringe.

'This is two weeks after impact.'

The hemisphere showed graphic vision of a primal Earth. Thick leathery vegetation, familiar and unfamiliar palms encrusted with dust and ash that was being turned to greasy slush. The whole area was being pounded by a fantastic deluge of brown gelatinous acid rain which already thickly coated the ground.

Jessy looked at the scene and shuddered, terrified as she considered the source of the vision. Who or what had taken these images? The scene changed to a fixed airborne shot showing several erupting volcanoes that had been spurred into action by the impact, spewing ash that was combining with dirt in the atmosphere. A space shot from a similar aspect as the first revealed the drama. Blue Earth was brown Earth, a thoroughly Venusian world, the surface, the oceans and the atmosphere choked by massive impact clouds that stretched high into the stratosphere.

Zamindar suddenly stopped moving his arms. He stood totally still with both outer limbs at his side and his axial appendage slightly bent at the upper elbow. An unusual posture, Jessy thought. He looked like he was ready to jump. Like a grasshopper, she reckoned, studying him closely. He looked like he was chock full of potential energy.

Zamindar gazed down at Sean with ashen eyes wide and staring. Pregnant with things we don't want to know, Jessy thought, shivering briefly and closing her eyes. She still found it hard to look at them. 'Jesus Christ,' she said, as quietly as she could, staring at the floor, wondering again how evolution had cooked them up.

'They have answered your question Sean. They could not have known whether mammals would rise to intelligence. True awareness, they indicate, and as we know, is not ingrained into any of the laws of self organization or evolution, simply because there are no laws. We know that, but they say it is not natural at all. The data before us contends the rise to natural intelligence was a unique occurrence. A singular fluke of such colossal rarity that it has happened only once. They continually restate this idea. Singular.'

They stared up at Zamindar, puzzling over what it meant, wondering what relevance the statement had on the big picture, for Earth, for the Virijians, and for everything else that resided in

222

the cosmos. How the hell did they know what happened or didn't happen in the deeper Universe…are they saying they've been everywhere? Jessy asked herself, gazing off in the distance, unseeing. '

Sean spoke first, struggling to get his words past his throat. 'Singular?' he snorted, 'what about us…that is you and I.' He looked at Zamindar. 'That's at least two examples of Nature's success. Sure, they interfered a bit, got us started, but does that mean they don't count us?'

Sean's face slackened as he considered his own question, '…yeah, well I guess that might rule us out…but how can they claim that intelligence is singular, don't they know about you?' Jessy could feel the hair stand up on the back of her neck. She knew, or at least she thought she did.

Both Virijians were now looking slightly to one side of each other, totally fixated, communicating silently and rapidly with each other only a metre apart. Their temple flesh was moving faster than they'd ever seen before. It was literally churning like the surface of a stormy sea, and their eyes looked painfully distended, bloated and swollen by whatever they'd just read. Jessy eyeballed both of them. Something was wrong. Their eyes were distended and they definitely had a yellowish tinge to their pasty white features

What the hell? Sean thought, feeling deeply shaken by what he was seeing, watching things that seemed distressingly human, that seemed deeply flawed.

They knew immediately that their friends had read something that was intriguing them, confusing them, perhaps had even shocked them. Scaring them? Mitch wondered, studying their eyes.

Their facial cast looked very different, tighter, less melancholy, less expressionless. There was something flickering behind their eyes that he couldn't define, that they'd never seen before, that they weren't sure they wanted to see. Was it anxiety?

The visual hemisphere suddenly jumped back to life and began revealing stark star maps, vision of galaxies, globular clusters, spirals, elliptics, irregulars, massive whirlpools and others; the frame changing every second or so. The staccato light was mesmerizing and within a few minutes a thousand galaxies skipped brightly over the screen. Then it went black and this time it stayed black.

Char swung his massive head toward Mitch, immediately cramming his brain with language. The ancient vessel from *God knew where* had now been deeply penetrated.

Char seemed to wind himself up and then pause before speaking. Although lungs and larynx formed no part of their language, the way he was holding himself suggested that he held a mighty chestfull of air, ready for an explosion of voice that would never come.

His toning was abrupt and loud, and oddly shrill, as though. With a flourish of rotating elbows and squirming contours, Char said. 'They created your minds.' ⋅

His body became totally still, like he'd been dipped in clay and rapid fired. The only movement was a slight twitching from the horrible anthracite vein that ran across his forehead. Char glanced at Zamindar with his callus working overtime.

'They set the ground work, sure,' Mitch managed, 'but give us some credit, we evolved and went forward…' He stopped talking midsentence and turned to the Virijians as he gained an inkling of what Zamindar might have been suggesting. Mitch continued staring unseeingly at the imposing critter that loomed in front of him like a towering fictional effigy. Surely it didn't mean what he thought it meant.

Sean and Jessy gazed up at him, guessing they were about to become privy to something else that would add to the already unbearable pressure brought by the Sphere's mathematical gizzard.

The revelations were running a course analogous to the death throes of a large star, the pinching off of age old energies that would lead to a collapse that ultimately crushes everything to virtually nothing. Making the former magnificence wink out as though it had never been. Ever.

Jessy nervously drew in a breath of air from the huge chamber that stretched around them. There was no escaping the stabbing feeling that they were totally out of their depth, primitive pawns in what was a fantastically complex game of show and tell. None of them knew what do or think.

They stared at the orb in various states of disbelief and reverence, watching and listening as the stark hemispheres swallowed many of Mankind's most fundamental theories. Like it or not,

223

they were getting answers to questions they hadn't even dreamed of asking. And perhaps would get solutions to those that had forever remained out of reach.

The voice returned, this time it was Char's, and the words came more slowly this time, as though he were carefully selecting each one. Jessy clenched her toes as the sound started. Her eyes were narrow and grave, surveying the incredible scene in front of her.

'After contributing a basic life design and having rid Earth of dinosaurs they returned to deliver a genetic revision on some of the mammals. On millions of them actually, which would select them to quickly overbreed the others and guaranteed, they thought, that pre-intelligence and early technology, their first goal, would develop rapidly.'

Sean's eyes spread a bit more. The real nature of their assistance was starting to gel in his mind. The whites of his eyes were headlights as he searched the faces around him. They all, all the humans that is, looked totally and utterly overwhelmed, doing their best to absorb the impossible.

'Deliberate selection,' Sean murmured. '...Christ, if that's true then their tampering probably led to Prosimians, the tiny primates, then to anthropoids and to hominids. My God, the natural lineage of Man doesn't seem so natural anymore, wasn't natural...artificial ...fake.'

The pinpoints of light disappeared. A white hot star suddenly ignited behind Sean's eyes, flooding his brain with the dizzying light from mingled disbelief and fear. He could feel the foundations of his mind creaking as the bricks of his own existence were forcibly chiselled away.

Mitch reckoned they might be storytellers, what sounded like truth, could be, well…crap. He wasn't convinced. He thought they were legit though, but he wasn't entirely sure. Location was difficult to reconcile with it being a fake.

The thought of them, whoever they were, carrying out some sort of heinous medical procedure, perhaps in the middle of a dusty African savanna, made Jessy feel like dry retching. If she wasn't where she was and surrounded by who and what she was, the ideas being spat at her would seem like a crazy fantasy. But it wasn't like that, was nothing like that, although she wished it was with all her being. Her mind was a mixture of fear and incredulity.

'You might cringe at the thought of your ancestors being tampered with, but because of it, and only because of it, are you here to ponder it. I can tell you that you were nearly not selected as the most likely species to succeed.' Char stopped toning and peered at them almost quizzically, seemingly waiting for the inevitable response from Jessy.

It came from Sean, in a broken whisper. 'You mean they nearly chose another animal...to bring to awareness...to intelligence? 'What the hell else was there to choose from, a reptile, a bird, you said they considered dinosaurs but that...'

'Not dinosaurs, but according to them there were others. They claim that two residents of the planet had the capacity to develop, with help, to real smartness. They say they had a choice of two. A four legged creature, a primitive ungulate similar to your cow, and a tiny tree dwelling mammal. That was the choice for Earth. They had to choose one of them, decide which one they would mould into a special creature, to go on to an intelligent destiny and become the owners of the planet. And also, which one would be dragged permanently into a sensory backwater. It was a critical judgement in the history of your world and one they stress was not taken lightly. The decision they made here would define the future destiny of Earth. Quite simply, they had to get it right.'

Sean was in mindlock, a state of total bewilderment as he hung on every stinging word that filled his brain. He couldn't help but think about it. A cow. An intelligent, upright cow for Christ's sake! With technology, cities, religion...maybe some sort of crazy bovine culture. It sounded insane, was insane, but maybe the current situation would seem equally as absurd to another species, had they been chosen instead of Man. What about bats or whales? He was pretty sure they were around at the time and nearing the end of their evolutionary cycle.

Did he believe it? He wasn't sure, but coming from where it was coming from, how could he deny it? How could he possibly doubt its authenticity? If he were anywhere else but right here, he would, but he wasn't and he couldn't. He wanted to, but no way he could. It felt very unreal. Perhaps if they did the decrypting themselves it would feel more real, he wasn't sure.

'Again, they state quite clearly that without their help neither would have become self-aware, not mammals, not ungulates, ever. They needed to haul one from the instinctive abyss. To rev it up, give it a genetic shove, hard enough to push it over the otherwise insurmountable chasm that lay between advanced instinct and true, thinking awareness.'

Sean glanced at Jessy and then Mitch and lastly, over at the orb and the Virijians. He was half mad with fear, the other half of him was just desperate for some detail.

Synthetic. Jessy was blinded by the word and couldn't shake it from her brain. But it was more than just a word, synthetic, it was a feeling, an unpleasant gnawing sensation that things around her were moving too fast. That things too private to mention were changing, had changed, and had done so in a millisecond and forever. And now it was too late. But too late for what? She suddenly wondered, peering around herself in a state close to panic.

What they were telling us had always been. We humans had just mucked it up, made assumptions about ourselves based on logic. In this case, logic didn't work. In fact, most of the assumptions had been right. It was just the big picture, the painter of the big picture that we'd missed. The causator. The Artist. Evolution had done the little things, the fine tuning, but they, whoever they were, had done the big things, including the biggest thing. That is, consummating some deeply buried potential they said we had. She wasn't sure whether to be thankful or downright resentful, or hopping fucking mad.

A thought suddenly struck her like a red hot poker. Were these beings God? They'd been to Earth, there was no doubt about that. Was that why it was built into religion? Were they the inspiration for the original Hebrew Bible?

She felt a strange sensation in her head, a buzzing, almost spiritual wonder-terror that seemed to swamp the very centre of her being. A feeling that made her feel sick with fear. It was an enervating, feeling she decided. It wasn't a feeling of divinity…or of revelation.

Jessy felt an intense irretrievable loss, almost as though she'd been abruptly stripped of her memories, of her soul. Like waking up from a glorious dream to find that you had lived your whole life inside that dream. Suddenly realizing that reality didn't exist, that reality was a dream. And now you'd woken up forever, into an ethereal mental nebula where everything you thought you knew had suddenly vanished, and been replaced by a brand new set of rules. By a brand new reality.

How could humanity cope with such overwhelming enlightenment, knowing it was just some meticulously engineered fruit, spliced and sown by an invasive alien pedagogues. A bastard race born of DNA rape. Her face was ashen. She felt disorientated considering it. Jessy was snapped back to attention by Char who had seen her drift off into thoughtful oblivion. He watched her closely.

'Once they set the groundwork Jessy,' Char directed his toning to her, 'they believed that ensuing natural selection would favor the primate. So, their ultimate decision was in favor of your ancestors, in favor of you, which is obviously no surprise. They sent them on the path to something grand and demobilized the others, the Condylarthra, and genetically sculpted them over time into streamlined ocean dwellers. They have ended their evolutionary days as your Cetacea, your whales and dolphins. Born and raised from an ancient but very real competitor to Mankind.'

Jessy croaked quietly, 'artificial life design, artificial selection, xeno fucking genesis. God almighty, nothing has been natural. I just…' She trailed off into silence, not sure what to say next.

Sean rattled off a question when it was quiet, 'How did they get to Earth?' He'd been trying to slip it in for ten minutes. 'Starship…Lorentzian space? Where do they come from, somewhere close, Barnard's, Wolf…Tau Ceti maybe?' His eyes pleaded. No response. Sean restated his questions more succinctly. Still no response. Fucking nothing…not a peep. He assumed they didn't know. That there was no answer to his question, yet.

Anyway, he was sure they probably came from further away, another galaxy maybe, based on what they said, another cluster perhaps. His stomach felt like it was about to boil, and burn through his skin like a red hot football bladder. It felt like he'd eaten something well past its due date.

Zamindar ignored Sean entirely and continued. He was focussed on the contents of the Sphere, not Sean's continual questions.

225

'They put Earth aside for thirty million years and some suggestions of early intelligence in their chosen species did develop. But it was slower and less successful than they had hoped. Physiologically their evolution was first rate, but in Mind it was far less than expected. They were forced to come back thirty-five million years ago and deliver a very precise chromosomal and DNA embellishment on your anthropoid apes. This they were sure would lead quickly to the rise of awareness and a real technical potential.'

Sean opened his mouth but Jessy beat him. They knew now. 'So, they made Man…humanity?' she stuttered incredulously. She knew this was where it was leading, but that didn't reduce the impact of the words actually being spoken, the revelation made, the detail and the frequency of their genetic interference announced. They did much more than just lay the groundwork. Christ, they'd put up the walls, roof and painted the interior. They'd done it all, including wiring.

Mitch was entirely lost for words. Hell, all that he'd learned, been taught, all the ideas and theories and postulations. Poor old Darwin. All the revered names in history that had formulated theses and contributed to Man's understanding of himself, and his place in the cosmos. Jesus Holy Christ, he considered. Man didn't know a thing about himself. Absolutely naught. Who are we? Strangers, Clones, a test tube society definitely. The manicured spawn from some higher technology. We're as alien as the Virijians…alien to Earth. Like the Liger. Mutants. Jesus Christ, Mitch groaned to himself, wondering how the population in general back on Earth would react.

'You said four times,' Sean croaked. 'You said they'd been to Earth four times…that's only…er, three so far.' He wasn't sure he wanted to hear more, but then he wasn't sure he didn't either. Zam's voice pierced his skull. Tough luck if you didn't want to know more. Any choice was gone. Backpedaling wasn't an option.

'Twenty-five million years after the last time, that's about nine million years ago, they reassessed your world, knowing only too well that it was delinquent and difficult, but apparently, a most remarkable case. They saw that the lineage they had tagged for consciousness had narrowed alarmingly and was headed for extinction. And they, the Sphere builders, were headed irrevocably for failure on this world. The small scampering hominids were still in the throes of building on pre-intelligence but they knew by observation that they wouldn't live long enough to fulfill their designed destiny. That is, to jump to the next critical level. Their ascent was happening too slowly. Natural selection was selecting against the artificial breed, almost as though there were a biological conspiracy on Earth, one that simply refused to concede intelligence.'

'So, they came back, again?' Jessy whined. 'To save us? Or to avoid the embarrassment of us dying out despite their best efforts, and ruining their track record? She sensed an aching pressure in the depths of her mind, and she recognized it for what it was. It was a question, and it felt jagged and hot as though it had sliced into her cortex with drawn teeth. Jessy tried to avoid it but couldn't. She repeated the question, were these beings, whoever they were…our surrogate parents? And God created Man…the biblical recollection rose into her mind. She'd never been "religious" but the Book of Genesis had just gained a terrifying relevance. She'd once posed the question to a "believer" along the lines of, what if God was an astronaut? Whilst badly worded they both knew what it meant. Maybe the premise was correct.

Zamindar abruptly straightened his bearish shoulders, in the process causing all three of his upper limbs to ripple slightly, like the surface of a mill pond roused by a gentle breeze. His toning came louder now, filling every crevasse of their minds.

'They returned to a popular birthing ground in east Africa, to seal your fate and invasively deliver the final mechanisms that would ensure the success of their flimsy line of hominids. They inserted designed amino sequences into Australopithecine DNA which by their account was successful. And fortuitously so, because they make it very clear that if it failed, they had decided never to return. They were prepared to write Earth off as a host to intelligence and instead leave it to develop naturally, come what may … had that happened, there would be nothing on your planet resembling intelligence or technology.' Zamindar paused and looked at the cube, inhaling more of its cryptic scent but showing nothing that looked remotely like a recognizable emotion. Was he awed,

226

sad, triumphant, bored? Who would know? Maybe none of them, all of them, or anything in the middle. He appeared little different, even his color was the same.

Zamindar continued 'Within a few million years, success was theirs. A single powerful lineage broke free from your Hominids. And in a short time, Broca's area in the brain emerged, allowing the first stirrings of speech and language. Then came ballistic muscle movements. All these were attributes that should have evolved from their earlier work on Earth. But for some reason they had not worked, requiring them to be forcibly created by their own hand.'

Sean stared at Zamindar with a cortex full to bursting with crazed thoughts and obscure, unsettling sensations. 'How do they know all the details, the names that we designated to our forebears, the names of our continents, they couldn't know all that could they? Although I suppose...'

'We added those details Sean and we got the details from you, from your brain and from Jessy's. You both have a knowledge of evolution and human physiology, particularly the female, who we also find easier to read. Of course, we already knew a great deal about your history from Earth's carrier radiation.'

Jessy cringed at the thought of Zamindar rummaging through her head, looking for slices of detail he could use to add weight to the commentary. She had a sudden image of the Virijian flicking through a file directory, searching for the right document, the right detail...in her head.

The two armers stared at each other, standing rigidly, like three human sculptures molded from metal alloy. They were smothered by a horde of spinning emotions. All their heads were heavy with questions they were too frightened to ponder, let alone ask, but Sean at least had become addicted to the cranial rush of revelation. He urged Zamindar on with his eyes. Jessy looked at the floor, ready to be swallowed up, to avoid more. The brain racket was immediate, and brief.

'Their impact has been profound in every aspect of life design and life selection on Earth, that is apparent.'

Stating the bleeding obvious, Mitch thought. What was possible or impossible? Answer was, everything and nothing. That is, everything was possible, nothing was impossible. They had just heard impossible.

Jessy had taken everything in and was overwhelmed by a crescendo of pounding memories and racing emotions. She tried to clear her mind, padding over to the wall behind her and sitting down on the warm alien floor, letting her gaze rest on the unbroken whiteness around her. Her eyes found a wall and she lost focus, and her brain followed.

Jessy drank a heavy lungful of air and peered around, taking in the strange alien world she found herself in. In one of those moments of thunderous realization she knew that her memory, whilst entirely accurate, was a recollection of fabricated emotions to think, apparently the very rarest power of all. What the hell was natural anyway? She still had her memories, they were real enough, but the feeling persisted that none of what she saw, felt, and treasured from those memories should have existed. Would have existed in a real world, an untouched world, none of it, including her goddamn brain. The location of the orb might give her pause, however. Why would it be placed there if it wasn't real?

The second hemisphere showed a starmap, as before, but this time it didn't change. It was the Milky Way and it showed the location of the Sun on the second to last spiral. A tiny dot on a tremendous arm of stars.

Sean cleared his throat, 'and you, they did the same with you. The word singular doesn't allow you to have evolved naturally either.' There was no response from either Virijian on that score. Because they knew. They were in exactly the same boat as them.

The starmaps started to change, slowly this time, showing other galaxies. Zamindar started toning. 'These maps show the location of cognitive life which they have been responsible for helping along. Not as much as Earth, but in providing the gentle push to consciousness that otherwise would not have been, so they say.'

Each galaxy had a single highlighted star and planet and they were all like Earth, near the edge of the galaxy, away from the active centres. Below them were tightly bunched lines that lay in various states of obliquity. They assumed that any meaning they had, lay in the degree to which they were tilted away from the vertical. In any event the nature of the maps was fairly obvious.

Sean moved closer and peered at them. 'They've apparently created, if that's the right word, one intelligence per galaxy. But where are these galaxies?' He looked closer, eyeballing the hemisphere, looking for anything he might have seen before. His mouth suddenly dropped open and his words vented like escaping atmosphere, '...that's M87...M51 and, that's got to be the Antennae Galaxy...see the ejecta...it must be...'

Sean stopped rambling as Zamindar suddenly and with blinding speed placed a single digit into one of the grooves. The hemisphere paused on a starmap. A huge anaemic pseudo spiral dominated space on the great circle. There was one star encompassed by a double isosceles triangle with a notch cut out near the apex. It sat near the absolute extremity of the group. They were all shocked to see Zamindar move so quickly. But he did it and did it dexterously. The movements they'd seen before were lumbering and slow.

Zamindar and Char were both communicating rapidly. 'This is our galaxy, and it seems to answer the question you posed. It appears they claim to have aided our ascent as well as your own.'

'But should we believe them?' Jessy asked, out loud for the first time, from far away. 'Maybe they're the equivalent of cosmic storytellers, pathological liars, who knows, how can we be sure?' She moved closer to Mitch as she spoke.

'I think we have to believe them,' Sean said. 'Taking account of all the facts presented, logic would suggest that they are conveying the truth.'

'Agree,' Jessy said, still looking down. Mitch nodded. They all agreed.

'But why?' Mitch said. 'Why tell us at all? What would their reasoning be? And why tell us at a particular point in our development...and not inform you at a similar time? After all, you've been around for a hell of a lot longer than us, and you had no idea. Doesn't that seem odd. Is it because we were so difficult that they've told us, boasted to us perhaps?' His image of the Principal's office shot back at him in a flash. Oh shit, Mitch snapped silently, chastising himself. They didn't do it because we were naughty. He felt like slapping himself. 'As if,' he piped, almost grinning.

'We simply do not know the answer. The cube has two cycles left so perhaps they will tell us why we have not been similarly blessed with a Sphere.'

The Virijians moved swiftly back to the cube and it cycled downward. The opposite hemisphere stayed blank this time. Mitch watched as they started toning copiously in what looked to be an increasingly agitated state of mind, behaviour that seemed totally wrong for these creatures.

Jessy closed her eyes. What now, she whimpered silently, unable to imagine, not wanting to imagine what might be behind their odd demeanour? Their manner was almost casual to the stunning news of some cognitive designer. So, what was it then? Her mind jackknifed, losing itself in the shadows of impossibility. 'Come on,' Jessy said upbeat and smiling, 'let's look on the bright side.' She thought about it and had nothing else to say, despite trying to think of something to back it up...she couldn't. There had to be a bright side...right? She was met with looks of confusion, Sean was scratching his head and Mitch had one eye closed, clearly trying to think deeply...and failing. Both were trying to think of something intelligent to say. Both failed.

Would there be a signature at the foot of the last cycle? Or some gloriously anointed Cosmic Seal? Who were they, where did they come from, how did they move around and just how unthinkably advanced were they? So many questions.

Char's skin was peculiarly discoloured. His normally pasty white flesh appeared distinctly yellow and was mirrored almost perfectly by Zamindar. It looked as though they were suffering from some sort of mutual jaundice. Mitch said no, but Jessy surmised that maybe they'd caught something from them, a virus or bacteria. Much more likely the other way around, she reckoned. She was certain the Virijians could deal with their primitive germs, take them in their stride, she was sure.

Jessy stumbled backward, aghast at the sickly stain that was bubbling beneath their skin. What the hell was wrong with them?' She hoped they were just sick. Her thoughts were abruptly drowned out by the Sulphur faced being.

'We have finished scanning the Sphere,' Char said slowly and somewhat distractedly. Their goitres were squirming like flames on a campfire. Clearly, they were more interested in talking to each other, than them. The jaundice had almost bled away but the final yellowish stain seemed to have set like pale ink in their lower dermis, for both of them.

'Are you okay?' Jessy asked of Char who to her eye still looked distinctly unwell. Cirrhosis? she wondered. It sure looked like it. He was still yellowish.

Sean hoped to hell it wasn't contagious.

Char ignored her question and toned rapidly, distinctly quicker than they'd heard before. The nonchalance was suddenly swallowed by an unsettling new urgency.

'There is something extraordinary within the message,' Char began. 'Something we could not have anticipated. We have contemplated not telling you, but minds greater than ours have decided you should know.' Char gazed at Zamindar without expression, the amber tinge deepening again.

Jessy groaned feebly to Mitch, 'if whatever they're going to tell us has had such an impact on them, what the hell will it do to us?' She wasn't sure she wanted to hear what was coming. In fact, she was certain she didn't want to hear it. 'What could be more insane than what they've already told us Mitch?' He looked at her silently and wondered the same thing.

Sean's face was like rendered porcelain as he waited for the words. He could tell they were coming by the sound of static that filled his brain.

'Do you want us to reveal the remainder of the message?' Zamindar asked, almost tentatively, as though he were hoping they would say no. He was still distinctly yellowish.

Sean looked at Mitch, then at Jessy, and replied in the affirmative. Jessy was visibly shaking, scared witless. Think of Christmas Trees, she whispered to herself. It wasn't working. She tried focussing on Josh, but that didn't work either. Jessy still felt light headed and dizzy.

Sean and Mitch wanted to hear everything, it was an addiction now, and anyway, what more could there be? Zamindar spoke quickly, recounting the latest data he and Char had collected.

'The authors of this message are a race of beings (he looked at Char in a rapid sideways movement that had all his limbs moving in concord) a race of beings, over twenty billion years old.' Both Virijians froze like storefront dummies, watching and waiting, knowing what sort of response the insane statement would probably bring.

'Come fucking on,' Mitch eventually spluttered, 'That's older than the Universe for God's sake. You said yourself that your calculations were...'

'Please,' Zamindar declared loudly. 'Wait and listen and you will understand.'

He winced at the earsplitting demand for quiet. They looked as one at Zamindar, now fully expecting anything. They'd never been berated by the Virijian, but seemingly that's what had just happened, or at least that's what it felt like. The Virijians had just told them to shut it. Jessy Mitch and Sean were now silent, frozen and waiting for the Virijian to tone. Not a muscle was moved. The silence was pervasive.

He toned quietly, slowly and clearly. 'These beings do not come from our Universe. They live around us, not actually here and now, but between us, over us, through us.'
More silence. Sprinting minds. Fading belief. What? What in God's name did he mean?

'You mean they live in another dimension?' Sean asked hoarsely. He'd heard of the concept but never, ever, related it to reality. It was only mathematical gobbledygook...wasn't it?
'More correctly they live obliquely to us, perpendicular, laterally if you prefer. They occupy an entirely different cosmos, an older and larger Universe that existed billions of years before ours was born, and which continues to exist today. Their Universe is more than thirty billion years old.' The towering alien stared at the humans, seemingly waiting for a voice. His contours were a twisting nest of spidery vascular quickening. Sean looked at Charijiok who was essentially yellow and getting yellower, which coupled with what he'd just said, made his heart hammer in his chest.

Jessy's body was numb. 'So they come from a different Universe, Jessy whispered? 'Jesus Christ,' she gurgled from the back of her mouth.

229

'Sweet mother of Mary,' Mitch said. His voice was barely a gurgle. The Many Worlds thesis floated into his mind, a bizarre theory that was actually based on real physics. He knew that, but then so was hopping back in time to murder your granny. Some things, whilst possible, were surely meant to stay on a physicist's blackboard...weren't they? What the hell did reality really mean, and how many of them were there? Mitch forced himself to keep thinking about it, fighting the need to gape at Zamindar.

Jessy could feel herself losing it. Despite the massive emptiness around her, she felt the ship crushing in, felt her mind sagging under the weight of annihilated philosophy on Earth. This revelation, these revelations would unbrick everything anyone had ever known or thought, or dreamt. Holy God, she thought, what of religion...of social structure...of science? What of anything? Jessy had heard enough. She hadn't been ready for any of it. Fear pulsed through Jessy and her mind froze with horror as she considered it all.

Char par rotated his axial claw and slid it upward and then downward in a fluid motion, clearly sending an instruction of sorts to his comrade. He looked directly at Jessy, then Sean and lastly at Mitch. Then he stood tall and glanced at Zamindar who nodded almost imperceptibly, an earthly gesture they'd never seen before.

'Jesus Christ,' Jessy whined, looking at the floor. She could hear the static, she knew voice was coming, but she didn't want to hear anymore. Like all of them, Jessy would somehow have to suck it up. Char continued, in the colour of a ripe lemon, and Jessy braced herself by clenching every muscle she could, and scrutinising him closely.

'These beings who seem to designate themselves with the numeral one, claim that they created our Universe. Conceived all that surrounds us...' Char continued toning over the exhortations of Sean in particular. He knew it was coming, but still...Jessy and Mitch just stared like long dead corpses. Their eyes were open wide and inspecting Charijiok carefully, watching his every move, seeing the saffron tones not only not improve, but get worse. Deeper.

'...they designed the initial quantum fluctuation in space. Planted the Planck seed from which everything, us, you, totality...inflated, grew and ripened into what we see around us. They set the laws of physics, meticulously tuned their values and engineered precisely, the overriding laws and constants that we see in the Universe; one's right for our kind of life.' The toning stopped, briefly. Zamindar gazed at them and slackened his torsal limbs against his body, making himself look something like a resting cuttlefish. Again, he looked ready to jump.

Looking at one another, the humans were shattered, faces soft with confusion, not knowing how to react or what to say. It was always past reason, but now it was beyond even a joke, beyond the most fantastical hallucinations. Jessy looked at Mitch, not daring to move. Her mind refused to register the latest raft of words. She felt drained and her mind empty. She switched off. She could almost hear herself creaking and shaking, speeding up before her mind wound down, into the terminal stages of unravelment. Still he went on. She concentrated on Josh who was asleep again, she knew the Virijians were responsible for his placid behaviour. They had to be, there was so little crying and the arm, always so active, was now so still. And then there was the sleeping. Sean did some tests and said Josh was in great health. So, there was only one reason. It was them, she was sure of it.

Jessy's focus wavered as she opened her eyes and looked at her son, her brain screaming in a rainbow of disbelief. She didn't believe it...but...she wasn't entirely sure.

Zamindar's toning was back like an excruciating migraine.

Here we go again, she thought, having heard quite enough. She was tired, physically and mentally...mainly mentally. Jessy felt like sleeping, but she also realised that there was no escaping this...awake, asleep...whatever. This would catch up with her sooner or later. Probably sooner.

'Ours is one of a thousand and thirty-two Universes which they have created. This is the answer to your dark matter. One, it would appear, they are the ultimate engineers and observers. Cosmic architects. They have the power and the technology, and we have already witnessed their ability to duplicate Nature, to create Nature. To be Nature.'

Jessy's breath was shallow. She stared, dumbfounded at Mitch who had an indecipherable look in his eyes.

Sean's mind whirled around the question of how? How the hell could they do all that? What manner of thing were they? "Technology" didn't seem an adequate description for what they were claiming to have done. It was magic, pure and simple. Physical sorcery on the highest level imaginable. Still, he wondered...how? Zamindar got his question and took hold of it.

'They created our Universe, they explain, by tunnelling a pocket in their own spacetime. They produced a specially configured quark sized glob that possessed perfect energy and symmetry. The minute glob pinched off from their own space, and energy screamed into being, with the pinchee Universe, us, having no effect, ever, on the pincher Universe despite their apparent proximity. In that sense, we or they, are in a different dimension, a different and totally separate layer of spacetime. We live inside an exquisitely manicured black hole, that they created.

'Every aspect of the glob was carefully prepared so that what came out of it, the forces and the particles, would eventually yield a home that was capable of sustaining carbon-based life, and capable...'

A hail of sparks smacked into Sean's mind, flooding him with a vision of such awe and scope that he abruptly stopped breathing. A thundering knowing hit him and dug to the floorboards of his mind. He finally drew in a breath and his words spewed into the space bay. He didn't mean to talk, but it happened anyway. His mouth just opened and the words vented.

'So that's it...' he exulted loudly. 'They aligned our physics with the requirements for life...our life. It always seemed so incredibly lucky, so finely tuned and contrived, and now we find out that our laws are contrived. Physics, math, chemistry...life itself, all the Laws. Now we know for sure. Jesus Christ,' he muttered, looking at the floor. Sean's eyes were huge and blind as he paused and savored what he was saying. He knew now, and the sudden realization was suffocating. It was almost too much. He wobbled, but caught himself, before he crumpled like a house of sand.

Jessy's eyes were wide open and frozen pretty much stiff as she stared at Charijiok. The riddle of dark matter solved, apparently. It was simply gravity bleeding from the other universes, designed for the right result. No wonder we couldn't find WIMPS or a brand new particle. We even looked for decay products of Higgs and other particles. More fool us, Jessy thought, grinning slightly as she thought of all the stupid experiments that were being conducted. If it wasn't there, it wasn't there. They were searching for something that wasn't there.

Sean continued murmuring under his breath, looking and sounding like a nutter, '...carbon resonance...forces...particles...flatness of space...fuck...fake. FAKE.' The word burnt into his mind, a word he knew that had grown a sudden new meaning, inherited a brand new power to destroy everything humanity had ever known, or thought it knew. Fake. It summed it up nicely. Every fortuitous law and constant in the Universe that allowed us to be here was prearranged by some Godlike race bent on erecting playgrounds for their dazzling technology.

Sean contemplated the insane paradox. 'Everything about the Universe is so acutely balanced in favor of life, we should have known. How could it have been just fucking luck? Or the crazy multiverse theory. We guessed there was something strange but perhaps we should have known. Just the most minute change in any one of the cosmic laws and Mother would have bypassed making any significant life capable atoms at all. No carbon, no life, no us.' Sean had heard and even read about the so called multiverse, that there were trillions of universes, all with chance laws, and carbon based life obviously inhabits the one that suits it. That tenuous theory had just been pretty much blasted out of the water. 'We're here by design. Because '*One*' made us and made our universe from scratch, like Carl Sagan and apple pies.'

Sean was suddenly struck by an overwhelming sense of loneliness, concurrent with a slice of divinity. He whispered "Mother" and chuckled out loud. 'Mother didn't exist, never had. Nature, natural...it simply wasn't right. Creator, that was right. What we called Mother was actually them. They'd baked her from scratch like a carefully prepared pie. As deranged as it sounds, we're currently in close communication with Nature's creator.

231

God, Mitch thought. Sean was right. But something else struck him. Something he'd read years ago that even then had set his mind thinking.

Mitch's words oozed from behind a swollen tongue, 'I remember reading that if the conditions in the first split second of creation had differed by more than one part in a trillion, trillion, trillion...that the amplifications over time would've spawned a barren Universe. Either totally starless, or one that would've crunched back together long ago if it was too lumpy. Meaning no us and no anything. Forget the multiverse.

They all stared at him, understanding with diamond clarity what he was saying. They should have known. It all seemed so obvious, Mitch thought. With those odds, how could that be luck? By Design. The words pierced him like hollow point shells. Luck had absolutely nothing to do with it. The Universe was produced, by them. Jessy sat on the warm floor with Josh and watched him crawl across it for a short distance before collecting him and starting the process over, again. She forcibly focussed on Josh, then gawked at Sean, who looked like he was at a prom as he rubbed absently at his arm.

Sean gushed, '...we should've realized that the coincidences were actually impossible. And yet we didn't...we wondered and we dreamt and we suggested, but we kept searching for "real" reasons. But now we know. Everything that allowed us to be here, all of it was done before creation, by the creators, our creators.'

Sean looked down at the floor, out of breath and almost out of mind. 'Fuck', he growled to himself and repeated it several times. 'Everything is counterfeit...everything. Totality is plastic, all that we see and all that we know, all that we have ever known. Will ever know. Holy Jesus!'

Nothing around him was as he thought it was. Was it the end of philosophy as they knew it, he wasn't sure? Would they be able to deal with it? Would Earth be able to cope with what they'd just learned? Paradigms lost. It never had more meaning.

'What you say is true Sean,' Char said, 'they mention this tuning a little further on.' The Virijian looked back at the cube, then back at them and almost smiled, or grimaced, it was hard to tell what meant what. Sean felt a renewed stab of energy.

'After their carefully designed seed is ready, conditions of pure energy inflate it and then expand it. If the preconditions are set just so, the mass joins eventually into what we see around us, stars, galaxies, planets, dark matter, dark energy and organic life. But not consciousness, not true thinking intelligence. One fabricated the beginning of our Universe in such a way, and thankfully for us, they did it right. It was successful. It was a living Universe.' Char stretched his middle arm forward and then back, letting it come to rest on the crystalline cloth of his hip. He walked away and then back toward the orb.

Sean continued to struggle with the lunacy of all he knew, simply being part of someone's experiments. The so called "fires of creation", the background radiation from the Big Bang that was detectable in the infrared, he realized, were actually the fires of *'One'*.

Every time he had looked up in Australia, at nighttime, he was dumbfounded by the number of stars in the sky. It was truly glorious. From Sirius to Eta Carinea. Breathtaking. Apparently they created it all, ·

Jessy inhaled heavily, almost gagging on the sharpness of her own breath. 'Fuck,' she whispered hoarsely, opening her eyes wide and ogling Char and the orb grimly. 'Our Universe was created by the hand of who...of God, are they any different from a god, from God himself?'

'I don't know Jess, but I can't envisage more powerful beings. The ability to create a Universe, Universes, by definition they are God. Who could deny it?' Sean returned.

Making matter, who would've thought? Sean felt the tingling start in his toes. Jessy moved her head slowly from side to side, and ended up looking at Zamindar. 'You said they live around us. Can they see us...like, now?' She continued bobbing her head around.

'They would no doubt be aware that we have penetrated their Sphere and although they would not watch any species all the time, they would be watching us now, I feel certain. This would

232

be a significant moment for them I imagine, given the difficult nature of the life on your planet and the pains they went to in bringing you forth.'

'Oh Christ,' Jessy wailed '...this isn't happening, Mitch, this isn't happening', she repeated the sentiment twice more. Her brain felt like it might split open at any second and vent a bloody spray of shattered memories. 'It can't be...can it?' Jessy muttered, still looking around. Padding unsteadily backward to the rear wall, she stood staring straight ahead, shoulders trembling and mind stalling. She was aghast at the prospect of almighty and insatiably curious overlords...voyeurs with unlimited powers to exercise their bent. 'Oh God,' she muttered, looking downward at Josh who still looked happy enough. She felt like her brain had come apart from her body. She gazed at herself from above her left shoulder. Swimming light was everywhere.

Jessy could feel herself going...wobbling visibly on legs turned to jelly, feeling her cortex winding down and seeing the Sphere swelling, becoming a tremendous dark smudge that swamped her horizons. Her head was leaden and her thoughts were coming in slow, gooey lumps as though gelatin crystals were slowing setting between her ears. Jessy's overworked mind had quite simply had enough. She squealed briefly and slid slowly down the wall, hitting the warm floor with a soft thud then rolling onto her side, completely unconscious. Josh stopped his crawling and looked over to his prone mother, giving a squeak and then totally unconcerned, resumed his explorations.

'Jessy, what the..!' Mitch cried as he heard her hit the floor with a dull thomp. Running over, he gently pulled her to a sitting position, propping her rubbery body against the wall.

'Wake up damn it,' Mitch shrilled, as she flopped lifelessly against the wall like a beached fish. He checked her pulse. She seemed fine, albeit with a sore head. She continued to just lie there, looking totally lifeless.

To Sean and Mitch, Jessy showed no signs of life and equally showed no sign of coming around. She was breathing but that was about it. What they couldn't see were the pulses of light that were flashing through her brain like sapient lightning.

As Mitch nursed her forehead, Jessy's cortex was hot with the energy of involuntary thought, abuzz with the power of intense dream state.

Jessy "woke" into a bizarre nighttime landscape. She wondered where she was, but only briefly and vaguely, a distant thought shrouded in mist. Ahead of her, a light turned on and started pulsing. Staccato bursts of purple, red and white strobed over a sea of creatures that were all hair and wide eyes.

The apelike creatures were dancing spastic like to a silent beat. Then everything stopped and there was abrupt silence and total, unremitting darkness. Then there was a well of pure white light, twisting, dazzling brightness, like a star turning on for the first time.

Someone or something started moving through the light, moving from the inside to the outside and Jessy knew immediately that it was one of them. *One of One*. She stopped breathing. For some reason she was terrified beyond thinking, almost beyond respiration. Her heart stopped beating in her chest as the thing slid out into the warm open air of what looked like an African savanna. She could see it clearly. Without doubt it was human. At least it looked that way.

'Oh fuck,' she eventually wheezed. 'A man, it's a man...Jesus Christ, a man!' Suddenly she couldn't think and then in a pulse of total recall, she remembered. Jessy looked at the erect figure and was overcome by a biblical knowing. She almost fell to the ground but managed to remain on her feet, whimpering out loud, paralyzed with terror.

'They made us in their image...in his image, *One* are fucking Man. Oh, sweet Jesus.' She clasped her hands and fell slowly to her knees, ending up crouching in the grass surrounded by the hairy ape things.

'In his image,' she repeated over and over. 'They are God...they are God.'

The being that emerged from the light was a man, clearly, unambiguously a Homo Sapien, in appearance at least. It stood there motionless, casting its critical eye, Jessy thought, over its failed stock. Did it see her? She tried to avoid being seen, she was sure she stuck out like the proverbial fish out of water.

Mitch had seen the first sign of life from Jessy since she'd passed out ten minutes ago. He crouched next to her and saw with relief that her eyelids were flickering, indicating that at least something was happening inside.

Perhaps she was on the verge of a grand mal siezure, but hopefully she was just edging her way up the ladder to wakefulness. He bent over and tapped her cheek as the tremors worsened. Mitch noticed with some distress that her breath was escaping in heavy gasps which shook her entire body.

'What the hell's happening?' he yelled, looking at Sean. Jessy's eyes slowly opened and her pupils, wide and dilated, shrunk back to alertness, to recall. Her hands flew to cradle her head as she remembered the dream terror in the first instant of consciousness.

'Oh fuck...damn...goddamn it, she swore through labored, shallow breathing.

'What happened?' Mitch asked softly. 'You were out for ten minutes, we were starting to wonder whether you'd checked out for good.' Jessy's eyes stared up into the pale void. 'Another stinking nightmare. Fuck it. I thought they'd gone, but they're worse than ever. Damn it all to hell. With everything else that's happening I don't need this.' She pressed her hands over her face and breathed deeply. Fuck, she repeated to herself.

Jessy related the bizarre nightmare to Mitch. He wasn't the least bit surprised that she was upset. Standing up on wobbly legs she struggled back toward the Sphere. It was still there. That wasn't a dream. Damn it. She wished it was a dream. She wished the whole thing was a dream.

With Jessy recovered, Sean's attention arrowed back to the Sphere, or more particularly to his tangled thoughts about the architects of the fabulous vessel.

'Can they cross over to, er...our Universe?' Sean asked, the wonder of the enquiry painted in his eyes. He thought he knew the answer, but it was the detail he yearned for.

Zamindar responded, 'They can and they have, many times, as we can tell from their interaction with the creatures of our Universe, with you in particular. They can inflate their link with negative mass and pass through them at will and can reach any part of the Universe, our Universe that is, instantaneously, or so it would seem.

'And what of the composition of this Sphere...the strange atoms, were our guesses even close?'

'...we know that *One* manipulate each of the seeds from which their cosmic environments spring. The individual universes are experiments remember, so as you would expect, each one has different building blocks...different quarks, different leptons, different atoms. Hence, we have in front of us an unexplainable Sphere composed of something none of us have ever seen before. They are not part of your supposed "Island of Stability" on the Periodic Table. Rather, this object represents the atomic nature of their Universe, the stable energy state of the parent Universe. The first from which all else came. In front of us are the real atoms of creation, created apparently without the input of a controlling being. Created naturally if you like, unless of course there is a species above *One,* who perhaps treat them as an experiment...'

Char looked almost confused, but he probably wasn't, although the vein in his forehead was thicker, engorged with pulsing purply blood. Jessy studied him closely, there was no feature about him that she didn't find ugly. Char and all the Virijians, were monsters in the truest sense of the word, physically. They were extremely smart though, with a tremendous technology.

Sean thought for a second and was aghast at the idea that there might be hundreds or maybe thousands of races of Superbeings who formed a colossal Universal pecking order. The one above forging playgrounds and homes for their children below, the inferior offspring as it were. Maybe that was the meaning of life, new playgrounds, new universes, creation.

'The creators of new universes are long living thinking beings. Hell, maybe one day, in a billion years time, we'll be inducted into the Cosmic Super club.' Sean let out a bursting breath of air. 'And we'll be making Universes.' He grinned and chuckled, the breadth of the concept was lightyears beyond his grasp. The thought of a limitless succession of gods stretching upward and outward, struck his mind and left a gaping axe wound. Surely not, he thought. It must end here, but

234

then he thought, why the hell should it? Maybe it didn't stop. What we thought before was wrong, why should we be right now? The lineage maybe went on forever.

Jessy thought that maybe *One* were the ultimate outworking of intellect, perhaps displaying the final biological purpose of awareness and mind. That is, the responsibility to build new realities, new life, to ensure the perpetuation of wisdom, by continually creating it. Jessy could feel the fear and the anxiety grating at her. It was slowly unbricking her sense of self, piece by piece. Ordinary, or what she and humanity would consider ordinary, what they took for granted, was finished. "Ordinary" didn't exist anymore. Everything around them, on Earth and beyond, was extraordinary, she reckoned.

'Thousands of Universes and thousands of superior species,' Sean muttered to himself as if to speak it out loud would make it sound less fanciful. He suddenly felt unspeakably inadequate, like a cave dweller barely able to fashion a stone tool or to put two decent grunts together. He forcibly blanked the ideas from his head and thought of nothing but puffy white clouds scudding over the swollen landscape of his mind. One last thought managed to sneak through, a quote actually, a favourite of his, the opening to a book which had fostered his youthful interest in space. '*The cosmos is all that is or ever was or ever will be*'. Sean thought about it and knew that Carl Sagan had gotten it terribly wrong. A forgivable mistake, he thought. After all, who would have thought?

Jessy turned from Josh and looked directly at Char, feeling ill and blinking rapidly. 'What do they, um, look like...are they, er... humanoid?' she asked tentatively, wondering what sort of nightmarish vision they might be. Couldn't be worse than you guys, Jessy figured, looking at Char and his rippling callus and then at Zamindar. Then she considered the mindboggling antiquity of the Sphere builders. They were older than the most distant quasar...beyond the most senile star or galaxy...billions of years older than the Universe. She pondered about their physical evolution, had it bumped up against some sort of inviolable end point, and if it had, what was it? I guess we'll eventually find out, Jessy assumed, thinking they'd again visit their planet, one day.

Would it be like God returning to Earth? She shivered, thinking about it. What the fuck would they do? What would we do as a people? Jessy struggled mightily with the mental visions it evoked. Maybe they were robotic.

Had their physical form been gradually swabbed away like annoying mucus, or were they still flesh and blood? What in the name of the Almighty did they, could they look like, given how old they were? Jessy could feel the questions and the fears, choking and hot, digging into her cortex. Exhaustion came knocking again, hard.

Sean wondered what Einstein would have thought if he was told that the laws he so brilliantly unraveled were no more natural than Monopoly rules. Sean's mind reeled again. Intelligent design, he said to himself. 'A dozen numbers, all preprogrammed...gravity, constants, Higgs... strengths...masses...,' Sean said quietly. 'Now we know, he repeated sharply.'

'They are God,' Jessy repeated. 'Engineering photons, the fucking speed of light, there is no limit to their powers of creation.' It was a statement now, no longer a question.

'If they can do all that, what's left to do?' Mitch added. 'They can spontaneously create Nature and as far as we're concerned, they are Nature. They gave birth to time as we know it, to everything we know, will ever know...'

'But why did they leave this capsule for us?' Sean asked suddenly, '...why didn't they just pop through a Lorentzian thingy and tell us in person instead of leaving a remote vessel. And why didn't they convey the message in an Earthly language. There seems no doubt they could've done that, updated it when syntax became established and made it easier for us, guaranteed that we'd understand it.'

Charijiok's callus presumably spoke with Zamindar and then turned to look at Sean.

'The mathematical language was a natural timer,' Char toned, 'a control placed on its activation and decryption, which of course we overcame. They also make it clear that they do not wish to personally interact, they see no point in it, yet. Hence the Sphere. They wish to create and direct life, structure new intelligences and different Universes, observe, assess, analyze, plan for their future and forge new ideas, projects, new frontiers of enquiry. To interact with us would serve no purpose. Remember, they are billions of years older and exponentially more technical than us. What would they say? Interaction is not their goal, yet.'

Jessy glanced up apprehensively. 'So, they could've wiped out Hitler, prevented JFK's murder, all the wars, the famines, the plagues, 9/11, and prevented a million other disasters and atrocities, they could've done all that couldn't they?' She peered at the Virijian knowingly, then glanced at Sean and Mitch, nodding.

'It is not their way, they are our creators, but once cognition is produced or clearly developing on a particular world, they are left alone to grow and develop.

The way society matures from that point onward is part of the reason they make Universes. Assessing those societies forms part of their research, as does the emergence and effect of an occasional tyrant or shattering planetary event along the way. Perhaps they watched your Hitler with an analytical interest and observed your Twin Towers disaster with a scientific curiosity, but interfere to stop these things, that is definitely not their way.' The Virijian fell silent. No headshake to accompany these comments. There was nothing human about the Virijians.

'Even if your planet were headed inexorably for destruction, they would not step in. They could, but they would not. Had our black hole penetrated your solar system, they would not have helped. They do not interfere. They are researchers, data collectors and statisticians, apparently with a strict scientific protocol. They will intervene on a genetic level to create intelligence, but only because they say they have to. And that is their only invasive act and unlike Earth, it is usually a single act. Ours and the other Universes, their own personal Multiverse, are simply a series of independent experiments...no more, no less.'

Jessy gulped, pondering the others that were out there amid the eternal dimensions of space. So many of them, she brooded uncomfortably, clutching an arm to her chest and peering down at the floor. There were billions of chances to produce something apocalyptically ugly...hideous and skin crawlingly terrible, where one look would equal everlasting madness. They were all thankfully a long way away. Probably too far for Sean, no doubt.

Zamindar continued, 'When one of their stock unlocks a Sphere, they demonstrate a certain broad technological capability. In some cases, they do not leave a calling card and choose to keep their presence hidden, continuing to observe and assess without revelation. They only communicate with certain of their kin, although why this is, we can only guess at.'

'And that's why you didn't find a Sphere, because there wasn't one to find?' Sean asked.

'It would appear so,' Zamindar returned. 'The information they have provided in this vessel is inadequate, it whets our curiosity and makes us hungry for more but it seems unlikely we will ever get any more.'

Jessy said, 'I find it strange they should decide to reveal themselves and then do it on such a level. Is it a test to see how we deal with it? To see what we do next? To see how it affects us moving forward?'

The Virijian didn't comment. He didn't know, or didn't want to answer. Probably the former, hopefully.

Jessy with Josh, Mitch and Sean all took turns with the Earthly accommodations so thoughtfully provided by the Virijians. They ate, drank and used the porcelain structure that still looked so very out of place.

Alone in the bathroom, Jessy tried to come to terms with what she'd heard. Out of sight of the Sphere and the Virijians, the whole thing took on a dreamy, ethereal quality. It was an experience that was profoundly shocking, unbelievable in the extreme, but with the Virijian oration it obtained a sense of credibility. It was believable, but back in more homey 'burbs, the craziness became exactly that, ludicrous and farcical. Back on Earth, if that ever happened, she was sure it would seem unbelievable.

What of religion? she wondered, it was finished surely? And what of humanity's motivation, goals on Earth and in space? What of culture, socioracial structures, economics, politics?

She could only imagine the stifling effect these revelations would have, but then she considered it further and thought well, maybe not.

Perhaps it would spur us on, make us more determined than ever to communicate with the other galactic communities that we now knew were out there. With the Virijians help, maybe Earth would find itself on the brink of a stunning and wondrous new era of cosmic interaction. Then again, possibly not. Her emotional state was waxing and waning, swinging like a gate in a storm.

Feeling only marginally more positive, Jessy returned to the others who were still huddled around the Sphere. To Jessy, the orb looked more foreboding than ever, a dark dull symbol of history lost and foundations crushed. Jessy was downcast, she, herself, looked crushed.

Sean looked up at Zamindar. 'The most important question is, what does all this imply about life per se in this Multiverse? They say that life on a basic level is not rare, uncommon, but not truly rare. It was that geochemistry to biochemistry thing again. Where nourishing conditions exist, life will normally follow five percent of the time or almost always where the system has been seeded with their protein pods.' Sean stopped and looked at Zamindar again, 'do they mention what types of life they have encountered, is all the naturally emerging life carbon based?'

'They do not mention specifics, to our disappointment as well as your own. The astonishing revelation is that naturally evolved intelligence has emerged only once. Once out of trillions of trillions of ecospheric planets. According to *One,* life on occasion has developed great complexity and advanced instinct but nowhere, nowhere at all, but on *One's* initial planetary home did the molecular ballet line up and score the equivalent of a trillion, trillion lottery wins in a row. Where complexification led to a life form that grew naturally to self-awareness. What they are saying is that the natural evolution of truly intelligent creatures was a fluke so incredibly unlikely it has not yet been repeated. Apart from *One,* simplicity has never complexified naturally to self-awareness. They believe soon, with the creation of new Universes, the odds will stack up and a brand new natural intelligence will emerge. They emphasize that before a species develops recognizable intelligence, they can determine whether or not they carry the potential. But so far, they haven't found it.'

Mitch looked at Char and spoke almost in a whisper. 'So, after a billion years *One* discovered they were the single bearers of intelligence in their Universe. That they were totally alone. And having discovered the underlying paradigm of evolutionary intelligence and having worked through the moral considerations, they took it upon themselves to engineer other intelligences and other Universes. So, they could watch, assess and analyze and eventually perhaps later, interact.'

Jessy shook her head and it kept shaking. She truly understood now. There was no confusion, not any more. All the impossible revelations had joined in a mountain of evidence that filled her mind like setting concrete. And she knew the others had arrived at the same conclusion, she could see it splashed in their eyes, the pallor of total disbelief, mingling with an uncomfortable knowing. The knowing was the greatest secret of all, not actually conveyed like the others, but nonetheless implicit in what they'd heard.

The knowing started as a gentle gnawing sensation, but now had swollen into a steel edged razor with a million cutting facets that now imbued the centre of their minds...strangling the synapses that held their human mindset. One single thought, glorious and terrifying in equal parts, now pervaded them, to the exclusion of everything else.

God existed. Actually existed...was real. That was fact now. These being weren't just gods, they were God. In the purest, biblical, religious sense, they were God.

Jessy had never known anything with more certainty in her life. She could feel the realization gripping her chest and slowing her breathing. He wasn't just a baseless fictional character, or a spiritual phantasm authored by some lonely and desperate society. He was *'One'* and *'One'* was real and His work was everywhere around them...from the trees and the soil to the most distant celestial object, and beyond. Nothing did not owe its existence to God. Fact.

She thought about it, religion, philosophy, science...the competing arguments, the age old conflicts...the rabid, vicious testaments were ended right here, along with everything else they'd come to know. God existed. End of story. They had proof undeniable. If we were going to pray to anyone, pray to '*One*'.

The Creator of the Universe, of humanity, had spoken to them...given them all the clues they'd needed to piece together the ultimate cosmic puzzle. The puzzle they never knew existed. It was the answer to the very paradox of mind and intelligence, evolution, philosophy...existence...

In fact, God was more real and more powerful than even the scriptures were held to believe, for he hadn't just created their Universe, he'd created a thousand others.

As their flailing minds digested the evidence, their neuropathways were crumbling and being rewired, connecting them to a vision that was far too broad to get a grip on, too multidimensional to fully appreciate.

What did it all mean for the unwitting people of Earth?

Mitch and Sean were as certain as Jessy. They had come to precisely the same conclusion. *One was God* in the truest sense of the word, the final outworking of their own humble human intelligence, boasting a science and technology, a celestial oneness that was so supreme as to be totally and utterly incomprehensible to them.

God was real...Jessy kept repeating it, hoping it would somehow root itself in the real time of her mind. She was a scientist and atheist, and didn't know how all this would sit with her yet. They were looking at the Real Deal, Creator, Maker...producer of everything. Sean swore quietly and held his forehead, feeling the heat below his skin, the warmth of screaming neurons, brain cells stripped of their protective sheaths by thoughts verging on the potency of molecular acid.

Jessy considered the billions of earthly souls who "believed" in a supreme being, in an eternal overlord, and she realized that every one of them was unquestionably right. Their ideology and their conviction, in the broader sense was entirely accurate. Their faith was based on fact, not on some ancient storytellers' whim. It was historical fact. Undeniable truth that was built into everything they had ever known or seen or touched.

Science and religion had both got Creation right, Jessy could see that. Both were inexorably joined at the quantum level, science was religion, because God was the ultimate scientist. He was the possessor of a technology beyond magic, beyond the scope of the most color soaked human fantasy. Beyond what the word "technology" was ever supposed to mean or describe.

That was it Jessy thought, God was science and science was God. That was the new philosophy. The philosophy of the Sphere. The unification of Discipline and Divinity. That which had always been...

238

13

Encounter

'Somewhere, something incredible is waiting to be known.' ~ Carl Sagan

They stood transfixed by the Sphere, unsure what to think of the madness that had been thrown at them. The three smaller beings looked pale and breathless, wobbling with the impact of knowing that everything they thought they knew had suddenly been flung on its head. Their brains were rebelling with thousands of years of pre-wired instinct that was being forcibly pried away. The rest of the population on Earth would feel the pain and the wonder soon enough. They too would eventually drink in The Word and feel the rush of emotion as they watched the houses of genesis crumble hopelessly around them, crumble to less than dust.

The larger, more imposing creatures looked thoughtful, pensive even, as they silently conversed, soundlessly pondered and curiously debated the Sphere's claims. Their most elementary assumptions about themselves had been similarly annihilated.

The grey cube briefly found new life, flooding itself with shifting figures but quickly falling dull and dark and apparently dead, having this time offered its last morsel of cosmic intrigue.

Glancing briefly at each other, the two Virijians locked eyes for a split second before turning away from the Sphere and gazing back at their human cargo.

'We must leave,' Char toned quickly. 'The Sphere has moved beyond the final cycle, there is no more to reveal, for the moment.'

Jessy broke her unfocussed gaze and looked up from the floor. Char's words were like sweet manna for her tired mind. Thank God, she lauded silently, comforted by the suggestion of finality, knowing what they'd already learned would keep them going forever, as it was.

Philosophers, historians, scientists, cosmologists, every splinter of human endeavor would have to start over, from the new foundation they'd been shown here. The real foundation. The only fucking foundation that had ever been. We'd just got it awfully wrong, Sean thought, a justifiable blunder. Zamindar looked deliberately at his towering comrade, half closing one eye with a greasy eyelid, like a slow motion blink.

'But before we leave,' he suddenly toned, 'the last cycle has exposed something you will consider important.' He glanced at each of the humans in turn.

Jessy's thanks turned to dust. There was something else. She felt the dread return in a rush of blood that flushed every pore of her body. She looked up at Charijiok, and for the first time wondered if he had a mate back home, if that's how it worked there. He was pig ugly, but that was to our eyes, maybe to them, he was a real looker. Doubt it, she shuddered, taking in his huge face and greasy, loose eyes. She averted her eyes, just avoiding a full blown shiver.

Charijiok said, 'it is an answer to something you have all been wondering about.'

Sean felt another stab of curiosity, but the Virijian suddenly stopped and apparently lost himself in thoughtful silence. As though he was waiting for some sort of response from the humans.

The pressure in Sean's throat became too much, 'Go on...please!' he blurted, having lost any semblance of patience some time ago.

Their eyes were focused as a single lens on Zamindar, waiting for another bizarre promulgation...but how much more could there possibly be? Jessy had lost count of how many times she'd asked herself that same question. And the brain-jarring revelations had kept flowing like a Derby commentary.

239

After what seemed like an eternity, and after first silently toning with Char, Zamindar proceeded. They were all none the wiser until Zamindar toned to them.

'The Sphere is a trans-dimensional duct.'

Shrill and rapid, the acoustic sounding came loud and clear. Zamindar paused while the term took on some sort of meaning which he was sure it quickly would. Sean, Mitch and Jessy eyed each other and despite the odd term they knew exactly what Zamindar was telling them. Tunnel!

'...they are able to access our Universe by moving through these Spheres. When so activated they can instantly multiply their mass trillions of times without effecting our space. Only space within the Sphere is distorted. It digs a hole in our Universe and extends a bridge, an instantaneous connection, to their Universe. These things, these Spheres, such as that before you, are dimensional gateways. One can pass through them at will.'

Jessy's eyes widened as she digested what he was saying. She scrutinised Zamindar, '...but you said they weren't big on face to face contact...so can we assume that this happens very rarely?' She prayed it was the case. She didn't want to see them. Not yet anyway. She'd had more than enough. It was surely time for some normality again. She swivelled her eyes upward, thinking deeply.

The thought of some horrendous god thing unfolding itself from the depths of the Sphere made her feel like vomiting, Jessy instinctively edged her feet backward. That would be the paralysing climax to this insane episode, she thought, the final straw that would fling her into the depths of irretrievable mental shutdown. Jessy peered at Zamindar hopefully.

He toned, 'the pressure of looking after such a huge family would likely dictate that from *One* world's perspective it would only be very rarely visited. Remember, there are several billion different civilizations and over one thousand living Universes. But in the broader context, they would be taking trans-dimensional visits almost continually.'

Mitch padded over to the orb and knocked silently on it. 'Um…what do we do with this thing now that it's served its, er…purpose? Do we set it back where we found it, or maybe take it to Earth with us, stick it in a museum, or just set it adrift in space? Are there any instructions or do we decide?' Maybe somehow cut it into small pieces, he grinned to himself wickedly.

Zamindar peered curiously at Mitch and toned just as Sean was about to speak.

'The Sphere has not satisfied its prime directive. Some of its objectives have been satisfied, but not its prime goal. That still remains.'

Jessy shuffled drunkenly on legs suddenly turned to warm rubber. Her voice was a rattle in the back of her throat, '...are you saying that by telling us they made our world, made our Universe, wasn't the main thrust of it?' Jessy spat the sentence at the Virijian, unconsciously holding him responsible for the ludicrous contention. She was agog at the very idea...what more could there be?'

'Yes, it was, but it was only part of it,' Zamindar said slowly. 'But it was not the Sphere's prime directive. You see Jessy, they, *One*, are coming.'

They all stared unseeingly at the lumbering creature who blocked space in front of them. '...as if we haven't heard enough,' Jessy whined. Her feet felt like islands of mortar. She staggered slowly backward. Fear boiled deep within her belly. What did it mean? Why were they coming? When were they coming?

Sean searched and finally found his voice after clearing his throat. 'You said they weren't interested, that they wouldn't bother, that they were observers, that they couldn't...'

'This was the final component of the message,' Char said, talking over Sean. 'They look in on their successful Cultures, but only after the Sphere has been found, and only after the data has been successfully deciphered. Meaning that they somehow know whether or not the information has been properly digested.'

'They probably watch and see,' Jessy said in a voice sharp with fear. She speculated where their viewpoint was, above, below, right behind her...inside her? Jessy shuddered at the sudden mental image, at the grotesque idea that these god beings might be standing inside her. Jessy knew that these assumption were the profoundly ridiculous, but accepted paradoxes of alternate dimensions and universes. They could share spatiality. Profound didn't do the idea justice she decided. It was all mad, the whole lot of it … but proven … apparently.

'This is the one concession to their offspring. *One* regard it as something akin to moral discipline that such a meeting occur after the message is absorbed, they say for the benefit of the newly informed intelligence. Questions raised by their message and the inability of the cognizant race to confirm any misgivings about themselves or their makers has, they explain, fatally unravelled many societies older than yours. *One's* "single contact" scenario has apparently been successful in preserving the longevity of their children.'

Sean didn't hesitate, forget *why*, he thought. 'when're they coming?' He said it so quickly it sounded like a single syllable. 'Could they pop through now?' His eyes were like saucers.

Jessy held her breath, gripping her temples with fists that were pulled into claws. She sure as hell hoped not. No, she screamed to herself, and turned around.

'According to their time reference, you cannot expect them for another twenty of your years. They designate that quite specifically. For them of course, twenty Earth years would only be minutes, perhaps not even that. These beings probably have individual life spans equivalent to millions of years or quite conceivably they may have no mass energy whatsoever, and are entirely immortal. They may literally live forever.'

'Twenty years!' Sean spat. 'Twisted shit, I'll be an old man, a seventy-year-old…if I'm alive. Hell, I might be dead, I'll have to watch myself, starting right now. Watch the triglycerides, regular exercise…' He looked thoughtful for a second and then grimaced. '…oh, fuck it! What's the point? I don't smoke or drink, that's something I suppose.' Sean frowned, as he glared down at his gut, wishing it would just disappear.

Jessy was doing all she could not to laugh in his face. He was hilarious.

Mitch grinned at Sean who was still looking seriously frustrated. 'Lighten up, you'll do it easily,' he soothed, just don't stress, that will definitely kill you.'

Sean was deep in thought and didn't even hear him. His thoughts were still wrestling with the probability of actually living to see the day. I have to be here, he repeated silently.

Jessy was instantly relieved, looking heavenward, taking solace in the fact that it was twenty years away. The brain-rending confusion receded a bit. There would even be time to prepare, to think and to plan, time to have a normal life for a while. She laughed at that last thought. Fantasy she knew but still, she could hope.

Time to prepare… hah … what a laugh, considering the alien living cargo they would arrive home with. Normalcy would be out the window. Thrown overboard. Normal didn't exist anymore, certainly for them. Think about it, she goaded herself. A pair of Virijians and a bizarre metal egg from another Universe for God's sake!

And a script of information that would keep humanity busy for centuries and its philosophers busy forever. Who was she kidding? She and the others would be hounded around the globe. Unmercifully hunted by a planet load of militant paparazzi. There would be no place to hide; they were all screwed if they thought they'd be living the quiet life back on Earth.

Zamindar placed a single pendulous digit on the skin of the Sphere, sliding it slowly into the middle groove. He withdrew it rapidly after a few seconds as though its insides had suddenly turned white-hot.

Almost immediately there was movement, no sound, but motion everywhere. The splayed orb gradually started to come together, to become whole again. The two hemispheres swung toward one another, sliding silently and smoothly over the alien floor until both sides kissed, leaving only a thin and fading line to show there had been any split at all. All signs of the divide rapidly vanished. The Sphere was whole again, a massive ball bearing, as it had been when they first saw it riding high above Titan.

Jessy tried to avoid it but couldn't, the dreadful inertia in her mind was too much, her thoughts were wrenched back to the question of exactly what would pop out the next time it opened.

She knew the haunting question would be horribly debated during her profoundly vivid dreams. Scratch that … nightmares.

***

Ben White sprung from his bed with an enthusiasm he hadn't known since before the news. Normally it was an effort just to haul himself out of bed, to shave, and to wrestle through the rituals of another day. Today though, he was pumped with an eagerness born of adventure, for the first time in months he awoke with a natural energy. His tasks at AASSA over the past year or so had devolved into a living nightmare, but this would make up for it all. Ben had sweaty palms and trembling hands, petrified that something would go wrong. It was up to him alone to make sure it didn't. He was at the Head of it all. Number one.

Today was January 8th 2061, a Red Letter day if ever there was one, a day more profoundly insightful than any other twenty-four hour period ever. Today, humankind would fundamentally change forever. Man would leave his signature on the cosmos and make contact with the intelligent representatives of an impossibly distant world. Incredible and astonishing, but it was happening. Today, humanity would truly stand up and be counted, as would Earth.

On this hot afternoon in the southern summer, a society born beyond the Galaxy was coming to visit. And Ben knew it would be the most consequential moment in the nearly two trillion days since his planet had hatched from its fortuitously positioned dust shell.

Today he reckoned, Man would genuinely come of age, assuming of course that everything went to plan. He'd already prayed to any God that might be listening, or looking in his general direction, hoping against hope that nothing would go wrong. Ben was terrified and exhilarated, throttled by a sense of divinity at the scope of what was about to happen. And the best part was he would not only see it, he would be part of it, right at the very top. Like the proverbial cream.

He was sure he hadn't slept at all last night. He'd dozed for a few minutes but mainly his mind was in overdrive, wired on the events and the myriad possibilities, not all of them pleasant, of the day ahead. It would be unlike any other day in his life.

Minutes and hours had plodded by until after what seemed like days of darkness the predawn glow had finally touched the distant plateau. With the first tendrils of light he fairly vaulted out of bed. It was finally the day, it seemed, that his whole life had led up to.

Sixteen hours ago, Ben received the extraordinary message from Cygnus and had immediately contacted Barry Lowman at USPA. The newly established Contact Protocol Team (CPT) had been on standby and was immediately briefed and was at this moment enroute to the Woomera complex.

Four thousand security "Techs" were on base, organized and dispatched with surprising haste, given the recent chaos on Earth. Security forces were all banded under the banner of the United Nations. Specifically, under UNSC Resolution 122822FP which fully empowered their leaders to execute its stunning minutiae. They were fully empowered to do what it took to protect the dignitaries of Earth, and beyond. They all knew well what "beyond" meant.

Ben realised that nothing was being left to chance. He clenched his jaw and frowned. But who or what would pose a risk to this event, to this moment? Ben swatted at the air, he had no idea but equally he realized there would be some in opposition to it, some who couldn't see past their own tiny minds, bloated as they were with human frailties and stifling one planet phobias.

There would always be minority opposition no matter what the occasion. They were ready for protests and chaos. At least they thought they were. The UN force boasted eight hundred federal agents from twelve countries, in addition to the thousands of Techs, most of whom would be invisible outside the Primary Enclave. In their selection, they were drawn from a hundred and ten different nations. It was a world show, down to the last detail. Today, Earth was on show. Guaranteeing the integrity of the perimeter barrier, the UN contingent would also provide blanket protection to the host of dignitaries. And more importantly, would enforce the massive "no fly zone", a twelve hundred cubic kilometre parcel of sky bull's-eyed on the AASSA base. Hopefully it wouldn't fuck up.

242

The privilege of being shot from the sky by an F32 Stealth was on offer to anyone who took their craft into the restricted zone without permission. There would be no beg pardons today, there was simply too much at stake. Transcend and die. It wasn't hard to understand.

Ben took comfort in knowing that every detail, every person present, and every preparation down to the finest detail were defined, affirmed and sanctioned by the UN resolution short titled "22FP", the Friendly Planet Proclamation. Ben stood tall and pushed his shoulders back … and it was him, right at the centre of the front row.

It was world treaty that would govern the behaviour of the planet and its people on the occasion of Monday, January 8th 2061. The Resolution was World Legislation. No one would be allowed to disobey.

Ben stopped thinking and looked in the mirror and then at his watch. There wasn't much time and he looked like hell, which set him thinking, what would they look like? He rubbed his jaw and gave a Hmmmm noise. Would they look like hell too? Shit, he thought and gulped heavily. He began shaving.

Ben's mind continued to wrestle with the details of what would definitely be a harrowing day. True, everything was organized and on track, but the schedule was daunting, and it was still very early. It would be a day of constant arrivals, unremitting activity on the highest possible plane of thinking. He tried to rest his mind, but it failed. Ben closed his eyes and tilted his head back, but that didn't work either. All he could do was think about the day ahead. It would be different than any other day in his life. By different, he meant unimaginable.

At 1330 hours the show would start and it would truly be a circus. The only redeeming factor was their power to exclude the Press, apart from those lucky few from GAPCNN who were privy to those most golden of cards, giving them restricted access to The Enclave that would telecast the event to the globe live.

First on the scene would be the President of the AusRepublic at 1330 hours. Hot on his heels would be the US President, the head of National Security Council and the Secretary of Defense, all due an hour later. At 1445 hours the Secretary General and others of the UN would touch down at the recently upgraded Menzies Pater airfield.

The rest of the congregation would arrive at 1515 hours. The rest included the Eminent Dozen, the twelve person Contact Forum who would try and embody humanity, and who would collectively form Earth's cognitive frontline. They alone would be responsible for embracing and consummating the initial objectives of 22FP, first communion, the actual structure of which only they knew. They would be the first to try and communicate, to try and find some level of basic understanding, some sort of fundamental comprehension on which they could hopefully build.

They would be the welcoming party, and would do so on behalf of the eight billion other residents of the planet. Could they communicate with their alien friends, even on the most basic of levels? Few knew if it was even remotely possible. Most believed it wasn't. Certainly, if you believed the newspapers or social media, it wasn't going to happen. Logic said no way. Ben knew it was possible and he fully expected to be able to freely communicate. Not just him either.

Also, enroute was the head of the United Euro States, the Chairman of the Chinese Republic, and the CEO and other heavyweights from the USPA. The President of Russia was coming, as were eight members and one camera crew from Global Associated Press. Plus, selected heads from NASA, JPL, ESA, Spaceguard's PCAC, and the NASA and Space Agency's SETI teams of STETA and OSAL. There were also representatives from the National Science Foundation, the Science Advisory Committee, the International Astronomical Union.

And of course, there was Ben and his loyal crew who had chosen to stay on base at AASSA, after the news had scattered so many of their kind to the wind. Fucking good riddance, Ben reckoned, grinning wickedly, thinking about all those that had left. Their loss, he surmised.

Ben knew who was coming, not only the most notable dignitaries on Earth but also the singularly overwhelming scenario of them. Dignitaries from another world, from another galaxy. It sounded impossible, the realization still took his breath away and made him feel giddy and light headed. And nervous beyond description. The job of coordinating the whole thing was his, with help of course, but it was still him at the apex, him at the helm. He was the captain of a young technical civilization on the brink of graduation from preschool.

He only wished that a certain Brooklynite could have lived to enjoy the extraordinary moment, a man who had kickstarted Ben's fascination with space when he was just a boy. A man solely responsible for elbowing Ben toward the Great Void, toward an education and a career he otherwise doubted he would ever have seen. And he had helped millions just like him, motivating them with his eloquent, captivating orations on others. Quite simply Dr Sagan deserved to be here, right at the very apex of the Eminent Dozen, and the whole world knew it beyond any shadow of a doubt. Cancer had a hell of a lot to answer for. Him, Mitch's dad, and millions of others. But Ben could feel a part of the great man still with him, could still hear him enthusing over the cosmos...pondering its stupendous potentials. Today, that which he so fervently believed in, would crystallize in front of Ben in a breathtaking rush, and Carl would be with him, in spirit at least.

Earth appeared to be organized and ready, but there were so many unknowns. How would the newcomers react? And significantly, how the hell would he and the rest of his people react?

Tension gripped Ben's heart and throat as he pondered the actual moment of confrontation. That moment when his eyes fell onto theirs. When their gaze fused for the first time and they stood in mute assessment of one another, only a few steps apart. Fear boiled in his belly as he considered it. It was almost too much to contemplate, even though he'd thought about this possibility many times before, it was now so close.

Ben shook his head and momentarily freed his mind, but the crushing thought was never far away, crouching at the back of his brain like a jumping jack. Maybe they had picked the wrong person to do this? He considered. But then he thought it was probably a natural reaction, to be scared shitless. Who really knew, this was the first time … but why me?

He knew why though, for he had been chosen by the occupants of the orbiting starship. Had been asked for by name.

The two pods that were destined for Earth, sat idle within the belly of the massive ship, synchronously orbiting above their touchdown point. A landing was scheduled for eleven hours and fifty-two minutes hence, at precisely 1700 hours CST.

Ben paced slowly down the dull corridor that led the three hundred metres from his room to the main control facility. He could hear his boots clanging on the Chiton tiles as he gazed through the dusty windows and saw the Number One Gantry slide into view. The metal edifice was just visible against the dim dawn sky, a stark geometric sculpture, in places bleeding ruddy blood from the touch of a still feeble Sun.

He slowed to a stop and leant on the narrow metal sill, pondering the surreal scene. It was just after dawn. There was no wind...everything was utterly silent. No birds, no crickets, no activity on base, nothing. A part of him wished it would stay like that.

He could feel the energy though, crackling in the air around him, copious latent energy soon to be released in a tremendous chain reaction. And nothing and no one would be able to stop it.

Ben knew it was the peace before the storm. It was about to start. His eyes were wide and his legs a little wobbly as he again considered the day ahead. What a day, he said to himself, dazzled at the tasks in front of him.

The silence and tranquility of the predawn moment seemed to feed the almost spiritual sense of occasion that he felt. Ben's nerve endings were stirring and tingling. Soon, he knew, all hell would break loose as the final preparations for contact swung into gear. The sense of anxiety and unreality that gripped him was steadily swelling in the silence of the stark corridor.

He was now in the grip of a genuine feeling that something almost supernatural was about to happen. 'My God,' Ben whispered, looking at the dim reflection in the glass. Blurred though it was he could still see the stiffness in his expression and the fear behind his eyes.

As he looked at the unruffled vista, a sliver of orange corona, then a piece of glowing torso broke above the ancient plateau in the distance. Stunning arrows of orange and crimson arced into the dawn sky, kneading the clouds and transforming them into boiling islands of color. Ben had seen sunrises before, but he'd never seen one quite like this. Grinning, he scanned the fabulous panorama, looking straight out at the low hills that hid Alice Springs.

The sky brightened quickly as Sol floated above the ancient desert. He could feel the heat already and he knew exactly what it meant. He whispered to his reflection, '...hope they like it hot.' He smirked and chuckled, then moved in favour if a more serious expression.

Ben continued his walk down the corridor and considered the events that lay ahead. Events, he thought, the word hardly seemed sufficient. The disbelief he was feeling deepened again. It was happening, but still it refused to assume the feeling of reality. The whole concept of the day's events was somehow faint, immersed in a hazy aura of fantasy and fiction. Once again, he felt unsteady as he pondered his reaction to their craft arriving; at meeting the visitors ... Jesus Christ, meeting them, touching them, communicating with them.

He checked his pocket. Finding a twisted cigarette, he grabbed for it, but something in the distance, something huge and bright caught his eye. Snapping his head up, he saw a massive plume of dust suspended above the only road in and out of the base.

'Holy fuck.' he said out loud. 'What is that?' Looking closer he knew exactly what it was.

The cloud of burnt soil was rapidly spreading but was still very distinct, hanging like a pall in the nearly windless sky. Ben knew that nothing in the natural world was responsible for this storm.

***

At the exact moment that Ben had been watching the sunrise on Earth, a single Ajiron fell free above him. He wasn't monitoring the mothership but NASA was, around the clock, not only remotely via the slowly recovering DSN, but also visually using its newly inserted Primo satellite.

The Ajiron was free falling synchronously with the mothership, lying low on its horizon, nine hundred kilometres to the east. The view from its wide facility TV camera was extraordinary to say the least. A view dominated by a tremendous gray prickle beast that was dancing in perfect synch with the world it was shadowing.

NASA knew within seconds that something had dropped from the larger ship. Primo gave them enhanced vision of a shining vesicular pod, plunging earthward like a fiery meteor and disappearing among the clouds in seconds.

Charijiok was piloting the bubble through the last of the thick cirrus which broke suddenly at six thousand metres. A glorious panorama of sunlit prairies and richly vegetated basins fell into view as he ambled over southern central Africa.

Char was astounded by the beauty and richness of the landscape, and by its pristine crudeness. It reminded him of the photographs from the old texts, the relics from the Ancients, the days of the pre-Morij, when houses were everywhere, on the surface and under the ground.

Char's craft was not alone in the sky. Only a few kilometres away, an airliner, a Boeing 7971800B, was on a shallow climb through four thousand metres, trajectory emanating from Mbandaka in Zaire.

The Virijian had unexpectedly come face to face with the Messiah of Earth's domestic aviation. Char knew precisely what it was, but he wanted, needed, to have a closer look despite what he and Zamindar had agreed. His dual hearts pumped his nickel blood slightly faster as he gazed at the metallic beast, and realized where he was and what he was about to do.

Charijiok looked slowly down, looked left and then flew right, a rapid manoeuvre that had Ajiron on the plane's winged tail in seconds. The visitor inched along the metal matrix superstructure until it hovered just off the split wing, looking like a shard of the finest opal. Sliding along the UES Jumbo, Char drank in the vague technical congruence, only a few metres from the four hundred portholes that pocked its triple decked chassis.

He could see several humans, pilots he realized, shaking their heads and talking rapidly, gesticulating in his direction. Charijiok realized that he shouldn't be engaging in any contact, but the

245

opportunity was so magnificent that he, or for that matter any of his race, would never have given it a second thought. And he was the first.

Char bathed in the gaping stares from the hundreds of pallid faces that were nosing against the misty portholes of their ancient vessel. He tried to imagine what these creatures might be thinking, what they must have thought when they woke up and glanced skyward at the newborn pinkness of another day and saw his vessel, and him, casually scud up to them.

The pilot's voice over the intercom would make interesting listening. If you look out of the portside windows...

Char took the craft away and in a second was gone, vanishing over the brightening dawn horizon in a heartbeat. The Jumbo ambled on to Detroit only later realizing that they were the among the first to set their eyes on the technology of the newcomers.

They were the first to see the technical wizardry of truly alien minds. The six photographs snapped by Chuck Boyden, a small claims clerk for Seattle Mutual, were later sold to the Smithsonian for a million dollars each...and to think he'd nearly left his OM901 at home. There was much to be said for a wife's memory, not to mention the benefit of being the first.

***

Within five minutes of its meeting with the Boeing dinosaur, Ajiron was motionless in the air. It was eyeballing a narrow granitic reef, a remnant of the partially digested surface mostly smothered by impenetrable primary rainforest. Char was hovering near the banks of the Tshuapa River in Congo territory, totally wild, virgin wilderness. The overwhelming impression was "alive".

The rear of the bubble became milky and then instantly cleared. Char tilted the pod until the Sphere simply rolled out and dropped onto the mullocky formation below, without a sound. Despite its apparent weight, the Sphere seemed to fall in slow motion, like an air balloon, and hit the slab of granite and stuck fast as though two velcro lashes had come together.

Different atoms from different Universes.

The strange coupling came without any sound. The cacophony of the forest played on around it, the trillers and chirpers seemingly oblivious to the bizarre new arrivals. Char held the pod stationary for a moment and watched, but nothing happened. Then the Sphere vibrated slightly and lost definition. Then it literally fell into the granite, sinking like an anvil through water.

The Sphere penetrated the granite as easily as neutrinos through a steel block. The atoms of the Sphere, Char knew, had the capability, amongst other things, to make themselves invisible or neutral to them and theirs, in all respects.

Now, somewhere under the volcanic ridge, rolling around beneath the Congo, totally unimpeded by Earthly atoms, was a message from the closest thing in the Universe to God. A message from *The Makers*.

More or less expecting what he had seen, Char's mind bounded forward to the scene that would unfold in twenty years time, assuming they made good on their promise, which he had little doubt they would

Satisfied that he had completed the task *'One'* had specified, Char exited rapidly from Earth's atmosphere, arcing straight up like a runaway lift, without a sound.

***

From orbit, Mitch gazed out at the cosmos, and breathed in the exquisite vista of Australasia and Antarctica which wallowed beneath his toes. Despite feeling at home in space there were certain things that never lost their appeal.

He was still agog at the image of Earth from space, the reds and browns of Australia, the bone white poles, the whirlpool clouds and the brilliant sapphires of the nitrogen sky and dazzling oceans.

246

All girdled by a depthless black backdrop. Even after all he'd seen, he knew Earth was a planet among planets, simply stunning on any scale he could reasonably think of. Mitch knew with excruciating clarity that the colorful rock below him would never be quite the same again. What they would do today would change it forever. In time, Earth and its people would change profoundly.

The very marrow of terrestrial philosophy would be hacked out and replaced by something stronger and richer. The human radio would change station permanently, from AM-Earth to stereo FM-Universe. Forever. And he was there when it first happened.

***

It was 1640 Hours CST. Both pods dimpled and closed off from the orbiter and departed into brilliantly painted space. Slipping slowly downward, they fought the gradually condensing wind of the atmosphere.

Opaqueness, orange, burning crimson, then clarity and panorama, they were among the clouds. Home. It was everywhere. Jessy looked like she might cry. Sean's mind was sprinting with thought and recollection.

'...wish Rhys had lived to see it.' Sean's eyes were downcast as he spoke.

No one had spoken of Rhys in weeks. The mere mention of his name brought back a stinging sadness.

They broke through the thin cloud cover at 1652 hours and were only seventy kilometres from the base that was suddenly visible in the distance, hugging the barren red desert.

Jessy was looking off to her right, staring at something. '...What the hell?' She extended her arm and pointed. 'Look.'

'Has there been an announcement?' Sean wondered out loud. He thought about it, of course there had been. No one in Langley or Moscow, or anywhere else could have kept this quiet.

Below the dawdling vessels was a stationary body of traffic a hundred kilometres long that stretched along the arrow-straight road that led to the base from the southeast. From their height Mitch could make out buses, cars, trucks, wagons, motor bikes, rigs, everything that could move mechanically was there.

A vast queue of auto motion terminated at the perimeter fence in a pool of amorphous glinting metal. Where the road hit the fortified front gates there was a collection of maybe a thousand vehicles and perhaps ten thousand people. AASAA had never seen anything like it.

They were all sitting, standing, or simply milling around in front of the razor-tipped barrier fence. They were all looking in one direction, up toward them.

'I'd be down there too if I wasn't up here,' Sean said staring down, gently biting his lip.

He wondered what they were thinking, was it a friendly gathering? He assumed so but what if it wasn't? Was Earth afraid of what might happen today? No doubt some would be terrified. Hiding under their bed scared. The aliens are coming!

Watching what was happening below, Zamindar seemed to be paying absolutely no attention to the piloting of the pod. Char was only a hundred metres away in the other bubble, flying in mirror perfect formation. They could see him easily, piloting what was a tiny and almost transparent craft the size of a Chevrolet sedan.

Jessy pointed forward, toward several blurry dark smears that were swelling in the sky. Mitch immediately recognized them for what they were, familiar old friends. Sean looked at what was approaching and looked over at Mitch, giving him a two fingered salute, which was returned.

'Well, how nice,' Jessy said, gazing at the lumbering trio. It seemed to suggest that Earth was on top of things. After all, they weren't fully loaded F32's in kill mode. They were old friends, slapping the air, guiding them in. We were being welcomed. 'Well...thank God for that,' Jessy said, looking upward at the choppers.

Sean watched in awe as the thundering beasts sidled up and slid over the top of them, hacking the air with their primitive metal. The strobing thud was deafening as they flew within a few hundred feet, but it was an exquisite aria to Jessy. Earsplitting and dissonant, but they were the precious sounds of their own homegrown technology.

AASSA's three aging Super Pumas had taken off from the base ten minutes earlier as the final preamble of 22FP came into play. They were the escorts. The Blacks were a military welcome to the newcomers.

Despite the pilots' bewilderment at the skimming alien sacs, they managed to eventually take up their prescribed formation. The re-engineered Aero-spatiales sat above and to either side of the two vessels. Twelve fully flapped F32 Stealths flew an arrow formation a thousand metres directly above.

***

Ben watched as the pods broke from the clouds and slid basewards, coming in at a thousand metres above the grit of the desert. He looked at his watch and huffed. It was nearly time for 22FP.

'Very prompt,' he whispered to the US President.

Jerry Walton was the most powerful man in the world and was starting to look a little pale.

Ben squinted as he surveyed the base, paying particular attention to that part being used for The Reception. Everyone involved in 22FP had arrived fairly much on time and without incident.

Only the Russian President had been late, in fact he wasn't coming at all, opting instead to send his workhorse deputy. Quoting a sudden bout of "ill health" for his last minute withdrawal, it was accompanied by copious apologies from Red Square. Ben couldn't believe it, although he admitted it was hardly a shock. Typical, he thought, muscles quivering. He was such a clown.

He knew the Russian chief wasn't ill, he never got sick. Unless he'd relied on Dutch Courage ,which had turned into a bender, on the lemon *Wodka* he was so fond of. More likely, Kolevskoy was just terrified of meeting or coming close to the newcomers. Ben knew what he was like and he wasn't fooled, his ill health was a ruse, a highly transparent one to those who knew him. His deputy had been refused permission to attend. Fuck him, he thought. He was a massive loser too.

Ben wondered how he'd feel when he finally slid into bed tonight, if he did that is, he assumed he would eventually. Would it be everything he'd hoped for, all that he'd dreamed of and imagined over the last few days? Would his millions of mind's eye visions come close to reality?

Ben looked out at Helipad 1, or what he knew was Helipad 1 because it was totally veiled by dull gray Acriboard partitions. One that he, Walton and UN chief J. Roben Thurles would pass behind exactly two minutes after they touched down. They would in some manner or form, welcome their occupants to Earth.

They would be the first to clap eyes on them, to gaze at their alien contours, the evolutionary mosaic of some distant world…of some distant galaxy. Sweet baby Jesus. He wondered how long he could keep a lid on his boiling emotions. He peered down, as his hands became tight fists. An unidentifiable sound came from the back of his throat.

22FP assumed that the initial welcome would be heavily reliant on the understanding and direction of the Cygnans, which Ben had no doubt it would be. Their first glimpse, some believed, would tilt them into electrochemical lock. Mute sensory arrest where they would stare blindly, seeing but not seeing, unable to move or to reason. Minds would race, then slow, then stall…choked by pelting images of the ineffably strange. All the preparation in the world could never get one ready, for the unknown. How long the meet and greet would last no one knew. Ben had little doubt that they would all suffer lockjaw, a condition he knew would rapidly shift upward into their minds as they gazed upon the impossible visitors.

They would then proceed out from behind the shields and along a military broadloom to the modified executive boardroom of AASSA. Here, the Contact Forum and selected others would attempt an informal meeting, the format of which only the CPF knew.

Irrespective of any format, initial contact would be momentous and profound, but as Ben often thought and said, in actual content and intellectual quality it couldn't be expected to be much at all. It was just a hello and performing other pleasantries. Today they would all be focused on the

248

extraordinary symbolic significance, meaningful interaction, well that would come later, perhaps much later. Perhaps never.

***

Ben was momentarily blinded by a piercing light from above. Pulling his head up he found himself looking at a shining lens, a television camera that was following him like a gunsight on its prey. Ben swore to himself. 'Of course,' he said, slapping his forehead.

He'd momentarily forgotten that the whole thing was being televised, literally dispatched around the globe live. He could just make out the two CBS Primevision cameramen hiding under their sunflex tarpaulins. They were concealed from the Sun in their yellow suspension cages that hung pendulously from two cranes on the end of their stable-cables. Both were well away from the carpeted area, but even so they had superb views over the entire area. A view of what was known as the Primary Enclave, the compound that lay ready and waiting in the middle of the baking desert. The two men and their infinitely lucky support crews had the job of sending the images to the Realcom satellite that would relay it through a dozen other orbiters to ultimately reach a good proportion of more than eight billion residents of Earth.

In poorer regions, televisions or at least access to them, had abruptly become more valuable than even the staples of life. Rice, wheat, bread and milk were being traded for broken down Technic's and old Sony's. Ones that with a bit of quick fix work could be brought humming back to life to be able to capture on screen what was to happen right here and now, this forever unique set in stone heartbeat in the history of their world.

Everyone knew. And understood. It was a global perception and it ran through every cultural, economic, racial and socioreligious moiety on Earth. Everyone, without distinction, wanted to be a part of the moment, wanted to see it.

The UN quickly realized the problem that such unrelenting demand for access was creating. People were literally trading away their lifeblood; and dying because of it. Some Governments had to be forcibly funded into providing or at least allowing the provision of access to the event. Into allowing the erection of massive satellite driven broadcasting screens in areas where television simply didn't exist or was damn hard to access.

The scene in Tanzania typified the extraordinary scene. A million people had descended on the Serengetti Plain to encompass ten mighty screens. An ocean of struggling humanity waiting for the moment. Waiting for that which had tugged them there despite the daily battle for kilojoules which inevitably ruled their lives. They all knew, and realised what was on offer today.

The telecast was to be the most monumental ratings winner in the history of television.

***

Sean, Mitch, Jessy and even Josh watched fixedly as they skimmed over the ancient landscape with its occasional stunted tree and terrified kangaroo. They were already past the perimeter fence and saw the security patrols that literally blanketed the area, both immediately inside and for kilometres outside the fence.

'Are they expecting trouble?' Jessy asked, looking with a quizzical smile at the dark pimples that interrupted the colors of the desert.

'...precautions I suppose.' Mitch stared straight ahead, toward the base, his eyes drawn to the AASSA base he knew so well...the base that used to be his. Still his, he hoped, looking at the buildings which were getting bigger and bigger in front of them, in fact they were almost there.

'That's for us,' Mitch said pointing, '... looks like they've erected some sort of shield, how considerate. Maybe they think Zamindar here is a bit shy.' He said it with wry smile and dancing eyes. Zamindar didn't change his stoic countenance. He looked grimly at Mitch, Jessy and lastly, Sean.

249

All their eyes were maintained unblinkingly forward now, fastened on the shimmering metallic edifice. They were on top of the base.

Below them on the ground was a veritable canvass of humanity. Straining eyes were everywhere, all focused upward. The throng of poached egg eyes were looking at the arrival of the New Age on Earth. The very beginning of the Age of Fullness.

'At least they're thinking,' Sean said, looking at the shielded helipads, 'That's a good sign.'

Not knowing what to expect of the reception, he was comforted by the view of preparations. 'Yeah, agree,' Mitch said quietly, peering downward with bugged eyes. He looked at Jessy and was surprised to see tears welling in her eyes, shiny pools of water that looked ready to flood downward.

'Come on Jess, it'll be fine, trust me. Look at Sean, he's like a dog with two bones.'

'Thanks a lot,' he said, pretending to look hurt. 'Prick,' he said in jest.

'Just don't go stealing the show down there okay?'

'I'll do my best...' He smiled widely at Mitch.

Jessy tried to smile as she watched the people near the helipad swell by degree until their rigid postures and trembling faces were obvious. She could see the wonder-terror blazing in their eyes. It was a new word that applied to every one of those present, all those unsteady faces, Wonder-terror. It was etched boldly and eternally into history, as were they, to be remembered and revered for as long as the human race existed...as actually being there when it happened. She gulped, realizing that it was them disembarking with the Virijians that would be forever immortalized in Earth's history..

***

'God Almighty,' Ben breathed as he watched the two vessels dip below the partitions. He was astounded by the tiny, simplistic craft. 'Fuck,' he thought to himself. He felt exhausted and it hadn't even started yet.

It was time.

He was struggling for breath as his heart hammered his throat with alarmingly sepulchral beats. Not the reaction he'd hoped for. He tried to calm himself, tried to resist his racing pulse and churning mind. He thought about the next few minutes, and wished he hadn't. He was terrified.

Ben stood with Roben Thurles and on the other side was the US President who looked uncomfortable to say the least. Ben was looking at a sweating, stooped POTUS who looked very uncertain of what to expect.

He'd always impressed Ben as an intuitive and capable leader, who carried himself with an eminently calm, casual disposition. Nevertheless, Ben still wondered how he would cope today. Who could predict how someone would react to the truly unknown, to a dip in the very deepest end of the twilight zone? It'd be a bit different from addressing Congress or the US public, the audience would be a tad different.

In tone with his personality, the President had a relaxed and almost painfully slow southern drawl, something he'd acquired during his childhood in Louisiana and hadn't been able to get rid of. For that and a few other reasons (related mainly to bouts of colorful language) he was known to all as 'that cotton-picking President'.

He didn't like it, but the name had stuck after his abortive campaign a few years ago. After resigning himself to a long hiatus in the Republican soup kitchen, Yorke had been suddenly atomized by the nuke in Chicago and everything changed. Walton suddenly achieved his dream, and to the surprise of many he was doing okay. Better than okay actually. His numbers had never looked so good.

'We're on Mr President.'

The President looked peaked and drawn and quite unwell. 'Are you feeling alright sir?'

'I'm fine Ben. Is it always this damn hot? Must be a hundred and ten in the shade for God's sake. And that wind. Jesus,' he grunted, looking around himself through thick dark glasses. He mopped his brow and looked briefly skyward.

'It's forty-two degrees sir and yes that's not unusual for this area, especially in summer.'

'Why we didn't do this at Kennedy I'll never know,' Walton mopped his brow again.

Well sir, I believe our friends made that decision for us, but of course Taylor is the head of this base so ... just what role he played in shaping that decision, well, I'm not sure.'

'Goddamn Aussies,' Walton murmured under his breath.

'Pardon me sir?' Ben said, having heard quite clearly. Walton's nerves, like Ben's were stretched to the limit, ready to split at their loosely knit seams. They may have already split.

'Let's get on with it son, I've been looking forward to this since I heard the news.'

His words of anticipation belied his harrowed and twitching expression. He stood like a sweating mannequin in the heated Australian outback, pasty faced, under a large red umbrella.

Both craft had now been on the ground for two minutes. They all knew what that meant. 22FP would now be executed.

'Oh God,' Walton said quietly, wishing he was back behind old Resolute signing off on expenditure. Wishing he was anywhere but here, actually.

Thurles nodded at Walton and the trio edged slowly down the scarlet carpet as the authorized GAP photographer ran and knelt in front of them, snapping slices of incredible history. POTUS Walton was in the middle, Ben was to his right and the Secretary General was to his left. The fully loaded UN military lined either side of their path as Sol pumped out its best, turning the Enclave into a sweltering blast furnace. It was bloody hot and getting hotter. The photographs would show three very nervous, very hot human beings, trying vainly to appear calm, and failing badly.

***

Behind the shields, the six had exited their craft and were milling in silence amid the stifling heat of the early evening. Zamindar and Char had been toning for several minutes, but the humans simply stood there, waiting and watching, wondering what the hell they were supposed to do.

Eventually drawing breath, Jessy's mouth fell open and the words cascaded into the air. 'We're home Mitch....trillions of kilometres...we're actually back!' She looked around, up, down and to either side. 'And it feels different, somehow more like home than before.' She stopped and thought about what she'd just said, and with a slight smile, bent down and picked up a pebble from the bitumen. 'After seeing all that we've seen, home isn't Woomera or Australia any more, home is Earth, home is our planet. What we've seen has given home a truer meaning. Right Mitch?' She looked directly at him, her mouth curving up becoming a smile which slowly crossed her face.

'I'm feeling it too. I think our sense of scale has faded a bit, I guess because of the way we've viewed the cosmos. Earth is our island, our home, our local address. That's the smallest scale we should consider.' His breathing slowed as memory took over.

Mitch stared at Jessy for a long time, knowing that their new mindset would be a wonderful thing for the entire planet to embrace. For them, it was Earth en evidence...a wider view.

'God, I've been in artificial atmosphere for so long I'd forgotten what heat was like,' Sean said, swabbing his forehead with the back of his hand. They were all sweating freely, all the humans that is. He glanced over at Char, 'Do they feel it?' They sure didn't look like they did, he thought.

'No, we do not,' Char responded quickly. 'For us, homeostasis works externally as well as internally, unfortunately yours does not. Your hypothalamus still has a way to go.'

Back on Earth and still learning, still being amazed, Sean thought. Of course, he didn't expect anything less.

***

Headed by Ben, the three were now at the dividing curtain. They hesitated long and hard but didn't speak. It was all heartbeats and high temperature. Their eyes said it all. Ben wondered if his legs would obey the directions of his motor neurons. When he said forward, he hoped like hell that's what happened. Looking at the grey fabric covering of the shield, he let his focus dwindle as he tried to imagine the other side. It seemed like his entire life had been spent thinking about it, waiting for it, fantasizing about it. He shook himself back to attention. It was time for fantasy and reality to meet head-on, and God only knew what the result would be.

Ben parted the entry drape and in single file they and a photographer stooped and stepped through to Helipad 1. Straightening up, they all stopped dead in their tracks on the circled bitumen. The scene in front of them was as extraordinary as they could have imagined. The contrasts before them, man, machine and...alien, couldn't have been more vividly painted by an artist pegged on psychedelic ether.

'Ben!' Jessy shouted. She ran up and bear hugged him, dripping tears all over his jacket and gripping him in a furious embrace that forced the air from his lungs.

Ben eventually sucked in a breath. 'Welcome home Jess,' he croaked feebly, feeling a bit self-conscious as he looked around.

Sean and Mitch toed up and melted into the emotional wrestle between friends who had been separated for over two years. The Cygnans felt proud, like warriors returning from battle, which in a sense they guessed they really were.

Mitch deflected the questions about the child with ease because there, towering in front of the two pods were two fantastic, astonishing creatures, motionless and staring back at them like storyboard characters. They were looking nonchalantly at the animated humans, their emotional hunger written in their fattened veins and tapping flesh. They just stood there, still and stiff, doing nothing, presumably waiting for the humans to do something. Actually, they were assessing the behaviour of their new human friends. Observing, studying and inspecting.

'Sweet Jesus of Nazareth,' Walton peered through eyes that looked like cracked china plates. His neck and head were tilted back at a strange angle and the veins in his neck stuck out like Nylex hose. Thurles and Ben were dazed by the images that hit them with a dizzyingly bright punch. They had prepared for it, they all had, but there was no preparing for … *this*.

Headless trout. That was the crazy image that jumped into Walton's mind. He hadn't thought of it or felt it, in years. The bowel gripping horror and sickening nausea he'd felt as a youngster when he hacked the head from a squirming trout with his tiny pocket knife. Throbbing and twitching, it had gone on living despite its decapitation.

The eyes had flickered and darted around, eventually focusing on him, eyeballing the bloodied knife he held in his hand, he'd thought. At that moment his terror was total. He'd wet his pants and screamed for ten minutes in total, inconsolable panic. He didn't sleep a wink for a week. Fish heads...fish heads...

Mitch had warned them in advance about the nature of the Virijians, but warnings and reality, Walton would say later, were two diametrically opposed concepts. It helped he supposed but it was still shocking. For the most powerful man in the world, who had seen so much, he was shaking on first sight of Zamindar. Definitely not the response he'd anticipated nor hoped for.

Ben was stunned to the extent that he became totally confused. What was 22FP? His mind had slowed to a mucid and useless dawdle. They looked intimidating and almost aggressive as they gazed unblinkingly in their direction. His first real thought was a question. What in God's name have we gotten ourselves into? I mean, fuck, look at them. For him, ugly didn't do them justice.

Ben had the impression they were staring at him, assessing him, although he admitted it was hard to tell. Their eyes were almost amorphous, and their size, Christ they were massive, broad and tall, like sculpted tree-trunks, pale and moist from want of bark. Yikes. It wasn't pretty.

He had to confess that he found them unpleasantly loathsome to look at, humanoid maybe, but very different. At first sight, Ben felt a chilling repulsion that bordered on nausea, feelings that even despite his discomfort, embarrassed him. They made him feel depressingly primitive. In the same breath he wondered whether he could ever get used to their looks. God, they were ugly. What would the population in general think? Jesus, he hated to think what Joe Average would reckon about our new friends. They'd be terrified, no matter how much prep work was involved.

'You look like sideshow clowns...close your fucking mouths,' Mitch said, trying to break the tension. He waited. Snapping his fingers several times, they eventually dislodged their gaze and blinked. Ben shook his head and looked at him.

Mitch wanted to introduce them but the humans were rooted to the asphalt and only after long seconds did they shed some of their stiffness and fish up the leg strength to inch forward and consummate a modest greeting.

The President continued to struggle with himself. He was only arm's length from them now...could see them looming like twin leviathans in front of him.

'Welcome...er...Zamdar...is that right Mitch?' Walton's steely eyes were downcast as he spoke, then to one side, then the other, he couldn't look at them. Not yet.

The President had solved regional wars and appeased national disasters, and unified his people during terrifying times with a resolve rarely seen through history. But even he seemed out of his depth with these insanely bohemian beings.

'Zamindar sir,' Mitch corrected slowly. 'Just shake their hands, there's no need for a formal welcome here, do what comes naturally.'

'If I did that son, I'd be back on Airforce 1 by now.' Walton said quietly, his grey eyes giving away his real feelings. Mitch knew he was deadly serious.

'It's time,' Mitch said deliberately as he strode over to Sean and whispered through his teeth, '...time to take history by the scruff of the neck and give it a hell of a shake.' Sean smiled and padded to the curtain, and as unobtrusively as he could, stuck his head outside.

'Good God,' He bleared. Ben was stunned by the plaintively expectant crowd which as one, was staring aghast at him. They'd all been staring at the curtain. Chuckling to himself, he realized they probably thought he was one of them.

Satisfied that everything was in order, Sean withdrew back behind the partition, and looked wide eyed at Ben, 'Okay, let's do it,' he said. Ben could hear his rapid breathing.

He motioned them forward. Mitch pushed slowly through the curtain and was trailed by the Earthly trio who had entered only minutes before. The rest of them followed and formed an informal garrison around the two bearish but effortlessly graceful Virijians whose head and shoulders towered above the bobbing human rim.

The reaction from the crowd of officials and scientific luminaries was an almighty and collective intake of breath, followed by an immediate and earsplitting hush. Silence was total as the human ensemble gazed fixedly at the visitors with unblinking, slack-jawed fascination. And utter disbelief. It was generally expected that a crowd would break into voice after being silent for a dedication or an anthem, or anything. Not today though. It was literally as quiet as a church in prayer.

A lot of people shed tears that day. The dazzling profundity of the moment wasn't lost on any of them, most of whom had in one way or another thought about, hoped, and dreamed that contact would come in their lifetime.

Most doubted it would. Of course, none had even considered that contact would come in the form of fifth kind encounters, well not seriously anyway. Fantasized maybe. Intercepting a radio or photon message from a distant star system, perhaps, but this, no one seriously considered it as even a vague likelihood. It was a cosmologist's dreamtime phantasm that simply wasn't possible.

Each of those present that day thanked God that they were lucky enough to be involved in such a monumental moment, a snapshot in time that would be stored and remembered with uncompromising reverence for as long as Sapiens trod the planet.

Ben was flabbergasted at the sight of the two aliens who breezed pliantly along the deep pile military red, between the two lines of sweating infantry. They in turn were surrounded by a staring multitude, with the dusty amber desert forming a stunning backdrop that stretched unbroken to the horizon. The whole scene was illuminated by brilliant, broiling sunshine.

Zamindar and Char seemed almost to shine in the unimpeded light from Sol. Their chalky flesh appeared to glow with a power of its own, as though the sparks of star energy lay buried somewhere deep within them. They both moved forward, looked left, then right and then fleetingly

253

glanced at each other, both of their cranial knots quivering in harmony. Both were clearly savouring the moment as the humans made their way toward the main administration block that lay directly ahead, their path flanked by their large new friends.

The nine figures ambled through the double doors of the boardroom and instantly disappeared from view. The doors closed behind them with a heavy cachunk and were immediately set upon by a dozen burly peacekeepers. The assemblage of officialdom that had initially hung back in hushed awe, unexpectedly surged forward in an effort to get one last look at the new arrivals.

They were politely blocked by the security cordon ten metres from the bomb-proof doors. A similar cordon encircled the two Ajiron whose shielding covers had been withdrawn entirely. Exposed on the asphalt like a pair of silver eyes were two hauntingly alien bladders that reflected the Sun in an arc of blinding white flame.

The first meeting between representatives of an extraterrestrial culture and those of Earth proceeded, perhaps a hundred, or a million centuries before anyone could have expected it would. Not surprisingly, the first stories to hit newspapers spoke emphatically of the absolute absurdity of believing that first contact would be direct, yet it had been. Articles and interviews by a host of SETI and astro-science notables were centered around its astonishing improbability. Yet it had happened. It was so very unlikely, yet it had happened.

UFO buffs were thrust into an ambrosial paradise that they thought would forever be beyond their scrabbling fingers. They made claims that they were vindicated at last, that if it had happened once, as it now had, it had surely happened before. Aliens must have visited Earth before. They were wrong but they were persistent, nothing had changed. '*One*' had visited Earth but that wasn't what they meant. They were referring to visits by tiny creatures in flying ashtrays.

Despite billion channel analysers and systematic searches of "most likely" stellar homes, SETI, META, STETA and OSAL had all failed to find the sneezes of intelligence beyond Earth. Some scientific professionals, even some of note, were becoming demoralized in spite of the fantastic tracts of space that were invisible to the Earth and Earth orbit ears. That would quickly change though, three new space telescopes were ready to blast off and while none were owned by SETI, they were there to hunt planets and dissect atmospheres.

To most astro-scientists it was lunacy to suggest that there were not others out there. Stellar statistics demanded it they said. That and quantum likelihood. And yet before this incredible happening, there was no evidence for them. None at all. Only logic and probability suggested that they were there. Logic and probability that was homespun, did it extend into the Universe proper, well…yes it did. Finally, that question could be answered.

Those who would dare to suggest that first contact would be direct and would follow from two alien vehicles setting down on a terrestrial helipad, well, that would be considered the product of a nutter….a UFO junkie who's hopes and dreams were well out of whack with reality and highly questionable.

And yet it had happened. The unthinkable had become fact, born from the sabotage of an alien super vessel in the next suburb down. Direct contact was undeniably unlikely, but so too were the complex and incredible chain of events that led to it.

In space and therefore on Earth, anything is possible. M. Taylor proverb #1.(Seated at the heavy oak table under the diffuse glow from the soft lights, the CPT, all twelve of them, tried like hell to formally welcome the Virijians. They were having difficulties, as expected. But the difficulties weren't related to comprehension and perception, in fact quite the opposite.

They were related to their very concise grasp of human language and their thirst to move quickly beyond simple banter and official pleasantries. Zamindar and Char made it clear that they weren't much for nebulous and unprofitable gatherings. Understanding though they were, they wanted to get down to business, immediately. They didn't seem to care what Earth wanted. Or more importantly, what it didn't want.

It was apparent to the Forum that the Virijians had an Agenda, and they wanted to discuss it and more than likely, implement it as soon as they could. The longwinded introduction by Rima

254

Chandra III, the chairman of the Forum, was cut short by Zamindar who simply toned over the top of him. And despite further attempts by Chandra to complete his much prepared task he was thwarted entirely by the large and determined visitor.

Each of the Eminent Dozen met the two Virijians personally. It was a profoundly poignant moment for those men who had done so much to raise the awareness of the planet to the probability of others. The men who had fought pitched battles with Congress to win funding to probe the cosmos. It was the ultimate coup de grace...the realisation of an impossible dream, and for them to so intimately join in the stunning encounter was a worthy reward.

Having convinced the Forum that they should begin discussion of the 'first cosmic objective', Zamindar stood like a bleached Goliath and toned for almost an hour without a break. They asked that Earth join them and allow them the license to put their ideas and blueprints into place, to allow their wants to come to fruition, to the benefit, they maintained, of both planetary communities.

Neither the Virijians nor the returned Cygnans had breathed a word of the Sphere or of *'One'*. Jessy could barely imagine how the planet would react, coming so close on the heels of this. Maybe they wouldn't even believe them, would think they were suffering some crazed post cosmic morosis, after all, where the hell was the evidence? Sitting under the Congo, yeah right, who'd believe that? She knew they would though, the Virijians were nothing if not nakedly convincing and believable. But what about the reaction. Maybe they should wait a long time before revealing it. Twenty years perhaps? Jessy didn't want to even think about it, let alone talk about it.

In her rare times of solitude Jessy couldn't help but burrow into the deeper rumples of her mind and ask...why? Why were *'One'* coming back? What did they want and what would they tell them? What the hell was left to tell, more to the point, how would they look? Her dream of *'One'* looking like Man was never far away, sitting and waiting like a splinter bomb at the back of her brain.

Did *'One'* want to observe, or did they want to *do?* That was what really bothered her. And it doggedly refused to be soothed by the small part of her brain where logic resided. That puny kink in her mind wielded no muscle at all. It was continually bullied by the chemical blunderings of her Limbus that saw Jessy's emotions run roughshod over any deeper reason. Her hand moved from her cheek to the back of her neck. Everything aside though, she felt she had good reason to worry.

'One' had inflicted so much directional surgery on human genetics, were they coming back to do more? Was that their reason for returning? A final tweak to chromosomes #12 & #17 maybe. A tune-up to human DNA, an adjustment to nuceltide polymer #8456 perhaps. Would their return to Earth herald another and perhaps final evolutionary makeover? Would they begin the process of hauling Dolphins back onto dry land and similarly start the ball rolling to rid man of his limbs, to slipstream his body and set an aquatic future in place? The ultimate reversal of fortune. Surely, they wouldn't do that, would they? Jessy was bug-eyed and looked truly terrified.

In fact, they had said not so, by referring to their minimalist theory of intervention. But deep down maybe *'One'* were still unhappy with the direction the species was taking. The direction we were taking. They claimed to interfere only to bring forth true awareness, and then that was that. But could they be believed? On that score, they all knew they had no idea.

They weren't just from another planet, they were from another Universe. Their visit to Earth could be for any one of a thousand reasons, and at least half of those could be to the detriment of the eight billion souls who currently walked the globe. That, she knew was a distinct possibility.

***

Mitch and Jessy were standing near the recessed water fountain adjacent to the doors that led to the helipad outside. They were watching the Forum as they tried to direct the discussions, and noticed with amusement just how poorly they were doing.

The Virijians would only respond very selectively, ignoring everything they considered irrelevant or inconsistent with their Agenda.

Watching the meeting unfold, they were gripped by enormous pride and sadness, for they realized that their intimate connection with Zamindar and Char was over. It was inevitable, but they were sad anyway. The baton of discovery had been ceded to the people of Earth.

Jessy looked away from Zamindar, who was still toning profusely to his fascinated audience, and looked squarely at Mitch.

'I can't believe this is over. I was thinking about it earlier and it seems like I've never had another life, that my life was spent entirely on Cygnus and with the Virijians.'

Mitch looked quizzically at Jessy. Confused, he whispered, 'you hardly seemed to be enjoying yourself at the time Jessy, you had your moments, but most times I'm sure you would've traded it all for a harbor view.'

'Come on, it wasn't like that, you...'

'Anyway,' Mitch spoke over her, 'you heard what Zamindar said. It sounds like the adventure is just starting, and one way or another we will be involved. You heard him, he wants to meet with our four best political scientists, planetary scientists, psychologists, medicos, sociologists, astrophysicists, and you also heard why they want to meet with these minds. I know you heard that, so any adventure Jessy, is only just beginning to crank up. We're on the threshold. It's going to be fantastic and we'll be a part of it...and by the way, will you marry me?' Jessy glanced up at Mitch and noticed the ring he held in his upturned palm.

'My God. I thought you'd never ask, but I er, didn't expect... '

Mitch placed the ring on her finger and kissed her.

'Well?' he whispered. He felt like tapping his foot, hoping like hell she would say yes. He thought she would but you never know, he worried. Jessy definitely had her own mind.

'Of course, of course I will, yes I will marry you. God, I can't believe it...but you might have picked a more romantic setting,' she laughed playfully.

'This is the perfect spot Jess, our own moment of history in the midst of the most significant moment in the history of our planet; very apt I thought.'

'Well since you put it like that, how could I say no.' Jessy smiled broadly at Mitch.

14

Symbiosis

'We can't help it. Life looks for life.' ~ *Carl Sagan*

Nearing the planet, it was obvious that it had a power of its own. The motion of the hydrogenous haze was unmistakable, as was the fabulous contrast of the bright white methane knots that floated high in its atmosphere like a sprinkling of snow.

Pocking one of the white cirrus, a black smudge resolved into a small polygon that leapt upward and sped toward a line of massive vessels. There were ten craft in all. One of them was lagging a full two million kilometres behind the others and was being shadowed by something extraordinary.

In its grasp, some thirty thousand kilometres behind, was a planet, a vivid cloud obscured globe that hung behind it, dwarfing the vessel. Rou had grabbed the little Mercury sized world, a moon, and tugged it fifteen hundred million kilometres to its new neighborhood. It had come a long way, but it was now close to its star. It started to warm up and was ripe for a new suite of life to grow.

The cosmos suddenly detonated in white. Fourteen natural satellites of the greeny-blue world were sent spinning away, taken out of orbits they had followed for nearly five billion years. Space slowly regained its blackness and the distant yellow pyre that had just lost a few of its kin, reappeared.

The five Rou reoriented themselves until they were almost touching, with all their pendulous limbs focussed planetward. In a second, the world was drowning in a ghostly phosphorescence that spun around it, faster and faster until the surface was lost in a fantastic super rotational blur.

Erupting outward, the radiance could be seen gradually retreating as a misty torus behind the disk of the planet. Rou had ripped away the useless hydrogen -helium atmosphere and chewed the once pretty world to its ugly hematitic core. From fifty thousand kilometres, its girth had been reduced to sixteen thousand kilometres, a bit bigger than Earth.

It would be this rocky core that the Virijians would bio form, but first the planet would be tugged to warmer climes. And during the trip, a unique moon harbouring primitive life would be placed in its care, gently slotted into a Librational shuffle around its midriff.

Within a month the purloined rock was on its way to take up a new life more than four billion kilometres closer to its star. It was moving to a much better neighborhood. Neptune had lost a hell of a lot of weight.

***

The star was a minute, inconspicuous dot. One amongst billions of others that hung like rough-hewn diamonds around them. Travelling at ninety-nine percent Luminal, the faint dot grew rapidly, taking on a form and quickly becoming a dazzling orange photo-sphere. Main sequence and friendly.

For those in the craft it took only a short time for the star to swell from nothing to everything, but outside the craft, back on Earth, the same process was achingly slow. Such was the nature of time at these close Luminal speeds which invoked several Lorentz factors to dilate time.

Decelerating, the craft gradually wrestled its own momentum until it was only paddling through space. It was on the edge of the orange star's family of planets. The outermost was now visible before them, a frozen dead ammonia world with a tiny orbiting potato moon.

The seven positronium starships had exited a wormhole only four light years away in the vicinity of a red giant on the verge of going supernova. Jumping into flat space, the craft journeyed to this galactic perimeter system in only three months ship time, using relativistic travel to huge advantage.

They were now inside the orbit of the eighth planet, ambling toward its ochreous parent. Slipping close to the sixth planet, they saw a gigantic "almost star", a brown dwarf swaddled by a striking saffron mist and replete with over thirty moons.

Another few gigatons of mass and the planet would have found the fires of fusion in its core to set two stars burning in the sky. As it was, the gizzard of the planet sparked and fizzed with the spastic rumblings of potential star life.

The fifth and fourth planets were pitted and scarred worldlets without atmosphere or hope. The fourth had a stupendous crater which had bitten off one of its poles in an impact that was nearly large enough to crack it, pole to pole.

Penetrating the particle nebula, the line of vessels came upon the third planet. This one looked very different, even from millions of kilometres away. Its blueness and whiteness was striking, as was its shining equatorial girdle. Coming closer, the geometricity of its surface could be seen between the clouds. It was clearly and unambiguously alive.

Part of the disc was in darkness and on that side, they could see the lights of a civilization, the lights of massive cities, the ponderous glow of intelligence and consciousness. They watched in awe. But they passed this vibrant world without even slowing. Only a brief hello and an even quicker goodbye. Despite the energy of life that rejoiced below, this was not the place they were searching for. But for those onboard it looked achingly beautiful. Goodbye, is all they could say.

It was the second planet that the neuron pads were searching for. And within thirty minutes it appeared from the blackness, a tiny dot in the clear hull that grew larger and more colorful with each heartbeat. Pink and red with greyish poles, the planet was hazy with the swirlings of a tenuous ether.

Lapping it was a ring, only partially constructed around its girth. This was obviously a planet under repair. Not one being brought back to life but one being literally brought to life, kicking and screaming. They came closer still and the small world seemed to beckon to the odd new arrivals.

It had primal beauty, not the naked magnificence of the third planet, but a basic raw attraction. As they approached, the molecular flurry of its biosphere started clawing at the skin of the intruding ships. Then they saw it, sprawled below them.

The line of vessels entered a stationary orbit more or less above the fantastic structure that sat hugging the desert world below. It was immense and astonishing and it reflected its parent's light in blinding bursts.

This primitive planet was their new home. They had travelled through light years of normal space and God knew how many light millennia of Lorentzian space to get here. But the real work was yet to begin. And begin it would, soon.

***

Mitch and Jessy walked hand in hand, descending the ramp that led to the lawned area in front of their modest living quarters. It was nighttime but the moonlight ensured good vision. Jessy opened her eyes widely, and could see pretty well. She pushed her glasses back against her eyes.
In the distance was only barren landscape, flat and desolate and mostly devoid of life. The charcoal silhouette of a colossal dead volcano lay on the horizon, and as they watched they saw the faint light from the Paris satellite whiz overhead. Jessy looked up and caught Mitch's eye.

'Sometimes I think we've been so lucky, but other times I think we've missed out on so much. I mean we've hardly led a normal life, have we?' What was a normal life, she wondered? Syrius changed everything for us, literally everything. I wonder where the hell we'd be if CX1 hadn't appeared in our skies. Certainly not here, that's for damn sure.' She gazed around, smiling and exposing perfect white teeth.

She paused and thought about it. 'Some days I think CX1 was good to us…other days I'm not so sure.' Jessy was confused, tilting her head down. Some things never changed.

Mitch's salt and pepper hair shone in the moonlight. Looking at Jessy he noticed, not for the first time, just how gracefully she'd aged and how beautiful she still was. Not bad for fifty-five, he thought. Of course, they were Earth years. With their jaunts at near Luminal speeds they calculated that they'd managed to avoid at least seven of them.

His shadows, cast by the twin moons of Argyle and Newton, stood opposed behind him, testament to the strange new world they found themselves on.

'I'm homesick Mitch.'

He looked at her without expression, seeing the familiar sadness gently pushing behind her eyes. 'God Jess, come on,' he said, grinning. 'You're only ninety-three million light years from Earth, how can you possibly be homesick?' He knew she longed to go home, she hardly had to remind him of that.

With that, the rest of the family Taylor came barreling down the ramp. Teenager Josh with his brothers and sisters, Nick, Daniel and Alysha joined their parents on the engineered grass at the foot of their organic homette.

They talked and played under a fantastic pall of stars that punctuated the night sky like crystals on a coalface. It was a massive band of galactic light that dominated overhead, competing with the twin moons that hovered like a set of eyes near the horizon.

In the earth year 2063 Mitch and Jessy had been chosen and had eventually agreed, to head up Earth's first permanent step out of the solar system. In fact, out of the galaxy ... way, way out. With the Virijians help, humanity had colonized their first extrasolar planet, known as Gaia Solaris.

They had gotten there via a Lorentzian GraviTunnel that hugged Trijicyon and which purely by accident gave access to this beautifully stable dwarf stellar system. It lay on the rim of an oblate elliptical monster galaxy that contained more than four trillion stars.

Man had agreed to join Virija in joint tenancy of this eight planet system as one of the founding doctrines of their early communion. A Sapien colony had been established on the second planet, in plain view of the Virijians who were already entrenched on the third, having bio formed it a full five thousand years before.

Detailed societal plans for joint habitation of the second and third planets, and other planets in other systems and other galaxies were in their formative stages.

The psychosocial and technological framing of the principles for cohabitation had been surprisingly made quite a bit easier by the tangible differences between the two races. Strangely, it was helped along by the vast gulf between their respective intelligences.

Humans were a chaotic mishmash of unpredictable emotional elements, societal divisions, religious contrarieties and racial discords.

On the other hand, the Virijians were almost entirely predictable, emotionally uniform and focused almost as one around accord and harmony. Scientific endeavor and exploration, curiosity, was their inviolable community bedrock.

Thankfully, the Virijians had a precise understanding of the human mind, they had been very similar once. And importantly, with the Virijians being as homogenous as they were, their nature and temperament were well within the scope of the human mind. Only their technology was not. So, there was a belief that some form of limited interaction might occur in the near future.

It was expected that a workable blueprint for a partial social integration would be completed within a few years. Social experiments were high on the list of new space priorities.

259

Bio-forming had already progressed significantly on Gaia even before the Sapien pioneers had arrived. The living, breathing bio-animators from Virija were everywhere and had already partially transformed a thick mantle of carbon dioxide and hydrocarbons into a more amenable and friendly medium.

They were forging lakes and oceans where only basins and furrows had existed before. Complex fluvial systems were incising themselves virtually before their eyes, digging their way through the ferro-magnesium pediments of the maturing crust. Two years ago, water struck bedrock for the first time in a momentous pre-biological merger. It was still geochemistry but it would soon be biochemistry.

The humans' astonishment at their new home was brought home to them by discretely placed "vision-crypts" that delivered vivid panoramas from more than two hundred parts of the blossoming planet.

Within two years they would be able to move out from under their clear metal hemisphere, the petri dish, and begin the second phase of their global occupation plan, with help from their friends on the next planet down.

Gaia was literally ripening around them. It was an inconceivable thrill for Mitch and Jessy to watch the ice gradually melt and disappear from the hills, the misty cyano-nitrides fade from the atmosphere and the murky sky turn from orange to pink and then gradually to violet and ultimately to familiar blue. Living blue. It was planetary detox on the most fabulous level imaginable.

Over a single year they saw the winds slow to a virtual standstill. They saw the incessant dust storms stop and watched the UV resistant grasses bloom and color the bleak hellscape with the greenness of life.

All of it happened in under six months. With atmospheric oxygen came a protective ozone layer that armored their new world along with a spinning core and gravitational field, and signaled the beginning of a vibrant planet, of a truly life-capable world. They were viewing the birth of a brand new home, almost as though they were watching the rise of life on Earth, which took eons but here was compressed into a few short, tantalizing years.

Although Gaia was still lacking in certain of the finer biophysical details, Jessy always thought of it as a proto Earth. The thought comforted her when she sat on the landing of her soft little home and looked up at the furiously alien sky.

She was always overcome by just how far from her own planet they really were. Ninety-three million years just for our light to travel home. Jessy would frequently shiver with disbelief as she looked at the sky, dominated as it was by the close fourth planet Rinjiel, tenanted by eighty million Virijians. Considered by them to be a planet full.

Still, Gaia had blue nitrogen skies, large and swelling oceans of water, a stable and growing temperature (already above zero centigrade), soils on the verge of fertility, and simple seeded flora in abundance.

There would soon be complete marine ecosystems released into the seas. Eight years after arriving, the two thousand minds from Earth had achieved an infrastructure and kindled a foundational blueprint that, with continuing help from the Morij, would allow them to quickly humanize the planet. Once they were freed from their ponderous artificial sky.

Jessy looked up at the twin moons. Argyle was so close to Gaia that both were in a tight synchronous and locked rotation. Newton was three times further away but its extra flab made the twins look almost identical from where Jessy was sitting. It was amazing, not Earth, but amazing all the same.

She looked at the mahogany crater that pocked Argyle like an excised tumour, and lost herself in thoughts of home.

Mitch could see the look in her eyes. He'd seen it almost nightly for several years now, painted, indelibly it seemed, like a neoplastic expression.

'We've only got two years Jessy, then it's over, we go home, back to Earth for good.'

Jessy's mood didn't lighten, her eyes were still fastened on the horizon, brooding.

260

'We won't even recognize our own system,' she muttered, 'I mean, the changes! I know I supported the ideas, the new solar blueprint, but it'll take time to get used to them. Jesus, we've ended five or so billion years of stability in our homeland. In times like this you wonder if we did the right thing, but they were so persuasive weren't they?' Jessy broke her stare and turned slowly to face him. Her eyes blinked as they adjusted to the light.

Mitch looked thoughtful for a moment and then chuckled quietly as he looked upward.

'Yeah, I know, just imagine, the Moon with a fully-fledged atmosphere...a blue Moon! Goddamn, just to see it, imagine the view from Earth. No more "Man in the Moon" I'm afraid.' His eyes were downcast for a moment.

Think about it Jess, you look up and there where Luna should be, is a blue planet. A living world with white clouds and blue seas, another Earth like planet.' He continued peering at the sky long after he stopped speaking.

'Incredible,' Jessy said. She wouldn't believe it until she saw it. It was too much to imagine.

Mitch shrugged. 'And don't forget green Venus, that's in a brand new orbit, twenty million kilometres closer to Earth, hell, at closest approach it'd only be arm's length away! They shot the sulfuric atmosphere straight out of the solar plane towards Canopus. Won't they be happy when a planet load of acid turns up...'

'Maybe they'll send it straight back,' Jessy offered, grinning weakly, quickly regaining a more somber expression.

'And the best one Jessy, Neptune. Fully bio-formed, de-ringed, de-mooned and de-atmosphered. With Titan wrenched from Saturn and placed in its care. And the whole lot wrapped up and stuffed into Mars orbit, ex Mars that is, together with an orbiting black hole that gives access to Virija and Trijicyon.'

Holy shit, Mitch thought. They certainly were some big, big changes.

Jessy shook her head disbelievingly, feeling the familiar pad thump of her racing heart. Her voice was cold and sad, 'The old system has been re-engineered by our friends and thoroughly upgraded, brought fully up to date with our, or more particularly, with their requirements.

'Our requirements,' Mitch added loudly.

'What the hell would Galileo or Kepler think if they could unfurl their telescopes now. God, it's mind blowing...the whole concept. Solar engineering. No matter how many times you think about it and just when you think you've come to terms with it, bang, in the middle of the night you can't believe it again. I just wonder if we should've agreed so quickly, it seems so unnatural.'

Mitch looked at Jessy for long seconds. '...how many times have we had this discussion?' Mitch asked as he clambered to his feet and started pacing. 'If it's natural to obtain intelligence, which it is, even if it happened only once, then anything we do or the Virijians do or *'One'* do, is natural. More to the point, whatever a particular technology is capable of achieving, say moving planets, bio forming or even creating intelligence in others is, by further extension, of natural origin. We're only made of simple star carbon Jessy, a common resource, and I say we are incapable of doing anything unnatural. So, don't sweat it. We should be grateful and thankful that we've lived through and been involved in the most exciting forty years in the history of the planet.'

'I'm not convinced Mitch,' Jessy murmured, shaking her head, 'and don't speak too soon or in the past tense about the most exciting years. We head home in two years, which with time reduction in mind, will be one year before 2081, the year of *'One'*. The year we meet our maker, the second coming, call it what you like but that could and probably should surpass all that's gone before it.' Jessy wondered if it would be what she thought it would? Maybe it'd be a fizzer. Who knew?

There was a long silence as neurons silently chewed and digested the giddiness of *'One'*

'What will they be like?' Mitch said distractedly. 'Probably totally beyond our comprehension. Maybe we won't even recognize them as life at all. Perhaps they don't even reflect visible light, possibly have no physical form whatsoever. Whatever they will be...they'll be nothing like we imagine, be sure of that if nothing else.'

261

Jessy slipped her hand into Mitch's, and looked at him wide eyes. 'Beyond belief,' she muttered softly. 'They could be totally beyond, as in totally outside, our terms of reference.' Like trying to converse with a cloud, she thought, almost giggling.

Jessy recalled her nightmare and wondered again if maybe they, *'One'*, were human, or at least looked human. Could they be? In the image of Man, she thought. It caught in her throat. She thought of the Bible and wondered again.

They sat down with their four children on the metal ramp and looked out at an alien world. Alien though it was, it had, to Mitch and his family, taken on a familiar, almost homey aspect.

They all wanted to return to Earth, none of them would dispute that, but equally they knew they would be saddened to leave their rapidly ripening world. They'd known it since it was born, had seen its pain as it grew, watched it mature into a living, breathing Nirvana...a cradle, their cradle, lavish and beautiful beyond description. It had grown to be a good friend.

Mitch had yet to return to the oxidised treasure at M3 on the Moon. He still thought about it from time to time, the extraordinary crystal groups still made his mouth water. The zone of nearly pure primary copper and lead/zinc sulfides was to the side of the oxidised zone, so maybe it was still there, waiting.

Hand in hand, Mitch and Jessy were surrounded by their children on the edge of their little organic neighborhood. They gazed as one at silver Argyle and orange Newton that hung ponderously in the sky, bathed in the soft glow from their close star.

It was just starting to make its presence felt, creeping slowly toward their side of the planet. The appearance of Altinh in under fifteen minutes would herald another fine and warm day on Gaia Solaris on the edge of a galaxy tens of thousands of light millennia from the blue skies of home.

They were the first family of Homo Galacticus.

Unbeknownst to the *'first family of Homo Galacticus'*, worlds away and simultaneously right there with them and part of them, *'One'* was well pleased with them and looked forward to meeting them *"in the flesh"* very soon.

The End

GLOSSARY

AANEAS	Anglo-Austraian Near-Earth Asteroid Survey
AASSA	Aust American Space & Shuttle Agency
AMOS	Australian Meteorological and Oceanographic Society
CLH	Compact Laser Heterodyne
CPT	Contact Protocol Team
ECON	European Confederation
ESA	European Space Agency
ESI	Earthshield 1
F=MA	equals Mass x Acceleration
GAPCNN	Fictional Media Company
GSI	Global Security Intelligence
HOLMES	Fictional Periscopic Gripper
JPL	Jet Propulsion Lab (NASA)
LIGO	Laser Inferometer Gravitational Wave Observatory
LONEOS	Lowell Observatory Near-Earth Object Searcg
NASA	North American Space Association
NSF	National Science Foundation
OSAL	Fictional - seach for Extra-Terrestrial Beings
PACS	Fictional - seach for Extra-Terrestrial Beings
PCAC	Fictional - Department of Spaceguard
PCDU	Fictional - Phase Change Distillation Unit
PCM	Protocoma Maintenance
PND	Pseudo-Novae Drive
RADES	Ranging Delivery System
SEM.	Scanning Electron Microprobe (microscope)
SETI	Search for Extraterrestrial Intelligence
SIS	Steinardt Intelligence System
STAT	Fictional - seach for Extra-Terrestrial Beings
STETA	Fictional - seach for Extra-Terrestrial Beings
UNSC	United Nations Security Council
USPA	The United Space & Planetary Agency

Scott Bywater lives in Adelaide near the southern coast of Australia with his wife Mary and two kids, Josh and Alysha. Scott has an Honours Degree in Geomorphology from Flinders University, and an obsession with anything astrophysical. While at University, he published four mineralogical papers in the *Mineralogical Record* out of Tucson, Arizona.

To help facilitate writing on the subject he taught himself the finer details of quantum field theory, General Relativity, and in particular, String Theory and anthropic cosmology.

Scott believes that anyone who has looked up at the night sky and wondered why, or contemplated some of the deeper reasons for their existence, will derive much pleasure from this book.